"A powerful but despairing struggle, doom on a grand scale, with mostly unlikable characters doing despicable deeds, but Douglass creates a memorable maze of events that somehow simultaneously repels and fascinates."

—*Locus*

"A soap opera for the ancient world." —*Kirkus Reviews*

"There is sex and violence aplenty...the taste for this mythic fantasy saga must be acquired, but acquirers will relish it keenly." —*Booklist*

DRUID'S SWORD

BOOK FOUR OF THE TROY GAME

Sara Douglass

A TOM DOHERTY ASSOCIATES BOOK
NEW YORK

This is a work of fiction. All of the characters, organizations, and events portrayed in this novel are either products of the author's imagination or are used fictitiously.

DRUID'S SWORD: BOOK FOUR OF THE TROY GAME

Copyright © 2006 by Sara Douglass Enterprises Pty Ltd.

Edited by Claire Eddy

A Tor Book
Published by Tom Doherty Associates, LLC
175 Fifth Avenue
New York, NY 10010

www.tor.com

Tor® is a registered trademark of Tom Doherty Associates, LLC.

ISBN-13: 978-0-765-34445-8
ISBN-10: 0-765-34445-9

First Edition: May 2006
First Mass Market Edition: May 2007

Printed in the United States of America

0 9 8 7 6 5 4 3 2 1

ACKNOWLEDGMENTS

Many thanks to my agent, Jim Frenkel; my editor, Claire Eddy; and to Tor Books for all their aid in helping to bring the Troy Game to fruition. I also owe a big debt of thanks to that small cadre of dedicated London map and Ephemera collectors who haunt eBay—without them so much of London would still remain undiscovered, and I would not have had half so much fun in researching this book as I did.

ACKNOWLEDGMENTS

We are in the middle of a conflagration which is not just a struggle between two countries. It is the struggle of two different worlds. There is no way for these worlds to exist side by side. One of them must perish.

—Adolf Hitler, speech of December 10, 1940

Abbreviations Used in this Book

ARP: Air Raid Precaution (i.e., ARP wardens, stations, or shelters)

BBC: British Broadcasting Commission

GPO: General Post Office

IB: Incendiary bomb

IRA: Irish Republican Army

mph: miles per hour

RAF: Royal Air Force

UXB: Unexploded bomb

DRUID'S
SWORD

Prologue

HE WOMAN KNELT KEENING IN THE SA-
cred glade. She was strikingly handsome despite
her grief-stricken face smeared with thick lines
of blue woad war paint. She wore a chest plate of metal
over a robe of sweat- and bloodstained tartan wool. A red
woolen cape lay on the ground just behind her. Her dark
hair, laced here and there with silver, was twisted into a
plait that hung over one shoulder, and her bare arms glit-
tered with metal armbands.

A sword lay discarded to her right, a gourd beside it.

Before the woman lay the bodies of two adolescent girls,
one of whom was heavily pregnant. Their bodies were still
warm, the tears on their cheeks still fresh, but whatever
beauty they may have possessed was disguised by their
twisted limbs and faces, a legacy of the poison they had in-
gested a little time earlier.

The clearing was encircled by two score warriors, both
men and women, most of them wounded, all of them
droop-shouldered with despair and bitterness. Some leaned
on spears thrust into the ground, others on the shoulders of
comrades.

They were the remnants of the woman's army. Twelve
hours ago that army had been more than sixty thousand

strong. Now it was reduced to a few desperate score, and even they would not survive much longer.

The sound of the Roman centurions could be heard to the east as they fought their way through the forest toward the sacred glade.

Her army had not been able to stop them, but Boudicca—the mother who wept over her daughters and the sad loss of her country to the invader—knew that the forest would keep them at bay long enough for her to do what she needed.

A year ago all had been so well. True, her beloved land had been invaded by the Romans, but Boudicca and her husband, Prasutagus, who ruled over the Iceni, had spent months in careful negotiation with the Romans, trying to come to a mutually agreeable settlement. Then, ten months ago, a terrible wasting sickness struck Prasutagus that reduced his tall, strong frame to a skeletal, shaking weakness in a few short weeks. He died, leaving a desolate Boudicca regent of the Iceni, and guardian of her daughters' inheritance.

For no reason that Boudicca could understand, the Romans attacked as soon as they heard Prasutagus was interred in his hill grave. They ravaged the lands of the Iceni, whipped Boudicca, and raped her daughters.

They took all night over those rapes, and so far as Boudicca knew, most of the Roman soldiers within twenty miles had enjoyed her daughters during that time.

The child that her eldest had been carrying was a Roman bastard.

Boudicca had been so devastated by their unwarranted attacks on her, her daughters, and her people that for weeks she had been incapable of doing anything.

Then anger took over, and, backed by the Iceni and many of their neighboring tribes, Boudicca raised a mighty army of over sixty thousand warriors, both men and women, and attacked the Romans.

She had stunning success. Death abounded. With Boudicca at their head, the Iceni decimated Camulodunum Colonia, then Londinium, slaughtering any they found in their path. Boudicca took particular care with Londinium, causing it to be razed to the ground. For some reason

which she could not articulate, but which she felt in every fiber of her being, she blamed the city for all her troubles. Perhaps if she razed London, all might be well.

Over a hundred thousand died in the resulting conflagration.

From Londinium, Boudicca hardly paused for breath as she drove her army toward Verulamium, where more than seventy thousand died.

The Romans were stunned by the success of Boudicca's advance and appalled by her savagery. One of them wrote back to Rome that the pagan queen appeared bent not on taking prisoners or on amassing booty but on slaughter, the gibbet, the fire, and the cross. All she wanted, he wrote, was to create a wasteland of death.

Boudicca had ravaged south aided by surprise and a lack of any substantial Roman force to stand in her way. But eventually the Romans rallied, and the previous day the two forces had met in a desperate battle atop an ancient fort in the center of Epping Forest.

The Romans had the better of the battle, and routed the Iceni during a desperate struggle that took the entire day.

As the Iceni fell about her, Boudicca retreated a mile or two away, to this sacred glade. Whatever else, Boudicca was determined that the Romans should take neither her nor her daughters alive.

Her daughters had willingly taken the poison—the night of their rape was still violently fresh in their minds.

Now Boudicca raised her face to the men and women who surrounded her.

"I will drink of the gourd now," she said. "Witness my death, and then burn my body and that of my daughters. Then flee, if you wish. You do not need to follow me into death."

She reached for the gourd, and none of the warriors moved or spoke to stop her. But as Boudicca raised it to her lips, a murmur of surprise and fear rustled about the circle, and Boudicca lowered the gourd to see what had disturbed them.

Pray to the gods that the Romans had not arrived yet!

A pillar of light—faint and hazy, almost a thin fog—had appeared to one side of Boudicca.

She gasped and, with every one of the warriors, bent forward in honor before the apparition.

Was it one of the gods, come to save them?

"Nay," said the apparition, now forming itself into the recognizable form of a man, "but only me, your beloved husband, come to guide you."

"Prasutagus!" said Boudicca, setting the gourd aside and holding out her arms toward the ghost. Now her initial shock had passed, Boudicca was not surprised to see him. Prasutagus had been a great king, but he had been a far more powerful druid. How like him, she thought, to oversee her journey to the Otherworld.

He drifted close to her, his insubstantial hand caressing her cheek, then he looked at the bodies of their daughters. "They have passed gracefully, Boudicca, and are now happy in the Otherworld."

Boudicca's eyes filled with gratitude. "Prasutagus, will you oversee my own—"

"Boudicca," he said, interrupting her. "I need you to do something for me."

"Name it."

"In death," Prasutagus said, "I have become aware of many things. Terrible things."

Boudicca's eyes widened in distress, but she did not otherwise respond.

"Evil besets our land," he said.

"The Romans," Boudicca said, glancing behind her as she spoke, as if expecting the centurions to burst through the shrubbery at any moment.

"No," her husband said. "They are evil enough, true, but there is a far deeper evil which has spoiled this land."

"What?" Boudicca said.

"A foreign corruption," Prasutagus said. "Something brought here many lifetimes ago, which has taken root in the soil of our land, and infected it with utter malevolence."

About them the circle of warriors shifted and muttered.

"It is like a great poisonous spider," said Prasutagus,

"which has ensnared the entire land in its web. This spider seeks fulfilment, and we must do everything in our power to stop it, for if it achieves its goal, then, oh, then the sky itself will fall, and the land will be buried under a mountain of tears."

"What can we do?" Boudicca said. "What do you need *me* to do?"

"In death," said her husband, "I have met a strange little girl. She has black curly hair, and dark blue eyes, and rustles about in silken garments the color of night. Her face . . ." He hesitated. "Her face is cold, and she has an icicle for a heart."

Boudicca stared up into the face of her husband. She knew him so well, and could see the doubt that beset him.

"You don't trust her," she said.

"She is our only hope," Prasutagus said. "She has agreed to aid us. She says she will be our sword, the *land's* sword."

"You don't trust her," Boudicca said again.

Prasutagus sighed. "No. I don't. But if we don't accept her offer, then I am afraid that the land will wither and die under this evil. It grows stronger every day. It is . . . vile."

"Who is this girl?"

Prasutagus took a long time to answer. "The spirits call her the White Queen, for the coldness that besets her. Who is she? I don't know. But she is powerful and she loathes this evil, and wants it gone."

Boudicca wondered about that. Every instinct within her screamed not to accept what her husband said. But she trusted his judgment so greatly that if he said this strange girl was their only hope, then maybe she should believe him.

"If this White Queen is so powerful," said Boudicca, "and wants this evil gone, then why does she need us?"

Again Prasutagus took a long time to answer, and Boudicca wished he'd hurry up, for the Romans sounded even closer. Maybe Prasutagus had no sense of time and urgency now that he was dead.

"She says she needs to be bound to the land—" Prasutagus started, and suddenly Boudicca, horrifically, knew what her husband was going to say, and what he needed of her.

"No!" she said.

"She is not bound to the land," said Prasutagus, "and needs to be if she has any hope of—"

"Prasutagus, you want me to use my death to construct a *Seething*?"

A Seething was the most potent of rituals a druid could construct—and Boudicca *could* construct it, for she was as much druid as was Prasutagus. A Seething could be used to bind anything to any cause, and, if this strange little girl could help, and she said she needed to be bound to the land in order to be able to do so, then a Seething would do that magnificently.

But a Seething needed a death to make it.

No wonder Prasutagus had appeared to her just as she was about to take her own life.

Boudicca didn't know what to say. The fact of her own death did not trouble her at all, but to use it to bind the land to this unknown White Queen? What if she was as bad as that evil Prasutagus said had infected the land? What if by constructing the Seething, Boudicca bound the land to an even more terrible fate than the one it already faced?

"Boudicca," said a new voice, a small child's voice, and Boudicca's head whipped about as the circle of warriors murmured again and, one by one, melted back into the trees.

The child Prasutagus had spoken of now stood a few paces away. She was just as he'd described her. A beautiful face, framed with dark curls that tumbled down her back, and eyes so blue that Boudicca thought the sky must spend its days in envy of her.

And yet she was so cold. Her heart *was* ringed with icicles, and Boudicca wondered why.

"No one has ever loved me," said the child, and Boudicca felt the breath of her speaking as keenly as she would the wintry arctic winds that blew down from the north.

"We do not trust you," said Boudicca. "Why should we trust you? And what *is* this evil that—"

The child slid forward, grasping Boudicca's wrist.

Boudicca gasped and tried to pull back, but she could not. She felt as if she were frozen.

A vision consumed her.

She saw a naked man, with dark curly hair just like this girl's and six gleaming bands about his limbs, dancing through a labyrinth atop a hill.

She saw a young girl run out from the witnesses who stood about, and plunge a dagger into the throat of a heavily pregnant woman who stood to one side of the labyrinth, watching the dancing man.

She saw fire and death and destruction at the hands of an invader, and for a moment she thought that it was he who was the terrible evil.

"Not he," whispered the cold-faced child. "Watch."

Boudicca saw bodies pile atop the labyrinth; then, as if years passed in an instant, she saw the bodies decay into dust.

The labyrinth sank into the hill, and Boudicca saw the roots of trees become ensnared in it, and the burrowing creatures of the land become its slave.

"We need to stop the labyrinth," said the little girl, "before it overwhelms the entire land."

"And why should you care?" said Boudicca, finally managing to wrench her wrist free. "I can sense that you are not of this land, either. Why should you care?"

"Because I loathe it," said the little girl.

Then she smiled, and Boudicca's heart flipped over in horror.

For an instant a death's mask had replaced the girl's cold beauty.

But there was something about this girl. Something about the White Queen. Something that Boudicca could not identify, but something which screamed at her to trust her.

Trust me.

Boudicca wondered if she were being ensorceled.

"For a good cause," whispered the girl, and Boudicca capitulated.

"Of course we will help you," she said, and the White Queen gave her death's-head grin again.

"Good," she said. "Now, where's that poison?"

Still feeling strangely alien, as if the White Queen had taken over her entire being, Boudicca took the gourd from the ground.

"Prasutagus, watch over me," she whispered, then lifted the gourd to her mouth as the White Queen stepped back.

The poison acted within moments. Boudicca felt it eating at her stomach, then slithering into her blood.

Agony coursed through her, and her limbs twitched, wanting to flail and twist.

But Boudicca held firm. She began to mutter in the ancient druidic language, using not only her dying, but the deaths of everyone over this past year, starting with that of her husband, to fuel the Seething that would bind the White Queen to the land.

Was she doing the right thing? As the agony intensified, Boudicca began to doubt herself.

But it was too late now, too late to call back the words of the Seething, too late to stop the slow, triumphant smile that twisted the White Queen's face.

Her body twitched to and fro, and something shifted in the earth of the glade. Boudicca's voice cracked, then fell silent as her body succumbed to the convulsions.

"Ah," sighed the little girl. "It is done, now."

AS BOUDICCA ACCEPTED THE ARM OF HER HUS-band so that he might guide her to the Otherworld, she turned to him and said, "What have we done?"

PART ONE

NOAH

PART ONE

Chapter One

Saturday, 2 September 1939

MAJOR? MAJOR? I'M SORRY TO WAKE YOU, sir, but the train has arrived at Waterloo and you'll have to disembark."

Jack Skelton jerked too fast from deep sleep into wakefulness, and for several disorienting moments stared into the face of the conductor leaning over him, his mind unable to let go the dream images that skidded through it.

Frank Bentley and his insipid wife, Violet. Stella Wentworth, standing beautiful and untouchable under the embankment light. Matilda and Ecub, suburban housewives in dressing gowns. Asterion—Weyland Orr—taking him to Pen Hill. Faerie Hill Manor, and both the Lord of the Faerie and the king of England, George VI, waiting for him.

Grace—everyone's doom.

"Sir, I must ask you to—"

"Yes, yes. I'm awake." Jack Skelton struggled to his feet, one hand clutching at the overhead luggage rack for support as his head reeled.

The conductor stepped back. "It's been a bad few days, sir," he said, watching the American major curiously as he straightened his tie and uniform jacket, then lifted his greatcoat down from the rack. He wondered why the American was here, and hoped that it might be some indication that the Yanks wouldn't leave it as long to help out in

this war as they had left it the last. "We've heard news on the wireless that the PM has sent an ultimatum to the Nazis. Get out of Poland or we'll go to war."

The conductor paused, his face glum. "No chance that the Germans will back off, d'you think, major?"

Finally fully awake and oriented, Jack studied the man, knowing there was no chance for peace, and wondering if the man wanted false reassurances or the truth.

"It is too late now," he said. "I'm sorry."

The conductor's face tightened, and he gave a small nod. "Let me help you with your bag, sir."

ONCE ON THE PLATFORM, JACK TIPPED THE CON-ductor then stood motionless, looking about. Because he'd been so deeply asleep when the train had pulled in, and had probably then slept for fifteen minutes or more before the conductor woke him up, most of the other passengers had departed, and now the great cavernous space of Waterloo Station was all but deserted. He shivered, and tried to put it down to the cold night air.

The conductor had got back on the train, and now the platform was empty save for himself and several baggage handlers at the far end of the train, standing about an empty trolley, smoking and talking.

About the forthcoming war, no doubt. The Germans had invaded Poland earlier today, and war was inevitable. Jack could *feel* it seeping over the vast stretches of land and water between where he stood and where the Poles battled desperately. It was only a matter of time before it reached London.

He shivered again, and hunched deeper into his great-coat, lighting his own cigarette then flicking the match away. He drew a deep breath, taking comfort in the smoke. Jack had first come to this land almost three and a half thousand years ago as Brutus, the exiled Trojan prince. With Genvissa he'd thought to resurrect the ancient Troy Game, but everything had fallen apart when his then-wife, Cornelia, had murdered Genvissa before they could com-

plete the game. For three and a half thousand years Jack had—as Brutus, then as William, Duke of Normandy, and subsequently Louis de Silva—fought to finish what he had started so long ago. But always events and people (and that mostly Cornelia in her rebirth as Caela and then Noah) conspired to prevent him.

God, how long had it been since he'd last been in England? Almost three hundred years, give or take a decade or two. Oh, he'd come back briefly now and then, stepping through the realm of the Faerie, to meet with either Coel, the Lord of the Faerie, or with his father, Silvius, but apart from those fleeting visits . . . nothing. He'd walked away from the smoking ruins of London in 1666, walked away from the disaster of his hopes and dreams.

Walked away from Noah, who had abandoned her love for him to live with Asterion, and give him a child.

Walked away from the Troy Game.

Walked away from it all.

To roam.

He'd wandered first in the form of Louis de Silva rather than in his magical form of Ringwalker. He'd gone back to his father's estates in France, and from there, desperate, restless, angry beyond knowing, he'd drifted through the forests and fields and pleasure halls of Europe. Then, as the years passed, he assumed the form of a priest, because in his anger that amused him, and desecrated his way through Egypt and Arabia. From there, to India, and then even farther east, and as the decades spun by and his resentment and bewilderment at what had happened deepened, he became a sailor in a Portuguese man-of-war that had berthed in the Philippines, and fought and squandered his way across the oceans of the world.

Then he'd landed in America—new and brash and uncaring—and here Jack had found a home. He settled in the Appalachian mountains, finding solace in their high mountain lakes and dark forests. He lived there for a hundred years or more, spending more and more time not as a man but as Ringwalker, the name he took when he assumed the mantle of the ancient Stag God, roaming the

wild paths and tracks through the wilderness as he had once roamed the forests in England.

He found peace, and a renewed purpose. It was about this time, perhaps almost two hundred years after the Great Fire of London, that Jack made contact with the Lord of the Faerie again. Just a touch, a glimmer of friendship sent through the Faerie, but it was enough to begin rebuilding the bonds between them. From that point they'd met once every five or six years, sometimes in the forests of America, sometimes in the Faerie. These meetings lasted only a short while, less than an hour, and they rarely talked. They just spent time together.

About forty years ago, when they'd met in a lonely spot of the Faerie, the Lord of the Faerie had put his hand on Ringwalker's shoulder, and said, "My friend, John Thornton is back, a prince of the realm now. Loth is back also, and as wedded to the Christian church as he was when last he walked."

Ringwalker had tensed. "The others?"

"None of the rest of us had to be reborn. We have all done much as you have for the past few hundred years—moved in and out of the Faerie and in and out of mortal form as it suited us. Apart from John and Loth, we've all gone too far to be trapped by birth and death now."

We're all way too powerful. Too fey.

"And *her?* Is she still with *him?*"

"Noah? With Weyland? Of course, for they love each other deeply. Ringwalker, please, the land needs you back. We need you back. All of us."

"I don't think I can—"

"You must," the Lord of the Faerie had said quietly, and Ringwalker had bowed his head in acceptance.

Five months ago dreams began to pervade Jack's sleep. Each night, over and over, he dreamed of arriving in London, meeting with a nervous man called Frank Bentley, then walking about London, meeting in turn each of the people who had become caught up in the Troy Game.

Everyone save Noah.

Jack never met Noah in his dreams.

He knew what the dreams meant. It was time to go back. Time to *move*.

Time to find Noah.

And so now here he was, Major Jack Skelton, standing on the empty platform at Waterloo Station at ten P.M. waiting for someone to meet him. Jack had sent word (together with a request he hoped the Lord of the Faerie could accommodate) a week ago that he'd be here. Surely they'd send someone.

Who?

Noah? No, they'd not dare. Stella, perhaps—the Lord of the Faerie had told Jack of the name Genvissa-reborn used when she stepped out into the mortal world.

Would the Lord of the Faerie come himself?

Would the Troy Game meet him?

Not the Frank Bentley from his dreams, surely. Please let Frank be a figment of his dreaming mind . . . please . . .

Then Jack saw him. A tall, imposing figure striding onto the platform from the gate that led to the station concourse. A black trilby pulled down low over his brow. Flapping overcoat, beautifully cut, over an equally well tailored two-piece, double-breasted suit. A red silk scarf rippling at his throat. Matching leather gloves which the man was even now pulling off and stuffing into the pockets of his coat.

A gleaming smile in a swarthy face, redolent with mischief.

Not Frank Bentley.

"Jack!" The man held out his arms, and Jack laughed, and stepped into them.

"Silvius!"

His father grabbed him into a huge bear hug, almost lifting Jack off his feet. Jack hugged him back, and then both men were laughing, and leaning back from each other.

"Jack! Is there ever an incarnation you're willing to make when you're *not* as handsome as the worst renegade pirate?"

"How can I help that, with *your* blood in me?"

They fell silent, both men grinning hugely, unable to help themselves. For many thousands of years there had

been nothing but hatred and guilt between them. During the Bronze Age Silvius had been a Trojan prince, living in exile in Alba after the Greeks had sacked and destroyed Troy. As a prince of Troy Silvius had also been a Kingman—one trained in the ancient Aegean mysteries of the Game, a labyrinthine enchantment that a Kingman and his female counterpart, a Mistress of the Labyrinth, constructed via dance and magic in order to protect a city. Brutus, Silvius' fifteen-year-old son, had wanted his father's titles and powers, and had taken the first possible opportunity to murder his father. Brutus seized Silvius' six golden Kingship bands of Troy, magical limb bands that enhanced the wearer's Kingman powers, and eventually found his way to the island of Britain, then called Llangarlia. Here, with Genvissa, a Mistress of the Labyrinth and Darkwitch, he had resurrected the Troy Game in order to found London. But Brutus had used his father's murder to infuse the Game with power, and for thousands of years Silvius had been trapped in the vile dark heart of the labyrinth which lay at the center of the Troy Game (and which, in its physical form, lay under St. Paul's Cathedral in the center of London). It was only during Jack's last life as Louis de Silva that Silvius had managed to escape from the labyrinth's heart. Silvius and Brutus could have continued their hatred, but instead they had managed to set their violent past behind them, and understand that all the other one had ever wanted was approval, and love.

Silvius' hands tightened on Jack's shoulders, and he sobered. "I'm glad you're back. We all are."

"All?"

"*All* of us, Jack."

Jack wasn't so sure of that. It wasn't just he and his father who had a history of discord; Jack had a complex history of love and betrayal with most of the people caught up in the Troy Game: Cornelia, the wife he had originally despised and then come to love in her reincarnations as Caela and Noah, had betrayed him with Asterion, the creature who had lived at the dark heart of the labyrinth on Crete and who now lived as Weyland Orr; Asterion himself, who

had not only stolen Noah from him, but had also spent thousands of years trying to wrest control of the Troy Game away from Jack; Genvissa, the Mistress who had originally allied herself with Jack and who had then betrayed him to Asterion; Coel, a Llangarlian man who Jack, as Brutus, had murdered but who was now Jack's friend and ally as the Lord of the Faerie; Loth, a Llangarlian priest who had always fought against both Jack and the Troy Game; Ariadne, the ancient Darkwitch who, as Asterion's lover, had begun the series of events that had culminated in the destruction of Troy; and, last but not least, the Troy Game itself, which had taken the form of a little girl called Catling, and manipulated everyone in her effort to finally achieve completion. Jack found it hard to believe that any of these people, save his father and the Lord of the Faerie, were really "glad" to have him back. They might need him—almost everyone save Jack himself, who remained noncommittal on the subject, needed Jack if they wanted any chance of destroying the Troy Game, which most had come to see as evil incarnate—but Jack did not believe for an instant they were happy to have him here.

"We need you, Jack," Silvius said softly, still holding on to Jack's shoulders.

Ah, that's better. Yes, you all need me, but I doubt all of you are "glad" at my return.

"You're a cynical laddie," Silvius said, finally letting his son go and bending down to grab Jack's holdall. "God knows where you picked that up."

Jack grinned again, his humor restored, and stubbed out his cigarette under his shoe. "And you, father? What is this form you step out in? Do I detect an *Italian* accent in your voice?"

Silvius nodded toward the concourse, and they started to walk toward the gate at the end of the platform. "Mr. Silvius Makris, esquire, at your service," he said. "And a vaguely Mediterranean birth, if you please, not Italian. Not in this milieu in which we live."

"And what does Mr. Silvius Makris do in this modern world, eh?"

Silvius grinned again. "He mixes with the best crowd, don't you know, flaunting vague hints of an industrial fortune at his back, and buying the jolly crowd at the dance halls and nightclubs as many cocktails as they can manage before management has to drag them out by their coattails and mink stoles."

"A somewhat jolly but shallow existence, Silvius?"

"Beats the hell out of living trapped in the heart of the labyrinth, sonny."

That silenced Jack, and dampened the mood between them, as little else could have done. He and his father may have reconciled, but Jack still felt deep pangs of guilt at the way he'd trapped his father in the labyrinth.

"I'm sorry, Jack," Silvius said as they walked through the gate—Jack handing the ticket inspector his ticket as they passed. "I could have said that a little more diplomatically."

"You had every right to say it any way you wanted, Silvius."

"Ah, Jack, we shouldn't have to spend the rest of our lives apologizing. In our time I've been a pitiful father and you've been a lousy son. We'll just have to live with it." They'd reached the revolving doors leading out from the station into the street. "Now, what say you we step out into London and see what the night has to offer, eh?"

AS HE HAD IN HIS DREAM, JACK PAUSED ONCE they stood on the pavement outside. There was a fair amount of traffic on the road—mostly lorries and taxicabs—but few pedestrians.

Most people would be home, glued to the wireless, waiting on news from Europe.

Or Downing Street.

And, as he had in his dream, Jack looked northward. It was difficult from this angle, but he thought he could make out the dome of St. Paul's across the Thames.

He shivered again, and cursed silently the fact he'd agreed to come home.

"The car's this way, Jack," said Silvius, nodding to a point farther along the road.

"You're driving?"

Silvius grinned. "Yes. Normally Harry would have given me a driver—God knows he's surrounded with enough lackies at Faerie Hill Manor—but I thought that for tonight we might like to talk. Catch you up on the news, so to speak."

They'd been walking along the pavement toward Silvius' car, but now Jack stopped again. "Harry?"

Silvius shifted the weight of Jack's holdall into his other hand. "Brigadier—retired—Sir Harold Cole." His grin spread a bit wider as he waited for his son's reaction.

Jack suddenly realized who Silvius meant, and gave a short nod of understanding. Coel, reborn as Harold, king of England, reborn as Charles II—the Lord of the Faerie. Harold Cole now, in this mortal world. Jack hadn't realized as the only times he'd met with the man was when he walked in his Faerie form.

"When he's in this mortal land of toil the Lord of the Faerie walks as Harry Cole," Silvius said as they resumed walking. "He lives as a sort of . . . oh, a sort of a 'boffin' up at Faerie Hill Manor in Epping Forest. No one—beyond those of us who have known him for the past few thousand years, of course—really knows what he does, but he is trusted within the highest echelons of both government and military, and is consulted by both on matters of intelligence and defense. He's a close friend of the king."

Silvius slid a look Jack's way. "You know . . ."

"That John Thornton has been reborn as George VI? Yes, I knew that." Jack gave a short laugh. "We've been handing that pretty title about our group fairly evenly, I think."

"Very democratically," Silvius agreed. Then he stopped by a huge black saloon car. "Here we are, then."

He stowed Jack's holdall in the trunk, nodding Jack to get in the passenger side.

When he was behind the wheel, Silvius took a moment to draw on his leather gloves again. "It's been bad without you, Jack," he said, looking ahead at the road rather than at

his son. "None of us know what we can do against the Troy—"

"I don't want to talk about that now," Jack said quietly, his own eyes fixed ahead. His hand fumbled about in the pocket of his greatcoat and he drew out his cigarettes and matches. "Smoke?"

Silvius shook his head. "Jack—"

"Not now, Silvius, please," Jack said, then struck a match and drew deeply on his cigarette. "Not yet."

Silvius sighed, started up the car, and drove off.

Within moments they were on Blackfriars Bridge, and moments after that Silvius turned the car right up Ludgate Hill.

"Silvius?" Jack straightened in his seat. "Where are we going?"

"To pick someone up," Silvius said. "Another reason neither Harry nor myself wanted a civilian driver tonight."

Jack tensed, his cigarette forgotten in his hand. They were driving directly toward St. Paul's Cathedral.

Chapter Two

LONDON

Saturday, 2 September 1939

SILVIUS PULLED THE CAR TO A STOP HALF ON the pavement, half on the road, just outside the quire at the eastern end of St. Paul's Cathedral. Jack didn't believe this was quite legal, but the last thing he wanted to do right now was argue parking etiquette with his father. His heart was thumping and his breath felt tight in his chest.

He wasn't sure he wanted to get this close, this quickly.

"What are we doing here, Silvius?" His cigarette suddenly burned at his fingers, and Jack gave an exclamation and stubbed it out in the car's ashtray.

Silvius glanced at his son. "I told you. We're here to pick someone up. Who do you think, Jack?"

Catling? No, not her. Neither Silvius nor anyone associated with him or the Lord of the Faerie would want Catling. The land, personified by the Faerie, loathed the Troy Game, believing it more likely to destroy the land than protect it.

Jack glared at his father, then wrenched open the car door and climbed out, slamming the door behind him.

Silvius had the sense to stay where he was.

Jack looked over the roof of the car toward where Cheapside branched off to run eastward toward the Tower. Traffic was heavy around St. Paul's, both vehicular and pedestrian, and Jack wondered that no one complained about Silvius' big saloon parked partway on the pavement.

But both people and cars flowed around the car without a second glance, and Jack supposed Silvius must be using a little of the Faerie to smooth out whatever blockage he caused to traffic.

Jack took a deep breath, and turned about.

St. Paul's loomed above him. God, it was massive. He'd seen photos of Wren's masterpiece, but nothing prepared him for the sheer enormity of the structure.

Cornelia's stone hall. This was it. The last battlefield. Finally.

Jack thrust his hands inside the deep pockets of his greatcoat, then clenched them. He thought of all the times he had met Cornelia—and then later, Caela, as she had been reborn, and now Noah—inside her visionary stone hall. All that rancor and bitterness and misunderstanding they had shared within it. The vision of her lying with Asterion, and his murdering her.

Well, Asterion had torn her to pieces, but he hadn't quite murdered Noah, had he?

And she still loved him? After all the agony he'd put her through?

Jack fought down the anger which, after so many hun-

dreds of years, still threatened to overwhelm him. Did *he* still love and want her? He didn't know.

He was terrified of meeting her.

A movement caught his eye. There were a score of people moving through St. Paul's churchyard at that particular moment, all bustling either from or into the cathedral, or taking a shortcut through the gardens, but this one movement grabbed at Jack's attention.

A man, still disguised by the gloom. Coming slowly toward Jack and the car.

Moving slowly, dragging a leg.

Jack let his breath out on a ragged sigh. *Walter Herne. Loth reborn.*

Walter had walked under the low light of a nearby lamp now, and Jack could see him clearly. A short and neat man, fair-haired with a chubby-cheeked face. He was in what Jack called "civvies": a faded Fair Isle hand-knitted pullover over a white shirt, topped with a tweed jacket. Somewhat threadbare trousers. A dog collar. He was using a walking stick, putting his left foot gingerly to the ground.

"Not permanently crippled, Jack," Walter said as he came close, and held out a hand. "Fell off the damn bicycle on the weekend and sprained my ankle. Be right as rain in a couple of days."

Jack hesitated, then took Walter's hand. "You preach *here?*" He flicked a glance at the cathedral.

Walter stared at him a long moment, a small amused smile on his face. "I'm not that brave, Jack. I've just been spending the afternoon in the cathedral library. I don't have a regular parish. Just fill in when and where needed. Now . . . well, at the moment I appear to be on sick leave. I'm sure I'll find enough to keep me busy, what with the war and all."

What war are you referring to, Walter? "And are you sure you want to participate in *this* war?" Jack asked, nodding at the cathedral.

Three hundred years ago, as James, Duke of York, Walter had done everything he could to deny his ancient past and heritage, including acquiring a fantastical devotion to

Christianity—a total contradiction to his life as a powerful pagan priest when he'd lived as Loth. Jack didn't hold out much hope Walter had improved in this life, not from the evidence of that dog collar, but why else would he be in this car tonight?

"I am sick to death of it, Jack," Walter said, all humor draining from his face. "I want it to end so that I might be at peace."

"Amen to that," said Silvius, who had opened his door and was now standing looking over the roof of the car toward Jack and Walter. "Now, unless you want to do some sightseeing, Jack, would you two like to get inside so that we can hasten with all possible speed toward that nice reception I know awaits us?"

That last earned him yet another cynical glance from Jack, but both he and Walter moved toward the car. Walter opened the back door and got inside, stretching his bad leg along the bench seat, but just before Jack slid down into his front seat he stopped, and looked skyward.

For a moment he thought he saw something hanging in the sky, almost a . . . shadow. He frowned, trying to concentrate. Whatever it was, it made his Kingman blood tingle, as if he were being summoned. Without thinking, Jack half raised his hand, as if to snatch at the shadow.

And then it was gone, and Jack thought it must just have been a shadow only of his nerves, and nothing more.

"Jack?" Silvius said, and Jack gave a tiny shake of his head and slid down into the car seat, closing the door after him.

A moment later Silvius pulled out into Aldersgate and headed north, turning in a more easterly direction once he was past London wall.

AS THE CAR VANISHED AROUND A CORNER, TWO dark figures stepped out from the shadow of St. Paul's southern face. Dressed almost identically in belted overcoats and with broad-brimmed felt hats pulled low over their foreheads, the men stared for a moment after the car, then both looked upward.

One of the men hissed in an excited breath. "D'you see? D'you see?" he said, one hand clutching at the other man's shoulder.

"Aye," said the other softly. "It's alive."

"Our mistress has done well."

"*He's* back. She said it would appear when *he* came back. When *he* and *she* were together in London."

His brother giggled. "It's a pretty thing, isn't it? A pretty dancing."

"Shush!" the other hissed. "Careful what you say!"

They fell into silence, now looking furtively about the streets, their shoulders hunched, hands thrust into the deep pockets of their overcoats.

"It'll want to feed, then," said one, eventually.

The other took his time in replying, but when he did his voice was rigid with excitement. "It'll want to feed *tonight!*"

Simultaneously both men grinned, their teeth sharply white.

Then they were gone, and the streets of London were suddenly far more dangerous than they'd been a moment earlier.

THEY'D BEEN DRIVING IN SILENCE FOR MORE THAN fifteen minutes, slowly wending their way through the eastern and northern suburbs of London, when Silvius finally broke the silence.

"You know where we're going," he said quietly.

Jack took a moment to respond. "Yeah. Epping Forest." He lit a cigarette, using it as an excuse to pause. "And Faerie Hill Manor. I've been dreaming of it for months now."

And of who will be there to meet me.

"You'll find the forest somewhat depleted since last you were there," said Walter from the backseat.

Jack pulled heavily on the cigarette. "I know." Epping Forest was one of the very few remaining stands of what had once been a great forest that had stretched for hundreds of square miles above northeastern London. When he had been Brutus, almost four thousand years ago, the great primeval forest had connected with all the other forests of

the island. Even when he'd walked under its branches as Louis de Silva (and then as Ringwalker), Epping Forest had still been extensive.

Now most of the forest was gone, murdered by urban sprawl and hungry tractors, and all that was left of the dappled, moody shadows where the Stag God had once roamed was this pitiful remnant. Eight or nine minutes in a car—providing you didn't stop for a beer at one of the quaint pubs secreted within the trees—was all you'd need to drive straight through it.

"How long has . . . Harry . . . been living in Faerie Hill Manor?" Jack said after a few more minutes of silence. They were well on their way now, traversing the A11 as it proceeded north, and Jack needed the solace of conversation to calm his nerves.

"Permanently, about eight years now," said Silvius. "But he's been using the house for, oh, probably close to ninety years, off and on."

"And no one comments on the fact that Sir Harry appears so long-lived?"

Silvius grinned. "Faerie Hill Manor and its master fade away into the Faerie from time to time, Jack. As do we all. Half of the doors in Faerie Hill Manor open directly into the Faerie, half into bedrooms and closets. It fades away and people forget about it, and then it is back again and it is as if both house and master are new. There are people alive now who live close by the forest who have lived when Faerie Hill Manor has faded back into the Faerie, and then, thirty years later, they have never realized when it reappears once more that they knew it previously. Faerie magic."

Jack opened his window an inch and tossed out the stub of his cigarette. "You're mighty acquainted with the Faerie, it seems."

"It has been a good home to me, Jack." *Better than the dark heart of the labyrinth.*

Jack went very still for a moment, then swiveled about so he could look at Walter Herne in the backseat. "And you, Walter? Are you more comfortable with the Faerie than you were last life?"

"As I said earlier," Walter said quietly, holding Jack's steady gaze, "all I want is to see this through. We finish it this life, Jack. Once and for all."

"And then . . . what? You can be Christ's man, once and for all?" *Don't forget who and what I am, Walter. I'm every-thing your damned Christ doesn't want to know about.*

They stared at each other a long moment, then Walter leaned forward a little and shifted his gaze to focus on something over Jack's shoulder.

"Look," said Walter. "Look."

Jack turned forward, and his stomach clenched. Somehow they'd left suburbia behind, and now approached a round-about with a small congregation of cattle standing half asleep on the central grassy island and blinking in the glare of the car's headlamps. On the right side of the roundabout stood a somewhat ugly tavern—the Robin Hood Inn. Several cottages crowded close by the whitewashed walls of the inn.

Beyond the roundabout and the inn, the A11 ran for per-haps fifty yards before it vanished into trees.

"We're home," whispered Jack, and Silvius glanced sharply at him.

Chapter Three

FAERIE HILL MANOR

Saturday, 2 September 1939

DO YOU KNOW WHERE WE ARE?" SILVIUS asked after they'd been driving through the forest a few minutes. The car's headlamps illuminated a small patch of road ahead and enough of the encircling forest to show the close-crowded trees and the occasional branch that dipped down from nowhere to scrape the top of the car.

Most humans found driving through Epping Forest at night an eerie experience. Jack found it unbelievably painful. He was overwhelmed with nerves (only partly caused by the confrontation he knew lay directly ahead); with guilt (he should have been back so much earlier than this); with an extraordinary excitement (only a few more hours, surely, and then he could walk out the door of Faerie Hill Manor and into *this*); and with such an overwhelming sense of love and companionship that he instantly hated himself for having alienated himself so long from this land and this forest.

This was his home now. He should have remembered that.

He had a cigarette in his hand, just drawn from the pack before they'd passed the Robin Hood Inn, and still unlit. Now it lay unnoticed, crushed and broken between his clenched fingers.

Do you know where we are?

Jack blinked, and his chest jerked in a long, shuddery breath. Epping Forest, yes, but . . .

"We're approaching Great Monk Wood to our right," he said.

"Indeed," said Silvius. "Great Monk Wood is where Harry built Faerie Hill Manor." As he spoke he turned the car right, off the A11, onto a dirt lane that led into the higher ridged ground to the east, and a few minutes after that—long, terrifyingly nervous minutes for Jack—they entered a cleared space at the top of a ridge that sat deep within Great Monk Wood.

Silvius pulled the car to a halt as soon as they'd left the trees, and turned off the engine.

They sat there, all three men, listening as the cooling engine ticked in the night, and stared ahead.

FAERIE HILL MANOR APPEARED AS IT HAD IN THE dreams and visions Jack had experienced over the past months, a sprawling, fanciful nineteenth-century over-the-top Gothic citadel, all turrets and spires and soaring windows set amid the gray stonework. Again, as it had appeared in his dreams, the building sat atop a small grassy

knoll, both house and knoll apart from, and yet integral with, the encircling forest.

It was a cloudy night, and yet the house and knoll were bathed in a faint silvery luminescence.

Golden light shone from every window, and as Jack, Silvius, and Walter watched, the double front doors opened, and two figures walked out.

Jack blinked again, and everything changed.

Faerie Hill Manor and the knoll still shimmered within that unearthly luminescence, but whereas before the grass slopes leading up to the house had been bare, now there were a score of cars and a lorry parked at varying angles to one side of the house.

There came a rap at Jack's window, and he jumped.

A policeman stood there. "Your papers, if you please, sir," he said as Jack rolled down the glass.

Jack sighed, and withdrew a thick sheaf of papers from the breast pocket of his greatcoat, handing them to the policeman, who studied them for a few long moments by the light of a small torch, and then handed them back.

"Very good, major," he said, then he nodded to Walter in the back. "A good evening to you, reverend," and smiled at Silvius. "And to you, Mr. Makris."

"The children well, Tony?" Silvius said.

"Very well, Mr. Makris, thank you for inquiring. You may drive on. Forgive the extra security, but—"

"I know who is here, Tony. A good night to you, then." Silvius started up the car, and drove the fifty or so yards to the graveled drive directly in front of the sweeping steps that led to the front terrace.

As he pulled to a halt, Jack took a deep breath, then opened his door and stood up, looking up the steps to the terrace.

Brigadier Sir Harry Cole and Stella Wentworth stood there.

The Lord of the Faerie and his Faerie Queen, the Caroller.

"Welcome home, Jack," Harry whispered, and it did not surprise Jack in the least that that whisper reached all the way down the steps and into his heart.

Welcome home.

Jack gave a small nod, acknowledging Harry's welcome, then, without waiting for either his father or Walter, took the steps two at a time until he stood before Harry and Stella.

There he paused, just a step away, and studied them.

Harry was much as Jack had remembered him from his dreams. Early fifties, graying fair hair, a face somewhat lined with care, faded blue eyes, and dressed in a combination of military and civilian: khaki trousers, and a military button-down shirt and tie underneath a hand-knitted ribbed pullover.

Stella? Jack looked at her. She was no different from his visions of her, either. Beautiful (far more so than she'd been as Jane, and as much as she'd been as Swanne) with dark wavy hair carefully caught in a clip at the nape of her neck, pale skin, dark eyes, a slim, elegantly clothed figure. Everything about her exuded sophistication.

There was also a faint air of distance and haughtiness about her, but Jack decided it was nothing new. That was Genvissa-reborn all over.

His eyes slid back to Harry, then he smiled and stepped forward, and both men embraced fiercely.

"Have I arrived back into a maelstrom?" Jack asked softly as he finally stepped back.

Harry gave a small, humorless smile. "When have you not, Jack?"

"Stella." Jack gave her a small nod. It wasn't much when considering their past—lovers, enemies, allies—but Stella didn't look approachable enough for a hug, nor even a quick peck on the cheek.

Her eyes crinkled in amusement, and Jack instantly regretted his initial assessment of her.

"A singularly low-key entrance for you, Jack," she said. "Where the invasion fleet? Where the pageantry, the triumphal entrance into London?"

"Burned in the ashes of all our ambitions," Jack said, but he said it with an answering glint of humor in his own eyes, and was rewarded with a small smile from Stella.

"There are people waiting for you inside," she said as Silvius and Walter joined them on the terrace, and when

Jack took a deep breath at her words, no one could mistake the nerves behind it.

"Let us inside, then," Jack said, taking his cap off and sliding it under his left arm, and with that, Harry beckoning Stella before them, they walked through the magnificent cedar and cut-glass doors into the entrance hall of Faerie Hill Manor.

A man walked down the sweeping staircase to meet them.

Jack stepped forward and shook the man's hand with a slight bow of his head.

"Your majesty," he said.

George VI gave a small smile. "I think we can dispense with the formalities, Jack. But, by God, I am glad you are here. I cannot stay much longer, a few minutes only, and I had feared to have missed you."

Jack nodded. That the king was here at all to greet him was amazing, considering that Britain stood on the brink of war. "Are you a happy man, John Thornton?" he asked softly, finally letting the king's hand go. "When last we met we were both somewhat upset."

Images of the Broken Bough, a tavern on the Strand in seventeenth-century London, filled both men's minds. They'd met there the night Noah had gone to Asterion. Jack, as Louis, had been distraught at losing Noah to the horror of Asterion; Thornton had been despondent at knowing she would never love him. Two men, both desperate for a love they'd both lost.

"Careworn at the present," George VI replied, "for these are difficult times, but I am loved, and love, and I never had thought to find that. So, yes, I am a happy and most contented man."

There were steps behind the king on the staircase, and Jack looked up. Several men were running lightly down the stairs—two military attachés, a policeman, and a well-dressed man with a decidedly aristocratic air.

The aristocrat glanced at Jack, dismissed him in that glance, and spoke to George VI. "Your majesty, we must leave. Mr. Chamberlain has requested that he meet with you tonight, and we face a good drive back to the palace."

"Ah, yes, the Prime Minister." George VI's face suddenly looked even more careworn and tired than it had a moment earlier. He reached forward, and put a hand on Jack's shoulder. "Finish it this time, Jack. *Finish it.*"

And then he was gone, surrounded and hurried by his entourage, and a moment later Jack heard car doors slam outside and the sound of engines starting up.

"So now we have the house to ourselves," said Stella.

"There's no one else here?" Jack said, turning to look at her. *Noah wasn't here?* He didn't know whether to feel an overwhelming sense of relief, or a gut-wrenching vast disappointment.

"Oh yes," Stella said, "there are others here. Noah, too. But they're all 'ours,' if you know what I mean. George's entourage were outsiders."

"Come this way, Jack," Harry said, and he led the group to double doors to the right of the entrance hall. He opened one of them, and gestured Jack inside.

Jack walked through into the large paneled drawing room, then halted, transfixed by what he saw against the far wall, even though he should have expected it.

Weyland Orr, Asterion-reborn, standing by a wingback chair set by a great fireplace in which flickered a small fire. He looked just as he had when Jack had last seen him in the seventeenth century, fair hair slicked back over a strong handsome face, but clothed now in a modern suave man-about-town style.

To one side of him, and slightly distanced from the chair, stood Noah, also wearing the same face that Jack remembered. She stared at Jack with clearly recognizable tension, her beautiful features strained and pale. She was dressed as elegantly as Stella in a well-cut suit of pale green with matching high-heeled pumps, her dark hair carefully waved and set into a bun at the back of her neck.

Jack realized he was staring, and tore his eyes away from Noah to the chair by which Weyland stood.

A girl, perhaps seventeen or eighteen, sat there. As Jack looked, the girl turned her face toward him, then as quickly looked away again.

Her face was tear-stained and contorted in agony. Some part of Jack's brain registered that she was lovely, and that she reminded him of Cornelia when first he'd seen her, but his eyes were drawn immediately to her hands and wrists.

They were held out before her as if tied, and to Jack's startled gaze it appeared as if they had been bound with red-hot wire.

"This is Grace," said Harry quietly, "and we love her dearly, even though she is our doom."

Chapter Four

FAERIE HILL MANOR

Saturday, 2 September 1939

*J*ACK HAD BEEN LOOKING AT GRACE AS HARRY spoke, but within the instant he was staring back at Harry. He couldn't believe Harry had actually said that! Did he introduce Grace in that manner to everyone? *Meet Grace, why don't you? She's such a sweet girl, but, oh, she's our doom.*

"Jack?"

It was Noah, and Jack forced himself to look back at her. Jesus Christ, it was even more painful than he'd thought, to see her standing there with Weyland.

"Jack," she said. "Welcome home. It's good to see you."

Jack wondered if the atmosphere could possibly get any more strained . . . or more surreal. Here was Noah trying to carry on social conversation while not two paces away her daughter suffered horribly.

He looked back at Grace, appalled by her suffering, and by everyone else's apparent disinterest, and Weyland spoke.

"Do you know about . . . ?" Weyland gestured down to Grace's wrists.

"Yes." Jack had heard from the Lord of the Faerie how Catling—the Troy Game incarnate—had cursed Grace. These terrible fiery bracelets bound Grace to Catling. Whatever was done to Catling (to the Troy Game), would be done to Grace. Complete the Troy Game, and Grace would live (although she, as everyone else, would be under the Game's total dominion). Destroy the Game, and Grace—as well everything Grace had touched, the Faerie, London, Weyland's Idyll, everyone who had ever held her, or cared for her—would be destroyed as well.

An impossible and terrible situation, and one that no one—not Noah, not Weyland, not the Lord of the Faerie and all the might of the Faerie—could do anything to fix.

"This is Catling's welcome to you, Jack," said Grace, and Jack's eyes jerked back to her face, surprised that she had managed to speak through her pain.

"Grace . . ." Noah said. She took a half step toward her daughter, and then stopped.

There was a tension there, and Jack wondered at it. Suddenly tired of all this standing about, Jack shrugged off his greatcoat, tossed it and his cap on a nearby chair, and walked over to Grace's chair.

God, he could smell Noah's perfume from here, could feel her warmth, could feel her every breath. . . .

He sank down to his haunches before the girl, concentrating on her, trying to set his awareness of Noah to one side.

She still had her face partly averted toward her father, but Jack could see her now far more clearly. His initial impression that she looked like Cornelia was wrong. Her dark hair—worn in a cap of short, loose curls—was her mother's, as were her dark blue eyes and pale skin, but her strong, angular bone structure, and the very look of her face, was all Weyland. Now that he was closer, Jack could see that although she wore the form of a young girl teetering on the brink of womanhood, faint lines about her eyes and mouth bespoke years (*hundreds of years*) of torment.

He looked at her wrists, and had to use all the self-

control he'd learned over all his lives not to flinch back in horror.

Glowing red lines cut so deep into her wrists that, as they writhed and twisted back and forth, Jack could see glimpses of bone. Intuitively he understood that Grace felt every particle of pain that such injury caused, but that once the fiery bracelets faded, her wrists would be left with nothing but faint scars.

Catling's intent was to cause agony, and to do it in such a manner that she could revisit the agony time after time.

"Grace . . ." he said, unable for the moment to come to grips with the enormity of Catling's cruelty.

She finally turned her face directly to him. "Don't pity me," she said. "Please."

"I am not pitying you," Jack said, holding the girl's eyes. "I am admiring you. Tell me, is there anything I can do to help?"

"Oh, Jack," Noah said, and there was a world of hurt and need and pain in those two short words.

"It's all we want of you, Jack," Weyland said. "To damn well help her."

Jack wondered what it must have cost Weyland to have to ask him for help. He flicked a glance at Weyland, but as quickly returned his eyes to Grace.

"No one can help," Grace ground out.

"Is it like this always?" Jack said, making a small gesture to her wrists.

"No," Weyland replied. "Catling can leave her alone for weeks and months on end. Then, when Catling needs to make a point, remind us all of her power, she . . ." He couldn't finish.

Jack didn't need Weyland to finish in order to understand. Catling was using Grace to punish everyone who she thought stood in the way of her completion. She would tease, making people think that perhaps she'd relented, and then, just as everyone was crawling back toward a state resembling happiness, Grace would again be dragged into such torment that peace of mind and contentment flew out the door.

He realized that his initial impression of disinterest in Grace was very wrong. *Everyone* here was tormented by Grace's agony.

"I am very sorry that my arrival has caused this," Jack said to Grace. He reached out a hand, thinking to lay it on one of her upper arms, but she flinched away from him, and so Jack let his hand drop back to his side.

He stood up. "When the fire has faded," he said to Noah and Weyland, "then I'll examine Catling's hex. Maybe I can help, maybe not, but it won't hurt to look."

Noah's face relaxed in relief. "Thank you, Jack."

There was another one of those tense, awkward silences. Jack wanted to look away from Noah, but couldn't, and hated that weakness. He knew Weyland was staring at him, *everyone* was staring at him, but he just couldn't tear his eyes away from Noah.

In her turn, Noah was regarding him with unusual intensity. He could see words forming in her mind, and then being discarded as useless for the occasion.

"Why," Jack said very softly, "have we always found it so damned hard to talk to each other, Noah?"

Noah's dark blue eyes went absolutely brilliant with emotion, but before she could speak there was a clink of glass behind him. Immensely relieved at the distraction, Jack turned about. Silvius had poured out several glasses of whisky. He handed one to Jack, offered one to Noah, who refused, then gave a glass to Weyland before turning back to a side table and picking up another for himself.

Harry, Stella, and Walter already had glasses.

"To your return, Jack," Silvius said, and raised his glass.

Weyland grunted, set his glass aside, and turned away.

Jack downed his whisky in a single draught. "It's no cause for celebration," he said. Suddenly all he wanted to do was to get away from this room, and all the tension it contained. "Look, it's late, and I—"

"We need to know where you stand," Stella said. "George was right. We need to finish this now. Soon. No one"—she glanced at Grace as she said this—"can survive another hundred or so years of this agony of indecision and

reprisal by the Troy Game. It is destroying us all, piece by piece. So tell us, Jack, where *do* you stand? Are you going to complete the Troy Game and condemn us all to hell? Or will you destroy it, and destroy us as well?"

"Stella," Jack said, "I walked away all those hundreds of years ago because Noah destroyed the very ground on which I walked."

Out of the corner of his eye Jack saw Noah wince, but he didn't care. He was too tired to hide behind diplomacy.

"She shifted everything when she chose to take Weyland as her lover," Jack continued, "give him a child, and decide she didn't want to like the Troy Game after all. I don't know where I am, or who I want to be. I don't *know* where I stand, and I don't know what choices are open to me, damn it!"

"Stella," Harry said, walking over to Jack, taking his glass and then putting both of their glasses on the tray on the side table, "Jack is tired. He has only just arrived back, and he needs to rest and find his balance. Then, eventually, we will all need to decide what to do. It is up to not a single one among us, but *all* of us, to find a way out of the disaster that threatens. Jack, what do you want to do tonight? You can have a room here, or . . ."

Thank God, Jack thought, that Harry had so adroitly salvaged this conversation. "Did you manage to obtain the lease I sent word to you about?"

Harry smiled, just slightly, the movement enough to crinkle the skin about his eyes. "Yes. Copt Hall is yours."

Jack nodded, and would have said something, but Walter exclaimed first.

"Copt Hall? But that is a ruin!"

Harry's smile broadened a little, and he walked over to a desk and opened a drawer. He drew out a vellum indenture, rolled up and bound with a soft pink light, and handed it to Jack.

"The lease agreement is between yourself and the Faerie," he said. "It has no binding on the hall as it stands within this mortal realm, but only how it stands within the Faerie. It was a good choice, Jack, and I was pleased to execute the arrangements for you."

"Thank you," Jack said as he took the indenture and slid it inside one of the pockets of his greatcoat, which he had just picked up.

He stood a moment, looking about the room, meeting the eyes of everyone there (save Grace, who still had her face averted). "I don't know what I am going to do," Jack said softly. "I don't know where to go and to whom to turn. I don't know what awaits any of us. All I know"—he stepped back a pace—"is that I need some solace, and I have no idea where I can ever find it."

With that, he walked over to the door leading to the terrace and let himself out.

"JACK! WAIT!"

Jack stopped just as he'd been about to walk down the steps leading to the lawn. He turned around.

Harry was hurrying toward him.

"Jack, we need to talk about—"

"For God's sake, Harry, I'm as tired as hell. Can't it wait?"

"I'm sorry. We can leave it until tomorrow, but I thought that as Walter will be leaving after breakfast, and we'd need to talk to him before then, I'd—"

"Okay. Okay. Let's talk now then, if you insist."

"Jack, you still need to take one more step to assume your full powers as Ringwalker—you need to be marked. Damn it, the forests—the *land*—needs you. Don't snarl about it."

All Jack wanted to do was to fall into bed and sleep, and hope that tomorrow would be a better day. But no, here was Harry fretting at him. Still, that gave Jack a chance to voice something that had been worrying him.

"Harry," he said, "I understand this needs to be done, but I also have concerns about it."

"In what way?"

Jack managed to keep the stunned surprise off his face. *In what way?* Coel had been indeed completely subsumed by the Lord of the Faerie if he needed to ask that. "I like who I am, Harry. I don't particularly want to become a

bloody deer full time." Jack had assumed the role of Stag God—the God who watched over the forests and who was closely associated with the health of the land—from Og, a magnificent white deer with bloodred antlers.

Harry burst out laughing, and Jack imagined he could hear the faint rumble of conversation within the drawing room stop at the sound.

"You can be who you like," Harry said. "Og *was* a deer to begin with, so that is the form he assumed as God of the forests. You can keep your far prettier form, if you want."

Now it was Jack who gave the wry smile. "Am I the first man to hold the job?"

"Actually, you are. The forests shall have to get used to the idea. Jack, I hadn't realized you were worried about it."

Jack gave a slight shrug. "Do you think Walter will be willing to help in the marking?"

"Walter will do whatever he needs to in order to escape his past. Is there a place you have in mind?"

Jack thought of the times he had roamed Epping Forest when he'd lived as Louis. "Yes," he said. "Ambersbury Banks."

Harry nodded. "It is a good site, if a little stained by blood. This needs to be done fairly soon, Jack."

He'd been such good friends with this man, Jack thought, Brothers, almost. But now he realized that much of that friendship had vanished. Coel—Harry—was now far more the Lord of the Faerie than anything else.

Jack felt a great sadness overwhelm him. "I'll speak to Walter about it."

Harry nodded. "Good." He put a hand on Jack's shoulder briefly. "Sleep well in your new home, Jack. Oh, and Jack? Join us for breakfast in the morning. The table is laid from eight."

At that he turned, and went back into the house.

INSIDE THE DRAWING ROOM, NOAH CAREFULLY avoided everyone's eyes as she walked over to the drinks table, poured herself a whisky, and drank it straight down.

Just then, as they heard Harry's steps coming over the terrace toward the door, and Jack's steps retreating down the steps toward the lawn, Grace gave a gasp of sheer relief.

The fiery bracelets had vanished with Jack.

Catling's little lesson for the night had ended.

Chapter Five

COPT HALL AND FAERIE HILL MANOR

Sunday, 3 September 1939

COPT HALL STOOD SILENT AND BROKEN IN the still, frosted night. The great wrought-iron gates hung slightly askance, and while the lawn before the hall appeared to be neatly trimmed, the blades of grass had been cropped by the hungry mouths of rabbits, not the scythes of tending gardeners.

A hall had stood on this site at the northwestern edge of St. Thomas' Quarter of Epping Forest for almost eight hundred years. Kings and queens had either banqueted or hidden here. Families had been raised within its walls, and families condemned within them. A community had thrived, their babies welcomed and their weary funeraled.

Now there was little left but a shell. Four-story walls reared into the night sky, a shifting mass of purples and silvers and grays in the faint moonlight.

The walls had no roof, nor glass to fill their gaping windows. Staircases wound upward into nothingness, fireplaces sat in walls with great chasms plunging just beyond their hearths. Mice nested in the drains, and foxes in the cellars.

Smudges of soot, left over from a disastrous Sunday morning fire in 1917, still besmirched the turrets.

Once, long, long ago, Copt Hall had lived.

Now it was a broken shell.

Once, deer had trodden softly through the gardens.

Now deer gathered again. One or two at first, moving nervously across the still-graveled but weed-pocked drive. Then two or three more, emerging from the shadows of derelict outhouses. Then a dozen, trotting apprehensively forward from the overgrown Italianate garden at the rear of the hall.

The night grew even more still than it had been, and the ears of the deer twitched as they stared at the iron gates.

Then as one they started, and wheeled away to their right, away from the hall and toward the forest.

At its edge they stopped again, and stared once more to the gates.

A man stood there. He was dressed in a greatcoat with a military cap pulled down low over his brow. In his hand he held a holdall.

He stared at the hall, then took off his cap so that his face became clear in the moonlight.

The deer, still as one, let out a great sigh.

"WELL," SAID STELLA, SITTING HERSELF DOWN IN A chair and crossing her elegant legs. She'd lit a cigarette and was looking at the others, smoke drifting lazily about her face. "I think that all went rather well."

"For God's sake, Stella," Noah said. "It was awful."

"Well, for you maybe," said Stella. "But then he and I didn't part on such bad terms in the last life as you and he. What did you think, Grace? Brutus returned. You're the only one here who hasn't met him."

Grace now had her legs curled under her in the chair, and she gave a disinterested shrug at Stella's question.

"Are you tired, darling?" Noah said. "Do you want to go to bed?"

"Oh, Noah," Stella said, "she's not a child!"

Noah flushed, and might have said something, save that Weyland shot her a cautionary look. He poured Grace an inch of whisky and handed her the glass without a word, ran

his fingers lightly through his daughter's loose curls, then went and sat on the sofa, accepting a cigarette from Stella.

"He's angry," Weyland said, then drew deeply on the cigarette.

"He's only just arrived back," said Silvius. He was now leaning on the mantelpiece over the hearth. "What did you expect? That he'd walk in here, grin easily, and say, 'All is forgiven and I'm your man'?"

"*I* think," said Harry, "that we should be damned glad he's back at all. Noah, with all respect for your reasons, you tore his world apart in 1666. Frankly, for decades I was worried he'd just abandoned us so completely that we'd never see him again."

There was strain in his voice, and for a long moment no one else spoke. For a long while, no one had expected him back.

"If he can't help Grace," Weyland said very quietly, "then I for one shall wish he *had* never returned."

JACK SKELTON WALKED SLOWLY TOWARD THE front door. Rather, he walked toward the gaping hole that had once held the door. He'd known about this hall from when he'd been Louis de Silva, transforming into Ringwalker, and running the forest paths. Epping Forest itself was the remnant—the heart—of the great forests that had once covered this land, and Copt Hall itself had been built on a patch of ground where the barriers between the world of the mortal and the world of the Faerie were so thin as to be almost nonexistent.

It was likely the reason a hall had existed on this site for eight hundred years. It served as a gatehouse between worlds, although the majority of the mortal inhabitants of the hall probably had no idea of what came and went through door and window, and what wafted through its spaces.

Jack's pace slowed even further as he came closer to the door. He didn't know why it had burned—what had caused the fire, or what purpose the destruction had served. The

owners had retired to London and had never rebuilt, although they had talked about it off and on for years. There was a small staff still living in the undamaged wing of the hall who managed the vegetable gardens, sending the food down to the owner's London townhouse.

Jack doubted he'd ever come across them. He had the Faerie lease, not the mortal lease, and would be using this home within its Faerie aspect, not its mortal. He could come and go amid the laboring gardeners, and they would never see him, nor know of his passing.

Save, perhaps, for the occasional shiver, and a glance over a shoulder.

A step away from the door the barren stone arch shimmered, and Jack's feet scrunched in the gravel as he halted. The stonework shimmered again, and now Jack found himself before a whole and complete entrance, the massive wooden barred door in place, a soft light glowing from a lamp to one side of the entry overhang.

The door opened—something Jack had definitely not been expecting—to reveal a man standing inside.

He was tall and well built, with graying brown hair slicked back from his brow. His face was peculiarly mild, as if he practiced exhibiting no emotion save blandness. Although he was dressed in a smart jacket and trousers, and with a beautifully knotted tie over his shirt, the man nonetheless projected an aura of servility.

Dear God, thought Jack, *don't tell me the lease comes with a butler.*

"Good evening, sir," said the man. "I presume you are Major Skelton?"

Jack gave a nod.

"And you have the lease with you?"

Jack drew forth the lease from the pocket of his greatcoat. He made to hand it to the man, but as soon as he'd laid sight of the rolled indenture tied with the pink light, the man waved his hand in satisfaction, and Jack pocketed the lease again.

The man now drew the door wide open and stepped back in a gesture of invitation. "My name's Malcolm, sir. I

watch over Copt Hall and welcome friends as they visit."
There was flicker of amusement in his eyes. "And I do indeed come with the lease." He paused. "You might say that I come with the land."

At that he smiled, and Jack saw that his teeth were stained very slightly with blue.

Jack relaxed. Malcolm was a Sidlesaghe, one of the most ancient creatures of the land. Normally they existed as the standing stones in the various circles, or Dances, about Britain, but over the past thousand years the Sidlesaghes had increasingly taken living form as they aided the effort to repel the Troy Game.

"I also valet, sir. Whatever you desire in this house, then ask."

"Thank you, Malcolm. I appreciate both the welcome and the offer." Jack stepped through the door, and Malcolm both closed the door and took Jack's holdall in one smooth move.

"It is late, sir. Perhaps if I took you direct to your bedchamber?"

"Thank you, Malcolm."

They stepped through into what had once been the main part of the house. There was little left but stark, soot-stained walls open to the night air.

Then Malcolm moved a hand, and the empty space shimmered, and Jack found himself looking at a comfortable drawing room, a fire crackling cheerily in the hearth, with sofas and wingback chairs drawn up about.

A decanter and glasses were set out on a lamp table close to the fire.

Malcolm saw Jack looking at the chair and fire. "Are you sure you wouldn't like a nightcap before settling, sir?"

Jack shook his head. "Another night, Malcolm. Bed for now, I think."

Malcolm led him on toward the ruins of a once fine staircase that, again at a movement from Malcolm's hand, shimmered back into their original glory.

At the top of the stairs Malcolm led Jack to an elegant bedroom. A full canopied bed, curtained with thick red drapes (now drawn back and tied against the bedposts),

stood to one side of a blazing fire, while a fat armchair sat on the other side of the hearth.

A dressing table, replete with silver-backed brushes and combs and a jug and basin, stood against another wall with a doorway leading into a dressing room and bathroom.

Malcolm set the holdall down by the bed, and folded back the bedcovers. "May I fetch some cocoa?" he said as he pulled the sheets tight.

"If you will, Malcolm."

Malcolm dipped his head, and left.

Jack wandered over to the bed and sat down. God, he felt weary. It wasn't the journey at fault, but the strain of the meeting in the drawing room of Faerie Hill Manor. All that tenseness, all that expectation, all their damned, damned history of conflict and love and disappointment swirling all about them.

And Grace.

Jack thought that she epitomized all that conflict and love and disappointment and all the mistakes they had made throughout so many lives. She was a lovely young girl, and should have been carefree and happy.

But what was she instead? A shell of a girl, wracked with agony, because of the blunders and screwups of others. Or was she their fate made flesh? Was she everything that had ever gone wrong turned into breath and blood?

Jack rubbed his eyes. *Grace. Our doom.*

He didn't know what to do. Why had he come back? *What did they want of him?*

What did *he* want?

It was such a mess. A morass of stupidity. What the hell was he doing here? What could he do? *What could he do?*

"Sir?"

Jack jumped, and looked to where Malcolm stood in the doorway, a cup of steaming cocoa in his hands.

"Sir, I am sorry, but there is a visitor at the front door. I—"

Jack felt his stomach drop away with dread. He knew who it was.

"Set out a chair for her by the fire below," he said. "I will be with her shortly."

Malcolm set the cocoa down on the table by the chair, and left.

Jack sat a moment, then stood, wandering over to look down at the cocoa.

"Fuck it," he whispered, and walked toward the stairs.

SHE WAS STANDING BEFORE THE FIRE, HER hands held out as if for warmth. She'd heard him approach, he knew it, and she must have sensed it the moment he started down the stairs, he knew that as well, but now she turned about as if caught unawares, an expression of pleasant surprise on her face as if his step had startled her.

The expression faltered and died within the moment at the sight of his face.

Jack felt a little sick. She was so lovely, and he hated it that he yearned for her now as strongly as he had three hundred years ago.

"I'm sorry, Jack," Noah said. "What happened at Faerie Hill Manor wasn't particularly pleasant. We were all too tense."

"What have you told Weyland? That you were stepping out to admire the stars?"

"I told him I wanted to talk with you alone," she said quietly.

"Ah. Then I suppose Weyland is lurking at the windows to make sure I don't throw myself at you."

"Jack," she said. "Don't."

He walked past her to pour himself a glass of whatever the decanter held. He didn't want anything to drink, but he desperately needed something to do with his hands. Malcolm had set out another glass, and he held the decanter over it, raising his eyebrows to Noah.

She shook her head. "Jack—"

"But it is good whisky," Jack said. "Are you sure you won't have—"

"Jack—"

"Shit," he said. He put the decanter to one side, stepped forward, and took Noah's face in his hands. She started to

pull back, but his hands tightened, and he leaned forward and kissed her with such an intensity that when Noah finally managed to wrench herself free, her face was flushed and her breath rough.

"Have you tired of Weyland, then?" he said. "Have you come to tell me that you've gotten over your foolishness? That you want what we both should have had four thousand years ago?"

"No," she said. "I love Weyland still." *More than ever I loved you.*

"Then what the fuck *are* you doing here, Noah? What do you want?"

"I wanted to welcome you home, Jack. I didn't get a chance at Faerie Hill Manor."

Of course not. She'd been bound and gagged and couldn't get a word in edgewise. So she'd had to come out here in the middle of the night.

He wondered if Weyland should be as sure of her as Noah thought he was.

"Jack, you *are* home. Oh, please, gods, we cannot be at odds like this. Everything is wrong. The land suffers, its people suffer, Catling"—she said the name with such vehement loathing that Jack's face stilled—"looms all over us with such menacing doom that each dawn increases our burden of dread. And we don't know what to do about it. We don't know *how* to stop it, save by destroying the damned Troy Game."

"But you can't, can you?"

"No," she said. "Not without you."

"And even then, *how,* Noah? Shall we destroy your daughter, as well? That should do it . . . but, oh, I forget, if we do Grace to death then we destroy the Faerie, and most of us—although I'm not sure that I'm included in that curse, am I?—and likely London and all of the land as well."

He saw then just how badly Noah suffered. Her beautiful eyes became so agonized, and her lovely face so drawn, that he instantly took one of her hands, and held it as softly as he could.

"I'm sorry," he said.

She pulled her hand from his and dashed away the tears that threatened to spill over. "You have no idea what it has been like, Jack."

"No, but you somehow want me to make it instantly better, don't you? Well, I'm sorry, Noah, I really am, but I don't know how I can do that. I have no bloody idea. When Catling trapped Grace with her hex then she trapped all of us. What the *hell* am I doing back here?"

He walked away, standing staring into the vast interior of the hall, hands on hips. After a long moment he turned back to look at Noah. "What if I said there *is* nothing I can do?"

"I can't accept that, Jack," she said. "I *won't.*"

He sighed, sat in one of the chairs and gestured to another. "Sit down. Tell me about the state of the Troy Game."

"It is unbelievably strong," she said, sitting on the edge of a chair. "You can feel that, surely."

He hesitated, then gave a small nod. He remembered that momentary impression of the shadow hanging over St. Paul's, but thought it more likely a figment of his nerves at that point than of anything else.

"You know what powers I command, Jack," Noah continued. "I am Noah, goddess of the waters. I am also a powerful Mistress of the Labyrinth. *And* I am a Darkwitch. I have three strengths and powers at my command, and I can combine all three of them into something so powerful, so lethal that, if I so choose, I could probably murder the entire world. But I can't murder Catling. I can't murder the Troy Game. It is too cunning for me now. Too deep. Too dark."

"But you are also Eaving, the shelterer," Jack said, calling Noah by her goddess name. "Wouldn't that contraindicate any and all of these murderous ambitions?"

She studied him, then laughed softly, realizing that he was attempting a small jest. "Oh, aye, you are right. My Eaving nature would probably preclude any attempt at my using my Darkwitch and Mistress of the Labyrinth powers to 'murder' anyone. Dear gods, I can't think why Catling hasn't asked me for shelter already!" Because her goddess name meant *shelter*, Noah was forced to shelter and protect

any who asked it of her, no matter what she thought of them, or how she feared them.

Now Jack smiled, and the tension between them relaxed a little. "Tell me," he said, very softly, and Noah didn't need any more words to know exactly what he meant.

"I thought I was being so clever," she said, "burning London. I thought it would stop the Troy Game—Catling—in her tracks for a while, give us enough time to prepare. But Catling had already trapped us."

She stopped, and both remembered that terrible day when Jack, in his form as Ringwalker, had battled with Weyland within the Idyll as Noah watched helplessly on. While they'd been so stupidly, pointlessly engaged, Catling had sent her two dark imps into the Idyll to twist the red wool hex around Grace's wrists, henceforth binding her fate to that of the Troy Game's.

"Afterwards," Noah continued, "when London lay burned and desecrated, and you had left, we did everything we could think of to free Grace. Everything." She paused, and Jack could again see the pain well up inside her. "Nothing worked. Not from any of us, gods or Faerie alike. Jack, it wasn't just that Grace had been so cruelly trapped, it was that Catling then wrapped Grace in agony whenever she felt like it or felt she needed to remind us how badly we were trapped, or whenever she had a particular message to get across. She has made Grace suffer all these years. *All* these years. And in the process . . ." Again she paused, and Jack realized it was to bring her emotions under control. "And in the process I lost my daughter."

That statement startled Jack somewhat, although earlier he'd recognized the tension between Noah and Grace. Surely Grace had lost a great deal more than Noah?

Noah hadn't noticed Jack's reaction. "Grace was never a baby. She was never a child. She has spent her entire life struggling to survive the anguish and the hopelessness. Jack,"—Noah looked over to him with eyes full of emotion—"all I had wanted was a daughter to love. I thought I'd have it with Catling, but look what she truly was. I was *certain* I'd have it with Grace, but then . . ."

"She doesn't like to be mothered, does she?"

Noah made a small gesture of unhappiness. "I fuss too much. All I want to do is to take her in my arms and somehow take some of that hurt into myself, but she hates that."

"She loathes pity."

"I don't know what to do anymore, Jack."

He wasn't sure what she meant those words to apply to, Grace or the wider disaster they were all involved in, then he decided it didn't matter. The statement held true enough for whatever subject.

"Do you think this looming war is Catling's doing?" Jack asked, wanting to change the subject.

"Who knows? Whether Catling is responsible for the war or not, I am sure she will grow in power from it. We are all sure she will use what is coming to force us to her will. Jack, there is a frightful despair winging its way toward us, and none of us know what to do about it."

"I don't have a magical answer for you."

Noah looked down at her hands.

Jack sighed. "I am not Catling's tool, Noah, but I am not yours either. All I know is that I want to be free, of this debacle we have created for ourselves, and of you. But I don't know how to do that."

AT FAERIE HILL MANOR, GRACE STOOD AT THE WINdow of her room and looked toward London.

She went white, and a hand flew to her mouth.

"My God," she whispered. *"What is that?"*

Chapter Six

COPT HALL AND FAERIE HILL MANOR

Sunday, 3 September 1939

S JACK AND NOAH TALKED, MALCOLM cleaned the kitchen and laid the table for breakfast. Just as he set out the plates, he heard a scratching at the door that led outside.

Malcolm's eyes flew to the door leading into the hall, as if he thought to find Jack standing there. Then, reassured that Jack and Noah were still deep in conversation, he opened the door and slipped outside.

Two dark, overcoated figures stood in the shadow of the porch, jittering from foot to foot in excitement.

"Malcolm! Malcolm! Malcolm!"

"Shush!" Malcolm hissed at the imps. "What are you doing here? *Why?* Don't you realize how dangerous it would be for Jack to see—"

"We saw it! We saw it! It's *alive!*"

"You shouldn't be here!"

"You're our friend," one of the imps said, *"and* hers. We thought you'd like to hear the news."

"Then I am excited for you. Now go."

"It was hungry, Malcolm."

Malcolm froze in horror. *Gods, no . . .*

"We fed it, Malcolm."

"Then that's between you and your dark mistress," Malcolm said, trying to keep the fear out of his voice. "I want no part of it."

As one, the imps shook their heads slowly. "It is too late, Malcolm. You have been a part of this a long, long time now. Would you like to hear how we—"

But Malcolm had stepped back inside, and the kitchen door shut firmly in their faces.

"—prepared the meal?" whispered the imps.

AT FAERIE HILL MANOR SILVIUS SAT BY THE DYING fire in the drawing room, sipping a last glass of whisky, staring unseeing at the coals.

Jack. Ah, gods, it was so good to have him home. Silvius' mouth gave a quirk of amusement. And so unsettling. He wondered, idly, how long it would take for the oh-so-carefully-constructed veneer of harmony that existed between all the players of the Troy Game to crack apart under the strain of Jack's presence.

Almost in answer to his thought Silvius heard the door open. He tipped his head slightly, to see who it was.

Weyland, in dressing gown and slippers, and looking as if he'd found Catling in his very bed by the glower on his face.

He poured himself a whisky then sat in the chair opposite Silvius. "She's gone to him," he said, then swallowed the whisky in one swallow.

"You couldn't have expected anything less," Silvius said, earning himself a further glower from Weyland.

Silvius got up and refilled both their glasses, making a note to himself to bring a couple of good bottles of whisky next time he came to Faerie Hill Manor to restock what he and Weyland were undoubtedly going to get through tonight.

"But surely you trust her," Silvius said, handing Weyland his whisky and sitting back down. "Weyland . . . she loves you."

Weyland gave a shrug.

Silvius didn't respond for a while, spending the time studying Weyland. Over the past several decades they'd gradually become good friends—apart from Noah, Silvius was Weyland's only real friend.

"Weyland, she *does* love you."

Weyland sighed. "Once I would not have worried. She turned her back on Jack three hundred years ago. But now . . ."

Now Weyland and Noah had drifted apart. Not much, just a little, but Silvius knew that "little" ate at Weyland's confidence.

"What will you do?" Silvius said.

"I don't know," Weyland said, but there was something in his face, something in the edge to his voice, that made Silvius wonder if Weyland knew very well what he was going to do.

UPSTAIRS, GRACE LAY IN HER BED. SHE WAS NOT asleep, nor had she slept all night.

She could not sleep.

This was not merely due to the shock of what she'd seen earlier, hovering over London, but because of the young woman—Catling—who sat in a chair in the shadows of the room, staring unblinkingly at Grace in her bed, her hands clasped softly in her lap.

Catling had begun to sit by Grace's bed at night a long time ago, ever since Grace was a toddler.

And, as Grace had grown, so also had Catling grown, so that now Catling resembled a young, beautiful woman with long black hair framing her porcelain skin and dark blue eyes.

Beautiful as it might have been, that face radiated nothing but coldness.

"Leave me be," Grace whispered as, somewhere deep within the Faerie, the Caroller sang in the dawn. "Have you not made me suffer enough this past night? Why sit here now, and torment me?"

Catling stared at her, her eyes wide, as if she thought to affect innocence.

Grace began to cry, silently. *Go away,* she mouthed and, eventually, as the inhabitants of Faerie Hill Manor started to rise for the day, Catling rose then vanished.

Chapter Seven

FAERIE HILL MANOR

Sunday, 3 September 1939

L OOK," SAID JACK AS HE SPOONED OUT SOME
scrambled egg onto his plate, and then moved along
the buffet to the toast and slid four slices next to the
egg, "I can't say or do anything until I've looked around
London. I need to know for myself what is happening with
the Troy Game."

He hesitated over the bacon, then forked several slices
of that onto the plate as well. Then he looked back to the
table. Everyone he'd met the previous night, except George
VI, was already seated about, pretending some interest in
their breakfast. Jack left the buffet and took a spare seat be-
tween Walter Herne and his father, Silvius.

Of them all, only Silvius looked as though he was actu-
ally enjoying the food.

Jack took a forkful of egg, and chewed on it, studying
his companions. Noah was dressed very smartly in a tai-
lored suit with a soft blouse beneath, and Jack managed,
only barely, to repress a wince when he saw the diamond
ring on the fourth finger of her left hand.

Weyland, next to her, was studiously ignoring Jack.

Harry and Stella, at the head of the table, were trying
their best to look relaxed. Stella had managed it reasonably
effortlessly, although she barely picked at her food, but
Harry looked almost as tense as Weyland.

Walter simply looked out of place, and as if he could
barely wait until he thought it was time enough to ask per-
mission to leave the table.

Grace sat at the far end of the table. She didn't even pretend to be interested in food, but sat, staring at her wrists in her lap.

Jack noticed she had on a very long-sleeved blouse. He also noticed the dark rings under her eyes.

"I need someone to drive me down to London," he said, "so I can wander around. And, if it is possible, can I ask for someone to arrange a car for me?" That shouldn't be too difficult, he thought, given the talent sitting about this table.

"Weyland?" Harry said.

"I'll be driving Noah and Grace back home this afternoon," Weyland said, not looking up from the tablecloth. "You can come with us, if you like."

"You don't live here?" Jack said.

"No," Noah answered, probably feeling that Weyland may have exhausted his store of politeness for the day. "We visit often, but we live in a private suite at the Savoy. I didn't want to move too far from central London."

Jack pursed his lips in a silent whistle. The Savoy? It was one of London's grandest and most expensive hotels, built on the Strand on the site of an ancient palace, from which it had taken its name. His lips twitched. "Only the best for Eaving?"

Weyland looked up. "It was my choice, not Noah's. I had grown sick of living in squalor."

"But which is better fitting for you, eh?" Jack said, holding Weyland's gaze.

"Jack," Harry said, "we can't afford to—"

Jack's head whipped around to Harry. "I can afford a little bitterness now and again, surely."

"You have just used up your allowance, Jack," Harry said. The tone of his voice was deceptively mild, and no one in the breakfast room missed the reprimand.

Jack's jaw tightened, but he dropped his eyes, and began to fork his eggs around his plate.

"I also have a car I can give you," Weyland said. "I have three garaged at the Savoy. Can't use them all now. You can take one."

Jack looked back at Weyland. "Thank you," he said. He

hesitated, then realized horribly that the pause was growing too long. "It was a bitter pill for me to lose Noah," he said, "and my tongue has become far too well used to that bitterness. My remark was uncalled for, Weyland. I apologize."

Weyland nodded, accepting the apology, but his face didn't lose any of its hostility.

Stella blinked, then looked at Noah, raising her eyebrows.

Noah caught the look, smiled, and then gave a short laugh of genuine amusement. "*I* find it amazing that we can all sit here at breakfast, and that the worst thing we can do to each other is exchange a few snide comments. Once, we would have hurled assorted knives, daggers, arrows, and murderous promises." She looked at Jack. "Jack, thank you for coming back. We have been longing for you for so many years . . . yes, even Weyland—"

"Absolutely desperately, old chap," Weyland said, and the mood around the table lightened even further as everyone managed varying levels of grins.

Noah shot him a grateful look, then returned her gaze to Jack. "—that to have you here now . . . well . . . it is relief beyond measuring."

"Don't expect too much of me, Noah," Jack said.

There was a small silence, broken eventually by Harry. "The PM is to make a radio broadcast this morning at eleven fifteen," he said. "I'm sure we will all know what he has to say."

Of course. War.

"None of us can prevent it," Harry said. "Nothing we have done has caused it." He gave a slight shrug. "Greed. Ambition. Brutality. It is all part of life."

Stella rose from the table and lifted the coffeepot from the hot plate on the buffet table. She walked about the breakfast table, refilling cups as people wanted.

"Jack," she said, "tell us where you have been. What have you been *doing* for so long? Founding empires? Destroying hopes and ambitions? Breaking hearts?"

"Learning to live with myself, mostly," Jack said quietly. "Learning about myself." He pushed his plate away, the food only half eaten. "For the past two hundred years I've

been living in America. Mostly alone, inhabiting the vast forests, roaming the mountains."

Stella sat down. "As Ringwalker?" Jack had only barely come into his responsibilities as Ringwalker, the ancient Stag God of the forests, when he had left England in the seventeenth century.

"For a greater portion of the time, yes. It was part of the journey into myself I needed to make. Other times I walked as a man—I took the identity Jack Skelton during the Civil War—and lived within a more human society."

"Aha," said Silvius, "and did you break hearts then?"

Jack gave a rueful smile, and slid a glance Noah's way. "A few, I have no doubt. It is, after all, what I've been good at."

"And the uniform, Jack?" Stella said. She'd lit a cigarette now, and was leaning back in her chair, studying him.

"I use it much as Harry uses his 'boffin' status, I think. It is useful, and it gets me entry to places and people I otherwise would not. It is a useful glamour—no one questions it. My 'papers' are all in order." Jack paused, his fingers toying with a fork. "Besides, I've always been more comfortable in uniform than out of it."

"Jack the Conqueror," Harry said with a smile, referring to Jack's previous life as William of Normandy.

"Speaking of whom," said Jack, "where is Matilda? And Ecub and Erith?"

"They live in London," said Noah.

"Highbury?" Jack said. "I had a vision that they lived there."

Noah shook her head. "Hampstead. They're all waiting to meet you—Matilda especially." When Jack had been William, Matilda had been his much loved and respected wife. "But they thought it might be a bit too much having *everyone* gathered here last night."

"What else can we do for you, Jack?" said Harry. "What else do you need?"

Jack felt a little resentful at the prompt, knowing Harry referred to their conversation on the terrace of the previous night. "A long talk with you, Harry. Perhaps you can walk about London with me this afternoon?"

"A pleasure. What else?"

Jack decided he might as well give Harry what he'd been waiting for. "Something Walter can do for me." He swiveled in his chair so he could look Walter in the face.

He did not immediately speak, but as soon as Walter lifted his eyes to Jack's, power *rippled* out of Jack, making most of the people about the table gasp and sit up a little straighter.

"There is one last task you need to perform for me and for this land," Jack said. "And when you have done this task, then perhaps both I and the land will let you go to your Christ, and we will never make any demand upon you again. A bargain, Walter Herne?"

"And this task?" Walter said. He was noticeably shaken, but his voice was strong.

"Do you truly not know what it might be?" Jack said. The power was now almost visibly dancing out of him, and there was not a person in that room who was not fixated by it.

"You need to be marked," said Walter. "You need your crown."

"Aye. Do you dare the crowning, Walter?"

"Do you?" Walter whispered, and Jack smiled, and the power abated.

"*Will* you do it, Walter?"

He nodded. "If you will let me go."

Jack looked at Harry. "Well, my Lord of the Faerie? Is that possible? Can Walter be given his freedom from all demands of this land, freedom to go to Christ, if he does this for me?"

Harry had been looking at Jack, a little awed by the power he'd just displayed and thinking he had used his time running the forests of the New World very effectively indeed, but now he switched his gaze to Walter.

"Yes," he said, and his appearance shifted subtly, so that for a moment it was not Harry Cole who sat at the head of the breakfast table, but the Lord of the Faerie wearing his crown of twigs and red berries. "Yes, I agree. If that is what you want, Walter, then do this one last thing for both Jack and the land, and you have your freedom to walk away. If you can."

Walter breathed out in patent relief. "Thank you. Jack, when?"

Jack gave a grin, and it was almost feral in its nature. "Not just yet. But soon. At a time and place of my choosing."

At the far end of the table Grace looked between Jack and Harry, then dropped her eyes before any noted the look.

Chapter Eight

FAERIE HILL MANOR AND LONDON

Sunday, 3 September 1939

THEY SAT IN THE DRAWING ROOM, AROUND a small side table on which sat a large wireless. Harry sat closest to it, fiddling with the knobs to fine-tune the set.

Then, just as everyone's nerves could barely stand the scratchy static one more moment, the voice of a broadcaster filled the room with last-minute news before the prime minister's announcement: a lorry had turned over in Highgate, spilling food too good to be wasted over half the road; the American ambassador had been seen leaving the residence of the prime minister at No. 10 Downing Street late the previous night.

A woman had been murdered, quite vilely (although the broadcaster gave no details), and her corpse left sprawled under the porch of St. Magnus the Martyr.

The broadcaster paused, then announced the PM, and the voice of Neville Chamberlain sounded.

I am speaking to you from the Cabinet Room at 10 Downing Street. This morning the British Ambassador in Berlin handed the German Government a final Note stating that unless we heard from them by eleven o'clock that they were prepared at once to withdraw

*their troops from Poland, a state of war would exist
between us.*

*I have to tell you now that no such undertaking has
been received, and that consequently, this country is
now at war with Germany.*

There was little reaction at the words. No one had expected anything else.

*You can imagine what a bitter blow it is to me that all
my long struggle to win peace has failed. Yet I cannot
believe that there is anything more, or anything different that I could have done that would have been more
successful.*

"There never is, really is there," Silvius said softly.

Chamberlain continued speaking about Britain's obligations to the Polish people, and how he expected the British would bear the burden of war with their usual fortitude.

*Now may God bless you all and may He defend the
right. For it is evil things we shall be fighting
against—brute force, bad faith, injustice, oppression,
and persecution—and against them I am certain that
the right will prevail.*

Harry and Jack exchanged a long, meaningful glance. In previous lives both of them had led the armies of a nation into war, and now neither envied Chamberlain very much his forthcoming experience.

" 'Evil things we shall be fighting against,' " Noah said. "He has no idea how evil."

THEY ATE A LIGHT LUNCH—MOST EATING AS LITTLE at lunch as they did at breakfast—and then Weyland brought around his car to the front to take his family, Harry, and Jack down to London.

Jack whistled in admiration as soon as he saw the huge

silver and red enameled Daimler. "Nice," he said, then he gave a small grin. "Bet it is going to make a spectacular target in moonlight."

"Weyland has been asked to paint it something more subdued," Noah said as Weyland put their small bags into the trunk. "He's been resisting until now."

"This morning has put paid to the silver," Weyland said, shutting the trunk. "I'll get one of the mechanics at the Savoy garage to dull it down somewhat."

He walked about to the driver's door. "Come on then," he said. "Load up."

Noah moved to the front passenger side, which left Harry, Jack, and Grace to accommodate themselves in the back bench seat. Jack found this a little awkward. Grace hadn't said a word all day, and frankly, he didn't know what to say to her. Very patently she wasn't one for light conversation, and in fact actively avoided conversation at all by refusing to look anyone in the face. She looked extraordinarily tired with pallid skin and dark rings under her eyes, and Jack wondered if there was any residual soreness left in her wrists after Catling's attack last night. He couldn't see them; the sleeves of her blouse, and now the cardigan coat she'd put on against the autumn chill, effectively hid any sight of her wrists, and he had no idea how to broach the subject.

Jack walked around to the driver's side of the car and slid into the backseat. On the other side, Harry indicated Grace should sit in the middle, and Jack barely stopped himself from squirming closer to the car door as Grace slid in beside him. He wanted to make a bit more room for her, but was worried she might take the movement as one of revulsion.

Her silence, her terrible introspectiveness, was beginning to intimidate him.

As soon as Harry had closed his door, Weyland pulled away. "London," he said.

THE JOURNEY WAS ACCOMPLISHED IN COMPLETE silence. By the time they drew close to the City, the inner

square mile of ancient London, Jack was ready to scream. The sense of awkwardness had grown by the minute during the drive, and Jack wasn't sure if it was due to Grace's extraordinary inhibition, or to the fact that what lay between Noah, Weyland, and himself simply couldn't stand a close confinement in a car for longer than two or three minutes.

Eventually, when Weyland pulled over close to the Tower of London, Jack had to restrain himself from throwing open the door and exiting with indecent haste.

Noah leaned over the front seat. "Harry, will you and Jack join us for dinner? Weyland needs to hand over the keys to Jack's car, and you might as well stay for a meal."

Dinner? Jack couldn't think of a worse way to spend the evening. All he wanted to do was get out of this car and get as far away from Grace and her oppressive silence and Weyland and Noah and their memories as fast as he could.

"We'd be delighted," Harry said, his voice sounding so natural Jack's mouth almost dropped open. *Hadn't he felt the tension?*

"Besides," Harry continued, "Jack said last night that he'd like to take a closer look at Grace's wrists, and Catling's hex. Perhaps he can do that this evening."

Noah looked over to Jack, who by now had his door ajar with one foot on the roadway. "Jack, that would be wonderful. Thank you."

Jack managed a smile, and slid even farther toward the world beyond the Daimler.

"You don't have to," Grace suddenly, extraordinarily, said, and Jack froze, staring at her.

She was looking at him fully in the face, the first time she'd done so all day, and Jack could see that strong emotion roiled inside of her, although he couldn't tell what it was.

He had a horrible thought that she knew full well how desperate he was to get away from both her and the car.

"You don't have to," she repeated.

Now every eye was on Jack, Weyland's as well, who had swiveled about in his own seat.

"I don't want to be a nuisance," Grace said, and now both

her words and the expression in her eyes (*terror that he would think her a burden*), made Jack instantly ashamed of himself.

He halted partway out of the car, then slid back in. He reached out his left hand, grasping her right hand gently, then slid his fingers under the cuffs of blouse and cardigan to encircle her wrist.

It felt like the wrist of a child, so thin, the bones so vulnerable.

"Anyone in this car," he said, "can tell you I've never bloody troubled myself with 'nuisances.' Not for three thousand years and more. I'm not going to start now." His face relaxed slightly, the skin about his dark eyes crinkling. "You are not a nuisance, Grace."

And then he was gone, the door closing behind him, and Grace was left with her right hand still a little extended, as if she could still feel Jack's fingers around it.

"SHE MUST BE TEARING NOAH AND WEYLAND apart," Jack said to Harry as they watched the Daimler disappear into the traffic.

"That's extraordinarily perceptive of you," Harry said. "Particularly when you're not normally so given to that quality."

"Is she always so difficult to reach?"

Harry nodded. "No one really knows her. God knows we've all tried." He paused. "I was her lover for a while, but even then—"

Jack's mouth dropped open. "I don't believe you," he said. Then, before Harry could answer, Jack grabbed Harry by the shoulder and turned him slightly, using his other hand to pat down Harry's back. "No. I *don't* believe you. You're not full of holes, and if you'd been Grace's lover I am certain Stella would not have hesitated to fill your back with puncture wounds. Did she know?"

"Well, yes," Harry said. "I imagine so. I'm sure I mentioned it to her." Then he laughed at the expression on Jack's face. "I doubt that there are too many other pretty young girls I could have taken as my occasional lover with-

out Stella turning slightly murderous, but Grace is the exception. Stella is probably closer to Grace than anyone, including Noah and Weyland."

"Stella doesn't pity her," Jack said.

"My," Harry said softly, "you *have* acquired some perception, haven't you? Now, Jack, let's walk about this damn city and you tell me what it is that we face. Noah keeps telling me the Troy Game grows stronger and darker, but, gods alone know, that's not what I want to hear from you."

They began to walk, slowly and silently, about the northern side of the Tower. Harry hung back a little, allowing Jack to take the lead. When they got to Great Tower Hill, on the immediate western wall of the Tower, Jack stopped and turned back to Harry. "I want to walk about the old route of London's wall, up north, then west, then south to Blackfriars Bridge. Then across that to Southwark and east along the river walk back to Tower Bridge. Are you up to it?"

Harry nodded. "Is it enough?"

"Not particularly 'enough,' but it will do. It's a broad circular route through the oldest part of the city, and it will give me Catling's strength." Strange, he thought, that now he could only think of the Troy Game as Catling. "Good Lord, Harry. This place has changed."

He looked down to his feet, and tapped one shoe against the tarmac. "There's a subway down here." He lifted his head, turning it westward toward the city. "They riddle the city."

"Aye. Since the late Victorian age the railroaders have been digging under the streets. Jack . . . are they . . . ?"

"A part of Catling? Yes. Every tunnel, every walkway, every subway, every street and laneway add to her web."

"You've been gone too long."

Jack lifted his eyes up to Harry's. "I couldn't have stopped this, Harry. I don't think anyone could."

They began to walk, skirting the Tower once again and moving onto the Minories, which led up to Aldgate. Harry expected Jack to cross straight over and continue northwest, following the ancient line of the city walls, but at Aldgate Jack stopped, and stared west toward the junc-

tion of Leadenhall and Fenchurch streets. The City was quiet. Not only was it a Sunday, but most people would have sought the comfort of family on this day of all days, and there was little to obstruct Jack's view. Suddenly he turned left down toward the junction.

"Jack?"

Jack held up a hand. *Soon, Harry. Give me a moment.* He strode down to the junction of the two streets, where stood an ancient water pump, and stood there, a frown on his face, looking up and about at the buildings, then into the sky, and then downward, a foot once again tapping at the tarmac.

"Jack?"

Jack gave a slight shake of his head. "There's something here, Harry. I don't know what. It feels . . . different. Sideways."

"What feels 'sideways'?"

"I don't know . . . I don't *know*. Last night I thought I felt something at St. Paul's, but I thought it just imagination. But now, whatever it is, it is just that little bit stronger than it was last night. More . . . *alive*."

Harry stood, watching Jack. "Is it the Troy Game?"

Jack shrugged. He stared down Leadenhall Street, then walked down it, crossing over to the north side as soon as a lorry rumbled past them.

It was full of military personnel.

Harry hurried after him. "Jack . . . ?"

"It's the same thing," Jack said, walking past a jeweler's, then a tailor's, then a bookshop, all closed for the day. "It's down here as well. A . . . a . . . *damn it* . . . there is something different. Something *odd*. Something I don't understand." He stopped, and gestured in frustration at his head. "Something that I just can't grasp. Something . . . elusive. But something that makes my Kingman blood tingle."

And then he was off again, striding—almost jogging—toward Cornhill, and then north past the Bank. Here he stopped yet once more, shook his head, then moved on.

For the next two hours Jack and Harry moved through central London. From the Bank up to London Wall, then

west to Aldersgate, which ran south toward St. Paul's, all the time ducking in and out of narrow alleys, into blind courts, up service laneways. Every few minutes Jack would stop, look around, look up, think, frown, then move on. By the time they reached Aldersgate Harry was so tense his shoulders had bunched up toward his neck, and his back was so tight walking had become painful.

What the hell is it, Jack?

"I want to go down to St. Paul's," said Jack. "Please, Harry, bear with me a while longer."

Harry wasn't sure he could live a moment longer, let alone "bear" with anything, but he grimaced and merely followed Jack as he walked down toward St. Paul's. Of all places in the city, the cathedral seemed the most active. People filed in and out, whether to attend a regular service or simply to sit in the nave or one of the side chapels to pray silently.

Jack halted in the churchyard, almost where he'd waited for Walter Herne the previous night.

"It is here as well," he said. "It is all over."

"Jack . . . talk to me," said Harry, who was relieved his voice came out normally instead of the scream that threatened.

Jack had been looking skyward. Now he looked back to Harry.

"Had Noah said anything to you? Stella? Ariadne, if you've had any contact with her? *Weyland?*"

"No. What *is* it?"

Jack took a deep breath. "From this brief walk, Harry, I can tell you that Catling—the Troy Game—appears healthy and vibrant and, yes, dark and dismal and so strong I don't think all the gods in their heavens could ever dislodge her. But there's something else hanging over and about and through London. Something *other*. Shadowy. Insubstantial. I'm sorry I can't explain it any more than that. Whether or not it relates to Catling and the labyrinth that Genvissa and I built . . . I don't know. If it did relate to Catling then I would have thought that Noah or Weyland, or any one of the others trained in the arts of the labyrinth,

would have picked it up. Maybe I *have* been away too long. Something has happened here, Harry. Something I can't even comprehend, let alone explain."

"Jack—"

"There's only one thing I do know, Harry, and that is that whatever *this* is, it is huge. What we've covered today is only a fraction of it. Tell me, what is happening in the Faerie? Is there any intimation of something 'different' reflected into the Faerie?"

"No. Only the growing presence of the Troy Game, bad enough as that is. Nothing else."

"None of the creatures of the Faerie have mentioned anything to you?"

Harry shook his head. All the lines had deepened in his face, making him look so physically weary, and so emotionally exhausted, that Jack reached out a hand and rested it on his shoulder.

"I'm sorry, my friend," he said softly, "but there is something very, very wrong with this city."

Chapter Nine

THE SAVOY

Sunday, 3 September 1939

Noah Speaks

OH, HOW TERRIFYING, HOW INCREDIBLE, how nerve-wracking, how relieving to have him back.

How wonderful.

I don't think I can possibly put into words all the emotions that surged through me when first we realized Jack—

as he called himself now—was coming home. Guilt—oh yes. Excitement—yes, I'll confess to that also. Terror, at what he would say to me, and what he would *think* of me.

During the seventeenth century I'd destroyed his world. He'd wanted me, had loved me, had thought to build a life together with me.

Believed he and I would complete the Troy Game together.

Instead I had abandoned him and the life together I'd promised him to love Weyland Orr, Brutus-Jack's hated enemy, and I had abandoned the Troy Game, to claim it would be our destroyer, not our savior.

He'd walked away, hurt beyond knowing, and bitter, and I am not the one to blame him for that.

Meanwhile, Weyland's and my own little paradise, so briefly enjoyed, fell apart around us. We'd had a beautiful little daughter, Grace, who healed so many wounds. Weyland's at losing the daughter Ariadne had given him so many thousands of years ago, and mine, at losing my own tiny daughter to Genvissa's malevolence.

Then Catling snatched, twisting her red wool hex about baby-Grace's wrists, and our daughter, our beloved, so much wanted daughter, became an open wound of her own.

These few hundred years between the terrible events of 1666 and 1939 had been . . . difficult.

Ah, let me be frank. They'd been a waking nightmare. Grace suffered so terribly, and we could do nothing. Our lovely daughter twisted in upon herself, losing all warmth and gaiety and love, until I think no one could reach her. gods alone know I tried, but I was too emotional, I think, too desperate, and eventually she pushed me away. The closest anyone came was Stella. I don't know why—what was it about Stella that I didn't have?—but I did not tax either Grace or Stella with it. If Grace found a little more companionship with Stella than with me, then so be it.

Yet even that friendship had waned over the past fifty years or so as Grace isolated herself more deeply than ever. She talked, she breathed, she occasionally came out with a sentence or two (her "almost conversation" with Jack in the

car on the way to the Savoy had stunned me; I hadn't heard her say so many words at one time in years), she washed and dressed herself.

She suffered whenever Catling chose to visit her with agony.

She didn't live. Not really.

Weyland and I were at our wits' end. We loved her so much, we wanted so much for her, *we wanted to help her so badly*.

And in the end we couldn't do a thing for her.

Yet now Jack was back. And he'd said he would look at Grace's hex! I tried not to think that somehow tonight Jack would make it all right, that he would find what everyone else had singularly failed to do—the means of removing the hex. After all, he was a Kingman, and he created the Troy Game, and maybe he *did* have the skill and knowledge to help Grace.

I tried not to hope too much, but I am afraid that after we dropped off Jack and Harry, and all through the day as we waited within the Savoy for them to arrive for dinner, I went around with a silly smile on my face.

Weyland commented on it as soon as we'd arrived back in our suite and Grace had gone to her room.

"Noah?" He didn't have to say any more. There was an infinite weight of questions in that single word.

"What do you think, Weyland?" I went to him, and slid my hands around his waist, leaning in against him. "Do you think Jack *can* do something for Grace?"

He studied me a moment, his hazel eyes clouded with something I couldn't quite read. "Is that hope all that's fueling the light in your face, Noah?"

Ah, gods, when would Weyland realize how much I loved him? "No," I said, and leaned closer and kissed him. "I'm thinking also of how we might entertain ourselves once our guests have gone for the night."

He smiled, but it wasn't convincing, and he extracted himself from my embrace and walked over to the sideboard in our sitting room and poured himself a drink.

"Weyland—"

He turned around. "Noah, I have been both dreading and hoping for this day for so long. We all need Jack if we're going to have a hope of destroying the Troy Game . . . if we're going to have a hope of saving *Grace*. But he's such a wild card. He can both save us or destroy us. He could take you from me with a single word—"

"Weyland, don't be ridiculous—"

"—with a single look. Gods, he is so much more *powerful* now than he was as Louis de Silva. Did you not feel the power rippling out from him when he spoke to Walter? And that was but a fraction of what I think he's capable of commanding."

"He's not Theseus, Weyland." In his first life as the loathed Minotaur, Weyland had been murdered by Theseus, who had been given the power to destroy him by Weyland's then lover, Ariadne.

"Really, Noah? Everything rides on him. Everything. Us. Grace. This land. The Faerie. He has the power to either save us or doom us."

I tried to joke. "But you must trust him if you're going to give him one of your cars!" Weyland loved his motorcars, and had allowed no one else but me to drive them.

He grunted, and drained the contents of his glass. "Do you think he will help us?"

"What choice does he have?"

I got nothing but a cynical look for that, and so I gave up on the conversation and went to the windows to look down on the Thames. We'd been living at the Savoy for about six years now. Because none of us, Weyland, myself, or Grace, died or aged (Grace had taken about eighteen mortal years to grow to her present height and maturity, and hadn't aged from that point on), we tended to move from house to house, and neighborhood to neighborhood, on a fairly regular basis, generally about every ten years. Every so often we moved into a village in the countryside surrounding London for a period of twenty or so years so that people in the city would forget our faces.

The Savoy was proving to be one of our favorite homes. The grand hotel had been built in the late nineteenth century, with no expense spared, and had been modernized sev-

eral times since. Although the majority of guests were short-term, there were many like ourselves who took one of the larger suites and turned it into a home, staying for many years at a time. Our suite consisted of a large sitting room, a dining room (with a small kitchenette off it, although we mostly had our meals provided from the Savoy's kitchens), three bedrooms, a box room, a luxurious bathroom, and a powder room, all, save for the box room, appointed and furnished with the utmost sumptuousness and elegance. The luxury of the hotel, and its convenience to central London, were attractions, to be sure, but so also was the sense of "family" among the staff, and most certainly also was the fact that our suite, on the floor beneath the attic level, had windows that overlooked the Thames.

I could stand there for hours, watching the water sprites at mischief among the pleasure boats.

We had no entrance to the Idyll from the Savoy. Hundreds of years ago, when Weyland had purchased the house in Idol Lane, he'd constructed a stunningly beautiful, magical faerie world on the top floor of the house. He called it his Idyll, and used it to retreat from the world. The Idyll had shown me a side of Weyland I'd never suspected—the creative, faerie aspect of him—and it was in the Idyll that Weyland and I had come to love each other. The Idyll still existed, but we could only access it from the Faerie, or from the steps inside the rebuilt spire of St. Dunstan's-in-the-East.

We rarely visited the Idyll. I think Catling's imps' intrusion into the Idyll in order to place that hex on Grace had destroyed some of its magic for us. As for Grace . . . I don't think she ever went back into the Idyll after the Great Fire.

Catling had caused a great blight on this land. She would prove its death if she could not be destroyed.

I had to believe that Jack would aid us, and would *succeed* in aiding us. I had to.

WE SPENT A DESULTORY AFTERNOON WAITING for Jack and Harry. I telephoned Matilda, and spoke to her

for a while about Jack's arrival, and all that he had said and done thus far. (I left out the fact Jack had kissed me; that was irrelevant, surely.) She asked me to send her best wishes, and the hope they could meet soon. Then I spent my time alternatively flipping through magazines, watching the river from the windows, and walking as silently as I could to Grace's room, standing outside her closed door with my hand raised to knock, then walking away again, too dispirited to risk a rejection. Weyland went down to one of the bars for a while, where fortunately he did not drink too much, then down to the garage, where I suppose he spent an hour or so either farewelling one of the cars or instructing one of the mechanics to get it ready for transfer to its new owner.

Just after six in the late afternoon the internal telephone rang, and Robert Stacey, the concierge who ran the residential guest's lobby (we did not enter through the main, glittering lobby of the hotel, but a smaller one just around the corner from the Savoy Court), said that two gentlemen were on their way to see us. He already knew Harry, and would have allowed Jack through on Harry's recommendation, but I wondered what Stacey had thought of him.

Stacey was a Sidlesaghe. He always appeared at whatever front door we kept in some form or the other as our doorkeeper and watcher.

I don't know who he watched more, me or Grace.

I put down the telephone, then realized I'd been standing there staring at it too long, and that Weyland was staring at me.

I smiled wanly. "They're on their way up."

Weyland looked at me a heartbeat longer, then gave a tight little nod, and left the sitting room. I heard him knock softly on Grace's door, then enter her bedroom.

I wish I'd had the courage to do that earlier.

Oh gods, the nerves were fluttering in my stomach. Please, *please* let Jack be able to help Grace.

I took a deep breath, walked slowly to the front door of the suite, and, by the time the knock on the door came, hoped that the smile on my face was steady.

"Harry," I said as I opened the door. "Jack." I kissed Harry on the cheek, as I always did, hesitated awkwardly, then greeted Jack in the same manner.

Both men appeared tense and tired, and I wondered what had happened while they'd been out walking the City. *Had Catling appeared to them?* I hadn't seen her since that terrible day she had dragged Weyland and me down to the heart of the labyrinth, but she'd surely approach Jack sooner or later, now that he was home.

Harry had led Jack straight through into the sitting room, and I followed.

Weyland and Grace were already there, sitting on the sofa, and I was glad to see Grace had changed into something a little less inhibited than her earlier blouse and skirt. She wore a flowered linen dress I had given her some months past, but which I always had to badger her to wear. I wondered whether Weyland had urged her to change, or if she'd shown some initiative herself.

Weyland stood up from the sofa to shake both Harry's and Jack's hands. Harry nodded a welcome at Grace, but Jack leaned down to shake her hand as well, which I thought a trifle too formal. But at least Grace looked him in the eye as they shook, so I was grateful for that small mercy, at least.

"Well?" said Weyland, not pausing for any verbal niceties, although he'd gone to the drinks cabinet to pour everyone a drink.

Harry and Jack glanced at each other, and I felt a premonition of dread.

"Sit down," I said, then sat myself as Weyland brought me my drink.

Harry and Jack took two of the armchairs, but Weyland sat back next to Grace on the sofa.

"There's something different," Jack said without any preamble.

I didn't know what he meant. Yes, London had changed . . . but surely he would have expected that? "Catling has grown," I said. "She is stronger than ever."

Jack stared searchingly at me as I spoke, as if he expected me to say something different, or as if I might be

hiding something. Then he turned his head toward the sofa. "Weyland?"

"What do you mean, Jack?" Weyland said. "What do you want us to say? *What* is different?"

Jack moved a hand, delaying his response to Weyland for a moment. "Grace?" he said.

She'd been staring at her lap, but now she raised her face to him.

"Different?" she said. "Do you mean wrong?"

Harry glanced sharply at Jack at that question, and Jack himself leaned forward in his chair. "*Is* there something wrong, Grace?"

She didn't answer immediately, but held Jack's gaze for a long moment, then looked back to her lap, where one of her hands was wrapped around her other wrist. "Everything has been wrong for a very long time."

It was no answer and it didn't satisfy Jack, but he let it go. For my part, I was amazed at how much Jack seemed to get out of Grace. Jack got sentences. The rest of us got little more than monosyllables.

"There's something different, or 'wrong,' about London," Jack said, passing a hand over his face as if very, very tired. "I can't define it, I can't describe it, I don't know what it pertains to . . . save that it touches in *some* way upon the Troy Game. But *what* I can't tell you. Noah . . . you are a Mistress of the Labyrinth, a powerful one, have you felt *nothing?*"

"No. Jack, what can you mean?"

He gave a confused shake of his head, and so I turned to Harry. "Harry?"

"I can't add anything more to what Jack has said. *He* can feel this, I can't."

Harry was frustrated, but I could tell he didn't disbelieve Jack.

"We walked all over central London," Harry continued, "from the Tower where you dropped us around the northern line of old London Wall, to St. Paul's, to Southwark. Jack says that whatever the wrongness is, it is huge."

"It has spread far further than just central London," Jack said. "Long fingers."

"Long fingers?" Weyland said, the instant before I asked the same question.

Jack waved a hand in the air, a gesture of utter frustration.

Weyland and I shared a look—one of utter dread.

"Is it Catling?" I asked softly.

He took a long time to answer. "No," he said finally. "I don't think so. It doesn't have the feel of the Troy Game about it although I think that this difference, this wrongness, somehow is connected to the Game. I don't know. To be honest, I don't trust my judgment on this." He took a sip of his drink. "It is all so ephemeral. So . . . shadowy."

Grace made a move then, just a slight one, a turn of her head, but given she was normally so still it attracted everyone's attention.

"Grace?" Jack said again. "Is there anything you know? Anything you *feel?*"

"I can't be of any help to you. I'm sorry."

"Grace," Jack said, and I swear before all gods I have ever known I have never heard his voice so gentle, "I value your opinion as much as anyone's in this room. More, in fact,"—his voice now became a little teasing—"as you have not yet given me the chance to distrust you."

My face flamed. Was that a barb aimed for me?

"I'm sorry," she repeated. "I can't help you."

Jack gave a nod of his head, then sighed. "I have never felt anything like this before, not as a man, not as a Kingman, not as Ringwalker."

"But it *is* threatening," Weyland said. "Yes?" He stood, and was now freshening everyone's drinks.

"I don't even know that," said Jack. "It is just there, it is just huge, and it is unknowable. So *I* find it threatening, but"—he gave a disarming smile, which made my heart give an uncomfortable little lurch—"it could of course be an early Christmas present left by . . . well, by whomever."

"It could be a trap," Grace said in a voice almost a whisper. Her gaze had returned to her lap.

Jack regarded her thoughtfully. "Sure, it could be a trap." He paused. "Ah, certainly it is a trap! When has anything good ever happened for us, eh?"

I was looking at Grace, but then caught Weyland looking at me. Grace was supposed to have been a gift to us, but then she had been trapped, and all of us with her.

"I can't sort it out tonight, or even tomorrow or the month after, I think," Jack said. "I need to think about it . . . explore it. Run the forests."

A peculiar sense came over him then, a wildness, and I knew he was longing for the dark secret spaces of the trees.

"I have ordered a meal from the restaurant," I said. "It should be here within the hour. Perhaps Weyland can take Jack down to the garage and sort out the car before then?"

I was babbling, but to be frank, right at this moment I was both so scared and unnerved I didn't know what to say.

"No," said Jack. "I can pick up the car later. For now, I think, I want to have a look at Grace's wrists."

Chapter Ten

THE SAVOY

Sunday, 3 September 1939

*J*ACK WAS GLAD OF HIS EARLIER PROMISE TO see if he could untangle Catling's hex, because now it gave him the perfect excuse to sit close to Grace and truly observe her. He'd been unsettled ever since arriving back in London—everything had been a strain—but since this afternoon's walk around London his anxiety had increased ten-fold.

Something wrong. Something undefinable. Something unexplainable. Something shadowy.

And something, Jack was certain, about which Grace knew something. He wasn't sure if she was deliberately

withholding information from him, or whether whatever she knew she believed so trivial it was of no importance.

As he sat down next to her, gently taking her wrists between his hands, so that she was forced to turn a little to face him, Jack wondered at what she said earlier. Grace had known instinctively something was wrong.

Everything has been wrong for a very long time.

Was it just the Troy Game? What *else* had been wrong for a very long time? . . . Jack certainly hadn't felt anything when he'd been in London during the 1660s.

Or had that remark been nothing but a grab for sympathy? No, he thought not. There had been nothing pathetic or piteous about it. Merely a bland statement of fact, and of resignation.

He put his thoughts of the "wrongness" aside for the moment, and concentrated on Grace.

Dear God, she was thin! Not just her wrists, but all of her. She was close enough to him that he could both feel her warmth and see the rise and fall of her body with each breath, and with both warmth and breath Jack could sense her essential fragility. Under his fingers he felt the fluttering of her pulse—she was very nervous having him so close.

She was so afraid.

The room was silent, everyone staring at Jack, save for Grace, who had her eyes downcast.

Jack had her wrists enclosed within each of his hands, and now he ran his thumbs very slowly along the raised scars that twisted around her wrists, and then ran up her arms, curling over and about, almost to her elbows.

What he sensed there stunned him, and his eyes flew to Grace's face.

She was staring directly at him now, but he could not work out if she was frightened or just . . . simply didn't realize.

Jack opened his mouth, intending to say something, but Grace's face closed over, shutting him out completely, and she averted her face.

"Jack?" Noah said.

"Nothing," he muttered, sliding his fingers back down

Grace's arms to her forearms and wrists, trying to drag his disordered thoughts back to Catling's hex about Grace's wrists.

Jesus Christ, he had to have a quiet word with Noah, and soon.

Jack took a deep breath, and finally managed to concentrate on the hex. He ran his thumbs over the scars around her wrists and forearms, feeling them, discovering their nature. He understood that every time Catling struck, these wounds opened anew.

Finally Jack raised his eyes to her. "Grace?"

She still had her face averted from his, and made no sound or movement.

"Grace, look at me."

Reluctantly, she turned her face to his.

"I am going to do something now that will cause you some discomfort. Not real pain, but it will be uncomfortable. I'm sorry."

She gave a jerk of her head.

I'm sorry, Grace. Jack moved his thumbs again, this time shifting them so that they both lay beside the largest line of scarring on each wrist. His hands tightened very slightly, then he slid his thumbs under the lines of red scarring, and lifted the scars away from Grace's flesh as if they were silken ribbons.

Grace gasped, and tried to jerk herself back, but Jack had a firm grasp of her wrists, and she could not move.

Behind her, Weyland put his hands on her shoulders, either to keep her in place or to comfort her.

"Take your hands away, Weyland," Jack said quietly, not looking up, and, very reluctantly, Weyland lifted his hands away from his daughter.

Hello, Jack. Welcome home!

Jack froze, and he jerked his eyes upward.

Grace had heard that as well, but no one else had reacted.

Isn't she lovely, Jack? Don't you want to save her?

Grace started to tremble under his fingers, and he used his fingertips, running under her wrists and lower arm, to stroke once or twice; gently, reassuringly.

Don't think you can work out the knots binding these sweet little ribbons, Jack. It'll kill her, and you, if you try.

"It's all right, Grace," he whispered. His thumbs had moved farther up under the scarring onto her lower arms, and Grace moaned very softly.

No. It is not "all right," Jack. Poor Grace suffers. You haven't seen how badly she can suffer yet. Would you like to now?

Abruptly Jack pulled his hands away from Grace.

"I'm sorry, Grace," he said. "I can't help you."

Her blue eyes went almost black with emotion, and to Jack's horror he realized it was despair. He reached forward again, and took one of her hands. "It is not because of what was just said"—*not because of Catling's threats*—"but because this hex is so intricate, so powerful, it has literally bound your life to the twists of the labyrinth. I can't help you. And I *am* sorry about that."

"Grace," said Noah, who had risen and now leaned over her daughter, "perhaps you need to rest."

"I don't need to rest," Grace said.

"She doesn't need rest," Jack said at precisely the same moment. Then, as an awkward silence descended, he said, "I wish I could help you, but I don't know how."

Grace turned her head away, and Jack had the feeling that it wasn't in dismissal, but once again, as he'd felt in the car, that she was withdrawing because she didn't want to be a nuisance.

SOMEHOW THEY GOT THROUGH DINNER. IT WAS A generally silent affair, punctuated only with some self-conscious conversation, and the sound of plates being pushed away, their contents barely touched.

It had been a bad day for eating, Jack thought, and he was torn between wanting desperately to make his excuses and return to Copt Hall and needing to have a quiet word with Noah. She was visibly upset, and Jack knew she'd allowed herself to believe that Jack could help her daughter.

Eventually the meal was over, and Harry said diplomatically that he and Jack were tired, that it had been an emotional day for everyone, and that if Weyland was still willing to hand a car over to Jack, perhaps he, Harry, and Jack could repair to the garage?

The sound of chairs scraping back from the table was indecently loud. Before Grace had a chance to bolt for her room, Jack managed a quick moment with her.

"I am sorry," he said again.

She looked at him with emotionless eyes, then turned her back and walked away.

What do you know? Jack thought, watching her, remembering what he'd felt from her arms. *And what are you?*

Friend, or foe?

Victim, or trap?

"Jack?" said Weyland, jangling a set of car keys in his hand.

JACK FINALLY MANAGED TO HAVE A HURRIED CON-versation with Noah as she helped him on with his coat.

"Noah, how did the four Kingship bands make it into the Faerie?"

"Why do you want to—"

"Noah, please, just answer."

"I turned them into golden ribbons and tied them around Grace's arms and legs. Then the Lord of the Faerie carried Grace, and the bands, into the Faerie. Why?"

Jack stared at her, but before he could answer Weyland walked up.

"Jack? Are you coming, or not?"

THE SAVOY'S GARAGE WAS SITUATED WITHIN THE basements of the hotel. It was filled with such an array of luxury vehicles that Weyland's Daimler appeared almost ordinary. Weyland led Jack and Harry to a spot partway down the garage. Here was his Daimler, and beside it a pale gray-green Austin convertible, its cloth hood folded back.

Jack stepped close, running his hand admiringly over the soft leather of its seats.

"You would trust me with this?"

Weyland tossed him the keys, and Jack had to twist quickly in order to catch them.

"If it gets you away from here," Weyland said, "then, yes, I will trust you with it."

He turned, walking away a few steps before halting and again addressing Jack. "I don't know what you did to Grace this afternoon, Jack, but I can't help feeling that she'd have been better off without you."

Chapter Eleven

CLAPHAM

Sunday, 3 September 1939

WEYLAND DIDN'T GO BACK UP TO NOAH and Grace once Jack and Harry had left. Instead he stood, staring blankly at the space where the Austin had been parked, before cursing under his breath and opening the driver's door of the Daimler.

He drove to a narrow, sad side street running off High Street in Clapham. Empty crates and overflowing rubbish bins lined the footpaths, most of the windows on the buildings had been boarded up; a small, thin dog lay curled up, shivering, in a doorway, and puddles of something thick and vile lay glinting on the road surface.

Weyland had never been here before, but he had long known of the street's most shadowy residents. Having locked the Daimler, Weyland walked up to a door and knocked softly.

Someone had tacked a wooden plaque to the wall by the door. Weyland glanced at it as he waited:

PHILPOT INVESTIGATIONS.
JAMES PHILPOT AND WILLIAM PHILPOT,
PROPRIETORS.

Footsteps crept cautiously toward the door, and Weyland tensed slightly.

"Come on, come on," Weyland muttered.

The footsteps halted on the other side of the door.

Weyland banged his fist on the door.

"We're closed," came a whisper.

"You're bloody not closed to me," Weyland said. "Open up!"

"We don't work for you anymore, Weyland," the voice whispered.

"Do you work for money?"

The voice hesitated. "Yes," it whispered eventually, the word riddled with caution.

"Then you're working for me," Weyland said. "Now open up, damn you!"

There was a long silence on the other side; then, just as Weyland raised his hand to bang on the door again, he heard the rattle of keys.

A lock was turned, then another, and then one more, and, achingly slowly, the door creaked open an inch.

"I haven't got all night," Weyland said, and pushed the door open with his shoulder.

There was a startled yelp on the other side as whoever had crouched behind the door was pushed onto the floor, then Weyland was in a dark corridor. He groped along the wall, hoping that the fools had at least had their establishment electrified, found a switch, and flicked it down.

Light flooded the corridor from a bare bulb hung high.

A thin man dressed in drab clothes was slowly rising from the floor, his hands fluttering at his trousers as if to brush from them the dust collected during his fall, his

bright black eyes wide with fright and fixed on Weyland. His dark hair was slicked back against his skull, his face was swarthy and marked with the ancient scars of acne, and his mouth curled as if wondering whether or not to snarl.

"So this is what you look like all grown up," said Weyland to the imp. "Which one are you, then?"

"Jim," said the imp, now fully risen. "And quite independent, thank you."

Weyland regarded him. He'd first created the imps almost a thousand years ago as a means to control Noah and Stella—Caela and Swanne, as they had been then. But during their last life Weyland had come to love Noah, and had set the imps free into London, tired of them and the agony they'd inflicted. This was a decision Weyland had regretted when the imps then became the servants of Catling, draping her hex about Grace's wrists. Every so often over the past three hundred years Weyland had occasionally sent his senses out scrying for the imps, seeing what mischief they were about, but he hadn't bothered himself with them otherwise. They'd simply faded into London's turgid underworld after the Great Fire, where no doubt they had created some limited mayhem, but not any major troubles, so far as Weyland could make out. "Private investigators, moreover," he said. "What do you investigate, Jim? Gutters? Sadnesses? Despair?"

A muscle twitched in Jim's throat, and he edged past Weyland. "We're entirely respectable."

Weyland sneered.

"If you'll come through," Jim Philpot said, nodding to a doorway at the end of the corridor.

THE OTHER IMP WAS SITTING AT A WOODEN TABLE in the back room, had just picked up a bread and dripping sandwich from a plate. There was another plate with a half-eaten sandwich pushed to one side; Weyland evidently had interrupted their evening meal. As Weyland entered, the imp put his sandwich down and stood warily.

"You must be William," said Weyland, noting that the

imp was identical to his brother, save that his face was slightly rounder and even more pock-marked.

"Bill," said the imp, wiping his hands on his stained vest and then holding one out to shake hands.

Weyland ignored it. "I need you to do something for me."

Jim and Bill shared a glance.

"He said he'd pay," Jim said.

"Money?" said Bill.

Weyland, who had been inspecting the contents of a filing cabinet, turned around. "I'll pay you in violence, if you like."

"We'd prefer money," said the imps together.

"Well, if you insist. What are your rates?"

Bill told him, and Weyland raised his eyebrows. "I'll pay you half that. You're worth no more."

"We're *very* good," said Jim.

"We can creep anywhere," said Bill.

"Discover anything for you," said Jim.

Weyland grunted. "I need you to display some manner of delicacy. Think you can manage it?"

The imps grinned, showing unexpectedly white, good teeth.

"Has Noah a lover?" said Bill.

"Do you need photographs?" said Jim.

"No! *Not* Noah," Weyland said, and the imps glanced knowingly at each other.

"Jack's back," said Bill.

"We can take photographs," said Jim. "Dig out receipts. Bribe hotel clerks. Present you with the evidence."

"Not Noah!"

"Of course not," said the imps as one. "Not Noah. Never Noah."

"Jack," Weyland said, his voice grating.

"Jack," the imps said, their eyes gleaming. "Now *there's* an interesting fellow."

Weyland's eyes narrowed. "And what do *you* know about Jack?"

"Absolutely nothing," said Jim.

"Never heard of him," said Bill.

Weyland drew in an irritated breath. "Jack thinks there's

something 'different' about London. Something that is possibly . . . malign."

"Sounds interesting," said Jim.

"Sounds like our kind of job," said Bill. "We can take photographs of the malign, if you like. Lots of them."

"*Shut up,*" Weyland said. "Just listen, eh? Jack is all over my wife and my daughter, and I don't like it."

Jim opened his mouth to say something, thought better of it, and closed it again.

"Everything has . . . changed . . . since he's come back," Weyland said. "Grown unsettled. I don't like it. Like as not Jack will destroy us all. Destroy Grace."

"Sweet Grace," whispered Bill, and Weyland snarled at him.

"*I said not to speak!* Can't you just *listen?*"

The imps both nodded vigorously.

"I don't like not knowing what he is doing. Not knowing what he's about. Discover it, can you? Follow him? See what he's doing? If he is seeing . . ."

The imps raised their eyebrows.

"Just follow him," Weyland finished. "And see if you can't find out what Jack is babbling on about when he talks about this difference . . . this wrongness."

"We can do that," said Bill.

"Be careful," said Weyland. "Don't reveal yourselves."

"We're very, very good," said Bill. "Jack will not realize our presence."

There was a silence, then Jim spoke. "You don't trust Jack, do you?".

"Would *you?*"

"Not if we had a daughter like Grace to protect, no," said Bill, and for once there wasn't a hint of cupidity in his voice at all.

WHEN WEYLAND HAD GONE, THE IMPS SAT DOWN at the table and finished off their dripping sandwiches.

"So Jack has discovered the dancing," said Bill. "What a good boy he is."

"He hasn't discovered all of it," said Jim, and both imps giggled around their mouthfuls.

"What do you think we should tell Weyland?"

"Not all of it," said Jim, and both spluttered with laughter. And within a breath, fell silent.

"It needs to feed again," whispered Jim.

"Soon," whispered Bill. "Soon."

Chapter Twelve

COPT HALL

Thursday, 7 September 1939

T HE WAR WAS ON, BUT AS YET IT HAD LIT-tle impact on Londoners' lives. The war had been expected for almost a year now, civil and defense preparations complete for months, evacuations from the city underway for the past weeks (although as yet most people had elected to stay). There had been a fission of excitement and emotion on Sunday when the worst was known, but over the past few days the excitement had died down. London had not been bombed (there had been one or two false air raid warnings), there had been no massed campaigns in Europe, the world had not ended.

Life went on largely as normal.

Jack Skelton spent the earlier part of the week at Copt Hall and its surrounds.

He settled in, altering the hall to his needs, Malcolm proving an invaluable resource. Neither Jack's nor Malcolm's presence was ever noted by the four or five servants and gardeners who still worked around the hall, keeping the one remaining wing in some semblance of working order, and attending the gardens to send flowers and vegeta-

bles down to London. When fires were lit in the hearths high in the burned-out walls, no mortal eye saw them. When a gramophone occasionally played music in what remained of the elegant drawing room, they did not hear. If any had the occasion to walk through the stark remains of the hall, then their feet encountered only grassy earth, not the beautifully patterned rugs, and their hips did not bump into the chairs and tables set about.

Neither did the servants ever notice the Austin convertible parked under the trees, and they did not realize the comings and goings of the major and his valet.

In the mornings they did note the deer spoor along the graveled front driveway, but so long as the deer kept off the gardens they did not mind their presence.

The strange heart of Copt Hall had awoken about them, and the servants and gardeners had not even a single intuition of it.

Epping Forest had once surrounded Copt Hall completely, but for scores of years now the forest had retreated, and the hall stood some three-quarters of a mile from the main body of the forest. But during the night, when Malcolm would open the front door so the major might set off for his evening walk *(his run through the forest),* the forest crowded all about, embracing the hall and its occupants, and Jack could move from front porch into forest depths with a single step.

He spent these nights roaming as Ringwalker, reacquainting himself with forest and land, and stamping his authority back on both. Others—strange creatures not either of the Faerie or of the mortal—had tried to nibble away at Ringwalker's influence in his absence, and on both Monday and Tuesday nights the forest rang now and again with the sounds of battles: brief, fierce, bloody encounters.

Malcolm always had cloths and a bowl of warm water redolent with antiseptic waiting when the major returned just before dawn.

Jack also ventured into the Faerie. He had hardly been here during the time he'd been away, but little had changed. The Naked, the central sacred hill of the Faerie,

still rose in the midst of the forest-covered hills that rolled away toward snow-capped mountains in the vast distance, the Lord of the Faerie's Faerie wood throne still sat on the eastern aspect of its summit. The Faerie folk continued to drift in and out of the mists that clung to the hills, and Jack spent hours talking or, more often, just sitting in silence with them, absorbing the Faerie.

The only difference Jack noted was that the Idyll, Weyland's creation that had once graced the top floor of the house in Idol Lane, now bordered the Faerie. If Jack stood close to the Faerie Lord's throne on The Naked, and looked east, then he could see rising on the horizon the myriad of walkways and spires and bridges of Weyland's extraordinary creation. The Lord of the Faerie told him that he'd walked close to the Idyll, but had never entered.

"That realm is of Weyland and Noah and Grace, all of themselves," the Faerie Lord had commented.

By Wednesday Jack felt he'd done enough to reestablish his dominance over the forest spaces, as well as renew his bond with the Faerie, and so on Wednesday he drove the Austin convertible down to London. He spent that day wandering again around the city, but came home in the evening no more the wiser.

There was something . . . *wrong* . . . but he could not define or isolate it.

On Thursday morning he remarked to Malcolm that they would have visitors in the late afternoon, and could Malcolm please prepare a tea for five guests.

NOAH ENJOYED DRIVING, AND SHE VERY PARTICU-larly enjoyed driving the Daimler. She enjoyed even more her success in wresting it from Weyland for the day, but in truth that had not been too difficult. When she'd said where she was going, and with whom, he'd rolled his eyes and simply handed over the keys.

Grace beside her in the front passenger seat, Noah drove north to Hampstead where she picked up Matilda,

Ecub, and Erith. None of these three women had been re-born this life. They had, as with Noah, Weyland, Stella, and Harry, merely moved back into the realm of the mortal from the Faerie, taking as their identities the names each had borne in their original lives. They shared a terrace house in a smart quarter of Hampstead, where they busied themselves in their local community, teaching music, history, and botany to private girl students. On some days, the ancient pagan festival days of the year, they joined Noah, and together Eaving and Eaving's Sisters walked the land, rejoicing in the eternal themes of rebirth and regeneration.

Once Grace had often joined them. Now she rarely did.

The three sisters who crowded into the backseat of the Daimler were in a high mood. Jack was back! Noah was slightly less exuberant, but still cheerful, and Grace was her usual introspective, quiet self, preferring to look out her window rather than take part in the animated discussion between the other women. Noah had already spoken to Matilda and Ecub on the telephone, telling the women what had transpired on Sunday (Jack's sense of something wrong in London, his failure to help Grace) and so now they chatted about more inconsequential things, like whether or not Jack could possibly be as handsome as Noah had said, or as charismatic as she intimated.

They arrived at Copt Hall close to five P.M.—their arrival, as everything else even faintly connected with the Faerie, totally unobserved by the hall's mortal servants.

"Mesdames," said Malcolm at the door, inclining his head as he ushered them through. "Major Skelton is waiting for you in the drawing room."

Grace was the last to come through, and Malcolm gazed at her a little more curiously than was polite, but she was herself looking about with so much inquisitiveness that she did not notice.

Just before he closed the door, Malcolm saw that several deer had emerged from the trees.

In the shadows behind them Malcolm thought he saw

three ghostly spears propped against a tree trunk, and he smiled.

My fellows, he said in greeting.

JACK GREETED MATILDA, ECUB, AND ERITH WITH evident delight, kissing each on the mouth, but Matilda with perhaps a little more depth and passion than the other two.

Noah received a peck on the cheek—"As you are a married woman," Jack remarked—and Grace a similar kiss on the cheek. She gave him no chance to kiss her mouth had he even wanted to, averting her face as he approached.

Jack gave Grace a strange look at that, but he turned away from her almost immediately without a word and ushered the women to the easy chairs grouped about the fire.

As they settled themselves, Malcolm bore in a large tray, laden with silver tea and hot water pots and delicate bone china cups and saucers. He set this down on a low table in the center of the chairs, and then moved a stand filled with cakes and dainties beside it.

"We can help ourselves, Malcolm, thank you," Jack said, and Malcolm inclined his head yet once more and withdrew.

Noah leaned forward to the table, ready to pour, but Jack waved her back.

"Grace," he said, "will you be 'mother'?"

She flushed a little, glancing around the other women, and Jack noticed that her hands trembled very slightly as she leaned forward. But, having once laid hand to teapot and cup and saucer, Grace then accomplished the pouring of the tea with considerable poise, handing out the cups of tea and passing around the milk pitcher and sugar bowl as needed.

Then she sat down, looked at Jack (who had been watching her keenly the entire time), and said, "Did I pass the test?"

"Grace—" Noah began, but Jack burst into laughter, surprised and delighted both by her unexpectedly direct gaze and her tart tone.

"Yes," he said. "You did. You may apply forthwith to Malcolm for a position on the staff."

For a moment he thought she almost smiled. Her eyes widened slightly, and her face relaxed, but then her customary guard went back up, and she dropped her eyes away from his. She refilled the teapot with the hot water, then rose, the now empty hot water pot in her hand.

"I'll ask Malcolm to refill this," she said, and was gone before Jack, or any of the women, had time to comment.

"I'm sorry, Jack," Noah said. "She can be so abrupt sometimes."

Jack stirred his tea. "She has reason enough to be, Noah."

"Yes, but . . ." Noah's voice drifted off.

Matilda had watched the exchange, her eyes narrowing, and now she spoke. "Enough of Grace, Jack. What of *you*? God damn it, man, we've missed you! Tell us all now, we demand it. What have you been doing, where have you been, what do you *know*?"

Matilda was sitting in the chair next to Jack's, and close enough that he could lean over and kiss her softly on the mouth. "And I have missed you, too, Matilda," he said, barely pulling his mouth away from hers. "How fortunate that you are no one else's wife in *this* life."

"Ah," she said, smiling, "but I have my eye on your man, Malcolm."

The group laughed, and Jack slid back into his chair, and soon they were buried in conversation and reminiscences.

GRACE STOOD UNDER THE OVERHANG OF A DOOR and watched as Jack leaned over and kissed Matilda. She was a distance away, but she had acute enough hearing to pick up their exchange.

"Miss Orr?"

She spun about, clutching the hot water pot close, her eyes wide with surprise.

Malcolm smiled at her. "Do you need more water?"

"Yes." A pause. "Thank you."

"Then come with me."

He led her through the ruins to a kitchen where an aga stove radiated warmth.

"Put the pot on the table," he said. "It will take a moment to boil some more water."

Grace obliged, and as Malcolm busied himself at the aga, she wandered slowly about the kitchen.

"This is a strange house," she eventually said, standing by a plate rack and running one hand lightly over the china within.

Malcolm, still at the stove, glanced at her, pleased that she'd spoken. "It has a deep past, Miss Orr."

She turned to face him. "A deep past? As have you, I think, Malcolm."

"Me? Why, I'm just Major Skelton's manservant, Miss Orr." Malcolm affected a rolling country burr as he spoke, but Grace did not smile.

"I don't think you're anyone's servant, Malcolm. Tell me, *what* are you?"

Now Malcolm turned fully from the aga. "Would you like me to show you, Grace? Just a little?"

He could see the indecision on her face: the slightly narrowed eyes, the corner of a top lip disappearing as she chewed on it.

"Do you *dare,* Grace?" he asked, very softly.

A long silence. "Yes," Grace eventually said.

"Then roll up your sleeves."

Grace took a step back, instinctively, defensively, crossing her arms across her chest. She was wearing a long-sleeved cardigan over a blouse and skirt, very much as she'd been wearing the day her father had driven her and Jack down to London, and now she automatically tugged a little at the cuffs of her cardigan, pulling their already stretched sleeves farther over her hands.

"Grace," said Malcolm, "do you think none of us know about your wrists, and the scars they bear? If you want to see what I am, then roll up your sleeves, and come naked-fleshed into my world."

* * *

NO ONE IN THE DRAWING ROOM HAD COMMENTED on Grace's continuing absence, even if they had noticed it. Jack had talked a while about where he'd been, and who, and what he had done in the years since 1666, and then Eaving's Sisters had explained what they'd been doing (not much, according to their report, apart from wandering the Faerie, and growing closer to the land).

Then Ecub asked Jack about what he'd said on the Sunday evening, about the "wrongness" within London.

Jack told them what little he knew. "I went back into London yesterday, but discovered little more. Whatever it is, is so ephemeral that I can barely grasp it. And you're certain that none of you have felt it? Not even walking the land, or within the Faerie?"

All of the women, including Noah, shook their heads.

Jack sighed. "Maybe it is nothing. Maybe I have been away too long. Maybe . . ." He shrugged, and smiled disarmingly. "Maybe it is but the taint of the modern world."

"What are you going to do now, Jack?" Matilda asked.

"Run the forest a little longer, bond with the land a little more deeply." His eyes, suddenly keen, switched to Noah. "Collect my Kingship bands." A pause, as he studied Noah carefully. "Will you keep them from me, Noah?"

Her chin tilted up. "No. They are yours whenever you wish."

A strange expression came over Jack's face as she said that, but then it relaxed away, and he stood up. "Good. Now, let me show you about my home, such as it is."

MALCOLM LED GRACE OUT THE KITCHEN DOOR and toward a grassy area that bordered the gardens. It was now evening, and a mist had moved in from the forest almost a mile away.

Grace shivered, wrapping her arms around herself.

The sleeves of both cardigan and blouse were rolled up well over her elbows, and the livid scars around her wrists and arms almost glowed in the silvery, damp light.

Malcolm nodded toward several shapes looming up from the mist. "See," he said, a hand on Grace's back pushing her gently forward. "They were once my companions."

Three deer moved out of the mist, their nervousness apparent in their quick, high steps.

Malcolm held out a hand, and they sidled up to him, moving themselves so that he stood between them and Grace.

"Shush," he said, his voice very soft, "don't you see she's been damaged as well?"

Grace stared at him then, as tense and as nervous as the deer.

Malcolm turned his face slightly so he could see her from the corner of his eye; one of his hands rubbed up and down the flank of first this deer, then the next. "Hold out your wrists, Grace. And come closer. Do."

Do, do, do, he repeated, over and over, his voice so soft and gentle and calming, and before she had quite realized it, Grace took a step forward, extending one of her wrists.

JACK FOUND HIMSELF STANDING ON A BALCONY with Matilda at the very top of Copt Hall.

Noah, Ecub, and Erith were somewhere else in the building.

"Jack, how are you? Tell me the truth, you can do that. You can trust me."

He slipped an arm around her. "Oh, aye, I can trust you." He moved slightly so he could kiss the top of her head. Matilda was taller than she had been in either of her previous lives, but still short enough that he could pull her in close and cuddle her under his chin.

"Well?" she said, leaning in close to him, and wondering if it was possible they might restart what had once been a great marriage.

"I feel lost and dislocated," he said. "Nothing is right. I *was* away too long."

"Noah . . ."

"I know. She is lost to me. I know." He gave a hollow laugh. "But can I accept it?"

"Jack," she whispered, her arms around him now. "Perhaps I can—"

"Look," he said, his voice lifting in surprise, and she felt his body tense fractionally away from hers.

Matilda looked down. Far below them, at the edge of an overgrown grassy lawn and a patch of tangled shrubbery, stood Malcolm and Grace, close to a clutch of deer.

As they watched, Grace lifted one of her wrists, and one of the deer leaned forward, achingly slowly, and sniffed at it.

"What is she doing down there?" Jack asked. He'd moved completely away from Matilda now, and leaned on the balcony railing.

"Finding a friend, perhaps?" Matilda said. "God alone knows she has precious few of those."

THE DEER LEANED IN TO GRACE, SO VERY, VERY slowly, and just as slowly Grace leaned toward it. The deer snuffled at Grace's wrist, then ran his damp nose up her arm. Grace gasped, and for a moment looked as if she were about to pull back.

"Be still, Grace," said Malcolm. "He will not hurt you. He just wants to know you."

"I am afraid . . ."

"I know, girlie."

At the gentleness in Malcolm's voice Grace looked at him. "I will destroy them—"

"You are talking of your hex? Afraid it will reach out to snatch them as well? Don't fear. If that were so then my friends here would not come near you."

The deer was now standing very close to Grace, close enough that it was leaning its body into the woman. The other two deer were now close, and sniffing curiously at Grace's other wrist.

"Malcolm . . . Malcolm . . . who are you?"

"I was once a king, my dear, and these lovely creatures my warrior-priests."

* * *

JACK WAS LOOKING AT MATILDA. "TALK TO ME about Grace, Matilda. She is a puzzle to me."

Matilda took her time in answering. "She's lost, Jack. She was so loved and wanted by both her parents, but from babyhood she was lost to them, and perhaps even to herself. She's isolated herself within a ring of fire and of suffering, and can't escape."

Jack's mouth gave a humorless twist. *She is everyone's "doom,"* he thought.

"Grace has no friends," Matilda continued. "She allows no one in, and besides . . ."

"Besides?"

"Jack, Grace has two such grand parents: one a goddess, a Darkwitch, and the most potent Mistress of the Labyrinth who has ever existed. The other is a creature so powerful and with such a dark, terrible past that he is, in his own way, as intimidating as Noah."

"Intimidating?"

"Jack, Grace is intimidated by Noah, and by us, Eaving's Sisters. We represent a past and a bond that she can't share. You say that you are lost and dislocated, but so is Grace. Worst of all, Grace feels she disappoints Noah. Grace knows full well she can't be the daughter Noah has always so desperately wanted."

"Noah suffocates her."

Matilda looked at him sharply. "Yes, she does, but can you blame her for it? If you had a child who suffered as Grace does—could you stand back and regard her with impartial coolness?" Then she looked down, and gasped. "Gods, Jack, look at that!"

GRACE WAS LAUGHING. WATCHING HER, MALCOLM had an enormous grin on his own face as he thought that was possibly the first time Grace had laughed in scores, if not hundreds, of years.

The deer were crowding Grace now, but she was not

afraid. She patted and rubbed at them, and smiled and laughed, and seemed oblivious to Malcolm's presence.

Suddenly Malcolm looked up, and saw Jack and Matilda watching from the heights of the hall.

She is accepted among the herd, he said in Jack's mind.

So was Judas part of Christ's herd, Jack replied, but there was no malignancy in his words, and they did not dampen Malcolm's grin.

"You are welcomed within the glade, Grace," he said, but he kept his eyes on Jack as he spoke.

The next moment Grace gave a cry, and twisted away from Malcolm and the deer.

Chapter Thirteen

COPT HALL

Thursday, 7 September 1939

Noah Speaks

J WAS WITH ECUB AND ERITH, WALKING THE gardens at the side of the house, when I felt Grace's pain. *Catling!*

As always, two emotions consumed me instantly: anger—*fury*—that Catling should so torment Grace; and a bleak impotence that was more devastating than the anger. What could I do? Nothing, really, for all I could do was fuss, and Grace so hated to be fussed over.

I knew from what I could feel that Grace was in the gardens around the back of Copt Hall, and I (as Ecub and Erith) were with her within moments.

She was not alone. Jack's valet, Malcolm, was standing

by her side, and, as I ran toward Grace, Jack and Matilda materialized directly before my daughter.

I couldn't look away from Grace. She was now half crouched, bent over her wrists, and I could *feel* the suffering radiating out from her.

"Grace!" I cried, and ran the final few steps between us.

Before I could reach her, Jack stepped between us. "It's all right, Noah," he said. "Malcolm can take Grace into the kitchen where it is warm and quiet—"

Quiet? What was he trying to say?

"—until her pain has passed."

With that he turned away from me, not even waiting for a response, and bent down and said something very quickly and quietly into Grace's ear. She gave a tiny nod, then rose and, still half crouched about herself, her wrists clutched to her chest, walked slowly toward the kitchen, Malcolm a half step behind.

"Jack," I began, irritated by the way he'd stepped between me and Grace, but he motioned to me to wait.

"Malcolm can keep Grace quiet company for the time being," Jack said to me. "He can be quiet for her."

I was grinding my teeth by this time, but I gave a jerk of my head.

"And while Grace endures," Jack said, "you and I can talk."

"Matilda and Erith and I," said Ecub, "shall clear the tea things from the drawing room—no, do not worry, we shall not disturb Grace in the kitchen—and then wait in the car." She looked at the other two women and winked. "I'm sure one of us has remembered to bring a flask of whisky with her, and we can spend the time quite pleasantly while waiting for Noah and Grace."

Jack smiled his thanks, then took me by the elbow and guided me toward a stand of trees beyond the grass.

The trees hadn't been there a few minutes previously.

Even this evidence of Jack's power did nothing to quell my ill temper.

"There was no need to step between us, Jack," I said, none too gently pulling my elbow from his hand.

"She didn't want you, Noah."

That was too much. I stopped in my tracks and turned to him, my mouth opening to let him know what I thought.

"You said to me that she doesn't like to be mothered," he said. "Look, I know you want to help her, but . . ."

Oh, that "but."

"Perhaps it is better to just let her be," he finished. "Let her endure alone. She didn't choose isolation by circumstance, Noah, but by choice."

"It is easy to see that *you* are not a parent," I said, and then wished I hadn't. When he had been William, Jack had been an excellent parent to his and Matilda's children, and he had been a loving father to our sons as well, even if he hadn't been the best of husbands to me. And he'd been gone almost three hundred years since last I'd seen him— who knew what children he'd fathered in that time?

"Walk with me," he said softly, and I briefly closed my eyes, and thought that if he'd said that to me when he'd been Brutus, and I Cornelia, and with that same measure of warmth and sweetness he'd just used, then all of our troubles would never have had the chance to start.

So we walked. Twilight was thick about us now, and a heavy mist clung to our clothes and hair. I was glad for the coat I had put on earlier to walk in the garden, and slid my hands deep into its pockets. Above us the trees twisted, their branches now mostly denuded of leaves, the earth to each side of our path humped into eerie mishappen swellings with the pressure of the roots below. Our feet crunched on dead leaves and forest litter, and as we walked deeper into the forest, and as the night settled about us, so all of the tension of the past minutes dissipated.

"It feels good," I said eventually, "to be walking thus with you."

From the corner of my eye I saw him smile slightly. "Aye, it does."

I stopped, turning to look at him. Ah, gods, he was so

handsome. I wish . . . oh, I could wish for so many things, and it couldn't make the world any better a place, would it?

"We should have walked thus a long time ago," I said.

The amusement dropped from his face, and he regarded me with an intensity that made my stomach twist with emotion.

"What we should have done a long time ago has been a hard and long lesson to learn," he said.

We fell silent, neither of us able to look away from the other.

"I—" I began

"We should—" he said at the same time, and we both laughed self-consciously.

Then he leaned forward, and kissed me.

Oh, my. This wasn't that hard angry kiss he'd given me when I'd met him the night he'd arrived at Copt Hall. This was something altogether different, and far more unnerving.

I drew back a little, just a little, but not far enough, for he merely closed the distance between us and continued the kiss, deepening it a little.

Eventually I managed to draw back enough to break the contact. Gods, of what had I been thinking?

The answer to that didn't bear thinking about.

He smiled a little, and way too intimately.

"Perhaps we should get back to the house," I said.

He didn't move. "I can scarcely believe that you will fetch those bands for me so willingly. For so many years you've hid them from me, and refused me access."

I was still so befuddled by the kiss, and so confused by my own reaction to it, I had to wonder if he was talking about the bands . . . or something else.

"And you will just fetch them from the Faerie for me? Whenever I ask?"

Just the Kingship bands, then. "Of course," I said. "Whenever you ask."

Again he gave that odd look he had given earlier when we'd talked about the bands inside.

"Jack," I said, "I'm so sorry that I kept them from you all these years. You know I had reason enough."

He gave one of those infuriating slight shrugs. "I know you thought to have reason."

I was about to snap, but he spoke before I could manage it. "And they're in the Faerie?"

"Of course they are, save the two I sent into the Otherworld."

And yet again, one of those strange looks.

"Jack?"

He smiled then, easy and relaxed, and changed the subject. "Have I mentioned today how beautiful you are?"

"Jack, don't."

He reached out a hand, and ran his fingers softly down the side of my face.

"Are you sure I can't win you away from Weyland?"

"Jack . . ."

He turned his face then, staring back to the Hall. "Catling has retreated," he said, "and Grace's pain had faded. We should go back."

I was disappointed at his words, yet at the same time relieved. Yes, we should go back.

Back to Grace.

I sighed.

PART TWO

GRACE

London, 1014

FOR SCORES OF YEARS THE DANES AND NOR-
wegians had fought the Anglo-Saxons for control of
England. First an Anglo-Saxon king sat on the
throne, then a Dane, then a Norwegian, and always there
was yet another contender sailing up the Thames to launch
an assault on London in order to gain the throne.

In 1014 the English King Aethelred, aided by the Norwe-
gian King Olaf, made a desperate assault on London, try-
ing to wrench it away from the Danes, who had seized the
city and elected Cnut to the throne of England. The Danes
had fortified the city well, constructing bulwarks and
ditches in Southwark, reinforcing their castle on the site
where the Tower of London now stands, and barricading
the wooden bridge that straddled the Thames between Lon-
don and Southwark.

By evening of the day of the attack the battle had
reached its most desperate. Neither Aethelred nor Olaf
could manage to breach the defenses at either the castle on
the northern bank of the river, nor the defenses on the
southern bank of Southwark.

Olaf, an experienced Norse warrior, didn't know what to
try next. His men were nearing exhaustion, the Danish de-
fenders appeared to have limitless supplies of ammunition
as well as men, and it appeared to him that they would be
beaten back to a humiliating defeat by star rise.

Olaf! Olaf!

Olaf was standing in the belly of one of his warships,

gazing in frustration upriver to the bridge, when he heard his name being called.

He frowned, looking about the boat. It was filled with Norse warriors, and yet that voice had sounded as if it had come from the throat of a small girl.

A movement on the south bank of the river caught his attention.

The bank was far distant, but Olaf found he could see as clearly as if the bank were no more than ten feet away.

A small girl, five or six years old, stood there. She had long black curly hair, the whitest face imaginable, and was dressed in a dark gown of what to Olaf looked like the most expensive and exotic material.

Then, suddenly, the little girl was standing beside him in the belly of the ship, and Olaf made a sign against evil, knowing he stood in the presence of a malignant spirit.

"Do you want to win this city or not?" said the girl-spirit. "Yes? Then set aside your fear of me. Listen to me, Olaf, and hear how you can take this city from the Danes."

FOUR HOURS LATER, UNDER COVER OF FULL DARK, *Olaf directed his fleet of fifteen warships upriver toward the bridge. As soon as they came within range of the bridge, the Danes cast down spears and arrows and great stones, but they bounced harmlessly off Olaf's ships, for Olaf had taken the spirit's advice and fixed thick screens of woven hazel over and around his ships.*

Once at the bridge, Olaf's men worked quickly, casting strong cables around the piles of the bridge. As they moved out from under the cover of the hazel screens, many were struck by missiles and fell into the river, but within minutes the cables were secured, and Olaf screamed at his men to row back downstream.

It took less than three minutes for the piles to give way. The bridge collapsed into the river, taking with it thousands of Danish warriors. Those who didn't fall into the river fled into London, or into Southwark.

Aethelred and Olaf then set their warriors against the

bulwarks and fortifications in a renewed assault. The loss of the bridge, and the thousands of Danes who had been crowded upon it, had broken the nerve of those Danes left, and by dawn London belonged to Olaf and Aethelred.

Once the city was secured, the Norwegians and the English set to feasting. Great quantities of drink and food were consumed and, as part of the celebrations, a Norse wit by the name of Ottar composed a short verse to celebrate the critical moment that had won the day.

> *London Bridge is broken down.*
> *Gold is won, and bright renown,*
> *Shields resounding,*
> *War-horns sounding,*
> *Hildur shouting in the din!*
> *Arrows singing,*
> *Mailcoats ringing,*
> *London Bridge is broken down!*
> *London Bridge is broken down!*

In her dark corner of existence, the little girl did not even raise a smile at the drunken revelry. There had been only one thing she'd wanted, and that was to destroy London Bridge.

London bridge is fallen down! *she whispered.* London Bridge is fallen down!

Now, let us rebuild it to what *I* want.

Chapter One

COPT HALL

Thursday, 7 September 1939

Grace Speaks

ALL MY LIFE, SO IT SEEMS TO ME, HAS BEEN spent watching everyone about me Waiting for Jack. It was like a parlor game that we all played whenever we had nothing else to do. When there was a lull in a conversation, whenever thumbs began to twiddle, if a book grew boring or an afternoon stretched ahead without a single amusement ready to fill the empty hours, then we played Waiting for Jack.

All my life. For almost three hundred years. Waiting for Jack. His name changed occasionally, of course. In my early years it was Waiting for Louis, or sometimes Waiting for Ringwalker. Occasionally someone would forget themselves entirely and play Waiting for Brutus. Life held its breath, Waiting for Jack.

It was a torment. Much of my life was a torment, but most particularly the Waiting for Jack part of it. I was the only one who didn't know him. Everyone else had an opinion and, more importantly, a long history with this mythical creature. My mother had loved Jack, and had then abandoned him for my father. My father had spent the greater part of his life hating him, and then the remainder of it terrified that Jack would somehow snatch my mother

back. Harry was Jack's friend, but that friendship was based on a peculiar mix of shared murder, women, and ambitions, and I had never pretended to understand it. Stella had been Jack's lover and (most importantly) his partner in building the Troy Game, Matilda had been his wife, Silvius his father, Ecub and Erith his lovers as well, while Walter had simply existed, so far as I could tell, on a diet of unrelieved dislike for Jack . . . which was a breath of fresh air amid all the other shared histories of love and betrayals.

Everyone waited for Jack, everyone knew Jack, and I was the only one so completely excluded from all this shared history that I had no idea at all what to expect, or what to wait *for*.

Jack assumed almost mythic proportions in the time he was gone. This just wasn't in my own mind, but everyone else's as well. The Troy Game dominated our lives completely—whenever people weren't playing Waiting for Jack, they were playing What Can We Do about the Troy Game. No one could get on with their lives until something was done about the Troy Game, and it appeared that the only person who knew what to do about the Troy Game was Jack.

When Jack arrived home, then somehow all would be well. I wasn't so sure about this, because from what I'd been told about all the adventures and trials of the past it seemed most apparent to me that Jack had as little idea as anyone else about how to tackle the Troy Game problem, but everyone else seemed to cling most desperately to the idea that somehow Jack could solve everything.

Jack would arrive home, and miraculously both Destroy the Troy Game and Save Grace within the first five minutes. That he didn't do either was, I am afraid, not much of a surprise to me.

Life at the Savoy and at Faerie Hill Manor was thrown into turmoil the day Harry announced that Jack Skelton would be arriving on the Saturday evening train at Waterloo. My father was terrified, my mother even more so, Stella was amused (more at my parents' reactions than at the idea that Mythical Jack was about to reappear and save us all), Harry was nervous, Walter resentful, Silvius genuinely pleased.

Me? I was the most terrified of all, because I thought that this long-waited-for and almost-mythical Jack would almost certainly manage to murder us all. I had lived for hundreds of years in abject terror of the next time that Catling might decide to visit her agony on me. It dominated my entire life. I could do nothing, go nowhere, without fearing that while I was out Catling might decide to amuse herself. But at least I knew I would always survive each of Catling's attacks, at least I was alive, and at least I knew I would stay that way while Jack was absent.

But when Jack returned, that terrible decision would need to be made: to try to destroy the Troy Game and thus destroy not only me but everything tied to me, or to decide to complete the Troy Game, and allow me (and everything tied to me) life, but in a nightmarish subjection to Catling and her whims.

When I'd been younger I'd tried desperately to free myself from Catling's curse. But there was no means of escape. I had tried to use my Darkcraft just once, and the suffering that Catling had inflicted on me for that single piece of independence had impressed upon me for all time never, ever to try it again. So, as far as I was concerned, Jack's arrival meant either one of two things: death, or a fate worse than death.

My wildest fantasy had always been that Jack would *never* return, and we'd all be kept in this appalling limbo. Yes, it was appalling, but it was in its own way a life, and for me it was surely better than either of the other two alternatives.

Jack would never be able to save us. I knew it. I had tried to tell my parents and Harry this, but they always metaphorically patted me on the head and told me they'd find a way once Jack arrived home. All they needed was Jack and his undoubtedly fresh ideas, and Grace, London, and, indeed, the entire world would be saved.

But we would never be saved, and could never be saved. I knew this, because I knew Catling far better than any of them did, and I knew Catling had laid a trap for Jack that our Newly Arrived Savior showed every sign of walking directly into.

I knew Catling had laid a trap for Jack, because I had

seen it hovering over London that first night Jack had arrived. Catling had thrown that hex about my wrists when I was a scant few weeks old. I could remember those weeks before I'd been cursed, and that memory was a torment. My mother had adored me unconditionally, my father loved me more than life itself. I'd grown in my mother's womb surrounded with that love, and when I was born then I inhaled it with every breath. We all shared the Darkcraft, we reveled in it, we used it to merge our existences so that often the three of us—mother, father, baby—were more like one indivisible individual.

Then Catling hexed me, tied my fate to hers, and that love and unity were corrupted. Other emotions crowded in—fear, guilt, blame, uncertainty, impotency, pity, a smothering protectiveness—and they drove me apart from my parents as almost nothing else could have done. I became "pitiful Grace," regarded still with love but also with boundless sympathy laced always with a vile little streak of fear. *There goes Grace, dear Grace, poor Grace, our doom.* I became a nuisance to everyone—at least that's how I felt. People had to look out for me, people had to try to ease my pain, people had to be nice to me. *Poor Grace suffers, we must try our best for her.*

Whenever I walked into a room, people would tense as if a great burden had fallen on their shoulders. I dragged in trial and disappointment and disaster at my heels, and I felt as if I made the world a wearier place for whomever I encountered. I was the outsider. Everyone else shared a past that I did not, and a companionship that I could not.

I retreated from my parents, and from everyone around me. I had no friends, not really, because everyone regarded me with that appalling combination of pity and dread, and it allowed no true closeness. Stella was the nearest thing I ever had to a friend, but I caught even her regarding me with that strange pity-fear expression in her eyes, and it killed any real friendship before it had begun.

I may not have had a friend, but I had a companion. Catling.

She came and sat with me, night after night, year after year. She grew up with me, appearing as a little girl when I was, as an adolescent with me, and finally taking the shape of a young woman as I matured. She did not appear every night, but maybe one or two nights a week I would wake during the night and see her lurking in the shadows of my room, a strange, cold presence. Sometimes she would stand, sometimes she would creep close enough to sit in a chair, but always she'd be there, silent, staring unblinkingly at me. Occasionally she brought her hateful, spiteful imps; mostly Catling came alone.

I screamed at her, I wept at her, I rose from my bed and tried to strike at her, but she ignored tears and words, and always faded away the instant before my fists could strike her.

She never spoke. She just watched me, sometimes allowing a small derisory smile to light her face.

Planning. That's the single perception I got most strongly from her. She had a cunning little plan going, the bitch. I could see it in her eyes, in the way her fingers constantly moved as if she were playing cat's cradle, in the way her lips occasionally moved in silent concert with fingers.

She had a plan to destroy us all, and all it needed was Jack.

Catling played Waiting for Jack as well. The only difference between Catling's playing of that game, and the rest of our fumbled attempts at it, was that Catling knew precisely how to win it.

OF JACK HIMSELF . . . WELL, HE WAS BOTH AS EXpected, and yet different. I heard all the stories. Brutus the hard-hearted, ambitious bully; William the kinder but still ambitious invader; Louis the impotent, angry man. To me Jack seemed a strange mix of lover-soldier-Kingman. Those who knew Jack seemed evenly divided into those who loved or had loved him, and those who hated or feared him. Without exception the women were all bound by some degree of love (save for Stella, who professed herself beyond such considerations).

And despite *her* protestations, I wondered if my mother loved him still.

I'D BEEN SO GRATEFUL TO HIM WHEN CATLING struck when I was with Malcolm and the deer. My mother had been rushing toward me, prepared to smother me with concern, and Jack had quietly stepped in, and ushered me away to enjoy some peace. I knew my mother meant well, I knew she loved me, I knew how much my pain hurt her as well, and, oh, yes I loved her as well, but all I ever wanted now was to be able to endure in some quietude, because that was the only thing that made the agony bearable.

I'd been enjoying myself. Stupidly, because I knew Catling would not be able to resist taking this opportunity to torment me. Strange, strange Malcolm had taken me out to the deer, and their simple presence, and the soft, tickly rasping of the deer's tongue along my skin, was just so undemanding, and so easy, that I felt all the muscles along my neck and shoulders and back relax, and I saw Malcolm grinning at me, and I laughed in sheer enjoyment.

Then Catling struck.

My flesh tore open. I have had many years in which to think about the best words to describe what this felt like, and the simplest and best way to try and describe it to someone else is to say, "Well, imagine that you had barbed wire, razor sharp, buried within the flesh of your wrists and lower forearms. Imagine also that every so often—no particular pattern to it, just on your tormentor's whim—the barbed wire tore through toward the surface, ripping your flesh apart. But only slowly. Not fast. Not like some kind-hearted nursing sister ripping a drain out of a wound in order to cause the least discomfort possible. No, this happens slowly. Worse, it happens continuously. You see, the barbed wire never quite makes it to the surface. It just continues to tear through your flesh. The terrible wounds are never actually *made,* they are continually *in the making.*"

The red wires that glowed around my wrists were merely

the external manifestation of pain. The real pain—that was inside. The continual tearing upward. The continual *causing* of the wound. Most people only saw the red hot wires glowing around my wrists, but I think that when Jack Skelton first walked into the drawing room of Faerie Hill Manor he actually saw inside, saw the wounds *in the making*.

And, in the seeing, did not pity me.

Then, today, when Catling bit again while the deer were licking me, he came to me, and bent down, and whispered in my ear, *I know*.

I'm not too sure that he really did, but the words were better than what anyone else had ever spoken to me. Then, before my mother could fuss, he ushered me and Malcolm toward the kitchen.

There, while he and my mother wandered off among the trees, I sank down in a corner. I didn't want a chair, I didn't want to sit in front of the stove. I wanted cold to somehow provide some comfort against the raging agony in my wrists, and I wanted solitude in order to find the strength to bear it, and the corner of the kitchen seemed like the best place available.

Malcolm paid me the compliment of ignoring me, wandering about from table to aga, then to the sink, clearing away the tea dishes that someone—Matilda, I think—had brought in. He didn't speak to me, he didn't look at me, but I knew he was very aware of both my presence and my pain, but was not made uncomfortable by either.

Always I tried to be alone when Catling struck. I never wanted anyone near me. The only reason I'd stayed in that drawing room for Jack's arrival was that I had refused to allow Catling to drive me away on this momentous occasion.

So I should have hated this, having this strange man as witness to my humiliation. But I didn't. I found his presence . . . comforting and consoling.

Despite the agony, and the humiliation, and the terrifying sense of being out of control that always accompanied these attacks, it was a good time for me. For the first time in so many long years I didn't feel quite so alone. For so

long too many people had fussed, and then Jack had appeared to know just what I had needed.

Then Jack ruined it all by returning from his little walk in the woods with my mother. Returned with his arm linked with my mother's, and with a glow to my mother's face and a light in her eyes that terrified me. I didn't want my father to be hurt, and I could see his devastation written all over my mother. I looked into her face, and saw there the ruin of all of us. The delicate balance that had so long preserved us against utter ruin was broken.

My mother, of course, hurried over to where I was standing. "Grace?"

"I am well enough, mother. Don't fuss."

She didn't. She turned directly away from me and back to Jack. "You have been very kind, Jack. Thank you," she said, and then gave him a lovely smile that I'd only ever seen her give to my father, and that not recently.

I was certain then that she still loved Jack, and I cursed her silently. Not merely for what she would do to my father but what she would do to all of us. My world was fracturing around me, as I had feared it would the moment I heard Jack Skelton was returning.

"I want to go home," I said. "I don't want to stay here."

Oh God, I sounded childish and selfish, but I couldn't bear it any longer. Malcolm was looking between Jack and my mother, as also were Matilda, Ecub, and Erith, who had just come into the kitchen.

"Thank you," I said to Malcolm as I walked toward the door leading outside. Then, over my shoulder to my mother: "I'll wait in the car."

"THAT WAS RUDE, GRACE," NOAH SAID AS SHE drove us back to London. She'd marched back to the car a few moments after me, Matilda, Ecub, and Erith trailing silently after her (as they had continued to maintain a diplomatic silence in the backseat as we drove south). Jack and Malcolm had remained in the house.

"Father will be waiting for us," I said.

"Jack was kind to you," Noah said, her eyes fixed firmly on the road ahead. "The least you could have done was to thank him."

She was right, of course. But I didn't reply, for if I had I thought I would have burst into tears. I loved my parents, they provided the only constant and stability in my life, I didn't want to see them torn apart, and I was terrified that my mother wouldn't be able to help herself.

And if they tore apart, then everything would tear apart. I knew it. Catling had set her trap, and Jack and my mother were falling into its clutches. My life as it was up to this point had been terrible enough, but it *was* a life, and I felt that with Jack's arrival I'd been sat down before some glum-eyed medical specialist who would fold his hands, and look over the top of his glasses, and say, "I'm sorry, my dear, but there's no hope. There is nothing to be done. I would give you six months, only."

My mother and Jack Skelton were going to murder us all with their disastrous love. Why couldn't they have learned that lesson a millennium ago?

Ah, but why should I hate them for that? We'd all been murdered, so long, long ago. There never was such a thing as hope, and I'd been foolish to ever believe it.

There was only ever the Troy Game, victorious.

Chapter Two

Copt Hall

Thursday, 7 September 1939

WHAT WERE YOU DOING WITH GRACE, Malcolm?" Jack said. He was leaning against some kitchen cupboards, arms folded, his gaze steady on Malcolm, still at the sink. Outside he could hear Noah's car pull away.

"I was introducing her to some of my companions."

"They weren't deer, Malcolm."

Malcolm turned around at that, drying his hands on a tea towel. "Frankly, I thought I'd done a good job of disguising them."

Now Jack's gaze verged on the openly hostile. The disguise *had* been good—good enough to fool everyone else—but when Jack had come downstairs and seen the deer close, their forms had appeared false.

Transparent.

A disguise.

There had been three men standing there. Warriors, wearing tartan kilts and a terrible expression of loss in their eyes.

And Malcolm had allowed one of them to stroke Grace's arm.

Jack was furious, but wasn't quite sure why. Because Malcolm was something *other* than he'd thought? Because Grace had been in danger?

"Who are you, Malcolm?"

Malcolm gave Jack a long, considered look. "You thought I was a Sidlesaghe."

"Who are you, Malcolm?"

"My ancient name was Prasutagus," he said. "I was king of the Iceni."

Jack's mind raced. As a man he did not know the name, but as Ringwalker . . . oh yes, the name was familiar. He could feel its significance seeping up from the soil beneath the foundations of the hall.

"You were Boudicca's husband," he said.

Malcolm gave a small smile. "I was far more than that." He shifted slightly, making a slight movement with one hand, and suddenly Jack saw standing before him a tall, thin man who, though he continued to wear Malcolm's clothing, exuded an aura of ancient power.

Faint blue lines marked his face—the woad markings of one of the ancient priests of the land.

Jack raised an eyebrow. "A druid, no less. So tell me, Druid Prasutagus, what were you doing with Grace? And why are you here"—one shoe tapped the floor—"in Copt Hall?"

"I am here to help save the land," Malcolm replied.

From the infection you brought to it. Jack didn't so much hear that thought from Malcolm as feel it.

"Should I trust you?" Jack said.

"Yes."

"What do you know?"

"Enough."

"That's no answer," Jack snapped. "And you have not told me what you were doing with Grace. Why show her to those warriors? Why allow them to *touch* her?"

"I wanted to know if I could trust her," said Malcolm, "and if I could trust her with you. So I introduced her to some of my warrior-priests, men whose opinions I respect before any other. They instinctively trusted her."

"There is more to Grace than meets the eye," Jack said, wondering why Malcolm needed to be able to trust Grace.

"Oh, I know that," said Malcolm. "Jack, I am not your enemy. I am your servant. *I know who you are.* I can do nothing but serve you. Don't make me the enemy."

Jack relaxed a little. "And your wife? Should I expect to see her dusting the stairs one day?"

"Boudicca still rests in death," said Malcolm. "She has not returned to this world to live."

Perhaps they needed someone in the Otherworld for whatever it was they were about, Jack thought. "What is the bond between you and Copt Hall?"

"The hall stands on the site where Boudicca killed herself and our two daughters," he said. "This"—now his foot tapped at the kitchen floor—"is where they died. I am tied to it by sorrow and by power. And now, by you. I am not surprised you picked this place, above all others, to make your home."

There was something else lurking behind his words, but Jack could not see it. *Why was he back? What had Prasutagus and Boudicca to do with the Troy Game?* Jack knew he could stand here all day and ask Malcolm questions and get little back in response but more puzzlement. So he studied Malcolm one long moment longer, stretching out the silence until it was slightly uncomfortable, then gave a nod, as if dismissing Malcolm, and left the room.

Malcolm stared after him. Then, when he was quite sure Jack was gone, he bared his teeth in a silent snarl.

"That wasn't very nice," said a voice.

Malcolm snapped around.

A young woman with long curling black hair and a cold face was leaning against the outside door, in almost the same position Jack had been leaning against the cupboard.

"When they discover you there'll be hell to pay," Malcolm said, recovering his composure.

"Ah, but isn't that what you and I and Boudicca have planned for, all along?" said the woman. Her eyes wandered over to where Jack had been standing but a minute previously.

"You can't wait to meet him, can you?" Malcolm said softly.

If possible, the woman's face became even colder. "I care nothing for him," she said.

"Of course not," said Malcolm. "Did you know the imps are murdering—" He went on, but got no further, for suddenly he found himself alone in the kitchen.

Chapter Three

MAZE POND, SOUTHWARK

Friday, 8 September 1939

VERA CLEMENTS FINISHED HER SHIFT AS A nurse's aide at Guy's Hospital far later than usual. The damned ward sister had been unhappy with the dressing trays, and had required Vera to do them all again—cleaning, laying out, wrapping, sterilizing, the entire bloody lot. No matter that Sister had known it would make Vera late. No matter that Sister *must* have known that it would be full dark by the time Vera left and Vera would have to walk to the train station along unlit streets.

Nothing mattered but the cursed dressing trays.

Well, now Vera had finished, but night had closed in, and Vera knew her parents would be worried. They hated her walking the streets at night, and, once they'd realized she'd missed her usual train home, they would be sitting around the kitchen table, a cold pot of tea between them, worried eyes flickering toward the little clock sitting on the dresser.

Well, at least London Station wasn't far. All Vera had to do was duck up Maze Pond, then nip across St. Thomas Street and she was there. Five minutes, six at the most, and she'd be inside the station and heading for her home.

She hunched down into her coat—Lord, but it was cold for this time of the year!—and walked so fast up Maze Pond it was almost a jog. Her heels clattered along the pavement, enough to wake the dead, but Vera didn't care. Just another few minutes and she'd be out of this dark, lonely street and inside the train—

A shadow moved, catching Vera's eye, and she jerked to a halt.

A man stood in the dark rectangle of a doorway across the street. Vera could make out nothing of him but the glow of his cigarette as he drew on it, and the outline of the hat pulled down low over his brow.

He wasn't looking at her—his head was bent low, as if studying the pavement—but Vera *knew* his attention was all on her.

She forced her feet to move. Silly man, she told herself. Lonely, no doubt. Thinking to chat up a nurse on her way home. Well, he'd not get a word out of—

She gasped in shock. She couldn't see it, but somehow she *knew* that another man was following her up Maze Pond. His footsteps were slow and stealthy, his movements slippery, his eyes fixed on her back.

Vera spun around.

A shape (*the man*) slipped into a passageway between buildings and was gone.

Trying to control her breathing, Vera glanced at the man across the street—still in his doorway, still drawing on his cigarette—then back at the now-empty street behind her.

Slowly, her every move a nightmarish effort now, Vera turned around again and began to walk as fast as she could up the street.

From the corner of her eye she saw the man in the doorway toss aside his smoke and step after her.

Vera broke into a run. *St. Thomas Street was just ahead! She could reach it in less than a minute!*

The second man stepped out of an alleyway directly in front of her and grabbed at her elbow.

Vera shrieked, the sound a harsh whistle in her throat, jerking her arm away, hearing the man laugh softly.

"Got you worried, have we, sweet?" he whispered.

She tried to step around him, tried to run, tried to drag her eyes away from his, but she stumbled in the gutter, sprawling painfully across the surface of the street.

A hand traced lightly down her back. Vera could feel its fingers burning through her coat.

Sobbing, terrified, Vera scrambled forward, trying re-

peatedly to get to her feet but stumbling back to her hands and knees every time.

Her hands and knees were bleeding, and the base of her chin throbbed from where it had slammed into the road.

One of the men stepped up behind her—Vera thought her heart would burst from fright—and buried his hand in her coat between her shoulder blades.

The next instant he had hauled her to her feet.

Run, he whispered in her mind. *Run!*

Vera ran.

Her feet slipped wildly on the road, but somehow she managed to stay upright. Her handbag had long gone, and her jaunty red woolen cap lay on the roadway where she'd fallen. Her hair escaped from its bun and wrapped itself about her eyes, blinding her, and her coat flapped madly as she ran toward the junction of Maze Pond with St. Thomas Street.

She could see cars passing along St. Thomas Street, could see the dim lights of London Station, could see the shapes of people moving around inside.

Vera knew she would never make it out of Maze Pond.

"Are we scared yet?" came a whisper in her ear. "Truly terrified?"

Vera spun around, hitting out madly, blindly, with her fists.

Something sharp, something nasty, sliced along her left ribs.

Can you feel her terror?

She heard that, although she knew her assailants weren't addressing her.

Rather, they addressed something large, something shadowy, something huge, something *seething* down from the night sky!

Vera screamed, her mind refusing to accept what she was seeing, or what was about to happen to her.

One of the men, laughing softly, grabbed at the collar of her coat, pulling her against him.

A knife, very long, very cold, very sharp, slid into her belly, then jerked to one side.

* * * *

MUCH LATER, THE IMPS, MOVING UNDER THE cloak of power, left Vera Clements' ruined corpse under the porch of St. Magnus the Martyr on the northern bank of the Thames.

One of them, Jim, held a scrap of flesh in his hand—still warm, bloody, and soft.

He sighed, as if regretful, then walked the short distance to the embankment and tossed what remained of Vera's womb into the cold, gray waters.

Then both Jim and Bill looked upward, their teeth glinting.

It had been a good night.

Chapter Four

FAERIE HILL MANOR

Saturday, 9 September 1939

JACK DROVE THROUGH EPPING FOREST THE night after Vera had taken her ill-fated walk along Maze Pond. Despite the cool weather, he had the hood of the Austin convertible folded back, and the wind rippled through the short curls on his head. He drove with one hand on the wheel, the other resting on the top of the door, occasionally lifting his hand to his mouth to draw on the cigarette he held.

The car zipped along the narrow roadways. There was a speed limit of only twenty mph in force to try to save petrol, but Jack ignored it. No one would see or hear him, for Jack drove that strange borderland between the Faerie and the mortal world, where distances expanded and contracted according to need, and where time passed only as requested. Trees crowded the verges of the roadway, dark

and impenetrable, their branches meeting overhead so that
Jack drove through a dark tunnel; occasionally the head-
lamps of the Austin would catch something strange drift-
ing between the trees or scampering across the road just in
front of the car.

Jack had been driving for hours. In the usual world it
would have taken but a few short minutes to drive from
Copt Hall to Faerie Hill Manor, but Jack wanted the time
and space to think. Tonight was a cliff edge. A night of be-
ginnings and endings. Never again would he be the same
once he stepped over that edge.

Tonight he would be marked. Tonight he would take that
final step into the forest.

Do I really want to do it?

Yes, of course he did. It would give him power beyond
knowing, and peace beyond anything he'd ever achieved, if
all went well.

Am I frightened?

Yes, of course he was. This was a step that could never
be retraced. Never again could he just walk away as he had
when he was Louis de Silva.

This was a night that would bind him to the trees. Once
and for all.

For the first time since he'd arrived back in England, Jack
was not wearing his uniform. Instead he'd dressed simply in
an open-necked white shirt, gray flannel trousers, and a
single-breasted jacket of the same material. Loose, elegant,
comfortable clothing.

He'd be sore when he came back.

Jack shifted in the driver's seat a little as he thought that,
and he forcibly shifted his train of thought to Walter Herne,
hoping that the man would be where planned, at the time
planned.

"Just this one thing, Walter," Jack whispered, "and then
you're a free man. Just this one thing. . . ."

IT WAS JUST AFTER NINE P.M. WHEN JACK PULLED
into the forecourt of Faerie Hill Manor. Unlike the first

night he'd arrived, the house was now under full blackout conditions. A sliver of light showed here and there from behind blackout curtains, but that was it.

Harry was waiting for him, opened the front door as soon as Jack knocked.

They nodded a greeting.

"Is all set?" Jack said.

"Yes." Harry motioned to the drawing room. "Come on through. There's time for a talk before you go."

Jack more than half expected to find Grace huddled by the fire again, as he had the first time he'd walked into this room, but although the fire crackled, the room was empty save for himself and Harry.

"Where's Stella?" Jack said.

"Gone to the Faerie for the night," Harry said. "Drink?"

Jack hesitated, then nodded. A drink wouldn't do him any harm at all.

As Harry walked over to the drinks cabinet, Jack idly glanced at a copy of the *Daily Mail* lying on a table.

There was a small article partway down the page. The body of another woman had been found under the porch of St. Magnus the Martyr.

"What do you know about this?" Jack said, tapping the article with a finger as Harry handed him his whisky.

Harry glanced down, then looked sharply back to Jack. "Why the interest?"

"There was another murder, wasn't there? The night I arrived. I remember the radio announcer mentioning it just before Chamberlain made the announcement of war. What do you know about it, Harry? Why your interest in my interest?"

Harry sipped at his whisky, taking his time in replying. "There's been some concern about the two murders at Scotland Yard," he said finally. "The murders were particularly brutal. Both women had their bellies mutilated—ripped apart. Their wombs were gone." He paused. "Some wit within the Yard has dubbed the killer the Penitent Ripper . . . the murders bear some resemblance to the Jack the Ripper murders fifty years ago—you have heard of them? Yes?— but because this time the women have been left on the porch

of St. Magnus the Martyr the 'Jack' has been replaced with 'penitent.' No doubt the papers will get hold of *that* sobriquet soon enough. Jack, do *you* know anything about them?"

Jack shook his head. "God, to be that brutal to do that to a woman." He gave a grunt. "Reminds me of Weyland . . ."

They fell silent, remembering that horrific day so long ago when, as Charles II and Louis de Silva, they had ridden back into London to the screams of Noah and Jane as Weyland tore them apart.

"Not Weyland," said Harry. "Not this time."

Jack gave a small shrug and set his emptied whisky glass to one side.

"Noah told me that you and she seemed to have . . . sorted out some of your differences," Harry said, breaking the small awkward silence that had risen between them.

"We talked," Jack said. "We didn't fight."

"Really?" Harry looked at Jack carefully. "Are you getting on well enough to make the Great Marriage, d'you think?" The Great Marriage symbolized the ultimate union between the land and the waters, bringing all aspects of the land and Faerie into harmony. If Jack and Noah, in their capacities as gods of the forest and waters, effected the Great Marriage, it would strengthen the land and the Faerie in their battle against the Troy Game.

"We have to do it, don't we?" Jack said.

"To give yourselves the best chance of saving the land, yes, you do. But somehow I thought you'd be more cheerful about the prospect than you seem."

"I'm sure I won't find it too difficult, Harry. But I don't want to talk about that tonight. Nor those murders. Tonight it is just me and the forest."

At that moment the telephone rang, and both men gave a slight jump. Harry walked over to the desk and picked up the receiver. "Yes?"

He listened a moment, carefully turning his back so Jack could not see his face, then said, "I'll let him know. Thank you for telephoning, Walter."

"He's not backed out?" Jack took a step toward Harry as he put the telephone receiver back into its cradle.

Harry shook his head. "No. There's been a bomb scare Hampstead way. A woman out with her boyfriend found what they thought was a UXB lying on the edge of the heath. Everyone panicked, half the neighborhood was evacuated, the ARP and the fire brigade became terribly officious, and the end result is that with the panic and the evacuation, as well all the personnel running around the heath, Walter has been caught up in the fuss, and said he won't be able to leave the area for a couple of hours."

Jack's shoulders clearly relaxed. "What was it, if not a UXB?"

"Apparently some schoolboys had made a papier-mâché approximation of what they'd thought a bomb might look like, painted it black, and stored it under a shrub to see if they could frighten evening lovers out for a stroll."

"So I have an hour or two to spare."

"Then feel free to relax here. I am needed back in the Faerie, although I'll be back in time for . . . well, in time for your adornment. Help yourself to another drink. Or two, if you think you need it."

ONCE HARRY HAD LEFT, JACK REFILLED HIS GLASS, wandered desultorily about the bookshelves for a quarter of an hour, then decided he needed space and air. He put the almost untouched whisky glass down on the table and headed for the set of doors that led onto the side terrace.

He slipped through, shutting the doors quickly behind him, and wandered slowly over to the stone balustrade that looked down the side of the hill on which the house stood. It was a lovely night, cool, but not cold, and with a little moonlight filtering through the cloud layer. Jack took a deep breath, staring toward the forest, his eyes picking out individual trees, and the slow movement of the forest creatures across the forest floor, sniffling out food and scent trails, and . . .

Jack became aware that he wasn't alone on the terrace.

It was an unsettling sense, for he felt that the other presence was either fearful or antagonistic, either about to run away or to attack.

He turned around, very slowly, his hands in the pockets of his trousers, as if he were merely taking in the view.

There, to his left. In the shadows where the terrace joined into a hip of the house. Jack strolled casually closer, always looking over the railing toward the view, his senses straining toward the shadows to his left.

"I'm sorry to have disturbed you."

He tensed, then turned easily, a smile on his face. "Grace. What are you doing here?"

She was sitting against the wall of the house at an outdoor table and chair setting, looking desperately uncomfortable at Jack's presence. She was huddled into a coat, so deeply that all that was visible of her was the pale smudge of her face beneath her tousled hair.

"I came to see Stella," Grace said, her eyes watching Jack's every move as he walked over to the table and sat down in a chair opposite her.

He didn't take his eyes off her, despite realizing that she was growing more self-conscious by the moment. "She isn't here. She's in the Faerie tonight. That's where you should find her."

"Oh."

Jack narrowed his eyes. *Have you come to see Stella,* he wondered, *or Harry? Come to see your lover?* "I didn't see another car outside when I pulled up," he said.

"I didn't come by car."

Already nervous at what awaited him later that night, Jack grew even more unsettled at the implications of that response. "Do you often sit out here and scare people?" he snapped.

"I didn't mean to scare you."

"What do you *want,* Grace? Don't feed me the Stella story."

She took a long time to respond, but finally answered directly. "I came to see you, Jack. I knew you'd be here tonight."

Ah, the truth at last. But how did she now he'd be here? Only Harry and Walter, and possibly Noah, knew about tonight.

Ah, but there was Malcolm. Malcolm knew he'd be coming to Faerie Hill Manor tonight, but—presumably—did not know the reason.

Will I see him atop Ambersbury Banks tonight? Jack wondered, and knew, without a doubt, that he would.

So. Malcolm told Grace. Interesting. What was there between them?

"Well, here I am, then." Jack shook a cigarette out of its pack, then slid the pack back into the breast pocket of his jacket. "What did you want to see me about?"

She ran her tongue over her top lip. "I needed to talk to you about my mother. I wondered what you and my mother . . . what . . . you and she . . . um . . ."

Jack lit the cigarette with a match, the glow momentarily lighting his face. "Yes?"

She shifted, even more uncomfortable, and would not look at Jack's face. Then she took a deep breath. "I wanted to know what you wanted with my mother."

"It's none of your business, Grace."

Now she looked directly at him. "Don't dismiss me like that. When you play with the Troy Game, you're playing with my *life,* Jack."

He watched her, hiding the expression of his eyes behind the drifting smoke of his cigarette. "I need and want a great deal from your mother."

"Do you love her?"

"Of course," he said, softly, wondering as he said it whether he really meant it, or if he'd said that only to goad Grace.

"Don't tear us apart, Jack! Don't *upset* things!"

"Oh, for God's sake, Grace! What the hell business is it of yours? What is between your mother and me and your damned father goes back a very long time before you were born. She and I . . . she and I . . . Ah!" He was too angry to go on.

"She loves my *father.*"

"*Really?*"

She was silent, again dropping her gaze away from his angry eyes.

"I have spent three thousand years loving your mother, Grace. Besides, she and I need to make the Great Marriage—"

Grace's face tensed at that.

"—and we need to close out the Troy Game together. Or destroy it together. She and I are so linked, and so closely—Christ, don't you know of the intimacy that must exist between a Mistress of the Labyrinth and a Kingman?—that I can't just . . ." Dear God, what was he doing, trying to explain himself to this girl? "I am not going to just walk away from Noah. Unless you give me a good reason, of course."

Jack was angry enough now to push Grace a bit too far. "Come now, what might that reason be? Ah, perhaps you think to offer *yourself* as compensation if I leave Noah alone? A suitable runner's-up prize to the sorry loser? Oh come now, Grace, you can't possibly think yourself any kind of replacement for your mother. You're only—"

It was precisely at that moment that she looked back at him, and Jack stopped midflow, appalled by what he saw in her eyes. He'd *never* once seen that in any person's eyes, not even in Cornelia-Caela-Noah's when he'd said the most vicious things to her. *This* he'd only ever seen in an animal's eyes, when it was trapped, and knew it was going to die.

A great withdrawing, deep into itself.

A passing from the world.

"Jesus, Grace, I'm sorry." Instantly contrite, and hating himself for what he'd said, Jack reached across the table and grabbed at the sleeve of her coat, certain in that moment that she *was* actually about to vanish. "I'm *sorry*, Grace."

She hovered there, at the edge of that bleak place, and Jack's fingers tightened on her coat sleeve. He had thought previously that he'd understood how terrible her life had been. Now he understood that he truly had no idea, and that he very likely never would.

What he *did* understand was her fright at the idea Jack would tear her mother and father apart. They must be one of the few constants she had; one of the only certainties she knew.

Not to mention that any drama between Jack, Noah, and Weyland, if it affected the Troy Game, had the distinct possibility of destroying any hope Grace had for freedom from Catling's hex.

I'm sorry, Grace. This he said both with his power and with pure emotion. *I'm sorry, Grace. That was a vicious thing to say, and I* am *sorry for it.*

"You'll destroy us," she whispered. "You'll destroy *me.*"

He tightened his fingers around her arm. "I don't want to. I won't, Grace."

He could see that she didn't believe him, but he felt her arm relax very slightly under his hand, and the terrible withdrawing in her eyes had stopped.

"You must love your father very much," Jack said, releasing Grace's coat sleeve and suddenly remembering his cigarette. He drew deeply on it.

"I don't want to hurt him," Grace said.

That response told him a great deal about Grace. Did she think everything her fault? Did she shoulder the responsibility for all the world's ills?

"He and I go back a long way," he said. "Many lives. I hadn't ever imagined Asterion could be a good father."

Grace had relaxed enough now that one of her hands had crept out from beneath the coat sleeve, its fingers idly drawing invisible patterns on the tabletop.

"Fatherhood is his redemption," she said. "He thinks he dare not fail at it."

Jack was watching the patterns her fingers made on the table, fascinated by their movement. "I'm surprised he and Noah have not had more children."

"After their tragedy with me?" Grace said. "I'm surprised they even dare to still make love."

That remark should have been bitter, but instead Jack found himself smiling at the rich layer of amusement behind it. *Who* are *you,* he thought, *behind that mask of fear?*

Grace's mouth lifted in a small smile as well, and for a brief instant they shared the moment of humor. Then her eyes dropped back to her fingers, and Jack's followed them.

And then he went cold as he realized what she'd been so idly doing, tracing out those patterns on the tabletop.

She'd been tracing out harmonies. Meaningless, idle harmonies, but harmonies nonetheless, drawing together the strands of existence of the night air about them, of the tabletop, of the threads that made up her coat, of the smoke dribbling out the end of his cigarette . . .

Grace could have sat there and done that before almost any man save Jack, and they would have had no idea what she was doing.

But Jack was a Kingman, and he knew *precisely* what she was doing.

And what she was.

"Who taught you the arts of Mistress of the Labyrinth?" he asked.

Grace snatched her hand back from the table, and it vanished up the overlong sleeve of her coat.

"Ariadne?" said Jack, hating it that his voice had now hardened, but so surprised and unnerved by what he'd just realized—*and by what he knew hovered beneath the flesh of her arms*—that he was unable to stop it. "Your mother?"

"Stella."

"Stella?"

"Why not?"

"Why?"

"She said I should learn, and so she taught me."

"Not your mother?"

Grace's tongue slid about her upper lip again. "I don't think she knows I've been trained."

Jack's mouth dropped open. "You're kidding me. How could she *not* know?"

"She doesn't ever see *me,* Jack. She only sees a tragedy. She just sees her mistake."

"Sweet mother of God, Grace." He paused. Noah didn't know? How blind *was* she when it came to her daughter? "Where did Stella teach you?"

"Where she was taught by her mother. On Tot Hill. There was a—"

Jack remembered back all those thousands of years. "There was a stone building on the hill. A meeting hall. Genvissa—Stella—took me there."

Grace nodded. "That stone building was what her mother used to transform into the Great Founding Labyrinth."

As a Kingman, Jack knew the process by which all Mistresses of the Labyrinth were trained. They were taken by the one who taught them to a building which, through the arts of the labyrinth, was transformed into a mirror of the Great Founding Labyrinth that had once stood in Knossos. There they learned to manipulate the harmonies of life, and to control the labyrinth itself.

So Stella taught Grace on Tot Hill. "Which House of Parliament did you use?" Jack said, referring to the fact that the British Houses of Parliament now stood on the exact site that Genvissa's stone hall had once occupied. Now that his initial shock was over at the discovery Grace was a trained Mistress, he was vaguely amused at the thought that either Commons or Lords had been transformed, without any mortal realizing it, into the Great Founding Labyrinth.

Grace looked him in the eye, and he saw for the first time a flash of confidence in their depths.

"Not the Houses of Parliament," she said. "Westminster Abbey. The altar."

Jack's unease returned. When he was William, Asterion had crowned him at the altar of the abbey. That thought reminded Jack that Grace was not only a Mistress of the Labyrinth, she was also a Darkwitch, bred twice by the father of Darkcraft himself, Asterion.

Just how vulnerable was Grace? Really? Was this a reality that sat before him, or an act? He couldn't read her, and it made him distrust everything she said.

"It seems I am surrounded by Mistresses of the Labyrinth," he said, lighting up a new cigarette. "Stella, your mother, Ariadne—who I believe is still about—and now you. Is there anyone else I should know about?"

Grace shook her head.

"And just one Kingman. All of you, to fight over me."

She didn't reply to that, and eventually Jack sighed and stubbed out his cigarette, wishing he was anywhere but here, and that Noah and Weyland had never conceived this complication of a child. "Grace Orr, Mistress of the Labyrinth, what *do* you know of this 'wrongness' that I have felt over London? You know something, I can feel it. What, for Christ's sake?"

She took her time in answering. "Catling comes and sits with me at night."

Jack was torn between irritation at her evasiveness and horror at her revelation. "*What?* Do your parents know?"

Grace shook her head. "I can't tell them. They already have enough of a burden to carry."

Jack wasn't sure whether to regard her as a supreme manipulator (*look at how pitiful my life is*) or a truly tragic figure. Or was there something else lurking there? *Who was Grace, truly?* "How long has Catling been 'sitting with you at night'?"

"Ever since I was a toddler."

"And? What does she say? What does this have to do with what I felt?"

Grace made a helpless gesture. "She just . . . watches. But she smiles at me, and, oh God, I know she has something planned. I can feel it *eking* out of her. What you have felt, your 'wrongness' . . . it must be her. A trap. Please, please, Jack, please don't fall into it!"

Jack again drew deeply on his cigarette, watching Grace's face through the drifting smoke, and said nothing.

There were traps everywhere, and Jack was sure he was staring at one of the biggest and most dangerous of them.

Chapter Five

AMBERSBURY BANKS, EPPING FOREST

Saturday, 9 September 1939

AN HOUR LATER JACK LEFT FAERIE HILL Manor. He'd come here earlier already unsettled at the thought of what this night held; now, after his conversation with Grace, he was so nervous that he found himself jumping at every noise.

The house was quiet when Jack walked out the front door. Harry had not reappeared, but Jack was not worried; he could feel the Lord of the Faerie watching, and knew he would be there to witness. Neither had Walter appeared, but Jack had felt him drawing closer, driving along the forest road north.

He, too, would be at the appointed place.

Grace had earlier gone up the stairs to the upper floor of the house, saying she was going to bed.

But Jack didn't believe her. *What was her real purpose in talking to him? Why this night of all nights? And what in God's name was he supposed to make of her words . . . and of* her?

He stood on the front terrace in the dark night, remembering her fingers idly twisting those harmonies out across the table top. Those harmonies had been so compelling, and he'd felt them thrumming through his blood. But he shouldn't forget she was also a Darkwitch. *Ringwalker had only one enemy, and that was the Darkwitch.*

That's what he had once thought, but Jack had made his peace with Noah, and with Stella. Should Grace then be feared?

"Why not," he whispered, "until I know different?"

Then, suddenly making up his mind, he ran lightly down the steps to where his Austin sat. Jack stood, stared at it, then he lifted his head, and looked northward.

The night encircled him, very still and dark.

There was no moon.

Jack took a step away from the car. His hands clenched, then released as he forced himself to relax. He took a deep breath, closed his eyes, then walked away from the car toward the edge of the forest.

EPPING FOREST HAD EXISTED SINCE THE LAND that was now Britain had first risen from the misty swamps of creation. It had once been much larger and much mightier, spreading eastward and northward across the land. Between its trees had roamed bears and wolves, hares and badgers, mammoth and aurochs, and stranger, wilder beasts that sometimes strayed out of the Faerie. By the midtwentieth century, after thousands of years of depredation by the axe and plow, the forest covered only some five thousand acres.

Yet the forest's power remained, as much of it as when once the forest had covered so much more of the land. Only now it was . . . concentrated.

Epping Forest was riddled with walkways and bridle paths, roads and forestry tracks, and the trails worn down by the tens of thousands of years of foxes hunting dormice and ghosts hunting resolution, but Jack walked none of these. He walked a strange causeway that had not been trodden since Og, the being who had walked formerly as the Stag God, had taken it over a hundred thousand years previously.

It was an easy path to follow, however, despite the dark of the moonless night.

The leaf litter marking the trail was speckled with drops of glistening blood. Og's blood.

When tonight was done, the path would be laid down anew for the next resurgent Stag God to walk down in perhaps another hundred thousand years' time.

This time it would be laid down in Jack's blood.

The blood, and what it implied, strangely settled Jack's

nerves. He was glad to be doing this, finally. It was the ultimate step—or the ultimate plummet, whichever way you preferred to view it—into his life as Ringwalker, God of the forests.

He walked north, his feet scrunching down firmly on the bloodstained leaf litter as if he drew comfort from the blood leaching up through the soles of his shoes. His path took him roughly parallel with New Epping Road—although sometimes he diverged, and wandered briefly into the Faerie, where Sidlesaghes and water sprites shadowed him—and Jack swung a little deeper into the forest when he passed the Wake Arms and the Fox and Hounds taverns. Within fifteen minutes of leaving Faerie Hill Manor Jack entered the section of the forest called the Long Running. The forest drew back at this point, and Jack strode through long, coarse rush grass. Here he took a deep breath, and quickened his pace slightly.

He didn't have far to go.

Another fifteen minutes, and Jack approached the ancient fort of Ambersbury Banks on the northwestern edge of Epping Forest. He wasn't far from Copt Hall, and for a moment his pace slowed, and his head turned westward to where he felt the hall rising, but then he focused forward once more.

Ambersbury Banks was a raised circular fortress, defended by earthen banks and ditches that had, over the centuries, crumbled and decayed under the onslaught of the forest. Historians and foresters had long argued over whether it was an ancient British camp, or one thrown up by the Romans, but in reality no human hand had built Ambersbury Banks. It was a part of the Faerie, one of The Naked's children that had lost its way and slipped into the mortal world, never to find its way home. It had a twin, Loughton Camp to the south, but Ambersbury was the older and more powerful of the two hills.

And with a far bloodier history. Ambersbury was a place of blood, and it attracted blood to it. Boudicca's army had been slaughtered here, but there had been lesser murders on Ambersbury, although no less tragic, as when Sulemaic, an Anglo-Saxon warrior, had raped then murdered twin

thirteen-year-old sisters on the primeval Faerie hill one dark, moonless night in the eighth century. During the fourteenth century two young boys had been found at Ambersbury with their throats cut and every drop of blood drained from their bodies into the ancient earth. In the eighteenth century a toddler had met a similar fate. Twice during the nineteenth century, in incidents separated by twenty-four years, two cuckolded husbands had slit their wives' throats within the fort's boundaries.

It was not a particularly pleasant place for the vulnerable to linger.

There had also been blood spilled on Ambersbury Banks that was not associated with either battles or tragedies. Almost four thousand years ago a young man, known as the Gormagog, had come here to be marked as Og's living representative. Thirty years after that, Gormagog had brought his son Loth to be similarly marked.

They had been tattooed with the mark of the former Stag God.

Jack was coming here to be marked with something far darker. He had come to absorb into his flesh the remnants of Og's being.

MOST OF AMBERSBURY BANKS WAS SPECKLED with ancient, gnarled trees which had, over thousands of years, twisted the lines of earthworks until it appeared that a gigantic plow had run amok over the hill, riding it into parallel lines of agony that mirrored its bloody history. On the summit, however, there was a clear space of perhaps a quarter of an acre.

In the center of this almost circular patch of grassland stood the stump of a tree that had been felled in a storm eight hundred years earlier. Over the centuries its top had been worn smooth by the rubbing of countless hands. It was known as the wooden stone, because when you looked down to its base, you saw that the stump's twisting, knotted roots were wrapped around and over a broad smooth-faced stone.

This stone was the heart of Ambersbury Banks; its

causeway, if you like, back into the Faerie. It was an altar, as old as the hill itself, and it had served almost as many religions and priests and druids as it had weathered storms.

Although the night was moonless, the cleared space on the summit of the hill was nonetheless lit with an unearthly silvery light. A man stood by the stump, carefully laying out instruments atop its smooth surface.

It was Walter Herne, now without his stick and standing full square on both feet.

He had removed both his dog collar and his shirt, and stood bare-chested in the night air, his skin goose-bumped against the cold. There was a shadowy tracery over his shoulders and chest, the memory of a mark that had lingered through several lives.

Loth, and all he had once been, and all he could once have been, was not quite dead, although Walter hoped to murder him once and for all this night.

Just this one thing, Walter, and then you'll be free.

Just this one thing.

There was a movement to the eastern quarter of the summit, and Walter froze and looked over.

Then he relaxed, if only a little. It was the Lord of the Faerie, standing forth from under a tree. Like Walter he was bare-chested, although rather than Walter's woolen trousers and shoes he wore well-fitted leather trousers, and his feet were bare.

On his head sat a crown of red berries set amid twisted twigs.

The Lord of the Faerie walked a point halfway between the encircling trees and the stump where stood Walter, then he stopped.

"We are glad you have come, Loth," he said, and Walter twitched.

"My name is not Loth," he said.

The Lord of the Faerie ignored his rebuttal. "I have brought the pestle and mortar," he said, and lifted his right hand.

That hand had been empty a bare moment ago, but now the Lord of the Faerie carried a crudely chiseled stone pes-

tle and mortar in his hand. As Walter watched, the Lord of
the Faerie squatted down and, with his left hand, grabbed a
handful of dirt and blown leaves from between his feet. As
he rose, he crumbled the mixture of dirt and leaves into the
bowl of the mortar.

Then he lifted his hand to his crown, and plucked from it
three or four of the red berries.

These, too, he crumbled into the bowl.

Once this was done, the Lord of the Faerie walked over
to Walter, looked him in the eye for a long moment, then
put the pestle and mortar on the top of the stump.

Before Walter could speak, or even move, the Lord of
the Faerie leaned very close to him, placing a hand on Wal-
ter's chest.

"How could you walk away from this?" he whispered,
his mouth almost touching Walter's ear. The Lord of the
Faerie ran his hand softly over Walter's chest, and then up
and over his right shoulder. "How could you leave? We
were such friends, once, you and I."

Walter didn't know if the Lord of the Faerie referred to
the friendship he had once shared with the Lord of the
Faerie when he had been Loth, and the Faerie lord had
been Coel, or if he talked of the more distant friendship
between the Faerie lord and his earthly servant.
Whichever one the Faerie lord meant, Walter had no idea
how to answer.

His mouth opened, but he could find no words to speak.

The Lord of the Faerie's hand tightened fractionally on
Walter's shoulder, and he leaned even closer to the man,
his mouth now touching Walter's flesh. *How could you
leave?*

Tears sprang to Walter's eyes, but he was saved from the
need to answer by the appearance of a man emerging from
under the trees on the western verge of the clearing.

Both the Lord of the Faerie and Walter's eyes slid
toward him.

The man bowed from the waist in deference to the Lord
of the Faerie, then stepped forward.

It was Malcolm, Jack Skelton's valet, but he no longer

wore the servant's clothes. Instead he'd come dressed as an ancient druid in a robe of tartan wool, and with woad marking out his face, his forearms, and the backs of his hands.

"It is a wakeful night," Malcolm said as he came to a halt a few steps away from where Walter and the Lord of the Faerie still stood so close together. "The forest is restless, waiting for its lord."

The Lord of the Faerie regarded him with unblinking eyes. "Well met, druid. I did not know you lingered within Malcolm's flesh. And at Copt Hall, no less. What role do you play in this?"

"I am bound to the land," said Malcolm, "as surely you must know, and I work in its interests. I am bound to Copt Hall by death, and similarly bound to Ambersbury Banks. I have come tonight to serve, if I may."

The Lord of the Faerie regarded him steadily, then abruptly stepped back from Walter and gave Malcolm a nod.

Then all three men turned their eyes to the south.

Jack Skelton had walked into the clearing.

HIS NERVES KICKED IN AGAIN THE INSTANT HE SAW the group—Malcolm included, as he'd expected—around the stump. It wasn't the forthcoming pain that troubled him so much as the realization that there would be no going back from this night. The Lord of the Faerie had reassured him that this would *confirm* his humanity, rather than subsume it, but that still did not help his qualms.

So he hesitated on the edge of the clearing. He thought he'd been sure, but now knew he wasn't.

Then the Lord of the Faerie walked forward. Very slowly, very surely.

"Jack," the Lord of the Faerie said, coming to a halt before him.

He said nothing else, just held Jack's gaze with such an easy surety, such a tranquility, that Jack felt himself relax.

The Lord of the Faerie's mouth moved in a small smile. "You can be who and what you want," he said. "Whenever you want. That is what tonight is about. You will be woven

entirely, forest to man. You choose the face you wear, you choose the power you wield. As Louis de Silva you gained the power and the knowledge. Tonight you gain the familiarity, and you will gain everything that Og once commanded, but you will lose nothing at all."

It was what Jack needed to hear, and he relaxed even further. The Lord of the Faerie stepped up to him, one hand running behind Jack's neck to cradle his head in its palm, and kissed softly first Jack's forehead, then both cheeks, and finally his mouth.

"Welcome to the strangeness of completion, Jack," the Lord of the Faerie said softly.

Then he was gone, back to the central ancient altar of Ambersbury Banks, and Jack, still at the edge of the clearing, began slowly to strip away his jacket and shirt.

MALCOLM CAME TO JACK'S SIDE, AND TOOK FROM him the jacket and shirt, then Jack's shoes and socks. He folded each article neatly, unhurriedly, then placed them behind a tree, out of sight.

Then he walked away to the western edge of the clearing, and stood, watching, hands folded before him, eyes shining.

Jack took a deep breath, then walked forward. He could feel the cold air upon his naked flesh of his chest, but it wasn't uncomfortable.

Through the soles of his bare feet he could feel the forest—feel the *land*—as a thrumming warmth, almost a breathing, caring curiosity. It would be a witness, too.

He relaxed yet further. *Tonight he would gain familiarity and completeness.*

Wisdom, too, he hoped.

And eyes, with which to see.

Walter stood behind the altar. Jack could see that he was tense and fearful. His shoulders were rigid, his eyes glittered, he held his arms stiffly at his side.

"Hello, Walter," Jack said.

Walter inclined his head.

"Can you do this, Walter?" Jack said. "Will you let go the Stag God entirely into my care? Do you *dare*?"

Something happened in Walter's face. A deep emotion flittered over it. Jack thought for a moment it was fear, then realized it was actually excitement. He remembered how the Lord of the Faerie, as Charles, had told him that James (as Walter had been in his former life) had been deeply excited at his return to England after all his years in exile, however much he professed a devotion to Christ, and now Jack could see a similar excitement in Walter's face.

Whatever Walter said, the core of his being still vibrated to the ancient rituals.

"Do *you* dare, Jack?" Walter said, and Jack grinned.

He glanced down at the top of the stump and saw what Walter had laid out there.

A surgical scalpel. Three razor-edged blades. Gauze swabs.

The mortar and pestle, and the dirt, leaves, and berries within the bowl of the mortar.

"Shall we begin?" Walter asked, and Jack jerked his eyes back to the man's face.

"Do you remember, Walter, how once we battled it out in the heart of the labyrinth atop Og's Hill?"

"How could I forget? I battled to save the land from you and your foreign magic. You battled to save your labyrinth. And you broke my spine."

"How stupid we were," Jack said softly, "when all the time we should have been standing here."

Walter moved away a little, fiddling with the instruments he'd laid out. "Let's get this done," he said, "and then let me walk away."

Jack gave a terse nod, then turned around—and gave a slight jump. While he and Walter had been speaking, the Lord of the Faerie had moved about silently and now stood directly facing Jack.

"How at home are you with the Ringwalk, Jack?" the Lord of the Faerie said.

"I feel it as if it is my own flesh," Jack replied.

"Really?" said the Lord of the Faerie. *"Really?"*

Chapter Six

Epping Forest

Sunday, 10 September 1939

Grace Speaks

𝕴 FOLLOWED. OF COURSE I DID. I KNEW SOMEthing was happening tonight, and I knew it involved Jack, and I knew also that Harry was somehow concerned. I knew that Harry and Jack had been planning Jack's marking, together with Walter. I knew that my parents knew something about it, but they did not speak of it to me. I'd never felt more the "outsider" than I had over the past week as I watched the small glances, and the occasional significant words, pass to and fro. It wasn't much said or done, but there was enough.

Oh God, I so much wanted to be a part of something, to not be continually pushed to the outer.

To *share*.

I was also terrified of what might be about to happen. I was so unsure of Jack, and of the desperately fine balance he could (almost certainly *would*) upset, that this sense of something momentous happening was enough to set my nerves on edge.

As well, over the past three nights Catling had sat grinning with such apparent satisfaction at me from her shadowy corner of my bedroom that I was certain that something terrible was imminent.

So, while my mother was out with her sisters, and my father had taken his shift atop the Savoy on ARP duty (earlier in the year he had volunteered as an ARP warden), I had sat in our apartment feeling such an ominous

weight of dread about my shoulders that I could no longer bear it.

I used my Darkcraft.

I rarely touched it. I had tried to use it once, many years ago, in an attempt to throw Catling's shackles from my wrists, but that had caused such a terrifying retribution that I'd never tried again. Somehow that failure had tainted the Darkcraft in my mind; I'd always associated it with the pain and terror of Catling's reprisal.

But tonight I was prepared to risk using it. To be honest, I think I might have torn my hair out if I'd been forced to use the trains or buses to get to Epping Forest (I had no doubt that Jack's marking would take place there), not to mention the goodly walk I'd have then been forced to take to reach Faerie Hill Manor once I'd arrived at either train station or bus stop . . . and I did not drive, so could not take one of my father's cars.

So I used the Darkcraft. I sat on my bed in our apartment, wearing the first thing I'd found to throw around myself, and allowed the Darkcraft to well up and consume me.

It was terrifying, if only because I thought Catling might reach out and bite. But she let me be, and I surrendered to the Darkcraft, closing my eyes against its power . . .

And opened them on the terrace of Faerie Hill Manor to find myself looking at Jack's back as he stood on the terrace. I knew he'd intuited my presence, and so I spoke, and he came over and sat down to talk to me.

I was more unnerved than ever, because I could feel his deep unease. He had, of course, wanted to know why I was there . . . I could hardly tell him it was because I was morbidly curious about this marking . . . and so I rattled on senselessly about my mother and how I feared he was going to upset things and . . .

Oh dear. I must have come across like a stupid young girl. I *knew* I'd come across as a stupid young girl because then Jack had snapped at me, and all I'd wanted to do was to run away, to cease to exist, because he was so angry at me, and I was so mortified.

Then he'd been apologetic (and appeared as if he

meant it, too), and from then on the conversation had oscillated between fear and candor and suspicion. I was furious with myself for allowing him to realize I'd been trained as a Mistress of the Labyrinth; he was furious to discover it.

And, I think, disappointed. He must have thought I was a pathetic Mistress of the Labyrinth.

I don't know why I told him about Catling sitting with me at night. I'd told no one for hundreds of years—why him, then? Jack had a terrible habit of just sitting and watching me from behind the smoke dribbling from his cigarette, and words seemed to tumble from my mouth.

Anything, to fill the silence.

We'd gone back inside eventually, and Harry, just arrived back from whatever he'd been doing in the Faerie, professed some surprise at my presence. He'd told me to spend the night, and that he'd have me driven back to the Savoy in the morning, and then he and Jack had, separately, left.

I waited ten minutes after Jack had left, then followed.

I FOLLOWED JACK RATHER THAN HARRY. HARRY had vanished from my perception, but I could sense Jack's movements through the forest, although I don't know what power I used to do so. It was hardly as if I had any natural connection with the forest, or with Jack himself, but once I left Faerie Hill Manor I turned around slowly in the driveway . . . and I felt a glimmer of Jack's movement to my north.

And so I trailed him. Very quietly, using every ounce of natural and magical quiet I could (although I was very circumspect in using my Darkcraft).

The forest was very dark and, for me, very unknowable. I rarely spent much time here at all. I'd been to Faerie Hill Manor a handful of times only in the past few years, and I don't think I'd ever walked in the forest itself. As soon as I stepped beneath the trees and felt the "foreignness" of the forest, its deep, mystical power, I realized how much of my life had been spent tucked away in some quiet room in

whatever house or apartment my parents had at the time. I'd been so sheltered (by both parents, although necessarily my mother had been the better at it) that I'd experienced very little of the outside world, let alone the Faerie magic of a place like Epping Forest.

I hadn't even been back to the Faerie since I'd been a baby. I think everyone had thought it might be unwise. Think of all the damage that Catling might wreak there through me.

I'd spent my life huddled in rooms, as if I were a prisoner.

Yet now, here I was, creeping through a forest that appeared to watch every movement I made.

I was more unnerved than ever, but paradoxically more determined. I would *not* be frightened. I had the Darkcraft. I could keep silent. Harry and Jack would never know I was following them.

I could *participate,* even if silently and unknowably, rather than be told six weeks after the event.

The journey through Epping Forest in Jack's trail took about half an hour, I suppose. We were heading north toward the town of Epping, and I did not know if Jack meant to go all the way to the town, or if he had a destination somewhere closer.

Somewhere closer, as it turned out.

I became aware eventually that he'd stopped moving, that he'd *arrived* at wherever he needed to be, and my own movements became far more cautious. I *crept* as best I could, every nerve straining for danger or chance of discovery, my Darkcraft simmering, begging to be allowed full rein.

Although the trees were well spaced, I had the sense that they were crowding about me, *watching* me, and, as I started up the incline of a hill that itself seemed to be a living, breathing entity. I could see a cleared space at the top of the hill, lit with the faint luminescence of magic, and my movements slowed even further, and I crept forward, careful silent step by careful silent step, taking cover behind every tree, every shrub, until I worked my way to the eastern edge of the clearing, and found myself a massive beech tree behind which to crouch. There was a small crab apple just to one

side of it that was more shrub than tree, and it enabled me to peer from behind the beech without chance of discovery.

TO BE FRANK, I HAVE NO IDEA AT ALL WHAT I WAS expecting, but to my eyes the group was quite extraordinary. Harry I was not so surprised to see, but I had so rarely seen him in his existence as the Lord of the Faerie that I stared at him for long minutes. Staid Walter Herne was standing half naked by a large stump, looking as if he wanted to be anywhere but. Malcolm lurked to the other side of the clearing looking like something from a history book, with blue paint smeared all over his face; his appearance did not surprise me at all, but his presence did make me feel uncomfortable. Then Jack . . . Jack, standing before the Lord of the Faerie, dressed only in his trousers, and as tense as one of the red deer that I'd stroked outside Copt Hall.

My eyes lingered on Jack, but eventually returned to the Lord of the Faerie. I'd known Harry all my life—but barely knew the Lord of the Faerie. The Lord of the Faerie existed only in the Faerie, where I'd spent so little time, and Harry had been . . . well, Harry had been Harry whenever he appeared in this world.

Harry I knew quite well. Perhaps a little too well. A few years ago we'd been lovers briefly. It had been Harry's idea—at least he'd been the one to suggest the liaison—and I'd acquiesced out of loneliness, curiosity, and a deep sense of needing to do something other than be Catling's victim.

It had not been a particular success. It had taken exactly one night to sate whatever curiosity I'd had (Harry had been my first, and thus far only, lover), and I'd sensed very quickly that Harry's heart had not been in it. He'd been kind, thoughtful, but, in the end, slightly distracted. I'd asked him why he'd wanted to do this, why, when all knew full well he had heart only for Stella, he'd decided to take me as a lover, and he'd shrugged and said only, "I was trying to help," which was no damned help at all.

So while I knew Harry reasonably intimately, during my adult life I'd never seen much of the Lord of the Faerie, and, crouching behind the beech and peering through the crab apple, I suddenly wished it had been the Lord of the Faerie who had taken me as a lover, and not Harry. The Lord of the Faerie had such vibrancy, such vigor, such *authority,* that I felt a moment's envy for what Stella enjoyed, and I had not.

Walter was fidgeting with something on the stump now—I could not see what—but Jack and the Lord of the Faerie appeared to be engaged in a brief but intense discussion. The Lord of the Faerie had his hand on Jack's shoulder, then abruptly he shifted it into Jack's hair, grabbing at it and giving Jack's head a little shake. It looked almost as if the Lord of the Faerie was trying either to ascertain Jack's agreement for whatever was about to happen, or was trying to talk him out of it.

I squirmed around so that I was sitting comfortably—I didn't want to be struck with a sudden and catastrophic cramp if I got too cold and stiff—and peered even more closely through the crab apple.

Walter had stilled now, and was looking intently at the Lord of the Faerie.

Everyone's attention was on the Lord of the Faerie. Even Malcolm on the other side of the clearing appeared to be transfixed by him.

Then Jack gave a small nod, and some of the tension dissipated.

"You are *sure,* Jack?" I heard the Lord of the Faerie say, and Jack nodded again.

"This can't be undone."

"I know," Jack said.

The Lord of the Faerie gave a small, tight smile, looked at Walter, and inclined his head.

Then, so suddenly I almost gasped with the shock, the Lord of the Faerie used his hand buried amid Jack's hair to push Jack facedown over the stump, his chest centered on its top. I am sure Jack wasn't expecting that, for he gave an audible gasp, and for an instant tensed as if he wanted to struggle.

Then he relaxed, although I could see it took a conscious effort.

My heart was thumping. Suddenly that stump no longer looked like a stump, but an altar, and Jack its sacrifice.

Walter lifted a hand, and let it rest flat-palmed between Jack's shoulder blades.

I could see Jack's muscles tense again, even from my distance.

With his other hand Walter lifted something from the stump to Jack's side. It was shiny but other than that I could not quite make it out.

Then Walter spoke, and what he said was so strange I assumed I had not heard right.

"I remember," he said. "I remember it all."

I stared at him, frowning, and then realized that somehow the dynamics within the group had changed. No one had moved—the Lord of the Faerie and Walter still stood either side of the stump with Jack pushed face-first down atop it, and Malcolm still stood to the far side of the clearing—but *something* had changed.

Everyone, Jack included, was focused on something to the south of the clearing.

I looked, and my heart felt as if it had stopped.

A ghostly white stag with bloodred antlers had stepped forth from the forest into the clearing. I wasn't so silly or so protected that I had no idea who it was. It was the ghost of Og, he who had been the God of the forests before Jack assumed that mantle.

And ghost surely, because the creature was so ephemeral that I felt a goodly gust of wind would blow him away entirely.

Welcome, friend, I heard—*felt*—the Lord of the Faerie say.

I felt Jack shudder (I have no idea how), and my eyes flew back to him.

Walter smiled, cold and terrible.

His right hand, that which held the shiny instrument, moved, and I saw that he held a scalpel.

I felt sick. More than anything I wanted to edge back from the clearing, and fade away into the forest, but I knew

that if I made a single movement now everyone would become aware of my presence.

And that would be dangerous. I understood that now so clearly that I felt as if a terrible, icy hand was squeezing at my stomach.

If they realize my presence now they'll kill me.

I shouldn't have come. I shouldn't be here. This wasn't for me. This was some nightmarish, arcane ritual in which I had no place. For the gods' sakes, I was Grace, tied to Catling, and I hexed everything I touched.

I should have run, but I didn't. I had a feeling that it was way too late now, anyway.

Walter finally lowered both his eyes and his right hand . . .

And began to slice into Jack's flesh.

I jumped, I couldn't help it. I jumped so badly that the crab apple shook and the leaf litter crackled under my body.

At the same moment that I moved (and created what sounded to me like my own little hurricane of noise), Jack cried out.

It was the most terrible sound I have ever heard. His body twitched, his hands, to either side of the stump, grabbed onto the wood, his head jerked back and he cried out with a haunting, hoarse cry of . . . oh God, it sounded like a man lost. There was pain in it, yes, but there was such an undercurrent of bewilderment, isolation, and uncertainty to the cry that I had to momentarily close my eyes.

If he was this uncertain, this isolated, this bewildered, then what hope had any of us?

No one within the clearing reacted to Jack's cry. Walter kept cutting. I couldn't see what he was doing, but his hand was moved as if possessed.

Only a slaughterman could cut that fast.

There was blood everywhere. It flowed over Jack's arms, and down his back until it stained his trousers. He hadn't made a sound since that initial cry, but I could see every muscle in his back and legs and arms tighten until I couldn't believe that the stump itself didn't implode under the pressure.

Walter kept on cutting.

I forced my eyes away from him and Jack, and saw that

the Lord of the Faerie and Malcolm stared not at Jack but at the stag.

I jerked my eyes in its direction.

And felt a wave of faintness sweep over me. *Dear God, I shouldn't be here, I had no business here, I shouldn't be seeing this . . . oh God, I was everyone's doom . . . had I brought calamity to this ritual as well?*

The stag was vanishing.

Curve by curve, line by line. His hindquarters had all gone, and his spine was dissolving as I watched. His back legs were there one moment, and gone the next.

Walter was carving the stag into Jack's flesh.

And as he did, so the stag disappeared, line by line.

I knew then I was witnessing the final marriage of Jack to his power and potential as the God of the forests. He was literally absorbing all that Og had been. After this ritual was completed, then so would Jack be absolute.

I shouldn't be here, I shouldn't be here . . .

But it was too late to run away now, and I thought that disrupting the ritual with a headlong flight (which all would be sure to notice) would, in its own way, be as cataclysmic as staying to watch.

Then a terrible sense of dread permeated my bones.

Something was standing behind me.

I didn't want to look, but I had to. I couldn't bear not to know.

I slowly turned my head.

She was standing about ten feet away, barely visible, but *there*. The despicable, terrible parody of the young woman, hiding her true nature behind that cold mask of beauty.

And then, for the first time in all these years, she spoke.

"Good girl," she whispered, the patronizing bitch. "You're doing just what is needed." Her face grimaced in a smile so cold that I cringed and clamped my eyes shut.

When I opened them again, she was gone.

Achingly slowly I looked back into the clearing, sure that all must be staring at my direction.

But, no. Walter was still carving into Jack's shoulders

and back, the Lord of the Faerie was now looking at Jack rather than the stag—which was virtually all gone save for his shoulders and head—and Malcolm was studying the bloody tableau at the stump.

I felt frozen, my life stilled. This *had* been Catling's plan, that I should be here, and perhaps so that my presence should corrupt Jack's final transformation.

The Lord of the Faerie was leaning down to Jack now, and I only barely summoned the interest to keep on watching. He'd taken hold of Jack's left arm, and was helping Jack to turn over so that he now lay with his bloody, mangled back against the stump.

I saw a glimpse of Jack's face as he turned over, and it was terrible. That he was in agony there could be no doubt, and it appeared as if he could barely control his limbs—the Lord of the Faerie had to grab at him at one point to stop him sliding off the stump.

Walter now began to carve into the front of Jack's shoulders and chest. Walter was doing what all good priests of every religion have done since the beginning of time.

He was acting as a conduit for the God power.

I looked to Jack. He was flexing his legs very slightly up and down, his hips swiveling from side to side, as if he was in so much pain he could barely restrain himself from leaping up from the stump.

I found myself rubbing my own wrists, and wondered that Catling had not thought to wrap me in agony while she was here.

Perhaps she hadn't wanted to interrupt the ritual taking place within the clearing.

The stag was now reduced to nothing but its spread of bloodred antlers, and as I watched even they disappeared.

Walter sighed, blinked, and tossed the scalpel to one side. His shoulders sagged momentarily, then he aided the Lord of the Faerie to pull Jack into a sitting position.

Jack's entire torso was awash with blood. I could see the darker scores of the lines Walter had cut into his flesh, but as there was so much blood around I could not make out their pattern.

As if I could not guess what pattern they would make.

I sunk as low as I could. My protecting beech and crab apple were in Jack's direct line of sight, and I was more scared than ever that I would be discovered.

Walter had now picked up a mortar and pestle, and was grinding away at whatever he had in the bowl. Then he set the pestle to one side, scooped up the ground ingredients in his fingers, and started to rub them into Jack's cut flesh.

Jack cried out again, and I winced. He twisted under Walter's ever rubbing fingers, but the Lord of the Faerie had him by the upper arms, and Walter continued to work away, rubbing, rubbing, rubbing, over Jack's shoulders, his back, down over his chest.

Occasionally a low moan came from Jack's lips, and his body flinched and shuddered as Walter's fingers rubbed too deep here and there.

Then Walter stepped back.

"It is done," he said. "I have made the mark."

"And the mark has made Jack," said the Lord of the Faerie.

Malcolm walked forward, and in his hand he had a pristine white towel. He rubbed away at first Jack's back, and then his shoulders and chest, removing the worst of the blood. He was not rough, but it could hardly have been a pleasant experience for Jack.

As soon as Malcolm had stepped back, the once white towel now hanging limp and bloodied from his hands, the Lord of the Faerie made as if to help Jack to rise, but Jack shrugged him off irritably.

"I am no cripple," he said, and he slid his feet down to the grass and stood upright.

He was still directly facing me, and thus I had clear sight of what happened next.

He stood, his head hanging down, his arms limp, his chest and shoulders looking as though they'd been through a mincer, then he shuddered, his arms jerked, and his head snapped up.

His body quivered, and appeared to blur for an instant.

Then, in the silence, I did gasp, because his shoulders

and chest (and back also, I knew, though I could not see it) completely lost their bloody aspect and appeared now as though they were covered with blue-black living lines. I had thought Walter to be carving the image of the stag into Jack's flesh, but that was not quite so.

I could see elements of the stag in the lines that marked Jack's shoulders and chest, but there was far more to those lines than just representation.

They lived. They had power of their own.

It was the forest woven into his flesh. *And something else, although I could not immediately make it out.*

Jack stood, his head cocked very slightly to one side, his entire presence so powerful and so beautiful I could not have looked away even if I had been commanded to do so. He shook his head very slightly, as if to clear it.

"Well?" said the Lord of the Faerie.

Jack straightened, and looked the Lord of the Faerie directly in the eye.

"You were right," he said, and his voice, although low, seemed to vibrate with . . . not power, knowledge, maybe. "I feel entire, at home with both myself and the forest. Complete."

Chapter Seven

EPPING FOREST

Sunday, 10 September 1939

THE SKIN AROUND THE LORD OF THE Faerie's eyes crinkled, the only sign of his deep emotion. "Then I am most pleased for you," he said, his eyes trailing over Jack's upper body.

The mark covered Jack's shoulders (and also ran a cou-

ple of inches down over the tops of his arms), the top part
of his back, and the front of his chest. Its wounds had al-
ready healed over into faded blue-black and slightly raised
lines, their meanderings partway between a tattoo and a
scar. Although it had been a scant few minutes since Walter
had finished, the mark looked as though it had been there
for decades, fading back into Jack's flesh as if it were a liv-
ing part of him.

The Lord of the Faerie ran one of his hands over the
mark. "If you look at it one way," he said softly, "you can see
the spread of the stag's antlers. But if you narrow your eyes
and look another way, you can see . . ." His eyes slid up to
meet Jack's. "Then you can see the Ringwalk. Tell me, Jack,
who are you now? Man, or stag? Kingman, or Ringwalker?"

Jack gave a slight smile. He opened his mouth, about to
answer, but then he stilled.

His entire *being* stilled. And then the marks on his body
moved slightly. It was as if they blurred, and then shifted as
if rearranging themselves more comfortably, but the move-
ment was so slight that the Lord of the Faerie, watching,
was not quite sure if the mark *had* moved, or if it was his
imagination.

Jack lifted his head, and looked toward the eastern edge
of the clearing, where stood a great beech, and a scrubby
crab apple. A moment later he strode over, leaned down,
and hauled out a white-faced Grace.

The Lord of the Faerie made a sound partway between
exasperation and surprise, and walked over to where Jack
held Grace, Malcolm following close behind the Faerie lord.

Malcolm had a small smile on his face.

Walter stayed at the stump. He appeared completely in-
different to what was happening at the edge of the clearing,
instead cleaning the instruments he had brought with him,
and putting them neatly back inside a leather satchel he
had left to one side.

Jack was not sure whether to be angry or disturbed. He
grasped Grace by both her wrists, the sleeves of her coat
pushed up to reveal her scars, his hands holding tightly
enough that she couldn't pull away, but not so tight that he

would injure her. She appeared frightened. Her face was white, her blue eyes brilliant and wide; her pulse jumped under his fingers, her breath was fast and shallow.

Jack wasn't prepared to go by appearances. Grace played the innocent well enough, but she was also a Dark-witch and a Mistress of the Labyrinth, and "innocence" did not sit well with either.

"Why are you here, Grace?" he said.

She swallowed. "I wanted to see what you and ... Harry—"

Jack wondered why wouldn't she refer to him as the Lord of the Faerie.

"—were up to. I knew something was up, and—"

"How did you know 'something was up'?" Jack said. The Lord of the Faerie had moved very close now, alternating his concerned gaze between Jack and Grace.

Malcolm stood slightly to one side, holding Jack's shirt, jacket, and shoes and socks, and looking considerably less worried than either Jack or the Lord of the Faerie. Indeed, he looked mildly amused.

Grace tried to pull away and Jack tightened his grip.

"How did you know 'something was up'?" he repeated, his voice harder now. "Why track me down, first at Faerie Hill Manor and then here? *How did you know?*"

Malcolm made as if to say something, but Jack shot him a hard glance, and Malcolm shut his mouth.

"I had seen you with the Lord of the Faerie, with Harry, talking. I—"

"We never talked of this before you," said the Lord of the Faerie. His entire being had tensed, and he had subtly aligned his body with that of Jack's.

"Yes, you did," said Grace. "You spoke of it over the breakfast we shared at Faerie Hill Manor."

Jack didn't know what to think. How had she known it was tonight?

"My parents knew about it," Grace went on, "but they did not speak of it to me. Oh gods, I just *knew*, Jack! Not any specifics, just that ... there was something happening. I could sense it."

To one side, Malcolm smiled again, very slightly.

"Why not just ask, Grace?" Jack said. "Why sneak about? Why hide behind the trees? Why didn't you just walk out and say, 'Here I am, may I watch?'"

"Because you would have sent me away," said Grace softly, and in this statement, at least, Jack could see truth.

"And so what did you think, Grace?" he said. "What did you make of what you saw?"

Again she tried to pull away from him, and again he had to tighten his hands. Her eyes flickered over his upper body, and he could feel her tense.

"That you are very strange," she whispered. "And that I am very much afraid of you right now, and of what I may have done."

"'What you may have done'?" said Jack.

"Everything I touch is corrupted with Catling," said Grace. "I tie their fate to hers."

"My fate is already tied to Catling's," Jack said. "I can't imagine anything you did would further damn me. The marking was perfect, Grace. It has not been 'corrupted.'"

He could see she didn't believe it, and he wondered again how much of this frailty was genuine, and how much an act. For God's sake, he should never forget that she was a Darkwitch.

"I'm sorry," said Grace. "But you should know . . . Catling was here, too. She witnessed this."

To one side Malcolm was looking anywhere but at Jack or Grace.

Jack's eyes narrowed, but he didn't immediately say anything. He was certain very little went on that Catling didn't know about. She *was* the Troy Game incarnate, after all, and her tendrils probably spread under most of the land by now. She would have known about this, in any case.

His silence had obviously further disconcerted Grace, for she stuttered on as if to fill the void: "She said . . . she said that . . . that I was doing only what was needed. By watching . . . I think."

"Well, then," said Jack, "at least we haven't annoyed her, have we?"

"Jack?" said the Lord of the Faerie.

Jack did not reply; not to the Lord of the Faerie. "Who are you, Grace?" he said, very softly.

Then his hands tightened about Grace's wrists so that she gasped, and the marks on his upper body blurred, and then shifted.

They moved, flowing down both his arms like living lines of ink, circling his wrists, then cascading over his hands and onto Grace's flesh.

She cried out, and jerked back, but could not free herself from Jack's grip.

Malcolm, his face intense, stepped forward, the Lord of the Faerie also moving closer. Both men had their eyes riveted on Grace's wrists.

Jack's marks encircled Grace's wrists and then seeped into her scars, filling them with their liquid-blue black.

Grace cried out once more, and renewed her twisting, but Jack had her so tightly she could still not free herself.

Then the liquid blue-black receded, climbing back over Jack's hands, up his arms, and, within a moment, reverting to its faded appearance about his upper body.

Abruptly, Jack let Grace go, and she stumbled back a pace or two, rubbing at her wrists.

"You are a mystery," Jack said, his voice puzzled. "I cannot make you out. Either you are completely shuttered, or you are utterly transparent. I cannot for the life of me *understand* you. But the marks see no harm in you. No harm at all."

"Of course not," said Malcolm. "Is that not what I discovered?"

Jack shot him a glance that was part exasperated, part irritated. Then he looked over to Walter. "You have your car here? Yes? Then will you drive Grace back into London."

"I have no obligation to you any more," said Walter. "I have done what you asked. I am free of you now."

"No, you have no obligation to me," Jack snapped. "I am asking this of your goodwill only, not from any sense of *damned* obligation owed!"

Then he looked back to Grace. "Go back to London, Grace. Go home."

"Jack," she said. "I'm sorry about Catling."

"Everyone is sorry about Catling," he said. "It is not a burden you need to carry alone."

She opened her mouth to speak again, but Jack tipped his head toward Walter. "Go," he said, and Grace nodded, and walked over to Walter.

Within a moment they were gone, walking westward through the forest toward the main road.

Jack finally took the shirt Malcolm had been patiently holding and slipped it on.

"Coel," he said to the Lord of the Faerie, using the man's ancient name, "why was Grace so unsure of you in this form?"

"Grace has not been to the Faerie since she was a baby," the Lord of the Faerie said. "She has not seen me as the Lord of the Faerie for a very, very long time."

"Why has she not been back to the Faerie, Coel?"

"We thought to keep her away because . . ."

"Ah," Jack said softly, doing up the buttons of his shirt. "In case she further contaminated you, yes?"

The Lord of the Faerie's face tightened, but he did not respond to Jack's jibe.

"And now, Jack?" he said.

"Now I need to go see Catling," Jack said. "Wait for me in Faerie Hill Manor, Coel, and ask Noah to meet with us there at dawn. Malcolm. My shoes, if you please."

Chapter Eight

THE CRYPT OF ST. PAUL'S CATHEDRAL

Sunday, 10 September 1939

ACK WALKED BACK TO FAERIE HILL MANOR with the Lord of the Faerie, and from there drove his Austin convertible down to London.

He did not see Walter's car—he and Grace were likely half an hour ahead of him.

London was quiet, blacked out and shut down against the expected air raids. Jack drove slowly—unlike on his earlier wild drive through Epping Forest—with only a sliver of light seeping out from the guards over the car's headlamps. There was almost no one about. A few blackout and ARP wardens, the occasional giggling couple heading home from a dance hall, an early milkman driving his horse-drawn van along Aldersgate.

St. Paul's was as still as a headstone.

Jack parked his car in Paternoster Row, one street to the north of the cathedral. He got out slowly, buttoning his jacket against the predawn chill, closing the car door quietly. He stood in the road, looking upward at the dome of the cathedral looming above the intervening buildings, and lit a cigarette, drawing slowly on it as he thought.

Jack should have felt unsettled, but he didn't. Grace's presence at his marking should have disturbed him, and, on some level it did, but not as much as he might have expected.

Instead Jack felt more at peace with himself than he had in . . . well, than he ever had. The marking had accomplished what the Lord of the Faerie had said it would. He felt *complete,* as if he had finally arrived at the end of a

very, very long journey. He had absorbed all that had been Og, but he was, most of all, still Jack.

And he felt more . . . sinuous. A strange word, but it described perfectly what Jack sensed about his altered state. It wasn't as if he knew more—knowledge had flowed into him when he became Ringwalker and that store of knowledge hadn't increased during the past few hours—it was just that he could insinuate himself into all the cracks and crevices of that knowledge where previously he had skimmed over them.

Jack glanced upward, higher than the dome of the cathedral. Again he sensed the "strangeness" that hung over London, so much like an ephemeral shadow always at the very edge of his vision, always shifting just before he could recognize it. Even his new perception made little difference to Jack's inability to grasp its extent and purpose.

A movement to his right caught at the outer edge of his vision, and he dropped his head and looked.

Farther down Paternoster Row, just where it intersected with Maria Lane, stood a shadowy figure. A young woman, too thin, with long dark curls, and dressed in an ankle-length black silk dress. Her hands were folded before her, and her face cast down, but as Jack watched, the cigarette burning unheeded in his fingers, she raised her head and stared at him.

It was too dark, and she too far, for Jack to make out her features, but he could *feel* her smile, and his flesh goose-bumped with the cold that emanated from her.

Jack blinked, and she vanished. Abruptly he tossed the cigarette down to the roadway and ground it out under the sole of his shoe.

Catling waited, and was impatient.

ALTHOUGH THE EXTERIOR OF THE CATHEDRAL had been as still as a headstone, the interior had more life. Jack entered through an open side door in the northern face of the cathedral—one used by cathedral personnel rather

than a public door—into one of the chapels to one side of the great dome.

There were people inside—one group of three men standing under the dome itself, others moving in the shadows farther down the nave—but none of them saw Jack, or realized his presence, for he had cloaked himself within Faerie magic. The last thing Jack wanted was to converse with Catling in full view and understanding of the cathedral's servants.

For several minutes Jack stood on the marble floor beneath the dome.

Here it was, Cornelia's stone hall. So many memories: watching a disguised Asterion make love to Caela; his own numerous confrontations with Cornelia-Caela within its spaces; all the dreams he'd had over the past three thousand years that had been centered within this cathedral.

Jack turned slowly about, trying to absorb everything that the cathedral was. It was huge, but it was far more than just a massive space. Most mortals walking in here must have been truly awed, Jack thought, but they could not have seen what he did, nor understood what he felt. St. Paul's was, after all, so much more than just a cathedral. Deep below twisted the dark heart of the labyrinth that Jack had created with Genvissa, in his life as Brutus.

But that dark heart wasn't just "deep below." Jack could feel it twisting up through all the columns and struts of the building, and could sense its dark veins throbbing through the fabric of the dome. For an instant he closed his eyes, taking a deep breath.

What had he and Genvissa done?

What a fool he'd been, and her as well. They'd had no idea how easily they'd been manipulated. How pliable they'd been in the snaking fingers of an ancient evil. All they'd thought about was their own immortality, their own power.

Their own gain.

And now the Lord of the Faerie, and Noah, and Asterion, and all the Faerie wanted him, Jack, to unwind the Game. To destroy it.

"It's not going to be that easy," Jack whispered.

Because the Troy Game can't be destroyed.

The thought hit him like a sledgehammer, and Jack's eyes flew open.

Again, there was a movement to his side, and again he saw the figure of the woman lurking in the shadows.

Again she vanished almost as soon as he'd caught sight of her.

Bitch, Jack thought, and he turned for the doorway in which the young woman had been standing.

It was the entrance to the stairwell leading down to the crypt.

Jack's mouth quirked. Catling could have as easily met him on the main floor of the cathedral, but no doubt she felt more comfortable, and more in control, in the crypt.

The crypt of St. Paul's stretched the entire length and breadth of the cathedral. Originally it had been the burial chamber of the cathedral—all and sundry within London who had any influence at all tried to ensure their burial within St. Paul's crypt—but Jack had heard that only a few years previously crypt burials had finally ended. Many of Britain's heroes had a tomb here: the Duke of Wellington's casket took pride of place in the center of the crypt under the dome of the cathedral itself; Admiral Lord Nelson's casket was only a little farther down, conveniently placed opposite the entrance to the cathedral treasury, perhaps so that his ghostly presence might thwart any attempted burglary; a dozen lesser generals and captains; Christopher Wren himself.

The space was surprisingly light, spacious, and welcoming.

It was also a hive of activity. To one end of the crypt were set bunk beds, as well what appeared to be a portable mess hall. There were several groups of men, some sleeping, a few playing cards at one of the tables, the larger number moving purposefully about the crypt, carting stores, boxes, and gas masks about.

They were the cathedral Watch, but they had no idea what truly they were guarding.

Just to the left of where Jack stood, at the base of the

stairs, was a notice board, and on it, prominently displayed, was a fluttering piece of paper.

Jack stepped closer to read it. It was a memorandum, issued the day before.

> *The Dean and Chapter, having reviewed the situation in the light of experience, have decided to make the following statement. It is their intention to carry on the life of the Cathedral as fully and as long as circumstances permit.*

Jack read that memo for what it was: a message from Catling. *You're not going to kill me, Jack. I can't be destroyed.*

"It *is* my intention, Jack, to carry on as fully and as long as circumstances permit."

Jack spun around.

A young woman stood a few feet away. Jack's first impression was that she was lovely—and that she looked very much like Grace, save that her hair was black, and very long and left to hang in curls down her back—but that initial impression was followed almost instantly with a sense of malevolence so powerful that Jack literally felt nauseated.

Catling. All grown up now from her life as a child in the seventeenth century.

She still affected the long, black dress, tight-waisted and full-skirted, which rustled about her like a graveyard wind.

Her face, though physically beautiful, was also so white, and her expression so hard and cold, that she had the appearance of a blank-faced doll.

"Nice to meet you after so many years, Jack," said Catling, her mouth twisting in a parody of a smile. She paused, and the smile became particularly malicious. "Father."

"I am not your father."

"Oh, but you are. You and Genvissa made me, that night you danced the Dance of the Torches. It wasn't the dance that was so important . . . but what you did after it. Remember?"

Jack kept his expression blank, but his mind raced. What

had he and Genvissa done after they'd completed the Dance of the Torches and founded the Troy Game atop Og's Hill?

Then his breath caught, remembering what he and Genvissa *had* managed within the megaron within the palace he had built on the White Mound.

They'd made love. They'd fled the celebrations atop Og's Hill and come back to his palace, where they'd fallen atop a pile of furs washed with torchlight and twisted and writhed in what Jack, as Brutus, had thought was a fairly close approximation to making love.

And they conceived a daughter.

Jack felt the breath still within him.

He had pulled himself free of Genvissa's body, raising himself on his arms above her, then kneeling between her bent legs, laughing with sheer joy at all the power that lay within their reach.

She, her hands splayed across her belly, saying, "We have made a daughter between us, Brutus. A daughter-heir."

And he had replied, so damned sure of himself, "You have blessed me."

Then came Cornelia, rushing into the megaron, her belly gently rounded out with the daughter she had been carrying, and discovered her husband and Genvissa.

And he, Brutus, had looked over to Cornelia, and laughed.

"Yes," said Catling. "You *do* remember, don't you? You made *me* that night. Both within the labyrinth on Og's Hill *and* on that pile of furs with Genvissa."

"I don't believe it."

"Why not? It makes sense enough, surely. I was supposed to have become flesh incarnate when Genvissa gave birth to me . . . but then Asterion"—her voice hardened into implacable hatred—"gave Cornelia that dagger with which to murder Genvissa, and my fleshly body, with it. I hated Genvissa then, loathed her for failing to carry me to term. So I picked Cornelia as my Mistress of the Labyrinth, and later used her—and you—to finally arrive into flesh. Better late than never."

Jack tried to make sense of what she was saying. "But why choose Cornelia to then become your Mistress of the

Labyrinth? She had ruined your chances when she murdered Genvissa. Surely you must have loathed her."

"And still do," said Catling. "But I saw that Cornelia would grow into a powerful Darkwitch, *and* goddess, and that she would be the best Mistress of the Labyrinth I could hope for. Besides, it makes a pretty revenge, don't you think? Choosing the woman who had briefly stymied me to then bear me, and complete me. It fulfills a nice circle."

She paused. "You're thinking of unwinding me, aren't you?"

"Would you blame me?" said Jack.

"You can't unwind me, Jack. Think to harm me and I will make Grace suffer so badly she will wish herself dead. And if Grace suffers, then all this land," she hissed the last word, "will suffer with her. Hate me all you want, but you will *not* destroy me!"

Jack did hate her at that moment. He hated her so much that he literally swayed forward, his hands half raised, determined to do her unto death.

"Besides," Catling said, "you are my creator and my father, Jack. It is impossible for you to destroy me."

Then she stepped back, and laughed. "You and your pretty God pretensions. I care not for what magic markings you have all over your skin"—her hand waved dismissively, and Jack felt his marks burn and slide, as if they were trying to escape her presence—"all I need is for you to do one thing, dance the Dance of the Flowers with Noah, and complete me. You'll never escape me, you'll never destroy me, so you may as well succumb to the inevitable and complete me. It will be sweeter for you, in the end."

Then she stabbed a finger at him. "If you try to harm me, Jack, then I will take this land and destroy it. I will *burn* it. And then I will do the same to the Faerie. Hark!" She put her hand to her ear in a parody of a pantomime gesture. "What is that I hear? The drone of bombers? The whistle of bombs? The shriek of flesh tearing? The—"

"Shut up, you vicious crone!"

Catling smiled at that, and stepped back. "I can't be un-done, Jack. Accept it."

Then she was gone, and Jack was left alone, save for the soft footfalls of the cathedral Watch treading about the crypt.

TWENTY MINUTES LATER, WHEN HE FINALLY FELT strong enough to leave the cathedral, Jack leaned against the Austin parked in Paternoster Row, and sent an urgent appeal to Harry.

CATLING STOOD IN THE DARK HEART OF THE labyrinth, very still. Nothing moved, not a hair on her head, not a finger, not a fold of her cold, silken skirt.

She was disgusted with herself.

She'd overreacted, threatened, made a scene.

Made a *fool* of herself.

All because Jack had been so much more than she'd expected.

It wasn't the power. Not really. Jack now combined his Kingman abilities with those of Ringwalker. Catling had expected him to be powerful.

What she hadn't expected was Jack to be so calm. So still. So at peace with himself.

That wasn't the man she'd relied on speaking to this night. That wasn't the man she'd known as Brutus, and then William, then Louis. Those men had been fractured, unsure.

They could never have harmed Catling.

But Jack was something different. Different enough to give Catling considerable pause. Different enough to reduce her to childish threats.

Catling was willing to admit to herself that it had been a mistake, perhaps, to make Noah and Jack so powerful. As just Mistress and Kingman they would have been so much more manageable . . . but, oh, as just Mistress and King-

man, without any of the powers of the land they now brought with them, Catling herself would have been so much less. Well, it was too late now. Catling would just need to ensure she stayed one step ahead of Jack and Noah.

She was glad to have discovered Jack's strength so early. It might have been disastrous if the first she'd realized it was on the day he thought to try to destroy her.

Despite her grandiose threats to Jack, Catling wasn't entirely sure she *was* totally invulnerable. After all, she still hadn't been completed, and total invulnerability would only come after that event. It was better not to underestimate Jack. Catling liked to anticipate possible attacks and challenges— that was why she had tied Grace by hex once Catling realized Noah would move against her. Even as Mistress, Darkwitch, and goddess combined, Noah may not have been able to destroy her, but Catling just liked to make sure.

It would be best to make sure now, too.

Finally Catling moved, just slightly. A tongue, running briefly about her upper lip. Eyes, cast upward, as if she could see through all the layers of earth and rubble and stone and marble to the sky overhead.

It was coming. War. Pain. Horror. Destruction, raining down on London. Everything Catling could ever have wanted, because she could feed from the devastation, grow strong on the pain and the horror, gobble and wax fat on the terror. Grow robust enough to thwart whatever means Jack and Noah used to attack her.

But the horror wasn't here *yet*. Oh, the war had started, and the horror was on its way. But it wasn't here yet.

Catling hoped Jack wasn't in any hurry to either attack her or complete her, because Catling needed all the strength she could muster in order to outwit him.

Chapter Nine

FAERIE HILL MANOR

Sunday, 10 September 1939

NOAH JUMPED, THEN LOOKED AT STELLA and Harry sitting on the leather chesterfield. "The car. He's here."

Harry and Stella shared a glance, then Harry sighed, and stood up. "I'll let him in."

"Stella," Noah said, "do you know what has happened?" Noah knew Jack's final marking had been planned for last night and she had not been surprised when the Lord of the Faerie had sent her a summons a couple of hours previously to meet with him and Jack at Faerie Hill at dawn. Noah had been so tense about Jack's marking she had spent the night wandering the Faerie with Eaving's Sisters, and had come straight from the Faerie to Faerie Hill Manor.

Now she wondered if that had been a good idea. Obviously something *else* had happened.

Perhaps she should have attended the marking as well.

"None, Noah," said Stella. "Only a half hour ago Harry asked me to meet him here." She glanced at her watch. "There's only an hour and a half until sunrise. I can't stay long."

Noah looked over to the chesterfield sofa. Silvius was sitting there, having arrived a few minutes previously. If Jack had asked both his father and Stella to come . . . then something *must* be wrong.

"Silvius?" Noah said. "Do you have any idea?"

Silvius shook his head. "I just received the summons. I came. I don't know what's happening."

"Perhaps I should ring home," Noah said, looking at the telephone. "See if Weyland and Grace are—"

"Noah, calm down," Silvius said. "I am certain if there was an impending disaster Jack would have let us know."

"And maybe that's why we're here now," Noah said, her voice edgy.

At that moment Jack walked into the room, Harry close behind.

Noah sprang to her feet. "Jack?"

Jack nodded, including everyone in that greeting, then looked to Harry. "Thank you for getting everyone here. Well, almost everyone. Where is—"

"I don't know," said Harry. "She should be here."

"Ariadne was delayed slightly," said Silvius. "She will be here shortly."

Noah's and Stella's eyes widened at Ariadne's name, and Jack frowned slightly at his father. He wondered how it was Silvius knew of Ariadne's invitation, let alone the fact she was delayed.

Silvius held his son's look, a bland expression on his face, and Jack sighed. His father wasn't about to offer up any information on the issue, and, considering the gravity of what Jack had to relate, how Silvius knew of Ariadne's movements wasn't of the greatest importance right now.

"It has been a long night," Jack said, "both good and bad. Did Harry tell you where I'd gone from Ambersbury Banks?"

"No," said Noah. "But the marking . . . it went well?"

Jack gave her a smile. "It went well, Noah." He hesitated, wondering if he should tell her about Grace, and then wondered why she didn't already know. Hadn't she missed her daughter at home?

"There is something I need to tell you," Jack said, "and we don't have much time before Stella needs to carol in the dawn." That last was more a question than a statement, and he raised his eyebrows at Stella as he said it.

She gave a nod. "I have an hour and a half, Jack."

"Very well." Jack walked over to the cold fireplace, and stood there for a minute or two, looking into the empty

grate, his hands deep in his trouser pockets. "I went from Ambersbury Banks to St. Paul's," he said finally, turning around, "to see Catling."

"And?" said Noah.

Jack's mouth quirked. "It was the first time I had ever seen her. My 'daughter.'"

"She is no real daughter, Jack," Noah said. "She was only ever a trickery."

Jack remembered when he and Noah had made love in the magical re-creation of her father's megaron. Noah had fallen pregnant, and for a time she and Louis, as Jack had been then, had thought her child a re-creation of the daughter they had made three thousand years earlier, and who had been murdered by Genvissa.

But she wasn't. In reality Catling had been the Troy Game incarnate, turned to flesh to more expertly manipulate all those caught up in the Game's machinations.

Jack held Noah's eyes. "Yes," he said softly, "she actually is my daughter. But not yours, Noah." His gaze shifted to Stella. "She's yours and mine, Stella. The daughter we made that night we created the Troy Game atop Og's Hill, when you were Genvissa."

A complete silence met this pronouncement. Everyone stared at Jack, their minds racing. Remembering.

"No . . ." Stella whispered.

"That is what Catling had to tell me tonight," Jack said, his voice suddenly weary. "She said that there was no means by which she could be destroyed, as I was both her father and her creator. She said that she'd meant to become incarnate when first we'd made the Game, Stella, when I was Brutus and you Genvissa. We'd gone back to the palace on White Mound, drunk with power and ambition, and we'd coupled, and, fools that we were, we had no bloody idea that what we'd done was to conceive the Troy Game incarnate."

"But . . ." Noah said. She'd gone to Stella, who was so white she looked as if she were about to faint, and had an arm around her waist.

"Ah, yes, that 'but,'" said Jack. "Then all Catling's initial plans were ruined when Asterion persuaded you,

through Mag, to murder Genvissa when she was only weeks away from giving birth. Imagine Catling's frustration." He paused, using the time to catch Noah's gaze. "And think of how much she must have hated *you*, Noah, for frustrating her plans. She chose you to become her Mistress of the Labyrinth not only because she could see how powerful you would become, but in revenge. In hatred."

Noah had now gone white as Stella, and she did not reply.

"Not only did she use your body to subsequently achieve flesh," said Jack, "but you were going to be the one to complete her. A final punishment."

"Stop for a moment," said Harry. He'd been standing listening to the conversation, growing more incredulous, and more terrified, with each moment that passed. "Jack, we can get back to you and Stella's ill-fated conception in a moment, but what I want to know is . . . why did Catling say you could not destroy her?"

"Because Jack is both her father and creator," Silvius said. He'd been listening quietly, his eyes locked on Jack, his face reflecting the horror of everyone else. "I don't know the intricacies of it, but I am guessing that the double role in 'creating,' whether Game or flesh, might tie Jack's hands somewhat. Who knows? It might just be possible."

Jack's shoulders slumped. "Yes. It might be possible. I just don't know."

Harry strode the distance between them and grabbed at the material of Jack's jacket. The lines on his careworn face had deepened until Harry looked as ancient as the forest itself. "What do you mean—*you don't know?*" he hissed.

"He doesn't know," said a woman's voice, "because in all the history of the labyrinth, we've never had a Game achieve flesh. We have no precedent to work from."

Harry let Jack go and, with everyone else, looked at the doorway.

A beautiful, dark-haired woman stood there, dressed in an elegantly cut scarlet suit and black leather high heels and with a matching purse tucked under one arm. Her hair was fashionably waved and set, and her makeup was impeccable.

Ariadne.

"Nice to meet you finally, Jack," she said, advancing into the room and giving Jack a peck on the cheek. Then she gave first Noah then Stella a kiss, took a step toward Harry, thought better of it, then sat down next to Silvius on the chesterfield, crossing her lovely legs. She and Silvius glanced at each other, but otherwise did not exchange greetings, which Jack marked as highly suspicious.

"Catling is a clever little minx," said Ariadne. "Very cunning, and from what I heard as I stood in the doorway I think I can say that she's had this planned for a very, very long time. Perhaps everyone *is* trapped."

"Ariadne," Jack said, "just tell us what you know, if you please."

"The Troy Game wanted to become flesh incarnate," said Ariadne. "Naturally she chose her Kingman and Mistress of the Labyrinth—first Brutus and Genvissa, then Brutus-Louis and Noah when the first pairing failed—to give her flesh. You are her parents. She is of your flesh. It is highly possible that she can't now be undone for two reasons: firstly her parents, flesh of her flesh, literally would be unable to unmake her—which is similar to what Silvius theorized—and secondly, because once a Game becomes flesh, maybe it *is* incapable of being undone. Who knows? As I said, no Game has ever done this before."

"Gods," Noah said. "It makes a terrible kind of sense."

"Any added comments, Silvius?" Jack said.

"I defer to Ariadne's knowledge," he said. "After all, what was I but a straight-down-the-line Kingman who never put a foot wrong?"

Jack noted there was some interaction between Silvius and Ariadne at this point, a faint frisson of amusement that passed between them. If their current conversation hadn't been so important Jack would have been hard pressed not to drag his father outside to ask him privately what was happening between him and Ariadne.

There was another long silence. Stella walked over to the drinks cabinet as if she were going to pour herself a drink, thought better of it, then sat down in a chair with a thump. Noah just stood, a shaking hand to her face.

"But think of this," said Silvius. "If Catling has been this invulnerable, all this time, then why hex Grace? Why tie Grace's fate to hers? If all this is true, then Catling didn't need a backup."

Noah dropped her hand away from her face, her eyes suddenly bright. "Do you think she was lying?"

Jack shared a look with Ariadne and Silvius, then shrugged. "I don't know, Noah. We all"—he waved a hand, taking in Stella, Ariadne, Silvius and Noah—"need to think about it. Games *can* be unwound. Look at Troy, and Jericho, and all the cities you destroyed, Ariadne."

Ariadne had the grace to drop her eyes.

"But none of those cities, *none* of them," said Silvius, "had Games that were incarnate. We just don't know. I don't necessarily believe anything Catling says, but there *is* a grain of sense in her assertion."

"Nonetheless," said Ariadne, "I feel that Catling hexed Grace because Catling is still vulnerable. There is no other reason to do it."

"Not because Catling has a malevolent and spiteful character, and it may have given her joy to see Grace, and the rest of us, suffer?" said Noah.

"No," said Ariadne. "Remember, Catling's fate is Grace's fate, but Grace's fate is also Catling's fate. The hex works both ways, and Catling would not have left herself exposed in this manner if there wasn't a damn good reason to do it. She needed a backup, Grace was it, and that means she must be vulnerable elsewhere. Maybe she can't be unwound or destroyed. Maybe. But maybe there's another chink in her armor somewhere."

"Hope," said Noah. "Thank the gods."

"May I ask something?" said Silvius.

Jack gave his father a small smile. "Sure. So long as I have an answer for it."

"*If* the Troy Game can be destroyed . . . then what happens to the majority of people in this room who have been caught up in its machinations, reborn life after life? Will you be gone as well?"

"No," said Jack. "We all exist independently of the Troy

Game, and we're all tied either to the land or to each other now. Only if the land is destroyed will we cease to exist."

"Thank goodness for that," said Silvius with a grin. "I was just starting to enjoy everyone's company."

Harry had been silent this time, listening to the Mistresses of the Labyrinth and the two Kingmen talk, but now he walked over to Jack, and put a hand on his shoulder. "Jack, I take it from this conversation that you *are* now prepared to commit to the Troy Game's undoing?"

"Yes," Jack said. "Not that it does you any good, but, yes. The Troy Game needs to be destroyed, unwound, undone, put away . . . whatever. It is a vileness, and . . . oh God, I *wish* I had never created the damned thing!"

"And *I* wish the land had never conducted its vile alliance with the Game," said Harry, "but wishes will do us no good at all."

"Catling knew what choice I would make," Jack said. "She had her threats all to hand."

"*I* still can't come to grips with the idea that the daughter we conceived was in fact Catling," said Stella. "Gods . . . all these years I have thought of her, and of what she could have been . . . and here she was before us all the time. Catling. *Gods!*"

"I wish my daughter had been born," said Noah softly. "Who knows what she may have been."

Stella dropped her eyes.

"Enough," said Harry. "There are no recriminations, no guilt. What has happened has happened, and we need to move forward."

"Straight over the cliff?" muttered Ariadne, inspecting her scarlet fingernails.

Harry shot her a black look, but did not otherwise respond to her. "The Troy Game is the greatest threat this land has ever faced," he said, "and it needs to be as strong as it can to face it. Jack, Noah, for three and a half thousand years you have been antagonists, one way or the other. Jealousies and ambitions have driven you apart. It is time, finally, to put a stop to it, because, *damn it,* you are causing this land almost as much damage as Catling!"

Harry paused, looking between them. "It is time to make the Great Marriage. Time to give the land the strength it needs to fight back. You will do this."

That was a directive, not a question, and it created an interesting undercurrent of emotion in the room: Jack and Noah looked at each other, and then as quickly away again. Silvius studied his son carefully, Ariadne grinned, somewhat lasciviously, and Stella sent her a glance of irritation.

Jack finally gave a tired little smile. "Noah?" he said. "*Can* we put our past behind us?"

"Of course," she said, her response quick, but her face and words underscored with a little nervousness.

"Will Weyland accept this?" Jack said.

Now it was she who gave the tired smile. "I will talk to him."

"He will not stand in its way," Harry said, and, again, that was not a question.

"I will talk to him," Noah repeated.

"Noah—" Harry began.

"I will talk to him, Harry, and he will agree. Okay?"

"Make sure that he does," Harry said quietly. "Now, as to the when. The sooner the—"

"No," said Jack. "Sooner is not necessarily better. The Great Marriage is best done on May Day, Harry. That's eight months away. We could do it sooner, yes, but if we do it on the strength of the rising spring, then it will achieve its greatest power."

"He's right, Harry," Noah said.

"But that's so far away," Harry said.

"Harry, I know," Jack said. "But we can't rush into this. We need to deal with the Troy Game, and we *will* do it, I promise you—"

To one side Ariadne gave a soft snort of laughter, then reached into her purse for a cigarette, which Silvius lit for her.

"We *will* do it," Jack said, glancing at Ariadne, "but we're only going to get one chance at this. If we delay the Great Marriage until May Day then we'll ensure the land, as well Noah and I, are at our strongest before we attempt—"

"The impossible," Ariadne muttered, and drew down deeply on her cigarette.

"God damn you!" Jack spun about, and marched over until he was standing directly over Ariadne.

She didn't flinch, merely regarding him calmly through the drifting smoke of her cigarette.

"You had your part to play in this mess," said Jack, "and you damn well have your part to play in its fixing. Yes?"

Ariadne gave a tilt of her head, which was as close as she could come to an apology. "I will help, yes. So, what do you have planned, great God of the forests?"

Jack caught his father's twinkling eye, and barely managed to repress a smile. Ariadne was taunting him, but she was doing it in good humor, and he was suddenly very glad she was here.

"Jack needs to get the Kingship bands," Harry said.

"Of course," said Noah. "Whenever he wants them, I will fetch them."

Jack slid Noah a quick look, then again just as quickly looked away.

Ariadne was watching him, and smiled to herself.

"We need to work out *how* we can get around what Catling has told Jack," Stella said. "Whatever she says, surely there is a way to unwind the Game."

"So what do we do first?" Harry said. "Jack? Do you want your bands?"

How the world had changed, Jack reflected. For two lifetimes Noah, as Caela and then Noah, and Harry, in his earlier incarnation as Harold, had spent much of their time trying to keep him away from the bands. Now they were his for the asking.

"Not until Noah and I have made the Great Marriage," he said. "I really do want to delay making any move for as long as I can—precipitous action is going to murder us all—and if I have the bands then Catling will want Noah and me to weave the final binding enchantment, completing the Game, immediately. Not having the bands will buy us time."

"Catling will get impatient," Ariadne said. "And once

Catling gets impatient"—she blew out a plume of smoke—
"Catling will get nasty."

"And thus we need to do some war planning," Silvius
said. "What *are* we going to do?"

"I need to discover just what it is that appears out of
place about London," said Jack. "I have no idea at all what
this damned shadowy difference is, save for the fact that it
clearly derives from the labyrinthine arts. Somehow. Given
that Noah and Stella have not detected anything, nor Sil-
vius nor Weyland, and all of you with your knowledge of
the Troy Game and the labyrinthine arts, should be able to
do so, I have no idea what it *could* be."

"Jack?" said Ariadne.

"Yes?"

"Would you mind filling me in? I'm not too sure that Sil-
vius knows anything about this, either."

"Oh," said Jack. "Sorry." He paused, trying to gather his
thoughts. "When I arrived in London a week or so past, I
felt something . . . different . . . about the city. Harry and I
spent an afternoon walking around the City. There is some-
thing hanging over London. A shadow—that's the only
way I can think of it. Whatever the shadow is, it involves
labyrinthine power, although there is a 'disassociation'
with the Troy Game. I'm sorry, I can't explain it better than
that, Ariadne, and I have no idea if it works against us or
for us. But we *do* need to know precisely what it is . . . and
it worries me that Noah and Stella can't sense it. You, Ari-
adne? Silvius?"

Both shook their heads. "But you can be sure we'll send
out senses scrying the instant we get back to London," Sil-
vius said.

Ariadne frowned. "Catling said nothing about it?" she
said.

"No," Jack said, "but then we didn't have the longest of
conversations."

"Have you asked Grace?"

"Grace called it a 'wrongness,' " Jack said, "but I can't
help thinking that she knows what it is."

"Grace wouldn't hide anything from you," said Noah.

Jack stubbed out his cigarette in an ashtray. "Grace hides many things."

"Grace is an innocent in all this," Noah said.

"There are no innocents in any of this," Jack said, "and certainly not Grace. She should, for instance, have mentioned she has undergone her training as a Mistress of the Labyrinth."

"What?" Noah said.

"You didn't know?" said Jack. "Grace is your daughter, and you a trained Mistress of the Labyrinth yourself, and *you didn't know?"*

"But . . . how? Who trained her?"

Jack looked pointedly at Stella, who was looking decidedly uncomfortable.

"She wanted to learn," Stella said. "So I taught her. She said she didn't want to ask you, Noah."

Noah could do nothing but stare at Stella.

"Did you know, Ariadne?" Jack said.

"She asked me if I thought Stella would train her," Ariadne said, "and I told her just to ask."

"I can't believe that you would have done this, Stella," Noah said, her voice low.

"Oh, come now, Noah," Jack said. "Why shouldn't she have been trained? She was bred for it, after all. She had the potential inside her. Did you ever *offer?"*

"But why not ask *me?"* Noah said.

"Ask her that yourself," Jack said. "Look, I appreciate that Grace is your daughter, but she's no child. She's been Harry's lover, she is a Darkwitch, she is a trained Mistress of the Labyrinth, she's had to contend with years and years of having Catling visit her at night, she knew about the marking tonight, and came to watch, *and* I am sure she knows what this shadow hanging over London really is. God knows what other secrets she has tucked away."

Now everyone was staring at Jack.

"Harry?" said Noah. "You were Grace's *lover?"*

"Catling has been appearing to Grace?" said Stella—and Jack noted that as she didn't seem to be in the least perturbed about Grace's affair with Harry, she obviously knew about it.

"Grace is at the center of the puzzle," Jack said, "and not in the least because of Catling's hex. Grace is a powerful force in her own right, and—"

"To get to the center of the great puzzle—how to destroy the Troy Game—you will need to get to the center of Grace," finished Ariadne. She and Silvius had been exchanging amused glances throughout this series of revelations, and the pair of them were by far the most relaxed in the room.

"Grace means no harm!" Noah said, and at that moment Jack admired her more than he'd ever done. She'd just heard a series of startling secrets about her daughter, all of which Grace had kept from Noah, and Noah's first instinct was still to protect her daughter.

"I don't meant to intimate that she did," Jack said. "But Grace is central to our cause. I think she holds a key that will either hand us a means by which to destroy Catling . . . or she will fracture us apart completely."

"Jack—" Noah began.

"Harry has given us our lecture about unity and strengthening the land," Jack said, addressing the entire group, "but think of this. What I have just told you about Grace represents all the fractures running through our group. Noah, you should have realized that she'd been trained as a Mistress of the Labyrinth, just as you should have realized she wasn't at home tonight, but you didn't. Harry, Grace is integral to our cause, but for hundreds of years you have chosen to keep her out of the Faerie, and have not shown her your face as the Lord of the Faerie . . . and you were her *lover,* for God's sake! No one realized Catling has been shadowing Grace's every footstep for the past three hundred years, and, damn it, every one of you should have realized, or at least intuited it!"

Jack paused. "I don't know whether to regard Grace as a threat, or to sympathize with her. She kept secrets, but were they secrets meant to deceive . . . or were they defensive strategies?"

"And yet, Jack," said Ariadne, "all this you learn within a week. You must be quite the charmer."

Jack gave her Ariadne a steady look. "I have open eyes," he said.

Chapter Ten

The Savoy

Sunday, 10 September 1939

NOAH WALKED SLOWLY INTO THE FOYER OF the private residents' entrance of the Savoy, nodding at Robert Stacey, the concierge, as she passed his office.

As always, he gave a slight bow as she passed.

Noah felt irritated and more than a little bit humiliated. But overwhelmingly she felt chastened. How had she not realized Grace had become a Mistress of the Labyrinth? How could she not have *felt* it?

Moreover, Catling had been spending her time making Grace's nights a living hell?

Catling had been in their apartment, night after night?

Not only had Noah not known (and she *should* have known, damn it!), Grace hadn't felt she could speak to Noah about it.

Noah felt sick to her stomach. She knew there had been distances in her relationship with Grace, but hadn't realized their extent and strength.

She's not a child, Jack had said to her, and Noah wondered if it was so damned bloody obvious that "a child" is how she'd thought of Grace all these years.

Noah stood before the lifts, slowly taking off her gloves and unbuttoning her coat, trying to put off the moment when she would have to enter the lift and face both Grace and Weyland—and, oh, Weyland . . . how would he feel, knowing that the Great Marriage had been agreed?

The fact that Grace had been Harry's lover for a while had been, in the end, the least of Jack's revelations. Noah

could understand why a daughter might keep that from a mother—who had also been the man's lover in a previous life. She couldn't, however, understand why Harry had so carefully kept it from her (but not from Stella, obviously).

And she hadn't once thought, until Jack had mentioned it, why it was that Harry had never shown himself to Grace as the Lord of the Faerie.

"Perhaps we are fractured, after all," Noah murmured, finally taking courage in hand and stepping into the lift.

Three minutes later, she stood before her front door. Without hesitation, she used her key to let herself in.

WEYLAND WAS SITTING ON THE SOFA, READING Saturday's *Times*. He looked tired and drawn, and Noah remembered he'd been on warden duty all night.

She bent and kissed him, and knew instantly that anxiety and tension hovered just behind the tiredness.

"You've been . . . ?" he said as Noah lifted her mouth from his.

"To Faerie Hill Manor," she said. She tossed her coat and gloves over the back of the sofa. "I will tell you about it, for, oh, there is much to say, but I need to see Grace first. Is she in?"

He nodded.

"Do you mind?" Noah said.

"Will you come back?" he said, softly, and Noah's heart almost broke.

"I will always come back," she said, then bent and kissed him once more. "I won't be long."

"GRACE?" NOAH HESITATED BEFORE THE CLOSED door to her daughter's bedroom, then decided to take the slight sound she heard within as an assent to her entry.

Noah opened the door, walked inside, then closed the door behind her, taking a moment to survey the bedroom, as if she were seeing it for the first time.

The room was large, as were all rooms in the Orr apart-

ment, and when Grace had first moved in here, it had been beautifully decorated with drapes and scatter rugs over the wooden floor, and with deep armchairs and cushions in the alcove by the window.

But now . . . Noah realized that over time Grace had stripped the bedroom clean of everything save that which had a purely functional nature: a bed, a single wooden chair, a wardrobe, a dressing table.

There was nothing else. Not a book, not a scatter rug, not a cushion.

Not a scarf or a frippery to be seen.

Nothing save functionality.

Dear God, why hadn't she seen this *before now, as well?*

Grace was sitting on the end of her bed, watching her mother carefully. She was dressed in a plain blouse and skirt, and Noah almost wept at the sight.

Grace was so lovely, she *should* be dressed in silks and velvets and brocades.

She *should* live in a palace, and have emperors sprawl at her feet.

She should live free, not a slave to terror.

"Hello, Grace," Noah said, and, after walking over to the bed, sat down next to her daughter and gave her a kiss on her cheek.

"Jack told you," Grace said, and Noah realized she looked nervous.

Noah looked down to her hands, which had begun to fidget in her lap. *Gods, what should she say?*

After a long moment—a long moment in which Noah could feel Grace physically tensing—Noah looked up, smiled as naturally as she could, and said, "I am so proud of you."

Then, as Grace stared, Noah lifted a hand, placed it against Grace's cheek, and leaned forward once more, this time planting a lingering kiss on Grace's mouth.

"What a fool I am for not realizing," Noah said.

Then she rose and left the room.

* * *

WEYLAND STOOD AS NOAH WALKED BACK INTO the room. "Noah?"

She sat down, but did not speak.

Weyland hesitated, then sank down beside her.

"Noah?"

"Jack spoke to Catling last night . . . and then he spoke to us."

"You and Harry."

Noah drew in a breath. "And Stella, Silvius, and Ariadne."

Weyland, if possible, stilled even more. Ariadne had betrayed him, and arranged his murder in Weyland's first life as Asterion. His loathing of her was monumental, and even though the ancient witch had been living in London for the past three hundred years, Weyland had avoided her as carefully as Ariadne had avoided him.

"Weyland, just listen to me for a few minutes, and then we can talk." In a hushed, terse tone, Noah told Weyland what had transpired at the meeting at Faerie Hill Manor (keeping silent, for the moment, about the discussion of the Great Marriage). Weyland was shocked by what Jack had to say about Catling (surely she could be destroyed, *surely!*), but when Noah revealed that Grace had trained as a Mistress of the Labyrinth, and that Catling appeared often to her at night, Weyland looked so ill Noah thought he might actually faint.

"Why didn't we know?" Weyland said.

"We were blind, Weyland. We were too busy trying to protect her, when what we should have been doing was encouraging her to fly."

"But . . ."

"I know," Noah said, taking both Weyland's hands in hers. "I tried to shelter her, it is largely what I lived for, and yet I think that 'shelter' was the last thing Grace needed."

Weyland did not reply as he tried to make sense of what he'd heard. They'd spent so many years, and so much of themselves, trying to keep Grace from any further harm, and trying to protect her, and believing that she was so fragile that she needed to be wrapped in as much parental security as possible, that to consider allowing Grace "to fly" was almost

incomprehensible. Even more than Noah's, Weyland's every breath had been devoted to safeguarding Grace. He had lost one daughter; to lose this one as well was unthinkable.

"She's trained as a Mistress of the Labyrinth?" he said eventually.

Noah nodded.

"And we didn't know." Weyland paused. "She's either very powerful or we are very weak."

Noah tried a small smile. "I prefer to think that she is very powerful."

"Who trained her?"

"Stella."

Weyland gave a soft snort of laughter. "All that time I tried to persuade Stella to teach you, and she wouldn't. Then, just for the fun of it, she trains our daughter. At least it wasn't Ariadne. I do not think I could have borne that."

"There are a couple of other things I should tell you."

Weyland's eyes, which had been lightening up, suddenly went cold and hard again, and Noah bemoaned the fact that even now, after so much time together, he found it so difficult to trust her love for him.

"Grace and Harry have been lovers," Noah said, and watched Weyland digest the information.

"Thank God Stella didn't murder her," he said, and Noah laughed, squeezing his hands, glad he had accepted it so readily.

"Talking of Harry . . . ," she said.

"Yes?"

"He has asked Jack and me to make the Great Marriage. Unite and strengthen the land as much as possible to face whatever Catling decides to throw at it."

"Of course you agreed," Weyland said, and now both his voice and face were flat.

"Yes, we did," said Noah. "Weyland, it will be a single night. It won't mean—"

He shot her such a terrible look, composed of equal parts fear and hatred and despair, that Noah quailed.

"I know," she whispered, and Weyland pulled his hands away from hers.

* * *

ALL IN ALL, NOAH THOUGHT LATER AS SHE SAT
back on the sofa, a whisky and soda in her hand, alone in
the room, it had been a frightful day. So many revelations.
Too much to absorb.

For the moment Noah was not thinking about Grace or
Weyland. Two other subjects consumed her: the Great
Marriage, and the revelation that the daughter Brutus and
Genvissa had conceived had been Catling.

Noah felt a little sick at the idea of the Great Marriage.
Seeing Jack again, after all these years, had confused her
deeply. She was so sure of Weyland, so sure she loved him,
so happy in her choice, and yet when Jack smiled, or slid
his eyes her way, or, damn it, kissed her, then doubts as-
sailed her. It made Noah realize that no matter how much
she loved Weyland, she could not simply set to one side
what she had once felt for Jack. As Cornelia and Caela, and
then again in her early years as Noah, she had loved Jack
with an all-consuming passion.

Then had come Weyland, and Noah thought she'd left
her love for Jack far in her past.

But now Noah wondered if it wasn't as far behind her as
she'd thought.

She loved Weyland. She truly did, and was happy with
him, and didn't want their marriage to fall apart, but, oh,
that moment when Harry had mentioned the Great Mar-
riage, and she and Jack had exchanged glances, everything
almost *had* fallen apart.

"Gods," muttered Noah, putting her drink down so she
could rummage around the room looking for a cigarette.
She didn't smoke much, but right now she felt a cigarette
might just save her life.

Five minutes and no cigarette later, Noah slumped back
on the sofa and drained her drink. She forced her mind
away from Jack, and thought about the child he, as Brutus,
had conceived with Genvissa.

Catling! Noah wasn't too sure whether to be glad she'd
murdered Genvissa when she had, delaying the Troy

Game's emergence into flesh, or to wonder if she'd only increased Catling's malevolence in the doing. *Did I only make things worse*?

For hours Noah sat there, drinking too many whiskies and sodas, thinking about Jack and Catling and, eventually, that daughter she'd lost in her first life. Genvissa and she had both lost daughters. Genvissa's had been Catling . . . but what had Cornelia been carrying? Just an innocent baby, the victim of Genvissa's (or Catling's, more like) hatred, or something *else*?

Noah remembered how her daughter had been conceived, using the power of Mag's Pond.

"Surely nothing bad could have come of that," she whispered eventually, when the apartment was cold and dark. "Surely."

Then she sighed, set the empty glass to one side, and went to look for Grace.

WEYLAND HAD GONE TO FIND THE IMPS. HE DIS-covered them wandering the Embankment, not too far from the Savoy, as if they'd known he would need them.

"Well?" said Weyland, leaning over the stone wall and looking at the Thames.

"My, we're in a fierce mood today," said Jim.

"I am in *no* mood for your witticisms," snapped Weyland. "*What* have you learned?"

"Jack has been doing what anyone who knew him, and you, and Noah, could have expected," said Bill, instantly professional. He reached into his jacket pocket and withdrew a small notebook, flipped through the pages. "He has established himself at Copt Hall. Spends many nights running the forests. Has an eccentric manservant."

At that Bill looked up from his notebook and both he and Jim intoned as one, "We don't like Malcolm."

"Why is that?"

"He is unreadable," said Bill.

Weyland gave a slight shrug. "He's working for Jack. Isn't that enough reason to dislike him?"

The imps grinned, and Bill went back to his notebook. "Your wife has been out to see Jack. Twice."

"I know that."

"She went for a walk in the woods with him."

"So?"

"We could have taken photographs, if you had asked."

Weyland felt like reaching out and strangling the damned imp. "Photographs of *what*?"

"They kissed," said Jim.

Weyland closed his eyes, taking a deep breath. "And?" he said, opening his eyes again.

"That's it," said Jim. "Just a kiss."

"But she *clung* to him," said Bill.

Then he fell silent, and both imps looked steadily at Weyland. For his part, Weyland suddenly wished he'd never set the cursed creatures on Jack's trail. He realized suddenly he didn't want to know what Jack and Noah got up to.

"And this wrongness that Jack has been carrying on about?" said Weyland.

"Don't know what he's talking about," said Jim.

"But it sounds scary," said Bill.

Weyland narrowed his eyes. "You're hiding something."

"Never," said Jim.

"You're looking way too pleased with yourselves," Weyland said.

The imps looked steadily, brightly, at him, but didn't say anything.

"What about these murders?" said Weyland. "What do you know about them?"

"Why ask us about them?" said Jim.

"Lucky guess," said Weyland. "Look at you, all bright confidence one moment and shifty-eyed discomfort the next. If there was one thing, lads, that you should have learned over the past three hundred years, it is a greater confidence in the art of dissembling."

"We don't know anything," said Bill. "Nothing."

This time his voice was surer, and both imps were back to regarding Weyland as if they'd never been guilty of

anything more foul than stealing a pie left to cool on a windowsill, but Weyland knew, with every piece of intuition available to him, that they were involved *somehow*.

He looked at them a moment, then nodded. "I've grown tired of you," he said. "I think we need to consider our association at an end."

"Wait!" said Jim. "What about some payment, then?"

Weyland looked back over his shoulder as he walked away. "I gave you life. Consider that payment enough."

Chapter Eleven

September to November 1939

ℑACK HAD COMMITTED HIMSELF TO DESTROYing the Troy Game—and if he was honest with himself, he had committed himself to it a very long time ago—but he wouldn't be pushed by anyone into moving precipitously. Catling was too powerful (Jack's mind shied away from invulnerable) and whatever chink she had in her armor (if it existed) would be so tiny, so transient, that Jack knew he not only needed to be very, very sure of it, but that he would only ever get one chance at it.

In Jack's mind there were two puzzles that needed to be solved. Firstly, he needed to discover *what* it was that hung over London like strange labyrinthine shadow. Every day that Jack rose from his bed he was more convinced that it concerned the Troy Game, even if it wasn't a direct part of it. Secondly, Jack needed to plumb the equally strange

labyrinthine shadows of Grace. She was so important, yet so unfathomable. That could be due to cunning, or, as he'd thought earlier, it could just as well be defensive.

Jack leaned more toward the defensive. God alone knew she had enough reason for it. More importantly, however, when he'd tested her on Ambersbury Banks the marks had seen no harm in her. He sensed no direct danger to himself from her.

Besides, Matilda liked her. *She's isolated herself within a ring of fire and of suffering, and can't escape,* Matilda had said to him. Jack was not always certain of his own judgment, but he *was* sure of Matilda's. If he had been Brutus, or William, or even Louis, Jack thought, he would have distrusted Grace on sight, and leaned toward blaming her for every dark cloud that scudded across the sun.

But now . . . no.

Grace was a puzzle, and she needed to be solved, but during September and October Jack spent almost every waking hour trying to discover as much as he could about the shadow that hung over London. In this he had to be very circumspect. If whatever was so different could be used against Catling, then Jack couldn't risk alerting her to its presence (and why was it Catling did not know of this? How could she *not*?). What Jack wanted to do was to walk every street of London, plotting out carefully what he saw, felt, and intuited along each of those streets, but this Jack could not do.

Nothing would have alerted Catling faster. Certainly Jack could take the occasional stroll down a street here, an alleyway there, but a systematic perambulation of all London—and beyond, if the difference stretched even farther than the metropolis? No. He was fully aware that Catling might be watching his every move.

It would be easier if Noah, Stella, and Ariadne could sense the shadow as well, because then four of them, wandering here and there about their daily business, would have been able to assemble a good picture. But none of the women could sense the difference, so they were useless to him.

But Grace could. Jack had absolutely no doubt of that. He meant to talk to her about it—perhaps even enlist her

aid—but for most of the two months following his meeting with Catling in St. Paul's crypt, Jack did what he could himself. He wanted to learn as much as he could by himself, before he spoke to Grace.

So Jack crisscrossed the city, one journey every two or three days, finding an excuse wherever possible to travel as widely as possible. There was a maze in Greenwich village he needed to view, and mazes in Peckham, Richmond, and Clapham as well. Every one of the ancient Veiled Hills of Llangarlia necessarily needed to be visited, as did the far newer docklands in east London.

Noah helped, handed an excuse by Queen Elizabeth, who made a radio broadcast urging women everywhere to do their bit for the war effort. Noah used this broadcast as the perfect reason to establish, as her very own effort, a mobile canteen (rather aptly named "Noah's Ark"). She purchased a van, had it fitted out as a canteen, and most nights she and Eaving's Sisters drove about, taking refreshments (tea, hot chocolate, and sticky buns) to the various air raid shelters around London.

Her mobile canteen gave Jack the perfect pretext to visit. Two or three nights a week he would find a reason to track her down and visit for five or ten minutes. Noah knew of the motive behind these visits, and cooperated by giving him a reason to visit: to talk about the arrangements for the Great Marriage; to discuss how and when they might do the Dance of the Flowers; and, in order not to make Catling too suspicious, to worry about what might happen after the completion of the Troy Game. *Could* they survive it? Was it worth risking the destruction of the land and Faerie to try to thwart Catling?

All this meant that Jack did, indeed, manage to visit a fair proportion of London, but there was a catch. The only way he could sense this difference that hung over the city was to *walk* the streets. To physically feel the city, and what underpinned it, throb up through the soles of his feet. Obviously Jack could not walk all these distances, because to do so would be to rouse Catling's suspicions. If he needed to go somewhere, he necessarily had to drive his Austin

convertible to get there, and thus the only time he managed to add to his store of understanding about the shadow was when he got out of the car.

Those few moments when he walked from car to building, or to Noah's mobile canteen. The longer moment when he could stretch his legs walking around a hill, or a block or two of a suburb. But Jack had to have a reason for all these walks. He couldn't just be *walking,* at least not too much.

He was desperate that Catling should have no idea about what he did.

Particularly after the night she tracked him down and asked him what he was doing.

Jack was in Peckham Rye, a suburb to the south of London, very late at night. His excuse for this excursion was that he wanted to visit the ancient site of Nunhead graveyard where, when he'd been William, two of his squires had been buried. The graveyard had been leveled (and its contents removed) during the nineteenth century when the train lines had come through the area, and terraced suburbia had leached out to either side of the twin rails like a black stain, but the faint memory of the squires' souls still lingered, and Jack knew that the journey would be no waste of time, no matter what he discovered about the shadow.

He was walking quietly up Ferndale Road, a nondescript street of late Victorian brick terraces, when he heard steps behind him.

Jack stopped, and turned around.

Catling stood a few feet away.

Her white face floated like a rotting moon within all the blackness surrounding her, and Jack had to swallow, suddenly nauseated.

"Well, well, Jack," she said, using a strange, sliding gait to move closer. "What do you here?"

"Visiting old friends," he said.

She raised an eyebrow, and moved to the side of him, forcing Jack to turn in order to keep her in sight. "Old friends?" she said.

"I had two squires when I lived as William," he said. "Henry and Raoul. They took wives after the invasion, and

settled here, in this parish." His shoe tapped against the tar-
mac. "They were buried here, a thousand years ago. I came
to pay my respect."

"How loyal. I am pleased. I like loyalty. I hope also that
you will remember your loyalty to me."

Jack inclined his head in an ambiguous gesture.

Her voice hardened. "You wouldn't want to forget it,
Jack."

"No. Of course not."

"Ah, you're looking for a means by which to destroy me,
aren't you? Grubbing about the streets, hoping lost souls
will whisper secrets into your ear?"

Jack went cold, but then realized that she knew or sus-
pected nothing specific. She was goading him, hoping he'd
let slip secrets himself.

He chose to change the subject. "Noah and I are going to
make the Great Marriage."

"Yes? What of it?"

"You should be pleased. The Great Marriage will unite
your chosen Kingman and Mistress of the Labyrinth to-
gether in such strength that your final completion will be
all the more powerful. After all, you did tie yourself in with
the land. The Great Marriage will enrich you."

Catling's face went expressionless, then she smiled.
"Then I am pleased." She resumed her peculiar sliding gait
down the roadway, and Jack followed, keeping enough dis-
tance between them that they did not inadvertently touch.

"When?" she continued. "Perhaps I'd like to attend."

Jack shuddered. *God, not that!* "In May next year."

Catling slid to a halt. "May? Next *year*?"

"The best possible day to conduct the marriage is on
May Day, Catling. That date, spring resurgent, will bring
the most power to the union. You've waited this long to be
completed. Another six or so months won't hurt."

"You want the time in which to plan to destroy me."

"Yes! *Yes,* I do. I admit it. You have been the greatest
mistake of all my lives, Catling, and I will do anything I
can to unwind you."

"I can't be—"

"I know what you have told me. Perhaps you are right. Perhaps all I can do is complete you and take what comfort that gives me."

Her eyes narrowed until they were bleak gleaming slivers. "And you *will* be comforted, Jack. If I am completed, then this land and the Faerie will be saved. Payment enough, I should imagine."

"Perhaps," said Jack. The idea of the land and the Faerie under Catling's complete dominion did not sound much like salvation to him.

Catling stepped very close, and put a hand on Jack's arm; he had to force himself not to flinch away as iciness crept down through the layers of his coat, jacket, and shirt.

"It won't be that bad, Jack. The ordinary man on the street, and the average woman at her knitting, will never know the difference. Besides, what has mankind ever achieved with his freedom? War, pain, brutality. What difference *me*?"

Come now, Jack. It won't be too bad. The Faerie will be safe, finally you can have Noah, and Grace can be freed from her pain. Isn't that a good deal?

Jack suddenly realized that Catling *did* think this was reasonable, and that he would truly be tempted.

And why shouldn't she believe this, eh? If he'd been either Brutus or William he would not have hesitated.

Although if he'd been Brutus he may have asked for some gold, as well.

CATLING WATCHED JACK WALK AWAY DOWN FERN-dale Road.

He'd wanted to delay any attempt to complete her.

The delay (if not Jack's reason for it) suited Catling perfectly. Gods alone knew *she* needed the time to bolster her own strength for Jack and Noah's inevitable attempt to destroy her.

But she wasn't happy. She glanced upward at the sky. Damn it, she needed to feed in order to strengthen herself. *When* would the horror start?

She looked back along the street.

Jack had disappeared.

What was he planning?

Coming to a decision, Catling vanished.

IT TOOK HER OVER AN HOUR TO INTUIT THE IMPS'
location, but once she knew precisely where they were,
Catling wasted no time in making her presence known.

"What are you *doing?*" she hissed, stepping forward to
see just what it was the imps crouched over under the porch
of the church.

Bill and Jim leaped back, mewing in their startlement,
and Catling's hiss turned into a gasp.

A woman's body lay sprawled on the stone. It was
naked, its torso torn and bloodied.

Catling crouched down beside the mutilated corpse,
keeping her skirts carefully drawn aside lest they be dirt-
ied. She studied it closely, then looked up at Bill and Jim.
"Just having fun, then?"

The imps hung their heads.

Catling stood up. "*Just* having fun?"

Their heads swayed slowly from side to side.

"We thought it would please you," whispered Jim.

Catling looked down at the corpse again. "You've torn
her womb out."

The imps nodded.

Catling giggled. "Where is it?"

"In the river," said Bill.

"Oh." Catling shrugged. "Never mind. Well, obviously
you have too much time on your hands. You need some-
thing to keep you busy."

"Yes?" Jim said doubtfully.

"I need you to keep an eye on Jack. You know who I
mean, surely. Brutus-reborn. He had come back as Louis
the last time—"

"We know who you mean," the imps said together.

"Good, then. He's up to something, walking about all

over London, much as he'd like to disguise it. I'd like to know what it is."

"You want us to follow him?" Jim said.

"Not obviously, you fool!" Catling said. "Just . . . *discover* what it is he and Noah plan, why can't you?"

"It'll be dangerous," Bill said.

"Not half as dangerous as I can be," Catling said.

The imps nodded, pretending to think about it. "Of course we can help you," Jim said. "Discover what Jack and Noah are about. Certainly."

Catling stared at them. "Good."

Then she was gone, and the imps were left standing under the porch of St. Magnus the Martyr with the corpse of their latest victim at their feet. They looked each other in the eye.

"Never any mention of payment," Bill said.

"Doesn't she realize we're professionals now?" said his brother.

"Even Weyland realized we're professionals," said Bill.

"Bet we won't get a penny out of *her*."

Bill sighed, then poked a foot into the corpse. "All we need now is for Jack to turn up and ask us to keep a watch on what he's doing."

Chapter Twelve

September to November 1939

HIS ENCOUNTER WITH CATLING BOTH UN-
nerved and relieved Jack. He was relieved that
Catling hadn't argued about the delay in completing
her, yet that very lack unnerved him. Why wasn't she an-
gry? Why hadn't she pushed for completion?

Jack was also unsettled by a third murder of a woman on
the night he'd met with Catling—the murderer had left his
victim's mutilated body under the porch of St. Magnus, as
he had the first two.

While the papers gave no details, they did allude to the
means of mutilation, and Harry's prediction soon proved
correct. The papers picked up on Scotland Yard's epithet,
"the Penitent Ripper," and now headlines once given over
exclusively to the war in Europe took a vacation into the
horror at home.

Ripper Rises From Grave!
Penitent Ripper Haunts the City!
London's Women Live in Fear!

Jack shuddered every time he read another lurid headline.
The murders disturbed him deeply, although he wasn't cer-
tain why. Surely he was inured to death and pain by now?

Four days after meeting Catling, Jack managed to have a
quiet word with Noah. He recounted to her what had hap-
pened in Ferndale Road.

"I am glad enough she didn't push for completion," he said, "but I worry about it at the same time."

Noah gave a shrug. "Perhaps she accepted your argument that the Great Marriage not only needs to be done to strengthen us both, but needs to wait for May Day." She gave a small smile. "And maybe Catling really believes that you will be happy enough to complete her if it means you will have me at the end of it."

He leaned forward—they were alone in the lee of her mobile canteen, Eaving's Sisters bustling food and drink into a community hall on the other side—and gave her a soft kiss on her cheek.

"Do I have a chance with you, Noah?"

"No." But she said it a little too quickly, her gaze sliding away, and Jack's eyes narrowed fractionally.

Finally he laughed, very softly, and leaned back, wondering why he didn't push the issue.

"I know the Great Marriage will cause difficulties for you at home," he said.

"Weyland and I will manage, Jack."

"Noah . . ."

She looked up at him then, and Jack's heart leapt in his chest. *God,* he thought, *I do have a chance.*

"Noah . . ." He leaned down to her, but just before his mouth touched hers they heard Matilda and Ecub approach the van, and they drew back from each other.

JACK SOUGHT OUT GRACE IN EARLY DECEMBER. He'd seen her on several occasions over the past two months, mostly with Noah's mobile canteen, with which she helped from time to time. She'd been at Faerie Hill Manor one day when he'd visited Harry, and similarly one afternoon when he'd gone to the Savoy to see Noah (Weyland being conveniently out). On that day Grace had been very tense and watchful of her mother with Jack, and Jack fully realized she did not like the idea of his trying to prise Noah away from Weyland.

Apart from that afternoon, when Grace had been clearly

tense, Jack had noticed a subtle change in her over the months. It was most apparent in her relationship with Noah. The wariness between the two had dissipated a little bit. It was still there, but both appeared more relaxed around each other. Certainly Noah was more relaxed with her daughter, although Jack suspected it was something that Noah had to work at assiduously.

And Grace was more confident within herself. Again, it was not a dramatic change, but it was there. Noah told him that Grace was going out more by herself, and that she and Weyland had taken to enjoying one or two nights dancing to the big band music of the Orpheans in the hotel's ballroom.

One afternoon, when he knew Noah and Weyland were out, Jack, dressed in his military uniform, waited patiently before Robert Stacey's desk as the concierge rang up to Grace to see if she wanted a visitor.

Stacey had to wait in silence a considerable time as Grace thought about it, and Jack half thought Grace would refuse to see him, but then Stacey spoke, put down the receiver, and nodded Jack toward the lifts.

"It is good to see Miss Orr receiving a young man, major."

Jack almost smiled as he realized Stacey thought he was paying court to Grace. "Do you have any advice for me, Mr. Stacey?"

Stacey's eyes wandered upward, as if he could see Grace through all the intervening layers of concrete and marble. Then he looked at Jack, his gaze flinty. "She a very special young lady, major. None of us here would like to see her hurt."

"Then I will take care, Mr. Stacey." Jack tipped his cap at the concierge, then made for the lifts.

"Major?"

Jack turned around, then drew a sharp intake of breath. Stacey's form shimmered, and suddenly there was not a man standing there, but a Sidlesaghe.

"None of us," said the Sidlesaghe, his mournful face drawn in long lines, half raising his long arms, "would like to see her hurt."

Jack wondered at this special protection afforded Grace, and became even more determined to discover her secrets. "Then, as I said, Sidlesaghe, I will take care."

The Sidlesaghe's form shimmered again, and Robert Stacey, staid and nondescript, once more stood before Jack. "Have a good visit, major," he said.

Jack nodded, and turned once more for the lifts.

GRACE WAS CLEARLY DISCONCERTED TO SEE JACK. She opened the door slowly, and stood, looking at him. "Yes?"

"Your mother told me you would be in. I wanted to see you, so I came to visit." He paused. "May I come in?"

She hesitated a moment longer, then nodded, and opened the door wide, standing back to let him through then walking past him to lead him into the apartment's drawing room.

Grace was dressed very differently from anything Jack had seen her wearing before—another change, and definitely for the better. Whereas Grace had earlier worn very demure, and often downright shapeless, skirts and blouses, now she wore a close-fitted blue linen dress that suited both her coloring and figure. She was wearing high heels, too, and Jack suddenly realized that Grace's legs were almost as lovely as Ariadne's.

The entire ensemble, Jack decided, was a remarkable improvement.

"Yes?" Grace said again as they sat down in opposite chairs in the drawing room.

"I won't bite, Grace."

She colored a little. "I'm sorry. I'm just surprised to see you. I thought you preferred my mother."

Jack ignored the remark about Noah and decided to waste no time on preliminaries about the weather. "I wanted to talk to you about the shadow I feel about London. It is labyrinthine, it somehow concerns the Troy Game, I can *feel* that"—he tapped at his chest—"and yet only I, and you, I suspect, can sense it. Grace, talk to me."

Grace fiddled with a fold of loose material over her

stomach, her eyes turned to the view out the window. "My mother has told me that you've been exploring."

"Yes."

Her eyes finally came back to him. "What have you discovered?"

"More questions than answers. It has, I think, a labyrinthine quality, but I have not been able to trace its entire extent, or anything like its true nature or purpose. Because it touches my Kingman blood, *calls* to it"—Jack tapped his chest softly—"then everyone else with training in the skills of the labyrinth should be able to sense some of it, too. But your parents can't. Stella can't. Ariadne and my father likewise. But I think that you can . . . Grace, *can* you sense it?"

Her fingers had stilled, and she watched him with wary eyes.

"Grace?"

Finally Grace nodded.

"But why *you*," Jack said, "and not your mother, or Stella? They are the two Mistresses of the Labyrinth most intimately connected with the Troy Game, and there's no other Game about that—"

Jack stopped abruptly, and at the same moment Grace tensed and looked to the window.

Something had shifted outside, something in the Embankment along the Thames beyond the Savoy's windows, but it was been so fleeting, and so ethereal, that Jack would have put it down to his imagination.

Save that Grace had clearly felt it as well.

"Grace?" He leaned forward in his chair, concerned. Grace was still staring at the window, her face drawn and pale, her hands clutching at the arms of her chair. "Grace? Are you all right? What was that?"

She didn't move, and Jack slid forward on his own chair enough that he could reach out and put a hand on her knee. "Grace?"

She jumped as he touched her, and jerked her face back to his. "Nothing. There was nothing." She gave a forced laugh. "Aren't most women in London seeing the Penitent Ripper behind every shadow these days?"

Jack winced. "Grace—"

"It was nothing, Jack."

"Grace—"

"Whatever this shadow is," Grace said, "I am *certain* it is a trap. I know it."

"And what if it is not?" he said. "It doesn't feel like a trap to me."

"What does it feel like to you, then?"

He hesitated, unsure about voicing the conviction that had been growing over the past few weeks. "I think it is a weakness within the Troy Game," he said finally.

"If it was a weakness, then my mother and Stella would feel it also."

"I don't know why they can't. It just doesn't feel like a trap to me."

"Jack—"

"Grace, I know you don't agree with me. But, is it possible that you could help me?"

Grace retreated into stillness.

"You can feel it. I can feel it. We're the only two. Grace, I need your help to trace out the extent of this strange shadow. I can't do it on my own, and Catling watches me too closely. You have a little more freedom."

Grace's mouth twisted at that last, but she gave a small nod. "What do you want me to do?"

Chapter Thirteen

November to December 1939

Grace Speaks

𝕴 DIDN'T TRUST JACK. I STILL THOUGHT HE WAS likely to destroy that fragile balance that had kept us alive for this long, and I thought he was likely to tear my parents apart, but, nonetheless, I agreed to help him. I had two reasons for this. I wasn't sure of the *how* of it, but I thought he was primarily responsible for the difference in the way my mother treated me. I had thought she'd rail at me, or demand explanations, or, worse, *fuss,* when she discovered that I had trained as a Mistress of the Labyrinth, that I had been entertaining Catling for years within my bedchamber, and, not the least, had been the lover of *her* former lover . . . but all Noah had done was walk into my room, kiss me once, and then twice, and say, "I am so proud of you."

Then she walked out.

I was doubly stunned by that: by her words and by the sheer simplicity of her actions. It broke down barriers as nothing else could have done. We didn't exactly become bosom friends overnight, but, after so many years of distance, we began to talk again. She asked me one day about my Great Ordeal, I found myself telling her in more detail than I'd originally intended, and then, most remarkable of all, we ended up laughing over some silly matter.

So I was grateful to Jack for that. I didn't know how he'd done it, or if he had consciously done anything, but he had certainly been the catalyst to the thawing in relations between me and my mother.

The second reason I'd agreed to help Jack was because no one had ever asked for my help before. Here was something that my mother, or Ariadne, or Stella could not do . . . but I could. It gave me a sense of purpose, of *usefulness,* that I'd never had previously. I thought Jack was very, very wrong when he said he thought this difference was a weakness, but I thought that if I helped, then perhaps I would be able to show him that he was wrong, and I was right.

Grace had a job, finally. My own contribution to the "war effort."

That night after Jack had come to see me, Catling did not appear beside my bed at night.

I took that for a good sign.

The next morning we met at a Lyon's Tea Shop just off the Strand.

"Catling watches me," said Jack, stirring his cup of tea and ignoring the stares of the women in the shop.

Although I'd realized Jack was a handsome man, I hadn't realized the full extent of his attractiveness until I saw the other women unable to keep their eyes off him for any longer than five seconds.

I'd never had tea with such an attractive man before, and was a little bit surprised to find I was actually basking in the envy of every other woman present.

"She watches me, also," I said.

"Ah," said Jack, smiling, and looking up from his tea, "but she only enjoys tormenting you. *Me* she expects to try and murder her at any moment. Her eyes are always keener when turned my way."

I inclined my head, conceding the point and wondering what the other women thought of me—a younger sister to the American major? His girl? "And so that's why you need my help?"

"Partly. You can do more than I can, simply because Catling will be watching me more avidly than you. But

that's not the only reason, Grace. The main reason is that you can actually *help* me. You're not just a decoy. You're a benefit all of yourself."

God damn it, he looked as though he meant that. I felt my cheeks flush, and dropped my eyes to my as yet untouched currant bun. I picked it up, put it down, picked it up again, then dropped it, feeling like an utter fool.

I raised my eyes, and saw that he was regarding me with such a gentle smile that my cheeks flamed anew.

I reminded myself forcibly that he'd spent a good few thousand years lusting for my mother, and still did, and that this was most certainly an act.

"What do you want me to do?" I said, my voice a little harder than I'd meant.

Jack's smile faded, and he spent a moment taking a swallow of his tea. Then he explained how he needed to trace out the extent of the shadow. It had to be done on foot rather than by car, or bus, or tube. It had to be *felt*.

"I need to know not merely its extent, but whether it has frail or strong points. I need to understand its . . ."

He stopped, struggling to put into words what he felt.

"Character," I said.

"Yes. Precisely. Can you do it?"

I shrugged, trying to regain the ground I'd lost with the silliness over the currant bun. "If you want," I said diffidently.

Again, that gentle smile. "I want, Grace."

I felt the flush threaten again, and so I hurried on with more prosaic matters. "I can mark out what I discover on a map, if you like."

The smile broadened, just a little, and I wondered if he was laughing at me. "I should have thought of that. Yes, that would be useful. Thank you, Grace."

Still unsure of myself, I started to toy with the cursed bun again.

"Grace?"

"Yes?"

"Be careful. I hesitated to ask you to do this because of . . . the murders."

There had been four now. Another just two nights ago. Yet

one more young woman, brutally murdered, and left under the porch of St. Magnus the Martyr. The police were doing all they could to calm the situation, including—according to Harry—setting up a close but surreptitious watch over St. Magnus, but the unease within the City was growing.

"Nothing can happen to me, Jack," I said. "I'm sure Catling will keep me safe. She can't have *me* be torn apart."

"Grace. Please. Be careful."

I wanted to laugh his concern away, but I couldn't. He was looking at me so intently I had to shift my eyes, stumbling for something to say.

Before I could make any bigger a fool of myself the tea shop lady bustled over and fussed over Jack (first she was on this side of him, then that, wondering if she could get him more tea, or asking him a silly question about New York, and even, God help me, wondering if he could explain for her, and all other ladies present, whether or not he thought Hitler really had the strength to invade in the spring). Jack took it all in good humor, but he did not once look at her, and answered only with brief (although polite) words, and eventually she subsided, sighed, wiped her hands on her apron, and drifted back to stand behind the counter.

"One of your conquests from a previous life?" I asked, vastly relieved at the interruption, and Jack roared with laughter. One of the other customers, a spindly woman in a faded red coat who had been watching Jack as keenly as the lady behind the counter, dropped her half-eaten scone into her cup, splashing tea all over her coat.

"One of the hopefuls," he said once his laughter had died down, "but I am pretty sure I refused her then, too."

" 'Pretty sure'?" I said.

He shrugged. "There were so many."

I grinned, and suddenly the sun shone a little brighter than it had hitherto. I wondered when last I'd shared a joke with someone, then realized that I never had.

Jack was still smiling at me, and I sat there, thinking how odd it was that I could laugh so easily with someone I was certain would destroy my life.

* * *

I DID WHAT JACK ASKED OF ME, AND DISCOVERED a purpose to my life that had been missing until now. For weeks, all through the late autumn, I traveled about London and its immediate environs (although never at night; despite my casual words to Jack I didn't want to put myself in the way of the Penitent Ripper). I moved about in no discernable pattern. In fact, I borrowed one of Ward Lock's little red guide books from Robert Stacey—the Sidlesaghe kept something of everything in his office—and opened a page at random each morning, and thus chose my day's excursion. I made sure I had a purpose in each day's excursion—a visit to a shop, a hairdresser, a theater, or an opportunity to wander down a river walk—and I only went two or three days a week.

Catling never appeared to me when I walked out, as she had to Jack, although every so often I would open my eyes at night, and there she would be, sitting shadowed in a corner. Watching.

Did she realize what I was doing? I don't know, but she said nothing to me, nor gave me any indication that she did understand. So I continued on my trips. Everywhere I went, I scried out with my power a little bit more of Catling's trap, and once I was home in the afternoon or evening, I traced out with red pencil what I had discovered on one of Bacon's wall maps of London. This map I kept secreted within the bathroom of our apartment in a magazine rack (my parents may have discovered it, but neither said anything). Catling had far-seeing eyes, but I had to assume they didn't follow me into the bathroom.

But, oh my, Catling *was* cunning. There was a clear labyrinthine intent forming from all these slowly connecting red lines. I could not only see that with my eyes, but also could feel it with my powers as Mistress of the Labyrinth. It was subtle (this was a surprise; I had never suspected Catling to be subtle), and of some considerable beauty. I felt instinctively that it traced out the path of a

labyrinth, but what I had was so fragmentary I could not distinguish the actual turning of the labyrinth's paths.

It was . . . oh, how shall I describe this? It was almost hypnotically enigmatic. The more I discovered, the more I wanted to discover.

A trap, obviously, designed to lure Jack (and, presumably, my mother, although why she couldn't sense it I have no idea) deeper and deeper into its dark heart. *Look at me, I am beautiful and exquisite and filled with so much potential that if only you sink deeper and deeper into my depths you can have anything you want, even your freedom.*

Every three weeks or so, Jack and I would meet somewhere. Generally as if by accident—perhaps at my mother's mobile canteen as it trundled about the air raid shelters at night, or at Faerie Hill Manor, and once more at another tea shop (Jack patently felt he needed to spread his charms about).

I did not ever bring my large wall map with me—that would have been too dangerous for prying eyes—but Jack would take one of my wrists, and somehow he would see with my eyes, *absorb* the information I had learned, and then sit back, and nod, and ask me what I thought.

Always I would say the same thing: *It is beautiful and exquisite, and more deadly than anything I could ever imagine. Be careful, Jack.*

And he would nod again, and withdraw his hand from me, and not share his thoughts.

WE ALWAYS SPENT CHRISTMAS AT FAERIE HILL Manor, and this year was no exception in that regard. What was so different about this Christmas was the sense of hope that pervaded the gathering.

No one had to play Waiting for Jack, because Jack was here, and while no one wanted to admit it, most people somehow believed that Jack would somehow manage to save them.

On this day even my father seemed slightly more relaxed about Jack, and I was happy to see that while Jack

gave my mother a kiss of greeting on her arrival, he spent
no more time with her than was appropriate. We did every-
thing that families are supposed to do at Christmas: ate too
much, played some silly parlor games, embarrassed our-
selves far too readily with some terrible Christmas jests,
and wore foolish hats.

We also did things that most families didn't do. We
spent Christmas afternoon strolling the borderlands of the
Faerie. We didn't go in, and I wondered if this was because
of my presence, but many of the Sidlesaghes came out to
join us in our walk, and later, Long Tom and two of his
brothers stayed to spend Christmas evening with us, which
was a great joy, for I liked the Sidlesaghes.

On that walk we strolled close to Copt Hall. Malcolm
joined us there, and Harry asked him back to Faerie Hill
Manor for the evening, which invitation Malcolm cheer-
fully accepted.

Deer shadowed us as we turned back for Faerie Hill
Manor, and I saw Malcolm looking at me intently when he
saw me watching them.

We only ate a light supper. The king (another of my
mother's erstwhile lovers), while not attending, had sent us
a beautiful platter of marzipan fruits, colored and shaped
to look like the real thing, and with stalks of cinnamon
sticks, the ends frayed where they met the fruit for an
added touch of reality. After supper, we gathered in the
drawing room, gods and Sidlesaghes and Mistresses of the
Labyrinth (save Ariadne, who was also not present), drift-
ing into three or four groups to either sit and converse over
cigarettes and whisky, or to play board games or cards.

I had not been so happy for years, and it was no surprise
at all, that Catling should choose that day, and that happi-
ness, to strike.

I was playing canasta with Long Tom, Stella, and Harry
when suddenly pincers of red-hot agony closed about my
wrists. The cards dropped from my fingers, and involuntar-
ily I leaned forward, my wrists held tight against my waist,
trying desperately not to groan.

No! Oh God, not tonight. Please, no . . .

But Catling could not have resisted, this, could she?

From the corner of my eye I saw my mother, who'd been sitting with two of the Sidlesaghes and drinking a little bit more whisky than was good for her, put her glass to one side, and start up.

She and I were closer now, and maybe she would fuss, and maybe not, but suddenly all I wanted was to get away. Not only from my mother, but from that warm, happy room.

I stumbled to my feet, muttered something about wanting to be alone, and managed to get out of the French doors onto the terrace without making a complete fool of myself and falling over. I moved away from the doors as fast as I could, wanting to get out of people's eyesight—

They must all be staring at me.

—now giving in to the luxury of groaning, clutching my wrists into my body so tightly I could feel their heat through my clothes, and wishing I were dead. Catling had left me alone for weeks. The last time she had attacked had been that day I'd been at Copt Hall and the deer had been nuzzling me. I'd grown too used to being left alone, too used to feeling useful, too used to *feeling*.

Damn it!

I burst into tears, lost in misery, and managed to make it over to where the outdoor table and chairs sat pushed against a wall. I sat down (almost falling in the attempt), and it was only then, as the cold of the chair penetrated through to my flesh, that I realized I'd come out dressed in only a thin silk frock, without even a cardigan, and that not only was the air close to freezing, but there was a dusting of snow over the terrace.

I was mortified. I was in agony from my wrists, but for the moment that mortification hurt worse. Everyone inside would be thinking . . .

How silly.

Poor Grace.

Perhaps someone should go out.

After all, it is Christmas, and she really shouldn't be alone.

And then, God curse it, someone *did* come out. I heard the opening and closing of the French doors, the brief mur-

mur of conversation while they were open, and then several sets of footsteps coming toward me.

I couldn't bear to look, tears were streaming down my cheeks, and I wondered if I would embarrass myself further if I made a dash for the lawns.

In the end the choice was made for me. As I tensed to rise, Jack and Harry pulled out chairs to one side of me, and Malcolm set down a plate of the marzipan fruit on the table, as well a decanter of whisky and several glasses.

Then, with no comment, Malcolm took a blanket he had over one arm and tucked it about my shoulders, poking it efficiently down the sides of my body, and folding it over my front, enclosing my entire body apart from my feet and head within its warmth.

Then he turned and walked back inside.

Jack and Harry—both well wrapped in thick coats and with hats pulled down low—took no notice of me. Jack poured out whisky for the two of them, Harry grabbed a piece of marzipan fruit and chewed away enthusiastically, and then, well fortified, both began to chat.

Thus began the most extraordinary hour.

Jack and Harry sat there, keeping me company on the terrace, chatting away about friends they had known in past lives, stupidities both had managed to commit, sharing humor and warmth and companionship.

And they included me in it.

They didn't once address me, and only rarely glanced at me (Jack once leaned over and, without missing a single beat in his conversation, matter-of-factly tucked in a corner of the blanket that came loose when I shuddered under a particularly vile spasm), but somehow they *included* me in everything they said and did. I felt a part of the conversation, even if I couldn't speak, and even if the two men rarely looked at me.

I felt included in their company.

Jack and Harry had a shared past that went back thousands of years. They had been enemies, they had been friends, they had shared wives and lovers and adventures and disasters too numerous to tally.

All without me.

By rights I should have felt such an outsider that this conversation would have been a misery for me. But it wasn't. They gossiped back and forth about people and events I'd heard of, and far more of people and events of which I'd never heard, and yet they somehow made me feel such a part of their conversation, of their entire existence, that anyone listening might have thought me their intimate companion for all these thousands of years.

It was the most amazing gift, and I had no doubt at all that it was Jack's doing (as I had no doubt at all that he'd somehow been the catalyst for my mother's transformation). Harry had never once done anything like this for me, not when we'd been lovers, not at any other time.

No, this was Jack, and I felt such a surge of gratefulness to him that I actually began to weep even more than I had previously.

The men were, by this time, engaged in a spirited discussion about the relative merits of the war stallions both had owned when Jack had been William and Harry had been Harold, and I sat there and wept with happiness as Catling's fire banded my wrists and the men argued about fetlocks.

It was the best Christmas I'd ever had.

And, as I sat there, and wept in joy, the pain abruptly vanished, and I gave a soft gasp.

The pain had lost its effectiveness. Catling had done her worst, and all I had done was weep with happiness.

Jack and Harry barely broke stride (they'd reached withers by this stage); Jack poured out a fresh glass of whisky, pushing it toward me, and Harry picked up a marzipan pear, put it on a plate that had appeared to one side, sliced it into thin layers, and likewise pushed that toward me.

WE SAT THERE FOR PERHAPS ANOTHER HOUR.
Gradually, I joined in the conversation, which Jack had steered away from his and Harry's shared past to the prob-

lems the Epping Forest keepers had trying to reestablish the resident fallow deer population. That was, surely, a topic I didn't have much knowledge of, either, but somehow Harry and Jack listened to what I had to say (while in no way appearing in the slightest bit patronizing), and laughed at some of my weaker attempts at jesting.

That made Jack remember our meeting in the Lyon's Tea Shop, and soon he had both Harry and me laughing uproariously with his vastly exaggerated account of how every woman within five hundred yards had offered him her body then and there.

"And yet you were resistant?" Harry said to me eventually.

I grinned at Jack. "Everyone needs at least one mountain left to scale."

"Is that a challenge?" he said, his tone light, those dark eyebrows raised.

"It most certainly isn't an invitation," I said, and he smiled, and our conversation drifted to other things.

WE WENT BACK IN, EVENTUALLY, TO FIND MOST OF the others had gone to bed. My parents and I were staying at Faerie Hill Manor that night, going back to the Savoy in the morning, and I walked toward the stairs, thinking to go to bed myself, when Jack called softly to me.

I'd walked up three or four of the stairs by this time, and I turned, and looked down at him.

He was holding out the plate with the remaining slices of marzipan pear on it. "Take this," he said. "A midnight snack."

It was already long past midnight, but I smiled, and thanked him, and walked back down the steps to take the plate from his hand.

As I did so I looked over to where Harry stood by the door leading to the drawing room.

As our eyes met, he gave a small, sad smile, then turned his back and walked through the door.

I looked back at Jack, who was watching me with eyes

so unreadable they had become as mysterious as the strange shadow that hung over London.

Suddenly uncomfortable, I took the plate and walked up the stairs.

When I got to my room, I put the plate of the sliced marzipan pear on my nightstand, thinking that I might eat some if I woke during the night.

But I slept the night through, more soundly than I have slept in years, and when I woke in the morning both the plate and its contents had gone, and I thought that one of Harry's servants had been in early, and had cleared it away.

I felt a small twinge of disappointment, but then forgot it within moments.

WITHIN THE DARK CRYPT, THE WHITE QUEEN PUT the plate with its marzipan sliced pear atop the altar. She stood a long moment, staring at it.

Then she gave a soft smile, and touched the marzipan fruit briefly, as if caressing it. She had been working so long for this, so long, and finally . . .

Then the White Queen's face lost its warmth, and grew cool and distant once more.

All depended on whether or not Grace would be prepared to offer her life for Jack.

"So tell me, Grace," the White Queen whispered into the chilly, dank air of the crypt. "Is he sweet enough to die for? Are you prepared to offer your neck to the return swing of the druid's sword?"

Chapter Fourteen

Hampstead and Kensington

New Year's Eve, December 1939

J**ACK SPENT NEW YEAR'S EVE WITH MATILDA,**
Ecub, and Erith at their house in Hampstead. Situated on Heath Road, the house had a commanding view of the heath, and once he'd parked the Austin, Jack spent several minutes standing, looking out over the heath, lost in memories.

He could remember riding through here, sitting behind Genvissa on her pony, as she took him to the Llandin, Llangarlia's most sacred hill. He could remember becoming drunk on her dreams of power, remember being drunk with lust for her.

And here he was, so many thousands of years on, more powerful than perhaps he could have imagined then, and yet so different, and coming to visit women that, as Brutus, he had despised.

Jack sighed, and turned for the house.

It was a modern brick house, sprawling and comfortable, and Matilda opened the door just as he raised his hand to knock.

"Lost in memories, Jack?" she said softly as she leaned forward to kiss his cheek.

"I have learned to hate memories," he said.

Matilda grinned. "Not all of them, I hope."

He laughed, and kissed her mouth. "No. There are a few I treasure."

It was an enjoyable evening. Despite what Jack had said to Matilda, the four of them spent several hours lost in memories. They did not discuss the great events that had

consumed their several lives, nor did they mention the Troy Game, but, rather as Jack and Harry had done on Christmas Eve, they remembered the little things that had made life enjoyable and worthwhile: fabrics and foods; walks and glades; jests that had survived through the centuries. They recalled their time spent in exile on the continent when Jack had been Louis, and the other three the wife and mistresses of Charles II, and they slipped naturally back into the closeness that all four had shared during that life.

"Sometimes I wish," Jack said as the hands of the clock crept ever closer to midnight, "that we could just sideslip into one of the harmless, comfortable times that we have all experienced, and leave the Troy Game and all that it implies behind us."

"If we did that," said Erith, "then we would lose too much."

Jack opened his mouth to protest, then shut it, realizing she was right. The good times they had shared would be as nothing if they were not all bonded by the terrors as well.

"I thought you might have been at Faerie Hill Manor tonight," Ecub remarked, glancing at the clock. It lacked but a few minutes until midnight. "Noah and Weyland will be there, and Silvius, too, perhaps. And Grace."

"I ruined Weyland's Christmas," Jack said. "I thought I'd leave him to his family for New Year's."

"But I hear from Noah," Ecub said, "and from Grace herself, that you have been spending time with Grace. That is well done, Jack. Inch by inch, Grace is emerging from her shell."

"I am not being charitable," Jack said, a little annoyed by Ecub's words. "Grace is somehow connected to this shadow. She can trace it. If I am to discover its true nature, then I need Grace."

"Let us not talk of this shadow tonight," Matilda said, rising from her chair to top up their glasses. "Look, midnight is upon us, and we need to farewell the past and look only into the future."

As the clock chimed, they toasted the New Year, sharing

laughter and kisses, then Erith and Ecub excused themselves, saying they were tired after so much conversation and alcohol and needed their bed.

Jack laughed softly as the door closed behind them. "They are not terribly subtle. Did you ask them to do that, Matilda?"

"No," she said. "But they knew I would like time alone with you."

She moved to sit on the arm of Jack's chair. "Jack, can I see your markings?"

He put his glass down, slipped off his jacket and tie, then his shirt, then took a deep breath as Matilda slid her hands over his chest and shoulders.

"They are very beautiful, Jack. Very powerful."

"Matilda—"

"Will you stay the night with me, Jack?"

It was tempting. Matilda's hands were firm and inviting on his body and, oh, how he'd missed both her body and her advice in his bed. Spending the night with Matilda meant not only making love with her, but spending hours in talk with her, confiding his fears and hopes, asking her advice, and all the while running his hands over her body . . .

Matilda smiled slowly as she saw his eyes darken. "Just this once," she said. "Just for comfort."

Jack's hands slid around her waist, then up her back. She leaned down and kissed him, and his hands firmed about her body and slid her down onto his lap.

"Thank God," she whispered. "For a moment I thought all you had come for tonight was tea and cake and conversation."

Suddenly all Jack could see was Grace sitting opposite him in the Lyons Tea Shop as the tea lady fussed over Jack, and then Grace's jesting about the occasion on Christmas.

"I'm sorry," Jack said, leaning back from Matilda, his hands falling away from her body. "I really should be going."

JACK'S FATHER, SILVIUS, HAD NO SUCH QUALMS about accepting the invitation offered him the same night. By one A.M. he lay in bed in a luxurious Kensington apart-

ment, running one hand softly over the waist and hip of the woman lying next to him, sated both with love and with alcohol.

Ariadne smiled, kissing Silvius softly, running her hand behind his head, tangling her fingers within his black curls.

"It was nice of you to keep a pariah like me company on New Year's," she whispered.

"It was an invitation I could not resist."

Her hand shifted from the nape of his neck to his bicep. "I can still feel the ghost of the Kingship bands of Troy about your flesh," she said, then leaned forward and softly kissed his arm.

"Ah," Silvius said, grinning. "It was not me you desired at all, then, but the gold I once wore."

"Indeed," said Ariadne, arching one of her beautiful eyebrows. "Think that I wanted *you*?"

"The things you have to put up with, eh, to remember your past glory days?"

Ariadne considered briefly being offended (*past* glory days?) but then decided she preferred laughing with this man than being irate at him. "I wish I'd met you a long time ago," she said.

"If you could have dragged me away the instant before Brutus plunged that arrow into my eye it might have saved everyone a great deal of trouble."

She smiled, and kissed him, and for a few minutes there was little said between them at all. But just as Ariadne was sure that Silvius was thinking of nothing but furthering his discovery of her body, he pulled his mouth from hers and pulled back just a little.

"I was talking to Weyland this morning, and—" he began.

"For all the gods' sakes, Silvius, if you *must* talk then let us not talk of *him*!"

She sounded truly waspish, and Silvius apologized to her. "I am an old man, Ariadne, and you know how old men's minds wander at the most inopportune moment. I'd started thinking about how Brutus murdered me, setting into motion all the events that led to the Troy Game, and

then . . . well, then, witless fool that I am, I forgot what a treasure I held in my arms."

Mildly mollified, but not yet prepared to forgive him entirely, Ariadne sat up in bed, reaching for her cigarettes. "Want one?"

Silvius repressed a sigh—*whose fault was this but his?*—and sat up as well. "Yes, thank you."

Ariadne lit two cigarettes, handed one to Silvius, then drew deeply on hers as she leaned back against the pillows. "All right then, so you have managed to drag Weyland into our bed. What did you wish to say about him that was so important you could interrupt a loving with *me*?"

She was still annoyed, but Silvius was relieved to hear a hint of amusement in her voice.

"He's set the imps to watching Jack," Silvius said.

Ariadne gave a small snort. "Fool."

"He fears for his family," Silvius said. "For his marriage . . . for his daughter."

"And so he has set those black imps to scurrying about after Jack?"

"They've grown up into private investigators," said Silvius, amusement riddling his voice.

Ariadne laughed at that. "What? Chasing down mischievous husbands?"

Silvius smiled, happy that Ariadne had finally relaxed enough to laugh. Gods alone knew what she might have done to him had she been truly annoyed. He spent a moment or two smoking before mentioning what had really bothered him about his conversation with Weyland.

"Weyland thinks the imps are involved in the Penitent Ripper murders," he said.

"Jesus God, Silvius!" Ariadne said, turning to look Silvius in the face. Details of the murderer's grisly method of ripping out the women's wombs had been leaked—if not into the press, then into enough ears that it had become the talk of London. Those details had been niggling at the back of Ariadne's mind, but it wasn't until Silvius mentioned the imps that they had firmed into horrifying clarity.

"What's wrong?" Silvius said.

"The imps!"

"What *about* the imps, woman?"

"The imps are doing the murders!"

"How can you know?"

Ariadne drew in a shaky breath, and, concerned, Silvius took her cigarette and stubbed it out with his in the ashtray on his bedside table.

"Silvius, have you not heard the story of how the imps were born?"

"Perhaps, Ariadne, but it would have been so long ago that—"

"Weyland put both imps into Jane's—now Stella—and Noah's wombs. Then, when Charles and Louis entered London, he commanded the imps to tear themselves out of the women's wombs . . . gods, Silvius, those imps tore and chewed their way into life! Both women should have died, save that Weyland forced them to live."

Silvius remembered it now—Stella had told him of this many, many years past. "The imps are recreating their own birth," he said, horrified.

"Tearing the women apart," said Ariadne, "save that these women die, they do not survive, as did Jane and Noah."

"But . . . why? *Why?*"

"Sheer damned bleakness," said Ariadne. "They are, after all, Weyland's creation."

She earned a sharp glance from Silvius at this, but he did not comment on it.

"Why didn't Weyland see the connection?" he said after a moment.

Ariadne's only answer was to shrug and reach for another cigarette.

PART THREE

THE GREAT MARRIAGE

London, 1170

ETER DE COLECHURCH, CHAPLAIN OF ST.
Mary Colechurch in Cheapside, was a worried
man. Peter's duties as chaplain were only nomi-
nal, for the greater part of his day was taken up in his du-
ties as Bridge Master of London Bridge. Peter had been
delighted when Henry II offered him the post of Bridge
Master seven years earlier, but the intervening years had
witnessed Peter's enthusiasm wane.

London Bridge was nothing but trouble.

The troubles had started more than a century ago when
the ever-cursed Norsemen had pulled the damned thing
down. A wooden bridge was quickly erected to replace the
one that the Norsemen had destroyed, but that succumbed
to fire within a few years. A new bridge was built, but that
was swept away in floods within a year.

It took fifteen years to secure the funds to rebuild the
bridge—which misfortune claimed within four years. When
Peter first came to the post of Bridge Master in 1163 his
initial task was to rebuild the bridge yet again. Peter was
an engineer of rare skill, which was the reason he'd se-
cured the post in the first instance, and over the course of
two years he designed and supervised the building of a
beautiful bridge made almost entirely of elm wood, known
for its strength and resistance to rot.

It had been up less than seven years, but already it was
badly cracked and beginning to lean.

It would need to be replaced soon.

Henry II was demanding answers. Moreover, he was

starting to murmur publicly about finding an engineer who could build a bridge that would last longer than a season. As much as Peter liked to moan quietly that the entire bridge was cursed, it was hardly an excuse he could present to the king.

Today Peter was walking the length of the bridge, something he did twice a day. He walked from London over to Southwark, pausing to lean over the balustrade every so often to wince at the fresh cracks that had appeared overnight, and was now on his return trip.

Halfway across he paused to look at St. Paul's.

The cathedral was itself in the process of being rebuilt, and the steeple was just starting to rise above the body of the nave.

Peter looked, awash with admiration. How he wished he could work on a cathedral . . .

"Why not?" said a little girl's voice.

Peter looked down. A five- or six-year-old girl in a black dress stood at his side, regarding him gravely. She was very pretty with her black hair and eyes, although her face appeared so cold that she might have stepped from the grave not a moment since.

Peter repressed a superstitious shiver.

"St. Paul's needs something to rival it," the little girl continued now that she had Peter's full attention. "It needs something to balance it out. Why don't you build a bridge to rival St. Paul's beauty?"

"Little girl," Peter began.

"Oh, I'm not really a little girl, you know," said the creature standing so close. "This form just amuses me. What would really thrill me is if you would build me a house, right here on the bridge. One that will rival St. Paul's in beauty and power."

Peter was very slowly backing away. She was a devil, a malign fairy, a—

"All I want is a chapel," said the girl. "Is that so bad?"

"A chapel?" Peter said, coming to a halt.

"Indeed," the girl said. "Imagine, if you will, a beautiful stone bridge, soaring over graceful stone piers—"

"*It can't be done. No one can build the kind of piers in this river needed to support a stone—*"

"*What if I showed you how?*" the girl said.

While Peter de Colechurch knew perfectly well that this apparition was a spirit of some kind, he was now wondering if, perhaps, it was an angel sent from God to guide him rather than a devil sent to tease him.

After all, what devil would want a chapel?

The little girl smiled, deepening the coldness on her face. "*I will show you how to build this bridge,*" *she said,* "*and Henry will shower you with favors, and your name will ring down the centuries. All I want is a chapel, Peter. In the middle of the bridge. You can dedicate it to whomever you wish. I'm not fussed. There is just one little thing I need in this chapel.*"

"*Yes?*" *said Peter, his suspicions again flaring.*

The little girl smiled sweetly. "*A crypt, Peter de Colechurch, with an altar laid out and dedicated to God. Do we have a deal?*"

"*Show me first how to build these piers,*" *said Peter, and the little girl laughed, and agreed.*

She knew Peter was hers.

"What can't be done. We care not what the End or price of this enterprise, or approve a vote——"

"What? I? I should just leave——" she stopped, aghast.

Worse than de Coulomb? Even perfect? And that this companion was a youth of some kind, he was now working. It is, perhaps, it was an illusion too, but too God to exist, him rather than a devil, or the less.

After all, what they would amuse a chapel.

"He had his caught, assuming the tenuous of her face. I will show you how to build this bridge," she said. "I'll help you. Show me your fingers, and your home, huh. Just draw the contours. All want is a copper. Rare. In the middle of the battle. For too stubborn it is, where you was wrong. I'm not bound. There is just one little shape I need in this charge."

"I'm good enough his emotions to the thing."

The little girl smiled, creased. "A copper. Rare," de Coulomb, with all that learned and dedicated to find. Do we have a deal?"

"Show me first how to build these piers," said Roger, and the little girl inspired, and cried.

She drew their fingers.

Chapter One

WITHIN THE FAERIE AND ATOP THE SAVOY

January to April 1940

HE WORST WINTER IN DECADES GRIPPED the land. Snow lay in great drifts, blocking many roads and making communications difficult, and ice formed over rivers, even freezing over the upper reaches of the Thames. Frosts crippled the fields, and raging winter seas washed mines ashore where they killed boys with too-curious fingers. Life continued on as close to normal as possible under the twin weights of the cold and the war, but most outdoor activities had to be curtailed, if not stopped completely, and people shivered within their homes under the twin restrictions of the severe winter and fuel shortages. When the ice and snow and frosts had ended, floods devastated large portions of southeastern England.

In late February and early March the IRA commenced a series of bombings in London. No one was killed, but a number of people were injured and the bombs caused extensive property damage.

While the war still raged in Europe, many people in London, and over Great Britain generally, had begun to relax away from their initial fears of invasion, massive bombings, and gas attacks. Most Londoners had stopped carrying their gas masks around with them, those who had built air raid shelters in their back gardens had to spend an

hour every fortnight dusting away the cobwebs from their doors, and Noah and Eaving's Sisters had parked their mobile canteen for the moment. London had suffered no attacks (although there had been several false air raid warnings), Britain had suffered no invasion, and on the fifth of April, the British prime minister, Neville Chamberlain, went so far as to announce that he thought Hitler had "missed the bus" and thought that a German invasion of the west was now highly unlikely.

It wasn't a view that the Lord of the Faerie shared. One frosty March morning he arrived at the door of Copt Hall and asked Malcolm to fetch Jack.

"Coel?" Jack said. It was still very early, and he'd only just risen. He was dressed, but his jaw was still unshaven, and he took the cup of tea that Malcolm offered gratefully.

The Lord of the Faerie shook his head when Malcolm asked him if he wanted tea, then waited until the valet had left the drawing room before speaking.

"Jack, we have a problem in the Faerie."

Jack drained his cup of tea and set it aside. "Yes?"

"It is better if you come. You have barely set foot in the Faerie since your return, and this you need to see."

Jack gave the Lord of the Faerie a long look, then nodded, fetched his coat, and led the Lord of the Faerie to the front door.

From the front door they walked straight into the Faerie.

The Lord of the Faerie was right, Jack thought, as he gazed over the misted wooded hills rolling away into infinity. He should have come back more often than he had. The instant his foot stepped onto the magical soil, Jack felt a sense of wellness, almost of nurturing, envelop his being.

And something else. Something . . . not quite right.

His marks moved slightly, drawing icy trails of uneasiness across his shoulders. "Coel?" he said.

In response the Lord of the Faerie led him toward the edge of woodlands that lead into the first of the forested hills. At first glance the trees and plants seemed healthy

enough, but the Lord of the Faerie pointed to a shrub, and then the lower branches of a tree.

"See, here, and here," he said.

Jack stepped closer. There were patches of blackness on the lower leaves of the tree, and many of the leaves over the top of the shrub were similarly dead. "What is it?" he said.

"Frost," said the Lord of the Faerie. "The iciness that grips the land had started to penetrate into the Faerie."

Jack pinched off one of the blackened leaves of the shrub. It crumbled into dust between his fingers. His marks moved again, and Jack's uneasiness increased. This shouldn't happen. The Faerie was cut off from the mortal world. The infections of the mortal world simply should not touch the Faerie.

"Catling," Jack said, very soft. What else could explain it? "Why?" he said. Catling already knew that Jack would do nothing until the Great Marriage on May Day, so why send these tendrils of attack into the Faerie now?

"Why not?" said the Lord of the Faerie, then he sighed, and pinched at the bridge of his nose. "It might be Catling, or it may be an indication of how sick and weak the land has become. Either possibility terrifies me, Jack."

"I'd lean toward the latter," said Jack. He touched another leaf, watching it crumble. "I just don't think Catling would move this early."

"Then if it is the latter, Jack, then we need the Great Marriage sooner rather than—"

"It should wait until May, Coel."

"Why?"

"Damn it, you know why! Done that day, during spring resurgent, it will have the greatest effectiveness possible!" Jack sighed, and moderated his tone. "My friend, I am not delaying, only wanting to wait until the marriage will be its most potent."

"I know, I know. It is just that when one of the Sidlesaghes pointed this out to me this morning . . ." The Lord of the Faerie looked up toward the summit of The Naked. "Noah tells me that Weyland is not . . . happy."

"Ah, damn it. I should have spoken to him sooner. I will, Harry. I will."

The Lord of the Faerie nodded. "Do that. Jack, there is something else."

Jack raised his eyebrows.

The Lord of the Faerie nodded to something over Jack's shoulder. "Look."

Jack turned.

When he'd come into the Faerie previously, he'd remarked to himself on the Idyll, which stood at the borders of the Faerie. Now he could still see the Idyll, but it appeared to have retreated. Between it and the Faerie was a blue haze, almost like a mystic ocean.

"The Idyll is retreating," the Lord of the Faerie said, very softly. "It no longer wants to touch the Faerie. Something is very, very badly wrong, Jack."

WEYLAND HAD VOLUNTEERED FOR WARDEN DUTY within the ARP as soon as they had called for volunteers when it appeared that war loomed. He wasn't able to say why he had done it—the last thing that Asterion was likely to do was to volunteer his services for defense of something he had spent thousands of years trying to destroy—but Weyland found a curious kind of peace when he was atop the roof of the Savoy, watching for possible enemy aircraft.

It felt almost like making amends, but that notion was so alien to him that Weyland tended to shy away from it.

Weyland stood duty one or two nights a week, as needed. As on this night, he was alone. Initially, the Savoy had posted two or three men (either employees who had volunteered, or similarly minded permanent residents), but as the initial months of the war had dragged on, and London had suffered nothing more than a scare or two, the manager of the hotel had decided that only one man need sit up each night.

And, being the Savoy, that man was well supplied with thermoses of the best coffee, thick sandwiches, and the lightest of sponge cakes.

Weyland enjoyed his nights alone atop the Savoy.

He'd settled himself down in a small canvas shelter, almost like a game blind, that the hotel manager had caused to be erected. Canvas it might be, but it was triple-layered canvas, and there was a small kerosene heater inside that kept the occupant cozy, and an armchair to keep him comfortable. There were small windows cut at eye level in its four walls and door, and the warden on duty need only scan the sky through these cut-out windows with his binoculars to check for aircraft, rather than actually venture out into the cold to wander the roof.

The shelter was also quite roomy (having been built originally to house two or three men), but even so, Weyland had nowhere to go when the door suddenly lifted up and Jack stepped in.

"May I sit down?" Jack said, indicating a stool set to one side.

"What are you doing here?"

Jack sat down on the stool. "I thought you might like some company."

Weyland grunted.

"And I wanted to talk to you. About the Great Marriage."

Now Weyland shifted uncomfortably in his seat. "I don't really want to—"

"When I leapt into the Idyll, when Grace was just a baby, and said that Noah would betray you—that betrayal was in her very blood—I was wrong, Weyland."

Weyland remained silent. He was staring out one of the windows in the canvas, carefully not looking at Jack.

"It was a stupid thing to say, and I was angry beyond belief," Jack said. "You *know* I was wrong."

Weyland sighed, and moved his head so that he was almost—but not yet quite—looking at Jack. "You had every right to be angry. And you had picked your moment too well. I was livid with fury as well, and when you appeared . . ."

When Jack—then in his form as Ringwalker—had appeared, Weyland had leapt for his throat, and both men had engaged in a bitter, hateful, brutal struggle.

"Then we engaged in disaster, Weyland," Jack said. "While we battled, and while Noah watched on, Catling

placed her hex on Grace. We can't afford to have that happen again."

"What do you mean?"

"If we are at odds, if we wallow in misunderstandings and jealousies, we are fractured and vulnerable. Weyland, you were right when we met the night Noah set the Great Fire. She and I never had a chance. Whatever we might have had was doomed from the start."

"But you still love Noah."

Jack gave a wry smile. "Oh, yes. I do. I will never stop loving her. But I think I am *tired* of loving her, Weyland. It has only ever hurt, and I know full well that I could never keep her." He gave a short, humorless laugh. "Do you remember that day that Noah first came to you in your house in Idol Lane?"

"Of course."

"I don't know what happened in your house that night, Weyland, but I and John Thornton met in a tavern called the Broken Bough on the Strand. There I drank myself into an almost-oblivion, and Thornton sat there and pitied me. We agreed on one thing, Weyland, and that was that we were both love-smitten fools who would never, never have the woman we both craved so much. I hadn't come close to accepting it at that point, but that was, I think, the start of it."

Weyland finally looked Jack full in the face. "And you *have* accepted it now?"

Jack hesitated fractionally before replying. "Yes."

"Of course you have. Nonetheless, you will happily engage in the Great Marriage with her."

"Of course. But, Weyland, the Great Marriage doesn't actually have to involve sex."

"Don't feed me lies. What kind of fool do you think I am?"

"A fool who is trying to make it easier for you," Jack snapped.

Weyland sighed, looking away. For a long minute there was silence.

"I don't want to lose her," Weyland said eventually, very softly.

"And you won't," said Jack, and surprised himself by

sounding as if he meant it. He made a move then, as if to rise, but Weyland forestalled him.

"Don't leave just yet," Weyland said. "There's something I need to talk to you about."

Jack sank back to his stool.

"The murders," Weyland said.

Something cold and black coiled about Jack's stomach.

"The imps are doing them," Weyland said.

"What?"

"I had suspected them, but Silvius came to see me a week or so back, and mentioned something to me."

"And it was . . . ?"

"Remember how the imps tore themselves out of Jane and Noah?"

Suddenly what had been worrying at Jack's mind about the murders fell into place. "Dear God, they're recreating their own births!"

Weyland inclined his head in agreement.

"Why?" said Jack. "What are they about?"

"I don't know," said Weyland. "But I intend to discover it."

Chapter Two

THE FAERIE

Wednesday, 1 May 1940

T HE GREAT MARRIAGE TOOK PLACE ATOP The Naked on the first day in May, 1940. All of the Faerie were invited, and select among those from the mortal world: Eaving's Sisters, Walter (an invitation he did not accept, although his wife, Anne, did come), and Weyland, among others. Ariadne was not invited.

But Grace had been. That had not been certain at first,

but Jack insisted she be invited, and finally the Lord of the Faerie had bowed to his request. Jack did not know if Grace would actually come, and was pleased when, finally, she turned up with the last group of guests to arrive.

The summit of The Naked was thronged with guests, but, as always when a court or convocation was held atop The Naked, even the tens of thousands of attendees did not make the summit feel crowded. The Lord of the Faerie and the Caroller, Stella as she was in the mortal world, mingled among the crowd, their presence easily marked by the glossy blue and black magpie that hovered over the Caroller's head.

Weyland and Grace stood to one side of the gathering. Grace was patently uncomfortable, while Weyland had assumed an air of boredom. Weyland was dressed not in his modern, dapper style but in a very old-worldly suit that was highly reminiscent of his seventeenth-century attire; his daughter had dressed herself in a simple white dress that clung to her slim figure and drifted softly about her calves. She stood very close to her father, her face grave, her eyes troubled, as she watched the crowds before her.

From time to time she would twist a little, and allow her eyes to drift over the magical landscape of hills and valleys.

Jack and Noah attended in their magical god-forms as Ringwalker and Eaving. As with the Lord of the Faerie and the Caroller, they mingled freely among the crowd—if separately—laughing with this friend, embracing another, giving the appearance of a joyful couple about to be united in marriage.

No one saw, or even intuited, the woman with long black curls hiding on a hill that rose two distant from The Naked. She crouched behind a tree, her white face occasionally peeping out from behind it, her dark blue eyes following either Ringwalker or Eaving, although sometimes she glanced toward Grace.

"ARE YOU ALL RIGHT?" GRACE WHISPERED, LEANing even closer to her father.

Weyland put an arm about her shoulders, wondering that she felt so cold. "It has to be done, Grace. There is little I can do about it. Besides, I have grown used to your mother's lovers."

"Liar," she whispered, and he hugged her a little tighter.

"Your mother is so beautiful," he said. "It is difficult."

At that moment Eaving passed close by, and she looked over and saw them. She came over, and kissed first Weyland on the mouth, and then Grace on the cheek.

She looked stunning. When she walked as Eaving, Noah generally wore a sleeveless loose-fitting robe of ecru, cream, and silver that drifted about her like a cloud.

On this day, she wore a gown of deep emerald shot through with flashes of gray and black. She wore the water, of which she was goddess, and which she would take into her marriage.

Her eyes, too, were different from her normal dark blue. Now they were a sage green, shot through with lightning flashes of gold.

Now Eaving smiled at Grace. "I am still your mother," she said.

Grace managed a smile, but it was obviously forced.

Eaving laid her hand against Grace's cheek, and shot Weyland an anxious look, but he gave a brief shake of his head, and Eaving sighed. "I love your father, Grace," she said. "More than anything in this world."

"Save Jack?" said Grace.

Eaving did not mind the question, understanding the anxiety behind it. "Oh, I love him, too, but not as your father." She looked at Weyland. "Ringwalker has never given me candied fruits to eat out of a human skull, nor has he presented me with a wraith from the Halls of the Dead on Christmas Eve. Only your father could ever think of that."

Weyland smiled at that, remembering their midnight feast in the bone house of St. Dunstan's-in-the-East when he had arranged for long-dead wraiths to serve them. That had been the night she'd told him she was pregnant with Grace.

Grace frowned, not understanding, and Eaving once

again laid a soft hand briefly against her cheek. "Your father can share that memory with you tonight, while I am gone. Maybe it will give you comfort."

Then she turned, and vanished into the crowd.

IT WAS NOT THE LORD OF THE FAERIE WHO opened and conducted the ceremony, as may have been expected, but the Caroller. At some point the crowds had formed a gigantic circle about a central table, and it was at this simple oak table that the Caroller stood.

As with so many others, she, too, was clothed in a magical raiment—this one of a rosy light that barely hid her figure. She was the one who caroled in the dawn and the dusk, and she stood, the center of all attention, as lovely as the sun as it crested the horizon.

"My lord"—the Caroller inclined her head to the Lord of the Faerie, who stood at the crowd's edge some distance away—"has asked me to conduct this ceremony, and it pleased me to accept. It also amused me"—her eyes did, indeed, dance with merriment—"because I spent so many thousands of years trying to keep these two apart." She gave an expressive shrug. "We can all make mistakes occasionally.

"I stand here also because I know this pair so well. I have known them for almost four thousand years—a mere blink in the lives of some of those present, but significant enough for our story. Ringwalker, once Brutus, once William, once Louis, now Jack when he walks the mortal land, has been my partner in dance and ambition and power. He has been my husband, my lover, my enemy, the focus of all my lives save in the last years of my last when"—the Caroller turned and looked at the Lord of the Faerie full on, her face so alive with love, so radiant, that Grace, who with Weyland had come to stand within the inner ranks of the circled crown, had to blink away tears—"I discovered that the greatest love of my life had been with me all the time."

The Lord of the Faerie smiled, and put his right hand on his heart.

"Eaving," the Caroller continued, "I knew first as Cornelia, whom I hated." She paused, as if needing time to remember the depth of that hate. "Then I knew her as Caela, and I despised and ridiculed her. Then she came to me as Noah, and I discovered a friend."

Again the Caroller paused, her face deeply reflective. "I had never had a friend before." She sighed, and shook herself .slightly, as if rousing herself from her memories. "And, finally, I came to know her as my sister, and as Eaving, the goddess of the waters. It has been a long journey.

"A journey that ends tonight—ends for me, but starts anew for this land, and for Eaving and Ringwalker. My friends, will you stand forward?"

The crowd parted at the eastern and western edges of its inner circle, and Ringwalker and Eaving stepped forth. Ringwalker, who walked forth from the western section of the summit, wore nothing save a white linen hip wrap, much as he had when he was Brutus. Otherwise his flesh was bare—save for the inky raised lines of black that writhed across his shoulders, back, and upper chest.

Eaving, who came from the eastern section of the crowd, still wore her dress that appeared to have been woven from water.

They met at the table, and Ringwalker gave the Caroller an amused glance. "Fine words," he whispered, "but how do I know you do not secrete a knife amid all your rosy prettiness, ready to finally plunge it into my, or Eaving's, back?"

She smiled. "There has been too much death between us, all three of us. No more death. Life only ever after."

She turned to the table, and indicated a shallow wooden bowl of water, and an identical bowl filled with leaves and fruit of the forest. "This is not a marriage that I can make," she said, "but only facilitate. Ringwalker? Eaving?"

And she stood back.

Ringwalker and Eaving stood a long moment, looking at each other, then Ringwalker spoke.

"We made a marriage a long time ago," he said, his voice very soft but nonetheless reaching to everyone atop The Naked, "and we made it very badly. This time, we

need to do it properly, and with love and understanding rather than with hatred and suspicion."

He smiled then, and it was so gentle, and so full of love, that hands reached surreptitiously to eyes all through the watching crowd. "Hades' daughter, Cornelia, I should have treated you as a jewel from the moment I first met you, and yet failed. Will you forgive me?"

Eaving reached out and touched his cheek as she had so recently touched her daughter's. "And I should have kissed you, and failed to. Will you forgive me?"

"Will you kiss me now?" Ringwalker said.

"And will you love me now?" Eaving said, taking Ring-walker's hands in hers.

Then, not responding in words, both leaned forward and kissed, deeply and passionately, as if they had been lovers parted for eons.

And Ringwalker's markings, the blue-inked scars over his upper body, flowed down his arms to where Noah held his hands. They touched her flesh once, twice, as if probing, and then retreated up his arms to once more writhe about his shoulders and chest.

ON HER HILL, THE BLACK-HAIRED WOMAN SAW, and smiled.

DEEP WITHIN THE CROWD, MALCOLM SAW ALSO, and he looked over to Grace, and gave a little nod, as if something had just been confirmed in his mind.

Then he turned his head very slightly in the direction of the hill where the black-haired woman hid, and his eyes crinkled in delight.

EAVING DREW BACK, SMILED, THEN REACHED FOR the bowl of water. She balanced it carefully in her hands, then raised it up to Ringwalker's face, that he might drink.

He took a long draught, then, as Eaving replaced the

bowl on the table, reached for a strand of leaves, and twisted it within her hair.

They kissed again, and as they did, so the crowd erupted in a great cry of jubilation.

RINGWALKER AND EAVING HAD DRAWN AWAY from the crowd now, making their departure, and Grace turned slightly to realize, with a start, that her father was gone.

Already feeling empty and desolate at the sight of her mother and Ringwalker embracing, Grace looked about, her heart beating fast.

What had happened to Weyland?

She saw him, finally, standing on the very far side of The Naked, as far away from Eaving and Ringwalker as he could get. Grace walked over slowly, coming to a silent halt by his side. She followed his eyes, looking out over the Faerie, then very quietly slipped her hand into his.

"I wish . . ." Weyland finally said.

Grace blinked away tears. "I know," she whispered, and leaned in against her father.

RINGWALKER AND EAVING WENT TO A PLACE VERY private and very secretive, a cave that existed at the borderlands of water and forest.

There they kissed again.

"We have made love in such a variety of places," Ringwalker said as she turned away from him slightly, and slid the gown from her shoulders, "and over so many thousands of years."

"And as so many different people," Eaving said. Naked now, she turned back to Ringwalker, running her hands over his body, untying the wrap around his hips.

"I was glad to see Grace at the ceremony," Ringwalker said, then wished he could have dragged the words back. He supposed that the last thing Eaving wanted to chat about now was her daughter.

"Mmmm," Eaving said, her attention on everything but her daughter.

Ringwalker opened his mouth to say something else, and then realized, with a jolt, that he was using words to delay that moment when he would need to *act* on this consummation.

Somewhat clumsily, he put his hands on her shoulders, then caressed her upper arms.

I wonder, he thought, *why I don't feel more joy.*

"Ringwalker," she breathed, resting her warm body against his, her hands on his lower back, then running up to his shoulders.

"These marks are so wondrous," she said, and kissed them. "So . . . seductive."

Then her hands ran down his arms, pausing at those spots were the Kingship bands of Troy would eventually rest.

"I can't wait for the moment that I slide the bands on your limbs," Eaving said in a voice so sensuous that she imbued the promise with such a depth of sexual overtones that Ringwalker *should* have responded.

But he didn't, not in the way he thought Eaving may have hoped. Everything felt . . . not wrong . . . but faded and pale. Muted. There was desire, yes, but it was but a faint ghost of what he'd once felt for this woman.

She looked up at him questioningly, wondering why he took so long to respond, and Ringwalker bent his head to kiss her so that she could not see the hesitation in his eyes. As their mouths touched, then clung, he understood very suddenly that what he had said to Weyland was true. He *was* tired of loving Noah.

"Ringwalker?" Eaving said. "Is anything the matter?"

"Nothing," Ringwalker said, and picked her up in his arms and carried her to the bed that rested between two lighted braziers.

All night, as he lay with Eaving, the marks on his shoulders remained quiescent, as if sleeping, and whenever Eaving moved her hands over them, Ringwalker shifted them away again, very gently.

* * *

NOAH RETURNED TO HER APARTMENT WITHIN THE Savoy the next morning at ten A.M.

Weyland was sitting on the sofa, not even pretending to read his newspaper, his fingers drumming lightly on the arm of the sofa. He stood as Noah entered, and tried to smile.

"So what did you do all night, my lovely?" he said.

Noah shrugged off her coat and kissed him softly on the mouth. She was very relaxed, very calm, very confident. "We spent all night laughing at how stupid we had been as Brutus and Cornelia, and admitted that we preferred a friendship to the constant strife of loving."

She said it so guilelessly that Weyland was tempted to believe her, but he wished before anything else that she had told him the truth.

AT COPT HALL MALCOLM WAS SETTING OUT THE breakfast things when Jack walked in the kitchen door.

"I would have expected more of a spring in your step," Malcolm commented as Jack sat down at the table.

"Last night was none of your business, Malcolm."

Oh, but it surely was, Malcolm thought. "You're very irritable this morning."

"It is *none* of your business, Malcolm!"

Unperturbed, Malcolm set down some toast and tea. "Great Marriages," he said, "need not necessarily be made in Faerie places."

Jack had no idea what Malcolm meant, but he knew the man well enough to know that if he responded it would only encourage Malcolm further.

He began to butter his toast with hard, jerky movements of his knife.

Behind him, Malcolm arched one eyebrow as the toast finally crumbled into disarray.

For him, the Great Marriage had gone better than he could have hoped.

Chapter Three

FAERIE HILL MANOR

Friday, 10 May 1940

SPRING MORE THAN MADE UP FOR THE TER-rible winter. Once May arrived, almost overnight—so it seemed to the bemused inhabitants of England—the skies cleared, what snow and ice there was left evaporated, floods receded, and mud and slush turned to newly sprung turf and emerging meadow flowers. Even in the concrete and tarmac City, flowers pushed their heads out of cracks in walls and butterfly bushes sprung out of gutters and old tiled roofs, producing their gorgeously-scented purple flowers a full six weeks early.

No one had ever seen a spring like it. The newspapers were full of reports of the bounty: the surge in crops, the record weights of vegetables, and the wonderful clear and warm weather. Old-timers shook their heads and said they'd not heard of the like, even in their grandparents' times. Many were seen to grin, and remark on how winter still lingered in the German Fatherland.

The results in the Faerie were as spectacular as those in the mortal world. All signs of frost damage vanished, and the hills and forests seemed somehow to lift: foliage became thicker, flowers more beautifully scented, shrubbery denser, the very air itself almost decadently sweeter.

The only troubling note was that the Idyll remained distant. It had not retreated any farther, but neither did it bond itself to the Faerie's borders once more.

Nonetheless, the lines fell from Harry's face, and as each day passed his mortal appearance more closely mirrored that of the Lord of the Faerie. Those mortals around

him, the people he worked with in military intelligence and some of the more obscure government departments, remarked on it, and he said only that the spring had provided him with a tonic so good it had soothed away all his cares and aches.

Stella laughed more often, and the Sidlesaghes took to wandering the bridle paths of Epping Forest, coming close to playing tag through the dappled shadows.

But the most extraordinary change resulting from the Great Marriage was in Noah.

The day after the Great Marriage she left the Savoy to visit with Matilda and Ecub. The instant she walked out into the street to catch a cab, she stopped, her eyes widening.

"My gods, Jack," she whispered, "I can feel it, too!"

ON THE EVENING OF FRIDAY, THE TENTH OF MAY, Jack, Noah, Weyland, and Grace met with Harry and Stella at Faerie Hill Manor. It was the first time they had all gathered together since the Great Marriage. Overall it was a happy get-together—after all, the Great Marriage had apparently done what it was supposed to—and all were relaxed.

All save Grace, who was very quiet. This was, however, so much her usual state, that no one save Jack, who had seen her far more animated, paid it much attention.

Once everyone was gathered, Harry asked if anyone had listened to the radio since lunchtime.

Noah shook her head, looking to Weyland, who also shook his. "We've spent the day in our apartment, reading," she said. "Grace?"

Grace just gave a shake of her head.

"Copt Hall didn't come equipped with a radio," said Jack with a grin, "and I doubt that Malcolm would allow me one if I desired it. What is it, Harry? Bad news, or good?"

"Good. Neville Chamberlain has resigned."

Chamberlain had been Britain's prime minister all through the lead-up to the war and during its initial months. He was a likeable enough chap, and a good prime minister during peace, but most people thought he was out

of his depth when confronted with the sheer enormity of Hitler.

"And?" said Jack softly. "Who has replaced him?"

"Winston Churchill," said Harry.

"This is good?" said Jack. "I'm sorry, I don't know him, although I've heard of him."

"Yes, it is good," said Harry. "I've met Churchill on several occasions, and know him well through other acquaintances. George," he said, referring to the king, "does not like him particularly, but I think Churchill will be of much benefit for the land. He has a touch of the Faerie about him—there must be ancient blood in there somewhere—and he has pluck, and those combined, will, I think do us all much good."

"And surely," said Stella, "we cannot fail to miss the significance of his rise to power so soon after the Great Marriage. He is the *land's* choice."

"I've called you together tonight," said Harry, "to work out where we go from here. I think that Jack needs to get the arm bands, and then—"

"Harry," said Noah, leaning forward in her chair, her eyes shining, and looking at Jack even though she addressed Harry, "before we talk about that, there is something else I need to tell you."

"And it is . . . ?" said Harry, who had a sudden horrible premonition that she was about to announce she was pregnant by Jack. Babies were all very well, but this, now, would be disastrous. He flickered a glance Weyland's way, trying to see if Weyland had any inkling of what it was Noah was about to reveal.

But Weyland had his face blank of all expression, and was no help to Harry.

"I can sense the shadow, Jack!" she said. "I walked outside the day after the Great Marriage, and suddenly, *I felt it!*"

Everyone in the room reacted, some far more than others.

Stella looked at Noah with some curiosity, but did not seem overly excited at the news. Grace stared at her mother as if she had announced an imminent Martian invasion. Harry just looked stunned, incapable of speech.

Weyland's face tensed, and he looked away from his wife.

Jack made a soft sound and sat forward. *"You felt it?* Thank god! Tell me, what? What did you feel? Do you understand it? Can you recognize if—"

"Jack!" said Noah, laughing and holding out her hands as if to fend him off. "Be still a moment, and let me tell it. Yes, I can feel what you do—it must have been the Great Marriage! A great shadow—I don't know what else to call it, either—hovering over London, its tentacles reaching deep within the city, something distinctly labyrinthine. I have not explored as you and Grace have done"—she finally glanced at her daughter to include her in the conversation—"but I have used every sense I have, as Mistress of the Labyrinth, as Eaving, and as Darkwitch, to scry out its sense."

"And?" said Jack. His sense of excitement had faded now, and instead he appeared palpably tense.

"I think it is a weakness in the Troy Game," Noah said.

"No," said Grace. "Not a weakness."

"Grace," said Noah, "I know that you think—"

"Can't you see that it is a trap?" Grace said. "Catling is too cunning for you! I *know*! She sits beside my bed at night, and what I feel in this shadow about London is what I feel emanating from her. *God damn it!* It is a trap." She brushed tears away from her eyes, muttering an inaudible curse, more at the tears than at what her mother had just said. "I'm sorry. I shouldn't have shouted. I just don't think this is any weakness. I wish . . ."

She drifted to a close, looked about, then sat back in her chair, looking miserable.

Jack watched her, his eyes narrowed in thought. *Was she so miserable at what she thought was his and Noah's misinterpretation of the shadow . . . or at the fact that now her mother could feel it as well?*

"Weyland," Jack said, "can you feel it yet?"

Weyland gave a terse shake of his head. "Obviously Noah's newfound ability is tied to the success of your wedding night."

Jack chose to ignore that remark—there wasn't much he could say to it anyway—and instead changed the subject.

"Harry, I hear you about the Kingship bands," he said, "but once I retrieve those then Catling will expect me and Noah to complete her immediately. Not having them buys us more time—I can give Catling some excuse or the other. But dear God, now that Noah can feel this weakness as well—"

To one side Grace looked away as Jack used the word "weakness" as fact.

"—then I am more convinced than ever we need to get to the bottom of this mystery before we do anything else. If we can exploit this weakness, then perhaps we have the means to unwind the Troy Game."

Harry nodded. "Yes, I agree. You are sure you can placate Catling?"

Jack gave a small shrug. "I will do my best." He looked at Noah. "Secreting those final two bands in the Otherworld was a master stroke, Noah. Unlike the other four bands, Catling will have no idea what needs to be done to retrieve those two, and must believe whatever I tell her."

Noah smiled at him, warmed by his compliment, then she looked at Grace, and her smile died a little. She stood up. "Grace, what say you and I go to the kitchen and make some coffee. I think we need clear heads now more than whisky-fuddled wits."

"GRACE," NOAH SAID AS SOON AS SHE AND HER daughter were alone in the kitchen, "I should have mentioned this to you beforehand. I apologize. That was not the way for you to hear."

Grace banged around in the sink, filling the kettle. "But what good points you scored with Jack."

"Grace—"

"I'm sorry," Grace said, now banging the kettle down on the stovetop so heavily water slopped out of its spout. "It is just that I don't believe it is a weakness. I am afraid that . . ."

"I know." Noah came to stand behind her daughter, who was standing staring at the kettle, and making no effort to light the gas burner. She put her hands on Grace's shoulders, and pulled her back into her body, holding her gently.

"I know you are scared, and I know you are scared about what Jack and I think. My darling"—she turned Grace around, and cupped one hand under her chin, tipping Grace's face up to meet her eyes—"I can only promise you that I will keep an open mind, and I and Jack will explore every possible avenue of explanation. Neither of us wants to make a mistake."

"I can help."

"Yes, of course." Noah was not sure what help Grace could be—mainly because she was worried that Grace was the one with the shuttered mind when it came to deciphering this particular puzzle—but Noah also knew very well that she could not say that. "Grace, I *promise* that I will keep an open mind on this."

GRACE AND NOAH SEEMED TO BE TAKING AN IN-ordinately long time to be making a simple pot of coffee, and as Harry and Stella wandered off to converse in low tones by the fire, Jack slipped over to sit next to Weyland.

"Weyland," Jack said.

Weyland gave a soft grunt.

"Weyland, I am sorry for your sake that Noah and I had to make the Great Marriage."

Weyland shot him a look full of cynicism.

"Believe it or not," Jack said, "I *am* sorry for it. Weyland . . ." He hesitated, wondering how to put what he wanted to say into words, and wondering just *what* it was that he wanted to say in the first instance.

"Jack, just leave it."

"Weyland—"

"*Leave it.*"

They lapsed into an uncomfortable silence.

Finally Jack cleared his throat. "May I ask you something? It isn't about Noah."

"If you must."

"Weyland . . . you spent thousands of years trying to kill me and steal the Kingship bands so that you could control the Troy Game with Noah. Can I assume that you have

Kingman powers? That you have Kingman knowledge? That if you *did* have the Kingship bands, and Noah, that you could step fully into the shoes of the Kingman?"

"Oh, my, what a loaded question. How should I answer?"

"Honestly, if you please."

"Then I will. Yes, I could do it. I do not have precise Kingman training, but on the other hand I lived so long in the heart of the labyrinth that I have absorbed many of its secrets. I could not do it prettily—perhaps you might offer me further training—but do it I could. Remember also that I would bring my Darkcraft behind whatever I could do as Kingman. I could be a very, very effective—and somewhat bleak—Kingman. Jack, why do you ask?"

"I don't know. I don't have any precise reason. I guess I'm just doing what all good generals do and working out precisely what my weapons are." He paused, drawing on his cigarette. "But think, here we are, surrounded by so many Mistresses of the Labyrinth. It just helps, I guess, to know that there are two possible Kingmen. Three, actually, with my father."

Chapter Four

EPPING FOREST

Friday, 10 May 1940

J ACK WAS WALKING HOME THROUGH THE forest, so completely absorbed in the exciting news that now Noah could sense the weakness that he was completely shocked when the figure of a tall, slim, dark-haired woman appeared before him on the forest path.

"Grace?"

As soon as the word left his mouth, Jack knew it wasn't

Grace. Her hair was too long and he'd never seen Grace wear a long black dress.

"Of course not," said Catling. "How could you possibly confuse us?"

"How indeed," said Jack. *Had Catling witnessed everything that had happened within Faerie Hill Manor?*

"You've been visiting with Harry," said Catling. "Noah was there, too."

"Yes," said Jack, watching Catling with careful eyes.

"You've made the Great Marriage with her."

"Yes." Jack was trying hard to retain his composure. Catling must want to know why they didn't move to complete her, and he started to formulate excuses in his mind.

Catling moved forward, *scurried* forward, and Jack took an involuntary step backward. "Was the sex good, Jack? Was the fuck worth the wait?"

"Yes," Jack said, his voice very quiet, his eyes very still. "It was."

Catling studied him keenly, her eyes narrowed. "Then you must be in a very good mood."

"I was until a moment ago."

"What's up, Jack?"

"In what sense?"

"What are you planning?"

"Can I be honest?"

"Please do."

"I'd like to find a way to destroy you, but it is proving damnably elusive."

"Then complete me instead."

"I'll need to fetch the bands of Troy to do that."

"Then fetch them, Jack."

"They're in the Faerie, and—"

"I know full well where they are. Four are in the Faerie and two are in the Otherworld. What I don't want to hear are your excuses for not fetching them. Jack, I am going to be honest with you here. I know you and Noah wish to destroy me, so you're desperately grubbing about, trying to find a means. Ah, let me rephrase that, I am sure you *have* a means—a Kingman and a Mistress of the Labyrinth can al-

ways unwind what they have created—but you can't figure out a way past the hex I've put on Grace. So you're trying to find the means to destroy me that won't also result in Grace's death, as well that of the Faerie, and everything else she has touched, and so on and so forth. Am I right thus far?"

Jack didn't respond.

"Yes," said Catling. "I *am* right. Now, I am a reasonable person, and I know I've put you and Noah in a spot—poor Grace, pitiful Grace—but reasonableness can only go so far before it is quite overtaken by impatience. After all, I have waited an awful long time for completion . . . I don't want to have to wait too much longer. So here's the deal, Jack. You take all the time you want, but know that the longer you take, the more people will suffer—"

"The murders. You've set the imps to murdering—"

"And that will stop once I am completed, Jack. I'll be in such a good mood I'll corral those imps once and for all. But it will get a great deal worse if you don't complete me. It is up to you, Jack, and your conscience."

Catling gave a small, terrible smile. "Just think . . . every death that results from your pitiful, fruitless hunt for a means to destroy me and save Grace shall rest on your conscience. If you think it is okay for a few more women to die terribly as either Bill or Jim rips their bellies apart . . ." Catling shrugged. "Then live with it. And if your conscience can deal with those murders, then maybe I'll escalate it a little further. Take the horror into new fields, so to speak. I can't force you to complete me, Jack, but I can make this land suffer terribly for your tardiness."

She paused, letting her words sink in.

"I'm sure Grace is worth all those lives, right? All the terror and suffering the innocent will endure?"

Then she vanished, and Jack was left staring, his stomach churning.

CATLING SEETHED THROUGH THE SPACES UNDER London, finally giving her anger full rein.

Jack was looking for a way to destroy her.

Oh, she knew he would, had been certain from the moment that Noah turned bad that Jack would eventually turn as well, but she *hated* it that he was trying to find a means to undo her.

Where would he be without her? A shifting pile of cold gray bone dust by now, that's where. Everything he was, was due to her intervention.

And she'd made him too strong. Too strong.

Catling was vulnerable. She needed to feed, needed to grow strong. Needed to be *sure* that she could outmaneuver whatever he threw at her and, knowing Jack, it would be the unexpected.

She needed to know what he was doing.

CATLING FOUND THE IMPS LOITERING IN COVENT Garden, shadowing a young woman carrying a basket of vegetables.

"Well?" she said, so startling Bill and Jim they almost stumbled from the footpath into the path of a passing lorry.

Its horn blaring, the lorry thundered past as Catling pulled them both onto the relative safety of the footpath.

"Leave the girl for the moment," Catling said. "You can always find another later. Victims are a dime a dozen in this city. I want to know what you've discovered. What *is* Jack doing wandering all about London?"

Jim and Bill exchanged a glance, then looked back to Catling.

"He's looking for a weakness," said Bill. "Something to pry open and make you bleed to death."

"And has he found it?"

Bill smiled. "No. All he has found is strength, but he is too foolish to see that."

Catling visibly relaxed. "I am too strong for him."

"Aye," said Jim. "That you are."

"*He* is weak," said Catling. "He has a conscience."

"Very foolish," said Jim.

"His conscience will drive him into my arms eventually," said Catling.

"Absolutely," said Bill.

"You still enjoying the murders?" said Catling.

"No doubt about it," said the imps simultaneously, their faces splitting in wide grins.

"Good," said Catling.

Chapter Five

LONDON

Late May 1940

Grace Speaks

I HAD BEEN FEELING SO MUCH HAPPIER, ALmost positive, and then doubts crept back in. I was unsettled and depressed by the Great Marriage. I had told myself—and Jack—that it was because I didn't want him destroying that fragile balance of our world, and that I didn't want him destroying my parents' own peace, but as the days and then weeks dragged on after May Day I had to admit to myself that there was more to it. I couldn't bear the thought of my mother sleeping with Jack, and my aversion to the idea had nothing at all to do with whether or not Jack would destroy any fragile balances, or what my father felt about it.

Jack and Noah had looked so happy atop The Naked, and all I could think of was how Jack had spent thousands of years trying to correct the mistakes of their first lives together and win Noah back. Why should he give up now?

My mother returned the next day. She appeared radiant. It was not just the smile on her face, but a myriad small things: humming a tune as she sorted through clothes that needed to be dry-cleaned; staring out a window for long minutes at a time at nothing in particular with a smile on

her face; falling into lengthy silences at mealtimes, also with a small smile on her face, when normally she would chatter on about anything.

My father did a very bad impression of not noticing.

Then came the little surprise she dropped at Faerie Hill Manor. That hit me on two levels. I was shocked, appalled, and, most of all, intensely jealous that she intruded so blithely into something that until now only Jack and I had shared. And I was shocked and appalled and desperately frightened that she, too, thought that Catling's trap was in fact a Catling weakness. Instantly, so it seemed, Jack's hitherto open mind (if only open a sliver on this matter, but it *had* been open) slammed shut. Yes, he agreed happily, it was a weakness. Noah had confirmed it.

Noah was his lover, she was the love of his life, she had shared thousands of years with him, and she was a goddess and a Darkwitch and a Mistress of the Labyrinth, and never, never, never could I compete on all those levels.

Of course he was going to believe her before me.

No wonder she had intruded so blithely.

Noah tried to make it all well with me in the kitchen. Considering the humiliating little scene I had put on, she was actually very nice. She promised to keep an open mind, but I knew that there was nothing I could do. Jack and Noah were so *intimate* (I don't mean that only in the sexual sense, but intimate because of all they had shared and on so many levels), and I so much the outsider . . . well, once they had jointly made up their minds on the issue, then I had no hope.

It didn't help that I had no proof, either. Sure, I was a Mistress of the Labyrinth, but I had nowhere the experience in the labyrinth that Jack and Noah had. I had nowhere the experience in *life* that they had. All I had was that deep sense that the shadow hanging over London was connected with Catling, and was somehow a vile trap that would ensnare us all, but I had no proof.

I was scared that Jack would ask me to stop helping him. After all, he had my mother on his team now. While I continued my work, walking about London, discovering what I could, I tended to avoid Jack.

I didn't want to know how well he and my mother did.

I didn't want him to suggest, gently, that maybe he and my mother could manage by themselves now, thank you for all your trouble.

ON THE LAST FRIDAY IN MAY I WAS OUT LATER than usual. I'd been wandering through Southwark, walking almost to Rotherhithe, and had lost track of the time.

I had also lost myself. I didn't have any maps with me, and I'd managed to stray into the wharf area—a warren of alleys and laneways, each indistinguishable from the other. It was dusk, gloom had enveloped the entire area, and I had no idea where I was. I couldn't even work out the location of the river. I knew it was close, I could hear the water and the occasional faint sound of barges and tugs, but no matter what turning I took, I could not catch sight of it.

I thought I would ask someone directions, but although half an hour ago the area had been bustling with lorries and handcarts and sailors and overalled women hurrying about, now the entire area was strangely deserted.

Rotherhithe shouldn't have been deserted. Not during wartime. It should have been bustling, even though it was coming on to full night.

There were no streetlamps.

No people.

No means to find my way home.

Power seeped around me.

Increasingly wary, I drew back against a wall, hiding in the darkness of the overhang of a warehouse.

I looked up. It was a clear night, and I could see the barrage balloons that hung over the wharves and river.

I could also sense the shadow, more powerfully than ever before.

Suddenly, although I *saw* nothing, I sensed the shadow gathering its strength, as if for a leap, then felt it rushing toward me.

I gave a soft cry, hating myself for it, and scrambled des-

perately along the wall, hoping to find a doorway, an entrance, *anything* to get out of the way of the—

"Hello, pretty lady."

Fear jolted through me. A man had come up behind me, grabbing me by the right elbow and pulling me against his body.

"What's a lovely thing like you doing out and about, hmmm, when a murderer is wandering the streets?"

There was something about the way he said "murderer," something in the vicious, cold jesting tone of his voice, that made me realize . . . oh God, oh God, oh God . . .

All my brave words to Jack were for nothing. I had never felt more terrified in my entire life than I did right then. Maybe he could not murder me—after all, Catling needed me alive—but what he could do . . . I had heard what these girls had suffered, what had been done to them, what—

Another man loomed before me, his hat pulled so low over his face I could make out nothing of his face save a well of darkness and some bright, gleaming teeth. He grabbed at my left arm, and then, no matter how I struggled, began slowly, lasciviously, unbuttoning my coat.

There were two *of them! No wonder the women hadn't stood a chance!*

The next moment his hand ran over my dress, over my breasts, over my abdomen, down to my groin.

I tried to kick him, but he responded by kicking my own legs out from under me, so that the only thing keeping me upright was their grip on my arms.

Then, the first man, still holding on to my elbow with one hand, produced a knife in his other.

I screamed. Then again, and yet once again. *Someone* must hear me, surely!

The second man laughed, low, soft, sibilant, and tore my skirt away.

My God, they were going to rape me first.

At that point I wished I *could* die. Surely it would be easier to just hold my breath, or suffocate myself against the coat of the man to my right.

The other man ripped away my petticoat, then I felt his cold fingers slide under the waistband of my drawers.

I wanted to scream again, but I was beyond it now.

His fingers slid low, rasping against my inner thigh.

"We were thinking," he whispered, now so close his mouth was almost against mine, "that we could whip a thing or two out—eh?—and who would miss it? It's not as if Jack needs it, right?"

I couldn't believe it. What did they know about Jack?

"After all," whispered the other—*Oh Christ, I could feel his cold tongue in my ear!*—"he has Noah now, right?"

Now the second man's hand rose up under my blouse and gripped one of my breasts, so painfully I whimpered.

"We're so happy we found you wandering about the streets, little girl," he said.

"We'd like to know what you're doing," said the other man.

Not man—imp! Suddenly I knew who they were! I remembered that moment, so many years ago, when they'd stood over me in my parents' bed, and wrapped Catling's hex around my wrists.

"What is sweet little Grace doing, wandering the streets, eh?" said other imp, and squeezed my breast with such renewed spite that I cried out in pain.

"Tell us, little Grace."

"Tell us, Grace, or you'll feel this cold blade sliding into regions until now only Harry has enjoyed."

I could barely force the words out. "I came down here to see a friend . . . I got lost . . . I—"

They wouldn't let me finish. I felt the flat, icy blade of the knife against my bare belly, then felt it turn, slowly, slowly, so that its edge bit into my skin.

I tore myself away. I don't know how I did it, but I tore myself away and stumbled up the street, hearing the soft, sarcastic laughter of the two men behind me.

Ten minutes later, clutching my coat around the ruins of my clothes, I hailed a cab back to the Savoy.

* * *

IN ROTHERHITHE THE IMPS PULLED THEIR CLOTHES straight, and Jim slipped the knife back into the sheath he had hung at his belt.

"D'you think we took it too far?" he said.

Bill leered. "I'd say we didn't take it far enough."

"We were told not to hurt her too much," said Bill. "I think a rape would have got us into hot water."

Bill grunted. "Perhaps we'll be asked to scare her again," he said. "Then we might as well notch up the fright a little further, eh?"

Jim laughed softly, his hand creeping back to caress his knife. "Yeah," he said. "Let's hope."

"Don't get your hopes too high," said their dark mistress, appearing so suddenly beside them that the imps jumped back in consternation.

Her mouth twitched very slightly at their fear. "You scared her well and truly," she said.

"We did!" the imps exclaimed together.

"But will she stay scared?" the woman whispered, then vanished.

Chapter Six

St. Margaret's Parish Hall

Friday, 14 June 1940

JACK HAD BEEN CONCERNED ABOUT GRACE for weeks. He'd sensed the withdrawal in her after the night of the Great Marriage, and that withdrawal had only got deeper as time passed. He knew she was upset about his involvement with her mother, and suspected that she was jealous that now Noah could sense the weakness where before it had only been Grace and himself.

Jack hadn't so much as laid eyes on her for almost three weeks, and had the distinct impression she was avoiding him. He was worried that Grace was tired of helping him, or believed that he'd prefer Noah to help to track down the extent of the shadow.

Preferences aside (and Jack was not entirely sure that he *did* want Noah before Grace), Noah wasn't much help. Yes, she could sense the shadow, but she couldn't discover any more about it. She could see what others had discovered, but she was not capable of discovering herself.

Jack could do that. Grace could.

Noah could not.

Jack had spent sleepless nights trying to work out the significance. He'd sensed the shadow the instant he'd stepped foot back in London. Grace had sensed it immediately as well. Both she and Jack could, by slow exploration, discover new elements of the weakness, slowly building up a greater understanding of it.

Then, after the Great Marriage, Noah had suddenly sensed it . . . but could do no more. She could not discover it, and Jack suspected that neither could she sense the shadow as strongly as he and Grace. Why? *Why*? What the significance of the Great Marriage? Why had the shadow opened up to Noah after that, if only fractionally?

Jack drove slowly toward the Savoy through the darkened city, the questions still tumbling about his mind, and still no closer to answering any of them than he had been over the past few weeks.

He needed to speak to Grace. Somehow, she was the key to all of this.

"Damn it," he muttered, pulling up outside the hotel, "why is she always so cursed elusive?"

HE RAN LIGHTLY UP THE STEPS TO THE PRIVATE residents' entrance of the Savoy.

Robert Stacey was standing a few feet inside the foyer, hands folded before him, demeanor calm, eyes steady, looking for all the world as if he had been waiting for Jack.

"You'll not find her at home tonight, sir," Stacey said as Jack came through the door.

"I'm not looking for Noah," said Jack, walking past the Sidlesaghe with a nod.

"I know," said Stacey.

Jack stopped halfway to the lifts, turning to look back at the Sidlesaghe. "You know?"

Stacey gave a small shrug.

Jack bit down his annoyance. "Where is she, Stacey?"

"You'll find Grace at the parish hall of St. Margaret's Westminster. There's a dance there tonight. Lots of young things attending. She wanted to go. She said she didn't want to be frightened, that she didn't want to let them scare her."

Jack looked at Stacey carefully, trying to sort through the implications of the Sidlesaghe's extraordinary little speech. What was Grace doing, suddenly deciding to go to a parish dance? If Grace had been a normal young woman, rather than one caught up in three thousand years' worth of hatred and ambition, then, yes, Jack could imagine she might have decided to go to a dance at the local parish hall.

But *Grace?* She was too withdrawn, too battered by all that had trapped her, and Jack could not for the life of him imagine her chatting gaily with numerous "young things" who could not, on any level, truly communicate with her. All in all, Jack thought a local dance would be hell on earth for such as Grace.

And . . . *didn't want to be frightened, she didn't want to let them scare her?* What the hell . . .

"Stacey? What has happened?"

"I am surprised you don't know, sir."

"What the fuck has happened Stacey?"

"Grace was attacked, about two weeks ago. Down in Rotherhithe, out trying to aid you. She came home, her clothes in tatters, her body bruised. She would hardly speak of it, and begged me to say nothing, but—"

"What happened to her?"

"So far as I can work out, two men attacked her, held a knife to her, tried to rape her. Threatened her with appalling violence." Stacey paused, watching the expression

on Jack's face very carefully. "I wouldn't be surprised if these two were the Penitent Ripper."

Jack went so cold he was surprised his heart didn't stop beating. *The imps. It must have been the imps.* Jesus Christ, what the *hell* was Catling playing at?

"I'm sure you'll see her safe home tonight, major," Stacey said.

"Why didn't you tell me about it earlier?"

"I'm telling you now, major."

Jack swore, then turned for the door.

THE PARISH HALL OF ST. MARGARET'S WESTMIN-ster had been carefully blacked out so that no light shone from window or door, but Jack could clearly hear the sound of music and laughter coming from within. In the first months of the war nighttime entertainments—the cinema, theaters, dances, restaurants—had largely shut down, either by government order or because people were too frightened to go out. But as the war had dragged on, and Hitler had neither invaded nor bombarded London with gas or fire, people had slowly relaxed, and the dance halls, cinemas, theaters and restaurants reopened again.

As he parked his Austin, Jack wondered how long this false sense of security would last. Neither Hitler nor Catling would leave the city entirely alone.

Not forever.

Inside, the parish hall was alive with music, light, jostling bodies, laughter and chatter. Jack paused just inside the door, tucking his military cap under one arm, surveying the scene.

Where was Grace?

He peered through the throng, trying to see her, but the dance floor was so jammed with tightly packed, moving bodies that Jack thought he'd have a better chance of spotting a distant star on a stormy night than of picking out Grace.

"Major?" said a voice at his elbow, and Jack turned.

A clergyman stood there, smiling at him. "Welcome to St. Margaret's, major. We weren't expecting our friends

from across the Atlantic just yet, however. You came here because . . . ?"

Despite the man's smile, Jack could see his suspicion.

"I'm looking for Grace Orr," he said.

The clergyman's face cleared. "Oh, Grace! Yes, of course she is here. I'm glad a friend . . . you *are* a friend, yes?"

Jack managed a smile. "Yes. I've been a friend of the family for more years than any of us care to remember."

"Of course. Well, I'm glad a friend of Grace's has managed to arrive. Maybe you can drag her out of the kitchen. Several of the young men here would love to ask her for a dance."

"The kitchen?"

The clergyman nodded toward a door at the back, and Jack nodded his thanks, and started to press his way through the crowd.

GRACE WAS STANDING AT THE SINK IN THE LITTLE kitchen, her arms in suds up to their elbows. As soon as she realized someone had entered—alerted not by the sound of the door, but by the sudden rush of noise as the door opened—she turned around, grabbing at a tea towel as she did so.

She froze as soon as she saw who it was, the tea towel draped over her arms.

Jack closed the door, slightly stunned by the depth of the relief that flooded through him as he saw she was safe. He flicked his eyes around the kitchen, half expecting the cursed imps to leap out of some shadow, but they were alone.

He looked back to Grace, taking a moment to study her.

She was wearing a pure white dress of some slinky material, sleeveless, and cut in close to waist and hip. A long-sleeved bolero jacket of the same material was draped over the back of a nearby chair, and Jack saw Grace's eyes flicker toward it.

He realized that the tea towel was not so much an aid to drying her arms, but a means of hiding her scars until she could slip on the jacket.

Grace gave an uncertain smile, glancing once more at the jacket.

"You do not need to hide your wrists from me," Jack said. He walked over to her, and tugged the tea towel out of her hands. "Want a hand with the dishes?" He thought she would flee if he suddenly demanded details of the attack.

She let the towel go, but with obvious reluctance. Jack had blocked her access to both jacket and door, and she leaned back against the sink, her face flushed.

"What are you doing here, Jack? My mother is out with—"

"I wasn't looking for your mother. But what are you doing in *here*?" He smiled, infusing a jesting tone into his voice, trying to relax her. "Isn't all the fun happening out there?" He tipped his head to the door leading back into the hall.

Another uncertain, unhappy smile. "I don't know why I came. It's stupid, really. I shouldn't be here."

No, thought Jack, *you shouldn't be here at all*. He had a sudden vision of Ambersbury Banks bathed in moonlight, and Grace standing there, still and waiting, her eyes wild with power.

"Grace, why *did* you come? At night. It's too dangerous. You could have been attacked again—" *Shit!* Jack broke off, wishing he could snatch back the words.

"Stacey told you," she said, very low.

"Yes, Stacey told me. Grace . . . Grace . . ."

"I am all right, Jack. They didn't hurt me."

Didn't hurt her? Torn clothing? Bruises? Knife? Threats of appalling violence. "Oh God . . . what happened, Grace? Please, tell me."

She drew in a breath, and he heard it shudder in her throat. "I was in Rotherhithe. It was late; I shouldn't have stayed out so long. Two men grabbed me, threatened me with a knife. I got away. That's all."

"No, there's more. Grace, those were the imps—you know that? Yes? Jesus God, they have been the ones doing the murders. Grace, what did they want?"

"Just to scare me, Jack. That's all. It was just Catling, finding a new way to torment me. I am *not* frightened."

And that was why she had come to this parish dance, Jack realized. To prove to herself and to the imps that she was not frightened. God, what *could* have happened. It terrified him.

Jack reached out his hands, resting them on her shoulders. "Grace, I can't have you going out and—"

"Jack, *please* don't ask me to stop helping you," she said. Her voice was steadier, and her eyes met his without flinching. "If I stop helping you then Catling will have won."

He didn't know what to say.

"I'll be careful, Jack. Really."

He gave a soft, disbelieving laugh. "I couldn't live with myself if anything happened to you, Grace."

"I know you have my mother to help you now, but—"

"Your mother can't do what you can. Noah cannot discover any more of the shadow. She can only sense what you and I have already discovered. Besides, Noah is not my life, whatever you think."

She dropped her eyes, and Jack could see she didn't believe him.

He tightened his hands fractionally on her shoulders. "Dance with me," he said.

"No, I—"

"Dance with me, Grace. It is a lovely night, and the music is good, and I have no idea why on earth both of us are spending the night tucked away in this wretched kitchen. After you, you wanted to come here to defy Catling, yes?" Quite suddenly Jack found the idea of dancing with Grace very appealing.

"Jack—"

"Dance with me, Grace."

Still she hesitated.

"Don't be frightened," he said, "not of the dancing floor." And with that he led her toward the door.

ONCE THEY REACHED THE DANCE FLOOR, JACK put his arm around Grace's waist, and held her firmly against him. The music, frenetic when he'd first arrived, had calmed and slowed into a soothing ballad, and Jack led

Grace into an unhurried, rhythmical ballroom dance. Grace held herself stiffly, uncertainly, and Jack had to coax her through every step.

The other dancers gave them their own space, not through any deliberate consideration, but because Jack and Grace's arrival on the dance floor had caused a not inconsiderable stir and most people wanted to be able to watch them. People had been gossiping ever since the handsome American major had arrived only to vanish into the kitchen to talk with the enigmatic Grace Orr, and now the talk, while muted, only increased in intensity. Jack was well aware that every eye in the hall was on them, and, from Grace's rigid stance, knew that she was, as well.

"Dance with me," Jack whispered, and smiled as Grace's body finally leaned against his, and her movements loosened so that their dancing became much freer.

She was a good dancer, and Jack remembered that Noah had said that Weyland sometimes took Grace dancing in the Savoy's ballroom.

But that was not the reason Grace danced well, was it? She was a trained Mistress of the Labyrinth, and she would have the rhythms and harmonies of the very stars themselves sliding through her veins.

Jack relaxed into the dance, enjoying the feel of Grace in his arms. He thought again of what those imps could have done to Grace, and his arm tightened fractionally about her.

Grace responded by leaning most of her weight against him, and tucking her head into his shoulder, and he smiled against the loose, springy curls of her hair. This form of dancing, coupled together so closely, was unusual to him. For most of his long, long life, dancers had been segregated by sexes and by distance. People danced in groups or lines or circles, not coupled together so intimately.

Jack wondered why it had taken so long for someone to think of this innovation.

Without thinking, the hand he had loosely clasped about Grace's back began to move. First randomly, gentle circles

in the small of her back, the silken fabric of her dress no barrier to the warmth and softness of her skin, and then, in more deliberate patterns.

Instantly Grace took a sharp intake of breath.

Before she could speak, Jack said, "Grace, you are a trained Mistress of the Labyrinth. But how good *are* you?"

Then his hand moved again, but far, far more deliberately than previously, and this time Jack underpinned its movements with his power as a Kingman. Using both his hand and his power, as well the movement of their dancing, Jack began to trace out harmonies, over and through her body.

Both Kingmen and Mistresses of the Labyrinth used dance to control the harmonies that made up all life—the harmonies found in the movement of the stars and the tides, the turning of the seasons, the running of water over land. Controlling these harmonies, even a fraction of them, was what gave Kingmen and Mistresses their power. In her training as a Mistress of the Labyrinth, Grace would have learned to touch and manipulate these harmonies, but she had never danced with a Kingman previously. She had never combined her powers with those of a Kingman.

Jack had never once danced this way with Noah, and it had been three and a half thousand years since he had danced with Genvissa. It had been a long, long time since he had allowed his powers as a Kingman free rein.

He did now, and he wondered how Grace would react—even if she was *capable* of reacting. Would this terrify her? Would she run from him? Would she not be able to counter his power and—

Sweetly, gently, infinitesimally quietly, Grace entwined her power with his, embracing and complementing his as if they had danced together a thousand times previously.

Jack trembled. He had expected everything but this. When he'd danced with Genvissa their powers had been complementary, yes, and they had been more than good together, but *this*? No. This was . . . extraordinary.

"What a surprise you are, Grace," Jack whispered. Then, his hold on her tightening, he said, "Trust me. *Trust me.*"

The parish hall about them vanished.

THEY DANCED ACROSS AMBERSBURY BANKS IN the thin moonlight. Jack wasn't sure why he had brought Grace here, only that as soon as she'd entwined her power with his he'd felt a need so powerful he'd been unable to resist it. They danced a little more wildly now, but still loosely entwined, and more wrapped in labyrinthine power than ever. Away from the parish hall, away from the stares, both could afford to expend a bit more power.

Music surrounded them, but the sound of the band had vanished, replaced by the music of the trees and the wind and the stars racing overhead.

Jack's sense of unreality grew as he realized the full significance of what he felt from Grace. During his training as a Kingman he'd heard stories (rumors, really) that for every Kingman there was one perfect match somewhere, a Mistress of the Labyrinth who would so seamlessly complement his power (and he, hers) that whatever Game they danced together would be flawless and unassailable. It was a rumor only, a legend, or so Jack had thought until the past few minutes.

What he felt from Grace he'd never felt from Genvissa, and his gut instinct told him he'd never feel it from Noah, either.

"Dear God, Grace," he said, and she tilted her head back to see his face.

She looked puzzled at his intensity, and Jack realized she could not feel what he did. Disappointment overwhelmed him, and she saw it, for her eyes clouded over, and she tensed in his arms.

"Grace, don't. It's all right. Please, dance with me here, dance with me. Don't go."

She relaxed against him once more, and Jack closed his eyes and rested his cheek against her curls. God, what was happening? Vivid images and emotions and desires flooded his mind.

It was, in the end, the desire that undid him. The pairing and dancing of a Kingman and Mistress was a marriage not only of power, but also of desire—the desire almost always begotten of the mating of their power.

He gave a short laugh, discomfited by his arousal, and, breaking off the dance and the flow of his power, stepped back from Grace.

"I'm sorry," he said.

The animation on her face drained away. "Jack? Did I do something wrong?"

He stared at her, still unable to believe that she had felt nothing. "No," he said eventually. "You have done nothing wrong, Grace."

She was very still, her eyes dark in this faint light, looking steadily at him. "Jack . . ."

"You're a surprise, Grace. You know that?"

A smile trembled about her mouth, then died. "Is that good, Jack? I don't know what you thought . . . if I . . . I know that I could not be as good as my mother, or Stella, but—"

"You're very good, Grace," he said quietly, finally realizing what she wanted to know. "You're very powerful, and you have *no* reason, *none,* to think that you can only ever exist in your mother's shadow, let alone Stella's." He gave a short laugh. "You stepped out of everyone's shadow tonight, Grace. Believe it."

She smiled then, relieved, and the smile was so lovely, and so transformed her, that Jack had to literally clench his fists in order to suppress the urge to kiss her. *God, man, this is one road you don't need to travel!*

"Stella said I was good, but I didn't know whether or not to believe it," she said.

Jack was incredulous that she had, most apparently, felt none of the powerful emotions he had. *Does she have no*

idea of her power, labyrinthine or sexual? Did I, until but a few minutes ago?

"Let me take you home, Grace."

APPARENTLY THEY HAD NOT BEEN MISSED AMID the dancers at St. Margaret's parish hall, for their "reappearance" there caused no great stir. Jack thought that somehow (amid his virtual total concentration on Grace) he'd kept a shadow of them dancing within the hall, and that their shadows had merely solidified back into a reality that had not disturbed anyone's perception of them.

All Jack wanted to do was to take Grace home, and then get back to Copt Hall, where he might sit, and think.

Grace fetched her jacket from the kitchen, then Jack escorted her outside to the car, both nodding their farewells to the clergyman as they left. Jack thought it highly likely that the man would telephone the Savoy within half an hour, to make sure that Grace arrived home unscathed.

They didn't talk in the car. Jack glanced at Grace from time to time as he drove, but saw they she sat apparently as reflective as himself.

She hadn't put the jacket on, and whenever Jack glanced at her, his eyes always slid down briefly to her wrists before looking back to the road.

"Grace," he said as he pulled up before the Savoy. "Can I talk to you about May Day?"

She stiffened. May Day had been the day of the Great Marriage.

"About you, Grace. Not Noah. May Day was your birthday, wasn't it?"

She looked at him, startled. "How did you know that?"

"Malcolm had mentioned it to me a while back, and, no, please don't ask me how he knew, because I have no idea." He paused, wondering how to put this. "I'm sorry we forgot that it was your birthday, Grace."

"There were grander events that day. My birthday didn't matter."

I wonder if that is really so, Jack wondered. May Day

was a powerful day for Grace's birth. "But still, we should not have forgotten your birthday. Grace, will you let me give you a present?"

She gave a small laugh, discomforted. "You don't need to do that."

"I do, I think. Did *anyone* remember, Grace?"

She looked down at her hands in her lap. "My father did."

Your father, but no one else? "Well, I shall make up for my tardiness. But give me a while." He grinned a little. "I need to think of the perfect gift."

Jack thought she'd protest once more that he didn't need to give her a gift, but instead she only thanked him, her face and voice grave.

He nodded, got out, opened her door, and escorted her toward the steps leading to the private residents' entrance. Just as they got to the top Jack caught gently at her elbow, stopping her before she opened the door. "Grace, I . . . ah, damn it. One half of me wants to demand that you stay here at home and keep safe, and the other half of me screams for you to continue to help me. I can't do this by myself, and Noah is no help."

"I will stay out of trouble, Jack. I won't stay out late by myself again."

"No more going to dances to prove yourself, eh?"

She smiled. "Not without you, Jack."

JACK DROVE A LITTLE WAY DOWN THE EMBANK-ment, then parked the Austin and sat in the car for hours, smoking and thinking, staring at the rising hulk of the Savoy.

It took him a long time to simply order his thoughts. To say that what had happened tonight was surprising was akin to saying Hitler had been a little bit naughty over the past year or so.

He was concerned about the attack—Grace had said very little about it, but Jack had fathomed enough to realize it had been terrifying. He wondered if Catling had indeed set the imps on to Grace—or if the pitiful creatures couldn't resist snatching at Grace when they had the chance.

Jack repressed a shiver. He *wanted* to demand that Grace not help him . . . but, oh, he needed that help so badly.

And he wanted an excuse to keep seeing Grace.

Especially after what had happened atop Ambersbury Banks tonight.

Grace was . . . astounding. Every little bit more he got to know about her simply increased her mystery. Darkwitch and Mistress of the Labyrinth; daughter of Asterion; his perfect labyrinthine partner *(Jesus God, the harmonies they could create between them!)*; a woman inescapably tied to the Troy Game; a woman admired by ancient druids; a woman, a Mistress of the Labyrinth, who was the only one apart from himself who was capable of discovering the secrets of this shadow.

And the bearer of four of the golden Kingship bands of Troy.

Jack had first realized that the day he'd come to the Savoy and tried to work out a means by which to free Grace of Catling's hex. The instant he'd taken her wrist and infused her with his power, he'd felt them, buried under her skin. He didn't think she knew they were there, but he had felt them, buried deep.

Noah may have thought Grace had merely carried them into the Faerie, but Jack knew that Grace had actually absorbed them.

This wasn't unusual. When a Kingman died, a Mistress of the Labyrinth often took his Kingship bands into her keeping so that she could pass them on to the dead Kingman's heir in a ceremony so imbued with power that it was second only to the creating of a Game as the most powerful thing a Mistress and Kingman could do together.

What this meant, Jack realized as he lit yet another cigarette, was that from very early on Grace had been "selected" as the Mistress to hand back to him the Kingship bands.

The Mistress who was also his perfect match, and who was the only one, with him, who could discover the puzzlement of the shadowed enchantment that hung over London.

That all these were connected was undoubted.

But *who* had done all this arranging and selecting? Not Noah. Noah had no idea of what she had bred.

Ariadne? Possibly. God knows, this had her stamp all over it, but Jack wasn't sure that Ariadne had the power to arrange it.

Catling?

Who else?

Yet none of this had the feel of Catling, either . . . and if Catling *had* arranged it then she'd be screaming at Jack to take Grace as his Mistress for the final dance of the Troy Game. Together they'd make a much more powerful completion than the pairing of Noah and Jack.

Ah! Jack stubbed out the cigarette. He could make no sense of the who behind the arranging, and thinking about what this all meant was just as frustrating.

If not nightmarish.

Jack recalled how he'd felt as he'd danced with Grace on Ambersbury Banks, and it terrified him.

"This is the last bloody thing I need," he muttered as he finally turned the ignition key on the Austin.

Chapter Seven

LONDON

June to September 1940

Grace Speaks

THERE WERE THREE THINGS ABOUT THAT night of Friday the fourteenth of June that made it memorable. The first was that Jack said to me, *You have no reason, none, to think that you can only ever exist in your mother's shadow,* and actually sounded as if he meant it.

The second was the confusion in his eyes as we danced. I had expected to see boredom, perhaps even some condescension. But not confusion.

The third was when Catling appeared to me once I'd gone to bed.

The night had started poorly enough. I have no idea what in the world made me think that going to the dance would prove my courage to anyone. It had been a stupid idea. Once I'd arrived, I'd realized I would hate it, but I didn't want to be rude and leave immediately. I didn't fit in, I couldn't share the gaiety, I didn't want to dance with any of the young men, I didn't want to chatter meaninglessly with the other women, and so I departed to the kitchen to wash out glasses.

My God, I am so hopeless.

When Jack appeared behind me I was so startled I thought for one horrible moment I would actually faint. Then I discovered that Stacey had blabbed and Jack knew about the attack and I was sure he would demand then and there that I stay home and be a good girl. He *wanted* to, I could see it, but he didn't. I suppose I should have told him of that terrible sense of the shadow "rushing" at me during the imps' attack, but I knew if I did, Jack *would* demand I stop helping him. So that I kept to myself.

Then he took me dancing, and then . . . oh, then he took me to heaven and back. That wasn't the dance or anything he said. He did that by paying me the ultimate compliment of assuming I had both the skill and the courage to be able to handle his Kingman power. He made me feel as though I mattered, as if I wasn't just a tragedy needing to be saved, and for that I think I would have given him anything, had he asked.

That melding of powers. It felt magnificent, and that mostly because it made me feel intimately close to someone, and I hadn't felt that since I was a tiny baby, and not yet under Catling's hex.

So, it was a good night, and particularly when Jack remembered my birthday.

I went to bed convinced I wouldn't sleep, that I had too

much to think about—and to anticipate, if I was to meet with Jack tomorrow to resume plotting out the course of this difference. But I did sleep, almost as immediately as my head hit the pillow.

About three A.M. I woke up suddenly and saw Catling sitting on a chair in the shadowed recesses of the room.

Instantly all the good feeling and the warmth vanished. I felt sick, and cold to the very marrow of my bones.

She rose, that hateful cold-faced woman, and came close to the bed.

Iciness radiated out of her, and I shivered.

"I thought you'd stay home and shiver," she said, "after what those imps did to you. What they *might* have done."

"I wasn't scared," I managed, stunned to hear her speak. I had managed to convince myself that her words on Ambersbury Banks had been an aberration. "*You* don't scare me."

My Lord, that sounded completely pathetic, and Catling laughed. "Very good," she said. "I like that."

I opened my mouth, wanting to goad Catling into revealing what she actually meant by those words, but she forestalled me.

"How did it feel," she said, "when he held you in his arms?"

That silenced me, and I gaped at her.

"Tell me, Grace. I want to know. How did it feel? How did Jack's body feel, pressed against yours in the dance? Did it delight you? Would you . . ." She paused, looking at me as if she were about to ask me something of the utmost importance. "Would you put everything else aside for him? Give your life for him?"

"Go away. Leave me in peace."

"No. Answer me."

What preposterous questions. "If I tell you, will you go away?"

"You want me to go away?"

I closed my eyes, not sure if I could put into words the fact that my entire life was *dedicated* to wanting her to "go away."

"Were you delighted, Grace?"

"Yes," I whispered, opening my eyes again. "I was delighted."

"And would you give your life for him, Grace? Would you live in darkness, if it would save him?"

"Would I be free of you, if I did?"

She smiled, so cold. "Yes."

"Then, yes, I would die for him, or live in darkness for him, if that would free me of you."

Something shifted in her eyes, and I hoped I hadn't made some horribly stupid vow with those words. I meant then to retract my statement, but suddenly Catling was gone, and I was left staring into the dark bedroom.

OVER THE NEXT WEEKS AND MONTHS I CONTINUED helping Jack plot out the extent of this shadow. I was careful never to stay out later than midafternoon, unless I was in the company of someone else (often Matilda, or another of Eaving's Sisters), and the imps did not bother me again. Jack gradually relaxed (I had noticed him trailing me on more than one occasion, keeping an eye on me), and he and I slipped into a quasi-friendship. It was an "almost" friendship, because even though Jack was friendly enough with me, there was a distance in his manner that hadn't been there previously. We talked about what we were doing and discovering, or of light and inconsequential matters, but often I caught him studying me with those unreadable black eyes of his, and I felt as if I was being judged in some manner.

If I grew too obviously uncomfortable under his regard, he relaxed it instantly, laughing and passing away the look with some light comment. Jack was very good at reassuring me, and I never worried until the next time I saw him watching me with that peculiar, inscrutable stillness.

He did not ask me to demonstrate my labyrinthine powers again, nor did he touch me with his Kingman power.

That disappointed me more than I had thought possible, but then I knew Jack had so many things to trouble himself with, that I must surely be the least of them.

He appeared to have forgotten my birthday present, but that did not concern me. The fact he'd remembered my birthday had been gift enough.

I met with him in tea shops, once or twice at Faerie Hill Manor, and several times at Copt Hall, where the enigmatic Malcolm served me tea and sandwiches. Occasionally Jack would drive me home to the Savoy, where he and Stacey nodded to each other warily. That amused me, mainly because it made me feel a little better to think that there were some creatures who could still unsettle Jack.

My mother often joined us. She was intimately involved with trying to decipher this puzzling shadow (I noticed now that neither Jack nor my mother ever called it a weakness in my presence), and what I discovered on my walks and explorations around London I shared as much with her as with Jack. I minded her presence, but not as much as previously. Every so often I would catch Jack's eyes on me, and the ghost of his words would cross my mind: *You do not stand in your mother's shadow, Grace.*

Then I would remember how well we had danced together, and the confusion in his eyes, and suddenly I did not mind the presence of my mother so very much at all.

Besides, however much I may have minded her presence, I couldn't deny that we needed her. Within a week of the dance at the parish hall, Hitler opened his air offensive against Britain. On the Wednesday night following the dance, Cambridge was bombed, and thereafter on most days and nights German aircraft appeared in the sky somewhere over Britain, dropping their payloads of bombs onto factories, airfields, ports, and, increasingly, houses and suburbs. The air of optimism—even gaiety—that had characterized the last few months now vanished. Day and night the RAF fighters went up against the bombers. People stood in fields, or outside their suburban houses, watching the dogfights going on overhead. I remember one day walking in the Greenwich area, and hearing in the far distance the drone of fighters overhead, and looking up, seeing the faint lines of combat far to my south.

The Battle of Britain, the papers had begun to call it.

During the night of Saturday, the twenty-fourth of August, eastern London was hit with what appeared to be a few stray sticks of bombs. There was damage in Stepney, Walthamstow, and Leyton, as well as Tottenham and Islington in North London as the aircraft flew on.

THE NEXT MORNING, SUNDAY, HARRY CALLED AN emergency meeting at Faerie Hill Manor. Once we'd all arrived—I and my parents, Jack, Stella, even Silvius, whom I hadn't seen for months—Harry did not bother to offer us a drink or ask us if we were comfortable.

Instead he opened a door that opened off the drawing room (one I'd not seen previously) and nodded us through into the Faerie. "If you please," he said.

It was so unusual for me to be invited to the Faerie that for the moment I was absorbed only in the strangeness of it. How often had I been here? As a baby, and then for the Great Marriage, but that was about it. The door led us through onto the slopes leading up to The Naked, and I turned about slowly, taking it all in.

Then I realized that most of the others (save Silvius, who was likely as much a stranger as I by the way he was looking about) were staring at a hill in the middle distance.

The Lord of the Faerie ("Harry" had been left behind on the other side of the door) was waving a hand at it. "Well?" he demanded.

I looked, and instantly felt coldness sweep through me. There were several dark patches on the hillside, as if the trees there had been burned.

"And here," said the Lord of the Faerie, now pointing to a hillside slightly to the north of the other one, and a little closer. Here there was just one blackened patch, but it was considerably larger, and it was now obvious that the trees had been set alight. The leaves had all burned away, and the trunks and branches stood blackened and dead against the azure sky.

Jack swore, which made me jump.

"When did this happen?" he said. "This is nothing like the frost damage you showed me in March."

"It happened last night," said the Lord of the Faerie. "When the bombs fell on London."

Everyone turned from the hillside to stare at the Faerie lord. The implications were so obvious, but so appalling, that I think everyone, like me, was too busy trying to deny the connection to actually speak.

"As the bombs hit the east end," said the Lord of the Faerie, "so this hillside"—he pointed to the one in the distance, in the east—"burst into flame. And as the bombs fell in the north of London"—now he pointed to the hillside closest to us—"so this detonated."

Still no one said anything.

"Imagine," the Lord of the Faerie said softly, looking at each of us in turn, "what will happen if the Luftwaffe mounts a blitzkrieg against London."

He and Jack exchanged a look then, and it was so bleak that I spoke, if only to break that terrible exchange between them.

"It's connected to the bombing?" I said. "But how? I didn't think that damage to the mortal world would have reflected here."

"Catling," said Jack. "This is Catling's doing."

"Somehow Catling is sending the damage through," said the Lord of the Faerie. "*Reflecting* it through."

"She's getting impatient," said my mother. She shivered, and wrapped her arms about herself.

"Aye," said the Lord of the Faerie. "But this damage is not all. Come with me."

We followed him up The Naked, and once on its summit, he pointed to the horizon. "What do you see," he said.

I frowned, for I couldn't see anything. There was merely a clear horizon. What did the Lord of the Faerie want us to—

"Oh my gods," whispered my mother. "The Idyll has gone."

"Aye," said the Lord of the Faerie. "It vanished, so one of the Faerie folk told me, the instant the first hillside burst into flame."

I felt sick. First the damage to the trees, and now my father's Idyll had been destroyed? "Is this my fault? I mean . . . I came here for the Great Marriage, and now this damage. Is Catling using me as a conduit to hurt the Faerie?"

Was that why the Lord of the Faerie had invited me here now? To judge me?

"No!" my mother cried, but before she could speak further Jack strode over to me, and took one of my wrists in his hand. He was wearing his military uniform, and while I could not see it, I felt those marks sliding down his arm, and an instant later saw them cascade over the top of his hand, across his fingers, and flow into my scars.

The instant they touched me I gasped and tried to pull away, but Jack had me in his grasp too tightly to allow me escape.

He stared at me, then, after a moment, his eyes crinkled in a slight smile. "No," he said. "Catling is not using you as a conduit. Do not blame yourself, Grace."

He let my wrist go, turning his attention to the rest of the group. "Catling is stronger than ever. This"—he waved his hand about, taking in all the damage in sky and tree—"she can do by herself."

Then he turned to my father. "Weyland? *Has* the Idyll been destroyed?"

My father shook his head. "No. It has just retreated into itself. Fled. I imagine the only way into it now is via the steps of the spire of St. Dunstan's-in-the-East."

"And if the Idyll is afraid," said the Lord of the Faerie, "then so am I. The only problem, my friends, is that, unlike the Idyll, the Faerie has nowhere to retreat."

Again there was a little silence as we all contemplated this, finally broken by Silvius.

"What did you mean," he asked the Lord of the Faerie, "by saying Catling was 'reflecting' the damage through?"

"Why expend effort yourself," said Stella, silent until now, "when you can merely reflect—or redirect—damage from one realm into another?"

"The how of this is largely irrelevant," said the Lord of the Faerie, looking at Jack and my mother. "What I need to

know is how and when you can stop it. Gods damn it, if Hitler sets London afire then the Faerie will burn as well!"

Jack and my mother exchanged a glance, then Jack sent a brief look my way before he answered the Lord of the Faerie. "Coel, we are still trying to discover what this weakness is hanging about the Game, and how best we might use it to—"

"Damn it!" shouted the Lord of the Faerie. "That is not what I want to hear! *When can you stop her?*"

Again Jack glanced at me before responding to the Lord of the Faerie. "The short answer to that, my friend, is that we can't. Not yet. I know you're desperate—so am I! But I have no idea how Noah and I can exploit this weakness and to attempt to do so before we understand it is to invite catastrophe!"

To that the Lord of the Faerie made no response, save a baring of his teeth in a snarl of sheer frustration.

Chapter Eight

ST. MAGNUS THE MARTYR, LONDON

Tuesday, 3 September 1940

WEYLAND HAD BEEN UNSETTLED AND unhappy ever since Jack had reappeared in London, but his sense of foreboding had grown stronger since he'd realized the imps were responsible for the Ripper murders. That the imps murdered occasionally, Weyland had no doubt, but this series of murders . . .

There was something about them. Something sinister.

Something purposeful.

Something shadowed.

Something, Weyland knew, that should scare him halfway to death.

All the bodies of the women had been laid out under the porch of St. Magnus the Martyr. Weyland had no idea about the significance of that location, although he worried at both himself and Silvius about it. The police had a constant but surreptitious presence around the ancient church, watching the porch and the streets and alleyways leading to it, but their presence had not stopped the murders, nor the bodies mysteriously appearing under the porch within the blink of an eye.

The imps were using power to lay the bodies out, but Weyland could match power with power, and he could see what police surveillance could not.

Unable to find the imps at their house, or anywhere else within London, Weyland had spent weeks, off and on, watching St. Magnus the Martyr. Noah had asked him what he was about at night, but he had merely shrugged, and passed his absences off as nocturnal wanderings, or extra ARP warden duty atop the Savoy. Noah didn't believe him, and her disbelief, as well as his absences, contributed to the growing rift between them, but Weyland didn't want to confide in her.

She was too close to Jack, especially now that she, too, could sense this cursed "shadow."

Weyland could bear, just, to watch Noah drift away, but he hated beyond anything Grace's growing closeness to Jack. To lose both wife and daughter to him. Ah! That was too much!

He was wandering within a block of St. Magnus late on the night of the third of September, cloaking his activities in power, when he felt the unmistakeable presence of the imps coming closer. He ducked down an alley, keeping himself cloaked in both power and shadows as much as possible, and crept closer to the church.

Weyland passed a policeman standing in the darkened archway of a door, but the policeman, half dozing, realized neither the presence of Weyland nor the closing presence of the imps.

He arrived at the church, clinging to the darkened recesses of an alley's entrance, just as the imps came down the main street. What he saw appalled him.

The imps were dragging between them a shrieking young woman.

Weyland stared, then looked back over his shoulder at the policeman. *Surely, even with his mortal-cursed blindness, he could somehow* sense *this horror?*

But the policeman merely yawned, and leaned more comfortably against the door arch.

Weyland looked back to the imps. They had dragged their victim to the porch, where Bill kicked her legs out from under her, seizing her disordered hair as she fell to the pavement.

Before Weyland could move, before he could run out and somehow try to save the woman from her fate, both imps looked skyward.

"Do you like it?" hissed Jim. "Do you like your meal?"

"Does her terror taste good to you?" said Bill. "Is it *enough* for you?"

To Weyland's horror he realized the imps were addressing the shadow. He froze where he was, unable to think, unable to act, wondering what in the gods' names it *was* hovering up there that demanded such a sacrifice.

He clenched his fists, knowing he should act, knowing he should do *something*, but just as his muscles tightened to dash out, Bill leaned down to the woman and, evading her hands which tried to stop him, buried the blade of a knife deep in her belly.

Weyland froze in horror.

Bill dragged the knife back and forth in the woman's abdomen, needing to use both his hands on the hilt to do it. Her heels drummed up and down on the pavement, shrieks bellowed forth from her throat, and her hands grabbed futilely at the knife—but none of it made any difference.

Bill was being deliberately slow, Weyland realized through a haze of sheer revulsion. He was drawing her death out, *drawing her terror out.*

So that the shadow could feed.

Jim was dancing about frenziedly, his face turned upward, his hands dancing about at his sides. "Do you like it?" he shrieked. "Can you *feel* it?"

The woman was still struggling, but her shrieks had died to moans, and her hands were now only moving feebly.

The ground beneath her was now soaked with blood.

Then Jim came to an abrupt halt, reached down with both hands into the ruined mess of the woman's belly, and started to rummage about.

Weyland took a step back, unable to watch anymore. Another step, and yet another one, and then he had turned and was running away.

Under the porch of St. Magnus the Martyr, Bill and Jim looked up, blood spattering their faces and coating their hands.

"What was that?" said Bill.

"A rat, nothing more," said Jim, and they bent back to their enjoyment.

Chapter Nine

COPT HALL

Friday, 6 September 1940

SILVIUS PULLED HIS CAR IN BEHIND WEY-land's Daimler, turned off the ignition, then sat thinking a few minutes as he finished his cigarette. He'd gotten a call from Jack earlier this afternoon, asking him to come to Copt Hall in the evening.

There was to be a council of war, apparently.

Silvius didn't envy his son. Jack had screwed things up royally when he'd been Brutus and had founded the travesty of the Troy Game. *Don't use my murder to found the Game*, Silvius had said to Brutus. *It is no way to start a Game.* But Brutus hadn't listened, and now here they all

were, desperately searching for some means to unwind the Game before it lost all patience and *bit*.

But it wasn't all his son's fault though, was it? Everyone had dirtied their hands in the matter: Brutus, Cornelia, Genvissa, Ariadne, Asterion, and, aye, even himself. Brutus had been his responsibility, his the hand that had fashioned the pot, and maybe, Silvius thought as he sighed and opened the car door, he was as much to blame as anyone else.

Only Grace seemed to be innocent, and Silvius felt terribly sorry for her. She was the one to suffer the most, she the one with all to lose, she the one at the heart of the dilemma and, because of it, terribly, terribly isolated.

Malcolm opened the front door of Copt Hall as Silvius approached.

"Is everyone else here?" Silvius said as Malcolm took his coat, scarf, and gloves.

"Yes, Mr. Makris. They're waiting for you in the drawing room."

Waiting silently, as Silvius discovered when he walked in. Weyland and Noah were seated on one of the sofas before the fire, while Grace and Jack were sitting in opposing armchairs.

Everyone had looked up as Silvius entered, and Jack rose, and walked forward to embrace his father.

"Silvius! I am glad you are here."

"Not too late, I hope," Silvius said. He glanced at Weyland—the man was wan, the skin too tight over his cheekbones, and his eyes avoided Silvius'.

"Not at all," said Jack. "Come, sit down and I'll get you a whisky."

Silvius nodded at the others as he sat down and took the whisky Jack handed him. He noted that there was a small satchel by the side of Grace's chair, and Silvius wondered what it contained.

"Silvius," Jack said as he sat down in his chair, "I've asked you to come here tonight to see if you can't offer any suggestions. You were a Kingman, and God knows we need every bit of help we can get."

"Then why is not Stella here?" said Silvius.

"It is dusk," said Noah. "She needs to carol in the twilight. Besides, she said that she could offer nothing more than I, or Jack."

Or Grace? wondered Silvius, having heard from Jack that she was also a trained Mistress of the Labyrinth. He saw Jack glance at Grace as Noah spoke, and knew his son had thought the same thing. *Interesting,* Silvius thought. *Noah forgets to include her daughter, but Jack remembers.*

"Then Ariadne should be here," Silvius said, swirling his whisky around his glass, and watching out of the corner of his eye as Weyland's face closed even further over.

"I can speak to her at a later time," said Jack.

"I will do it for you," said Silvius.

Jack raised an eyebrow, remembering other times Silvius had demonstrated a knowledge of Ariadne's movements.

"I see her from time to time," Silvius said.

"Is that so," Jack said.

Silvius shrugged. "We like to talk over old times," he said. "But we are not here now to talk of myself and Ariadne"—Jack sent him a look at that which Silvius interpreted to mean that Jack, at least, fully intended to speak to him about it sooner rather than later—"but of your problem in trying to unwind the Troy Game, Jack."

"Yes," Jack said. "Grace, Noah, and I have been trying to work out what this"—he glanced at Grace—"shadow is that hangs over the Troy Game. Grace thinks it a trap of Catling's making, Noah and I are more inclined to think it a weakness of the Troy Game."

Silvius noted with some interest the play of emotions between the three of them at that point. Grace studiously examined her hands in her lap. Noah glanced first at Jack, then at her daughter, looking strained, while Jack looked steadily at Grace, as if willing her to raise her eyes and meet his.

Intriguing, Silvius thought. Then he looked back to Weyland, saw the expression on the man's face, and his stomach curdled. He didn't know if it was because of the emotional interplay between Noah, Grace, and Jack, or because of what they'd said.

Look at *me*, man, Silvius willed Weyland, but Weyland kept his eyes averted, although he must have known of Silvius' silent plea.

Then Jack spoke again, distracting Silvius away from his concern about Weyland. Briefly Jack explained how initially only he and Grace could discern the difference, then how Noah could sense it after the Great Marriage.

"But only Grace and I can discover *more* of it," Jack concluded. "It is as though it is a pattern etched into glass. Grace and I are the only ones who can rub away the years of accumulated grime to reveal more of it—at which point Noah can see the newly exposed section of pattern."

"But I am, most apparently," said Noah with a disarming grin, "no-good at cleaning myself."

"And you can't discern it at all," Silvius said to Weyland. *Talk! Tell me what is wrong!*

But Weyland just gave a terse shake of his head, still averting his eyes from Silvius, and it was left to Noah to explain.

"I have taken Weyland outside," she said, "and tried to show it to him, but he felt nothing."

Silvius might have stood up and walked over to shake Weyland at that point, save that Jack asked Grace to explain what she'd discovered of the shadow.

Grace sat forward and laid a hand on the satchel at the side of the chair. "Are you sure it is safe?" she asked Jack. "Catling spends her life peering over my shoulder."

"Copt Hall is closed to her," Jack said. "It is the site of an ancient druid magic, designed to keep prying eyes out. Catling cannot see in here, Grace, nor hear what you say."

Grace nodded, and lifted the satchel to her lap. She opened the flap and pulled out a folded map, which she proceeded to unfold and spread out on the rug between the chairs and sofa.

Despite his growing concern about Weyland, Silvius leaned forward and studied the map. It was a large and detailed map of Greater London—so large it virtually filled the space between the chairs and sofa—and it had been marked in a myriad of places with red ink.

"Jack and I have spent the past months walking the city," Grace said, "tracing out what we have felt." She explained how it was that they actually had to put foot to pavement to be able to trace out the pathways of this strange phenomenon, and thus the slowness in their accumulation of data.

"We've done nothing systematically for fear of alerting Catling," she said, a hint of apology in her voice, "thus the haphazard nature of what we've discovered."

Haphazard, indeed, thought Silvius, although he acknowledged the reason behind it. There were groups of lines splotched here and there around the map. A group to the east centered on Greenwich, another to the south around Peckham, yet another to the west around Clapham. Besides the center of London, which they had mapped out in some detail, in all there were some nine areas where Jack and Grace had discovered manifestations of what they called their "shadow." But all their work had thus far covered only about a fiftieth of London; there wasn't enough on the map, there wasn't enough *known* about this shadow, to be able to clearly define it.

Yet there was enough to tantalize.

"It's labyrinthine," said Silvius, one hand extended as he slowly traced out the lines with his forefinger.

"Aye," said Jack. "But it makes no sense. None! If it is labyrinthine, and it is, then it must, *must,* be connected to the Troy Game. There is no other reason it could exist." He hesitated. "I should have asked Ariadne here. Her input would have been valuable, and I will make sure to ask her the next time I get people together to discuss this. Now, Silvius, what I can't make out, nor Noah nor Grace, is how all these separate sections"—he waved a hand over the ten areas they'd mapped out thus far—"connect up. Look"—he leaned over to the hearth and picked up a poker, which he used to trace over the map—"if we extrapolate this group of lines here, and here, then nothing makes sense. If this is some kind of reflection of the Troy Game, which it *must* be, damn it, because nothing else can explain it, then it simply doesn't 'fit' the Troy Game. It is . . ."

"Skew whiff," said Grace, with an apologetic shrug for her unscientific term.

Jack grinned at her, the casualness of which sent a jolt of surprise through Silvius.

"Aye," said Jack. "It is skew whiff."

"And that's why," Noah said, "Jack and I think it is a weakness of the Troy Game. Something has gone wrong with it."

"Do you think that because the Game has been left so long for completion," Silvius said, watching out the corner of his eye as Grace slid back in her chair, once more studying her hands in her lap, "it has . . . warped? Grown thin? Started to deteriorate?"

"Yes!" said Noah. "Jack and I both think that it is a weakness."

"But Grace doesn't think so," said Silvius.

"Grace," said Jack, "believes it is a trap set by Catling. Something designed to fool us." He turned to look at Grace directly. "Grace, I acknowledge your point of view, but Catling's behavior—the fact she hasn't pushed for completion as hard as I expected—indicates some vulnerability."

"The shadow *is* malevolent, Jack," Grace said.

Jack narrowed his eyes, suspecting that Grace kept something from him. He opened his mouth to ask, but she dropped her eyes away from his, and Jack knew Grace well enough by now to know she would not give him an answer.

"Jack?" said Silvius, interrupting Jack's train of thought. "Yes?"

"There is one person we haven't heard from today . . . and I think we need to. Badly."

Jack frowned at his father, then his expression cleared. "Oh. Weyland, do you have any input?"

It was very clear to Silvius that neither Jack nor Noah thought Weyland had anything to say at all. In fact, Noah's expression was so lovingly indulgent it bordered on the condescending.

For the longest moment Silvius thought Weyland wasn't going to speak. Then, staring into the fire, refusing to look at anyone, Weyland finally began talking.

"The imps have been murdering the women to feed the shadow. It feeds from terror and death. The imps work for it, or worship it, I don't know."

"Weyland—" Jack began.

"I watched them," said Weyland, his voice horribly flat. "Several nights ago. Murder a woman by means so slow that she died in degrees in agony and terror. The shadow fed from that terror."

Finally he looked up, the expression in his eyes terrible. "I'm with my daughter. I don't think this shadow is a 'weakness' at all. I think it is something constructed by Catling and designed to trap or destroy us."

There was a lengthy silence following Weyland's words.

"Weyland," Jack said eventually, his voice surprisingly even and calm, "what do you know of the imps? What have they been up to these past few hundred years?"

"I have barely registered them," Weyland said. "I knew they were around the city. Occasionally I could sense them up to some mischief—nothing dramatic, just mischief— but nothing spectacular."

"They're still Catling's instruments?" Jack said.

Weyland gave a small shrug. "So far as I know. They're not *my* instruments. Not any more."

"We need to speak to the imps," said Noah. "Perhaps they can tell us—"

"They're hardly likely to spout forth helpfully," snapped Weyland. "Besides, I *have* been trying to find them for the past few weeks, and it was only because I'd been keeping an eye on St. Magnus the Martyr that I eventually saw them. If the imps don't particularly want to be found, then they won't be."

"Father?" Grace said. "Why St. Magnus the Martyr? Why leave the bodies there?"

Again Weyland shrugged, but his expression softened as he regarded his daughter. "It isn't like the imps to be neat and tidy. There must be a good reason for that church, for its porch, but I don't know what it could be."

"I don't think any of us can know what to imply from what Weyland has told us," said Silvius. "The imps could

be trying to repair a weakness with fresh blood, or they could be strengthening a trap. They could even have sensed the shadow, decided to worship it, and have been offering it some kind of sacrifice."

"Or they could be feeding something monstrous that we have as yet no idea of," said Weyland, his voice hard-edged.

"Or they could be feeding something unknown and monstrous," Silvius agreed. "But unless someone can find the imps, and they actually talk, then we're still in the same dilemma we've been in for months. Only Jack and Grace can discover anything new about this shadow, and that only at a snail's pace. Weyland, can you continue to try to find the imps? Try to discover the reason behind their actions?"

Weyland gave a curt nod.

"Jack," Silvius said, "I don't think you really have any option, unless you want to wait another twenty years until you and Grace have mapped out this shadow in its entirety. You're going to need to probe the shadow. See what happens."

"The Faerie won't survive the twenty or so years it will take for Grace and me to map it entirely," Jack muttered. "Frankly, at the moment I'm almost more scared of the Lord of the Faerie than I am of Catling . . . or of whatever monstrosity that shadow is."

"Besides," said Noah, "too many women are dying."

Jack nodded, his face grim. "We need to move, and we need to do so soon."

"For all the gods' sakes—" Weyland began.

"We'll be careful, Weyland," Jack said. "I promise you."

Weyland looked at Grace, hunched back into her chair, and the expression on his face made tears spring into Silvius' eyes.

No one saw Malcolm at the door, edging back into the shadows.

THE GROUP BROKE UP WITHIN MINUTES, AND while Noah was talking to Jack, Weyland managed a few words with Grace as they waited in the Daimler.

"Grace, are you sure you want to keep on helping Jack? I am terrified for you." Weyland was leaning over the back of the driving seat, looking at Grace seated in the backseat.

"I enjoy helping Jack, father. I know it is risky, and I am careful, but I think I would go mad if I stayed in the apartment."

"I do not know," Weyland said softly, "if I am more afraid of what the imps might do to you, or of what Jack might. Grace, Grace, please be careful."

She shifted forward on the car seat and kissed his cheek softly. "I will be careful."

LATER, WHEN THE OTHERS HAD GONE, SILVIUS SAT back in his chair, his whisky glass refilled, and regarded his son speculatively.

"What do you think about what Weyland said?" he said.

Jack sighed, rubbing tiredly at his eyes. "I don't truly know. I don't doubt what he saw, but there are so many interpretations. God alone knows what those imps may think they are doing. They could just as easily have seen the shadow and decided to worship it, and sacrifice to it. It doesn't mean that the shadow is connected to the murders at all."

"On the other hand . . ."

"On the other hand, if it *is* connected . . ."

Silvius downed his whisky. "Jack, be careful. Not only of the shadow, but of Weyland. Weyland fears for his daughter, and he fears losing Noah. Be careful."

Jack grunted, refilling Silvius' glass.

"Now," said Silvius, "for something a little lighter, if no less worrying for Weyland. What's going on with you and Grace?"

Jack managed an easy grin, which didn't fool his father for an instant. "She's helping me to discover—"

"Don't feed me that line, Jack. Something else is going on. And I'm intrigued about the girl. She's at the center of this puzzle. How is it that she can help you plot out the difference, and not Noah? What's going on?"

Jack sighed. "I don't really know, Silvius. She's . . . I

don't know what to think of her." He paused, thinking, then leaned forward in his chair.

"I should have spoken to you of this earlier," Jack said, "but I thought that perhaps if I could discover more about Grace myself, then . . . Ah, gods, she's such a troubling conundrum. Silvius, I remember you telling me once, and Membricus . . . remember him?"

Silvius nodded. Membricus had been Jack's tutor and lover when he had lived as Brutus and had been involved with Brutus' initial training as a Kingman.

"Well," Jack said, "Membricus also told me that sometimes a Kingman encounters a Mistress whose power precisely fits his. A perfect, harmonious match. A hand-in-glove fit, and whatever other cliché you want to use. A Mistress who would so seamlessly complement his power that whatever Game they danced together would be flawless, more powerful beyond knowing."

Silvius' mouth had dropped open. "You're not telling me that . . ."

"Aye. Grace is my match. Her power, that is. She is my perfect dancing partner."

Her power, that is. As stunned as Silvius was, he couldn't help but wonder why Jack felt the need to add that qualifier.

"Not Noah?" Silvius said.

Jack sat back in his chair, and studied his hands as Grace had studied hers earlier. He did not respond.

Silvius' sense of astonishment deepened. All Jack had ever wanted was Noah. They'd been tied together with such bonds of hate and love, power and ambition, that he could hardly believe now that Jack just sat there and studied his hands indifferently at the question.

"When you returned home from your exile," said Silvius, "you appeared determined to get Noah back. I don't see that man sitting before me now."

Jack took a long time in responding, and when he did his voice was very soft, and he would not look at his father. "I am tired of it," he said. "Tired of loving her and wanting her and never managing to achieve her."

He looked up. "And when I slept with her on the night of the Great Marriage . . . all I felt was disappointment. A wish to be somewhere else. Noah keeps dropping hints, subconscious or not, I am not sure, that if I put a little effort into it, well, then, maybe I might have a chance."

"And you haven't roused yourself for that effort?"

"Catling spoke to me after the Great Marriage," Jack said. "She asked me, and forgive the vulgarism, but I only repeat her words, whether the fuck was worth the wait. And you know what?"

"It wasn't?"

Jack shook his head. "I told Catling that it had been, but, no. It wasn't. Not really. Three thousand years is too long to yearn for someone and never achieve her."

"And especially when that someone has such a lovely, enigmatic daughter. Who is your perfect, harmonious match."

Jack was silent.

"Jack, what's happening here?"

"I don't know."

Silvius doubted that very much. "Grace is very important, isn't she?"

Jack gave a half shrug. "She's at the center of everything. Tied to Catling by hex; my absolute match in power; the only other one besides myself who can prise open the secrets of this shadow hanging over London; beloved of ancient druids—"

"What?"

Jack told his father about Malcolm. "He has an astounding interest in her, but won't tell me why. And . . ."

"And?"

"You know that Noah secreted four of the Kingship bands inside the Faerie?"

"Yes."

"They're not there, Silvius. They never left Grace. They're resting within her flesh."

"Jesus Christ!" Silvius was so shocked his empty whisky glass slipped from his grip and rolled over the carpet.

Jack rose, picked it up, refilled both it and his own, then sat down again, handing Silvius his glass.

"She's an enigma," Jack said with a wry grin.

"Is she dangerous?"

Jack hesitated. "No." He saw his father's raised eyebrow. "I hesitated only because I honestly can't believe she is *not* dangerous, but she isn't. Did you hear that she'd appeared at my marking?"

Silvius nodded.

"Well, I tested her then. My marks, which come from the land itself, examined her, and they found . . ."

Silvius understood what it was Jack wasn't saying. "And they found her instantly"—he paused, wondering how to put it—"compatible?"

"Yes."

Silvius took a hefty sip of his whisky. "Jack, I really don't know how to ask this, or even if I should, but . . . what do you feel for Grace?"

He thought Jack would never answer. Jack sat back in his chair, his eyes on his whisky as he swirled it about his glass.

"Silvius," he said finally, "I don't want to fuck up again. I really don't."

"Are you sure you can break the habit?"

Jack laughed softly. "No, I'm not sure." He sobered. "And thus . . . Christ, Silvius, I don't want to hurt Grace, and I don't want to mess things up any more than I already have, and I don't know if I can bear the pain of loving again. I don't know if I have the *energy* for it."

"And yet she is your perfect, harmonious power match. And she can understand this strange labyrinthine puzzle in a way that Noah can't. *And* she seems to have the bands concealed within her flesh. Jack, does she know they're there?"

"I don't know. It isn't something I've broached with her. I can't believe that *Noah* doesn't know."

Silvius let that last pass. "Jack, I don't think you can risk letting Grace slip away. I also think she's likely a great deal

stronger than you think she is. I also think you're terrified to get too close to her in case you learn to love her."

Silvius thought Jack was already mostly there, but thought it better to carry on the pretense that Jack might actually have some say in whether he tipped over the edge or not.

"Dear God, Silvius, what do I do?"

"Jack, let me give you some advice. You need to make perfectly clear to both Grace and to Noah what you have made clear to me tonight—that Noah is no longer the center and meaning of your existence. Both Grace and her mother need to know that. That doesn't mean committing to Grace—"

Jack grunted.

"It bloody doesn't, Jack. Stop trying to find excuses for procrastination. You need to do it if for the only reason that knowing that is the *only* thing that is going to bring Grace out of her shell. Damn it, from what you've told me and from what I've observed tonight, Grace is so intimidated by your and Noah's history—and, yes, there's jealousy there as well, but that's only a small part of it—that she is never going to *fly*, until she knows there is room in the sky for her."

"You've become quite the lyricist, father."

Silvius grinned. Jack only called him "father" when he was truly annoyed. "You've got to make room in the sky for her, Jack. You're the only one who can do that."

"How? What do you want me to do?"

"Court her, Jack. Over the past three thousand years you've raped and bullied and threatened and taken women. Have you ever taken the time to court one?"

"Matilda—"

"Matilda you just decided you wanted, and she you. I doubt there was any 'courting' involved at all. Courting takes time, Jack. It means that either of you can pull back, think, inch forward again if you want to. It doesn't mean commitment. It just means taking a very close look at it."

"Is that what you're doing with Ariadne?"

Silvius roared with laughter. "We're circling warily, laddie. We're both too jaded for courting."

"As am I."

"No. I don't think you are, and Grace certainly isn't. Try it out, and, who knows, you may enjoy it." He paused. "I also think you'll discover a great deal more about her."

"I don't want to trick her."

"Then don't say or do anything you don't mean, Jack. But I think Grace is the only one who can solve the problem of this shadow labyrinth hanging over London." He grinned. "And don't forget she has four of your Kingship bands embedded in her flesh. She isn't going to give those to you if you're not very, very nice to her."

Jack grunted, and busied himself with his whisky.

"Jack, can I say something else to you? Something about this labyrinthine puzzle? Open your mind, and consider this: what if this shadow is not a weakness, and not even a trap? What if it is something *else*?"

MUCH LATER THAT NIGHT, ALMOST DAWN, THE imps were disturbed from their hiding place in an abandoned warehouse in London's wharf district by a soft call.

"It's *her*!" whispered Bill. "Jim! Jim! It is *her*!"

Jim scrambled to his feet, dusting down his clothes. "Get yourself presentable, man!" he hissed at his brother. "She hates it when—"

"No need for fuss," said the dark-haired woman, walking silently into the little backroom the imps had bedded down in. "I don't stand on ceremony."

The imps both were standing now, hands folded before them, heads hung guiltily.

"Have we done something to offend?" said Jim.

The woman tipped her cold, white face to one side, regarding them. "You mean the murders?" She considered it a moment. "Of course not. It was needed, and I thank you for it. All my plans would have gone awry if you hadn't . . . helped."

The imps beamed.

"But now," the woman continued, "the murders must stop. Weyland has seen you."

"Oh!" cried the imps as one, their faces falling.

"And Weyland has told all his friends," the woman continued. "Malcolm came to me this past night, and told me that Jack wants to speak to you."

"We won't be found," said Bill. "Promise."

"Indeed you won't," said the woman. "I am sure I can find some mischief for you across the Channel. But the murders must stop. It is enough."

"But the dancing needs to feed!" cried Jim.

"And it shall," said the woman. "Tonight it shall have all the food it needs to grow strong and healthy."

"Tonight?" said Bill. "But you told us that—" He broke off, watching his mistress's face. "Oh, it is to begin, then."

Both the imps smiled and, after a moment, so also did the cold-faced woman.

THE NEW DAY DAWNED CLEAR AND BRIGHT, A beautiful early autumn day.

There was little enemy aircraft activity over England during the morning, but in the early afternoon Luftwaffe aircraft, numbering more than a thousand planes in total, formed up over Calais.

In midafternoon, with Reichsmarschall Hermann Göring watching by the seashore, the planes turned for England.

And London.

The bombs first fell in the East End, lighting terrible infernos. Then, as the afternoon and evening wore on, the bombs and fires spread to the central part of the city. The fires lit the way for successive waves of Luftwaffe bombers. Through the night enemy aircraft continued to drop bombs into the massive firestorms raging through London. The city's defenses, faced with their first test, could not cope with the onslaught and the complete chaos on the ground. There were too few firemen and engines for the firestorms, and what effort they could make was compounded by an almost complete failure of the city's water

mains and the thousands of people, covered in blast dust, wandering dazed and shocked through the streets.

When Sunday morning dawned, much of the City and East End lay in ruins, the docks were almost completely destroyed, and over eighteen hundred Londoners were dead or terribly injured. Burned corpses littered the streets or lay dismembered amid the rubble of homes.

In France, Göring gave a triumphant radio address to the Germans, claiming a historic victory for the Fatherland.

The war had come to roost in London.

CATLING RESTED REPLETE DEEP IN THE HEART OF the labyrinth. She had fed well during the day and night, drawing nourishment from the pain and terror that had consumed London.

The German offensive over London had begun, and Catling knew that over the following weeks and months she could grow strong enough to counter whatever Jack and Noah might throw at her.

"Just a few more months," she whispered. "Just a few more months, and then I will be unstoppable."

OVER LONDON, THE SHADOW THROBBED.
It, too, had feasted well.

PART FOUR

MISTRESS OF THE LABYRINTH

London, 1205

THE PHYSICIAN SIGHED, LEANED DOWN, and closed Peter de Colechurch's eyes. The man was in God's hands now, and there was nothing anyone on earth could do for him. The physician stepped back and allowed the brothers of St. Mary Colechurch access to their venerable brother's body, thinking that Peter had lived an exceptional life, and an exceptionally long one at that. It had been a good life, and a good death, and no one could wish for better than that.

The new stone London bridge was almost complete. It would stand as monument to Peter—an elegant and strong series of gothic arches straddling piers built on foundations dug deep into the bed of the Thames. The bridge was the amazement of Europe—it was the longest stone bridge that anyone had ever seen, and everyone commented on Peter's extraordinary engineering skills.

No one else could have designed and built such a bridge. There was only one problem.

Peter had designed and had caused to be constructed a beautiful chapel on the bridge. Situated almost at the center of the bridge, the chapel straddled the ninth pier from the London bank. Dedicated to St. Thomas, the chapel projected almost sixty feet from the side of the bridge, and boasted graceful stained glass gothic windows, and entrances both from the road level on the bridge and from the starling below, so fishermen could tie up and worship when they needed. The best craftsmen had fitted out the interior of the chapel, and it had been dedicated only a few months before Peter's death.

The problem lay in the crypt Peter had insisted be incorporated into St. Thomas' chapel.

In itself the crypt was not unusual—most churches and chapels had them. But St. Thomas' crypt was unusual in two respects.

First, Peter insisted it be dug deep. So deep, in fact, that it lay well under the riverbed. Even though it was underwater, the crypt had been so well constructed that it was utterly watertight. It ran the entire length of the chapel above, had a spectacular fan-vaulted roof, and an altar at the east end.

As a crypt it was one of the best examples in London, and was easily accessible from the chapel above via a twisting stone stairwell in the ninth pier.

But . . . in that "but" lay the second problem. Even though it was bone dry, and even though it was commodious, the crypt was unusable.

There was something wrong with it.

Peter could never sense it, but from the day the crypt was completed, whenever someone else went down there they left almost immediately, complaining of a sense of foreboding so terrible they felt the world was about to end. Some people claimed to have seen a lovely young woman down there, huddled by the altar and weeping inconsolably as if she had been trapped and left to die by those she loved most. Others said the young woman had a terrible aspect, as though she were the most malevolent witch imaginable.

On the day after Peter's death, a workman went down to collect some tools, and never returned.

When his comrades went looking for him, they found him lying dead before the altar.

He had been strangled with a twisted length of red wool, and his face wore an expression of such terror that everyone who saw him instinctively looked over their shoulder as they hurriedly stepped back.

The bridge wardens decided immediately to seal the crypt. What bridge needed a crypt, anyway? Certainly not this bridge, and most certainly not this particular crypt.

Within hours of the decision being taken, stonemasons

were at work sealing the staircase that wound down to the crypt. Once one sealing layer of masonry had been built, the wardens decided to inter Peter de Colechurch in the space before the next layer of masonry went down. It would be a fitting resting place for the man, interred in his beloved bridge, and who knew, perhaps his bones might assuage the anger of whatever malign evil inhabited the crypt.

There was a short religious ceremony held at the site of the internment, and then a full funeral mass held above in St. Thomas' chapel while stonemasons laid down the next layer of masonry.

Once the priests had gone, and before the masons laid down the next coursework, they held a small ceremony of their own. One of them opened a large bag, withdrawing from it several small dead animals, as well as the detached limbs of some larger beasts, all with red wool tied around their legs and claws.

These he placed atop Peter's shrouded corpse, and then on top of the small animals another workman left a charm, given to him by a wise woman.

These added measures, they hoped, would assure that the malignant spirit stayed where she was.

Hours after they left, and when the stairwell was in darkness, the figure of a small girl, black-haired and cold-faced, materialized above the several layers of stonework meant to inter her below. She looked upward, a sneer on her face for the foolish efforts of those who thought to contain her, then she looked down to her feet, as if she could see Peter's corpse beneath the stonework.

Thank you, Peter, *she whispered.* May your journey to the Otherworld be sweet and gentle.

Chapter One

FAERIE HILL MANOR

Sunday, 8 September 1940

THEY GATHERED, WITHOUT SUMMONS, AT
Faerie Hill Manor. No one had slept the night
before, but of them all, Noah and Eaving's Sis-
ters looked the worst. They had spent all of Saturday after-
noon and the entire night in their mobile canteen, traveling
through the City and West End, visiting shelters and, even-
tually, helping transport the shocked survivors of the dev-
astation to relief centers. Matilda, Erith, and Ecub were
disheveled, their faces white under smudges of dirt and
soot, their clothes torn, their hands shaking as they ac-
cepted glasses of whisky or brandy from Stella.

Noah had not seen Weyland since the morning before,
and when she trailed in after Eaving's Sisters, he en-
veloped her into a tight embrace, weeping in relief, sure
he'd lost her the night previously. Noah clung to him as
tightly, then reached out for Grace, who was standing wan-
faced to one side, kissing her cheek before pulling her into
a shared embrace with Weyland.

"I have never imagined such horror," Noah said, her
voice strained and cracking, "Nothing . . . nothing I have
seen . . . ever . . . I can't . . ."

"Weyland, sit her down," Harry said, indicating a sofa.
As soon as Noah had lowered herself, Weyland beside her,

he thrust a glass of warm milk and brandy into her hand. "Drink it, Noah."

Glad to have something to do, Noah raised the glass in trembling hands to her mouth, and sipped at it. "Harry—"

"In a moment," Harry said. "Finish your drink. Let's all just get settled, and then we can talk."

Grace had been left standing in the center of the room when Noah and Weyland had gone to the sofa, and now Jack walked over to her, put a hand under her elbow, and guided her over to another sofa. He hesitated, as if he was going to sit beside her, then walked over to the fire and stood before it, as if he needed to warm himself.

Silvius was also present, as were Malcolm and Ariadne. She and Weyland had glanced at each other, but there had been no other interaction—both were too worried or traumatized to be bothered with hostility.

"Harry?" Jack said. "What has happened in the Faerie overnight?"

Harry and Stella exchanged a glance, and Jack felt his stomach turn over at its bleakness.

Harry flopped down in a chair. He passed a trembling hand over his eyes, and Stella sat down on the arm of the chair, and slid a comforting hand behind his neck.

In the end it was she who responded, not Harry. "Wherever a bomb dropped in London, Jack, so devastation spread over the Faerie. It isn't as bad as here, in the mortal world, but tracks of forested hills have now been left blackened and smoking. We . . . we don't know if they will ever regenerate."

"Christ," Jack muttered.

"The Faerie folk," said Harry, so quietly everyone had to strain to hear him, "were terrified. They sat huddled atop The Naked, crying out every time another section of the Faerie exploded. Gods . . . I had no idea what to say to them."

"It was terrible in London as well," said Noah. She swallowed, taking a moment to collect herself. "It was not just the infernos, and the death and mutilation, the *destruction*. It was the chaos . . . the realization that there was no effectual help, that there was no escape. It was the people, terrified, running hither and thither, scurrying ants in the

shadows cast by the flames, with no idea of where to go, or what to do . . . no idea what the hell was happening. *No one* knew what to do . . . no one expected . . .''

"And the noise," Matilda said as Noah drifted into silence. "The noise. The whine of the bombs falling, the *cruu-uuuump* as they exploded, the blast winds. The screams. The gasps. The sobs. The sound of ripping flesh. Oh gods, and the smell—the stench of burning buildings and people, of high explosive and molten metal. Noah's right. I don't think any of us could have imagined such horror. We had no idea."

"Grace?" Jack said suddenly. "Where were you?"

"In the Savoy's shelter," she said. "I was safe enough."

Jack smiled, relieved, then for the next few minutes they talked about the raid, what they'd seen, and what they'd seen of the devastation in London this morning.

"Did anyone see Catling?" Jack asked.

"I saw her in my bedroom," Grace said "just before I went down to the shelter. She didn't even seem to notice me. She stood at the window and stared outside. Then, just as I was leaving the room, she turned to me, and smiled."

Grace paused. "It was horrific. I have never seen anything so cold."

Jack remembered what Catling had told him—that every death that occurred until the day he and Noah closed out the Troy Game would be on his conscience. Jack didn't feel guilty as such—this was Catling's guilt to bear, not his—but all the same he knew they needed to make faster progress. Find out once and for all if this shadow was a weakness of the Troy Game—or something else.

He looked up toward his father. "You were right," he said. "We need to probe this labyrinthine puzzle and discover once and for all what it is. We need to know if we can use it against Catling, before she murders half of the land."

"Then be careful *you* don't murder half the land with your probing," said Weyland, his voice flat. "I'm with my daughter on this one. I think this shadow is something other than a weakness, and I fear it is more malevolent than you give it credit."

Chapter Two

LONDON

Wednesday, 11 September 1940

"NOAH?"

She'd been helping Matilda and Grace load the mobile canteen in the garage of the Savoy, but turned as Jack walked out of the shadows.

She smiled. "Jack."

Matilda and Grace had stepped down from the back of the van and were standing, watching. Jack nodded to Matilda, giving her a brief smile, then looked at Grace. "I didn't know you were helping your mother, Grace."

"It is better than staying in the apartment at night," she said. Then, for the first time, she spoke to him with her power, sharing what she didn't want to say aloud before her mother, or Matilda. *Don't worry, Jack. The imps won't attack me while I'm with Eaving's Sisters.*

Jack studied her uncertainly. He *was* worried about the imps, but he was also thinking about what his father had said. He wanted to spend more time with Grace, but he simply had no idea how to go about it, or even *if* he wanted to go about it. Every time he saw Grace he worried about what to say, or how to say it, and how either she or he might be hurt by it, and then the moment always passed, and Grace was walking away.

To one side Matilda raised her eyebrows a little, both at what Jack had said and at the way he was standing, looking at Grace, clearly indecisive about something.

Catling won't harm me, said Grace. *She can't. To harm me would be to harm herself.*

He looked at her a moment longer, gave her an irresolute smile, then turned back to Noah. "Noah, will you come with me tonight? I thought . . ."

Noah took a deep breath. "You want to try . . . ?"

"Yes."

Grace went white. "No," she said. "That's too dangerous!"

"Grace," said Jack, "I promise we'll be careful, but we *do* need to do this. We need to probe whatever this labyrinthine puzzle is, or at the very least we need to probe Catling's strength. We *will* be careful, but we can't hang about gathering information piecemeal. Too many people will die."

She stared at him, and turned away.

Jack looked after her, then sighed. "Matilda, can you and Grace cope alone tonight with your canteen? Where are Ecub and Erith—can they help you?"

Matilda nodded. "They're already waiting at the Elephant and Castle for us, Jack." Then, more quietly: "I'll watch out for her, Jack. We'll be fine. But *you* be careful, okay?"

"Okay, Matilda," Jack said. He grinned, gave her a peck on the cheek, and turned back to Noah.

THEY STOOD IN CARTER LANE JUST SOUTH OF THE cathedral. The lane was narrow and bounded by four-story buildings, but even so St. Paul's loomed over them. Even when they kept their heads low, and stood in the shelter of a doorway, they could feel its presence in every sinew of their bodies, and with every breath they took.

They could feel it *calling* to them. It was subtle, but it was unrelenting, and within an hour of coming to stand so close to the cathedral both Jack and Noah were feeling slightly sickened by it.

The labyrinth knew they were close.

They stood in a doorway of a solicitor's office. As doorways went it was reasonably commodious, but its overhang did nothing to impart any sense of safety either from the labyrinth's call or from the terrible menace of the Luftwaffe planes overhead. For four hours they had stood in

this doorway, barely moving, listening as wave after wave of bombers swept over, tensing every time they heard the whistle of bombs falling, jumping at the terrible crump of bombs detonating.

Jack had his arm around Noah's shoulder as she leaned in against him. Apart from the occasional movement they'd been standing almost motionless for the entire four hours.

They'd been immersing themselves in the power of the labyrinth that Brutus and Genvissa had made atop Og's Hill and which now rested deep within the earth beneath St. Paul's.

They were not Jack and Noah so much as Kingman and Mistress of the Labyrinth.

By two A.M. they'd tested the strength of the labyrinth itself, as well as tested their own combined abilities to use it. Additionally, and very, very carefully, they'd been probing at the Troy Game's defenses, trying to identify any chink in its armor.

All without alerting Catling to what they were doing, although both believed she must have known of their presence.

Feel the life of the city, Jack said in Noah's mind.

Aye, she said. *Feel the movement of its peoples, mirroring the winding of the labyrinth. Feel the waters of the Thames, the purr of the traffic, the dreams of the sleepers. Feel the labyrinth, winding its way through everything.*

"Harmonies," Jack whispered, aloud this time. Everything was harmonies, and every overlapping and intertwining layer of harmony increased the power available both to the labyrinth and to Jack and Noah.

Noah closed her eyes, leaning even closer to Jack, feeling the heat of his body through the thick material of his uniform. It felt so good to be here with him like this, in such accord, merging her powers so tightly, so cleanly, with his.

Finally, after so many missteps, so many mistakes, so many long, terrible years . . .

"Jack," she whispered, "can we use the shadow?"

Jack had spent the past hour probing at it with his and Noah's combined power. But whatever he did, he couldn't touch it, couldn't understand it any better, and, if he was

honest with himself, he was slightly relieved about that. Despite being almost certain that the shadow was a reflected weakness of the Troy Game, that "almost" niggled at him. If it wasn't a weakness, and he woke the shadow from its sleep . . . and if it was as malevolent as Grace and Weyland believed . . .

No, that was too awful to contemplate.

No, he replied. *It is closed to us. But if we can use the harmonies to influence one of those bombs to penetrate Catling's defenses, then we will be that little bit surer that the shadow is a reflection of a weakness in the Troy Game itself rather than anything . . . else.*

There was nothing else that it *could* be.

Surely?

"Jack . . ."

"I know," he murmured against her hair. "I am frightened as well."

"If we mishandle this . . ."

"I know." Jack paused. "But we've got to try."

Do we? she wondered, but there was no strength behind that thought, and Jack ignored it.

Can you feel the squadron flying over head now? he said to her. *Feel the plane on the northern flank? Sense the bombs in its belly?*

Aye, she replied.

Do you feel that bomb that lies cradled in the heart of its rack, feel its intent?

Aye. She could feel it as if it were her own child. She knew its history, knew its sorrows, knew its joys.

Do you want me to use my Darkcraft? Noah asked Jack.

He trembled, and she thought he might pull away, but almost immediately he relaxed again. *Will it help?*

Yes.

Then use it.

She reached out and took his hand, squeezing it gently.

Are you ready? he said.

Yes.

Then let us do it, said Jack, and Noah felt his arm tighten around her shoulder, felt his heart begin to race through the

layers of material between them, felt his power surge into her, and embrace hers . . .

And together they wrapped the bomb with harmonies.

GEORGE HEALL, ONE OF THE MEMBERS OF THE cathedral Watch, was sitting on the west steps of the cathedral enjoying a smoke when he suddenly lifted his head, the cigarette frozen halfway to his mouth.

Far above he could hear the whistle of a bomb.

It was strange, because the sound of the planes overhead, combined with the *ack-ack* and the explosions, as well as sirens and the creak and crackle of distant flames, meant that the whistling of bombs should be all but drowned out.

But this one was so clear it could almost be directly—

"*Christ!*" Heall said, tossing his cigarette to one side as he leapt to his feet. He took one step back toward the door into the cathedral when an enormous blast threw him off his feet, and tumbled him down the flight of steps to the pavement.

He managed to stop himself just before he rolled over the side of a massive crater. Heall lay there, fingers gripping the fractured pavement, his body and hair coated with fine blast debris, coughing in the thick dust, and staring deep into the crater where, so he swore later to his wife, he could see the glowing fins of the German bomb embedded in the earth some twelve feet down.

He thought the bomb was still alive, and ticking toward a cataclysmic detonation. He thought he had only seconds to get out of there if he wanted to live.

But still he could not move.

When, three minutes later, eight other members of the cathedral Watch clattered down the steps toward the crater not fifteen feet away, Heall was still lying there, body heaving as he coughed the dust out of his lungs, staring as if transfixed at the bomb.

* * *

AS SOON AS THEY FELT THE BOMB IMPACT JACK and Noah vanished, reappearing a moment later under the stand of trees to one side of Copt Hall.

Both were laughing.

"Why are we laughing," Noah said, "when it didn't go off?"

"It may not have exploded," Jack said, "but if Catling had been as strong as she wants us to believe, the bomb shouldn't have come anywhere near St. Paul's."

"Then the Game *is* weakened?"

Jack sobered. "Yes. I think so. No, I'm *sure* so. There's no other explanation either for the success of our little enterprise tonight or for that echo of the labyrinth about London. That shadowy presence is a reflection of the power of the Troy Game leaching out. It *has* to be."

What *else* could it be?

"Then the Troy Game is vulnerable."

"Yes. *Yes.*"

"Jack, you need your Kingship bands. With those you'll be infinitely more powerful."

He nodded slowly. "The spring equinox will be the best time to hand them over—the equinox is a time of power, and will be a good day to regain the Kingship bands. That isn't far away." He drew in a deep breath. "The Kingship bands. After all these years . . ."

She leaned a little closer to him. "I will fetch them from the Faerie for you."

He stepped back, his face losing much of its animation. "Of course. Soon. At the equinox."

LATER, WHEN NOAH HAD GONE, JACK STOOD UNder the trees staring south toward London, smoking one cigarette after the other. The sky was slowly lightening toward dawn, but still he could hear the sound of aircraft.

It had been a busy night for the Luftwaffe, and it sounded as if they would not let up until full light.

Jack sighed, taking a long draw on his smoke. On one

level the night had been a great success. The Game *was* vulnerable. Why else should he and Noah have been able to direct that bomb in so close?

On the other hand . . .

On the other hand, the night had been greatly unsettling.

Jack had drawn the greater part of his power from the labyrinth, but he felt as if he'd been spiraling power from somewhere else, as well. But from where? Not the forests or the land—the power Jack had used during the night had been pure Kingman power. But not all of it had derived from the labyrinth.

Something else had been feeding his abilities, and Jack had the highly uncomfortable feeling that if it hadn't been for this unknown source of power, he might not have managed as well as he had.

Noah, he was sure, had only drawn power from the labyrinth, and certainly hadn't been aware that Jack had been using power from a different source.

Jack felt as if something had reached out for him, and he had no idea what it was.

The shadow itself? No. No, he was sure of it.

Ah, maybe he'd imagined it.

But then, just as uncomfortable as the sense that he'd used power from another source, was how he'd felt about working with Noah.

It had been the first time that he and Noah had worked together as Kingman and Mistress of the Labyrinth. The first time they had merged and used their powers as a team.

It had gone favorably. They worked together well, their powers were unbelievably complementary, and Noah was powerful beyond anything Jack could have hoped for. They'd enjoyed great success, and had been happy with the result.

But . . .

If it hadn't been for that night when he'd danced with Grace, Jack would have been perfectly happy. If it hadn't been for that night when he'd tested Grace's powers, Jack would have been a content man.

During all his lives, from his time as Brutus to his current

incarnation as Jack Skelton, Jack had danced—or merged his powers—with three Mistresses of the Labyrinth.

Genvissa, Grace, and now Noah.

Genvissa he'd thought was wonderful when he was Brutus, but she was only a shadow compared to Grace and Noah.

Noah was the most powerful of all three, bringing behind her as she did not only the arts of the labyrinth, but those of Eaving and her abilities as a Darkwitch as well.

But Grace. Stronger than Genvissa, but weaker than Noah, Grace's abilities had, nonetheless, matched so flawlessly with his that, even given Noah's spectacular power, she simply could not compete with her daughter.

Not when it came to what Jack *wanted*.

As a Kingman, Jack longed for Grace. No other Mistress of the Labyrinth would ever do for him. Having tasted Grace, any other Mistress of the Labyrinth, even Noah, would only ever be a disappointment.

Yet there was no way Grace could possibly aid him either to destroy the Troy Game, or to complete it. She was so closely tied to the Game through Catling's hex that its fate was hers . . . she simply could not, under any circumstance, partner him in its destruction or completion.

But, oh God, as a Kingman he wanted her to partner him, so badly . . .

And as a man?

At that point Jack imagined he could hear Silvius' lightly mocking laughter.

"Jesus *Christ!*" he muttered, grinding out the cigarette under the heel of his shoe.

Then he looked south once more, this time directing his attention toward Kensington, where he sensed the object of his interest.

Ariadne, breakfast with me, if you please.

Chapter Three

COPT HALL

Thursday, 12 September 1940

ARIADNE WAS FLIRTING WITH MALCOLM, WHO was responding in kind quite outrageously, and Jack felt his temper simmering so close to the surface that he thought that if Ariadne simpered *one single more time* in Malcolm's direction he would pick one or both of them up and toss them outside.

"Jack," Ariadne said from her seat on the sofa, smoothing her dress down over her knees and dragging her eyes away from Malcolm, who hovered close by with a coffeepot in his hands. "I'm annoying you. I do apologize."

Jack contented himself with a hard look at Malcolm, who took the hint and retreated into the kitchen.

"But," Ariadne continued, her mouth curving in humor, "I find myself so thrilled at the idea of being wanted, of being *useful,* that I—"

"Cut it out, Ariadne." Jack had been standing by the fireplace. Now he sat down in a chair, setting his empty coffee cup to one side, and looked Ariadne over.

As ever, she looked both stunningly beautiful and dangerously poisonous, and Jack had to admit a moment's admiration for his father if he was actually engaged in a romance with this witch. The dress she wore was similar in cut and color to the scarlet dress she'd worn when he'd seen her at Faerie Hill Manor; close cut, hugging every curve, inviting and threatening all in one.

"I want to talk to you about Grace," he said.

Ariadne inclined her head, only her dark eyes showing

the faintest touch of wariness. "A delightful girl," she said. "Noah and Weyland must be so proud of her."

"She has been trained as a Mistress of the Labyrinth."

"Indeed." Ariadne paused to light a cigarette. "Stella trained her."

"A poor choice, given that either you or Noah could have done far better."

Ariadne shrugged. "But she chose Stella."

"You did not think to—"

"I was not asked."

Jack lit up a cigarette as well, using the action to think. "I have heard that during the Great Fire, when Catling had trapped Noah and Weyland in the heart of the labyrinth, you instructed Grace when she walked through the fire to rescue them."

"I may have done."

"Did you or did you not?"

"Yes, I did. For God's sake, Jack, where is this inquisition leading?"

"How powerful was she, Ariadne? How much potential did Grace have?"

Ariadne smoked her cigarette, studying Jack through narrowed eyes. *Well, well.*

"She had—*has*—enormous potential," she eventually said.

"As much as you?"

Ariadne thought about it. "More. Grace has a very powerful mother—Noah is Mistress, goddess, and Darkwitch—and Grace was conceived and grew in Noah's body during the time that Noah trained as a Mistress." She paused. "Rather, Grace grew in Noah's womb during the time that Noah opened herself up to the arts of the labyrinth—and Grace was an aware child. What Noah absorbed, so also did Grace. As well, her father—who is also her forefather—was the monster at the dark heart of the labyrinth, and, as you well know, she is twice bred with Darkcraft in her veins. All this means she has the potential to be"—she smiled, the expression that of a striking

falcon—"a very dangerous Mistress of the Labyrinth indeed."

"As powerful as Noah?" Jack said.

"Is that what you want, Jack?"

"Just answer my question, if you please."

Temper, temper, thought Ariadne. "Considering Grace's heritage, her parents, and the influences that shaped her in the womb, she could probably be Noah's equal, although she would not be able to bring in the powers that Noah controls as Eaving. More than that? I don't know."

"I tested her some time ago. She has potential, yes, but at the moment Grace is very weak."

"'She has potential,'" Ariadne repeated. "That's not quite what Silvius told me you'd said."

Jack froze in the act of lifting the cigarette to his mouth. *Silvius had repeated his conversation to Ariadne?*

"No need to be cross, Jack. It was pillow talk only." She grinned, and quoted the message emblazoned across countless posters on streets and in the Underground. "Loose lips . . . never know who's listening . . . careless talk costs lives, and all that. Look, calm down. He's told no one else."

Jack gave a short, humorless laugh. "No one else, but look who he *has* told."

"And I have told no one. So get to the point, Jack. Whatever power Grace has, and whatever strength it may one day obtain, she is your flawless match. Good for you. So why am I here?"

"Can you train her—"

"She's been trained."

"Then can you *deepen* that training, God damn it! Can you give her experience? Can you take whatever shitty job Stella did and—"

Ariadne burst into laughter. "I like Grace. She intrigues me, and not many people manage that feat. Yes, I can do that for you, although she'll have to agree."

Jack tipped his head as if he thought that was a foregone conclusion.

"What do you want her trained for, Jack?"

Jack took a long draw on his cigarette, then slowly ex-

haled the smoke. "Can I assume that Silvius passed on most of that conversation we had?"

"Probably, but you never know if he left something out."

"Grace carries four of the Kingship bands within her flesh."

"Yes. He told me that. But I already suspected something of it, anyway."

"Of course. Then you should know what I need Grace trained for."

"She needs to know how to hand the bands over to you."

"And you can be sure that was likely a piece of her training Stella left out. Damn it, Ariadne, why has neither Noah nor Stella, who took Grace through the Great Founding Labyrinth, not realized she has the bands within her?"

"Because most people are blind when it comes to Grace. Tell me, Jack, have you told Noah about the bands?"

Jack shook his head, drawing slowly on his cigarette.

"My goodness," said Ariadne. "Then she still assumes *she's* going to be the one to 'fetch' the bands for you? Yes?" Ariadne burst out laughing. "What will Noah do when she finds out, eh?"

He shrugged. "It won't be the end of the world for her. Besides, she has no choice."

"I always thought you would turn out okay, Jack."

"We don't have long. Can you get Grace ready in time?"

"Yes. I like a challenge. But we need to start soon."

"Meet me at dusk tonight." He named a place.

"I can be there. Jack, you need to tell Grace about the Kingship bands, if not Noah. Grace *has* to know, if she doesn't already."

"I'll do it tonight," Jack said. "There's one other thing."

"Yes?"

"You've been hanging about London creating mischief and having a fine time of it for three hundred years now. You must know the place inside and out. Can you give me the name of a good jeweler?"

"Of course," she said. "I have just the man for you."

Chapter Four

LAMBETH

Thursday, 12 September 1940

Grace Speaks

THERE WAS A BOMB. OUTSIDE ST. PAUL'S. A UXB. It fell early in the morning, blowing a huge crater just outside the west steps of the cathedral, and then, happily, failed to detonate.

It created a nightmare for the authorities. How to get it out without blowing half of St. Paul's to smithereens? Eventually a Lieutenant Davies tied the tail fins of the bomb to the back of a lorry, dragged it fifteen feet out of the crater and into the tray of the lorry, and then drove it to a tip outside of London where it was safely detonated.

His courage and selflessness so impressed the king that shortly afterward he announced he'd created the George Cross for acts of extreme bravery.

If only my worries could have been eased so efficiently as that bomb had been disposed of. I'd spent the night worrying, sure that Jack and my mother were about to bring the shadow bearing down on us all. I kept remembering the feeling of the shadow rushing toward me, as if it were about to eat me, and knew that not only was it not a reflection of Catling's weakness, it wasn't the slightest bit a weakness of *anything*. My relief when we got through the night without the world ending was immeasurable, but I wondered what consequences would flow on from that bomb hurled at Catling's throat.

My mother came back from that night's excursion eyes a-gleaming. She told me and my father what had hap-

pened, what it felt like blending her powers with those of Jack's, their excitement as they managed to direct the bomb down to St. Paul's.

"Of course, it missed, but only barely, and it didn't explode," she said, "but we managed it . . . and we shouldn't have been able to! Grace, I know that you're afraid that this strange shadowy labyrinthine puzzle is Catling's trap, but Jack and I are now convinced it is a reflection of some inherent weakness within the Game."

I glanced at my father as she said this, wondering how he was taking all this Jack-inspired enthusiasm.

He had his face closed over, but this was so much a part of his normal wariness I simply couldn't read him.

"Catling hasn't done anything," said my mother, still looking at me. "She hasn't reacted. *Surely,* sweetheart, this indicates a weakness on her part?"

I thought back to last night. I'd spent it with Matilda, Ecub, and Erith, doling out cups of tea and chocolate and ladles of sympathy for people cramped into shelters in the Southwark area.

I'd seen Catling. Just once, and that briefly, but enough to send a chill down my spine. We'd pulled into the lee of a building by the entrance to a shelter. Eaving's Sisters had all hurried about to the back of the van to unload their trolleys and trays, but I'd been distracted by a run in one of my stockings, and had paused by the open van door. Standing upright I'd slammed shut the door . . . and found myself looking directly into Catling's face as she stood in front of the van.

I went cold. I wanted to run, but didn't have either the will or the strength.

Jack is doing well tonight, she'd whispered in my mind, her face a mixture of excitement and anticipation, *although both of you still have a way to go.*

Then she'd vanished.

What had she meant by that? I spent the rest of the night sorting through various translations, and liking none of them. If nothing else, it didn't sound like a "weak" Catling.

Now, as my mother explained that now she and Jack were *certain* this shadow was a weakness, I began to doubt

myself. Maybe I had been wrong. Maybe I had misread Catling for all these years. Maybe . . .

"Grace?" my mother said. "Surely you're coming around to thinking it is a weakness? After Jack's and my success last night?"

"Perhaps," I said to my mother, mainly to stop her arguing with me, and she smiled, patently relieved.

"We'll be careful," she said, and I nodded, and that was enough for her.

She turned to my father then. "Soon I'll fetch Jack's Kingship bands from the Faerie," she said.

"Well," Weyland said, "Jack's welcome to them. And the other two? The ones you sent into the Otherworld?"

Noah shrugged. "Either the Lord of the Faerie can take him through, or Jack, like as not, will be powerful enough with four in his possession to get them himself." She smiled. "Soon, surely, we can start to make a move."

She reached forward over the table, and took one of my hands in hers. She turned it over, and her thumb stroked very gently at the scars and welts on my wrist.

"Soon, Grace, perhaps you will be free."

I didn't say anything, for the simple reason that I simply could not imagine freedom.

LATER THAT DAY JACK TELEPHONED.

"Grace," he said, "can you meet me at five this afternoon?"

"Why?"

"I need your help. Can you meet me the Surrey side of Westminster Bridge at five?"

"Yes, but—"

"Good, see you then." He rang off.

I put the phone down and spent the rest of the afternoon wondering.

AT FIVE TO FIVE I WALKED ACROSS THE NORTHERN side of Westminster Bridge. I tried to slow my steps, tried to while away those five minutes so that at least I'd arrive

on time and not too early, but by the time I had a clear view of the end of the bridge I could see that Jack was already there.

It was a cold, blustery day, skittering rain every five minutes, and he was well wrapped in a military greatcoat, its collar turned up, his cap pulled down over his brow, his hands thrust deep into the coat pockets. I guess I looked much the same, closely swathed in a calf-length camel coat, a scarf about my neck, but without the cap—a lack I'd been regretting ever since I left the Savoy as the wind snapped my curls back and forth over my face.

"Grace," he said. His face and the collar and shoulders of his coat glistened with raindrops, but he smiled easily, and leaned forward to brush his lips against my cheek as I walked up to him.

"I'm glad to see you well," I said. "After last night."

"I know you were worried, Grace, but—"

"I saw Catling last night."

Jack went very still. "And?"

"She seemed to know what you and my mother were doing, Jack, and she wasn't worried. She said that you were doing very well, but that both of us had a way to go. She didn't appear *weak*, Jack."

Jack stood silently, looking at me.

As always, I responded to his silent scrutiny by talking too much. "I was so worried for you last night. On—" *Damn it, why couldn't I keep my mouth shut?* "On the night the imps attacked me, I felt the shadow rushing toward me, as if it was going to snatch. It was so malevolent, so alive . . . and I thought that it might attack you and my mother . . ."

"Oh God, Grace. Why didn't you tell me this earlier?"

"You don't want to hear anything save that the shadow is a weakness of the Troy Game, Jack."

"Ouch. I suppose I deserved that. But, oh, Grace, I wish you'd told me . . ."

He sighed then. "I'm sorry, Grace. I wish . . . I wish you could trust me more, and that's not your fault, but mine."

I was starting to feel very uncomfortable, and I wished

I'd never opened my mouth. "Why did you want to see me tonight?"

He gave a funny little smile. "I can see I am going to have to work hard to retrieve the situation. I want to talk to you about something, but not here, not on this bridge. Will you stroll with me a little way?"

He gave me no chance to answer, but slid an arm through mine and guided me down the steps which led to the pedestrian subway under the bridge and onto Lambeth Embankment.

We walked in silence for some time, my mind churning. I always felt guilty when someone said they wanted to talk to me, and at the same time hated it that I did feel guilty. I wished I could be more confident, more like my mother, or Matilda, or even Ecub. Jack must find me so tiresome. I wished that I had told him earlier about my sense of the shadow rushing in toward me. He wouldn't think so poorly of me if I'd told him sooner.

We were walking along that part of the embankment directly opposite the Houses of Parliament by this point when the wind suddenly gusted. I had to pull my arm away from his to get my hair out of my eyes, and he stopped, turned to me, and slid both his hands about my face, holding my hair back for me.

I started to pull back, but his hands tightened.

"Don't move," he said. "Please . . ."

His face went very still, and his dark eyes became far keener than usual. I trembled, for I felt the marks over his shoulders start to move, sliding down his arms.

I shivered as they flowed over his fingers onto my face.

"There has been something troubling me about you ever since I first met you," he said.

I tensed, and knew he could feel it under his hands.

"I've never been able to read you," he said. "I've never been able to understand you."

I tried to pull away again, and again his hands tightened.

"Please don't be afraid of me," he whispered, and the touch of his hands became infinitely gentle.

"It took me a while to realize that this didn't have any-

thing to do with you, but with me," he continued. "I thought you were the shuttered one, but *I* had been." His voice became teasing. "I hate it when I realize I've been an idiot."

He was being too kind, and I was sure it was because he was about to tell me that he and my mother had decided to abandon all caution and renew their love affair. "Jack—"

"Do you remember," he said, "what I said to you atop Ambersbury Banks?"

"You said many things."

"The night you watched me being marked. I said you were either the most shuttered person I'd ever met, or the most transparent. I'd almost got it with the transparent, but not quite. Grace, you're the most extraordinary person. You have no artifice about you. Absolutely none. I've *never* met anyone, *no one,* in all my time on this earth like you. You have nothing to hide. You don't even try."

The marks were moving slowly about my face now, so soft, so caressing, and I think that I could not have moved had Hitler personally leaped up from behind the embankment wall and thrown a hand grenade or two in our direction.

"I didn't trust that at first," Jack continued. "I couldn't believe it. Surely everyone has something to hide. Some artifice needed to promote their own agenda. But you don't." His thumbs were stroking very slowly against my cheeks. "You don't. You're . . ." he paused, seemingly trying to find the right words. "You're as clear and as pure as the peal of a temple bell through a snowy night."

He stopped, giving a half embarrassed laugh. "Now I'm getting as lyrical as my father."

I didn't understand that last (and, in truth, I was having some difficulty with the rest of it, as well), and he laughed again, more confidently this time.

"See?" he said. "Your confusion is written all over your face. Everything is written all over your face. You let it shine forth."

"I thought you were angry at me," I said.

"I'm not angry," Jack said. "I know why you didn't tell me about the shadow."

He smiled a little then, his fingers moving very gently

against my face. I didn't know what he wanted, or where this was going, and, oh God, if what he was saying was true then surely he could read this all over my face.

His smile broadened, just very slightly, then I felt the touch of the marks withdraw, and a moment later that of Jack's hands. He slid his arm back through mine, and we resumed walking along Lambeth Embankment toward Lambeth Palace, the ancient stronghold of the archbishops of Canterbury.

My thoughts were so confused I felt numbed. For the past months Jack had been friendly, but somehow distant. Now all that distance had gone. In fact, Jack seemed hell bent on closing it as fast as he could.

"On the night of the parish dance," he said, "I said that Noah was not my life. I meant it, Grace."

I couldn't understand what he was saying.

Surely he really meant that—

"I'm tired of loving her, Grace. I can't be bothered any more."

I blinked. I had heard the words, but wasn't sure I had actually understood them.

"That sounds pretty damned selfish and self-centered, doesn't it?" Jack went on. "But during the night of the Great Marriage, Grace, I discovered that I'd been yearning for a dream . . . and it wasn't your mother." He paused again, while I concentrated very hard on my breathing. For some reason it didn't seem to be coming and going as easily as it should.

"Can I tell you a home truth?" he continued. "It was a relief to leave Noah the morning after the Great Marriage. That night was an ending for us, Grace. It wasn't a beginning or a promise or anything else. It was an ending. A completion."

"I don't think it was for my mother."

"Ah." We walked in silence for a while. I wished I knew where Jack was going with this conversation.

"That sense of ending was underscored last night, Grace," Jack said, neatly evading the implications of my statement. "Noah and I matched powers beautifully . . . but it was as nothing to what I felt with you."

"But . . . but . . . Jack. Stop. Please. I don't understand why you're telling me this."

"Because you needed, and deserved, to know how I felt about Noah. You also need to know how I feel about you."

I stopped, staring at him.

"I am both fascinated and terrified by you, Grace." He gave a small, lopsided grin. "Much, as I suspect, you feel about me."

I couldn't breathe now. Not at all.

"Recently my father gave me a bit of advice."

Finally I managed to take a breath, but was somewhat dismayed to find I couldn't look at Jack. I was instead sliding my eyes up and down the Thames as if I expected to see the first wave of German invaders at any moment.

God knows what he must have thought.

"He said I should get to know you better," Jack continued.

"Why should he say that?" My voice squeaked at the end of that sentence. I couldn't believe it.

Jack reached out a hand and took one of mine, pulling it close to his chest.

"Because we dance together so well. Because we're the only ones who can work out this shadow. And because you are . . . so . . . damn . . . beautiful."

At that my breathing gave out completely.

Jack gave a funny little smile, and squeezed my hand very slightly. "And because you have something I want very, very badly. And of all these things, Grace, even I don't know which is the most important to me. I suspect it might be the third thing I mentioned, but I need to be sure. Okay?"

"Okay." I wasn't sure what he wanted me to agree to, but I seemed to say what he wanted.

"Good." He gave my hand one more squeeze, then let it go. Again he slid his arm through mine, and again we resumed walking along Lambeth Embankment.

Everything was taking on a slightly surreal quality. I was aware that it was misting rain, and that it was very cold. I was aware of the occasional barge that puttered up the river, and of the birds that lifted off the embankment walls as we passed.

But none of it seemed real.

I wanted to believe that Jack had just said those words to me, but I couldn't quite manage it.

"Silvius made one other suggestion to me," Jack said as we walked past Lambeth Palace.

"Yes?"

I saw him smile from the corner of my eye.

"He suggested I hand you the sky, Grace."

AFTER THAT STRANGE LITTLE STATEMENT THERE was nothing said for a little while. At the end of Lambeth Palace we turned east away from the river toward the little church of St. Mary-at-Lambeth that crowded against the palace's southern wall.

I thought we were to go inside the church, but Jack led me toward the gate in the dilapidated paling fence that encircled the churchyard.

"Why—" I began.

"Wait," he said, leading me into the graveyard.

The wind continued to blow icy and uncomfortable, but the rain had dissipated. Even so, the graveyard of St. Mary's was a singularly cheerless place. It was unkempt, roses and weeds competing for space between dirty, leaning headstones, while broken shards of headstones past had been used to make an uneven path which wound through the graves and around the church.

"Jack?" I murmured.

He didn't answer, merely leading me farther along the path until we had come to the back of the church. Here there were several large tombs, and we wandered past them.

I pulled Jack to a halt at one.

"Captain William Bligh," I said. "This seems such a sedate home for him."

"Far from the wind-tossed mutinous seas," Jack murmured, and led me to the next tomb.

This one made me shiver, for it was decorated in part with verdant trees and acorns, and in part with a multi-snake-headed monster writhing triumphant over a skull.

"It is the tomb of the two John Tradescants," Jack said.

"And they were . . . ?"

"Famed gardeners of the late sixteenth and early seventeenth centuries," Jack said. "Many of the plants now so beloved of English cottage gardeners were originally imported by the Tradescants."

"Why are you showing me this, Jack?"

He didn't immediately respond, reaching out with one hand to run his fingers over the carved flowers on the Tradescant men's tomb. "Look at this," he said, his fingers now running over the snake-headed monster. "Amid the flowers, the monster."

I was feeling more unsettled than ever. "Jack?"

"It reminds me of the Flower Gate," he said, glancing at me. "You know what that is?"

"Of course. Catling needs you and Noah to dance the Flower Gate enchantment which will finally complete the Troy Game."

He grimaced, lifting his hand away from the tomb. "Amid the flowers, the monster," he repeated.

It was now starting to grow dark, and colder with every passing moment. *What in God's name was Jack up to?*

He looked at me directly. "Could you dance the Flower Gate into existence, if I asked, Grace?"

The world stopped around me. I don't think I even breathed for a very long minute. "I can't do that."

"Can't? Or won't?"

"Can't *and* won't, Jack. I'm just not good enough. And, for God's sake, you have my mother. *She's* the powerful one! I can't do it! Dear God . . . not the Troy Game. No. I can't. I'm bound to Catling, and I can't—"

He pressed his hand against my mouth, stopping the flow of my fear.

"If I handed you the sky, Grace, would you dare to fly?"

What was he suggesting?

"Grace, if I asked you to deepen your training and experience in the labyrinth, would you do it for me?"

He finally removed his hand, and I could speak. "Why? I mean, why would you want me to do that? I can't—"

He made an exasperated sound. "Jesus Christ, Grace. You could dance both Ariadne and Stella into the dust, if you so desired, and I suspect your mother also. I want you to fly, just for the sheer beauty of it, and because I think you're going to be so damned, cursed useful that—"

He stopped, looking away, a muscle moving slightly in his jaw.

Then he turned back to me, took my hands in his, and slid his hands up my arms, rucking up my coat sleeves.

"Grace, there is something I suspect you are not truly aware of." His fingers were running up and down each of my forearms, and now they halted just above my elbows. "Don't you know what you have? Don't you know what you hide?"

I frowned at him. The wind was frigid now, and the churchyard dark, and all I wanted was to get back to the Savoy and think over everything he had said, search out every hidden meaning, discover what he might have—

"Grace, within the flesh of your upper and forearms, you carry four of the golden Kingship bands of Troy. Did you not know that?"

I shook my head slowly, not believing, not even understanding, what he had just said. "Those bands are in the Faerie."

"No. Those bands are in you."

"No."

"Yes," said another voice.

I gave a low cry, and spun about—or so far as Jack's grip would allow me.

Ariadne stepped into view. She was closely bundled in a fur coat and with a silk scarf over her carefully coiffed hair. "You wore the bands as ribbons into the Faerie," she said.

"Yes," I said, "but then . . ."

But then what? I couldn't remember. I was a very aware baby, and I remember when my parents met with the Lord of the Faerie on London Bridge, and my mother handed over to the Lord of the Faerie the four Kingship bands of Troy that she possessed. Then . . . the Lord of the Faerie, I think, had turned them into ribbons about my limbs, and then he'd taken me into the Faerie . . . but then, then every-

thing had collapsed, Catling had caught my parents during the Great Fire, pulled them into the dark heart of the labyrinth, tortured them, tortured me when I went to save them . . .

What had become of the bands?

"They never left you, Grace," Jack said gently. "Don't you feel them?"

For the moment the idea that I held four of the golden Kingship bands of Troy within my flesh was too much to even start to comprehend, so I concentrated instead of Jack's request for me to deepen my training in the arts of the labyrinth. "So that's why you want me to learn greater skills with the labyrinth," I said. "You need the bands back."

"I want a great deal more from you than those four bands, Grace," Jack replied gravely.

"Oh, for goodness sake," Ariadne said. "Stop doubting yourself. The bands didn't just 'forget to leave.' They picked you to hand them back to Jack. They've been match-making. None of this is a mistake, or an error, or something we'll all regret horribly in the morning. Just say you'll come train with me, Grace, and let me get out of this Godforsaken graveyard before I freeze to death."

I gave a little smile. "Does Catling know about the bands? Is that why she's been sitting with me all these years?"

"Catling thinks they are in the Faerie," Jack said. "I don't think she has any idea they never left you." He gave a slow smile. "Imagine, something she *doesn't* know."

I laughed. Just a little bit, but I laughed. He was teasing me gently, knowing that I'd think he'd use Catling's misconception as further indication of her weakness.

"All right," I said. I looked at Ariadne, and for the first time in centuries remembered what it had felt like when she had talked me through what I had needed to do when St. Paul's burned down in 1666. The power, the strength, the sense that, both literally and metaphorically, I did not walk alone. "If Ariadne agrees to deepen my training, then I'm willing."

Jack grinned and Ariadne laughed, clapping her hands.

"Come with me tonight, then," she said, "and let me drag you down into darkness!"

"You have such a way with words, Grannie Ariadne," I said, "but I'd prefer to leave it until tomorrow when I've had time to have a bath and warm up."

SO THERE IT WAS. JACK WANTED TO "GET TO KNOW me better" having declared he found my mother "not quite what he was after," and Ariadne was going to deepen my training in the arts of the labyrinth.

I went back to the Savoy that night very, very happy. Overall I felt useful, but I also felt wanted.

I felt *valued*. Not just by Jack, but by the Kingship bands as well.

I sat in the bath that night, and ran my hands slowly up and down my arms. Jack had told me that though the ribbons had appeared on all my limbs, because the four bands Noah had handed over to the Lord of the Faerie had been the four armbands, then the bands were buried in the flesh of my arms, above and below my elbows.

I pressed against the flesh, and imagined I could feel them. *I was the one to hand them back to Jack.*

Once I would have worried about that. Worried that somehow I'd mess it up, or worried that somehow I'd corrupt the ritual because of my ties to Catling.

But I didn't worry about any of that. All I felt was a growing excitement.

And all I saw, as I sat there in the warm water, running my hands slowly up and down my arms, was Jack's face as he said to me, *You are . . . so . . . damn . . . beautiful.*

Chapter Five

COPT HALL

Friday, 13 September 1940

*J*ACK HAD LEAPT FAR OUT INTO THE DARK, dark unknown that afternoon and evening, risking much of himself and all he hoped to achieve. Despite this, all he could feel on his return to Copt Hall that night was a great relief and a growing kernel of excitement deep within his being. What he was doing was a massive risk, affecting not merely himself, but this entire land and all who lived in it, but at least he had a direction and, for once, it felt as if he'd made a good decision.

And so much of it depended on Grace.

Jack sat in the kitchen of Copt Hall, finishing a plateful of food. He couldn't get the image of the temple bell on the dark snowy night out of his head. It was an image that combined terrible fragility and stunning strength, and Jack thought it probably described Grace as well as anything.

But which would dominate? The fragility, or the strength?

"Major?"

Jack looked up. Malcolm was standing before the table, holding a delicate plate filled with sponge cakes.

"No, thank you," Jack said, and stood up. "I'll turn in for the night, I think."

He left the room, Malcolm grinning at his departing back.

THAT NIGHT JACK DREAMED. HE DREAMED HE stood in the middle of London Bridge, Catling standing before him.

The Great Marriage was well done, said Catling, *but you need to know that the greatest marriage you can ever make is in my dark heart.*

And then she was gone.

When Jack woke the next morning it was to find himself in a state of painful arousal coupled with a deep bitter anger that Catling should have so spoiled his memory of the day.

THAT DAY GRACE MOVED OUT OF HER PARENTS' apartment in the Savoy.

"Ariadne has asked me to come live with her for a little while," she explained to her dumbfounded parents.

"I'm sorry," she added.

Noah and Weyland exchanged a glance, and Grace could see a world of anxiety in that look.

Noah looked back at her daughter. "Why?" she asked.

"Ariadne has offered to teach me a little more of what she knows about the art and craft of the labyrinth," Grace said.

"I could teach you that," said Noah.

Grace looked deeply uncomfortable. "I know. It's just that Ariadne asked me last night, and I—"

"Don't apologize," said Noah. "I could have offered myself, and didn't." She smiled. "Ariadne is a taxing teacher, Grace, but she will teach well."

Weyland grunted. "All the art and craft *she* knows is that of murder," he said. Then he sighed, and apologized. "I just don't understand why you'd want to leave us."

Grace gave a quirky smile. "It is time I left home. Three hundred years is too long."

Noah laughed. "Aye, that it is," she said. "Will we still see you on the canteen run, Grace?"

"I don't see why not. Some nights, anyway."

"Then from where shall we pick you up? Does Ariadne still reside in the Tower?"

"No. She has a flat in Kensington, off Cromwell Road." Grace gave Noah the address. "Mother . . ."

Suddenly Noah wanted to stop whatever Grace might have been about to say. She leaned forward and hugged

Grace to her. "And when you tire of Ariadne's archness, my darling, remember there's a home for you here."

"What's happening, Noah?" Weyland said as Grace retired to her room to pack.

"I don't know," she replied. "I don't know." She shivered, and wrapped her arms about herself.

WEYLAND DROVE GRACE TO ARIADNE'S APART-ment later that afternoon. He felt he had to face Ariadne, to impress on her that Grace was everything to him and that if she harmed her, or allowed harm to touch her . . .

He'd also been ruminating on what Silvius had said, that he needed to put his animosity toward Ariadne aside. Until recently Weyland had not set eyes on Ariadne for over three and a half thousand years, not since that day she'd inveigled his return from the halls of the dead in order to bargain her share of the Darkcraft. In his mind she'd assumed almost mythical proportions—the great black witch committed always, totally, to his destruction.

And now she was taking his daughter.

"Gods, Grace," he muttered as they rang the doorbell to her apartment. "Be careful."

Grace turned to him, tears in her eyes, and gave him a brief hug. She opened her mouth to speak, but just then the door opened.

Ariadne stood there, dressed in her usual scarlet, a cigarette in one hand, and an expression of, unusually for her, some trepidation on her face.

She and Weyland stared at each other for a long moment.

"It's been a long time," she said.

"It's been a hellish time," Weyland said, and Ariadne's mouth twitched.

"I'll take care of her, Asterion."

"Be sure that you do."

Silence. They didn't look away from each other, nor did they blink.

Then Weyland gave a funny little laugh. "I can't believe I'm allowing you to take my daughter," he said, then he

turned and walked back down the stairs to the building's foyer.

"So much wasted," Ariadne said softly, watching him.

"What do you mean?" Grace said.

"He and I . . . everything. So much hatred, so much ambition. So much wasted time when we could have had . . ." She broke off, then shrugged. "I'm getting maudlin in my old age, my dear. Now come in, why don't you."

As Ariadne stepped back, Grace lifted her suitcase and walked in the door.

Straight into the swirling maelstrom of the Great Founding Labyrinth.

Chapter Six

KENSINGTON

Friday, 13 September, to Monday, 16 September 1940

ARIADNE REALIZED SHE HAD MADE TWO GIgantic errors of judgment the instant the front door closed behind them.

The first error of judgment was that Ariadne had assumed that even though Stella may not have been the most powerful person to teach Grace the intricacies of the labyrinth, she had at least done a competent job.

The second error was that Ariadne had assumed the very worst mistake she'd ever made was when she'd pledged Asterion her soul, and that of her daughter-heirs, if ever she tried to restart the Game.

In fact, Ariadne realized very suddenly, and very horrifically, by far the worst mistake of her life was propelling Grace directly into the Great Founding Labyrinth when in fact she wasn't able to cope with it.

Damn Stella to all hells for not training the girl properly!

As the door closed behind them, Grace crumpled over, dropping her suitcase, a low moan of agony escaping her mouth.

For one sickening, heart-stopping moment, Ariadne thought the Great Founding Labyrinth was going to kill Grace.

But Grace should have endured this when she went through her Great Ordeal! She should be able to cope!

Ariadne cried out, one hand reaching for Grace, the other fumbling for the door as if she thought she could drag Grace back out.

But the Great Founding Labyrinth would not allow her to go now, not when it had her in its maw.

Oh why, why hadn't she thought that Grace might not be able to cope?

Because she'd assumed—big, big mistake, the worst of her life—that Stella had trained Grace *well,* if not brilliantly.

But then Grace twisted around, and Ariadne saw that her wrists were crossed before her, and that wires of glowing red encircled them.

Catling had attacked the instant she felt Grace walk into the Great Founding Labyrinth.

Ariadne abandoned her attempt to open the door, and instead grabbed at Grace's shoulder. "Use the pain, Grace. *Use* it to concentrate your mind and power!"

It was a struggle, but Ariadne felt both intense relief and admiration for the girl sweep over her as Grace's eyes hardened with determination and power.

"The pain is a harmony as any other," said Ariadne. "*Dominate* it, don't allow it to dominate you, and then use it."

Grace drew in a deep breath, straightening her body, her eyes locked into those of Ariadne, drawing strength from her foremother.

"*Use* the pain," Ariadne said one more time.

Another deep breath, then Grace's body relaxed a little, and she gave a single nod. The red lines still glowed around her wrists, and Ariadne understood that they still caused Grace agony, but now the girl was using the agony—using

the harmonies spun out by the agony—as an accelerant to her own power.

Ariadne took a deep breath of her own. *Dear gods, what a fright!* "You have control now?" she said.

Grace nodded, although Ariadne could see that control was taking the girl considerable effort.

"Did Catling never attack you when Stella trained you? When Stella took you into the Great Founding Labyrinth? When you underwent your Great Ordeal?"

"No." Grace's voice was quiet, but it was underpinned with strength, and Ariadne decided she could let go the remnants of her anxiety.

"Interesting," said Ariadne. "She wasn't concerned when you underwent your initial training, but now she thinks to attack you."

"I don't think Catling likes you very much, Ariadne."

Ariadne laughed. "Then I'll take it as a compliment that she's upset now. But enough of Catling. You can cope with the pain? Good. Now, young lady, let me see what you're capable of."

THEY SPENT THE ENTIRE AFTERNOON AND EVEning deep within the Great Founding Labyrinth which Ariadne had raised in her drawing room. Ariadne, having recovered from her initial fright, took things more slowly than she'd originally intended.

No need to tempt fates any more than she already had.

As she'd suspected, Stella had done a competent job of teaching Grace, but she hadn't even begun to plumb the depths of Grace's abilities. Ariadne remembered when she'd trained Noah. Noah had been so extraordinary, so capable, so instinctive, that Ariadne had radically revised her original training schedule. Noah had not needed training so much as a gentle prompting now and again in the right direction.

Grace, as Ariadne quickly discovered, was similar. Her power was also instinctive, and she should have also been trained with gentle prompts. But Stella obviously had not

recognized this, and had instead adhered to a more traditional program of training—a far more restrictive program—that simply had not allowed Grace to open herself up to her true abilities.

Stella may also simply have not cared very much, Ariadne thought. As the Caroller her mind was on far different things, a far different world, and Ariadne doubted that Stella had used her abilities as Mistress of the Labyrinth very much at all in the past few hundred years.

"Tsk, tsk," Ariadne found herself muttering over and over as she discovered yet another door that had been slammed in Grace's face. "I should have taken you in hand many years ago."

For this initial session Ariadne contented herself with exploring Grace's powers herself, and working out just what was needed to open Grace up to her own potential. At midnight, when she sensed that both of them were close to exhaustion, she put her hand on Grace's arm, and muttered, "Enough!"

Instantly the Great Founding Labyrinth vanished, to be replaced by Ariadne's drawing room.

And the moment that the Great Founding Labyrinth vanished, so also did the fiery lines around Grace's wrists.

Grace almost collapsed, surprised by the sudden cessation of pain (which she had been using almost as a prop during the past few hours), as suddenly overwhelmed by exhaustion.

"Let's get you to bed," said Ariadne.

FOR THE NEXT TWO DAYS ARIADNE TOOK GRACE into the Great Founding Labyrinth every morning. There they spent several hours, Ariadne doing what she had done with Noah, prompting Grace, nudging her (sometimes literally with an elbow in Grace's ribs) in the right direction, praising her when she made a huge leap forward.

These leaps became more and more frequent—by mid–Sunday morning all Ariadne had to do was to stand back and watch.

Dear God, how had Stella missed this?

Grace was powerful. As powerful as Noah, although in a different way. She had a darker and far more instinctive grasp of the power of the labyrinth. She didn't bring at her back the powers of Eaving as Noah did, but she more than made up for that with her command of the Darkcraft.

The Darkcraft was twice bred in Grace as Weyland was both her forefather and her father.

But it was more than that, Ariadne finally, stunningly realized. It wasn't just that Grace commanded the Darkcraft in twice the measure that someone like Noah did; she commanded it an infinity of times more. It was as if Grace could somehow touch all the wielders of Darkcraft in her heritage (Noah, Weyland, Ariadne, and all the daughter-heirs of Ariadne's up to and including Genvissa-Stella), and draw on *all* their power. Grace didn't actually realize she was doing this—frankly, Ariadne believed that Grace had no idea at all of her potential or her power—but do it she could.

And all of this tied to Catling by that cursed hex.

Catling had not struck again after Friday afternoon, but Grace told Ariadne she could feel her watching, which made Ariadne worry.

If they spent the mornings inside the Great Founding Labyrinth, then they spent the afternoons talking.

Neither Noah nor Stella had told Grace anything of the heritage of the Mistresses of the Labyrinth (and Ariadne was not going to berate them for it, for she, too, should have attended to this), and so Ariadne took Grace for a long meander through history during these long afternoons.

She did this not so much as part of Grace's training (which, indeed, it was) but because Jack had asked Ariadne to prepare Grace for that moment when he would ask her for the Kingship bands.

Ariadne was not the only one who taught Grace her history. Silvius attended to this as well.

Silvius and Ariadne had enjoyed (although that was, perhaps, too strong an emotive expression for it) a sexual relationship, off and on, for some years. They'd gradually drifted together, drawn not merely by a strong sexual at-

traction, but by the fact that, as a Mistress of the Labyrinth and as a Kingman (if minus his Kingship bands), Ariadne and Silvius were naturally drawn together.

Besides, they had lived at roughly contemporary times in the Aegean world, and had shared memories and friends.

Ariadne had not asked Silvius to attend simply because they could get chummy over old times. She asked him in part because he could help as much as she in teaching Grace the history and antiquities of the labyrinth, but mostly because he was a Kingman, and Grace needed contact, and interaction, with a Kingman. She'd had interaction with Kingmen before, of course. She'd known Silvius all her life, and Weyland (who was close enough to being a Kingman to do), and had over the past year had contact with Jack.

But, apart from those few minutes with Jack atop Ambersbury Banks, she'd never interacted with a Kingman as a Mistress of the Labyrinth, and she needed to have as much experience in that contact as possible.

Admittedly, Ariadne thought that Jack would be giving Grace a reasonable amount of experience in that matter in the not too distant future, but Ariadne could also see that many other emotions would be caught up in that experience, and she thought it would benefit Grace to have contact with a Kingman with whom she wasn't increasingly emotionally bound.

What Jack had told Ariadne about his encounter with Grace atop Ambersbury Banks convinced Ariadne that Grace needed some fairly intense tuition in the art and craft of Kingmen. Jack had realized immediately that Grace's power and her abilities were a flawless match to his own, but Grace had not realized it.

She'd probably not even realized Jack's arousal, Ariadne thought in some disbelief. Dear gods, what had she been missing all these years?

So Silvius played a dual role in these afternoon sessions. As with Ariadne, he could give a firsthand account of the history of the labyrinth, the rise to power of the Mistresses

of the Labyrinth and Kingmen within the ancient Aegean world, and the uses to which the labyrinth had been put—forming protective wards, or Games, around cities and city-states.

Silvius could also gently touch Grace with his own power during these talks, slowly acclimatizing her (almost without her consciously realizing it) to the touch of a Kingman.

Grace certainly benefited from this, but in the end it was Ariadne who ended up being astounded by Silvius' power. She and Silvius may have been lovers, but even their sexual encounters hadn't opened Ariadne's eyes to just how good Silvius was, and she was aghast at how magical he must have been when he also wielded the power of the golden bands of Troy. *Damn it! Why had she been so blinded by Theseus?*

On Monday afternoon, after another session in the Great Founding Labyrinth during the morning (during which Ariadne had just stood back and watched in admiration as Grace expertly manipulated the harmonies of the labyrinth), Ariadne and Silvius took Grace back in time. They did this using their own power, but their own power significantly boosted by what Grace was able to lend them.

Without her, they could not have managed it.

Silvius led the way, directing their consciousnesses back through space and the centuries to a small Aegean city that sat atop a hill whose lower slopes were swathed in the gray-green of olive trees.

Where it is does not matter, Silvius said into Ariadne's and Grace's minds. *Its name is neither here nor there. Who and what it is does not affect us. What does matter is what happens within the temple attached to the palace. See.*

They were still seated in the chairs in Ariadne's drawing room, but none of them saw the luxurious appointments with which Ariadne had surrounded herself. Instead, as Silvius extended his hand, they saw the interior of a columned temple, painted in rich hues of blue and green and red, and gilded. Before the altar, on which stood a gruesome statue of a horned beast, stood a young man

dressed only in a white hip wrap. Before him stood a woman who all three watchers instantly identified as a Mistress of the Labyrinth both by the power that exuded from her, and by the manner of her dress, a long white linen skirt draped from her hips and proudly bare breasts.

Not one of my relatives, Ariadne said with a dismissive air, *but competent enough.*

Note the young man, said Silvius, ignoring Ariadne. *He is a Kingman, but his father died before he could hand over his Kingship bands.*

Ariadne and Silvius paused, sensing what Grace was understanding.

A father usually hands on Kingship bands? said Grace.

Yes, said Silvius, *although in my case Brutus simply snatched them from my dying limbs.* He chuckled. *No wonder he was to lose them so easily.*

Who, other than a father, can hand over the bands? said Grace.

It can be done by anyone who wields the power of the labyrinth, said Silvius. *Look here, and see.*

The Mistress of the Labyrinth, a woman of some thirty or thirty-five years of age with a face made striking more by her power and experience than by physical beauty, moved forward to lay a hand on the young man's naked chest.

He trembled, and for an instant looked as if he might move away.

The Mistress' mouth curled, and her eyes narrowed as she waited.

The man relaxed, and as he did so her hand caressed his skin.

"You are very beautiful," she said, and he smiled.

"Give them to me," he said, and Silvius, watching, gave a guffaw that only Ariadne and Grace heard.

He's as impatient as was Brutus! Silvius said.

Both Grace and Ariadne smiled.

"Take them from me," the Mistress of the Labyrinth whispered, and the young Kingman shuddered, although whether from desire for the woman before him or from desire for the bands the watchers could not tell.

He raised his right hand and took the Mistress' hand, which lay on his chest, moving it away, then running his hand slowly up her still outstretched arm.

Now she was the one who shuddered, and her lips parted fractionally.

The young man's hand moved, so slowly, so caressingly, up her arm to her biceps, his eyes holding hers in an unblinking stare. Then, just as his hand reached the very top of her arm, the pressure of his fingers changed. They dug down into her flesh, and the woman winced.

Then, suddenly, stunningly, gold gleamed between the young man's fingers.

Do you see? said Silvius. *Do you understand?*

Yes, said Grace. *The Kingman takes the bands from the Mistress, but she must allow him to do so.*

Good, said Ariadne. *Why, do you think, might this be difficult?*

Grace thought several minutes before responding, keeping her eyes on the vision before her as the young Kingman took band after band from the flesh of the Mistress of the Labyrinth.

"It is the ultimate intimacy," Grace whispered in her physical voice rather than her mental. "To allow a Kingman, *any* man, to draw something from your flesh. It is far more intimate than a sexual coupling. To allow someone to draw something so powerful from you . . . that would take such trust, such confidence."

"Such love," Silvius said, very softly.

"That would help, yes," said Grace, and both Ariadne and Silvius laughed.

"This is the first time I've seen my blood in you, my dear," said Ariadne.

Before them, as the Mistress cried out (with loss rather than with pain), the young Kingman drew forth from the flesh of her biceps a magnificent golden armband. It rose into his touch, as if it had been waiting, all this time, just below the surface of her skin.

Waiting for the touch of the Kingman.

Chapter Seven

MARBLE ARCH UNDERGROUND STATION

Tuesday, 17 September, to Friday, 20 September 1940

ARIADNE OPENED THE DOOR OF HER APARTment, and saw Jack standing there. She arched an eyebrow.

"Is Grace in?" Jack said.

"No." Ariadne let Jack in and showed him through to the drawing room. "Matilda dropped by earlier this evening, and Grace has gone with her to help her mother in her little van."

There was deep, rich amusement in Ariadne's voice at this, and Jack thought that running a mobile canteen would be the very last thing Ariadne would allow herself to be caught dead doing.

"Grace will be fine," Ariadne added.

Jack wasn't so sure. He was worried about Grace being out when the imps were undoubtedly prowling, but realized that he couldn't wrap up Grace in cotton wool. Grace needed to take risks, and Jack needed to accept that.

Ariadne sat herself down on a sofa, but Jack continued standing, turning his cap over and over in his hand. "Well?"

That damned eyebrow of Ariadne's arched even further than normal, and Jack realized she was looking at the cap turning over and over in his hand rather than at him.

Irritated, he tossed it onto a chair.

"I know it has only been a few days," he said, "and you will have had little chance to do much with Grace, but—"

"She's superb, Jack."

He stared at Ariadne, unable to say anything.

"As good as Noah, although using a different combination of powers." Ariadne paused, her face assuming a

thoughtful look. "Well, when I say superb, her *talent* is superb, but of course she needs much experience, which she hasn't had."

"And can she—"

"Hand over the bands? She is capable of it, yes."

Jack let out a long breath of relief. "Thank you, Ariadne."

"Jack, Catling attacked Grace the instant I first took her into the Great Founding Labyrinth."

Jack narrowed his eyes.

"Catling is worried, Jack. Watch out for her."

"Did she continue to attack? Grace has been with you four or five days, Ariadne. You must have taken her into the Great Founding Labyrinth more than that once."

"True," said Ariadne, "but Catling only attacked the first time. Maybe it was just . . . a reminder. But I still caution you to be careful."

"And Grace, of course."

Ariadne looked at Jack carefully. "You have far more potential to do Grace harm than she does to herself, Jack. *You* are the one who can save her, or damn her, whichever way your hand swings. *Be careful.*"

JACK KNEW NOAH'S GENERAL ROUTE WITH HER mobile canteen, and he finally found her van outside Marble Arch underground station by Hyde Park. He parked his Austin convertible a block or so away, then started to walk toward the van. He could see Matilda, Ecub, and Grace lifting trays out of the back, and he raised his hand, intending to call out to them.

But hardly had the hand left his side when it was snatched in an icy grip.

He tried to step back, but Catling's grip was viselike, and he found he couldn't move.

She leaned close, and snarled in Jack's face. "I didn't like that bomb, Jack."

"I don't know what you're—"

She hissed, her face contorting into such ugliness that Jack flinched.

"The little present that you and Noah dropped on me a week ago. It didn't go off, Jack. The will was there, but not the skill, eh?"

"Catling—"

"Don't do it again, Jack."

"I—"

"Do it again, Jack, and I will retaliate in kind."

"There are bombs dropping all over the place, damn it! Is it so unlikely that one would fall close to St. Paul's?"

Something changed in Catling's face. It became much harder, and, if possible, much colder. "I can see you need to be taught a lesson, Jack."

"Don't you—"

"Can you hear it, Jack?" Catling whispered, and then she was gone, and Jack was left standing staring at the van, seeing Grace and Matilda moving toward the entrance to the underground station with trays of food in their hands.

All he could hear was the whistle of the bomb falling through the sky.

He tried to move, tried to get his legs and arms and body moving forward, but it seemed to him that they only responded sluggishly.

"*Grace!*" he screamed.

LONDONERS HAD BEEN USING THE UNDERground train stations as makeshift shelters for weeks. Despite being underground, and despite the popular belief that the stations were better than official shelters, the government had been trying to discourage their use. Engineers worried that a bomb might broach a tunnel wall, causing the Thames to flood the entire system. Health officials worried because in most of the stations there were no toilets as they were too deep to connect to the sewer lines. Train authorities worried about sleeping people rolling off platforms and onto tracks: most of the people who sheltered were usually in their bedrolls four or five hours before the underground shut down for the night, and platforms were becoming so crowded with the sleeping that an accident

could easily occur. The police worried about crime and security risks.

But Londoners were increasingly settling down in the underground stations at night, and Marble Arch, right in the heart of London, was one of the more popular stations.

This night it was crowded; the platforms packed with the sleeping and many who were still awake: neighbors gossiping, parents trying to settle tired children; men playing cards. Noah, Ecub, Erith, and Matilda, with Grace helping, were ferrying trays filled with food and cups of tea down the stairs toward the platforms.

The bomb struck directly overhead with enough force to burst through the ticket station and several layers of concrete reinforcing, exploding just before it reached the platforms themselves.

The concussion blast blew scores of people onto the tracks; it was fortunate that the train system had already closed down for the night. Some rubble fell through from above, but that was not the bomb's deadliest gift.

Like so many other underground stations, Marble Arch was lined with hundreds of thousands of white ceramic tiles. The concussion blast blew thousands of them from the walls; some remained intact, the majority splintered into a deadly fusillade of razor-sharp fragments.

Twelve people were killed instantly, another seven or eight were fatally wounded, fifty or sixty more horrifically injured by the ceramic splinters.

Ecub, who had just emerged onto the platform from the stairwell, was blown fifteen feet to her left and momentarily knocked unconscious. Noah, Matilda, Erith, and Grace, still in the stairwell, were tumbled down the remaining ten or twelve steps, their trays and plates and cups and saucers scattering everywhere. Both Erith and Noah received minor scalds from the hot tea, while all four of them were heavily bruised and slightly lacerated.

JACK, WHO HAD BARELY REACHED THE ENTRANCE when the bomb exploded, thought they were all dead. He

scrambled down the stairs as best he could, climbing over rubble, shunting aside blocks of concrete that were in his way, choking on the thick blast dust that fogged the air.

He literally fell over Erith first, who was struggling to rise, and tripped down the final few steps. Jack muttered an expletive, managed to get his balance, then started feeling about in the gloom. "Noah? Grace? Gods damn it, *where are you*?"

"Here, Jack," said a voice, and he reached out in its direction and grabbed an arm.

"Noah? Noah, are you all right?"

"Yes." Noah's voice was strained. "Grace?" she said. *"Grace?"*

"Here," came a soft voice.

Jack moved toward the voice, but Noah was closer, and scrambled over to hug her daughter tight.

Erith and Matilda stood up, murmuring that they were unharmed save for some bumps and bruises.

"Ecub," said Noah. Jack could see a little better now—the dust was finally settling—and he saw Noah crouched close to Grace, her arms still about her daughter, both of them white with dust and marked with thin lines of blood trickling down foreheads and cheeks. He was relieved to see the blood was from nothing more than superficial scratches.

"Ecub," said Noah. "She'd gone through . . ." She couldn't continue.

Jack nodded. "I'll look for her," he said, and stepped through to where had once been the platforms.

IT WAS A SCENE HE'D NEVER FORGET. JACK HAD seen many disasters, participated in many battles, been present for a handful of slaughters, but this . . .

The actual physical damage to the station appeared relatively minimal. There was a gaping hole in the roof of the tunnel, and the tiles on the walls had fallen off or shattered, but apart from some rubble Jack could not see too much structural destruction.

Nonetheless, the scene that met Jack's eyes was one that

could have bubbled up directly from hell. The station lights sputtered on and off, bathing everything in a surreal yellow glimmer. Thick clouds of dust drifted through the intermittent light. Bodies lay sprawled across the platforms and over the tracks, covered with bloodied dust. Some people lay still, others moved sluggishly, still shocked by the blast.

There was relative silence, although one or two people moaned, and somewhere a child whimpered.

For a long moment Jack could do nothing but look on, appalled. Then a movement to his left caught at his attention.

It was Ecub, lying on the platform, partly crumpled against the wall. Jack could not exactly see it was Ecub, she was so covered in dust, but he nonetheless knew it was her.

"Ecub!" He bent down beside her, carefully brushing dust and fine rubble from her face and shoulders.

She waved a hand, indicating she wanted to rise, and Jack helped her up. Ecub wavered a moment, but she caught her balance quickly.

"You're injured," said Jack, concerned at the wound on the side of her head.

"I will live," she said. "Where's Noah? The others?"

"In the stairwell. Slightly scraped and shaken, but otherwise unharmed."

"Thank the gods."

"We need to leave," said Jack.

"No," said Ecub. "We've got to help these people."

"She's right," said Noah, appearing at Jack's side. "We need to help."

Jack took both women by the elbow and, over their protests, directed them toward the stairwell. "I'm sorry," he said, "but we are going to get out of here *now*. Listen to the sirens above. The fire engines and rescue crews have arrived. We'd only get in the way."

"But—" Noah began.

"We leave *now*," Jack said again. "This is Catling's doing, Noah, in retaliation for the UXB outside St. Paul's. We leave now, and we find somewhere to talk. The people here will be well enough without us."

* * *

THEY GATHERED FINALLY AT FAERIE HILL MANOR.
This was not accomplished without some trouble—Noah
had to drive her van back to the Savoy under difficult con-
ditions, Jack likewise with his car. Once they got to the
Savoy, to the relief of Weyland, who was almost beside
himself with worry, Jack asked Noah to use her skills as
Darkwitch to move them all to Faerie Hill Manor. Just be-
fore they left, he sent a mental message to Ariadne, asking
her and Silvius to meet them there.

By five A.M. they had gathered in Harry's drawing room,
Stella the only one not present as she needed to carol in the
dawn in the Faerie.

The women had cleaned themselves as much as possi-
ble, although none had changed, and Noah and Matilda
had applied plasters where needed to superficial cuts.

Now, coffee in hand, they sat down in the chairs and so-
fas grouped around the fire.

"Jack?" said Harry. "What has happened?" Noah and
Jack had already given Harry a brief account of the night's
adventures, but now, no fool, he wanted to know the real
reason behind Jack's barely suppressed impatience and
Noah's worry.

In as few words as possible, Jack told them of his meet-
ing with Catling just outside Marble Arch station, and of
subsequent events.

"It was a warning," he concluded. "If Noah and I try it
again . . ."

"She's scared," said Noah. "What she did tonight proves
it. We came too close, Jack."

Jack glanced at Grace, who was sitting in a chair, her
head resting back, her eyes closed. A small vein throbbed
in her throat, and Jack wished he'd had a chance to speak
with her alone without either her mother or the entire tribe
of Eaving's Sisters about. They hadn't had a chance to
speak since their walk along Lambeth Embankment, and
Jack needed not only to reassure himself that she was all

right after the incident at Marble Arch, but that she hadn't had any second thoughts.

He was mildly appalled at how anxious he was regarding the latter.

"I don't want Catling to come closer," Jack said.

Noah had seen the direction of Jack's eyes. "Jack, Catling can't hurt Grace! Their fates are tied too closely. Tonight was bluff only."

"A 'bluff' that has killed a score of people and injured many more," Jack said. "And you're not included in whatever Grace's and Catling's co-fate might be. Any of you, Noah, could be killed by Catling's malevolence."

"Not me," said Noah quietly. "She needs me to execute the final Dance of the Flowers with you."

"Then Ecub or Erith or Matilda, damn it!" Jack said.

"This was going to get bloody sooner or later," Harry said. "There is only one question. What to do?"

"I get the bands of Troy," said Jack. "I need the power."

Silvius, who had expected Jack to say this, watched with some wry amusement the interplay about the room at Jack's words. Grace tensed, opening her eyes and looking first at Jack, then at Ariadne. Ariadne smiled—one of her better, predatory smiles—and, having acknowledged Grace's glance, winked at Silvius. Noah noticed none of the interplay involving Grace and Ariadne, and merely smiled at Jack.

Oh dear, Silvius thought, *I expect that Jack has forgotten to take Noah aside for a quiet word about this.*

"I agree," Noah said. "When?"

"Sunday," Jack said. "The spring equinox. Noah—"

She had smiled at his words, then broke in before he could continue. "Jack, I have waited so many years to give these bands back to you. I—"

"Noah," Jack said, "Grace will be the one to hand them to me. I'm sorry. I should have said something earlier."

Noah's face froze. Her eyes twitched over to her daughter, who had flushed and was looking studiously at the hands in her lap, then she looked back to Jack. "You can't

want Grace . . . ," she started to say, then drifted to a halt in confusion.

There was a silence. Noah's face suddenly flamed a far deeper color than her daughter's. "I apologize," she said, looking first at Weyland—who was looking stolidly ahead at the wall as if he found it fascinating—then around the circle of faces. "That didn't come out the way I meant it. I, um, meant that . . . oh, gods . . ."

"Noah, stop, please," Jack said. "Grace needs to do it because the bands never left her. They're resting within her flesh."

Noah stared at him. She'd just made a total fool of herself, and for no reason. *Gods!* She wanted to be angry at Jack (he should have told her earlier, he should have said instantly why it was Grace needed to be the one to hand over the bands) but all she felt was more stupidly foolish than ever.

That was a little outburst befitting Cornelia, not Noah. Not Eaving.

"I had no idea, Grace," Noah said, wincing internally at how stiff that sounded. "There is so much I have no idea about."

With that she rose with as much dignity as she could summon, and walked to the door.

Jack spoke before she got there. "I should have said something to you earlier, Noah. I meant to, before that damn bomb fell. I apologize again."

Noah nodded, and put a hand on the door knob.

"Nonetheless," Jack continued, his voice a little firmer, "I want Grace."

Having been silently congratulating his son on his apology, Silvius drew in a silent breath at that last. Jack had phrased his response in the same way as Noah had originally objected, and, when all was said and done, Silvius knew that neither had been referring to the Kingship bands of Troy at all.

Well, well, so now all was out in the open. Silvius met Ariadne's eyes. She was very watchful, very careful. One of the greatest, if most difficult, alliances in history, that

between Brutus and Cornelia, had just been shattered. A new alliance would need to be built, and soon, if there was even the slightest chance that they could win out against the Troy Game.

"Grace will do very well," Ariadne said, as if everyone had been talking of nothing more dramatic than who should arrange the flowers for the Sunday church services.

Noah finally opened the door, and walked out.

Grace started to rise, but Weyland waved her down.

"No," he said, shooting a baleful glare at Jack, "let me talk to her."

Chapter Eight

FAERIE HILL MANOR

Friday, 20 September 1940

"ℐ CAN'T BELIEVE I SAID THAT. I JUST CAN'T BElieve it."

Noah had retreated to the downstairs cloakroom, and it was here that Weyland found her.

He leaned against the wall, arms crossed, looking steadily at Noah. He didn't know what to say. Rather, Weyland didn't know how to phrase what he was feeling without making the situation infinitely worse.

"I'm sorry," Noah said again, barely able to look Weyland in the eye.

"I didn't realize you still loved Jack so much."

Noah closed her eyes briefly. *Oh gods, what could she say?*

"I don't love him, Weyland. Not in the way I love you."

Weyland's face twisted. "Ah. That makes it all better, then."

"Weyland . . ." All Noah really wanted to do was to walk back into that drawing room and deliver Jack a stinging slap across his face. Telling her in front of everyone else, with no warning, all stated so baldly (*"I want Grace"*) was vintage Brutus. *Damn it!* She'd deserved some warning, surely?

What Noah knew she needed to do right now was to repair all the vast cracks which had appeared in her relationship with Weyland with that one, stupid remark.

You can't want Grace.

"Weyland . . ." Noah thought about reaching out to touch him, then reconsidered it with one look at his stony face. "My pride has been hurt today, Weyland. Not my heart."

"Really."

Noah couldn't blame him for being so hurt, for closing himself off. Gods, but had that been scripted she could not have done a better task of ruining the fragile trust built up between them.

She twisted her mouth ruefully. "I don't love him, Weyland. Not as Cornelia once did. Not as Caela did. Not even as I did before I'd come to know you. I think what has happened"—she gave a rueful laugh to match her expression and hoped it sounded genuine—"was that I had grown used to the idea of Jack pining for me. Jack had fled England after I'd rejected him for you. Then he'd spent almost three hundred years yearning for me. He'd come home, desperate for me. And what does he do? Toss away all of that tradition for our daughter."

Noah stopped there. She hadn't even come close to thinking about that. *Jack wanted Grace. Their daughter . . .*

"Aye, it is dented pride, Weyland. Nothing more, although that is great enough. One of the pillars of my life had been Jack's useless yearning for what he could not have—me. Now I discover he yearns for something, some-*one,* he can well have. My world is out of kilter, both as a woman and as a mother." *Please believe me, Weyland. Please. I don't want to lose you.*

Weyland, who had caught her mind-sent message, more than anything wanted to believe her. His entire world depended on believing her. But *could* he?

And Grace. Jack wanted Grace. Like Noah, Weyland hadn't even come close to thinking about that, and he didn't think he was capable of doing so right now.

"I do not want to lose you, either," Weyland very softly. "But I am terribly afraid I already have."

JACK STOOD WITH GRACE ON THE TERRACE OUT-side the drawing room. It was cold, and they were well wrapped in coats, but their pale faces and pinched cheeks had less to do with the weather than with what had happened earlier.

"I didn't do that very well, did I?" Jack said tiredly.

"I feel so guilty," Grace said. "My mother . . . I feel as if I shouldn't even think of stepping into her shoes."

"Grace, don't say that. Please. Don't feel guilty." ·

Grace gave a small, hollow laugh. "I am a daughter, Jack, and daughters always feel guilty when it comes to their mothers."

Jack didn't know what to say. He *had* meant to talk to Noah beforehand, but then came the bomb, and he hadn't thought before he'd mentioned the bands, and then Noah spoke up . . .

He lifted a hand, sliding it under the collar of Grace's coat so he cradled the back of her head.

"Are you all right?" Now the fingers of his other hand were running lightly over the abrasions on her temple. "The bomb didn't hurt you?"

Grace was looking at some vague point over Jack's shoulder. "I'm fine, Jack."

"Ariadne said you've done well with your training."

"Yes."

Christ! This was going badly. "I wish we'd had a chance to speak earlier. I wanted to talk to you about Thursday night last week. You know. On Lambeth Embankment." Now he was sounding like an insecure teenager. "I meant what I said about Noah. I meant what I said about you. But I wonder . . . I'm afraid that . . . perhaps after some time . . . I meant to

talk to you earlier, but didn't get the chance and . . . oh *Jesus,* I am not doing well here."

At least now she was looking at him, her eyes brilliant in her pinched face.

"Is it still okay with you," he said, "that I get to know you better?"

"Yes. Of course."

"Are you happy to hand over the bands to me?"

She smiled. "Yes."

"Don't worry about Catling," Jack said. "Between Malcolm and me, we can wrap Ambersbury Banks in so much druidic magic even Catling won't be able to penetrate it."

"I wasn't worried about Catling," Grace said.

"There is something else I need to tell you. Something good," he added. Jack was reading Grace better now, and he recognized her instant wariness whenever he mentioned he needed to talk to her about something. He wondered what series of childhood grave "talks" had so inhibited her.

"When we danced together on Ambersbury Banks, Grace, you shook my entire world. As a Mistress of the Labyrinth you are my perfect match. Your power not only matches mine, but it fits in beside it so seamlessly that together any Game we danced would be so flawless, so powerful, that nothing could ever attack it. Grace, our labyrinthine powers and abilities are perfectly harmoniously matched. Your mother and I together are good, but you and I . . . you and I will be legendary."

"Oh."

Jack realized suddenly what that must have sounded like: *Grace was immaterial. All Jack wanted was her power.* "And, oh," he said, very softly, both his hands cupping her face now, "to find this in a woman who is . . . so . . . damn . . . beautiful. It is not the Mistress I want to get to know, Grace—I already know her—but the woman. It is those brief glimpses of the woman that you allow me that tie my tongue in knots."

"Oh," she said again, but at least that time she sounded a little happier than the last.

"Can I take you out to dinner sometime, sometime soon?"

She smiled. "Yes."

Grace looked so sweet at that point, and her face felt so warm under his hands, that Jack found himself leaning slightly toward her.

Then, just before he kissed her, the French doors to the drawing room opened and Noah walked out.

NOAH SENT JACK ONE OF THOSE BLANK, DEEPLY meaningful looks, and asked if she could speak to her daughter alone. Jack's hands tightened briefly around Grace's face, then he smiled at her, stepped back, and left.

Once he had gone, Noah took a deep breath, clenched her fists deep inside her coat pockets, and hoped she hadn't lost her daughter as she was very much afraid she had lost Weyland.

"Grace," she said. "I have made an utter fool of myself, and I need to apologize to you as much as I do to Weyland."

Grace made no response, but at least she was looking at her mother, and from that Noah took some heart.

"I have grown too used to having Jack pine for me," Noah said. "It was a horrible shock to my pride to realize he'd abandoned me to pine after you instead."

Noah gave a small, wan smile. "And it was a terrible shock to realize that I have been so blind when it came to you."

"Mother—"

Noah pulled her hands out of her pockets and pulled Grace into an embrace. "I have no call either on Jack or on the Troy Game, whether it be its destruction or its completion. Grace, the world is yours if you want it. Take it, please, with all my love."

Grace hugged her mother tightly, then leaned back a little. "Ariadne has taught me what she knows, but you could teach me so much more. Will you?"

Noah took a deep breath. "No. Grace, I don't think I should. I think you and I . . ." What Noah wanted to say was that she thought there were too many barriers between her and Grace, not the least of them being Jack, and those

barriers would make teaching impossible. But she could hardly say that. "I'm too close to you, Grace. Too *blind*. Gods, I should have known Catling had been coming to you, and that the bands never left you, and I *didn't*. Ariadne has the clarity of distance." Noah gave a soft laugh. "She'll drive you hard, which is what you need, whereas I'd always be watching what I said around you. Grace, I love you dearly for asking, and I didn't deserve that, but Ariadne would be better for you."

"And Jack . . . do you mind?"

"I am worried about my daughter. I would worry whatever man came courting her. And Jack has so much baggage." Noah let a mischievous smile spread over her face. "But he's a great deal better than Brutus. Just don't let him push you, Grace. Do what *you* want, not what he wants for you."

Chapter Nine

LONDON

Friday, 20 September, to Saturday, 21 September 1940

Grace Speaks

SO MUCH HAD HAPPENED OVER THE PAST week or so for me that it proved difficult to process it all properly and put it in calm order. Everything from that strange walk down Lambeth Embankment with Jack, to going to live and train with Ariadne, to discovering that I had four of the Kingship bands of Troy buried within my flesh, and, on top of all this, to have Jack tell me that I was apparently his perfect labyrinthine match as well.

I found it so difficult to believe that I, who had lived her

entire life at the edge of the circle, was now very much in the heart of it.

Most of all I found it difficult to believe that Jack—Brutus-William-Louis-Jack—who had spent the past few thousand years aching for my mother should now abandon that ache to profess an interest in me.

I don't think I *would* have believed it, save for that painful scene at Faerie Hill Manor when my mother said, *You can't want Grace* (mirroring my own belief, precisely) and then Jack had replied, *I want Grace*. It wasn't just the words, but the expressions on everyone's faces, as well. There was disbelief, amazement, intrigue, and, as eyes slid my way, *interest*.

None of that had been staged, none of it rehearsed, all of it an open, painful wound. Jack had told my mother he didn't want her anymore.

That he wanted me.

I spent a great deal of time sitting on my bed in Ariadne's apartment, just thinking, learning to *feel*.

I was changing, becoming more confident, learning to live, learning who *I* was, and that was due almost as much to Ariadne as it was to Jack. Hitherto I'd spent my life cringing in corners; Ariadne, through both her training and the fact she treated me as an equal, gave me the confidence to dare on my own.

I had never believed that I could ever be anything other than the most mediocre of Mistresses. I had never dared hope that any man might bypass my mother for me. I'd never hoped to be important to anyone in anything other than a negative way.

What really surprised me was how much I liked this new state of being. People were beginning to *see* me.

I had feared Jack's arrival so much, and while I certainly could not pretend that it hadn't been painful, in a variety of ways, since his arrival I had begun to live.

I began, inch by inch, to believe there might be some hope for me. That somehow, Jack might be able to find a way to destroy the Troy Game, and save me in the process.

* * *

ON SATURDAY JACK TOOK ME OUT TO DINNER.
Ariadne took one look at the clothes I had brought with
me, sniffed, and produced something from her wardrobe
that I might wear. Amazingly, it wasn't scarlet, and not
even too revealing, but a lovely ice blue dress of some
clingy material that I actually felt comfortable wearing—
although I knew a year ago I would have cringed in it.

Jack took me to a restaurant in Chelsea.

I had a wonderful time.

We didn't talk about anything that had been said be-
tween us at Lambeth Embankment, or about what had been
said at Faerie Hill Manor the day he'd told everyone, my
mother included, that I carried the bands within me.

We didn't even talk about the Troy Game.

Instead we chatted very much as we had that Christmas
when Jack and Harry had kept me company in my pain on
the terrace. I discovered I liked talking to Jack very much,
and that he found it no effort talking to me. We talked
mostly about what he'd done and what he'd seen over his
lives. Nothing too demanding—funny, humorous tales, as
well some more reflective ones.

Partway through the evening I realized, with a jolt, that
Jack wasn't going to push. He would leave it up to me,
whatever I wanted, then all I needed was to ask. I felt a
weight lift away from my shoulders and, remarkably, I dis-
covered that I was enjoying myself, and that I was very,
very at ease with Jack.

We talked a little of tomorrow, when I would hand four
of the bands of Troy to Jack. It was a very brief discussion,
merely going over the technicalities of the ritual, but at the
end of it Jack asked me if I was afraid.

"No," I replied. "I'm not scared of you at all."

That wasn't what Jack had asked me, but I think it was
the answer he was hoping for, because his eyes gleamed
with pleasure, and he smiled.

"You're not scared of *yourself* any more," he said, and I

realized it was true. I'd spent my lifetime being scared of myself, and of life in general.

I stared at Jack, and took a deep breath in wonder.

THAT NIGHT, AS I LAY IN MY BED IN ARIADNE'S apartment, Catling appeared to me.

The horrid cold-faced malevolence. She stood at the end of the bed and stared.

And then smiled, as if she actually approved of what was happening.

I hated her, and *loathed* it that she had tainted what had otherwise been a wonderful night, but for once I did not rail at her, or beg her to go away.

I rolled over, settled myself comfortably, and went back to sleep.

PART FIVE

THE ENTWINED BANDS

London, 1670

THE SKYLINE OF LONDON WAS VERY GRAD-
*ually inching upward after the disaster of the
Great Fire four years previously. Houses and
warehouses had been the first structures to be rebuilt (beds
and businesses, as always, came first), but now the
churches and chapels were rising one by one through the
tangle of homes and warehouses.*

*Christopher Wren, although primarily responsible for the
design and rebuilding of St. Paul's Cathedral, had also de-
signed fifty of these churches as well as a myriad of private
and public secular buildings. He also supervised the build-
ing of about half of these churches and private buildings.*

Wren was a busy man.

*Still only in his late thirties, Wren worked a staggering
eighteen or nineteen hours each day, rising well before
dawn to head off to whatever building site commanded his
attention that day. He'd taken rooms in Southwark, which
meant that every morning, at dawn, he walked across Lon-
don Bridge heading for his work in London.*

*Always he paused by St. Thomas' chapel, sometimes to
enter for a few minutes' prayer, sometimes to stand on the
bridge, staring at the skyline before him, and sometimes to
pass the time of day with a small black-haired girl who
would wait for him in the shadows of the chapel.*

*Wren had come to accept, somewhat grudgingly, the
presence of this odd little girl in his life. They shared an in-
terest in the rebuilding of London, but they did not share a
friendship. For a little girl, she was strangely knowledge-*

*able, supernaturally knowledgeable, and Wren knew that
she was far more than just a "little girl." Exactly what
more she was Wren did not like to contemplate.*

*The Great Fire had razed London to the ground and, in
the doing, exposed ancient plague pits and burial grounds.
Sometimes, in his nightmares, Wren saw the little girl
climbing out of one of these exposed pits where she'd been
buried for a millennium or more. He would have liked to
have been able to avoid her completely, but Wren needed
the girl.*

As an assistant she was utterly extraordinary.

*Every time Wren thought a problem insolvable, the girl
had the answer.*

*Every time he thought he'd go insane with his workload,
he'd rise one morning to find architectural plans finished
and a detailed list of design ideas to one side for whatever
new project had been sent his way.*

*Every time Wren thought he had no ideas left, he'd have
a brief chat with the girl and, suddenly, inspiration struck.*

*Her input was invaluable. She had interest in the
strangest of things: this church, that warehouse, this
wharf. Whenever Wren saw her waiting for him, he knew
that she would have a new suggestion for him. Perhaps she
might suggest he realign a hospital or house he was design-
ing, just slightly. Maybe she would suggest the height of a
chimney stack, or the orientation of windows. Possibly this
steeple could be realigned, just a fraction, to match the an-
gle of a street that ran alongside it.*

*The only building the girl was no help with whatsoever
was St. Paul's.*

*"St. Paul's is none of my concern," she told him once
when he'd asked. "It is a foreign land to me, and I am not
welcome there."*

*While St. Paul's may not have interested her, the small
girl did have a lively interest in the church of St. Dun-
stan's-in-the-East. On one morning in early 1670 Wren was
crossing the bridge when he saw the girl waiting for him.*

*He was not surprised, for in his leather satchel he had
the plans for the new spire of St. Dunstan's.*

"Well?" The girl stepped forward, her eyes bright. She'd been badgering him for weeks to see this design. She'd made several suggestions as soon as she'd heard Wren had been commissioned to rebuild the spire, but out of sheer bloody-mindedness Wren had not yet shown her his final design.

For a moment Wren did not respond. Then he sighed, and pulled a rolled-up piece of paper from his satchel.

Before he could speak, the girl snatched the paper from Wren's hands, and unrolled it. Her eyes brightened as they ran over the design. "It is very beautiful," she said.

"Very different from my other spires."

"And there are stairs?"

"Yes." Wren turned the paper over. "Here. See?"

The little girl drew in a deep breath, then she nodded, and handed the plans back to Wren.

"It is very fine," she said. "Thank you."

Wren rolled up the paper, regarding her quizzically. "Why is St. Dunstan's-in-the-East so important to you?"

"It will be a tomb one day, Mr. Wren, and I wanted it to be an especially fine one."

"A tomb?" Wren suppressed a shudder. "Why the stairs, then?"

The girl smiled, the expression so cold Wren actually took a step back. "Because every tomb needs a way out, don't you think?"

Chapter One

The Faerie and Ambersbury Banks

Sunday, 22 September 1940

EPPING FOREST LAY QUIET AND STILL UNder the warm sun. Pollen motes danced in the shafts of sunshine lancing down through the forest canopy, and the leaves of the trees stirred gently, turned by the warmth of the air rather than by any breeze. It was a quiet, still, warm September day in Epping Forest.

Several score cyclists, hikers, and horse riders made the most of the warmth, moving languidly along the forest paths. Some of them approached Ambersbury Banks, thinking either to partake of a picnic lunch atop its rise, or to take in the view, but without fail every one turned back when they approached within a hundred yards or so of the Banks.

They'd suddenly thought of something better to do, or a movement to their flank distracted them, or they abruptly remembered they should be turning for home right now.

The mortal world left Ambersbury Banks well alone on Sunday the twenty-second of September 1940.

The ancient battlefield and pagan center of worship was shrouded with druidic magic. Here the shafts of sunlight were wider and brighter and more numerous so that the summit of Ambersbury appeared as if bathed in a golden, dancing waterfall. The wood-bound altar stone gleamed, and periodically shafts of sunlight refracted off the stone

and shot silver and gold splinters of light back into the tree tops.

Figures moved slowly around the edges of the summit. Members of the Faerie, gods, and those once-mortals who had been entangled in the machinations of the Troy Game had gathered here to witness, finally, the handing back to the Kingman, to Ringwalker, four of the golden Kingship bands of Troy.

The gathering consisted of Sidlesaghes, water sprites, many of the forest deer, as well as Noah, Weyland, Eaving's Sisters, the Caroller (who stood slightly apart from Eaving's Sisters), Malcolm (who had a briefcase sitting on the ground several feet behind him), and Silvius. They stood in a rough circle about the central altar where waited Jack Skelton—Ringwalker.

Jack was dressed in the white linen hip wrap he'd once worn as Brutus, bound with a scarlet and gold corded waistband. As Brutus Jack had worn sandals, but now his feet were bare so that he might keep constant contact with the land.

Across his shoulders, the markings of the stag God appeared very dark. Occasionally they became a little indistinct, as if they quivered.

As Jack waited, he walked slowly about the altar stone, keeping his eyes averted from all the watchers. He felt peaceful and very still, a state of being he'd never enjoyed as Brutus, or as William, or as Louis. Everything about the day felt *right*. Today four of the Kingship bands would return to his flesh, a homecoming for which he'd been aching for over three thousand years.

And yet all he felt was stillness and peace, and a sense of such well-being and warmth, both physical and spiritual, that Jack thought he could wait here for hours (days, months, years) and still not fret.

Jack understood that this sense of peace and well-being and stillness had very little to do with the knowledge that within an hour or less four of the bands would be his once again. Instead, it had everything to do with Grace. He knew that if it had been Noah to hand the bands to him, he would have felt anxious and impatient, and would have spent this

time pacing up and down wondering what *else* Noah might possibly do to upset him, to hinder, to create chaos.

From the moment he'd first met her as Cornelia, Noah had brought nothing but disarray and disharmony to his life. Oh, there had been joy and love there as well, but those had been such fleeting moments, they'd been all but lost within the turmoil.

Grace was the temple bell, ringing out amid the disorder.

Jack stopped his slow wandering about the altar stone. He stood still, centered in a broad shaft of sunlight, struck by the realization that Grace meant very much more to him than just a perfect, harmonious match of power, or a desirable woman. She was what he had always lacked along his series of tumultuous lives—his keystone. A kernel of peace to which he could always return.

At that very moment Grace appeared at the edge of the summit. Ariadne—who had spent this past hour preparing Grace for the ritual—stood just behind her.

Grace was dressed as a Mistress of the Labyrinth, wearing a long white linen skirt, bound at her waist with a match to Jack's scarlet and golden waistband. Her breasts were bare of any covering, her limbs of any jewelry, her short curls brushed loose and free.

"Grace," Jack said.

She walked toward him, slowly, gracefully, and if she was nervous she did not show it. She came to within a pace of him, her eyes direct on his, then halted.

Jack could not believe how composed and how lovely Grace looked. She was still a little too thin, but held herself with enough poise that it did not detract from her overall loveliness.

Thank God it is Grace standing here, and not Noah. The thought rocked Jack, and made him realize as nothing else how radically his life had altered in the past year.

Thank God, he whispered into Grace's mind, *that it is you standing here, and not your mother.*

Then Jack stepped forward and took Grace's right wrist in his right hand.

Chapter Two

Sunday, 22 September 1940

Grace Speaks

T HANK GOD, HE SAID, *THAT IT IS YOU standing here, and not your mother.*

I'd been nervous to that point, not much, but enough to unsettle me. I'd never been so much the center of attention, I'd never had such a vital role to play, I'd never been all but naked before Jack, and what we were about to do would be such an intimacy (atop the semi-nakedness) that I hadn't been able to quell a flutter of nerves in my stomach as I'd walked out from the cover of the trees into the glade.

But, oh, what a wonderful thing for him to say. Suddenly there was nothing for me but him. All my awareness of the watchers vanished as if they were not there. All my self-consciousness vanished. All my doubts faded, and I was overwhelmed with the sense that I was doing something very, very right.

He reached out, and slid his hand about my right wrist, and with that touch he became my entire world.

His hand moved up my forearm, his fingers very lightly tracing out the lines of the scars.

His eyes didn't move from mine, nor allow mine to drop away.

His hand slid over my elbow, then up to my biceps. There it stilled, and I felt both its warmth and its pressure increase.

Grace . . . he whispered in my mind, and I felt the power of the labyrinth curl about me.

Through me.

Grace . . .

I closed my eyes momentarily—surrendering to the power—then let my own power rise to meet his.

Grace.

Oh, gods, it felt good. During my time with Ariadne, Silvius had occasionally touched me with his Kingman power, but it was a pale shadow compared to how Jack's power now enveloped me. I remembered how I had felt when last we'd been together atop Ambersbury Banks, the night of the parish hall dance, and that also was a pale shadow to what I experienced now.

Jack touched me, and tears misted in my eyes, because I had never, never thought to experience anything this beautiful.

Or this intimate. I can barely explain it, the sense of someone pervading deep into your being. It should have felt intrusive, and maybe if it had been anyone but Jack, it would have been.

But Jack took so much care. Everything—his expression, his touch, his power—was so gentle that I felt nothing but serenity. I trusted him utterly, and he me, for we were both completely open to each other, both completely in the other's hands and power.

The warmth and pressure of his hand increased, and I felt that sensual thrill that, so Ariadne had said, always existed between a Kingman and Mistress of the Labyrinth when they entwined their powers. I hadn't felt it before with Jack—oh, there'd been attraction, but I hadn't experienced this sexual connection that a Kingman and Mistress experience when they touch each other with their power.

I'd never been this relaxed with anyone before in my life.

Jack's eyes had darkened, and I knew he was feeling it as well. But along with that sexual awareness came a sense of humor. I saw the skin about the corners of his eyes crinkle a little, and I smiled, and we shared humor and peace and thrill and stillness.

The pressure of Jack's fingers increased yet further. Their touch burned through my skin—

Grace.

—and I surrendered to it, and surrendered into what it demanded.

The first of the golden bands of Troy.

The golden metal rose up through my flesh from where it had been resting.

Oh gods, the *arousal* of it! What had I said to Ariadne when she and Silvius had shown me the vision of the ancient Kingman drawing forth the bands from a Mistress of the Labyrinth? That this was the ultimate intimacy a Kingman and Mistress could share? I understood that statement now as I hadn't been capable of understanding it then. It was a sexual intimacy, and thus the arousal, but it went far beyond that.

Way beyond it.

It was the absolute opening of yourself to another person, and it involved the absolute trust of each of those people in each other.

We both felt it. We stared at each other, sharing completely this astounding experience, and the fact that the golden band had now risen almost into his hand was almost irrelevant. Far more important was this opening and sharing.

The band had formed completely now; I felt its cool weight encircling my right biceps. My eyes filled with tears—at the overwhelming sensations flooding through me, and at the expression on Jack's face—and thus I could not see very well, but I felt Jack's hand slide between the golden band and my skin, and then I felt the band begin to move.

Infinitely slowly, but move it did, sliding over Jack's hand and somehow, in the process, separating itself from my own arm. He kept his hand resting on my biceps, his eyes on mine, but both of us *felt* that band move up Jack's forearm, over his elbow, slowly, slowly up his arm until it reached his biceps.

Where, waiting to greet it, were Jack's marks, slithering about almost in a frenzy, wrapping themselves about the band, caressing it, bedding it down so that it would never move again.

Never again be taken from his flesh.

"Oh gods, Grace," I heard Jack whisper, and then I felt his left hand reach out and slide up my own left arm, up to my biceps, so that Jack now stood very close to me, his arms crossed over—and grazing against, with every breath I took—my breasts.

The second band, that which lay deep beneath my upper left arm, began to rise up to meet Jack's hand.

Again, that almost overwhelming sexuality combined with the far greater intimacy of complete trust.

When that band had risen from my flesh and had moved to Jack's left biceps, then Jack slid his crossed hands down my arms—so slowly, so sensuously—to just below my elbows, where waited two more of the golden bands of Troy.

They rose together, the sensations now so overwhelming that I think I would have fallen were it not for Jack's gentle grasp on my arms, moving over Jack's hands up to a point just below his own elbows where, again, his marks waited to greet them.

When it was all done, I had to swallow in order to find the strength to speak.

"It is done, Jack," I whispered.

There was something in his eyes, something unknowable. He was a different man now. He had four of his Kingship bands, and they empowered him, *deepened* him, more than I'd thought possible.

At that point I wanted badly to move away from him, to somehow cope with all the emotions and sensations that still surged through me. To evaluate what had just happened.

I tried to lean back, to break the contact between us, but his grip firmed a little.

Trust me, he whispered in my mind.

"No," he said, "we are not yet done."

Then he finally lifted his eyes away from mine and looked to where Malcolm stood.

"Prasutagus," he said, "will you bring forth the box from the briefcase?"

Prasutagus? I'd heard the name somewhere previously. It had a strange familiarity about it, and it made my stomach turn over, but I had no idea why.

Why had Jack called Malcolm "Prasutagus"? What was happening?

There was a sound behind me, then Malcolm appeared at my side. In his hands he bore a wide leather box of some six inches in depth. It was beautifully made, its hinges and clasp of twisted gold, and I felt Jack shudder as he looked at it.

About us I felt the watching circle stir. I had been unaware of their presence until now—all I'd seen was Jack, all I'd felt was Jack—but now I sensed their curiosity and bewilderment.

Finally Jack's hands slid away from me, and now it was I who shivered.

He ran his hands over the box, lovingly, then, one hand still resting on the box, he looked back to me.

"Grace," he said, "do you remember I said I would give you a birthday gift?"

It had been that night we'd danced here, that night he said he'd felt how our powers matched.

I nodded. I was so overcome with emotion that he *had* remembered, and thought to give me a gift now, before all these people, that I didn't think I could speak.

"Then this is my gift to you," he said, and with his hand he opened the box.

My eyes must still have been misted with tears, because for a moment all I could see was a blur of brilliant light. Then Jack lifted something from the box, and, as I heard Ariadne laugh and my mother gasp, I blinked away my remaining tears and looked at a piece of jewelry that was so extraordinary I simply could not immediately comprehend it.

It was a bracelet of exquisite delicacy. From a thin wristband of diamond-set platinum, tendrils, or sprays, of diamonds radiated out in a complex and not immediately discernable pattern. It was like nothing I'd ever seen before. I must have frowned, trying to make it out, for from the corner of my eye I saw Jack smile, and reach out with one hand to take my right wrist and with the other slip the bracelet over my right hand.

The wristband fitted perfectly about my wrist. From there the tendrils, some fourteen or fifteen of them, spread

up my arm like twisted rivulets, some of the tendrils almost to my elbow.

They followed precisely the lines of my scars.

"Grace," Jack said, "these lines of diamonds track the lines of your scars, but they do not hide them, they *celebrate* them. Do you know what I'm saying to you? Do you understand?"

I couldn't think. I didn't *want* to think. I had no idea what Jack meant with this gift.

"Grace," he said, "I know of very few people, I know of *no one,* who could have survived what Catling has done to you with the same courage and dignity that you have managed. I couldn't do it, *haven't* done it; neither has your mother, not anyone else who has been caught up in this terrible Game. Everyone has made mistakes, taken missteps, and created havoc as they've done it. You've managed to exist within a purity and a grace and a clarity that is extraordinary. Grace, these bands"—now he lifted another one from its box and slipped it over my left wrist, where the sprays of diamonds again aligned themselves perfectly with the twistings of my scars—"celebrate your courage and your dignity. The diamonds are for your clarity, your sheer *brilliance,* the platinum celebrates your courage and dignity."

And they also replace what I have taken from you, he spoke into my mind. *You gifted bands to me, now I gift these to you.*

I couldn't speak.

He smiled, the expression very gentle, very sweet. "Can you see what I've done to them? Can you feel it?"

I shook my head. I felt numb. I had no idea what he was going to say now.

The grin widened very slightly. "These diamond bands were made by a jeweler in the West End to my design. He thought I was a crazy Yank." That smile stretched just a little further. "When he gave them to me yesterday morning I brought them to this spot and here I put something else into them. Something of me. A glamour. Grace, if you accept these bands from me they will never come off. They will cleave to your flesh as closely as do the Kingship bands of Troy to mine. But what the glamour enables you to do is to hide them or display them as you wish. *Do* you feel it?"

I was still numb (I was actually thinking that he'd arranged all of this yesterday, and then taken me to dinner and had said nothing of it), but now he'd pointed that out to me, yes, I could sense the glamour.

"They will not stop Catling from touching you, Grace, but when she does fire up her hex, and encircle you with agony, the diamonds will flare into light, and everyone about you will know of your courage and your grace."

I wish he'd stop speaking. I didn't think I could stand any more.

"I wish I could stop the pain, Grace," he said, and I saw tears in his eyes. "I wish I could, but I am powerless in that."

I tried to take in a deep breath, felt it tremble alarmingly, and stopped it before I could embarrass myself with tears.

"Will you accept the diamond bands, Grace?"

I looked at him then, and thought of everything we had shared and felt in this magical place on this day. "Yes," I said.

Chapter Three

FAERIE HILL MANOR

Sunday, 22 September 1940

NOAH STOOD IN THE DRAWING ROOM AT Faerie Hill Manor and watched as Grace, now dressed in more modern and modest clothing, slipped out the French windows. Noah glanced about the room.

Jack was nowhere to be seen.

She looked back to the French windows. It didn't take much imagination to work out that Grace had gone to talk to Jack.

Noah was torn. She needed to speak to the two of them,

and now would be the perfect chance as everyone else remained in the room, but on the other hand she didn't want to disturb them.

Or to walk in on something that might embarrass everyone.

Noah, as everyone else, she thought, save the strange enigmatic Malcolm (or Prasutagus, as Jack had called him), had been stunned by what had happened atop Ambersbury Banks. Not merely by Grace's sheer beauty and power and competence, but by what Jack had done for her afterward.

Those diamond bands. Stunning. And, oh, their meaning. The gift itself was extraordinary, but Jack could have chosen to give those bands to Grace at any time. His timing was no fluke, and it was deeply meaningful. What had happened atop Ambersbury Banks was a virtual exchange of bands, of rings, and all that symbolized. When it happened between a Kingman and a Mistress of the Labyrinth it added further layers of meaning and symbolism.

Until today Noah had not suspected the depth of what Jack felt for Grace.

Gods, she needed to talk to them both so badly. Noah put down her glass and slowly moved around the room, heading for the glass doors. What was Jack planning? And why was she so concerned? Did her uneasiness come from her role as woman, mother, or Mistress of the Labyrinth?

"What a mess," Noah muttered, and, taking a deep breath, slipped out to the terrace.

Jack, now back in his military uniform, and Grace were standing not very far away and, to Noah's relief, they weren't engaged in anything even vaguely embarrassing. In fact, they were merely standing together, talking.

"I'm sorry to interrupt," Noah said. "I wanted the opportunity to speak with the both of you."

Jack looked wary, but Grace smiled, and Noah leaned forward, gave her a hug, then took Grace's hands in hers, using the opportunity to inspect the diamond bracelets.

"They're *beautiful*," Noah said. She gave her head a little shake in wonderment. "And so powerful. Jack, these are so extraordinary. As is what you said to Grace when you

gave them to her. Thank you, from my heart. You have done more for her in the year you've been back than I've managed in three hundred."

Noah gave her daughter's hands a little squeeze, then let them go. "Jack, how does it feel, to have four of the bands back?"

Noah was genuinely curious. Jack had hunted and lusted and fought for those bands for well over three thousand years, yet now he seemed so calm. She could sense the change in him, the *deepening* and shifting of power, but to be so calm? He had changed, indeed.

Jack's face had relaxed a little. "They feel warm, Noah." He laughed a little at the expression on her face. "Really. They feel warm against my skin, and they feel . . . happy. Glad to be home, perhaps."

"And have they given you a greater understanding, Jack?" Noah asked, and Grace looked inquisitively at Jack as well.

Jack hesitated before replying. "I need to get down to London to see if the bands help any more with the strange shadow hanging over London. But I won't do that until I retrieve the other two bands."

"And you'll do that . . . when?" said Noah.

"Tomorrow," Jack said. "The Lord of the Faerie will take me into the Otherworld tomorrow."

Noah looked at him carefully. It seemed to her that Jack was torn between two competing emotions—excitement and worry.

"Jack," she said quietly. "Where are we going?" Before Jack could answer, Noah hurried on. "Please don't take what I say amiss. I just don't know . . . Jack, what you did for Grace today was wonderful, and I begrudge neither you nor her whatever awaits you . . . but I don't know where we, *I,* stand now with the Troy Game. Grace is a powerful Mistress of the Labyrinth, and she matches you, Jack, anyone can see that, but she can't help with the Troy Game. Grace"—Noah turned back to her daughter—"please don't think I am trying to—"

"Mother," Grace said, smiling, "don't worry. Jack and I were just talking of the same thing when you came out."

"Grace is pivotal," said Jack, "but no one seems to know why. You're right. Grace can't help with the Troy Game; she's too tightly tied to it. Catling's fate is hers."

Noah reached out a hand and laid it gently against Grace's cheek. "Gods damn it," she said softly, "I wish I could protect you." Her mouth gave a rueful quirk. "But I know I can't, and I know I've tried too hard to shelter you. Fly off with my blessing, Grace, but don't ask me to stop worrying about you."

Then she looked back to Jack. "And remember always that she is my daughter, Jack, and that I love her above anything else. Don't hurt her, *please don't hurt her*."

Then, before either Jack or Grace could respond, Noah turned and walked back inside.

THEY WATCHED HER GO, WAITED UNTIL THE DOOR closed behind her, then lapsed into a momentary awkward silence.

"Noah has a highly uncomfortable way of talking truth," said Jack. "And I have a terrible reputation with women, Grace—"

"I trust you, Jack."

"Surely Matilda and Ecub have brought you up with some terrible tales."

"I trust you, Jack."

I'm not too sure I trust myself, Jack thought, keeping the thought from Grace.

"Shit," he muttered. "I've been doing this for at least three thousand years. You'd think I'd be a bit better at it by now."

"Jack?"

He reached out a hand and cupped her face, then leaned forward and kissed her very softly, very quietly.

Grace's mouth twitched. "That's *all* you've learned in three thousand years?"

He laughed, once again taken by surprise by her sense of humor. "Grace Orr, I am going to enjoy getting to know you very, very much."

"I'm glad to hear you say that, now that you'd had what you wanted from me." Once again, rich humor ran through her voice.

"I said, Grace, that there were four reasons I wanted to get to know you better, and the fact you carried the four bands within your flesh was the fourth and least of those reasons."

She held his eyes easily, but when she spoke, it was to change the subject, and Jack realized that this getting to know her process would necessarily be done slowly.

Surprisingly, for a man who had once been Brutus, the thought caused him no impatience at all.

"Why did you call Malcolm Prasutagus?" Grace said.

"Do you know the name?"

"It is familiar, but I don't know why."

"King Prasutagus was Boudicca's husband."

Her eyes widened. "Malcolm is *Prasutagus?*"

"Aye. It is why he came to me at Copt Hall."

Grace frowned. "I don't understand."

"You don't know the legend of Boudicca?"

"I've heard of it, yes. But the details? No."

Jack leaned back against the wall of the house, folding his arms. "Boudicca and her army faced the Romans in Epping Forest. Ambersbury Banks was her last stand. She lost, and some sixty thousand of her soldiers died on the ancient fort."

Grace's mouth dropped open, but Jack continued before she could say anything. "Boudicca survived the slaughter and fled, the Romans harrying at her heels. She went to the site of Copt Hall, and there, with her daughters, took poison. Both Ambersbury Banks and Copt Hall are important sites for Prasutagus. He's not merely a king, Grace, but a powerful druid as well."

"Why is he back, Jack?"

He sighed. "I don't know. I sense he is trustworthy, and that he is for the land, but Malcolm—Prasutagus—is none too forthcoming when asked a direct question."

"Why did you call him Prasutagus today?"

Jack hesitated a little before replying. "Because I wanted him to hand me those bands in his capacity as a druid, not a servant."

"Why?"

"Because I wanted those bands to be as special as possible." *Because I wanted them infused with druid power.*

She took a deep breath, her eyes bright with emotion.

Jack could see she was struggling to find the right words to say, so he slipped his arm around her back and pulled her to him gently. "Just dance with me, here on the terrace, with no one to witness but the stars and the trees."

"Tell me you know where you're going, Jack."

He knew she referred to so much with that question.

"Grace," he said very quietly, resting his cheek against her curls as they started to dance slowly around the terrace, "I will go wherever you lead."

Chapter Four

THE OTHERWORLD

Monday, 23 September 1940

WELL, JACK, ARE YOU READY?"
Jack stood with the Lord of the Faerie on top of The Naked, dressed as he had been the previous day atop Ambersbury Bank in his white linen wrap. He felt very calm, and curiously detached. He'd been worried about the first four bands—*could Grace truly do it?*—but these . . . these would be easy. The Lord of the Faerie was so powerful that not even a trip into the Otherworld would tax him. The bands were an hour away at best.

"You're sure you remember where you left them?" he said. When the Lord of the Faerie had been merely Harold of Wessex, Coel-reborn, he'd taken the remaining two bands, the leg bands, into the Otherworld at the time of his death in order to keep them safe.

"Of course. Are you sure you can handle the power?"

Jack grinned. That final comment had been pure Coel. He raised his arms, crossing them over in front of him and running his hands over the bands on his biceps and upper forearms. "Are you afraid of what I might do with the power?"

The Lord of the Faerie laughed. "Aye, indeed I am. Tell me, Jack, *do* you feel different?"

"Every breath feels sweeter, Coel. The sun shines more warmly. I feel complete. Almost."

Jack had not slept at all the previous night. Instead he'd lain awake, feeling the four golden bands with every sense that he had. They felt so *right*. They felt as if they had never been away. And, aye, he did feel almost complete. In the past twenty-four hours every sense of his had sharpened, those he commanded as a man, as a Kingman, and as Ringwalker, God of the forests. He felt as if he understood more, and when he thought on the shadow over London, its truth seemed so close, as if all he needed to do was reach out and grab it . . .

Those final two bands, and he'd have the truth, once and for all.

Another hour, and his path ahead would be clear.

"Let's go," he said to the Lord of the Faerie.

THEY STEPPED OFF THE NAKED AND DIRECTLY into the road for the Otherworld. Jack was awed by Coel's power, for Jack could not have done this so easily.

The road stretched out before them, a faint trackway through a grassy field.

Jack looked around curiously. This wasn't the first time he'd traveled the road into the Otherworld—he'd died as Brutus and as William—but this roadway was different from either of the two roads he'd taken before.

"The road is different each time and for each person," said the Lord of the Faerie, who walked a half pace ahead of Jack. "For us, now, it will be short. We have not come to stay, but only to visit."

"We won't go entirely into the Otherworld?"

"No."

"But then how will you find the bands?"

The Lord of the Faerie grinned a little at the anxiety in Jack's voice. "I gave them to someone who has kept them safe. He knows we're on our way and will meet us at the border. With the bands."

"Who did you give them to?"

The Lord of the Faerie nodded ahead. "Him."

Jack looked forward. There was a faint line of trees in the distance, and he could just make out the shape of a man standing beneath them.

As they neared, the man stepped forth into the open, and Jack saw that the man had shoulder-length black curly hair, and wore the costume of an Aegean prince.

"Do you recognize him, Jack?" the Lord of the Faerie said.

Jack nodded. "Oh, aye," he said softly.

WHEN THEY GOT TO THE MAN THEY HALTED, AND Jack bowed slightly. "Greetings, Aeneas," he said. *Aeneas, his forefather, son of Aphrodite and a prince of Troy.*

Aeneas stared a long moment at Jack, then he stepped forward, put his hands on Jack's shoulders, and kissed him on each cheek.

"Greetings to you, Brutus. I have been watching you, off and on, for all these years."

Jack grimaced. "It must not have been pretty viewing."

Aeneas grinned. The Lord of the Faerie thought that he looked strikingly similar to Jack, although his forehead was broader and his nose blunter.

"None of us lived pretty lives, Brutus," Aeneas said. "You have been no worse than any of your line."

"Not even in recreating the Troy Game," said Jack, "in such a vile form that—"

"Brutus," Aeneas said, "the Troy Game was always vile. What do you think destroyed Troy?"

Jack stared, shocked.

"It wasn't the Greeks," said Aeneas. "Not in the final count. Our Game, she who was supposed to protect us, de-

cided she wanted to destroy the city of Troy and all who lived in it."

Jack was still staring at Aeneas, unable to speak, so the Lord of the Faerie asked the obvious question. "Why?"

"She wanted to move on," said Aeneas. "She saw in the land of Llangarlia, and the site that is now London, far greater power. Brutus, be careful."

"God," Jack muttered. "But you think that she can be destroyed?"

"Who knows? I cannot see that from here."

Jack took a deep breath. "I need the Kingship bands, the final two. Coel"—he nodded at the Lord of the Faerie—"said that he gave them to you."

Aeneas smiled at the Lord of the Faerie. "Of course he did. And I kept them safe for thousands of years."

Jack looked carefully at Aeneas. " '*Kept* them safe'?"

"I no longer have them. I gave them to the young woman in the black dress."

Jack did not think he had been so profoundly shocked, or horrified, in all his lives. "You . . . did . . . *what*?"

Aeneas' calm demeanor altered in the space of breath. His face contorted in anger, and he leaned forward and dealt Jack a slap across the chest. "I gave them to the young woman in the black dress. Your daughter. She—"

"*She is not my daughter! She is the Troy Game incarnate!*"

"She said she wanted them," finished Aeneas. "She said she would keep them safe for you. I believed her."

"What have you done?" Jack said, then he turned and half ran, half walked back down the road into the Faerie.

Aeneas looked at the Lord of the Faerie, who appeared almost as shocked as Jack.

"She was his *daughter*," Aeneas repeated. "Of course I trusted her."

THE LORD OF THE FAERIE GRABBED AT JACK'S ARM as Jack started to run down The Naked.

"Jack! Jack!"

"How could you have done this to me?" Jack snarled, and the Lord of the Faerie stepped back, horrified, letting go of Jack's arm.

"Jack, I had no idea that Aeneas would give them to Catling!"

Jack stared at the Faerie lord. "I can't believe that Catling had the power to do that. I can't believe that Aeneas *handed her the fucking bands!*"

He paused and visibly collected himself. "Coel, I am sorry. I should not have shouted at you, and you are not to blame for what has happened. But Aeneas . . . Aeneas *should have known!*"

There was a long silence.

"Gods, Jack," the Lord of the Faerie said, "what are you going to do?"

Jack ran a shaking hand over his eyes. "I don't know. I just don't know."

Chapter Five

St. Paul's and Faerie Hill Manor

Monday, 23 September 1940

HE WENT STRAIGHT TO ST. PAUL'S, TO THE crypt, to Catling. It was midafternoon, and the crypt of the cathedral was filled with workers, staff, and members of the cathedral Watch, but none of them saw the dark-haired man who stormed down the steps from the nave, nor did they see the young woman dressed in black who waited for him by the Duke of Wellington's tomb.

Jack was still dressed only in the white linen wrap of the Aegean Kingman, and Catling's eyes gleamed in pleasure at the sight of the four golden bands that glowed on his arms.

"You have done very well," she said. "I am pleased. When will you retrieve the final two?"

Jack's temper shattered. "You have them! Why? *Why?* What is the point? Give them to me, Catling."

Catling's eyes widened and she leaned back, a hand to the base of her throat, as if she were afraid. "I? I have not taken them. What is this, Jack? What manner of excuse?"

"You went to the Otherworld and you tricked Aeneas into giving you the—"

"I did not! Have you lost the bands, Jack? Have you lost the remaining two Kingship bands?"

They were standing close, and the air between them crackled with anger. Jack raised a hand, stabbing a forefinger at Catling.

"You *bitch*! What game do you play, then? What point first in taking the bands, and now in this pretense of innocence?"

Catling had gone very white, far paler than normal, and the black of her gown rippled, as if it were as furious as the entity it clothed.

"Don't speak to me like this, Jack."

"I want those bands!"

"And I want you to have them. Damn you, what kind of a fool are you! Did you think I will believe this tale of 'Oh, the bands are gone, and you have taken them, Catling'? No, no! I have not taken them! *You* have *lost* them!"

Jack forced himself to take a breath before answering her. Dear gods, this pretense of innocence was so transparent!

"You're holding them to blackmail me," he said. "Holding them to ensure I do what you want. Holding them to make sure I don't try to harm you. Holding them to force Noah and me to come down here to dance your final completion. Where are they, then?" Jack spun about, his eyes searching out every corner of the crypt. "Where have you secreted—"

Catling stepped forward and seized Jack's wrist.

"I don't like this, Jack. I don't like this at all. I am going to be very angry indeed if you can't find those bands."

Her grip tightened until Jack, despite himself, cried out in pain.

"I need you to have those bands, Jack. I don't believe

this prattle of 'Oh, you have taken them, Catling.' You could, surely, have come up with something a little more believable. Now—" Her grip tightened yet more so that Jack's knees sagged, and he managed to prevent himself from sinking to the floor only with a supreme effort of will. "—I have been very patient. Too patient. I've had enough. All my good temper has evaporated. I need to impress on you my authority, I think. What I do now, Jack, is merely the beginning. You need to find those bands. The longer you leave it the more those closest to you will suffer. The longer *London* will suffer. *Find those bands, Jack!*"

She released her grip, and Jack finally sagged to the floor.

The next moment he heard a cry of such agony it tore through to his very soul.

JACK DIDN'T HAVE THE FINAL TWO BANDS!

Catling didn't know what to think, even *how* to think. Who had them? *How* could they have vanished from the Otherworld?

Her instinctive reaction had been to wrap Grace in as much agony as she could, simply because that would keep Jack occupied for a while.

Catling needed to think.

"The imps," Catling muttered. "They might know where they are."

But no matter how much Catling hunted through London, she could not find the imps.

GRACE HAD BEEN WAITING WITH HER PARENTS, Stella, Ariadne, and Silvius at Faerie Hill Manor. When the Lord of the Faerie materialized before them (forgetting in his anxiety to assume his mortal form as Harry), they all rose from their seats, but the Lord of the Faerie spoke before they could ask him the question.

"They're gone," he said. "The final two bands have gone. Catling has them."

Noah gasped, while Grace took a step back, then sank back down to the sofa.

Her face was stricken.

"Catling took them?" Noah said. "Why? And how? Oh gods, if she has the power to reach into the Otherworld . . ."

"Who knows the how or the why," the Lord of the Faerie said, finally morphing back into the gentler form of Harry. "Jack has gone to St. Paul's to confront Catling."

"That is not such a good idea," said Grace softly.

Noah sat back down beside her. "Grace—"

"Not such a good idea," Grace whispered, raising her wrists to her chest.

"Grace—"

Before Noah could say anything more, Grace cried out, then convulsed, falling to the floor with the extremity of her pain.

In an instant Ariadne joined Noah at Grace's side, the others standing close about.

"Gods," Noah whispered. "I have never seen it so bad!"

Ariadne had to admit to herself that she couldn't think of seeing anything worse herself. When Catling had attacked Grace in Ariadne's apartment, only Grace's wrists and forearms had been involved.

Now it appeared as if all of Grace's body was wrapped in fiery lines of suffering. Her wrists were encased in a vicious red glow, and out from this glow spun lines and tendrils of fire that curled all over and about Grace's body.

Saving her face—left clear if only so everyone else could witness her anguish.

Ariadne put a hand to Grace's shoulder, then seized it back instantly. Grace's body felt as if it were on fire. Ariadne wanted to tell Grace to use the pain, as she had that day Catling had attacked her in Ariadne's apartment, but Ariadne realized that what Catling did now was so much worse, so extreme, that it had consumed Grace completely.

Grace had no chance, no time for thought, to turn the pain to her own use.

Suddenly Jack was there, pushing none too gently through the circle of watchers and dropping down beside Ariadne.

He reached out to touch Grace, then jerked his hands back as Grace cried out.

"Dear God," he whispered, his voice breaking, "what can I do? What can I do?"

Ariadne looked carefully at him, looked at the bands about his limbs and then down to the diamonds twinkling through the fire about Grace's wrists.

"There is something," she said. "Something I did once for Noah and Stella."

Chapter Six

SILVIUS' PALACE, ALBA

Monday, 23 September 1940

Grace Speaks

I FELT IT RATHER THAN HEARD IT, A VOICE THAT intruded into my pain.

Follow me.

I hated it. I wanted to try to concentrate on bearing the agony, to try and concentrate enough that I could use the pain as Ariadne had taught me, and this voice was a distraction.

Follow me.

Catling had never attacked me in this fashion before. I hadn't realized she had the capability. I wasn't happy to discover it now. She'd taken over every square inch of my body—at least that's what it felt like—and poured kerosene over it, and put a match to it. My skin burned and bubbled and—

Follow me.

Go away! I screamed at it. *Let me alone!*

Grace, please, follow my voice. I have found a cool, cool place for you.

It was Jack, I knew that, but I really didn't want him now. I just wanted to concentrate on overcoming and then using the pain.

But it was so extreme. So consuming. I didn't know if I could . . .

Grace, Grace, please. Trust me.

Trust Jack . . .

Come with me, Grace, please.

I followed him.

"WHERE ARE WE?" I SAID.

I was amazed I could manage even those three words. The pain had vanished, and I was almost delirious with relief.

We stood in a courtyard, furnished only with a bench under an apple tree and a pond full of flashing gold and silver fish.

"This was my father's house in Alba," Jack said, sitting down on the bench.

"Silvius' house?" I said, taking a seat beside him.

"Aye. This courtyard was his inner sanctum, his favorite place. I only came here for the first time relatively recently, during my transformation into Ringwalker."

That was significant, but I wasn't sure why. "It was nice of you to bring me," I said, then gave a soft laugh. "I'm sorry. That was a little banal. But I'm just so relieved that the pain has gone, and I do thank you for it from the depths of my heart. How did you manage it?"

"Ariadne suggested it. She used this enchantment to bring your mother out of her body during that time . . . um, during that time . . ."

"When my father tore her apart. I know about it, Jack."

"Well, she told me how to bring you out of your body to a place of sanctuary. To somewhere you could endure without pain. A peaceful, cool place."

I remembered what my mother had told me about that terrible day when my father had torn apart her and Stella, or Jane as she had been then. Ariadne had dragged them to Tower Fields, but only in spirit. Their bodies had been left bleeding and torn on the kitchen floor of the house in Idol Lane.

As my body would still be writhing in agony on the floor of the drawing room at Faerie Hill Manor. But *I* was gone, *I* had escaped that tormented body, as Noah and Stella had once escaped theirs, and I felt boundless gratitude to both Ariadne, for suggesting it, and Jack, for calling to me.

I do not think I would have followed any other voice.

"And she told you to bring me here?" I said.

"No. She actually suggested Tower Fields. I thought this was nicer."

I was pleased.

Jack took one of my hands, raising my arm slightly.

"Look," he said, "the fish are mirrored in your diamond bands."

Indeed they were. Flashes of gold and red and silver skittered up and down the tendrils and sprays of diamonds.

"Silvius told me he loved me in this courtyard," Jack continued. "I had never realized that he loved me. It was a shock. I thought I was a disappointment to him."

The significance of why he had brought me to this place now hit me.

"Grace"—his other hand now trailed fingers over my face, softly, slowly—"whatever you want is yours."

Everything I had ever heard about this man had taught me to believe that he stampeded people, and bullied and pushed to get what he wanted.

This man here was so different.

"How can you be so sure that I am what you want?" I asked.

"Because when I was waiting for you on Ambersbury Bank I realized that I would want to wait for no one else."

I trusted Jack completely, but I also knew that I needed to take what he offered—a long, slow, gradual slide into whatever awaited us.

He smiled, very slowly, reading my thoughts, then let go my wrist and leaned back against the trunk of the apple tree. "Catling says she does not have those bands."

"Do you believe her?"

"I don't know. She was furious. Completely. She said that my accusation was merely a ruse to hide the fact that I'd lost the final two Kingship bands." He swiveled his head a little so he could look me in the face. "That's why she attacked you. She told me I need to find those bands. That if I don't, then this"—he indicated my wrists, but meant the entire agony Catling had caused (was still causing) me—"was just the beginning. The longer I leave those bands, the more those closest to me will suffer. The more London will suffer."

"God, Jack . . ." It was the threat to the people of London that concerned me. They had suffered so much already, and it appalled me to think what Catling might do next.

"I will find the bands, Grace," he said. "Whoever has them, I will find them."

"But if Catling doesn't have them," I said, "then who?"

"I have no idea. Aeneas said it was Catling. For Christ's sake, Grace, who else would be wandering into the Otherworld, masquerading as Catling, persuading a long-dead Trojan prince to hand her two of the most magical items in existence, and then wander off with them again?"

"I'm sorry, I didn't mean—"

"Don't apologize for my ill temper, Grace. I wasn't irritated with you, but with myself. God, how could I have let this get so out of control? How could I have lost the bands?"

That was an unanswerable question. He hadn't, of course, "lost" the bands at all. He'd merely left them buried around the labyrinth atop Og's Hill and then my mother had managed to take them and hide them.

That thought made my mind lurch in another direction. "Jack, isn't it only someone who is associated with the Game . . . who the bands associate with . . . who can touch them? You, my mother, Aeneas—for he would once have worn them—Silvius for the same reason."

He looked at me with narrowed, speculative eyes. "You."

"What do you mean?" I asked.

"Grace, don't look like that. You're right. It is only someone associated with the Game who can touch them. Your father couldn't, could he?"

I shook my head. "He said they burned him."

"But you *could* touch them. You carried them within your flesh all these years. So . . . how are you associated with the Troy Game? What part are you fated to play?"

"Catling tied me to her with her hex—"

"Perhaps. But you're central in another way, I'm sure of it . . . and yet just can't see it." He grinned. "Guess I'll just have to hang around you, and try to discover it."

I was so relieved he wasn't angry or suspicious that I laughed.

He smiled also, then sobered. "Who could have got them, Grace, if not for one of a very small band among us, or Catling herself? And Aeneas *said* it was Catling. What is she playing at, then, to hide them, and then accuse me and plague you with pain?"

Chapter Seven

FAERIE HILL MANOR

Monday, 23 September 1940

GRACE SIGHED, THEN SAT UP FROM WHERE she'd been lying on the floor. "It's all right. The pain is gone."

"Thank the gods," Noah said, finally relaxing and helping Grace back to the sofa. She looked over to Jack, now standing by the fireplace. When he had taken Grace "away," both of them had remained in the room in body, but it was obvious their spirits had fled.

I wonder where he took her, Noah thought. *I wonder what place was special to him.*

Ariadne nodded to Jack, sharing with him a very small smile, then she looked around the room. "Well, then, what to do? The final two bands have been . . . misplaced, shall we say."

"Lost," Weyland muttered, casting a black look in Jack's direction.

"Stolen," said Harry, firmly.

"*Nothing* can be done without them," Weyland said.

"I have four bands," said Jack. "It is better than nothing. Far better."

"Will you be able to scry out the nature of the shadow?" said Noah to Jack.

He gave a little shrug. "I'll go down to London today. I won't know until I'm down there."

"*Do* you think Catling has them?" Harry said.

Jack looked around the room, considering his answer. "Grace said something to me just now . . . there are very few people who could touch the Kingship bands. Catling is one, and the others are all in this room: Noah, Silvius, Ariadne, Grace herself. Does anyone here want to confess to stealing them? No? Then Catling has them. There is no one else who could take them."

"Why would she take them?" said Noah.

Jack threw his hands up. "Who knows? I have no idea why she'd take them, then claim all this innocence and anger at my 'loss' of them."

"Perhaps she just wants an excuse to act," said Grace.

At that Weyland turned to Jack.

"Why the hell *have* you lost them, Jack? For all the gods' sakes, this is my daughter's *life* you're playing with! Couldn't you have managed to—"

"It not really Jack's fault—" Noah began.

Weyland sent her a glance of simmering anger, and Noah looked away.

"You care nothing but for your own gratification," Weyland went on, addressing Jack once more. "You do nothing but tear lives apart and—"

"Fine words from a man who personally tore apart Cornelia and my three sons when Troia Nova fell!" Jack snarled.

"You haven't thought about them for three and a half thousand damned years," Weyland shouted. "Don't pretend to be feeling a loss now!"

"That's enough!" Silvius roared, making both Weyland and Jack step back. "That's enough," he repeated more moderately. "Catling has played her cards well, eh? To have you two at each other's throats? United you're her doom. Separated by anger and jealousy, you're her triumph. Try to remember it."

Jack and Weyland stared at Silvius, then looked to each other. They didn't say anything, but both nodded, then looked away.

Noah, watching, sighed.

"WELL, WELL," SAID CATLING. "THAT WAS VERY pretty, wasn't it?"

Jack was in his bedroom in Copt Hall. He paused in the act of draping his jacket over the bedpost of his bed, and turned around.

Catling was standing in the door, leaning nonchalantly against its frame, her arms folded.

Jack raised his eyebrows. "Pretty?" He undid the cuffs of his shirtsleeves, then very slowly rolled them up to his elbows, exposing the lower of his armbands. "What was pretty?"

"What you did for Grace," said Catling. "Dragging her away from the pain like that. Very pretty trick. I should have remembered Ariadne might tell you about that; she wouldn't have had the power to drag Grace away from me, but you . . ."

"I'll do it again, Catling. If I need to."

"You've become quite attached to Grace, haven't you, Jack?"

He didn't answer, turning to his side table where Malcolm had laid out a late night whisky, and picking up the glass.

"Whatever you can do for Grace's pain, Jack, you mustn't forget that her fate is tied to mine. Grimacing in pain or smiling happily, she'll go down with me if you think to unwind me."

Jack sat down on the side of his bed, sipping at the whisky. "I haven't forgotten it."

"My, my," said Catling, very softly, very threateningly. "You think you're so clever, eh? Well, so maybe you can rescue Grace from her pain—I've grown a little tired of that trick, anyway—but you can't stop me from wounding you in other ways, Jack. Don't ever, ever forget that."

"Don't think you can—"

"*Don't think to harm me, Jack!* If you do, if you try one more trick like that UXB outside my front door, then I'll *destroy* you!"

"You can't destroy me. You need me."

Catling stared at him. "You have no idea what I can do to you, Jack."

Then she vanished, and Jack was left sitting on the bed, whisky in hand, staring blankly at the now-empty doorway.

Eventually, he roused himself, drained the whisky, then turned out the light, lying down atop the bed fully clothed.

He didn't sleep all night.

NEITHER DID CATLING REST. SOMEONE HAD THE final two bands, and, having thought a little about it, Catling was beginning to think Jack had them, whatever he said.

He wasn't wearing them at present—Catling would have felt that—but no doubt he'd secreted them away at some point, where he could snatch them and use them once he was ready to attack her.

Taken in that context, Jack's little display of indignation and anger was rather amusing. Convince Catling he didn't have the bands, and then strike when she least expected it.

Perhaps she shouldn't have gone to Jack and threatened him again, but the entire day had unsettled Catling just the littlest bit. Best to remind Jack of what she might do if truly riled.

And best for her, she thought, if she started to make some backup plans. Turn all that strength she was gaining from the Blitz to useful purpose. Make sure, absolutely certain, that when Jack and Noah moved they wouldn't be able to snatch her.

Grace was the key.

Grace was the perfect backup plan.

Catling finally managed a small smile, relaxing as she considered her options and how she might use Grace to full effect.

She still didn't like it that the imps had vanished, though.

Where could the dratted black-hearted creatures have got to?

Chapter Eight .

LONDON

Tuesday, 24 September 1940

ACK ROSE BEFORE FIRST LIGHT, DRESSED, took coffee and toast in the kitchen, then drove down to London.

He parked in central London, in the ancient City, and then . . . walked.

Feeling. Feeling the city almost as if it were the first time he'd stepped foot in it. Feeling it as if it were a stranger to him, and he to it. Feeling it with the force and power of the four Kingship bands of Troy that he wore.

He could sense Troy in the city. Sometimes he caught sight of a rampart out of the corner of his eye, and he turned to look, and would think for a moment he saw the walls of Troy rising behind one of London's grim nineteenth-century warehouses.

Sometimes Jack heard the distant wail of an air raid siren, or caught the far distant drone of aircraft as the RAF drove back a Luftwaffe bomber raid, and hear as well the war cries of the Greeks, and the thud of horses' hooves as the besiegers drove their war chariots against Troy's walls yet one more time.

How had he missed this before? Ah, it was the Kingship bands, Jack knew that, but still he was overcome with wonderment as he wandered the City. Had he done this, infused London with the ghostly presence of Troy, or had it been the Game, resurrecting once again its birthplace?

Was this his work, or Catling's?

And what did it mean for London's fate? Was it destined to die like Troy, be *betrayed* as Troy had once been—

By the Troy Game itself, Aeneas had said.

—or would London manage to escape its predecessor's fate, and become master of its own destiny?

To none of these questions could Jack find an answer. All he could do was wander and absorb the greater understanding, the greater reality, of London. It amazed him, enthralled him, terrified him, and comforted him, all in one.

The shadow hung heavier than ever over the city *(had such a shadow hung over Troy? Was it a precursor to destruction?),* and try as Jack might to garner a greater understanding of it, all he could manage was to garner a greater sense of the *hugeness* of it.

Damocles' sword, he thought, had nothing on this.

Toward the evening, when he was worn out from wandering and the frustration of not being able, despite the bands, to scry out any understanding of the shadow, Jack sent a message to Grace.

Grace, are you free? Will you meet me this evening at seven at the corner of Knaresborough Place and Cromwell Road? I need to speak with you. Please, Grace.

He wasn't sure if she would agree, but within moments he received a faint assent, and he smiled, pleased.

And the next moment froze in anger, as Catling once again stood before him.

Jack was moving through the empty back streets of

Covent Garden, heading back to his car. He had almost reached the Austin, when Catling appeared before him.

She stood in the twilight some three or four paces down the street, in the center of the road. She smiled once she realized Jack had seen her, and drew her hands out from behind her back.

She held one of the golden Kingship bands of Troy in each hand.

Do you see these, Jack? Do you want them?

"Damn you," Jack said, taking a step forward. "What is this? First you say you don't have them, and now you *tease* me with them? Why the torment? Just *give* them to me, damn you! I am little use to you without them!"

Catling's form shimmered, as if it had lost strength at Jack's anger, and the bands faded completely from view.

They're in my dark heart, Jack. Waiting for you. All you need do is—

Jack made a grab for the bands, but Catling vanished the instant before he touched them. As Jack stumbled and almost fell, he heard, in the distance, the sound of the air raid sirens starting up again.

The Luftwaffe was back.

GRACE WAS WAITING AT THE CORNER OF KNARES-borough Place and Cromwell Road in Kensington by the time Jack got there just after seven. She had on a dark coat, and a cap pulled down low over her brow, but the top of the coat was open enough for Jack to see that she wore a pretty frock underneath, and he smiled, pleased.

"Ariadne let you out for the night, then?" he said as he bent down and gave her a quick kiss on the cheek.

He wondered when she'd move on from Ariadne's apartment, and his stomach gave a little flip as he imagined her arriving at Copt Hall one day, suitcase in hand.

Grace glanced back down Knaresborough Place to the white stuccoed portico of Ariadne's apartment building. "She and Silvius had enough to occupy them," she said. "I doubt they realize I've gone. Jack, what have you discovered?"

Both her voice and face were a little strained, and, as Jack slipped his arm through hers, he gave it a slight squeeze of comfort.

"No more or less than I expected, Grace. Is there a tea shop or café near here? It is cold and dark, and I fancy the reassurance of some light."

Not the best thing to say, perhaps, if you wanted to comfort someone, but Jack thought Grace would better appreciate the truth than a mouthful of platitudes.

"The White Queen Café is just up Cromwell Road," Grace said. "I believe Mrs. Stanford keeps it open until ten, even through air raids—"

Both glanced up at that. Planes had been droning overhead for an hour or two now, but as yet no bombs had been heard in central London.

"—and I've heard the cake alone is worth a visit. Jack—"

"Wait," he said. "Let's get a table and some tea, and then we can talk." He paused, thinking as they walked for a few more steps, then added, "Of shadows and bands and cold-faced women dressed in black."

THE WHITE QUEEN CAFÉ WAS OPEN BUT EMPTY, and the proprietor, Mrs. Stanford, perked up cheerfully when the door opened and the man and woman came in.

"I thought I'd not see a soul tonight," she said as she took their coats, then guided them to a table, not near the blacked-out windows, but toward the rear of the rooms where it would be safer in case a bomb hit nearby. She glanced upward, as if she could see the planes that droned so far overhead. "Now, what can I get you, major? Miss?"

When Mrs. Stanford returned with a tray of tea and slices of marmalade cake, she nodded over to the radio that sat on a table close to the register. "The king is to give a speech tonight. Did you know? Ah, then, I'll turn the radio on then, low like, for you, so you can listen. Then"—she straightened up from their table, the empty tray now tucked under her arm—"I'll leave you two to it, then, shall I? Courting couple and all." She winked, first at Jack then

at Grace, then switched on the radio, and "left them to it," as promised.

Jack grinned. "Just remember Grace, you were the one who suggested this place. Have you been here before?"

"No. I heard about it from . . . well, from someone recently. Can't quite remember who . . . oh, never mind. They said Mrs. Stanford's marmalade cake was worth the visit, if nothing else. And they said it would be quiet. A good place for a talk."

"Well," said Jack, looking about the empty café, "I doubt it could get much quieter."

As they fiddled about with their tea, adding milk and sugar, selecting a slice of marmalade cake, Jack surreptitiously studied Grace.

She was wearing a lovely soft gray dress, which suited her coloring perfectly. It had three-quarter-length sleeves and, as Grace raised her teacup to her mouth, the diamond bands—hidden until now—suddenly twinkled into sight.

It warmed his heart; this was a far different woman from the one he had first met on coming home to London.

She colored a little as she saw the expression in his eyes as he regarded her, and so he put down his cup of tea, and brought matters from the personal to the more practical.

"I walked about London all day, Grace."

"And?"

She leaned forward, eager for news, and Jack wished he had something better to tell her. "I can understand no more about this shadow, although the enormity of the thing, its sheer gravity, is more impressive than ever. Damn it, Grace, I wish I had better news for you, but I need those final two bands. Without them . . ."

Grace's face fell, and Jack hurried on. "Grace, you haven't been out much, out in London, since Ariadne has taken you under her wing, right?"

She shook her head slowly.

"Look," Jack said, "I know it is a long shot, but can *you* try to sense more about it? You and I, we're the only ones who

can trace out its pattern . . . and since you've been with Ariadne, you've opened yourself up to a great deal more power."

He saw the surprise in her face, and he gave a little grimace. "Yes, I'm still worried about the imps, but there hasn't been a murder in weeks."

"Not since the night my father saw them."

"No," Jack said slowly. "Maybe they realized his presence and . . ."

"What?"

"The next night the Blitz started."

"Jack?"

"Ah, I don't know. There's something there, but"—he smiled—"I am so distracted by your loveliness my mind refuses to work." He allowed the moment to linger a little, then went on. "Keep safe. Don't stay out after late afternoon. And take someone with you if possible. Okay?"

"Okay, Jack." She smiled, and it was a slow and lovely thing. "Maybe my two bands will help in understanding the shadow."

In the kitchen the White Queen paused with her arms up to their elbows in the sink, then inclined her head very slightly toward the door through to the shop.

He smiled. "Thank you."

They listened to the radio for a few minutes as they drank their tea. There was an amateur variety show on, and its abysmal offering was slowly driving Jack toward considering a murder of the radio set. There were moments when he truly yearned for a resurrection of some ancient Aegean entertainments.

"I saw Catling today," he said, not wanting to tell Grace about Catling's visit last night and her ominous message.

Grace stilled.

"She appeared to me in the streets, an hour or so ago, flaunting the two remaining bands before me, telling me they rested in her dark heart, and were mine if only I decided on a visit."

Grace's blue eyes had grown very large and round. "Why? Why is she doing this? What does she *want*?"

"For me to visit her dark heart, I suppose."

"And will you?"

Jack sighed again, the fingers of one hand now rubbing at his forehead. "To be honest, Grace, the thought terrifies me." He tried a small smile and failed miserably. "I am not the Kingman I once was."

"She will kill you if you go down there."

"Not 'kill,' precisely. She needs me alive. But something much, much nastier."

At that moment both jumped, and Grace spilled tea out of her cup.

In the distance had come the faint muffled *cruuuuuump* of a bomb blast.

Then, a moment later, two others.

"It is going to be a bad night," Mrs. Stanford said, making both Grace and Jack jump again. She wiped her hands on her apron as she came through into the café, turned up the radio a little, then retreated back into the kitchen.

"What is Catling going to do?" Grace whispered once Mrs. Stanford had gone.

Jack gave a despairing shake of his head. "It isn't the first time Catling has spoken to me of her dark heart. After Noah and I made the Great Marriage, she appeared and told me the greatest marriage I could ever make was in her dark heart. She wants me there. Badly. Perhaps that's why she took the bands. But why, *why*, all this pretense of one moment she's all innocence, and then the next is literally standing there before me, bands in hand . . . Ah. I don't understand her."

The distant bomb blasts continued to come, now punctuating the night air with even regularity.

"Jack—"

Before Grace could continue, the voice of an announcer broke into the variety show.

"Ladies and gentlemen, this is a message from our king, George the Sixth . . ."

Jack and Grace fell silent as the king spoke. It was surreal, Jack thought, as he visualized the self-effacing George sitting in front of a radio microphone somewhere in Buckingham Palace, talking of the sacrifice and honor

and bravery of the British troops and the civilians at home, when all about him—and London—sticks of bombs continued to topple over and over lazily through the night sky, exploding all around the city.

Mrs. Stanford had come to the kitchen door to listen, and so Jack kept his voice quiet when he spoke to Grace.

"Do you ever see him . . . the king?"

"Rarely, Jack. He finds it difficult to get away from his palace and the court."

"You know who he is reborn?"

"Yes. John Thornton."

"He loved your mother very much."

Grace looked at him quizzically. "Why so pensive, Jack?"

"I was remembering what your father said to me yesterday."

"He didn't mean to—"

Jack smiled. "Oh yes, he did. He's terrified for you, Grace, and I cannot fault him for that. He thinks that I am as much a threat as Catling."

"No, surely he doesn't—"

"What he said about my three sons cut to the quick."

Grace didn't answer.

"Noah—Cornelia as she was then—and I had three glorious sons, and have I ever thought about them? No. How could I not have ever thought about them, Grace?"

"What were their names?" she asked softly.

"Achates," Jack said, and grimaced. "He was the eldest. Got on your mother the night I first raped her."

"Jack, there's no need to—"

"I think there is, Grace. I need to say this to you . . . not for your sake, perhaps, but to acknowledge those three boys."

"And the names of the others?"

"Idonale and Charistes. Those I got on your mother when I had imprisoned her within hatred."

"Did you love them?"

"As much as I was capable of loving when I lived as Brutus . . . and that was not very deeply. Not enough, I'm afraid. God, Grace, I was so hideous."

Grace had tears in her eyes, and neither of them were aware that the king's address had ended and Mrs. Stanford had turned off the radio and gone back into her kitchen.

"Your father has every right to be afraid of what I might do to you, Grace."

"I am not afraid," she whispered, and Jack gave a short laugh.

"*I'm* afraid of what I might do to you, Grace."

She didn't respond for a long minute. "And your daughter? The one who died at birth?"

In the kitchen the White Queen stirred, and raised her head, her nerveless black eyes gleaming.

"She had no name," Jack said. "And isn't that the greatest tragedy of all, that she had no name? That I cared so little for her that I thought not even to name her?"

"Jack . . ."

"If I had one wish, one wish that I could make come true, Grace, I think I would want to be able to hold that girl, and cuddle her, even if she were dead, tell her I love her, and name her. Give her that, at least."

In the kitchen the White Queen lowered her cold white face, and wept black tears into her bubbling pot of marmalade jam.

Chapter Nine

LONDON

Tuesday, 24 September, to Wednesday, 9 October 1940

Grace Speaks

I FELT SOMEWHAT GUILTY THAT JACK HAD TO ask me to go out into London again, and see what I could discover about the shadow. Since I'd been living at Ariadne's, I'd done little but work with her, or explore and develop my abilities with the labyrinthine harmonies by myself. I'd also been so involved with Jack's growing presence in my life that I had put virtually everything else aside. These were, however, pitiful excuses when considering the desperate battle we were all involved in, and I should not have needed Jack's prompting.

I went out the very next day. So much had changed, not merely about the city, but about me. Ariadne's training had deepened my power and my perception, but Jack's influence had bolstered my self-confidence and courage. I walked out into a city that I saw with different eyes, and I walked with bolder steps than I had ever hitherto.

Jack's diamond bracelets felt warm and comforting, a constant reminder not only of him, but of my own abilities. I didn't allow them visibility when I walked the streets, but they were always there, part of my flesh as the four bands of Troy had once been a part of me.

I did not fear Catling as once I had. I was still very much aware that she held my fate in her hands (or, bound by my wrists, as it were), and I very much respected her power and malevolence, but fear of her no longer dominated my life. Jack had taken my scars and my feelings of shame and

failure and burden, and (with his belief in me more than his gift) gave me back my life and my heritage.

Neither did I fear the imps. It had been weeks since their last murder, and I wondered if they were growing tired of their deadly activities.

For the sake of the young women of London, I hoped so.

Thus, with my newfound abilities and confidence, I discovered a new city. It opened up to me in a way it had never done before. I was far more aware of the labyrinthine shadow that hung over London, but I was also aware of all the labyrinthine twistings of the city itself, the paths and harmonies and strange meanderings that gave the city its life. I looked at the way cars and lorries and people moved about the city and saw underlying patterns and purposes. I watched the way racing pigeons flew in their flocks about the tops of the buildings, and saw a reflection of the way a Kingman danced about the labyrinth. I looked at the barrage of balloons moving in the breeze, and saw new possibilities of manipulating harmonies.

Suddenly I was more than Grace. I was a Mistress of the Labyrinth, and I was a Darkwitch, and I had the power to create my own future, rather than allowing others to create it for me.

Still, I encountered difficulties as well as new possibilities, and those mainly due to the war. Wandering about was no longer quite as easy as once it had been. Large areas had been bombed and were closed, or too difficult to access. Other areas were officially off limits, although a simple matter for me to assume a glamour and wander unseen. Yet more areas were unofficially off limits. These were areas where there was so much residual pain and fear and distress from bombing that I found myself walking past them quickly. I hadn't been affected by the sorrow and pain of others before, and I realized just how introspective (even selfish) I'd been before Jack arrived.

I still disguised what I was doing as much as possible. Catling appeared to have no idea of this shadow hanging over London (and I admit that this bothered me deeply, and made me wonder anew if this was all a distraction planned by

Catling herself to fool us) and I didn't want to be the one to make her suspicious. The war made disguising the true purpose of my meanderings easy. There were many people, all over London, who needed comfort and relief and help, and I spent a great deal of my time with either my mother or, increasingly, Matilda and Ecub (I was, finally, feeling more confident with them, as I was with my mother), traveling about with my mother's mobile canteen in the evening and night, visiting those who needed comfort during the day. It all gave me a chance to get out and about, and to open myself up to this shadowy possibility overhanging the city. But I also enjoyed meeting people, laughing and crying with them.

Again, it was all part of this new experience for me: *living.*

Mostly I kept to the central areas of London—both Jack and I were well aware that the shadow spread over the entire Greater London area, but it was at its most potent over the old City. It would be here, I thought, that I'd have more chance of discovering anything more of its nature.

FOR A WEEK I WALKED HERE AND THERE, VISITING a shop in this street, helping out at a shelter or a kitchen for the homeless in the next. On one occasion Ecub came with me, on another my father accompanied me. For that week I concentrated on opening myself up as much as possible. As each day passed I became more and more sure I was on the verge of a breakthrough. Each day the shadow seemed "closer"— not in a physical sense, but almost in an emotional one. I felt as if I would discover something significant very soon.

I was only slightly wrong. I didn't discover anything. *It* discovered me, and once it did, my newfound serenity shattered completely.

One day I met Matilda at Leman Street station. We meant to walk through the East End to see if we could be of any assistance. Both of us had spare food coupons (God alone knows where my mother had "found" those), cards giving directions to hostels for the homeless, and, we hoped, a store of sympathy and empathy for the wretched people of

the East End who had borne the brunt of the bombing thus far. As the morning wore on, we moved through that part of the East End closest to the Tower of London, stopping here and there to help as we were able.

I grew increasingly uncomfortable as the morning wore on. I felt as if I was being watched the entire time. That wasn't entirely unexpected—both Matilda and I were too well dressed to go totally unnoticed among the East Enders—but I didn't feel as if I were being watched by human eyes. I thought initially it was Catling . . . but it didn't feel like her, either.

It didn't have her malevolence, but it was watchful, cold, judgmental, greatly discomforting.

Matilda kept an eye on me. She knew something was unsettling me, but she didn't probe, for which I was grateful.

As the day passed I gradually opened myself up, using all the added knowledge and understanding that working with Ariadne had given me.

Finally, about midday, with a sickening turn of my stomach, I realized that the sense of being watched was caused by the shadow itself. *It* was watching me.

And it was whispering to me. That scared me so much that the instant I first realized it I gasped and leaned against the brick wall Matilda and I were passing. We'd been wandering along St. George Street, close to where it turned into Shadwell High Street, moving toward a community hall a few blocks farther up when suddenly I realized that all the "strangeness" I'd been feeling, and increasingly so for the past hour or more, was in fact soft words whispered at a frantic pace into my mind.

GraceGraceGraceGraceGraceGraceGraceGrace.

I leaned against the wall, my stomach now heaving over, and barely stopped myself from gagging. Along with the whispering I could sense the shadow, as if it were leaning close. The feeling was similar, if not quite as horrifying, to that I'd felt on the night the imps attacked me.

GraceGraceGraceGraceGraceGraceGraceGrace.

"Grace?" Matilda slid an arm about my shoulders. *"Grace?"*

*WatchmeGracewatchmeGracewatchmeGracewatch-
meGrace.*

"Oh gods, Matilda . . ." I whispered, desperately want-
ing her to stay near and yet not sure I could actually force
out the words to tell her what was happening.

GraceGraceGraceGraceGraceGraceGraceGrace.

"Grace?"

*WatchmeGracewatchmeGracewatchmeGracewatch-
meGrace.*

I finally managed to dampen the noise a little, for which
I was profoundly grateful. At least I could do that.

"Grace?" Matilda all but hissed.

"Matilda . . . the shadow is whispering to me. I don't be-
lieve it . . . sorry, I only just realized what was happening
and it overwhelmed me."

She was silent for one long shocked moment. "*What* is it
whispering?"

"It calls my name over and over, and begs me to watch it."

Both of us at that moment firmly fixed our eyes on the
pavement. Neither of us wanted to look up, although gods
alone knew what we might have seen. The shadow was not
visible as such; it could only be sensed.

The whispering continued—

GraceGraceGracewatchmeGracewatchmeGrace.

—but I found it far more bearable now that I'd damped
it down.

"What do you want to do, Grace?"

What did I want to do? "Continue on, I think, Matilda. I
don't want this to stop us."

Matilda looked at me searchingly, but eventually she
nodded, and we managed to continue walking down St.
George Street toward the community hall.

THE WHISPERING CONTINUED OVER THE NEXT FEW
days. Sometimes it was barely there, sometimes it was al-
most a scream in my head. On those occasions I shut it out
completely, closing myself off from my powers as a Mis-
tress of the Labyrinth as a last resort.

It called my name, it begged me to watch it.

And it asked me to come to St. Paul's.

That last made me revise my initial belief that it wasn't Catling. The shadow *must* be her—why else would it try to get me close to St. Paul's?

There wasn't much else I could discover about the shadow, but the whispering was enough for me.

I rang Copt Hall that first day, in the evening, when I'd returned to Ariadne's apartment. Jack was out. Malcolm was vague about where he was, but I gathered he was in the forest somewhere.

Jack rang me back the next evening, and we arranged to meet the following night. He'd wanted to come straight down to talk to me, but I'd demurred. It was late, I had a terrible headache, and I didn't want Jack to think he had to dash down to save me from every bump in the night. I told him what the shadow was saying to me (just calling my name, begging to meet me at St. Paul's), and he reluctantly agreed to leave it until the following evening.

I was a little surprised by how pleased I was to see him waiting outside the White Queen Café. As I approached he turned, saw me, and grinned, taking my hands (then running his own a little way over my wrists and up my forearms) and planting a soft kiss on my cheek.

We sat once again at the back table, Mrs. Stanford hovering happily in the background, feeding us marmalade cake and forcing us to listen to some execrable variety show on the radio. As before, there was no one else in the café save us.

"What do you think, Jack?"

He looked at me with worried eyes and shook his head slowly. "I have no idea. I can't hear it."

"It is Catling. It must be."

"Perhaps."

"*Jack.*"

"I know, I know. I haven't shut myself off to the idea that this entire shadow is Catling's construction, Grace. But . . . why would she want you to come to St. Paul's?"

I shrugged. Now that I was settled in the café and the initial euphoria of seeing Jack had passed, I felt close to tears.

The past few days of listening to the constant whispering had worn me down.

"I'll come out with you tomorrow," Jack said. "Maybe together . . ."

I nodded. Maybe together . . .

At that moment, we *both* heard the whispering.

GraceJackGraceackrajacgrajackjacejracegrajace.

Jack went white, and without thinking I reached out and took his hand.

Yes!Yes!Yes! GraceJack GraceJack Come to St. Paul's. Come to St. Paul's.

Now that it had both of us together (hand in hand) the whispering became clearer, less urgent.

Come to St. Paul's, Grace. Come to St. Paul's, Jack. Come to St. Paul's together, GraceJack.

Why? whispered Jack.

Because I have something to show you.

HOURS LATER WE STILL SAT IN THE WHITE QUEEN Café. Mrs. Stanford had come out to refresh our tea, and to call us her best customers, although I was starting to think we were her *only* customers.

No one else had entered during all this time.

"I don't know if I want to go," I said.

Jack was looking down at the snowy linen tablecloth, slowly drumming the fingers of one hand.

"I don't think it is Catling," he said.

I closed my eyes in mingled horror and desperation. "Jack—"

"Sweetheart," he said, that hand now sliding across the tablecloth and taking mine, *"I don't think it is Catling."*

My heart turned over when he called me sweetheart, but considering my stomach was also doing slow, queasy turns in fear, the mingled effect wasn't particularly pleasant. I knew I should trust him—gods alone knew Jack had so much more experience with the Troy Game than I did— but, oh, the fear . . .

"Please," he whispered. "Trust me."

God help me, I did. "All right," I whispered, and his hand tightened about mine.

IN THE KITCHEN THE WHITE QUEEN SMILED, AND the pot of marmalade dropped from her fingers and shattered over the floor.

WE WENT TO ST. PAUL'S THE NEXT WEEK. HAVING made the decision, we then lingered. Partly this was because of the weather, which had closed in (a poor excuse!), and partly because we both were more than a little hesitant.

Strangely, even though we took our time about arriving at the cathedral, the whispering stopped completely that night we'd made the decision to go.

We would arrive, eventually, and the shadow was content.

The night we did go, Wednesday, was a cold, blustery night. Jack picked me up from outside Ariadne's apartment at ten P.M. (we hadn't wanted to go during the day as night seemed safer for those who might use the cathedral, if not for us), then drove to a street two or three away from St. Paul's where he parked and turned off the ignition. We were both so tense we hadn't even spoken when I got in the car, and now, as we sat in the cold and dark, listening to sleet pelting against the car windows, we remained silent for long minutes. I had my hands thrust deep into my coat pockets, Jack had his still resting on the steering wheel of the Austin, as if he wanted to be ready to drive off at a moment's notice.

Eventually he sighed, and looked at me. "Ready?"

"No," I said.

He gave a faint laugh. "That's good enough for me. Grace, Catling won't hurt us. Neither of us. We're too important to her. She can taunt, but she won't hurt us."

I turned my head so I could look at him. Maybe he was right, maybe not, but we were here now, and we might as well get on with it.

I took a deep breath, opened the door, and stepped out into the freezing wet.

* * *

ONE OF THE AISLE DOORS IN THE WEST FACE OF
the cathedral was ajar. A member of the cathedral Watch
stood just inside, and looked at Jack and me incredulously
as we entered and shrugged off our wet coats.

"There's an air raid on," he said. "Are you sure you want
to come in? There's a shelter on Ludgate Hill."

"We'd like to stay for just a while," Jack said. "If you
don't mind."

He shrugged, and we were in.

THIS WAS THE FIRST TIME I'D EVER BEEN IN ST.
Paul's. The first time, that is, since I'd gone down into the
dark heart of the labyrinth where Catling had imprisoned
my parents while London burned in 1666, but that had
been a different cathedral entirely.

After that occasion, when Catling had first revealed the
horrific extent of her hex, I'd not been back. I'd had no de-
sire to visit, and neither of my parents had ever suggested
it. I had, of course, been completely terrified of the cathe-
dral, and I wasn't feeling much more confident now.

We walked very slowly down the south aisle, Jack taking
my hand as soon as we'd passed the sentinel by the door.

I was getting used to it, this holding of hands, getting
used to being with Jack as a matter of course, getting used
to being comfortable with him.

What I was not comfortable with was being inside this
great, terrible, cathedral.

I shrank closer to Jack, wanting the comfort of his
height and warmth and strength, looking about. To our left
lay the nave, but we didn't enter it, keeping instead to the
aisle.

Everything was very dim. A few lights shone, mostly in
the aisles, but they were spaced very far apart, and there
were pools of darkness between them. Every time we
walked into one of those pools of darkness I'd shrink even
closer against Jack and hold my breath until we'd regained

the light. From the tenseness of Jack's body, I guessed he wasn't feeling much more comfortable.

We couldn't see anyone else, although we could sense that there were some fifteen or more men of the cathedral Watch either in the crypt, or patrolling the cathedral's upper spaces. Occasionally we heard a soft step in the far distance, but it was always too distant to trouble us.

We continued to walk down the south aisle, very, very slowly, pausing occasionally to look about, until we reached Sir Christopher Wren's great dome.

Here we halted, just where the dome met the south transept, and stared upward.

The top of the dome was hidden in darkness, but we could *feel* it.

"So much has happened here, in dream and vision," Jack said very softly. "Here, in Cornelia's stone hall."

I had heard some of this from either my mother or Ecub over the years, but I am certain they had never told me the full extent of my mother's and Jack's meetings in here.

I wondered what had gone on, if ever they had made love under this dome.

"I have shouted words of hate and love to Noah here," said Jack, his voice now so quiet I had to strain to hear it. "I have seen your father make love to her here."

That was new to me, and I lifted my face and studied his.

"Your mother, whether as Cornelia or Caela or Noah, also saw visions of the little girl she thought was her daughter in here, running toward her, calling her name . . . and all that little girl ever was, was a lie we now call Catling."

I shivered, and he squeezed my hand.

"And to think," he said, "that this was my creation. Mine and Genvissa's."

"Well," I said, thinking I had to say something, "it is very *big*."

He started to chuckle.

"I'm sorry," I said, and he laughed harder, pulling me back into the south transept where there was but one weak lamp glowing amid all the vast dark.

He dampened his laughter and took my face in both his hands. "That's one of the things I like most about you, Grace," he said. "Your terrible, terrible sense of flattery."

I grinned. "That's my granny Ariadne coming out."

His thumbs were stroking along the side of my face, and I have to admit they felt very good. I decided to take my courage in hand and, standing on my toes, kissed him softly on the mouth.

"Very sweet. I have to admit, I didn't predict this particular development."

We sprang apart, although Jack snatched at my hand again to stop me from darting off into the vast dark spaces of the cathedral.

Catling laughed. She was somewhere in the darkness, but neither Jack nor I could quite make out the direction of her voice.

"What are you doing here?" she said. "Come to *pray*?"

"Come to walk the cathedral," I said, "to measure your worth."

Catling drew in a theatrical breath of shocked surprise.

"Ooooh! Such brave words from such a faint-hearted girl! Come on then, what do you here, eh?"

Footsteps sounded from the dome, shuffling closer and closer to us, but they kept to the dark spaces, and still we couldn't see the hateful creature.

"Come to measure your worth," said Jack in a voice flat with hatred, "and to measure our courage."

"And do you have such measure?" she said. "Of both worth and courage?"

"The visit has firmed in my mind," he said, "the conviction I would do anything to save Grace."

Catling laughed again, and I wondered if there was a hint of relief in the sound.

"Good. That's good, Jack. You'll do anything to save Grace. And you know there's only one way to do that, don't you, Jack?"

Silence. "*Don't you,* Jack?"

"Aye," he said, his voice still flat. "Aye. I know that."

"Good," Catling said. "Then your visit was worth it. Stay a while, why don't you, and enjoy the ambience."

And then she was gone. Although we could not see, we knew it instantly.

Catling had left us alone.

AN AGE SEEMED TO PASS WHILE WE STOOD THERE, silent, staring into the dark.

"Was that why we were supposed to come, I wonder?" I said eventually.

No, Jack said into my mind. *She knew nothing about it. Be careful what you say, Grace.*

I bit my lip. *If the shadow is connected to Catling,* I said, *then perhaps she has delivered the message she wanted.*

"She could have done that at any time," said Jack, his own voice irritated now. "Look, Grace, let's stay awhile longer. At least the place is full of benches."

He led me into the space under the dome, then into the nave. "Here," he said, pulling me toward the vast acreage of benches and pews in the nave. "We can sit here." *And wait.*

What if nothing happens? I said, sitting down next to him on a pew some three or four back from the dome. "What if—"

"Then we can just sit, Grace. Okay?"

We sat in silence for some time, both of us looking forward. I began to hope that nothing would happen, because even though we sat in St. Paul's under Catling's eye, and even though Jack was in a tired and cross mood, I was enjoying greatly this still silence with him, feeling his warmth and his slow breathing next to me. Just enjoying being with him. Normally I hated it when someone became cross and irritable, but Jack's mood didn't bother me at all, or spoil my enjoyment of being with him.

After a while, Jack sighed, slid an arm about my shoulders, and pulled me close. "Go to sleep, if you want, Grace," he whispered. *I will keep watch.*

But I didn't sleep. I didn't want to. I much preferred staying awake, feeling his warmth and closeness, feeling his chest rise and fall under my cheek.

We waited.

HOURS PASSED. I DON'T KNOW HOW MANY, BUT long enough for both of us to grow chilled and stiff. I had fallen into a limbo somewhere between wakefulness and sleep, and I think he had, too. Even the commencement of bombing for that night did not make us stir. We were far too used to it.

Time passed.

GraceJack! GraceJack! Are you awake?

We were both startled.

Look up, GraceJack. Look up.

We looked up.

It was as if the entire roof structure and dome of the cathedral had vanished. We could see the night sky—the churning clouds of the weather and the successive rolling waves of rain, although they did not touch us.

And we could see something else, something so faint we had to strain our eyes.

We saw faint luminescent lines tracing through the sky.

"Jack?"

Shush. Use your mind voice, Grace.

Damn it! Jack, what are those . . . I wouldn't say it. I knew he could see them as well as I.

I don't know.

Watch, came the unknown whisper, and the clouds parted as if by a divine hand, and we could see far, far into the night, so far we could distinguish the bombers circling overhead.

As the bombers appeared more clearly, so the faint luminescent lines (*of the shadow! We were being shown the shadow!*) glowed ever brighter, as if they were taking sustenance from the German aircraft.

Jack fumbled for my hand, and I clung to it. *It's the shadow,* I whispered into his mind, and he gave a terse nod.

A bomb came down.

We knew there were many bombs coming down, but we saw only one. It twisted lazily through the sky, gusting this way and that as the wind caught it, and, as we watched, it seemed to be that the luminescent lines reached out to the bomb, and brushed against it.

Turning it this way, and now that.

As the lines touched the bomb, they glowed anew, as if taking strength from the bomb.

I had eyes for nothing but the bomb, falling straight for the cathedral.

"Grace!" Jack said, then lurched to his feet, pulling me with him.

We stared a moment longer, mesmerized by the deadly sight, then Jack pulled at my hand and arm, tugged so hard I felt my shoulder joint groan and almost give way, and then we were running down the nave, running back toward the west doors, running for our lives . . .

This was a trick of Catling's, after all. She'd merely been toying with us. Playing with us for her own amusement.

We'd almost got to the doors when we stopped, and turned around. I don't know why we did this, but we both seemed impelled to turn around right at that moment.

There was a terrible crashing and thunder noise, and then *we saw the bomb, saw it as if it were only a few feet away,* tumbling through the roof above the quire, then falling free of slate and rafters and stone, falling through the air.

And striking the high altar, where it exploded.

The blast threw Jack and me off our feet. My head hit something, and I blacked out.

Chapter Ten

FAERIE HILL MANOR

Thursday, 10 October 1940

*G*RACE SAT ON THE SOFA IN THE DRAWING room of Faerie Hill Manor, two plasters on the left side of her forehead. Her face was wan, her clothes stained and dusty and torn in places. Jack sat next to her, an abrasion on his chin, his jacket and trousers streaked with blast dust.

Noah, Weyland, Ariadne, Silvius, and the Lord of the Faerie sat about in chairs, cups of coffee in their hands, looking at Grace and Jack.

For a long time no one said anything.

Grace had blacked out only for a few seconds after the blast, then she and Jack had stumbled out of the cathedral, somehow avoiding the scurrying members of the cathedral Watch, and made it back to Jack's Austin. He'd driven straight to Faerie Hill Manor, sending a mental request to the others to meet them there.

He'd not said why, nor given them any indication that he and Grace had been so close to disaster.

In truth, Jack thought, he'd been closer to disaster when Noah and Weyland saw the state of their daughter. There had been a few tense moments as Noah fussed and Weyland went very still and silent. Ariadne and Silvius, arriving a few minutes later, had taken one look at the tableau and had just sat down silently, wisely deciding to wait for explanations.

Harry, who had opened the door to them, had instantly and instinctively metamorphosed back to his greater self as the Lord of the Faerie.

Once Grace had assured her parents she was but scratched and shaken, Silvius went off to organize some coffee.

Now everyone waited.

Jack sighed and set his coffee aside. He described briefly what had happened, from the voices he and Grace had heard, to watching the luminescent lines above St. Paul's and the descent of the bomb.

Once he had finished, there was a silence as everyone stared at Grace and him.

"Jack?" said Noah eventually. "What does this mean? Who *is* this voice? A shadow doesn't have a voice. A weakness doesn't have a voice."

"I still think it might be Catling," said Grace.

Knowing how Grace felt about the shadow, Jack was not surprised at this statement, but he was surprised at the level of doubt in her voice.

"Catling didn't know anything about it," he said. "On that I would stake my life. Besides, it just doesn't make sense for it to be Catling."

"There are very few possibilities," said Silvius. "Everything this shadow is indicates it is labyrinthine in nature. Whoever this voice is *must* be trained in the arts of the labyrinth. Dear God, how many people could that be?"

"Most in this room," said Ariadne, "save Stella." She raised her eyebrows at the Lord of the Faerie.

"Stella is in the Faerie," he said. "She rarely enters the mortal world now. Besides, I don't think she has enough interest in the Troy Game, and what may or may not destroy it, to go to these elaborate lengths. It isn't Stella."

"Could it be a member of the Faerie?" Jack asked the Lord of the Faerie, glancing at Noah to include her in the question. "Or some faerie spirit of the land? So ancient and unknowable we may not know of it?"

"It is possible," said the Lord of the Faerie. "God knows enough fey spirits and beings have walked through this land over the millennia. I don't know them all—there are just too many shadows in the night. Noah?"

"I think it is likely," she said. "I mean, who *else*?"

"But whoever it is must be trained in the labyrinth," Sil-

vius said. "Doesn't that cut out any faerie spirit of the land?"

"Not necessarily," said Noah. "The land and the Troy Game conducted an alliance thousands of years ago, and the labyrinth had been burrowing deep into the earth since Brutus and Genvissa first constructed it. Some of the stranger and older faerie spirits may well have learned enough from the labyrinth to become skilled in its ways."

Jack turned a little so he could look directly at Grace. "Grace?"

She chewed her lip, and Jack could see indecision and doubt in her eyes.

"Perhaps," she said, and Jack grinned. Grace seriously doubted any of this but was trying to be polite.

"No," he said. "Not 'perhaps' at all. What do *you* think? What do you *feel*? Catling? Some ancient Faerie spirit we've all missed? Something else?"

Grace shifted a little on her seat. "Everything inside me screams Catling, but I doubt myself because, as you said, Jack, it just doesn't make sense for her to have done this. I'm also afraid that because of the hex that binds me to her, every time something goes bump in the night I automatically ascribe it to Catling." She gave a small shrug and a self-effacing smile. "Catling is my very own personal bogeyman."

"A member of the Faerie, then?" Jack said.

Grace thought about it. "I don't know enough about the Faerie to be able to say either yea or nay, Jack. Mother? What about the Sidlesaghes? Might they know?"

"Oh, moon and stars!" Noah said. "Why didn't I think of that? Yes, they might know. Gods alone know how many lifetimes they've spent being literally a part of the land. They can certainly still teach me things I never knew. I'll ask Long Tom. If he doesn't know who this is, then he can investigate."

"Good," said the Lord of the Faerie. "Noah can ask Long Tom, and maybe he can sort out this mystery for us. Jack, Grace, what do you make of the bomb? What were you shown, and why?"

"We were shown the vulnerability of the Troy Game," said Jack. "We were shown that it *can* be destroyed."

"That shadow must be a weakness," said Noah.

"I'm not sure," Grace said slowly. "The path of the bomb was changed by the shadow that hangs over London. The bomb was directed. I don't know if that actually indicates a weakness on Catling's part. Perhaps . . ."

"Perhaps?" said Jack.

"Perhaps we were being shown a weapon," said Grace.

"The bomb?" said the Lord of the Faerie.

"No," said Grace. "The shadow itself."

There was a short silence as people thought about it.

"Grace," said Noah finally. "What do you mean?"

"What if . . . what if the shadow is not a shadow, or a reflection, or a message. What if it is a *weapon*?"

Jack sat back, studying Grace. A weapon? Was it feasible? "The only kind of weapon capable of affecting the Troy Game would be . . ."

He drifted off, his mind racing. What kind of weapon *could* be effective against the Troy Game? "It would need to be of the Game itself," he finished. "Of the labyrinth. *Born* of the labyrinth."

Ariadne, who had been silent until now, leaned forward. "You're right, Jack. Only something *of* the Troy Game could be used *against* the Troy Game."

"What do you mean?" said the Lord of the Faerie.

Ariadne considered a moment, trying to clarify things in her own mind before she tried to explain them to the Lord of the Faerie. "The Troy Game was constructed to protect. In that purpose it has succeeded magnificently, *too* magnificently. Rather than protecting London, it protects itself. Moreover, the Game protects by absorbing evil . . . anything sent against it would merely be absorbed. To be destroyed, the Troy Game must be destroyed from within, if you like. By something of the Game itself."

"Catling has created the weapon of her own destruction?" Silvius said, incredulous.

Ariadne sighed. "I don't know, Silvius. I was just theorizing."

Jack laid a hand on her shoulder in support. "Lord Jesus, I need some sleep. This is too confusing for my addled mind. As I understand it, all that has been suggested is that some 'being,' perhaps a member of the Faerie, is trying to show Grace and me something. This something may be a weakness in the Troy Game . . . or perhaps it is a weapon to be used against the Troy Game. But if it is a weapon, then it must firstly have been constructed *of* the Troy Game itself . . . Ah! I can't figure it."

"I hope Long Tom has some answers," Noah said quietly.

"Me, too," said Grace after a moment.

CATLING COULD HARDLY BELIEVE JACK AND Grace had dropped a bomb on her. She couldn't decide whether to succumb to incandescent rage or icy dread.

Why was Jack so confident he thought he could attack her so blatantly?

And from where had Grace got such nerve? What was she *thinking* of?

In the end Catling decided not on either rage or dread but on action. Jack had ignored all her warnings. Very well. Perhaps now it was time to demonstrate to both him and Noah just how vulnerable they were.

And it wouldn't hurt to destroy Grace's irritating new-found confidence, either.

Catling retreated into the dark heart of the labyrinth and began to marshal her powers. For two days she sat, motion-less save for the winding red wool between her fingers.

On the third day she moved, as deadly as a viper.

Chapter Eleven

Sunday, 13 October 1940

LONG TOM, LIKE MOST OF THE SIDLESAGHES, had buried himself so deep within the Faerie to escape the war that it took Noah three days before the Sidlesaghe answered her call. They met in the Faerie, on a hill five removed from The Naked, under a great stand of trees where the Sidlesaghe felt safe.

Noah almost wept when she saw Long Tom. He looked so despondent, far more than his usual forlorn demeanor, and she hugged him tightly in greeting.

"Has the war stopped yet?" Long Tom said.

"No, my friend. I wish I had better news for you."

Long Tom sighed. "The land suffers."

Now the tears did come to Noah's eyes. "I know, Long Tom."

"What do you here, Noah?"

"Tom . . . there is something strange happening in London."

Long Tom looked nervous, and Noah laid a hand on his arm. "We need your help. Please."

Long Tom sighed again. "In what manner 'strange'?"

Noah told him as best she could about the shadow, its labyrinthine sense, and the voice, the being, that had communicated with Jack and Grace.

"Long Tom," she concluded, "we have no idea what this shadow is, or what its purpose is. Moreover, we do not know who this voice belongs to. Is it a creature of the Faerie, perhaps? Do you know, Tom?"

The Sidlesaghe hung his head and took a long time over his answer.

"I have heard whispers," he said eventually.

Noah almost ground her teeth at the obtuseness of his answer, but instead managed to infuse her voice with nothing but light query. "You have heard these whispers, too? Or you have heard whispers of this creature's identity?"

"I have heard whispers of the woman who calls to Grace and Jack."

Noah waited for as long as she could bear it. "Yes?"

"Some say it is the White Queen."

Noah frowned. *The White Queen?* She searched the ancient memory bequeathed to her by Mag, and found only shadowy elusiveness.

"Who is the White Queen, Long Tom?"

"She who has not lived."

"Tom, what do you mean?"

He shrugged helplessly. "I do not know what I mean, Noah. All I know is that some Sidlesaghes, and some others among the Faerie, have for many, many years been aware of a woman who is so shadowy, so unknowable, that no one has managed to understand her. She is fleeting. She is a shadow. She has become known as the White Queen because her cold, white face reminds all who see it of the winter landscape. Black eyes like the night. She's cold, cold, cold. Never lived. We don't know who she is, but some among us think she may be the one who has raised the shadow over London and who whispers to Grace and Jack."

Noah stared at Long Tom, unable to make any sense out of what he was saying. "Why haven't I seen her? Why don't I know her?"

"She is lost to you, Noah."

"What do you mean, Tom?"

"I don't know what I mean, Noah."

"Damn it, Tom—"

"I have to go, Noah. I don't like it here. There's trouble afoot. Magic and murder. I don't like it at all."

Suddenly he was gone.

* * *

NOAH WALKED ALONG THE ROAD LEADING FROM
Epping Forest toward London. Soon she would use her
power to transport herself to the mobile canteen, which
was working the northern suburbs, but for the moment
Noah just wanted to rub her head and walk and think.

Long Tom had a history of being obtuse, but this time
Noah didn't think he was deliberately trying to be vague.
He simply did not know any more than he'd told her.

He was also scared, although Noah had no idea whether
of this White Queen or of the general situation.

"Gods alone know our general situation is pitiful
enough," Noah mumbled as she wrapped herself in her
coat and strode along the verge of the road. It was cold, just
gone night, and even from this distance Noah could hear
the drone of bombers over London.

It was going to be another bad night.

Even worse than it currently was? She and Jack and
Grace, as everyone else, had wrestled with the problem of
what the shadow was, and no one (save Grace) had consid-
ered the possibility it might be something of which to be
afraid.

Noah did not like the sound of this White Queen very
much at all. She was too secretive—and why be secretive if
you had nothing to hide?

A cold, cold, fleeting shadow.

Noah shivered.

*There's trouble afoot. Magic and murder. I don't like it
at all.*

Noah's head sprang up and her eyes blazed.

The next instant she was gone.

GRACE HAD COME OUT TO HELP MATILDA, ECUB,
and Erith with the mobile canteen. She didn't want to have
to think any more, didn't want to have to speculate about
what the shadow might be and what the bomb may have

meant. She just wanted to *do* something, and Noah's Ark seemed like just the thing. Mindless work, offering pleasant companionship, taking her out of Ariadne's apartment, which Grace was beginning to find a trifle claustrophobic.

She didn't know where Jack was tonight. They'd spent yesterday together, wandering aimlessly, talking of little, and they'd parted without making arrangements to meet again. He'd seemed preoccupied, and Grace thought he may have gone back to stand outside St. Paul's (temporarily closed to the public for repairs) and stare up at the sky, and wonder.

"Grace?"

She jumped a little, then laughed guiltily. Matilda had come upon her standing at the back of the open van, staring up at the night sky.

"Do you think you should go look for him?" Matilda said.

"No," Grace said. "I'd waste my time if he doesn't want to be found. Now . . . sandwiches or the coffee?"

"Bring the sandwiches," Matilda said. "Half of the people in the shelter are children, and most are starving."

Grace looked up at the block of flats. They were a dreary lot, blank walls, featureless windows and architraves—clean and comfortable, no doubt, but such a heaviness of spirit lay over the building that Grace wondered how any soul could thrive while living here. The block's shelter was in the basement, and Grace thought it must be gloomy indeed, if that above ground was so dreary.

"Sandwiches it is, then," she said, and hefted a large tray in her arms.

"This way," said Matilda, and Grace followed.

She glanced up at the street plate on the building.

Coronation Avenue.

For no reason—it was such an innocuous name—Grace shuddered.

Then, tray in hand, she walked toward the entrance, trailing Matilda by a few steps.

* * *

THEY WERE HALFWAY DOWN THE STAIRS TO THE basement when the bomb hit.

It came straight in the roof, piercing through five floors with a terrifying noise before it detonated just inside Public Shelter No. 5 of Coronation Avenue.

Following immediately on the blast came the full weight of five floors of bricks, concrete, mortar, furniture, and debris plummeting downward and, along the way, breaking every water and sewer pipe that serviced the building.

Half the people inside the shelter were killed instantly. The rest were left trapped under tons of rubble that had sealed every exit.

Water and sewage started to trickle down into the basement.

THE BOMB STRUCK THE SAME INSTANT NOAH WAS materializing on the roadway just outside Coronation Avenue. It threw her off her feet, covering her in blast dust and shards of glass. For long moments she lay completely stunned, not merely by the physical effects of the blast, but by a sense of loss so powerful it completely overwhelmed her.

All she could sense from the ruined building not thirty feet away was death. Intimate death. The death of someone she loved.

She felt a sudden, terrible iciness, and knew the paths of the Otherworld were opening up.

"*No!*" she screamed, and, unable to rise, began to crawl painfully through the debris toward the building.

JACK HAD BEEN WANDERING EPPING FOREST, MAL-colm at his side. He'd been doing nothing in particular, just walking, thinking, exchanging the occasional word with Malcolm, when he, also, was hit with a wave of loss so stunning he became literally nauseated.

"Who?" said Malcolm, grasping at Jack's arm as he bent over, dry retching.

"Sweet Jesus . . ." whispered Jack.

"Who?" Malcolm snapped.

"Just about everyone," Jack said, but there was only one name consuming him.

Grace.

NOAH HEARD THE SIRENS OF THE APPROACHING fire engines, but she didn't care. Her hands and arms and knees were bleeding where they'd shuffled through shattered glass, but she didn't care about that, either.

She could feel Weyland and Jack coming closer, both using their power to transport themselves to the disaster, and she almost didn't care about the fact that both men who meant so much to her would shortly be here to help. What use were they when so many were dead?

Or dying.

GRACE WAS AWARE ONLY OF THE WEIGHT SUR-rounding her, and of the fact she could barely breath. Every intake of air was a gigantic struggle, every exhale made her head swim with agony. Her chest and abdomen hurt terribly, the air was thick with brick and concrete dust, and moving this thick, gritty air in and out of a chest that itself barely condescended to move required every effort of will she possessed.

Weight packed in about her. Her legs felt both warm and dead at the same time. She couldn't move them. Her left arm was trapped under weight (the same weight that made breathing so difficult), her right lay spread outward from her body, white with dust.

Her face lay cushioned on a pillow of gritty sandwiches, and Grace's first coherent thought was that she had dropped the damn sandwiches, and wasted so much valuable food.

Matilda would be cross.

Matilda?

Grace opened her mouth and croaked. She wet her lips, spat out some grit, and tried again.

"Matilda?"

"NOAH!" WEYLAND GRABBED HER AROUND THE waist and lifted her into his arms.

She wailed as he did so, her bloodied arms reaching out toward the mountain of rubble, but Weyland ignored her plea and carried her some fifty or sixty feet away, to a clear area of roadway.

He didn't need to ask where their daughter was.

"MATILDA?" GRACE COULDN'T SEE A THING, BUT she could move her right arm very slightly, and she felt around with her hand.

She gasped—and then flinched at the pain in her chest—as two of her outstretched fingers touched flesh. *"Matilda!"*

There was no reply, and Grace could not tell by touch whether Matilda was alive or not. She tried to reach out with her power, but it failed her, and Grace wondered if he had been so terribly injured that all her abilities were draining away with her blood.

Oh, she suddenly thought, *no wonder my legs are so warm. All my blood is escaping.*

With that thought Grace gave Matilda's face (at least she hoped it was Matilda's face and not a stranger's dismembered limb) a final tap with her fingers, then she sighed, and drifted off into a welcome unconsciousness.

JACK RAN OVER TO WHERE WEYLAND WAS crouched over Noah. "Is she . . ."

Death lay all about, and for the moment his sense of loss was so immense he couldn't distinguish who it was who had died, and who survived.

As Jack spoke to Weyland, he glanced over to the huge

smoking pile of rubble that had once been a block of flats, and his stomach turned over in horror.

No, no, surely they weren't beneath that!

"She's alive," Weyland said, his face and voice flat with what Jack assumed was combined hatred and pain. "She's alive, but the others . . . oh gods, all I feel is death."

Jack stared at him in horror. "No . . ." he whispered. "No."

Weyland sprang to his feet. *"My daughter is under that!"* he screamed in Jack's face. *"What have you done?"*

"I haven't . . . I . . ." Jack turned once more to the rubble, his mind registering dimly that several fire engines, ambulances, and police cars had screeched to a halt and that emergency personnel were now scurrying over the site.

He still couldn't think clearly. Everything overwhelmed him: Weyland's anger and distress; his own sense that death had taken someone very important to him, and was hovering over others; Noah's tears and faint cries; her blood-covered limbs; the massive pile of smoking rubble; the remains of Noah's mobile canteen, blown over fifty feet away and now nothing but a twisted pile of blackened metal.

Where is Grace? No, please God, she isn't under that! Please, please, please . . .

"Gentlemen? Madam?" One of the firemen had come over. "Madam, how badly injured are you? Sir . . . you're her husband? Good, then best get her to the ambulance over there. I—"

"My daughter is under there!" Noah cried, struggling to rise. "And my friends, my friends . . ."

Oh, Jack thought. *That's what I can feel. The death. Eaving's Sisters. Are they dead?* He couldn't feel it, couldn't isolate all the different strands of loss that had twisted about his soul to determine who was alive and who was dead.

The fireman glanced over at the rubble, and the look in his eyes made both Weyland and Noah cry out. *"No!"*

"Madam," the fireman said, "sir. You can do nothing here, and, ma'am, you need those cuts looked at. We'll get her out. We will."

Weyland gave the man a long stare, then picked Noah up in his arms again and carried her toward one of the ambu-

lances. Jack started toward the rubble, thinking only that if he just moved one piece, and then another, and then one more, then maybe he could reach down, and grasp Grace's hand, and pull her out.

"You won't, you know," said the fireman, and Jack stopped and looked over his shoulder. "I've buried them very, very thoroughly."

Jack's head swam, and for an instant he almost fainted with horror.

The fireman now wore Catling's face.

Chapter Twelve

STOKE NEWINGTON, LONDON

Sunday, 13 October 1940

"T HAT BOMB WAS TOO MUCH," SAID Catling, stepping closer to Jack. "What did you think you and Grace were doing? Did you think you would actually hurt me? Did you—"

"You wouldn't have done this if you weren't scared."

"I did it because I have grown tired of your lies and procrastination. Listen to me, Jack: Grace is trapped in there. She won't die—she can't, because *I* don't particularly want to wink out of existence just yet—but I've injured her quite badly. Terribly, in fact. And no one can get in to her. Can you see the rubble? There are five floors of bricks atop her, Jack. It is going to take a while to dig through all of that, yes? Now, I *could* hurry along the process, but I'll do it under one condition only."

Jack could barely breathe for fury. He hadn't been responsible for the bomb, but there was little point in arguing the matter with Catling.

"And that condition would be . . . ?" he ground out. He was aware that his fists were clenched, and only the realization that somewhere beneath this mask of vileness a real man lived stopped him from hitting Catling with all his might.

"I want you and Noah to vow, here and now, to complete me. No more dilly-dallying about trying to find a way to destroy me. Set a date, Jack. Until I get that vow Grace will remain trapped, and London will suffer more horribly than perhaps it need do under the German bombs. I'm going to make her suffer, Jack, and, while I'm at it, I'll make London suffer. Not just physically, but mentally and emotionally and spiritually as well. She's not going to be the same girl when she comes out. If you want the girl back that you love, then *promise me* a date of completion. *Now!*"

Jack found it difficult to believe he was still standing still. All he wanted to do was to wrap his fingers around Catling's throat . . .

"You'll kill her if you do that, Jack. Now, where's that promise, then?"

Oh God, what had he done? For an instant Jack recalled his brash, stupid belief as Brutus that the Troy Game would be so wonderful, would make him immortal, grant him so much power.

The promise, Jack.

"I don't have all the bands," he said.

Catling's face twisted. "I think you do. I think you're just saving them for the right moment to use against me."

"For God's sake—"

The promise, Jack.

"I need to speak with Noah. She will need to agree."

"Make sure she understands. Make sure she understands her little girl is going to agonize every moment she delays. Make sure she knows that there are many more I can kill the longer you delay. All these deaths, as Grace's agony, are *your* responsibility, Jack."

And then Catling was gone and the fireman was back, his eyes blinking in confusion.

* * *

GRACE CAME TO SLOWLY. SHE FOUGHT AGAINST waking because the pain was so bad. It wasn't like the agony caused by Catling. In some measure she'd grown accustomed to that, and had inured herself against it, but the weight of tons of rubble on her chest, and crushing her legs, was so different, so *final*, that Grace didn't think she could bear it. This was not something she need endure until Catling grew tired of it, this was something she'd need to endure until someone physically came along and pulled the weight of the rubble off her.

And all Grace could think about was that the rubble consisted of at least five stories of blank walls and featureless windows, and that pulling it off her was going to take many hours, maybe even days.

She started to sob, then stopped the instant the rucking of her chest caused her such distress she almost fainted again.

Then, suddenly, miraculously, she felt Matilda's face move under her outstretched fingers.

NOAH SAT ON A PILE OF BRICKS TO ONE SIDE OF the ambulance. Her arms and legs were bandaged, and she had plasters over her forehead and one cheek.

Her eyes were horribly dull.

Weyland stood by her, his eyes shifting between Noah and the emergency workers now crawling uselessly over the mountain of rubble.

Jack walked over, every step dragging.

He sat on the ground next to Noah, avoiding looking at Weyland's face.

"Catling," he said, needing to say no more.

Noah gave a soft cry. "*Why?* Why now?"

"She says she will keep Grace trapped until we agree to complete her. Until we set a date.'"

Weyland muttered an expletive, turning his face away.

Noah began to cry. "Jack . . . Ecub and Erith are dead."

Jack stared at Noah, unable to speak. No wonder he'd been so consumed by the sense of death.

Ecub and Erith. They'd been through so much together, and when he'd been Louis, they'd been his lovers.

"And Matilda?" he croaked, hardly able to ask. *No, not Matilda.* Not *her.* He couldn't feel them. They may have been lovers, and Matilda his wife, but Noah had the closer bond with them.

Noah swallowed, the movement making her wince in pain. "Close to death, Jack. I'm so sorry."

Jack's hands sank into his face. Grace was suffering, yes, but Catling had ensured that Noah and he would suffer as badly.

He wiped at his eyes, his hand trembling. "When you say 'dead,' Noah, how dead is that?"

"They won't come back, Jack. I don't know how Catling has managed it, but she has cut their ties, not only to life, but to us and to this land. They're gone completely."

Jack gave a low cry and buried his face in his hands. *No!* And Matilda hovered close to death. *No . . . not Matilda.*

After a moment he raised his head, and reached out to take one of Noah's hands.

"MATILDA!" GRACE CROAKED. "PLEASE, *PLEASE,* answer me."

She felt an exhale of breath, and perhaps a groan, but it was enough.

"Matilda!"

Another groan, and Grace felt the woman's face contort under her fingers. The movement caused her to scrape her wrist across a piece of rubble. It wasn't much of a movement, but it was enough for Grace to suddenly remember her diamond bands.

"Oh gods," she whispered. *Oh gods, oh gods, oh gods . . .*

Surely she had enough ability left to dredge the diamond bands to life? Grace closed her eyes and concentrated with everything she had. Surely she could manage this, at least? This tiny bit of magic?

There was a faint flicker of light, which Grace felt rather than saw. She opened her eyes.

The diamonds had appeared about her right wrist, the only one free of the rubble, and now faintly illumed the space in which she and Matilda lay.

Grace was initially overwhelmed with relief that she'd managed it, and then that relief was almost instantly swamped with horror as she realized just how dreadful was her and Matilda's situation.

They lay in an air pocket within the rubble roughly eight inches high and some four feet long. The entire space sloped downward, probably following the line of the stairs, with Grace lying at its upper limit and Matilda farther down. Both of their bodies were buried within the rubble; only the left half of Matilda's face was showing, while Grace at least had her entire head and one arm free.

What little part of their flesh that showed was covered in pulverized brick dust and small pieces of rubble and marked here and there with drying rivulets of blood.

Matilda's left eye blinked, once, slowly, then again.

"Matilda?" Grace whispered. "Matilda?"

"Oh Grace," Matilda managed to whisper. "What are you doing here?"

A POLICEMAN CAME OVER TO JACK, NOAH, AND Weyland. Weyland had slumped down on the ground beside Noah and Jack, each of the men holding one of Noah's hands.

Jack looked up at the man, wondering if he was truly a policeman, or Catling come to taunt them.

But it was just a young, ashen-faced constable. "Madam? Gentlemen? My sergeant sent me over. Do you know anyone inside the building?"

Noah made an incoherent sound, and it was Weyland who answered. "Our daughter is in there," he said. "Grace Orr. And three dear friends." He gave the constable their names.

"Why hasn't anyone got them out yet?" said Jack, standing up. "Do you want a hand?"

"Sir," said the constable, "we're doing everything we

can. All available emergency workers have been called in. But . . . it is difficult. The shelter was in the basement, and at least five stories have come down on top of it. The rubble is so compacted that we can't—"

The constable stopped abruptly, realizing he'd said too much.

"We'll do our best, sir," he concluded.

"Jesus Christ," Weyland muttered.

"YOU'LL LIVE," MATILDA SAID IN A HOARSE VOICE. "Catling can't have you die."

Grace wept. "Why can't I help you, Matilda?"

Matilda closed her eyes. Talking was difficult, breathing was harder, and something had so completely crushed her right shoulder and arm she wished she could lapse into unconsciousness again just to escape the pain.

But then Grace would be left alone in here.

Matilda suddenly missed Jack very, very much. She'd seen so little of him in this life, and she regretted not making the time to see him and talk to him more since his return to London. She wished desperately Jack were here now—not crushed under the rubble like herself and Grace, but just close enough so she could hear his voice, and pass the time of her dying with some happy memories of when she had been the duchess of Normandy, and he its charismatic duke. Times when they had been married, and happy.

She knew she was dying. She could feel death tugging away insistently at her, but Matilda wasn't ready to give in just yet. Best to hang on until they came for Grace. Best to wait until Grace was out. Then she could give in.

"Why can't I help you?" Grace whispered again, and to that Matilda had no answer save the one she was sure Grace already knew.

You're too badly injured, Grace. You're as close to death as me. You have as much power left as you have life.

Chapter Thirteen

STOKE NEWINGTON, LONDON

Monday, 14 October 1940

𝓙UST AFTER DAWN THE FIRE CHIEF CAME TO speak with Noah, Weyland, and Jack. "Every entrance down to the basement shelter is buried under tons of rubble," he said. "And the bomb shattered both the water and sewer mains. I'm afraid the basement is flooding." After witnessing so much death over the past month the chief was physically tired and utterly emotionally exhausted. He'd watched his words at the beginning.

Now he couldn't be bothered. He wasn't unsympathetic to the plight of the two men and woman standing before him (the parents and sweetheart of a girl buried in the nightmare that had once been Coronation Avenue, so he'd been told), but he had no more resources left to even try to summon tact or to wrap the terrible news in vaguenesses.

Noah laid a hand on his arm. "You must be able to do something." Her words were softly spoken, but underscored with a terrible anxiety.

"We're doing all we can," the fire chief said. "I'm sorry. Perhaps it would be better if you went home and waited for news."

His expression gave no doubt as to what news he thought that would be.

"We're not leaving," Noah and Weyland said together, and the fire chief gave a tired shrug, then walked away.

Weyland turned to Jack. "Surely you can do something!"

Jack was so tired and so overwrought that his eyes filled with tears. "Do you think I haven't thought of it? That I

haven't wracked my mind for every possible thing I could do? God *damn* it, Weyland, I can't shift tons of rubble on my own, either with my hands or with my power, and . . . and, Jesus Christ! There is *nothing* I can do!"

Noah shook her head slowly from side to side, then sank down to the ground again, head lowering into her hands. "Grace . . ." she whispered. "I can't reach her. Always before this I could feel her, touch her. Now there's nothing but a great darkness."

None of them could. Under normal circumstances any one of the three could easily have communicated with Grace with their abilities, but now . . . nothing. They'd tried, tried desperately, but nothing.

Like Matilda, they all knew what that meant.

Unlike Matilda, none of them were willing to admit it, even to themselves.

Jack dropped to his haunches beside her. "Noah, we need to talk about what Catling said. What she *threatened!* Ecub and Erith are dead, and Matilda is dying. Grace is suffering God knows what and probably wishes she were dead. Jesus, she is crushed under rubble! She—"

Noah grabbed at one of his hands. "What will hurt worst, Jack? Completing the Troy Game, or watching Grace suffer?"

"May I make a suggestion?"

Jack and Noah looked up. Malcolm had appeared, carrying a tray on which rested a plate of sandwiches and three steaming cups of tea.

"Not now, Malcolm," Jack said tiredly.

"Yes, *now*," said Malcolm, setting the tray down on the ground before Jack, Noah, and Weyland. "I have been speaking with the king," he continued, and none of the others wondered at that. Malcolm had the air of someone who would damn well talk to whomever he wished whenever he wished. "George is making an effort to come view the situation for himself. Harry is also on his way. May I suggest that you commit to nothing until both those men arrive? Between them they head the mortal and Faerie worlds, and their input is not only needed, it is required."

Jack resented Malcolm's lecturing tone, but knew he spoke sense. "Grace suffers," he said, and Malcolm rested a hand on his shoulder.

"I know," he said gently.

"MATILDA? ARE YOU STILL THERE?"

That was such a silly thing to say, Matilda thought. Where would she go, then? But, oh, Grace's voice. So lost and alone. So desperate.

"Yes," she said. "I am still here."

"How are you, Matilda?"

Well, I'm buried beneath tons of rubble. My shoulder and arm and abdomen and pelvis are crushed. My legs scream.

"My feet are wet," Matilda said. It was the least troublesome of her burdens at present.

Grace took in a hiccupy breath, and Matilda realized she was trying hard not to cry. *Oh, how I wish I could touch her. Reach out to her.*

"I wish Jack were here," Grace said.

"Me too," said Matilda, unable to keep the desperate longing out of her voice. *Oh, to have Jack here one last time. To have him hold me one last time.*

"What was he like as a husband, Matilda?"

Matilda thought about laughing, but knew it would crucify her with agony. "He was a trouble," she said, and there was enough humor in her voice for Grace to give a short, breathless laugh.

"I'm a little scared of him, Matilda."

Matilda thought about that. "Not of him, you're not. Of life, maybe."

There was a long silence. Finally, Grace spoke in a whisper. "What should I do, Matilda?"

"Take a damn risk," said Matilda. "That's what I did. I never regretted it."

"But you lost him."

"Grace?"

"Yes?"

"I am dying, do you know that?"

Grace began to weep. "Yes."

"Then hear me out, for I speak with the clarity of death. If you do not take the risk, then you will lose him. If you risk all for him, who knows?"

Grace didn't answer.

"Grace . . . risk it all."

AT ELEVEN A.M. THE KING AND HIS QUEEN AR-rived. Word had spread around London about the tragedy at Coronation Avenue, and crowds had been gathering since dawn. The site swarmed with rescue workers, but no matter how much rubble they shifted, they had still not even gotten near the stairwells leading down to the shelter, let alone started to clear them.

The area was cordoned off by police. To one side the Red Cross had erected a tent, and in that tent sat the relatives of those trapped.

Among them waited Noah, Weyland, and Jack. Harry and Stella had joined them after dawn, and now all five sat slightly apart from the other ashen-faced relatives. Malcolm was still there, but spent his time helping the Red Cross distribute tea and sandwiches.

Harry brought the news that the Faerie had not been troubled during the previous night's bombing. Catling had reserved all her ire for Grace, it appeared.

Jack's face was less ashen than it was gray. "I can't believe it has all come to this," he said. "Sitting huddled in a tent by a mountain of rubble, being fed tea and sandwiches by charity workers. I'm sick to death of it. It has to stop somehow. God, Stella, where did we go wrong? What did we start?"

Stella sighed. "I don't want to spend my time revisiting the sins of the past, Jack. Brutus and Genvissa simply don't matter anymore. I'm just grateful that now it isn't my decision."

Jack was about to say something more, but just then Harry looked out the tent flap at a convoy of cars arriving and straightened from where he was leaning against a table. "George is here," he said. "Thank the gods."

They all rose to their feet, huddling together but staying

in the tent as the other relatives and members of the Red Cross went outside to watch the king and queen.

"He'll come in to see us," said Harry. "He knows we're here. Wait."

MATILDA WISHED SHE COULD DIE. HER PAIN WAS growing too intense for her to ignore it, or wish it away, or concentrate on thinking of something else. To make matters worse, icy water was creeping slowly up her body. The coldness intensified and clarified the pain, and Matilda wondered if Catling had fated her to die not from her crushing injuries but from a slow drowning.

She thought this very likely. It would be just what Catling would do. The effect on Matilda was nothing—the effect it would have on Grace was everything. For hours Grace had tried everything she could, tried to summon every particle of power she had, in order to help Matilda.

Grace had been able to achieve nothing. She was so terribly injured that all her abilities as either Darkwitch or Mistress of the Labyrinth were as nothing.

Even had Grace been able to use her power, Matilda doubted she could do much.

After all, what was the power of gods when compared to the unmoveable force of hundreds of tons of masonry?

THE KING AND QUEEN TALKED QUIETLY WITH THE relief workers for twenty minutes, then they split up, Queen Elizabeth to talk to the relatives standing huddled in a teary-eyed, haggard-faced group to one side of the Red Cross tent, the king to duck inside the tent, waving back his courtiers and minders as he did so.

George VI stopped immediately inside the tent, his face haggard with months of care, and looked at the group standing a few feet away.

"Who is in there?" he asked.

"Our daughter," Weyland said. "And Matilda, Ecub, and

Erith. Ecub and Erith are dead, Matilda is dying, and Grace . . ." He couldn't go on.

"Dear God," George said, then went to Noah and hugged her tight. "I'm so sorry," he whispered, cradling her head against his shoulder.

Then he looked over the top of her head to where Jack and Weyland stood. "What has happened?"

Weyland motioned for Jack to answer. Jack gave a sigh, then, briefly, told George VI of what had happened over the past night.

"What do I do, George?" In his exhausted emotional state Jack didn't even care about the appropriate honorifics. "Catling has the power to murder this city, this entire country, if she doesn't get her way. But if Noah and I do what she asks . . ."

"Ah, God . . ." The king let Noah go and rubbed a hand over his face. "Harry?"

"The last thing I want is to see the land tied by the Troy Game," he said. "I am opposed to Jack and Noah completing the Game."

But what about Grace? Jack wanted to scream at him. In the end he spoke mildly. "Catling is only going to get worse. The idea of what she might do after this appalls me."

"You want to complete the Game?" Weyland said, aghast.

"You want your daughter to suffer any more than she is? Or this land?" Jack countered.

"Stop," said the king. "What are the alternatives? For Christ's sake . . . my wife and I have toured the bombed-out areas of London week in, week out. The grief and destruction—not just of buildings but of lives—is more than I think I can bear. Do I want Jack and Noah to complete the Game and condemn this land to subservience to that *thing* who calls herself Catling? No. Do I want Catling to crucify my people because you refuse to complete her? No. Give me an alternative."

"We thought there might be a way . . ." Jack began, then drifted off, not knowing how to explain about the shadow.

"Gods," Noah said. "I forgot to tell you what I'd heard

from Long Tom. George," she said to the king, "can you stay ten minutes? You need to hear this."

Jack, Weyland, and Harry all opened their mouths, but Noah waved them to silence. "George?"

He chewed his lip and looked over his shoulder. "I have already stayed too long. Elizabeth and my minders will be wondering what I am doing. Can you come to the palace in two hours' time? Yes, yes, I know you don't want to leave here, but there's God-all you can do, and we need to discuss this in more detail than we can in this tent. Somewhere more discreet. I'll talk to my private secretary on my way back to the car. He will stay behind and get you to the palace. Okay?"

"I can't leave Grace—" Noah began.

"I'll stay behind," Weyland said. "The king needs Harry, Jack, and you, not me. I'll stay."

Noah nodded, although she was clearly still unhappy.

Jack looked at Weyland. "Thank you," he said.

Chapter Fourteen

THE RUINS OF CORONATION AVENUE, LONDON

Monday, 14 October 1940

Grace Speaks

I LAY THERE, LISTENING TO MATILDA DIE, AND couldn't do anything for her. I *should* have been able to do something: ease her pain, move some of the rubble, still her breathing into the relief of death if that was what she wanted. I should have been to do that for myself.

But I couldn't do a thing. The rubble not only trapped me physically, but crushed and trapped most of the Darkwitch and labyrinthine powers I had as well. I had enough

to dredge some light out of the single diamond band that was free, but that was all, and I wondered if that was not *my* power, but something residual of Jack in the diamonds. Even that died, after an hour or two, and we were left in the dark.

So I lay there, in the dark, and listened to Matilda die. I could hear her anguish in every breath; each harsh inhale, each ragged exhale. I could hear it in the way she cried sometimes, or the pitifully tiny movements I heard her head make as she struggled uselessly against the weight of the rubble about her. I kept calling her name. It annoyed her, I know, but oh gods, I so desperately wanted to hear her voice, to know that she *was* still alive.

To know she was still with me.

I couldn't bear to think of what lay even farther beneath us in the basement shelter. Ecub and Erith were dead. *Truly* dead. Gone forever, and both Matilda and I cried for them. But there were others, and in the first hours after the bomb blast, they were still alive. I knew, because at first I could hear pitiful cries for help coming from below us, or desperate scratchings at the rubble.

Oh, the image, those trapped people scratching away with broken fingernails at the bricks atop them.

I could also hear the trickling of water and, after some time (how long? Hours? Days?) the unmistakeable stench of sewage.

All the cries for help below us ceased, and I no longer heard the pathetic scratchings at the rubble.

When Matilda said her feet were wet I wept, because I knew that somewhere a water pipe had been broken, a sewer, too, and that whoever had been left alive after the blast had now drowned. Now that horror threatened Matilda.

"Matilda?" I whispered. "Matilda?"

She didn't answer, and after a moment I realized I could no longer hear her ragged breathing.

"Matilda!" I stretched out my fingers, trying to feel her face, thinking only to jab at her cheek and remind her to breathe, but my fingers encountered not dry flesh, but cold, watery rubble.

Matilda had slipped away, down farther into the rubble, down, down, down into her grave.

I started to sob, not caring about the pain it caused my chest, calling out Matilda's name over and over until I could barely breathe.

All about me there was silence, save for the gentle lap of water against my fingers and the gentle grinding of rubble, as it settled deeper into the water.

After a while, Catling came to me.

Chapter Fifteen

BUCKINGHAM PALACE, LONDON

Monday, 14 October 1940

THEY CONVENED IN THE EARLY AFTER-noon in a study in the private quarters of Buckingham Palace. The queen had already gone back to Windsor, where she and George slept (the government feeling that Buckingham Palace was too great a target for Luftwaffe bombers), and George dismissed his secretary as soon as he had shown Noah, Jack, Harry, and Stella into the room.

Without asking if they wanted it, George poured each of them a large whisky, then waved them into deep, comfortable chairs.

"Jack," said George, "what's been happening?"

As briefly as he could, yet not omitting any necessary detail, Jack told the king about the labyrinthine shadow that hung over London. "We don't know truly if it is a help or a hindrance, if it is a trap or a weapon, and we call it a shadow because it is too insubstantial for any of us to see it clearly. After what has happened in the past night . . ." Jack paused, collected himself, and went on.

"After what has happened over the past night I am inclined to think more hindrance than help. If not for that bomb . . . Noah, for God's sake, tell us now what you heard from Long Tom."

Jack looked at George and lifted his hands in a gesture of despair. "She said she would wait until we got here."

"I'm sorry, Jack," Noah said. "Long Tom told me that he'd heard that the shadow, and thus perhaps the voice, belonged to a creature, a woman, so shadowy, so fleeting, that none could know her. He said she had not ever lived, and when I asked why it was that I could not sense her, or know of her, Long Tom said it was because she was lost to me." She paused. "Long Tom said she is known as the White Queen for her face as cold and pale as the winter landscape. She—"

"The White Queen?"

Noah stared at Jack. "You know her?"

"Jesus Christ!" Jack said. "Yes, maybe I do. While Grace has been staying with Ariadne we have met on several occasions at the White Queen Café on Cromwell Road in Kensington. We were, so far as I could tell, the only customers. Certainly no one else was ever there when we were. There was a woman who ran the café . . . Mrs. Stanford."

Now everyone was staring at Jack.

"I don't know any more," he said. "Sorry. Grace and I would go there to meet, have tea and"—he gave a faint smile—"Mrs. Stanford's specialty, marmalade cake, and talk. But she was so ordinary . . . and nothing much ever happened there . . . except, of course"—he sighed—"that this strange voice spoke to us both in that place."

"So we have a creature, the White Queen, who masquerades as a Mrs. Stanford who makes marmalade cake," said Harry, "and, in her spare time, strange labyrinthine shadows that hang over London. Marvellous. What does any of this tell us?"

"It raises more questions than it answers," said Noah. "Who *is* she, this cold, unborn woman? *Why can't we know her?*"

"Because she is somehow attached to Grace," said Jack.

"I think it is Grace she is interested in, or drawn to. None of us, not really."

"But she called to you as well," said the king.

"Maybe only because I am 'attached' to Grace," Jack said with a shrug.

Stella had been sitting back, listening to the conversation, her brow creased in thought, the fingers of one hand tapping against the arm of the chair. "No, no. I don't think you're incidental, Jack. I think she is interested in you as well as Grace, although not perhaps *as* interested. *Damn it!* I wish we had Grace here. She must have the key. She must know something. . . ."

"I wish we had Grace here, too," said Noah, looking at Stella with steady eyes. "But not for any information she might give us, but merely so I can hold her again, and know she is safe."

"This is getting us nowhere," said Jack. "All we're doing is blowing useless words about this room. Catling has clearly given us a choice. Promise to complete her, and get Grace out of that nightmare that is Coronation Avenue—as well, please God, anyone else who may still be alive—or Grace will continue to suffer, as well London." He shook his heads. "Catling is going to escalate the violence, the death, the destruction, if we don't agree, Noah. I told her I lacked two of the Kingship bands, but Catling didn't believe me. She believes I do have them, and am just trying to deceive her. God, Noah, what choice do we have? *What?*"

No one replied immediately.

"Grace. . . ." Stella said slowly.

"Grace is buried under several score tons of rubble and can't get out until Noah and I—"

"I know, Jack," Stella said. "I'm sorry."

"Is there any way of contacting the White Queen?" George said. "Jack? Apart from Grace, you are the only one who has had any contact with her."

"*She* contacts us, we don't contact her," Jack said. "Look, if someone can arrange a car, I can drive around to the café from here. Maybe . . ."

"It's a start," said Harry. "But if it fails?"

"My advice," said George, "is to give Catling the promise, but to somehow delay the completion. Is that possible?"

Jack and Noah exchanged a glance.

"Yes," said Jack. "Catling herself has made it possible. When she allied herself so closely to the land she managed to tie herself so closely to its restrictions. That's even more the case since she 'arranged' that Noah and I take on such vital roles within the life of the land."

"The December solstice," said Noah. "That would be the best time to complete her, and it is two months away. It would buy us time."

"But if you promised," said the Harry, "would you need to go through with it?"

Noah shrugged. "No. But I dread to think of the consequences if Jack and I didn't turn up for our 'date.'" She grimaced. "We need to use those two months well."

"And *I* need those final two bands," Jack said. "Catling will be neither completed nor defeated without them."

"Jack . . ." Noah said, sitting forward.

"Yes?"

"Do you think this White Queen might have them?"

For a moment Jack stared at Noah. "But Aeneas said . . ."

"Aeneas may have been duped."

"Christ," said Jack. "You might be right. Now it is even more important to either manage to contact the White Queen, or, better, to get Grace out of that rubble."

"Then are we agreed?" said George. "Jack tries his best to contact the White Queen, and if that doesn't work, then Jack and Noah give their promise to Catling . . . and hope to God that once Grace comes out she can give us more information, or gives Jack and Noah the key that will destroy Catling. Yes?"

No one looked very happy about it, but eventually everyone nodded. After a little more desultory conversation, Jack, Noah, the Lord of the Faerie, and Stella rose to leave.

After he farewelled the others, George pulled Jack to one side. "I will send for a car for you," he said, "but first I wanted to ask you something."

"Yes?"

Having initiated the conversation, George now hesitated. "I was watching your face as you talked of Grace," he said. "I wanted to ask . . . if . . ."

Jack smiled. "Are you remembering that night in the Broken Bough, when we both lamented the fact neither of us would ever have Noah?"

George's face relaxed. "Yes."

"Well . . . I thought then, and thought for too many years afterward that I would never find another woman I could possibly love as much as Noah. But . . . maybe I have. As you have."

Now George smiled, honestly and truly. "Yes. As I have. Jack . . . good luck."

Jack wasn't sure if George wished him well with Grace, or more generally with the battle against the Troy Game. But he smiled, shook the king's hand, and left feeling marginally better than when he had entered the room.

HALF AN HOUR LATER HE DREW UP HIS BORROWED car outside the White Queen Café in Cromwell Road.

Very slowly Jack got out of the car and closed the door behind him.

Both windows and door were boarded up, and the café looked as if it had been abandoned for many months. Cobwebs were strung between the boards, and, through a gap in the boards covering the door Jack could see a pile of mail on the floor.

He felt very cold and, for a moment, closer to despair than ever.

There was a postman walking past, and Jack stopped him, asking him if he knew how long the café had been boarded up.

"Mrs. Stanford took herself down to her sister's place in Devon at the beginning of the war," the postman said, watching curiously the expressions crossing Jack's face. "The café hasn't been open in over a year."

"Of course it hasn't," said Jack. "Thank you."

As the postman continued on his road, looking back over his shoulder once or twice at the American who had stopped him, Jack looked up to the sky.

The shadow had vanished.

There was nothing left.

"Grace?" Jack whispered.

He received no reply. Whatever he'd been able to sense of Grace previously had now vanished.

Grace was as gone as the White Queen and the labyrinthine shadow.

It was then, also, that Jack realized Matilda was dead, and he turned to the car, and, leaning against it, crossed his arms on the car's roof, bent his face down into them, and wept.

Chapter Sixteen

THE RUINS OF CORONATION AVENUE, LONDON

Monday, 14 October 1940

Grace Speaks

*J*F I HAD WANTED TO ESCAPE PREVIOUSLY, IT was nothing to how I felt now. My right hand scrabbled desperately among the rubble, scraping and cutting my fingers, but there was little I could do.

I could *feel* Catling drawing closer, a terrifying malignant presence, far worse than anything else I had ever felt from her, seeping down, down, down through tiny cracks in the rubble.

How are you feeling, sweet Grace?

I gave a single sob, loathing myself for the weakness. The feeling of evil was so overpowering that every sense I had was screaming at me to run, run, run . . .

I'd never felt this before, and I wondered at the fact she'd been saving this for so long.

I asked you how you were feeling, Grace.

I could see her now, although this made no sense in the confined (and pitch black) crack I had as a space about me. Catling sat on a pile of rubble a few feet away, a young woman of malevolent air and a horrible, childishly spiteful face.

"I am not at my best," I whispered, amazed that I could even speak.

Catling laughed. "You're about to get even worse, sweeting. Tell me, can you feel the weight of bricks crushing you?"

"Yes."

"Do you know that you'd be dead now if it weren't for my intervention?"

What did she want? My gratitude? "Yes."

"Your parents and Jack are quite distraught. Did you know that?"

"No."

"Are you happy about it?"

Gods, what does she want? "No. I wish they didn't suffer or worry."

"Well, I *want* them to suffer and worry. It is good for them. Might concentrate their minds. I've told them that if they don't agree to complete me, then . . . well, here you'll stay. Given that I think they rather want you out, I have high hopes they'll do what I want."

I was crying again, silently this time, feeling the tears trickle down my grit-covered cheeks.

"So I expect they'll get you back, dear Grace." She paused, and in that pause I could hear malevolence gathering. "Of course, they're not going to get you back *quite* the way they want."

As soon as she finished speaking, I heard it. What sounded like a huge boulder tumbling down through the rubble. There shouldn't be space for it, no boulder should be able to force its way down through the rubble.

But one did nonetheless.

"It is the lintel from the doorway into the flats, Grace.

Heavy concrete. Able to do much damage, I imagine. Poor Jack, won't he weep when he sees you?"

I struggled, crying out in horror as I heard the lump of concrete tumbling closer and closer, over and over, over and over . . .

"I'm going to say to you what I once heard your father saying to Jack, when he was welcoming him back into London after an unfortunate period of time spent in exile. I only need you alive, Grace. I don't need you whole."

The concrete slid closer, rasping and rumbling, and it was the most terrible thing I have ever heard in my entire life.

I only need you alive, Grace. I don't need you whole.

Now the concrete was sliding toward me at a frightful pace. I was screaming, not caring about the pain that tore through my chest with the effort, when I felt a sudden rush of warm air, and then something terrible, something appalling, slammed into my head.

Chapter Seventeen

THE RUINS OF CORONATION AVENUE

Tuesday, 15 October 1940

NAUSEATED WITH FEAR AND WORRY, JACK rejoined Noah and Weyland's vigil at Coronation Avenue.

It was late at night now, almost midnight, but still the emergency personnel worked away over the rubble, shifting it piece by piece by hand, desperately searching for the entrance to the stairwell leading down to the basement shelter. It had been more than twenty-four hours since the bomb had struck, and most of the initial crowd of onlookers had gone home to bed or their shelters, but a score or

more still huddled about, sharing thermoses of tea or chocolate, transfixed by the horror before them.

The tent was still there, its interior still as stark with despair as it had been when Jack had left it hours earlier. There was a table set out with the remnants of tea and sandwiches, but the Red Cross staff and volunteers had gone home an hour or so earlier. Noah and Weyland, the only two left within, had stood up when they heard the car pull up, its door slam, and then footsteps walking toward the tent, pausing as their owner stared for a long minute at the rubble.

When he entered, his uniform disheveled, his face stubbled with beard, his eyes haggard, Noah gave a soft cry and turned her own face into Weyland's shoulder.

"You didn't find the White Queen," Weyland said, his voice flat and emotionless. He looked even worse than Jack, his face gray, his eyes bloodshot, and he wavered slightly on his feet, as if exhaustion was but a few minutes from claiming him completely.

Jack gave a terse shake of his head. "The café was boarded up. A passing postman told me it had been since the beginning of the war. What Grace and I entered had been a construct of the White Queen."

"Who *is* she?" Noah said, turning her head to look at Jack although she kept it resting against Weyland. "What does she want. Why? *Why?*"

Weyland's arm tightened about her, and Jack looked away briefly before carrying on.

"There's worse. The shadow has gone."

"What?" Noah and Weyland said together.

"You didn't feel it?" Jack said to Noah.

She shook her head. "I was concentrating only on Grace," she said. "And I . . . we . . ."

Noah burst into tears, and it was Weyland who finished what she'd been trying to say. "We lost any sense of her about an hour ago," he said.

"Aye," Jack said, then sat down abruptly on a nearby chair. "Matilda is dead—"

He'd been about to add "too," and stopped himself only just in time.

"Oh gods . . ." Noah said brokenly. "Not Matilda. Not Matilda as well."

Weyland sat down in a chair, pulling Noah down into one beside his. "They can't all be . . ."

"She isn't dead," Jack said, and Noah and Weyland understood he wasn't referring to Matilda. "She *can't* be. Catling can't kill her without killing herself."

They were empty words, and he knew it. Catling patently had the capability of making things far worse than death for Grace.

Noah straightened up, wiping away her tears. "Jack, we've got to—"

"I know," he said.

"Dear gods," Weyland said. "Complete the Troy Game? But—"

We will promise only, said Jack into Weyland's mind, holding the man's eyes with his. *And, in promising, free Grace from whatever hell Catling has constructed for her.*

"We must, Weyland," Noah said.

Then pray to all gods and heavens you can get out of the promise when you need to, Weyland said.

JACK AND NOAH WALKED SLOWLY THROUGH THE crypt of St. Paul's. Again, while there were many members of the cathedral Watch about, none of them were aware of the man and woman—of the two ancient gods—who walked among them.

Jack and Noah had come straight from Coronation Avenue. Both looked terrible, close to exhaustion both physically and emotionally. They walked hand in hand, their steps dragging, their faces pale and drawn.

As they neared the tomb of Florence Nightingale, Catling emerged from the shadows.

This was the first time Noah had seen her in centuries, and she instinctively drew closer to Jack as they came to a halt a few paces away from Catling.

"Well," said Catling, "for a Kingman and Mistress of the

Labyrinth, you're looking rather dilapidated. Where your pride? Your elegance? Your might?"

"Buried with Grace," said Jack, "as well you know."

Catling smiled, the expression terribly cruel. "And look what it has brought me, eh? What I wanted. My Kingman and Mistress, at my feet. So, tell me, what do you here? What do you have to say?"

"You know why we are here," said Jack. "We've come with what you want. A promise to complete you, to raise the final Flower Gate."

Something came over Catling then, and it took Noah and Jack a moment to realize it was intense excitement. Her entire form blurred, became a dense mass of darkness, before she returned to her usual form of the white-faced young woman.

"When?" Catling said.

"The winter solstice," said Noah.

"No. No delays. Do it now."

"Blame yourself for the delay!" snapped Jack. "You bound the Game to the land, you bound both your Kingman and Mistress to the land, and if you want this done properly then you will need to wait until one of the nights of power which will bring the entire land behind us. The winter solstice it will have to be . . . unless you want something *less* than what we're capable of delivering."

Catling went very still, so much so that for a long moment she appeared to be a statue capable of neither breath nor movement.

"Two and a half months," she said finally. "I'll tell you what, Jack. If you don't mind me pushing Grace deeper and deeper into torment during those two and a half months, then I'm happy to wait. It's no trouble on my part to strip Grace's soul a little barer for each hour you delay. Your choice, Jack. Your choice."

Jack wanted nothing more than to reach out and strangle her. "You *said* you'd give Grace back to us once we'd promised—"

"And so I will. Most of her, anyway. The best bits I may

keep. Play with a little bit, if you understand my meaning. Whatever happens, Jack, Grace is not going to be the same girl if ever she wakes up."

Suddenly Catling's face twisted. *"Complete me!"*

Then she was gone, and Jack and Noah were left staring in horror at the space where she'd been.

THEY FLED BACK TO CORONATION AVENUE, USING their power rather than more conventional means.

It was a vastly different place to that they had left but an hour earlier. The rescue efforts were now frantic, and directed in one spot, whereas previously they had been desultory and spread over most of the mound of rubble.

"Weyland?" Noah said as she and Jack appeared at his side (it being well that everyone's attention was now concentrated on the rescue effort, so that their sudden appearance raised no eyebrows).

"They've found the stairwell," Weyland said, his voice tight. "You've promised, then."

Noah and Jack glanced at each other, their faces gaunt.

Then they looked back at the rescue efforts, not bothering to answer.

AN HOUR LATER CAME A SHOUT, THEN THE ACTIV-ity became even more frantic. Noah moaned and would have started forward, save that Weyland held her back.

"They'll bring her out soon," he said. "Wait."

The waiting was the worst thing any of the three had ever endured. It took another three hours before enough of the rubble had been removed that the rescue workers could lift a limp, bloody figure onto a stretcher. Medical and rescue personnel leaned over her and, after several terrible, long minutes, the fire chief trudged over to where Noah, Weyland, and Jack stood.

"I'm sorry," he said, and Noah burst into tears.

* * *

CATLING SEETHED. ICY DREAD BE DAMNED, SHE'D
succumbed to incandescent rage. Jack was delaying.

Very well. If he wanted to delay then he was going to pay
the price.

When he finally got Grace back he was going to wish she
had died instead.

PART SIX

THE WHITE QUEEN

London, November 1703

THE WEATHER HAD BEEN SHOCKING OVER *northern and western Europe throughout mid-November, but no one had anticipated the fury of the storm that blew in over Europe in the early hours of the twenty-sixth of that month. A fleet of one hundred Russian ships in the North Sea was scattered, and many lost. Four hundred coal barges that had just left port in northern England were sunk. In Norfolk fire swept through a town as chimney stacks were blown over.*

London was devastated by the storm. At one A.M. most residents woke terrified as hurricane force winds swept through the capital. Over two thousand chimneys toppled in the first ten minutes of the tempest, and the air became a lethal mix of flying shards of glass, bricks, slates, and nails. The lead on the roof of many churches rolled up like parchment, and spire after spire cracked, leaned, and sometimes toppled in the raging winds. On the Thames, every single ship moored at wharves, save for four, was torn from its moorings and driven downriver, to collide and break apart as the wind drove it ashore. Scores of houses blew down completely, thousands more had walls topple and roofs fly off, so that by next morning it appeared as if the city consisted only of the skeletal framework of houses.

Every building appeared to have been damaged.

Save one.

St. Dunstan's-in-the-East.

Alone of all the churches in the city it had survived completely intact.

When, later in the day, Sir Christopher Wren, now an old man, arrived, he stood for long minutes gazing up at the spire.

"You don't appear amazed," said an onlooker, "that a miracle has saved St. Dunstan's spire."

"Not a miracle," murmured Wren, "but the genius of a tiny girl."

And with that strange remark Wren turned his back and stumped down the wreckage of Idol Lane toward Thames Street.

Chapter One

THE NURSES IN THE LITTLE ANNEX OF ST.
Bart's that housed the long-term patients—those
waiting to die, or those so chronically ill they
could not be looked after at home—tried as best they could
to get as many early morning shifts as possible. It was then,
during the early morning, that Major Jack Skelton came to
sit by the bed of the girl who lay in the veranda ward.
Every morning, without fail, as soon as the dawn light
stained the sky, he could be found sitting at her bedside.

There he would stay for most of the morning. No one
ever saw him arrive, no one witnessed his departure, and
the ward sister had long since stopped asking him to con-
fine his visits to regular visiting hours.

Everyone on the nursing staff, from the ward sister to the
most junior aide, had long since fallen under the man's spell.

It wasn't so much his looks, or his charm, although both
these attributes were undoubted. It was the major's silent
vigil by Grace Orr's bedside that won the nursing staff's
hearts, and broke them, all in one. The girl's parents came
every day as well, but Major Skelton affected the staff so
much more deeply.

Most, although they would never have admitted it, were

thoroughly in love with the man, and spent many of their daydreaming hours wondering if they might possibly be the one to comfort him when Grace Orr died, as she undoubtedly would.

Grace Orr was lovely (or at least she had once been, from the photographs that her mother showed around), but everyone knew that she would not survive. It was a miracle she'd clung to life this long; there was no hope she'd continue to do so much longer.

So they brought the major cups of tea, and the sisters engaged him in conversation, and the nurses offered to sew the buttons on his jacket, although all were in perfect order and placement, and polish his shoes, although they already shone brilliantly. From time to time the more daring among them suggested an afternoon in a café somewhere, perhaps, to take his mind off things, to which the major always suppressed a wince, then smiled and rejected the offer with endearing charm.

His loyalty to the girl lying motionless on the bed was enchanting, and every nursing sister or aide who came into contact with Jack Skelton wondered what it would be like if they were the recipient of that loyalty and devotion.

Although they suspected some degree of despondency in the man, none suspected his level of despair.

ALTHOUGH THE EMERGENCY WORKERS HAD pulled Grace Orr from the rubble alive, none thought she would survive more than a few hours. Both her legs were crushed, as were her left arm and most of the ribs down her left side. Her left lung had collapsed and her right one was in imminent danger of following suit. Her spleen had ruptured, her heart was bruised so badly it was a wonder it still continued to beat. Her aorta leaked into her abdomen.

All of these injuries were critical, but it was the trauma to her head that was fatal. A huge wedge of concrete had crushed the top of her skull, penetrating deep into the

brain. It was not merely the physical damage done, but the resulting, inevitable infection that would surely kill the girl.

No one, including the fire chief who had given the news to her parents and Jack Skelton, had thought she'd survive longer than the day.

The ambulance had taken her to St. Bart's, where Grace's injuries were cleaned and she was placed in a bed to die. None of the doctors thought there was any point in doing anything more. Her parents and the major were given access, much sympathy, and left to watch Grace die while the doctors and nurses bent their efforts to patients who might actually live.

Grace survived.

None among the staff could quite credit it. She *shouldn't* have been able to live more than a few hours. Almost a third of her brain had been destroyed, and the damage to her aorta and heart should have killed her within hours of it being inflicted. Grace Orr simply should not have lived through her burial in the rubble, let alone a day or more outside.

When Grace continued to cling to life, and after much pleading from her parents and aggressive arguing from the American major, the doctors decided they would do what they could for her. She went to surgery—the surgeons warning that the anesthetic alone would likely prove fatal—and set her bones as best they could, stitched up her aorta, reinflated her lung, cleaned her intracranial cavity (with many a wince) and, discarding the shattered fragments of her skull, inserted a steel plate over the gaping hole and stitched her scalp back over it.

Grace survived both surgical procedures and anesthetic. She went into traction for those broken bones not able to be set in plaster, she had intravenous therapy and a nasogastric tube inserted for feeding, and was then shunted into the veranda ward of the annex to die.

She didn't die.

The doctors warned her parents and Major Skelton that if she survived she would be a vegetable.

They nodded, thanked the doctors, and settled down to wait.

Many long weeks passed.

JACK WAS SLOUCHED DOWN IN THE WICKERWORK easy chair the nurses had brought in for him weeks ago, elbow on arm rest, head resting in his hand.

His eyes did not leave Grace's still form.

She was long out of plaster and traction now, and her external injuries had healed. Her limbs once more lay straight by her sides, the drainage tube into her lung had gone, her scalp had grown over the steel plate, *grown over emptiness,* and her curls had sprung back, covering the raised red scars on her scalp. The doctors said her aorta had healed well.

They shook their heads whenever Jack or Noah and Weyland asked about her brain.

The ravages of her trauma and deep coma had left their own marks on her body. Grace, always slim, was now skeletal. Her body fat had vanished, and her bones poked out vast ranges of hills and valleys in her skin. Her color was either yellow or gray, depending on the time of the day.

Her chest rose and fell, slowly, in desperately shallow, inadequate breaths.

The red rubber of the nasogastric tube looked like a line of blood running down her face and over her shoulder.

Grace had gone. Jack could feel nothing of her. The doctors told him she was in a deep coma, a vegetative state, but even so Jack would have expected to be able to sense *something* of Grace.

But there was nothing. Jack could not even sense, let alone see, the diamond bands.

They had vanished with Grace.

Catling had her. Catling was playing with her, and Jack's guilt was now almost unbearable.

Grace, Grace, I am sorry, I am so sorry, I don't know what to do.

In the afternoons and evenings, and the long, long

nights, when he was alone, Jack often gave into his despair and wept. But tears were something he refused to give into before Grace. He thought that if she woke, and turned her head and opened her eyes, the last thing he would want her to see were his tears.

So, stoic Jack came to St. Bart's. Despairing Jack inhabited the rest of London and Epping Forest, alternating between anger and frenetic guilt-ridden activity, searching out the solution to Grace's terrible coma.

To the Troy Game.

He found solutions to none, save that the Troy Game continually whispered in his ear. *You can have her back, Jack, but only when you and Noah complete me.*

In his darker moments, and they were ever more frequent, Jack wondered if this fight against the Troy Game was worth it.

Perhaps they should just complete her and have done with it.

GRACE WAS LOCKED IN A NIGHTMARE SO TERRIBLE *she did not think she would survive it sane. She existed in a hell of jumbled, ancient memories that appeared to be those of her parents and Jack in previous lives, as well as the memories of the Troy Game itself and of all it had eaten.*

None of the memories was pleasant. She lived through the sack of Troy, and the rape and murder of all those Trojans who had not managed to escape the Greeks.

She endured each violation, each death, as if it were dealt to her own body.

She endured through Ariadne's Catastrophe, suffering along with the tens of thousands who were the Darkwitch's victims.

She suffered with her mother, at the hands of Brutus, and then at those of her father, Asterion.

She despaired with all those who had been Asterion's victims—the women he had raped, the men he had murdered (and, oh gods, these included her own half-brothers,

the sons of Cornelia and Brutus!), the children he had tortured and sodomized, the girls he had prostituted.

She suffered under her father's hands every indignity, every vile nightmare, he had visited on other women.

She felt every stab, every hurt, every wrench to flesh and spirit and soul.

Grace knew what was happening. Catling was tormenting her in order to destroy her.

And Grace thought the only way she could survive this was to lose her sanity.

TODAY WAS ONE OF THE WORST DAYS FOR JACK, and, sitting here with a faraway Grace, he'd sunk into his deepest despair yet. He'd picked up a copy of the *Daily Express* on the way in, and sat in the waiting room and read it while the nurses bathed Grace.

The paper reported on a speech Hitler had made yesterday. It included a translated transcript of the speech, and Hitler's opening words made Jack's blood run cold.

We are in the middle of a conflagration which is not just a struggle between two countries. It is the struggle of two different worlds. There is no way for these worlds to exist side by side. One of them must perish.

The struggle of two different worlds, for whom there was no hope of existing side by side. Jack wondered who had sent this message, for no matter what Hitler himself may have thought, those words were put into his mouth by someone, or something, else.

A message from Catling? Why not? It would serve her purpose well enough, and the bearer even better.

But it might just as well have come from the Faerie . . . perhaps even from this mysterious White Queen.

No matter who had sent it, the words held no comfort.

The winter solstice was fast approaching, and Jack had no idea what to do. No matter what he and Noah (and Weyland and Ariadne and Silvius and the Lord of the

Faerie) tried or investigated, no matter how hard anyone prayed or pleaded, there was no solution. No answer as to how they might destroy the Troy Game rather than complete it.

Catling had continued to escalate the terror on London (as Jack had no doubt she continued to escalate the horror for Grace). The nightly air raids on the capital, as, increasingly, around all Britain, became far worse. Tens of thousands perished in blast and fire and rubble. The Faerie suffered along with London. Huge patches of devastation had spread through the forests on the hills adjacent to The Naked, and many of the Faerie creatures were sickening.

Some were dying.

Jack and Noah either had to find a means to destroy the Troy Game, or they had to complete it. Otherwise, London, England, the Faerie and, likely, the entire world eventually, would turn to dust under Catling's malevolence.

Jack was more sure than ever that Grace had the key. Both the shadow and the diamond bands (as also the White Queen Café and its strange mistress) had vanished when Catling had taken Grace. Somehow Grace *must* have, or be, the key.

But Grace was gone, and her only way home was to do what no one wanted.

Complete the Troy Game.

Jack sat in the hopeless annex at St. Bart's and watched what remained of Grace, and despaired.

"Grace, Grace," he whispered. "I'm sorry, but it is the only way I know to save you."

Chapter Two

December 1940

Grace Speaks

I WAS LOSING TOUCH WITH REALITY, AND WITH my sanity. I was caught within a maelstrom of hate and spite that forced me to endure every sin committed by all those I had ever loved—my parents, Jack, Harry, Matilda, Stella—as well, so it felt to me, those sins of the rest of humanity besides. The memories, the horrific *actualities,* overwhelmed me, and I thought that the only way I could survive the memories, the rapes, the murders, the injustices, if not to lose all sanity, was to succumb to a vicious hatred of everyone I loved.

Catling's malevolence tossed me hither and thither, and as every moment passed I felt myself sliding closer and closer to utter despair. I had no rest, no comfort. Who were these people? How was it I could ever have thought to love them? They were vile, disgusting, the damage they had caused to each other, and to all the innocents whose lives they touched, to *my* life, was so gigantic it was completely unforgivable.

Amid all this that cold-faced bitch intruded into this maelstrom of hatred.

So what do you think, sweet Grace, of your inheritance?

I tried to close my ears, but it was no use.

These are difficult experiences for you to endure, eh?

I wept and struggled, but she wouldn't leave me be. She drifted closer, her terrible white face close to mine.

Why don't you talk to me, Grace? I'm here to help, you know.

I flailed out at her, but she wouldn't go, she wouldn't go, and I was so lost. No one would come for me, no one could aid me. I was here, in this not-quite-death, caught in Catling's torment, and I could do nothing about it.

Grace?

"Let me be!" I shouted at her. "What purpose does this serve?"

None, I grant you, save to torment you.

"You cow!" I yelled, furious now, not caring that I sounded like a petulant child (couldn't I find something more appropriate than "cow"?) and Catling just laughed.

Anger is good, Grace. You should use it more.

THE MEMORIES TOOK OVER, AND FOR THE longest time I did not resist. I saw Jack, as Brutus, rape my mother, then torment her for decades with silent horror. *I* felt it. *I* endured it. My half-brothers . . . I saw them in life, with their wives, their children, and I saw them die, tormented by my own father.

I wept.

Family is important, Grace. It is good that you weep for them.

Why wouldn't she leave me alone? Didn't she have something better to do?

I watched as the man I knew as Harry, the Lord of the Faerie, lived a life as Harold of Wessex in Saxon times. I saw his love for Swanne, now Stella, and saw her turn against him, betray him, murder him.

Please, please, Catling, let me sleep.

Don't call me that.

I didn't care what word games she used with me. I just didn't care. *Leave me alone, Catling. I am sick of you.*

And I am sick of you! I shall leave you alone for a while, and let you ponder your misfortune. When you're ready, call me.

She left, and I was glad.

The assault of images and sound and horror continued. I

fell into the life of a boy called Melanthus, a boy my mother had once thought to love, and a boy that Brutus, my beloved Jack, had murdered.

Would I never stop weeping?

Chapter Three

COPT HALL

Friday, 13 December 1940

THEY SAT IN A GROUP AROUND THE FIRE in Jack's drawing room, a heavy, tense silence hanging between them. Noah and Weyland had come straight from St. Bart's, followed shortly thereafter by Ariadne and Silvius, then by the Lord of the Faerie. Stella had remained within the Faerie to carol in the dusk. Apart from those around the fire, Malcolm stood in gloomy silence by the door to the hall, hands folded before him, his unblinking eyes on Jack.

Jack was getting sick of both Malcolm's silent regard and everyone else's silent tension.

"For Christ's sake," he said, "there must be something . . ."

"What?" said Weyland. "Something to *do*? Something to *say*? Something to *hope* for?"

Over the past few weeks Catling had tightened her grip over the land, and throughout Faerie. Winter had come early, and had deepened into a forbidding iciness across the country.

Snow had fallen in the Faerie, for the first time.

Trees on even undamaged hills were dying, and there were some creatures—the cavelings, the sylphs—that no one had heard from or seen in months.

The bombing continued, with the Luftwaffe campaign of terror and destruction now spread across Britain.

Complete me, or extend the suffering was the uncompromising message from the Troy Game.

Jack thought he was going mad. His mornings spent with Grace trapped him in a never-ending downward spiral of despair and guilt, while the ever-worsening bombing campaign and the Lord of the Faerie's news from the Faerie merely deepened both despair and guilt.

There were days he hated life, and wondered if death were a possibility.

"What can we do?" whispered Noah. "I have done everything I can. Turned every stone and peered under it, sought every opinion, from those ten thousand years dead and those still alive, seeking a solution, and yet there is nothing . . . nothing . . ."

"If you complete the Troy Game, and Grace wakes, could she then provide us with some kind of weapon—" Weyland began.

"Don't be a fool!" Jack snapped. "*Nothing* will be able to touch the Troy Game once it is completed."

"But Games have been unwound before," Weyland said.

"This one is too powerful, Weyland," Ariadne said softly, and Weyland turned to her, his face tight with anger.

"If it wasn't for you—" he said.

"Stop it," said Silvius, wondering if his entire life would be spent keeping the peace between these two. "Jack, Noah, what are our choices?"

Jack looked at Noah, and wondered who would be the one to say it first. "We have no choices," he eventually said, "save that we either destroy the Troy Game, or we complete it, and we do not have the knowledge or the tools to destroy it. Ergo, we must—"

"Gods, don't say it," said the Lord of the Faerie. "*Don't say it!*"

There was a short silence, then Jack spoke softly. "Noah and I will need to begin the preparations very soon," he said. "The solstice draws near. Catling needs to see that we

are preparing, and . . . and, if we are to do this, then we need to be ready."

Jack couldn't believe he'd said that. The very thought of completing the Game sickened him physically and emotionally—and yet somehow imparted a sense of relief. If he completed Catling, then the death and horror would cease.

"Grace is the key," said Malcolm from his doorway. "She and the White Queen."

"Grace is lost to us!" Jack shouted, half rising from his chair before Silvius put a hand on his shoulder. "And the damned, cursed White Queen, whoever the *fuck* she is, has vanished as well!"

"Jack . . ." Noah said quietly.

"And the shadow is no more," Jack continued, his tone slightly less aggressive now. "We have nothing left. Nothing."

"Not to mention the final two Kingship bands," Ariadne put in helpfully.

"Jesus Christ, woman," Jack said, his voice now horribly tired. "Have you nothing positive to contribute to this conversation?"

"Well," said Ariadne, "surely someone needs to point out to you, Jack, that without those final two bands you can't even complete the Troy Game."

Jack leaned his head back against his chair, and put a hand over his face. "Will someone *please* make a helpful suggestion?"

"Jack," said Noah. "You made those diamond bands for Grace. They are magic. Can you not use those?"

"They're gone, too," said Jack. "Gone to wherever Catling has incarcerated Grace."

Another momentary silence. Everyone capable of it, the Lord of the Faerie, Ariadne, Jack, Noah, had looked for Grace wherever they thought she might be: trapped in this world, in some forgotten corner of the Faerie, wandering the paths of the Otherworld, and yet she was nowhere. Catling had taken her somewhere no one could discover.

"Can't you make some more?" said the Lord of the Faerie.

Jack's face twisted, but Ariadne spoke before he could answer.

"It isn't that simple, Faerie lord. A new *set* might be made, although we have neither the time nor the resources for that to be done—we'd need the original Great Founding Labyrinth, not a recreation of one, to do it—but replacement bands? No, especially not for a set as important as the Kingship bands of Troy. Jack needs to use the same bands he started with, the same set, not a combination of four of the original ones plus two new."

"So are you saying," Weyland said, "that we can neither destroy *nor* complete the Troy Game?"

"That would be about it," said Jack, and let the bleakness overwhelm him.

Chapter Four

December 1940

Grace Speaks

J REMEMBERED SOMETHING. I SHOULD HAVE remembered it earlier. Sometimes I am very stupid.

When I went with Ariadne so she could further my training in the arts of the labyrinth, Catling struck me with agony the instant I stepped inside Ariadne's front door. The violence of the attack crippled me, and I know that Ariadne thought her re-creation of the Great Founding Labyrinth, which she'd set up in her drawing room, was close to killing me.

Then Ariadne had called to me. *Use the pain, Grace. Use it to concentrate your mind and power!*

I had. I used the pain. The pain still existed, but it did not

trouble me; indeed, it became a valued asset, fueling my concentration.

Very good. You should have remembered that earlier.

She was back, and my moment of hope evaporated.

I don't know why I try to help you, Grace. You are so stupid on occasion.

I tried to marshal what vestiges of intelligence I had left. The trouble was, I could not believe what my intuition screamed at me.

I could feel her watching me, keenly, and I felt a terrible flash of embarrassment at the things I had said to her.

"You're not Catling," I whispered. "My God, who *are* you? Who are you?"

The terrible visions still swam before me, but I realized that while Catling may have sent me to this hell, she hadn't followed me here.

She had, after all, more important things to do.

Who are you? I said, now using my power.

Never mind that for the moment. Remember only what you were considering before I disturbed you.

It was difficult, for all I wanted to do was to discover who this cold-faced woman was, but I managed to turn my mind back to the original problem. I had used Catling's torment when Ariadne had thrust me into the Great Founding Labyrinth to concentrate my mind. Not only that, I had literally used it as a power source within itself.

Ah, I breathed, relief and hope flooding through me. *I can use this hell, too. How stupid I am, indeed.*

She smiled, this creature who stood just within reach of the corner of one eye, and I felt from her a glimmer of sheer happiness. She didn't say anything, but that glimmer was enough.

I laughed, and, summoning my power (why had I forgotten it? Was despair truly the greatest enemy a person had?), began to bend this overwhelming cacophony of images and memories to my will.

Show me what I need to know, I commanded.

Everything changed.

Chapter Five

Monday, 16 December 1940

NOAH STOOD BATHED IN MOONLIGHT UNder a tree in the forest just north of Faerie Hill Manor. Jack thought that if it wasn't for the terrible expression of hopelessness on her face, she would never have looked so beautiful.

"You know," she said, "you and I have never talked about Grace. What you had she, um . . . what your . . ." She stopped and, remarkably, blushed.

Jack almost managed a smile. "What my intentions are, Noah?"

She looked embarrassed. "Yes."

"Strange that you and I should be having this conversation."

"It is certainly a long way from our initial conversation in Mesopotamia."

They both thought about that for a while, their first disastrous life together.

"It is strange how life turns out," Noah said eventually, and Jack gave a short laugh.

"Aye, that it is. I remember when I first heard you'd given Weyland a daughter. I was so furious. *So* furious. I could never have imagined what that daughter would have come to mean to me."

Noah waited.

"I have treated you so badly, life after life," said Jack. "This time around being no exception. I was angry at first because I'd convinced myself I could win you away from Weyland, then discovered that wasn't possible. And then

Grace began nibbling away at all my preconceptions of her, and, one day I woke up—probably with a push from Malcolm—"

Noah smiled.

"—and realized I loved her, and that love was a peaceful thing compared to what I felt for you."

"But better."

"Yes. You don't mind?"

She shook her head. "I don't begrudge my daughter your love, Jack." She paused. "Although it took me some time to come to terms with it."

"And that is my fault. I could have let you know in an easier manner than I did."

"Jack, we have spent all our lives in an eternal cycle of love and anger and apology. Can we break that cycle now?"

"You don't want me to apologize?"

"No. I . . . I just want you to save Grace, and this land, and Faerie, and me besides."

"Oh well, thank God for that. I thought you were going to demand something hard from me."

Noah tried to smile, but sudden tears glittered in her eyes.

Jack pulled her gently into his arms, and held her close. "Noah, this isn't much, but—"

She pulled back. "What?"

He hesitated, and his uncertainty frightened her.

"*Jack . . .*"

"When I agreed with Weyland last Friday that without the final two bands we could neither destroy nor complete the Troy Game . . . I wasn't quite correct. Silvius had a word with me afterward . . ."

"What did the damn fool say?" Noah said in a tight tone.

"He reminded me that I could actually close out the Troy Game with only four bands."

"But Catling thinks that you need the six bands. Wouldn't she know?"

He gave a shake of his head. "She's only insisting on the six bands because I've been insisting on it. I don't know if she really knows the full intricacies of how a Game is woven through to completion. Closing the Game is nowhere

near as difficult as opening it. Opening a Game requires the full strength of the bands."

"Get to the point."

"You and I could complete the Troy Game with just the four bands, Noah. It would be difficult, and we'd need to use every ounce of power we commanded, both as Kingman and Mistress and as gods of this land. But . . ."

"Jesus, Jack," Noah whispered, suddenly realizing where he was heading. "Don't say it!"

"But," Jack whispered, and now the tears glistened in his eyes as well, "I just wouldn't survive it, Noah."

Chapter Six

December 1940

Grace Speaks

*I*MPOSSIBLY, THE IMAGES BECAME EVEN MORE jumbled, but their nature changed entirely.

I continued to see images of my mother and of Jack's past lives, and while many of these were uncomfortable, they were not of the horrific variety Catling wanted me to see. I saw also fractured memories of people I didn't know, all associated in some way with London: builders and craftsmen, ferrymen, priests, architects.

I saw faint memories of a little girl with black curly hair and a cold face—but I was now not so foolish as to be certain of her identity.

I saw a tall man with a lovely, gentle face, peering into the ruins of . . . a church, I think.

I saw Jack, Brutus as he had been then, and my mother making frantic love inside a circular hut somewhere close to where Lambeth is now.

I saw Jack's two lost bands, but indistinctly. They looked to be lying on an altar, next to what appeared to be a plate of food.

They were waiting for him.

I saw Christopher Wren inspecting, not St. Paul's, nor any other of his famous churches, but what was probably Greenwich Hospital.

I saw the gentle-faced man again, now standing next to a printing press, arguing with a typesetter. *Londina Illustrata,* he was saying, *not Londinia Ilustratum!*

I saw the shadow, writhing over London, and I saw what it was, what it *could* be, and I wept for all our stupidity.

"I don't know how this can be," I said to the woman who now stood closer to me. "It *shouldn't* be."

"You and Jack have to sort it out," she said, and I studied her very closely as she spoke. She looked so much like Catling—the beautiful, cold face, the thick tumbling curls of black hair, the slim body clothed in tight black silk.

"Who are you? Why do you look so much like Catling?"

She smiled, although it never quite reached her eyes, and did not reply.

"Why are you so cold?"

"I have never lived. Never drawn breath. You'd be cold also, if that was your fate."

"What is your name?"

Again, that terrible smile. "I have never lived and have never been named. Some call me the White Queen, others call me the druid's sword."

I latched onto the first name only. *The White Queen . . . Café?* "Mrs. Stanford?"

"No. I appeared using a glamour of the real woman."

I realized what had been tickling at my mind, and now I felt sick with stupidity. When we decide to see things one way, we are then incapable of seeing them any other way. "It has been you, at night, sitting with me all these years."

"Yes."

"Why?"

"To get to know you."

"Why?"

She didn't answer that question. "Jack is going to do something very silly, Grace. You need to stop him, and for that you need to be able to break out of this little hell Catling has built for you *far* more than you need to know all my indifferent whys and wherefores."

"Why do you talk to me here and yet not when you have come a-visiting?"

Her eyes glittered with anger, and, oh, she looked so much like Catling then. "Why would I want to talk to you when you kept calling me 'bitch'?"

I winced, and could not reply.

She took pity on me, and her face softened fractionally. "It is only very recently that you've been prepared to see me any other way than as the hated sister."

Far too recently. "I'm sorry."

She shrugged. "Grace, listen to me. Catling fatally wounded you in the rubble of Coronation Avenue. If it wasn't for Catling's need to keep you alive, even if so indifferently alive, then your broken body would not still be drawing breath. She doesn't need you whole, Grace, she just needs you alive. But *you* need to be whole, you need to be alive and walking and speaking, because you need to get to Jack as soon as you can, and stop him before he condemns all of us to an everlasting hell of the Troy Game. Grace, only you can break free of this. I can't do it for you. Only you can. And you *can*. You just need to believe in yourself."

Chapter Seven

EPPING FOREST

Monday, 16 December 1940

*Y*OU THINK IT IS WORTH IT, TO HAVE YOU dead?" Noah said. "The Troy Game completed, and you dead? That is a double tragedy."

"A worse tragedy than seeing the land suffer as it is now?" Jack said. "A worse tragedy than watching the Faerie sicken and die? Better to complete the Troy Game and hope that, somehow, Grace returns from the living dead with some means of subsequently destroying the Game. Better I dead, than this nightmare continue."

"The Troy Game will not be able to be destroyed once it is completed. Ariadne said—"

"Ariadne has been wrong before. All Games can be unwound, even one so powerful as the Troy Game. You're a powerful Darkwitch, Noah, as is Grace. Between you—"

"Between us there would be nothing but grief if you were dead," said Noah very softly. "Do you think Grace wants to return to find you gone? What will it do to her?"

"She will cope," said Jack, but his face was terribly tight, and Noah could see the effort it took him to remain calm. He, as Noah, knew that if he died during the completion of the Troy Game, it wouldn't just be a death . . . it would be an eternal damnation to whatever the malignant forces of the dark heart of the labyrinth chose for him.

Catling would not let him rest easy.

"Perhaps Grace can . . ." Jack's voice drifted off.

"Perhaps Grace can pull you out of *death*? Jack, there are too many perhaps. This is such a stupid plan. We—"

"It is the only plan we have Noah. Can you think of something better?"

Noah was silent.

"We have almost no room left to move, Noah. Catling will eviscerate both land and Faerie *and* Grace if we don't complete her. We don't have any means by which to unwind her—she is too powerful and I don't have the final two bands. Besides, doing that will kill Grace more certainly than anything even that Catling has done to her. Noah, we must complete the Game, with whatever consequences, and pray that Grace returns with *something*."

"Grace may not return, Jack. We have only Catling's word that she will, and we all know what her word is worth."

Jack did not reply, staring instead with dark, unfathomable eyes into the forest.

"We need to discuss this with the Lord of the Faerie and Weyland and—" Noah said.

Jack's gaze swung back to her. "No. We don't discuss it. We just do it, Noah. There is nothing left to discuss."

Chapter Eight

St. Paul's Cathedral, London

Sunday, 29 December 1940

THE WINTER SOLSTICE WAS LATE. A WEEK late, and that week was an indication, as nothing else, that Catling was spiraling not merely the Faerie and the land, but the entire planet downward into oblivion.

There was no choice, in the end, save to do what she wanted. While the Lord of the Faerie, Weyland, Stella, Ari-

adne, and Silvius did not know that the day could prove fatal to Jack, they did know that he and Noah meant to complete the Troy Game. Given the circumstances, and despite their terrible misgivings, they reluctantly agreed that completion of the Troy Game was the only option left to them.

No one would survive another year if Catling did not get what she wanted.

When Brutus and Genvissa had started the final Dance of the Flowers atop Og's Hill three and a half thousand years previously, it had been a grand occasion with virtually the entire population of Troia Nova and the Sacred Hills in attendance. Hundreds of Trojan youths, men and women, had accompanied Brutus and Genvissa in the final dance. It had been held in light and openness and majesty, and Brutus and Genvissa had come very, very close to competing the Troy Game then and there.

But Cornelia, now Noah, had stepped in and plunged Asterion's horn dagger into Genvissa's neck. Genvissa, dying, had cursed everyone to continual rebirth until she had her revenge.

But it hadn't been Genvissa who had passed the real curse, had it? That had been the manipulative Troy Game itself, maneuvering everyone it needed to do just what it willed.

Now, more than three thousand years later, Jack and Noah were about to do what the Troy Game wanted. They were sick at heart, and close to physical nausea with what they were about to do, but they had no choice. It was not merely Grace's life that rode on the night, but the life of the entire land and Faerie besides.

This was no glorious spectacle as the original Dance of the Flowers had been. No one attended save Jack and Noah. There were no dancers, no witnesses, no crowds.

Shortly after dusk Noah and Jack entered St. Paul's. They were clothed in magic and mystery, and as on those occasions Jack had come to the cathedral to talk with Catling, none among the cathedral staff saw them.

They walked very slowly up the nave toward the space under the great dome. Both had dressed in the simple white linen, a hip wrap for Jack and a long skirt for Noah. Nei-

ther wore any shoes, and they were bare of adornment save for Jack's four golden Kingship bands on his arms.

The markings about his shoulders writhed desperately, as if they wanted to escape.

Noah carried in one hand a small posy of flowers, sad insipid things, which had been the best she could find at this time of year.

Halfway up the nave she reached out her free hand and took one of Jack's.

"I can't believe it has come to this," she whispered.

"Noah, we have to do it."

"Jack . . ." Her voice choked with emotion, and Jack stopped and faced her, taking both Noah's shoulders in his hands. "Noah, *we have no choice.*" He paused, taking a deep breath to steady his own nerves. "We have *never* had a choice."

"I—"

"It should have been me you plunged that knife into so long ago, Cornelia," Jack said, his mouth quirking a little as he called her by her original name. "Without me, we would have had none of this mess."

She tried to smile at him, but it trembled and vanished before it had any chance at life. "This is so stupid. Here we are about to condemn the world to a nightmare, and there is no one around to watch."

"Ah," said Catling, stepping out of the shadows, "but there is me. Glad you could come. Happy you're here." Her voice hardened. "Now get on with it."

Then she took another step closer. "Jack? No leg bands? What is this?"

"If I could find them I'd wear them," said Jack. "But I can't find them—and if you don't know where they are, Catling, with your power, then don't blame me for not being able to locate them."

"Ah, don't give me that! I know you have them! You just want me to believe you're weak. I'm sorry, Jack, but I am not letting down my guard. Just get on with it, but know I'll be watching for the first sign of treachery."

Catling looked at Jack very carefully. "If I sense any du-

plicity in you, Jack, then what I have done thus far will be but a foretaste of what I *can* do. Try to trick me if you will, but you—and everyone else—shall live to regret it."

"The land already regrets you," Noah said.

"Don't interrupt," Catling snapped, her eyes not leaving Jack's face. "Well?"

"No trickery," Jack said. "I just want to get this over with and done with."

Catling stared a moment longer, then gave a small nod. "Good, then get on with it. I've waited way too long for this moment."

THE WHITE QUEEN HAD GONE, AND GRACE WAN-dered alone in her hell.

Save it was not quite a hell any more, for now Grace knew she had the means not only to control it, but to use the power behind it.

"Jack is about to do something very stupid," she whispered to herself. "And I must stop him."

To do that she must manage two tasks: escape this hell, and escape it whole.

Grace sighed, and let her Darkcraft flow forth. Catling had used the power of the dark heart of the labyrinth to create this nightmare, and so Grace used the same power to manipulate it.

Show me, she commanded, and she saw before her a terrible sight.

Herself, fractured and wasted, lying still on a hospital bed. To one side sat Jack in a chair, his head in his hands. The vision shifted, and Grace saw her parents on the other side of the bed, her father's arm about Noah, their faces flat with misery.

"Oh," Grace murmured.

The vision shifted a little more. Now Jack was back, and Grace saw several nurses, peering out from the nurse's station, their eyes on Jack, their faces hopeless with love.

Grace smiled.

* * *

NOAH AND JACK STOOD UNDER THE DOME OF ST. Paul's. Evensong service was in progress around them, the cathedral almost full with worshippers, and yet it was as if two cathedrals existed: the cathedral of the mortal world, where people sang and prayed and clerics preached; and the shadow cathedral, where ancient beings bowed their heads, and began a dance of such great antiquity that both physically and metaphorically undermined everything the mortal worshippers believed.

Jack and Noah were aware of the worshippers, but paid them no regard save for a mild ironic thought that they were to have an audience, however unknowing, after all.

They stood at opposite aspects of the dome: Noah in its eastern sector, Jack in its western.

For the moment Noah stood still, watching Jack. Before they could begin the Dance of the Flowers, creating the Flower Gate that would trap evil within the dark heart of the labyrinth and complete the Troy Game, Jack had to raise the labyrinth.

As Brutus, so many thousands of years ago, Jack had buried the labyrinth deep within Og's Hill, where St. Paul's now stood. He'd done it to preserve the labyrinth, to save it until he and a reborn Genvissa could raise it again and finish what they had started.

It was difficult work, not merely because Jack had only four of the bands, but because it had been so long since he'd created the enchantment that had hidden the labyrinth. As Brutus he'd been wracked with grief for Genvissa and consumed with anger at Cornelia, and Jack now found it difficult to remember precisely what he'd done through the mists of both time and overwhelming emotion.

Noah, watching, found it almost unbearable. She could see the difficulty Jack was having, but she was almost overpowered with her sense of loss. This man, who she had hated and loved in equal measure, and who had been so much to her for so very long, was calling into daylight the means of his death.

Tears slid silently from her eyes. Noah was devastated at her sense of loss, but she was far more affected by the realization that at some point in the last hours she had come to accept it.

Better Jack's death than that of the land's.

"Cornelia must indeed be dead," she murmured, "and Eaving rampant, if I can think thus."

Across the dome, Jack suddenly stepped back, raising his face to Noah.

She gasped. The black and white marble flooring under the dome had become translucent, and she could see, from far, far below, a huge labyrinth rising toward the surface.

GRACE SIGHED AND, REMEMBERING HOW SHE HAD used the power of the pain of her wrists, directed the power that had created the nightmarish world of fractured images and memories to release her.

Back to my body, *she commanded,* and a body that works, if you please.

As she left the hell that Catling had built for her, Grace saw Catling herself, deep in the dark heart of the Troy Game.

For a moment Grace stilled, not frightened, but curious, wondering if Catling saw her.

But Catling was oblivious. Grace was the last thing on her mind. Catling only had eyes for what her Kingman and Mistress of the Labyrinth were doing.

THE MARBLE FLOOR UNDER THE DOME OF ST. Paul's vanished, replaced now by the ancient unicursal seven-circuit labyrinth of Crete, laid out in cream and brown stones as it had been when first built by Brutus.

The dancing floor.

Noah took a deep, shaky breath, and raised her head to look at Jack.

He was staring at her. Very slowly, he raised his hand toward her.

Noah swallowed, summoned her courage, and allowed the power of the labyrinth to infuse her.

GRACE ROSE FROM HER BED, AND THE NURSES started back, shocked.

She stumbled, clutching the back of a chair for support. "Damn these legs!" she said. Then Grace's face tightened in concentration, and her form seemed to glow for an instant; she straightened and, although still weak and uncertain on her feet, was nonetheless stronger than she had been a moment ago.

She looked at the nurses. "Can you help me? If someone could take out this feeding tube from my nose . . . and I need a coat, and perhaps some shoes, and I need to get to St. Paul's very, very quickly. Does anyone have a car?"

The ward sister, a marvelously stern woman called Sister Marr, had experienced many crises and challenges during almost forty working years on the wards of St. Bart's, and although slightly put out by the girl's apparently miraculous recovery, she was determined not to let the strangeness of the request unsettle her before the junior nurses.

After all, a lifetime's reputation was at stake.

"Is this absolutely necessary, Miss Orr?" Sister Marr said.

"Absolutely *vital*," Grace said.

"Well, then," Marr said, "I do not have a car, but I can requisition an ambulance for you." She looked Grace up and down. "After all, you still look as if you need it."

Grace smiled, so sweetly it took the nurses' breath away. "Sister Marr," she said, "you are a saint."

THEY DANCED ABOUT THE PERIMETER OF THE labyrinth, their movements graceful yet charged with a powerful sexuality. About them, unknowing, the congregation sang a hymn, and the slow, measured beat of the hymn penetrated into the magic surrounding Jack and Noah, and they danced to its rhythms and tempo.

The golden bands around Jack's arms glittered as his arms moved slowly through the dance, his face kept turned to Noah.

He kept hold of the dance and the labyrinthine power which consumed him only with the most extreme effort. The lack of the final two bands was now beginning to exhaust Jack, and he could feel, flickering at the edges of his consciousness, a dark and hungry presence.

As Noah danced, she allowed single flowers to fall from the posy she carried, and they drifted here and there about the labyrinth, apparently falling at random, yet somehow forming a pattern all their own.

Something sinister started to rise from the dark heart of the labyrinth.

SISTER MARR SAT IN THE BACK OF THE AMBU-lance and stared at the girl who sat opposite her. Someone had found her an ancient hound's-tooth coat, and she had it wrapped tight about her body.

The coat was meant for a large man, and it was so bulky on Grace Orr that it highlighted, rather than hid, her painful thinness.

No one had been able to find shoes to fit the girl, and so her legs emerged from under the hem of the coat like white, knobbly sticks, her bare feet overly large for her skeletal limbs.

Every so often the ambulance rocked as it rounded a corner, and Grace had to brace herself against the partition that divided the driver's cab from the back of the vehicle.

"Who the hell are you, Grace Orr?" said Sister Marr.

The girl smiled, and Marr was struck by how lovely her face was, despite being crowned by a head of hair that had been terribly decimated by the surgery on her skull.

"I am the White Queen's sister," she said.

* * *

THE FLOWERS THAT NOAH HAD SCATTERED ABOUT
the labyrinth began to move, sliding toward the entrance.
Jack and Noah continued their dance, but now they were
approaching each other, gravitating, like the flowers,
toward the entrance to the labyrinth.

As they came to within ten paces of the entrance, the
flowers rose one by one, weaving themselves into the form
of a gate.

And as the Flower Gate rose, so the darkness at the
heart of the labyrinth slid along the labyrinth's paths,
toward the gate.

THE AMBULANCE DREW TO A HALT OUTSIDE THE
west door of St. Paul's, and Sister Marr asked Grace if she
needed help.

Grace smiled sweetly again. "You have already been a
wonderful aid, Sister Marr. Thank you."

And then she was gone into the evening gloom, hob-
bling slowly on bare feet up the steps toward the doors, the
coat clutched about her.

NOAH LOOKED AT JACK WITH DESPERATE EYES.
The Dance of the Flowers was almost done, the Flower
Gate within a few inches of being completed, and some-
thing loathsome approached from the dark heart of the
labyrinth. This was to be expected . . . to a point. The entire
purpose of a Game was to protect a city from evil by trap-
ping such evil within the heart of the labyrinth. When the
Game was opened, it began to attract the evil that naturally
gravitates to the life and vibrancy of any city into its heart.
Then, when the Game was closed with the Flower Gate, the
evil would be trapped within the labyrinth for eternity—or
so long as the Game lasted. During the final Dance of the
Flowers, when the Kingman and Mistress of the Labyrinth
raised the Flower Gate, Noah knew that it was to be ex-
pected that the evil within the dark heart should panic and
try to escape.

But it shouldn't be able to escape very far from the dark heart through the corridors of the labyrinth, and it most certainly shouldn't, as this creeping darkness was, be inching closer and closer to the entrance.

Already tense, Noah began to feel panic chip away at the edges of what little composure she retained.

Jack? Jack? What is happening?

THE SUNDAY EVENSONG CONGREGATION STARED, incredulous, as the thin, battered girl with ragged hair and dressed only in a hound's-tooth coat, shuffled on precarious legs up the center aisle of the nave.

She was staring intently at the space under the dome, a frown on her face, and the farther she advanced up the aisle, the faster became her pace.

And the more precarious. Several people half raised from their seats as more than once the girl stumbled and almost fell. But as she regained her balance, then they sank down again.

In his pulpit, the reverend delivering the sermon stopped speaking and stared over the rims of his spectacles, mouth agape.

No one thought to stop her.

"JACK?" NOAH WHISPERED. "JACK?"

He didn't respond. He was staring through the weave of the gate toward the approaching miasma of evil, and his face was gray and pale, as if he was holding on to life by a mere breath.

Gods, though Noah, *that evil is coming for him!* Jack was vulnerable without the final two bands, and the rising blackness knew it.

The Flower Gate was almost complete, the final five or six flowers now slowly raising themselves from the floor toward the top bar of the gate.

As they did so the creeping evil reached the gate where it seethed momentarily as if confounded, then formed it-

self into a gigantic hand that reached slowly, slowly, for the handle of the gate.

"*Jack!*" Noah screamed.

THE GIRL REACHED THE MARBLE FLOOR UNDER the dome. Her face was now screwed up in such tight concentration that her eyes had virtually vanished. One hand was still clutched desperately in her coat, holding it against her, the other reached forward, as if for salvation.

She took another step forward, then another, tottering so badly she almost fell, then she reached out her hand and brought it down as if on someone's shoulder, saying in a tone as clear as a temple bell on a snowy night, "Jack. Don't. Stop this now."

And then all hell broke loose under the dome of St. Paul's Cathedral.

Chapter Nine

LONDON

Sunday, 29 December 1940

AT FIRST NOAH WASN'T SURE WHAT HAD happened. Jack suddenly reeled back, as if someone had grabbed him from behind.

Jack. Don't. Stop this now.

Simultaneously the enchantment of the Dance of the Flowers was broken as Noah and Jack lost all concentration, and the gate collapsed into a tangled heap of flowers scattered over the floor of the cathedral.

As the Flower Gate crumbled, so the huge black hand that had hovered behind it closed momentarily into a fist,

then leaped forward, past the heap of flowers, toward where Jack was only just managing to regain his balance.

Then Noah saw the pathetic figure that stood behind Jack, and she shouted out with all her strength, *"Grace! Grace! Get back!"*

Jack reeled around, as if only realizing at Noah's shout that someone stood beside him. His eyes widened—*Grace!*

"Hello, Jack," she said softly.

He started to lift a hand, reaching for her, but before he could touch her, before he could say anything, before he could even *smile* at her, the black hand that had emerged from the heart of the labyrinth lunged forward and grabbed Grace, fully enclosing her in its massive maw.

There was a single moment when both Noah and Jack leaped for the hand, still hovering in the space between them, and then it was gone, Grace with it, and Jack and Noah found themselves standing on the marble floor under the great dome of St. Paul's Cathedral, the entire evensong congregation staring at them.

Silence. Then, in the heartbeats after the barely dressed man and woman had appeared in the midst of evensong service, bombs started to rain down around the cathedral, and the entire congregation rose and fled for exits to the shelters.

CATLING AND GRACE FACED EACH OTHER IN THE dark heart of the labyrinth.

Catling was furious, so angry her eyes and clenched hands blurred in and out of focus with each breath she took.

She was shouting incoherently at Grace, who stood before her, wan and exhausted, but preternaturally calm.

None of the words that streamed from Catling's mouth were intelligible, but that hardly mattered. Grace did not need intelligible words to understand what Catling was trying to vocalize.

"Stop it," said Grace. "You don't frighten me anymore."

Catling stopped midinvective, her mouth remaining open for a heartbeat before she slowly closed it.

"You have only one weapon against me," said Grace. "Only one *effective* weapon, and that is death. But to kill me you need to murder yourself as well, and, frankly, I don't think you're up to that right now."

Catling's eyes glowed an intense silver, then settled back to a seething blackness.

"Anything else you try to use against me," said Grace, her voice now very quiet, "I will simply use to further my own power." She slid her wrists out of the long sleeves of the coat, holding them up before Catling.

The diamond bands glowed and sparkled in the dark evil of their surroundings.

"Behold the agony you visited on me," said Grace. "Now celebrated and used. The hell you sent me to, understood and managed, and then utilized likewise. Believe it, Catling, whatever you throw at me, short of your own death, I will likewise make use of to further my own power. Do you really want that? Do you *really* want me to grow much stronger?"

"What the fuck do you think you're going to gain from this?" said Catling. "I will rain destruction on both land and Faerie! Do you want that?"

"Better that than you holding complete dominion over land and Faerie," said Grace quietly.

"Yes?" said Catling. "Really? Come with me, then, and see what I can do."

IN THE PANIC TO GET TO SHELTERS, SEVERAL PEO-ple had left their coats behind in a vestibule, and Jack grabbed them for himself and Noah as they fled St. Paul's via a small door on the south face of the cathedral.

"Sweet Jesus," Jack muttered as he stared heavenward, "has Hitler sent the entire Luftwaffe?"

Noah hunched into her coat, standing as close to Jack as she could. "Not Hitler," she muttered.

London was alight. The German bombers were dropping massive quantities of incendiaries intermixed with the high

explosive bombs, and wherever Jack and Noah looked, they could see fires glowing in rooftops and within the windows of buildings.

"We've got to get out of here," Jack said, pulling Noah forward.

"*Jack——*"

"I know. We'll talk once we get out . . . *Jesus Christ!*" A huge blast from a warehouse not fifty yards away almost knocked them off their feet.

Jack slid an arm around Noah's waist, pulling her toward the street. Ordinarily he would have used his power to get them out of there, but both he and Noah were exhausted from their exertions in the cathedral—he far more than she—and Jack thought that even trying to use their powers would probably result in more injury to themselves than if they attempted to flee through the burning buildings.

"Grace . . ." Noah said, trying ineffectually to pull herself from Jack's grasp.

"Grace will have to look after herself for a time," said Jack. "For now, our hands will be full enough trying to save our own lives."

"DO YOU RECOGNIZE THIS PLACE, GRACE?"

She shook her head, looking about. Catling had brought her to the top of a hill that appeared to be in the northern suburbs of London. The summit was gently rounded, and its perimeter was marked by a score or more of standing stones.

"This is Pen Hill," said Catling, "as once it was. Now, of course, it is smothered in dull terraced housing and, so I believe, a murky little reservoir. But this is how it once was. One of the sacred Veiled Hills. Your mother had a fine time here, once."

Grace did not comment.

"Do you recognize the standing stones, Grace?"

Again Grace did not comment.

"They're Sidlesaghes. Been good friends to your mother over the years. Been *important* to her."

"Don't do it, Catling," said Grace. She had now turned and was looking steadily at Catling, her face as calm as it had been in the dark heart of the cathedral.

"I want to impress upon you," said Catling, "just how much I am going to make you pay for what you did in the cathedral." Again, as it had in the dark heart of the labyrinth, Catling's face suffused with anger, then blurred very slightly. "I want your mother, and your lover, and all the Faerie besides, to know just how disappointed I am, and I want them to know it is *your* fault! *You* will get the blame for this, Grace! *Yours* will be the guilt!"

Again, Grace just looked steadily at Catling, which only increased Catling's rage.

"I am going to murder them, Grace. What do you say to that, eh?"

"That it is something you will spend eternity regretting," Grace said. "As it is something which will sadden me for the rest of my days. But I refuse to bear the blame or guilt for your deeds, Catling. Do what you will, but bear the blame entirely."

Her astounding aura of calm had, if anything, deepened.

LONDON HAD SUFFERED SOME DISASTROUS BOMB-ing raids since the start of the bombing offensive, but this night would go down in history for the ferocity and destruction of the raid. Within days the press had labeled it the second Great Fire of London.

But for this night, anyone caught up in it had only one thought.

Survival.

The high explosive bombs caused massive damage wherever they fell, but the true horror were the small and seemingly inoffensive incendiary bombs. About the length and diameter of a forearm, they fell in their thousands on rooftops and down chimneys and into gutters where they

fizzed out a shower of molten sparks for several minutes. At almost one thousand degrees centigrade, these sparks set fire to anything flammable within several yards' diameter from the bomb.

The incendiary bombs were easy enough to put out. All one had to do was dump a bucket of sand on them and they would go out.

But there were not enough buckets of sand, nor enough people to dump them, for the hundreds of thousands of incendiary bombs that fell that night.

It was a calculated tactic on the Luftwaffe's part. It was the Christmas weekend, a Sunday, and the City would have very few people about to fight the incendiary bombs. If ever the Germans wanted to burn central London to the ground, this would be the best night of the year on which to attempt it.

What they hadn't counted on was additional support of a maddened Troy Game. Catling had been within a breath of completion—*Jack had actually been going to complete her, not destroy her!*—and had had her goal snatched from her at the last possible moment. She took what the German High Command sent, and made it infinitesimally worse.

Catling wanted London, as well Jack and Noah and all associated with them, to pay.

London burned.

When the firemen tried to pump water from fire hydrants, they discovered that the high explosive bombs had shattered most of the city's water mains, and there was little to no water available.

When they tried to pump water from the Thames, they discovered a supernaturally low tide, and there was little to no water available from the river, either.

Within an hour of the bombers first appearing overhead, central London was ablaze.

CATLING SEETHED. SHE TWISTED AROUND AND around in the center of the ancient circle atop Pen Hill, her form moving so fast it blurred. Her arms were flung out, her head twisted back, and from her throat emerged a

stream of noise so vile it appeared almost as if it would rend apart the very sky.

Grace stood to one side of her, looking not at Catling, but at the surrounding stones.

They were changing.

Cracks appeared in their bases, then zigzagged up the faces of the stones.

Grace was in touch enough now with her own power, both as a Darkwitch and a Mistress of the Labyrinth, to know what Catling was doing.

She was unwinding the Sidlesaghes' existence.

"Don't," whispered Grace.

Catling only increased her efforts, and the stones began to crumble. As they did so, a great wailing filled the air, and Grace knew it was the death screams of the Sidlesaghes.

"Don't," Grace whispered again.

Your fault, came Catling's whispered reply. *This is your fault. If you hadn't stopped Jack and Noah, then the Sidlesaghes would not now be being torn apart.*

"This fault is not mine to bear, Catling," said Grace.

The stones were now metamorphosing into the shapes of the Sidlesaghes, and as they did so, Grace, despite her calm, cried out in horror.

All of them, all of the beloved ancient sad songsters, were being torn apart before her eyes. A Sidlesaghe directly in front of her screamed as his right arm was wrenched away from his body, then fell to the grass as his right leg was torn away.

"Grace!" came a tortured voice, and she whipped around.

There, crawling toward her across the grass, came the wretched body of the Sidlesaghe she recognized as Long Tom.

"Grace," Long Tom said, his voice cracking as badly as his body. "Take my hand."

And he held out to her a hand from which Catling's power was slowly flaying the skin.

* * *

JACK AND NOAH HAD MANAGED TO MAKE IT TO
Blackfriars Bridge. There were some forty or fifty people
already on the bridge, all standing next to the railing as if
they needed the security of knowing they could plunge into
the waters of the Thames any time they needed, and all of
them were staring transfixed back toward the massive
flames that had now engulfed the city.

Jack and Noah joined them standing close together,
Jack's arm still around Noah, leaning against the balustrade
of the bridge, staring.

As they watched, the smoke cleared a little, and there
came a break in the flames, and they saw the dome of St.
Paul's rising amid hell.

The cathedral was untouched.

Noah abruptly twisted in Jack's arm, leaned over the
side of the bridge, and vomited.

When she finally straightened, she glanced at Jack's
face, and was stunned to see there a faint smile.

"Jack?"

He glanced at her then nodded at the sky. "Do you see it,
Noah? Do you feel it?"

Noah frowned at him, then looked up at the sky over St.
Paul's cathedral.

She gasped. The shadow was back, and it was stronger
than ever Noah had felt it previously.

"Grace is alive," said Jack. "Damn it, she is still
alive!"

TEARS SLID DOWN GRACE'S CHEEK AT LONG
Tom's horrific dying, but she did not hesitate to step for-
ward and reach for his hand.

Don't touch him, Catling seethed.

Too late, said Grace, and grasped Long Tom's bloody
hand in hers.

ST. PAUL'S WAS SURROUNDED BY EIGHTEENTH-
and nineteenth-century warehouses and offices, tightly

packed together and separated only by twisting, narrow streets.

All of them were ablaze.

As Grace took Long Tom's hand, a shower of sparks rose from the conflagration and blew northeast, landing on the ancient Guildhall.

It exploded into flames.

Inside, the ancient beings Gog and Magog stirred, and shook their spear and sword.

LONG TOM HAD GRASPED HER HAND SO TIGHTLY Grace could feel his flesh sinking into hers.

"D'you see?" Long Tom whispered in a horrible rasping tone.

"Yes," whispered Grace. "Yes, I see. Thank you, Long Tom."

THE ROOF OF THE GUILDHALL COLLAPSED, showering the wooden forms of Gog and Magog with sparks.

They caught alight instantly.

The wooden statues, alive with ancient power and with fire, stepped from their pedestals and began a slow dance about the flame-puddled floor of the Guildhall.

"Hello, Grace," they whispered.

WHAT ARE YOU DOING? CATLING SAID, COMING TO stand next to where Long Tom lay semiprone on the grass, Grace bending over him, their hands still entwined. *What are you doing?*

Seeing, said Grace. *Seeing that you don't wish me to know.*

Let him go! shrieked Catling, her hands grabbing those of Long Tom and Grace.

Way, way too late now, said Grace.

* * *

ROBERT STACEY, SIDLESAGHE AND CONCIERGE of the private residents' wing of the Savoy, slowly rose from his desk in the foyer of the residents' entrance.

Outside bombs rained down, and he could hear the roar of the inferno within the ancient City, even though it was many blocks away.

He was alone. Everyone else had fled for the shelters long since.

Hello, Grace, he said, and the next moment a nearby bomb blast shattered the glass door of the entrance foyer, and a sheet of glass fully five feet long and almost two wide impaled the Sidlesaghe.

ACROSS BRITAIN, THE ANCIENT STONE CIRCLES, or dances, that had stood so many thousands of years, shuddered as one, and then lost . . . life. They became shapeless, gray, lichen-covered stones, and nothing else.

The dances were dead.

LONG TOM LAY LIFELESS AT GRACE'S FEET. VERY slowly, reverentially, she let his hand go, and straightened up.

"You bitch," said Catling. "You can't beat me."

"I know that," said Grace. "I won't even try."

With that, she turned her back, walked down the hill, and vanished, leaving Catling standing amid the tattered remains of what had once been Sidlesaghes.

BENEATH BLACKFRIARS BRIDGE THE WATER sprites screamed.

"Jack!" Noah gasped, grabbing onto his arm for support. "Gods . . . *Jack!*"

"What is it?"

Noah gulped a huge, shocked breath. "The Sidlesaghes are dead," she whispered. "Every one of them. Catling has murdered the Sidlesaghes."

Before he could answer they were both reeling back as Catling appeared not a pace away.

"The Sidlesaghes tonight," she hissed, "and whoever I feel like in the morning. I will work my way through the creatures of the Faerie until you come back and finish what you started. How long will it take, eh? How many deaths?"

And with that she was gone.

THE STREETS AND BUILDINGS OF THE CITY, THE ancient square mile of London, largely had been replaced by an impenetrable firestorm. Firemen did their best, but combined with the ferocity of the blaze, its extent, the abnormal low tide of the Thames and the fractured water mains in the City, there was very little they could manage to accomplish. The incendiary bombs set roofs and gutters alight, and then the following high explosive bombs tore buildings apart, scattering burning fragments far and wide and setting hitherto untouched buildings ablaze.

Many fire crews had to abandon their equipment and run for their lives, holding their breath against the searing, ember-choked air.

One of the escaping firemen had an IB fall and embed itself into his back.

He burned alive, and no one could do anything to save him.

THE WAVE AFTER WAVE OF GERMAN BOMBERS RE-turned to refuel and reload bombs at their airfields in France. The first raid of the night had been a stunning success, and as aircraft were refueled, their crews chattered excitedly about their experiences flying over burning London.

"Like flying over bubbling pea soup," one pilot exclaimed, referring to the sight as each new dropped stick of bombs "bubbled" up through the churning clouds of smoke and flames. Others remarked on the stomach-dropping experience of having their aircraft suddenly hurtled thou-

sands of feet into the air by the super-heated air over the City, only to just as suddenly drop thousands of feet once the aircraft were past the conflagration.

At the planes, ground crew struggled with the payload for this return raid. Gone now were the IBs—they had already done their task; now the bombers were loaded with Satans, massive eighteen-hundred-megaton bombs that would be used to literally blow central London apart.

As the air crew chatted, and the aircraft were refueled and reloaded, something strange began to happen on the beaches of France.

A YOUNG WOMAN DRESSED IN NOTHING BUT A heavy hound's-tooth coat walked barefoot along the sand at tide's edge, the gray waves of the Channel foaming about her ankles. She walked heavily, as if exhausted, or as if she had been weakened by some serious illness, but nonetheless carried about her an air of serenity that counteracted her heaviness of gait. She held her forearms a little out from her body, waving her hands and fingers to the beat of a melody only she could hear.

The beat of the land.

She smiled as she walked, occasionally humming, occasionally speaking a few words as if murmuring a conversation to someone, sometimes laughing out loud.

At one point she tipped her head back, shook out her loose mop of curls, and ran lightly—stunningly lightly, considering the heaviness of her gait to this point—along the sand, the waters splashing about her bare legs.

Diamonds flashed and glowed around her wrists and lower arms.

After a while, her form became indistinct, as if a fog coalesced about her.

IN LUFTWAFFE AIRFIELD AFTER AIRFIELD, CREW raced back to their aircraft as the signals sounded that indicated the refueling and loading was complete. The

crews clambered aboard, and the engines of the aircraft roared.

One after another, the bombers taxied onto their runways, their crews looking forward to an easy bombing run.

As the aircraft took off one by one, circling their respective airfields until their entire squadrons were in the air, phones began ringing in airfield control rooms.

ON THE BEACHES OF FRANCE, THE YOUNG WOMAN had vanished, hidden within the thick, yellow fog which now blanketed the coastline, rising to almost nine thousand feet.

She may have been invisible, but as the fog thickened even more, coiling and twisting up from the Channel waters, there came a faint laugh, and some merry, whispered words.

Just like bubbling pea soup.

ONE AFTER ANOTHER, LUFTWAFFE PILOTS SWORE as the hastily radioed orders came in.

Return to base! Return to base! Flying conditions now extremely difficult.

Not to mention landing conditions, thought pilots as they exchanged glances within cockpits.

Now they'd have to get their bombers safely back on ground . . . without their satanic payloads exploding.

AT MIDNIGHT, PRECISELY, EXHAUSTED FIRE CREWS and emergency personnel in London were astounded to hear the all clear sound.

All had expected the Luftwaffe to return and finish what they had so devastatingly started: the IBs had clearly been dropped to create fires to act as beacons for returning bombers.

No one had any way of knowing that the reason those bombers didn't return was walking slowly through the surf in the churning, thick yellow fog that had suddenly, inexplicably blanketed the Channel coast.

Chapter Ten

LONDON

Monday, 30 December 1940

WHILE SUBURBAN LONDONERS COULD not fail to have been aware of the massive air raid overnight, because of reporting restrictions very few had any idea of the amount of damage resulting from the raid. All that the BBC reported that morning was: "Enemy aircraft attacked towns in the south of England during the night causing some damage. Fires were started and casualties have been reported." Unknowing, tens of thousands of people caught trains into work in the City as usual on Monday morning, only to stand outside London Bridge railway station, or Waterloo station, mouths agape in horror at what they saw.

Twisted, blackened, smoking rubble where once there had been buildings.

Where once there had been a city.

Almost without exception, every one of those workers tried to find their way to work. They picked their way through streets littered with debris—masonry, twisted steel beams, shattered glass, still smoldering bodies—to their places of work . . . if they were still standing. It took some workers almost five hours to reach their workplaces only to stand for ten minutes talking with comrades before starting the painful homeward journey back to the railway station once more. Others managed to get to their work in more timely fashion, to spend the day sorting out debris, tidying what they could, rescuing what remained, and, if practicable, setting down to the day's business in what remained of their offices. Still others, deeply moved by the exhausted

firemen about them, silently took sandwiches and thermoses from their lunch boxes and handed them out among the fire crews.

The GPO sent out the mail as usual, and postmen picked their careful way around fire crews and over rubble in order to deliver their letters.

Determined not to allow themselves to be cowed, Londoners did their best to resume their normal routines as soon as possible.

JACK AND NOAH STAYED ON BLACKFRIARS BRIDGE until well after dawn, looking north to where the dome of St. Paul's still rose from amid the destruction.

"No doubt the papers will claim it a miracle," Jack said dryly.

"Jack . . . what are we going to do?" Noah looked exhausted. Her shoulders were slumped, her face was smudged with soot, her hands trembled slightly where they clutched her coat.

"Indeed," said a new voice. "What *are* you going to do?"

The Lord of the Faerie had appeared behind them, and Jack and Noah turned about at the sound of his angry voice.

"The Sidlesaghes have *gone!*" said the Lord of the Faerie. "Murdered! And I heard what Catling said to you—sweet gods, she will work her murderous way through the entire Faerie! I didn't agree with you completing the Troy Game, but I think I agree even less with your abandoning the attempt!"

"Coel—" Jack began.

"What happened?" the Lord of the Faerie continued. "Why *did* you stop? *Look!*" His hand cast out at the destruction beyond the bridge. "Can you even imagine what the Faerie looks like this morning? Can you—"

"*Coel!*" Jack reached out and seized the Lord of the Faerie's shoulders. "Be still a moment. Listen to me. Grace is back. She—"

"*Grace* cannot fix what you have so gloriously mangled!" the Lord of the Faerie said.

"The shadow is back, too," said Noah quietly.

The Lord of the Faerie sent her a furious glance. "And what good has that cursed shadow done any of us to this point? None!"

"Please, Coel," said Jack. "Please. I know how you fear. But *listen* to me ... there is something happening, something ... *good*. The all clear sounded at midnight ... Why? Sweet Lord, Coel, the Luftwaffe should have returned, but they didn't. And the Sidlesaghes ... I'm not entirely sure they *are* completely gone. When Catling spoke to us she was unsettled, badly so. She only hauls out the huge threats when she feels threatened. She—"

"You didn't complete her," the Lord of the Faerie said. "She wasn't threatened, she was *angry*."

"She didn't use Grace as a threat," Jack said. "Catling snatched Grace from before Noah's and my eyes within the cathedral ... but when Catling came to us here she didn't use Grace to threaten us as she did when Grace was buried under Coronation Avenue. That means she didn't have Grace. And if Grace could have escaped the terror that was Catling last night, if she could have *risen from her deathbed*, then Grace has managed to access some power, or some knowledge, that thwarted Catling. Coel, let me talk to Grace. Believe me, *trust* me, there is hope, and her name is Grace."

The Lord of the Faerie stared at Jack, then gave a tight nod. "Gods help you if you're wrong on this, Jack."

With that he vanished, and Jack and Noah were left standing on the footpath of the bridge, staring at the space he had inhabited.

"What did you mean," Noah said, "when you told the Lord of the Faerie that the Sidlesaghes had not completely gone? *I* can't feel them ... What can you sense?"

Jack paused a bit before answering, his eyes focused on the dome of St. Paul's in the distance. "I can't feel them either," he said eventually. "It was just that, when we felt them die, I also sensed ... a *passing*. I don't know how else to explain it. They've gone, but I am not sure they've gone quite into death."

Chapter Eleven

COPT HALL

Monday, 30 December 1940

Grace Speaks

J FOUND MYSELF ON THE ROAD TO EPPING
Forest somewhere around Leytonstone. I had no idea
how I had come to be there—the last thing I remembered was the French beaches—but I knew there was only
one place I wanted to be right now, and that was Copt Hall.
Somehow the combination of Malcolm and Jack felt so
right, so comfortable, that I almost wept at the thought of
the distance I had yet to go.

I didn't think I could use anything save my shaky legs to
get me there. Whatever power I commanded had been totally
exhausted with the efforts of the past hours. *I* was completely exhausted. If I had managed to get myself off a bed
most people expected me to die in, then it had only been at
the greatest effort and expenditure of power and whatever reserves of strength remained to me. It was December, I knew
that, I could *feel* it rising through the soles of my feet and in
the sharpness of the air, and that meant I'd spent weeks,
months, wasting away in that hospital. I hadn't managed to
bring myself back to full vitality. I'd managed only to get
myself awake and up, and after what I'd done over the past
night, I wasn't going to be able to walk to the nearest telephone box, let alone the final five or six miles to Copt Hall.

I slumped down on the verge of the road and huddled
as deep inside the hound's-tooth coat as I could. It was
freezing, although thankfully not raining, and the coat
was all I had. My feet were bare, my scalp stung where it

had healed from Catling's nasty gift of that concrete lintel, my cheeks and nose felt as if they were succumbing to frostbite.

I had to get to Copt Hall soon.

I sighed, and looked about. It was mid-morning, and while the war had thinned out traffic, a lorry or bus must come along sooner or later. I had no money for the bus fare, but surely a kindly lorry or bus driver would give me a lift to the gates of Copt Hall. I wouldn't even need to explain away my strange appearance—disheveled and disoriented victims of the bombing were an all too frequent sight in and about London. The driver would merely assume I'd escaped the raid of the last night and was traveling to . . . a kindly uncle, perhaps, who would give me shelter.

Just then I heard the purr of a motor on the road leading from London. I struggled to my feet and moved to the side of the road, peering in the direction of London, hoping the driver, whoever it might be, would be kind enough to stop.

A big black sedan drove into view, and I recognized it instantly.

It appeared to glow a little in the early morning light, as if its driver was very, very angry.

I swallowed, momentarily considered darting for the cover of some nearby shrubbery, then discarded the thought. I wasn't strong enough to dart anywhere.

So I straightened up, wondering whether looking exhausted would work better for me or if I should go for the calm and confident and "delighted to see you so unexpectedly" look. In the end I had the choice made for me when Harry pulled his car over beside me, opened the door, got out, and glowered angrily at me.

Exhausted it would be. It certainly wasn't a look I would have any troubling maintaining.

"Harry?" I said.

"Grace," he said, and instantly metamorphosed into the Lord of the Faerie, which made me realize just how angry he was. "What have you been doing?" he said.

Well, I've been lying mostly dead on a bed for months, my Lord of the Faerie, and if things have gone wrong, then think not to blame me for it.

"Not much," I said.

He moved around the side of the car and came to stand directly before me, so close I had to crick my neck painfully to look him in the face. Intimidated, I tried to huddle a little deeper into the coat. Catling might not scare me any more, but her I loathed. The Lord of the Faerie was someone I respected, and I hated it that he was angry toward me.

"Why did you stop Jack and Noah from completing the Troy Game?" he said.

"Because it would have been tragic if they had completed it."

"And it isn't 'tragic' that now Catling had vowed to destroy every creature in the Faerie until she *is* completed? Damn you, Grace, the Sidlesaghes are gone, and within hours she will start on—"

I sighed, which was the wrong thing to do, because the Lord of the Faerie went almost into apoplexy.

"The Faerie is being destroyed and you can only sigh in irritation?"

"I'm sorry. I'm *sorry,* Harry . . . or Coel, or whoever you are. Look, I can stop her, but I don't have the strength to blow out a match right now. If you want me to stop her, I can, but you're going to have to help me."

I don't think that was what he expected me to say.

"You can *stop* her?"

"I can stop her from murdering any more of the creatures of the Faerie, at least. More than that I don't know. But . . . I . . . need . . . you . . . to . . . help . . . me."

He realized then that I was close to collapse, and he put a hand onto my shoulder. "What do you need?"

"I need you to take me to Catling."

He stared at me. "And will *I* be able to walk away from that, Grace?"

Oh, damn him. "Yes. I promise you she won't touch you. Now, *help* me, curse it!"

* * *

HE DID. HE TRANSFERRED BOTH OF US INTO THE crypt of St. Paul's, cloaking us in a glamour of invisibility.

Catling was waiting for us.

She didn't say anything, merely watched with narrowed eyes as the Lord of the Faerie and I walked (well, the Faerie lord walked, I hobbled, leaning heavily on his arm) over to her.

I wasn't in the mood for long conversational niceties. "Don't," I said.

Catling raised an eyebrow.

"I have heard," I said, very quietly, "that you have threatened to destroy the creatures of the Faerie, one by one. Do you not recall what happened when you thought to murder the Sidlesaghes?" At that I saw the Faerie lord look sharply at me, but I couldn't pause now for explanations.

"If you do that, Catling," I said, "then I will be the stronger for every Faerie death you cause. Do you understand?"

She paled (if that is possible for someone who affected so white a face under normal circumstances). "Are you threatening me?" she said.

"Yes," I said.

"If I die," Catling hissed, "so do you!"

"I know that."

We fell into silence, staring unblinkingly at each other.

Then I turned my face slightly to the Lord of the Faerie. "I am tired," I said. "Take me home, please."

"If I die, so do you!" Catling seethed at me as the Lord of the Faerie removed us both back to the roadside at Leytonstone.

"WHAT DID YOU MEAN," HE SAID, "BY SAYING THAT you would be the stronger if she destroyed any of the creatures of the Faerie?"

We were standing by his car. It was cold, fully light, and I was so drained I felt nauseous.

"Can I sit in the car, please?" I said.

"Grace?"

"May I call you Coel?"

He nodded.

"Coel, I want more than anything, *need* more than anything, to get some rest. Then I need to talk to Jack. Then we will talk to you. I promise."

He looked at me for a long moment, his face unreadable. "Is there any hope, Grace?"

I smiled. "Yes, but it is a strange one, and thus my need to talk to Jack."

He drew in a deep breath. "Where do you want to go?"

"Copt Hall."

I STOOD ON THE PORCH OF COPT HALL AND knocked at the door. I'd drifted into the unreality of Jack's Copt Hall and, while I was aware of the gardeners and caretakers who still lived and worked about the hall, there was no one and no reality for me save Malcolm's unsurprised face as he opened the door.

"I knew you'd come here," he said. Then, without asking, he stepped forward, picked me up into his arms, and carried me inside.

"I would really, really like a bath," I said.

"I have one steaming," he replied, and I was not surprised at all that he should be so considerate.

I SAT IN THE BATH AND SOAKED, BLISSFULLY happy. For the moment there was nothing for me save the bath, its warmth and its comfort. Malcolm had carried me up the stairs to a little wood-paneled bathroom that opened off one of the bedrooms, and there, indeed, was a wonderful claw-footed bath, steaming with crystal clear hot water. Malcolm helped me out of the coat—I was completely comfortable with him, and felt no awkwardness that he could see the horrors of my wasted body—then aided me into the bath.

There he left me, saying only he would fetch me some brandy, as he thought I could do with it.

There was a bath shelf sitting across the bath, with a flannel and a bar of clear, brown soap, but I was too tired to be bothered washing. I just sat, soaking in all the comfort the bath could offer, and eventually I heard footsteps ascending the stairs slowly.

They stopped just outside the bathroom, then entered.

Only then did I look up, and smile. "Hello, Jack."

He looked almost as exhausted as I did, his fatigue underscored with uncertainty and dispiritedness. He was also terribly dirty, smudged with soot and ash, and he had several small abrasions on his face.

He was dressed in a coat as poor as mine had been, and I reflected that it had not been a good night in the sartorial elegance stakes.

I nodded at a stool. "Sit down, please."

He did, with a thump, still staring at me. "Grace?"

"No," I said. "Merely a phantom passing through."

I regretted the jest as soon as the words left my mouth, because his eyes filled with tears and he had to bite his lip to keep the emotion contained.

"Grace," he said again, this time the word emerging on a breath fraught with such deep emotion that now *my* eyes misted up.

I took a deep breath, rubbed at my eyes with the back of my hand, and managed to speak calmly. "Thank you for sitting beside my hospital bed for so long."

"Your parents were there, too."

"I know, but right now I am thanking *you,* Jack."

He swallowed. "I can't believe you're here."

We fell silent. There was so much to say, and neither of us knew how to start. I began to feel a little bit awkward about sitting naked in a bath before him, and wished that my body didn't look so awful.

"You look beautiful," he said. Then he gave a soft laugh. "I can't believe you are *alive*! Grace, how? What has happened? How did you manage to get out of that damn hospital bed? And get away from Catling? And the shadow has returned! What do you know about that? Do you know about the White Queen? Oh, I have so much to say to you,

to ask you . . . And the Sidlesaghes, something has happened. Did you . . . oh, curse my damned mouth, I am sorry." He grinned, finally relaxing. "I'm just glad you're alive, Grace. And here."

"Here is where I want to be," I said, and before either of us could say anything really stupid, Malcolm made one of his fortuitous entrances with a tray bearing a decanter of brandy and two glasses.

He also had a pair of Jack's trousers over one arm, and as he set the tray down on the floor by the stool, Jack rose, shucked off the coat, discarded the hip wrap he had worn as Kingman, and slid the trousers on, buckling up the belt and then sitting down on the stool as Malcolm left. He reached for the tray, poured out some brandy into the glasses, then handed one to me.

We sat for a while, saying nothing, sipping the brandy.

"I'm sorry I have been away so long," I eventually said, handing Jack the empty glass.

He took it, raising his eyebrows to ask if I wanted a refill. I shook my head, and he set both our glasses on the tray.

"Where have you been?" he said. "Where did Catling take you?"

I shuddered. "Into hell, Jack. I will talk about it eventually, but not now, please."

He nodded, his eyes downcast. "How did you escape?"

"I learned how to use what Catling sent against me. I have been silly, I should have learned earlier."

He smiled, very gently. "Of all the silliness in this stupid adventure, Grace, you have been responsible for very little of it. Is that how you managed to escape her when she dragged you into the labyrinth after you stopped me?"

I nodded. "Everything she sends against me I can use." I lifted my wrists a little out of the water, and for a moment the diamonds gleamed. "I learned how to take the pain she wrapped about my wrists, and use that. I learned how to take the hell she had sent me into, and use that. I can't believe it took me so long to realize I had the ability to do that." I let my arms sink back into the water. "She can't

touch me now, save to murder me, and she needs to murder herself to kill me. That she won't do."

I smiled suddenly. "I feel free of her, Jack, even though I'm not. She has no hold over me other than the threat of both our murders, and that is no hold at all."

He looked at me very carefully at that. "No threat at all? Why not? Her fate is your fate. Whatever you have touched will share your fate. I—"

"Jack, please, stop." I thought of everything I had seen while in my coma, but I was too exhausted to try to explain it to him now. There *was* hope, I was certain of it.

Jack must have seen that hope in my face.

"Grace, what have you learned?"

I smiled, remembering, and Jack leaned forward.

"The shadow is back," he said. "It reappeared when you reappeared."

Indeed it had. It only manifested itself when Jack and I were together and present in London. We were the only reason it existed, and the reason it had only appeared for the first time Jack and I were present together in London.

"Grace?"

"Jack, I will tell you, but I need to sleep first. Not only because I am so very tired, as I see you are, but because I need to mull things over in my head."

And because what I have to tell you is so very, very difficult, Jack.

"Of course." He studied me, his eyes traveling down my body as it lay in the bath. "You're not very well, are you?"

I shook my head, close to tears again because he understood both that I did not wish to talk now, and because I was, indeed, "not very well."

"Well, then." He smiled. "I see that both flannel and soap are yet dry. Would you like me to wash the stink of hospital from you?"

He must have been desperate to discover what I had learned, but he was willing to wait, and for that, at this very moment, I was indebted to him. "Thank you," I said.

Jack sank to his knees by the bath, picked up flannel and soap, and proceeded to wash me down.

He touched me as a father would a child. There was nothing sexual or even intimate about it. Frankly, we were both too tired to care, and I wondered only that he had the energy to bathe me in the first instance.

Malcolm came back in carrying a tin urn of clean water, and Jack soaped his hands, and washed out my hair. He massaged my scalp gently, exploratively, his fingertips kneading into the spot where the concrete lintel had punctured my skull.

"The doctors thought you would die," he whispered. "Grace, how did you survive this?"

"Because I wanted to live," I said.

His fingers stilled, then the knuckle of one of them rapped against the plate in my skull. "Well, you have a tin head, now," he said, and I laughed, and then he with me, and I have never, *never*, been as happy as I was at that point.

Jack helped me out of the bath, and dried me off, his hands exploring my recently knitted bones in my legs and left arm (oh, such lumpy devils they were now!), then he gave me a silk dressing gown that Malcolm had set out, and then, wordlessly, carried me to a bed in one of the spare rooms. He tucked me in between the sheets, leaving me in the dressing gown, then laid his mouth very softly against my forehead, and told me to go to sleep. He said he needed to bathe, but that then he would be back, and he would watch over me.

I slept. I drifted off immediately, but, as is so often the case when you are so very tired, I did not sleep soundly. I woke every hour or so, dragging myself up from dreams that were vaguely unsettling but not threatening.

Every time I opened my eyes I saw Jack sitting in an armchair by the bed. Sometimes he was dozing, sometimes reading a book, sometimes sipping from a cup of tea that Malcolm had brought in to him.

Sometimes the lamp was on, and I saw him in a glow of warm, rosy light, and I knew that the entire day had passed and we were well into the night.

And still Jack watched.

I saw Malcolm with him on one occasion. He sat on a wooden chair he'd pulled close to Jack's armchair, and was leaning forward on it, talking in a low but urgent voice. He was saying something about New Year's Eve, and Jack was frowning, but as I watched the frown cleared, and Jack nodded, to Malcolm's undisguised relief.

"If Grace agrees," said Jack, and Malcolm seemed to accept that.

After that I did not remember anything else, so I must have drifted off finally into a sound sleep.

AFTER HE HAD SPOKEN WITH JACK, MALCOLM WENT into the bathroom to clean it, and clear away the brandy decanter and glasses.

But while the towels were still there, and the damp patches where a wet Grace had stood, the decanter and glasses had gone.

Malcolm thought nothing of it. Jack must have taken them down to the kitchen himself.

Chapter Twelve

THE DARK HEART OF THE LABYRINTH

Monday, 30 December 1940

CATLING HUDDLED IN THE HEART OF THE labyrinth and wondered what had gone so wrong.

She *should* have been completed by now, but instead she found herself still incomplete and more vulnerable than ever.

Who could have thought that Grace would have found the gumption to break free of her hellish prison? Who

could have thought Grace would have found the courage to stop the Dance of the Flowers and *then confront Catling?*

And confront her with real power.

To say that Catling didn't like it was a massive understatement.

Too many things were going wrong.

For the first time in her existence Catling wondered if completion was all she'd dreamed of. Surely she had enough power now? Why push for completion at all?

Because if left incomplete she was stunningly vulnerable. Catling simply could not allow herself to remain incomplete for too many more years, because then Jack and Noah (and Grace, curse her!) could grow even more powerful, and might discover the means to undo the hex that bound Grace. If that happened Catling could look forward to nothing but a rapid unwinding into oblivion.

As much as Catling was sure Jack and Noah would use any subsequent Dance of the Flowers to somehow trick Catling, and try to unwind her, Catling *needed* to be completed. She would need to risk the Dance of the Flowers.

But, oh, that day would be littered with trickeries.

Catling reviewed her weapons. She truly only had two: her continued destruction of the Faerie, which meant the Lord of the Faerie would put incredible pressure on Jack and Noah to complete Catling, and the hex on Grace. Even if Jack and Noah might be prepared to risk losing the Faerie (and that was a major if), Catling was certain they would never risk losing Grace, particularly after that touching scene she'd witnessed in St. Paul's the night Jack and Grace pulled the bomb down atop her.

"All I have to be certain of," whispered Catling in the desolation of the dark heart, "is that the hex can't be broken. That it is so powerful that *nothing* can thwart it."

She glanced upward, looking through all the layers of earth and rock and masonry to the sky above.

She had time. Neither Jack nor Noah would move against her just yet—not while Grace was in such a pitiful condition. She had some weeks, perhaps even months, in

which to wind down the bleakness and horror of the Blitz and use it to bolster the hex that bound Grace.

Bolster it so that no matter what happened, what Jack and Noah tried to do, *nothing* could possibly break it.

Chapter Thirteen

COPT HALL

Tuesday, 31 December 1940

ACK SAT ON THE SIDE OF THE BED, WATCHing Grace sleep. She looked terrible—dark shadows ringed her eyes, her flesh had shrunk against her bones, her skin tone was ashen and faintly yellowish where stretched over bone. On the other hand her breathing was deep and slow and comfortable, and her face relaxed.

He still couldn't quite believe she was alive. He kept thinking of the moment he had walked into the bathroom and saw her sitting in the bath, enclosed in steam and serenity. He remembered the gut-wrenching sense of relief and joy, combined with a terror that somehow the vision wasn't real and that any moment she would evaporate before his eyes.

Now, watching her sleep, Jack found it difficult to believe she would survive, or that she would not be snatched from him again.

There was a noise behind him, and Jack turned his head slightly.

It was Malcolm carrying a tray with two bowls of hot soup.

"Did you do this for Boudicca?" said Jack quietly as Malcolm set the tray down.

"Of course," said Malcolm. "I adored her." He looked at Grace. "She will need to wake soon."

"She will wake when she is ready," said Jack, but then he saw Malcolm's smile, and looked back to Grace himself.

Her eyes had opened, and she was smiling at Malcolm and then at Jack as his eyes turned to her.

"Chicken soup," she said, "with which to set the world to rights?"

"Chicken soup," said Malcolm, "with which to set you on the road to rights. The world can look after itself."

Jack helped Grace sit up, Malcolm plumping the pillows behind her, and Grace laughed and commented on what fine nurses they both had become.

Then Malcolm handed Grace and Jack their bowls of soup, told them he expected them to eat before they talked, and then departed.

"I wonder from where he got these chickens," said Grace. "Have the gardeners of Copt Hall missed one or two of their flock?"

Jack smiled, but did not answer, and, as instructed, they ate in silence.

Once they'd done, Jack took the bowls, set them aside, and sat once more on the side of the bed, taking Grace's hand.

He opened his mouth to speak, but she forestalled him.

"I'm so sorry about Matilda," she said.

Jack's eyes filled with sudden tears, not merely at the loss of Matilda which still ate at the edges of his composure every moment he was awake, but at Grace's care for his feelings. She was the one who had suffered alongside Matilda, she the one who had watched Matilda's terrible dying, and yet she only thought of him.

He nodded, unable to speak.

"Have they recovered her body, or Erith's and Ecub's?" Grace asked.

Jack closed his eyes momentarily, forcing tears to slide down his cheeks. "No. The rescue teams got you out, but by the time they'd managed to clear out the entire basement almost three weeks had gone past. The basement had flooded—"

"I know," Grace whispered.

"—and together with the weight of the rubble and debris, bodies were unrecognizable. They had . . ."

Decayed, he wanted to say, but didn't know how to say it without speaking in cold, bald words.

"It was impossible to determine who was who," he finished. "Most were buried in a mass grave, including whatever was left of Matilda, Ecub, and Erith."

"Oh, Jack . . ."

He took a deep breath. "Matilda and I . . . she . . ."

"She loved you, and you her."

"Oh God . . ." Jack wiped away his tears. "I wish she'd never been caught up in this damned . . . damned . . ."

"Ah, no you don't," Grace said. "Where would you have been all these years without Matilda?"

Jack laughed. "You're right. Thank you for making me smile." He wanted to ask Grace how Matilda had died, but he realized he didn't want to know, and he knew also that Matilda wouldn't have wanted him to know. "I'm glad you were there with her," he said.

"Well, she's probably chatting up Aeneas as we speak."

Jack blinked away the last of his tears. "Aye, she probably is. Grace, please talk to me of what has happened."

She sighed, and for a moment her eyes wandered away from his. Then, hesitantly, she told Jack of how Catling had tormented her in the rubble, and then sent her into the hell of memory.

"I saw too much, Jack. *Experienced* too much. Far too much. Catling hoped it would send me mad."

Jack felt cold. He could imagine what Catling had showed Grace, and imagine what Grace had experienced. Oh God, the terrible things he had done as Brutus . . . and yet still Grace could smile at him. "But she didn't drive you mad." *Nor did she drive you to hate me, and I have no idea what I have done to deserve such a gift.*

"No. Almost, but before I succumbed someone came to me. Someone who called herself the White Queen. *She* tormented me with possibilities until I finally figured out how to save myself." Grace looked carefully at Jack's face.

"You remember, don't you? The White Queen Café where we met, and where the woman's voice spoke to us?"

"Oh, aye. I remember that. But I, via Noah, have also heard the name elsewhere. The night you and Eaving's Sisters were trapped in Coronation Avenue, the Sidlesaghes told your mother the shadow belonged to a woman called the White Queen. Later that night, not knowing what to do, only desperately seeking some means by which to save you, I went around to the café. It was boarded up, had been for a year or so. This White Queen has been playing with us, Grace."

"Oh, aye. That she has. She has been the one to come sit by my side at night, all these years. Not Catling. They just look so much alike."

"*The White Queen* has been sitting with you?"

"Yes. Oh, and she called herself something else. The druid's sword. This is something about which I think we need to talk to Malcolm."

Jack grunted. "That doesn't guarantee any answers from him." He thought Grace was holding something back from him about the White Queen, but before he could ask her about it, she hurried on.

"I also discovered the true nature of the labyrinthine shadow."

Jack held his breath, waiting.

Grace sat up a little straighter, the effort bringing a flush to her cheeks. "The shadow is a new Game. Rather, it is the potential for a new Game. It has been laid down by the White Queen for you and for me to use, as Kingman and Mistress of the Labyrinth. That is why it only appeared when you and I were in London together, why it vanished when I 'died,' and why no one else, save my mother who can glimpse it, could sense it."

Jack was aware his mouth had slowly dropped open, but he didn't care. *A new Game?* Should he be terrified or intrigued? And how? *Who* was this White Queen that she had the potential to build a new Game?

"Why?" he whispered, barely able to speak. "How?"

"To use against the Troy Game," Grace said.

"But how hasn't Catling sensed it? Surely . . ."

"She hasn't sensed it for the same reason no one else has. This Game—or its potential, rather—was built exclusively for you and for me. *We* are the only ones it cares about. *We* are the only ones it reveals itself to. I'm not even sure that Catling will know once the Game is opened . . . it shadows her so perfectly, is so close to a mirror image of the Troy Game, that Catling may simply not see it. Ah, at the moment the *only* thing I know for sure is that the shadow is a new Game waiting for us to open it, and to use it, somehow, against the Troy Game."

Jack gave his head a little shake. "I don't understand. I don't understand *anything*. The imps could sense this shadow Game. My God, they were *feeding* it through their murders."

"I don't know the why of the imps' involvement, Jack." Grace paused. "Have there been any more murders since I was injured?"

Jack shook his head. "They stopped completely after early September. Perhaps the Blitz . . . ah, I don't know. But Jesus God, Grace, what do we make of a Game that requires murder to feed?"

"We don't know they were working on the behalf of the new Game, Jack. They just may have been worshipping it."

Jack shrugged his shoulders in frustration. There were too many things left unknown. "Who is this White Queen that she should care . . . and that she should be able to build this massive 'potential' Game?"

"A friend of the druids, obviously."

"Even so, the druids could not ever construct a Game, or show someone how to do it. So how could this White Queen do it? *How?* And you say that it should reveal itself only to you and to me, but Noah can also sense it, if not so strongly. I don't understand that. Grace, I'm sorry, but none of this makes sense."

Grace's hands tightened very slightly about Jack's hand. "Jack, the only reason my mother can sense the shadow is that she has a close connection to the White Queen. My

mother cannot sense the shadow because she has any connection to the new Game as such, but because she has an ancient bond with the White Queen."

"Look, I'm sorry, Grace, I am not following a word of this."

Grace's eyes filled with tears. "Jack, Noah is the White Queen's mother."

Jack stared blankly at Grace, his mind refusing to accept the logical implication of that.

"Please, please understand the rest before I am forced to tell it to you," Grace whispered.

"No . . . no . . . it can't be possible . . ."

"The White Queen is she who has never lived, Jack. She is your and Cornelia's daughter, conceived in the magic of Mag's Pond, and forced stillborn from Cornelia's body by Genvissa's ill will."

Jack stared at Grace.

"Jack, Jack, please, gods, just say something . . ."

"I . . ." There wasn't anything *to* say. Jack felt as though someone had snatched his mind and made away with it.

His daughter? His and Cornelia's? A faint memory came back of something Noah had said on his return to England. *I wish my daughter had been born. Who knows what she may have been.*

Prophetic words, indeed.

Jack tried to order his thoughts, to think this through logically. A daughter of his and Noah's would have the ability to construct this "potential" Game. Also, the White Queen was born of Noah, born of the line of Ariadne, which meant she was both Mistress of the Labyrinth and Darkwitch bred. She would naturally have the talent to construct a shadow labyrinthine Game.

And she would have built it of *Darkcraft*.

No wonder it required murder to feed.

Then Jack's heart skipped a beat as he thought of something else. The White Queen and Catling looked almost identical—gods, they shared identical parents—and Grace had mistaken the White Queen for Catling when she'd come to sit at Grace's side at night. Did that mean that the

woman Jack had spoken to had sometimes been the White Queen, *not* Catling? God, it all made so much sense now!

"*Jack?*"

He blinked, refocusing on Grace's face. She looked distraught, and more than anything else it was that look that cleared Jack's mind. "Grace, I'm sorry." He put his free hand about the back of her head, cradling it, and drew her closer until he could kiss the top of her forehead and then her mouth. "I'm sorry. I . . . I just can't believe . . . I can't fathom this."

"I know so little, Jack. I don't know her reasons, or her motive—save that I am sure she wants us to destroy the Troy Game—I don't even know how this new Game works . . . it looks so different to what I learned as a Mistress of the Labyrinth, or what I understand of the Troy Game. Dear gods, I don't even know if I completely trust the White Queen." Grace took a deep breath. "I remember once she asked me if I was prepared to die for you, and I said yes, if only to get rid of her."

Jack went cold all over again. "Jesus, Grace." He remembered how he had felt watching her sleep, wondering if she was to be snatched away from him again, and foreboding overwhelmed him.

Jack forced the presentiment away and kissed Grace's forehead once more. "I kept hoping that you'd come back with answers, Grace, but *this*?"

"The White Queen has the bands, Jack."

"Of course." *She had them in her dark heart. She'd told him that day she'd appeared before him with the bands in her hands. And he'd thought her Catling, and cursed her.* "Aeneas said my daughter came and asked for them. I'd assumed Catling."

"What else were you supposed to assume?"

"Where are they?"

"On an altar somewhere. I have no idea where. They're waiting for you. I think the White Queen took them so that you wouldn't be able to finish the Troy Game. She had no idea you'd try without them."

"My daughter . . ." He drifted into silence, thinking,

then spoke again. "But Noah couldn't sense the shadow at first. It was only later that she could. Why?"

"It was after the Great Marriage, yes?"

Jack nodded.

"Her parents had made the Great Marriage, maybe that made my . . . *our* . . . mother a 'part of the team' in a casual way. Or perhaps it made the White Queen happy, to see her parents at peace."

Grace leaned in against Jack's body. He still had no shirt on, and she lifted her hands to his shoulders, and played with the markings. She slid her fingers underneath them, lifting them slightly away from his skin, then allowed them to snap back into place.

"Grace," Jack said very softly, wondering if she was trying to distract him away from his worries, "unless you want to take this a great deal further, right now, then please don't do that."

"Sorry." She leaned back, the mischievous expression on her face anything but apologetic.

"You've changed," he said.

"I've grown up."

"And . . . ?"

"And at the moment I am all skin and bone," she said, "and I couldn't manage much more than I have just done. I need more of Malcolm's soup, I think."

Jack knew what she was saying—*I still don't want to rush*—and wondered at the sense of pleasant anticipation that gave him. He had spent almost four thousand years taking what he wanted, generally at a *great* rush, and the thought of drawing closer to Grace only at a pace best measured in inches rather than leaps and bounds should have frustrated him beyond measure. But it didn't.

"We've both grown up, I think," he said. "And you've deflected the conversation very nicely away from my daughter."

"I think she, as this Game she has made for us, is something that needs to be taken at leisure, as well. I don't know whether to trust either the White Queen or her Game."

With that Jack thoroughly agreed. He ran a hand over

Grace's shoulder, and down one arm. She was so thin. She literally did need more of Malcolm's soup, and as much other nourishment and rest as she could manage. The months spent in a coma would need months of recuperation. If what she said was true, that a new Game awaited them, then Grace would need to be very strong in order to be able to manage it.

A new Game. How could it be used?

"We need time, Jack," Grace said.

He sighed. "And is Catling going to give it to us? She has threatened to destroy every creature in the Faerie—"

Grace interrupted him with a finger over his mouth. She told him what had happened on her way to Copt Hall.

"She will not touch the Faerie creatures," she concluded, "and she cannot use me as an effective threat anymore, but what else she can do . . ." she shuddered.

"But we won't rush," he said.

She smiled. "No, we won't rush."

"Grace, what of the Sidlesaghes? What happened? We knew that Catling had attacked them, *murdered* them, but it did not feel to me as if they had passed completely. Grace, are they the reason you were able to stop Catling from touching any other Faerie creature?"

"Yes. Catling forced me to watch their deaths. I think she hoped that would drive me insane when her previous attempt had failed. Or perhaps she thought I would go mad from guilt. But I didn't. There is no blame to me or to you or to anyone else save Catling over the Sidlesaghes' deaths. And, yes, they *are* dead, and yet you are right to say they have not passed completely."

She paused, and Jack gave her the time she needed to continue.

"As Long Tom was dying, he crawled toward me, and gave me his hand. With his dying breath, and that of every other Sidlesaghe, their knowledge and their 'oneness' with the land passed into me."

He put his hands on her shoulders and leaned her backward a little so he could look at her full in the face. He studied her for a long moment. "So now you *are* of the land."

"Oh, aye. A bad mistake for Catling to make. She worries that if she kills any other Faerie creature then their knowledge and oneness with the land would pass to me. She won't take that risk."

"I don't doubt." Jack paused, suddenly thinking of something. "And the reason the Luftwaffe didn't come back last night?"

"A sudden fog on the Channel coast, Jack. Most unfortunate."

"And that . . ."

"And that I could not have done without the Sidlesaghes' knowledge, their oneness with the land, at my back."

"Ah, Grace . . ."

They sat in silence for a while, holding hands, taking comfort in each other's presence.

Finally Jack sighed, and spoke. "One of the first things we may be able to clarify is what connection the White Queen has to Malcolm."

Grace raised an eyebrow.

"Malcolm—Prasutagus—and Boudicca want to meet with us tonight. Do you feel well enough?"

Grace took a breath, then nodded.

Chapter Fourteen

COPT HALL

Tuesday, 31 December 1940: New Year's Eve

LATER THAT NIGHT JACK WRAPPED GRACE IN a thick blanket over her dressing gown, picked her up, and carried her down to the front door of Copt Hall.

Malcolm was waiting there, but not in his usual guise.

He'd lost his gentleman's clothes, and was instead dressed in leather trousers with a thickly woven tartan woolen cape thrown over his bare chest. His feet were likewise bare, and he had painted his face—a bland mask of austerity—with lines of blue woad.

"Prasutagus," Jack said.

Prasutagus nodded, then looked at Grace, staring curiously at him from the safety of Jack's arms.

"You are not afraid?" Prasutagus said.

She smiled. "No. I have grown sick of fear."

"And thus you are here," Prasutagus said. "We have waited a long time for this night."

"We?" said Grace.

"My wife and I," said Prasutagus. "*Britain* has waited a long time for this night. You are sick of fear, and we of the invader."

His eyes slipped to Jack as he said that, and Jack grinned.

"The barb no longer sticks, Prasutagus. I am now as much of this land as you."

Prasutagus' face relaxed from its sternness. "Naturally. If not I would have taken the opportunity to slip nightshade into your evening cocoa long before this."

That earned Prasutagus a sharp glance from Jack, but he chose not to respond to the remark. "Grace is not strong, Prasutagus. I can't think why we can't do this indoors."

"My wife does not want to move far from the trees," said Prasutagus, and tipped his head toward the door. "If you please."

OUTSIDE THE NIGHT WAS COLD AND SO STILL IT seemed as if life had stopped. There was a light sprinkling of snow on the ground which had frozen into a crackling crispness. While he had wrapped Grace well, Jack was himself dressed only in trousers and a pair of leather slip-on shoes, leaving his upper body bare. Now, standing on the threshold of the door, Jack shivered, and hugged Grace a little tighter to him.

There was silence to the south from London. For the past

two nights, ever since the terrible raid of the twenty-ninth, the Luftwaffe had stayed away.

Jack walked slowly onto the driveway. To his left was a stand of trees, the remaining remnant of Epping Forest's once close embrace, which sheltered his Austin convertible. Before him were low shrubs separating the driveway from a field. To his right another stand of trees, but at a greater distance than those to his left.

It was from these trees that the deer emerged.

Jack turned slightly to watch them, balancing Grace more firmly in his arms. She was no weight at all, but he worried that the pressure from his arms would discomfort her almost fleshless frame.

There were six of them, three fallow deer and three roe, all cautious, if not nervous.

Prasutagus came to stand at Jack's side, his eyes fixed on the trees just behind the deer.

A woman emerged from underneath the trees, and Jack heard Prasutagus draw in a sharp breath.

She was in her early thirties, tall and lithe with the muscular arms of a warrior, and long, dark, silver-laced hair twisted in a loose rope that hung over her left shoulder. Her face had a wide and high forehead, and was marked with lines of woad.

Her eyes were a lively hazel, and Jack could distinguish their sharp intelligence even at this distance.

She wore a tartan woolen sleeveless robe, sashed about her waist with a belt of blue leather, and splashed about its hem with blood.

The woman reached the deer, paused long enough to lay a hand on one's shoulder, then she stepped forward.

Jack walked to meet her, Grace watchful and tense in his arms.

"Boudicca," Jack said as he halted before her.

Boudicca acknowledged him with a tip of her head and an assessing glance from her sharp eyes, then turned her attention to Grace.

"Can you not stand?" Boudicca said.

"I'm sorry," said Grace, struggling a little in Jack's arms,

and he set her down carefully, keeping a hand on her waist for support. "She has been ill," he said to Boudicca. "She is weak."

Again a glance from those sharp eyes. "I know that," said Boudicca, then she looked past Jack and Grace to where Prasutagus had stepped up, and smiled so gloriously that Jack felt his heart stop for a brief moment.

"Prasutagus!" Boudicca said, and her husband moved past Jack and Grace and took Boudicca in his arms, kissing her brow, her eyes and then her mouth before hugging her tightly to him.

"We have not seen each other for some time," said Prasutagus, finally letting his wife go. "Not since I came back as Malcolm."

"Why didn't you both come back?" Jack said.

"Prasutagus was always the stronger druid," said Boudicca. "He had the strength, I not."

"And why *are* you back, whether in flesh or spirit?" said Jack. "Is it to reclaim your sword? To wield it?"

Prasutagus put a hand on Boudicca's shoulder, and looked at Jack and Grace. "We did not wish to speak to you until you knew of the woman you call the White Queen."

"Your sword," said Jack. "The druid's sword."

"Your daughter," said Boudicca, "and Grace's sister."

"Tell me of her," said Grace. She was now leaning against Jack for support, and he had an arm about her waist. "How is it she is involved in this? And what is your role?"

Prasutagus briefly told them of his and Boudicca's background. How they'd ruled over the Iceni, and how they'd attempted to negotiate a settlement with the invading Roman army.

"But then something poisoned my husband," said Boudicca, "and he died."

"In death," Prasutagus said, "I became aware that a terrible calamity had befallen this land. It had been infected with a presence so loathsome that I despaired. But then a little girl came to me, a girl with a cold, cold face and an icicle for a heart, and told me she could be my sword, the land's sword, if we conducted an alliance with her."

Jack almost could not breathe. He wondered why Prasutagus had done this, why he'd taken this risk.

"Because nothing else could have saved the land," Boudicca said. "*You* couldn't."

Jack winced at that.

"Why did she need you?" said Grace. "Why approach you?"

"She needed to be bound to the land in order to create what she needed," said Prasutagus. "She needed me and Boudicca to arrange a Seething, a druid ritual of binding, so powerful it needs a death to work it. We trusted her."

"But I think we may have been ensorceled," said Boudicca. "Just to ensure we did what she wanted."

Jack closed his eyes momentarily, his hand unconsciously tightening about Grace. "And thus, ensorceled and trusting, you killed yourself," he said finally, looking at Boudicca.

She shrugged a little. "I thought it was for good reason."

"For God's sake," Jack said. "Are you here to tell us that this White Queen, your sword, is as bad as that you'd hoped she'd destroy?"

"No, actually," said Prasutagus. "We have watched the White Queen for two thousand years. She's not particularly likable, and some of her methods are damnably frightening, but we think we were right to trust her."

"Then why are you back now, in this lifetime?" said Jack. "Why here now, to talk to us? Why drag Grace out in the middle of the night, when she should be asleep?"

"I am back in this lifetime to guide you, and to serve you," said Prasutagus. "This is the lifetime in which all will be won or lost. Boudicca would have returned also, but she did not have the power for rebirth."

"And we called you out here tonight," said Boudicca, "because it is a night of power, the turning of the year, and we wanted to bless you, and wish you well. Do what the White Queen asks of you. It is your only hope, and it is the land's only hope."

"There's another reason you're here, isn't there," Grace said.

"Aye," Boudicca said softly. "Do what the White Queen asks, but remember always that she is the druid's sword."

"And?" Jack said.

Boudicca looked steadily at Grace. "A druid's sword was always double-bladed. Twin-edged. On the cusp of the old year and the new, I am here to deliver to you a warning. Be careful. Look out for the return swing of the sword, because it may take your head."

PART SEVEN

LONDINA ILLUSTRATA

London, Christmas 1739

ONDON HAD SET ITSELF TO RIGHTS AFTER the great storm of thirty years earlier, although it had taken several years to find enough tile to reclad all the roofs and enough bricks to rebuild the chimneys. Now, Christmastime, the city was in full festive mode, even though London was in the grip of one of the coldest winters in living memory.

The Thames had frozen over, and Londoners took the opportunity to hold a Frost Fair on the ice. Colorful canvas tents dotted the ice selling food and drink, bowling alleys were established in the middle of the river, daring youths tied dogs to carts and held races from the bridge to Blackfriar's, fiddlers and pipers wandered among the crowds, playing popular tunes for a penny a time.

At times it appeared that the entire population of the city was having fun on the ice. Nevertheless, once dark fell and the revelers returned to their homes and warm fires, two lost urchins were left to huddle together, desperate for warmth and comfort, under the eaves of St. Thomas' chapel on London Bridge. The youths were thin and poorly clad, their hair black and curly, their complexions swarthy, as if they were coal miner's children who had made their way down to London to find their fortunes—and failed dismally.

There was no one else about. Everyone else was at home and at cheer, and bundled up before warm hearths.

Just after midnight, one of the shivering youths opened his eyes, then gasped. "You said you didn't want us!" he exclaimed.

His brother woke with a start, then trembled as he saw the little black-haired girl standing before them.

"I said no such thing," said the little girl.

"You did! You did!" said the first.

"Never," said the girl. "I wouldn't throw away such as you."

The second imp looked carefully at the little girl. "Hang on," he said. "You're not—"

"No need to speak names," said the girl. "After all, none of us have them."

The two imps looked at each other, then simultaneously shrugged their shoulders. True enough.

"Nonetheless," said the first imp, "you are little Mistress Surprise, aren't you?"

Now it was the girl's turn to shrug. "I've lived under this bridge for years. Can't think why no one seems to know I'm here."

The imps giggled. "Do you want us then? She has grown tired of us."

The girl pouted as if she wrestled with heavy thoughts. "Well, now, I'd hate to have you tell on me. I wouldn't be Mistress Surprise, would I, if she knew about me?"

The imps giggled some more. "We won't tell."

Suddenly the little girl vanished, replaced by a sense of such a terrifying oppression that the imps shrieked and huddled down on the ground, their spindly arms over their heads.

"Don't! Don't!" they cried. "We won't tell! We won't."

"Good," said the little girl, now returned to her less threatening aspect. "Be sure you don't. I can be just as nasty as my sister when the inclination takes me."

The imps sulked silently for a while, and the little girl let them think about it.

"On the other hand," she said, "I can be a great deal nicer, too."

"Why would you want to be nice to us?" said one of the imps.

"Because I am engaged in a project," said the girl, "and it is getting too big for me to manage by myself. I am in grave need of assistance."

"And you'd trust us?"

"Trust is not quite the word I'd use . . . but I do need you, and you can be a help."

The imps thought about it for several heartbeats.

"Do you have a nice warm room to keep us?" one of them asked hopefully.

"Of course," said the little girl, "and not far from here, actually."

She held out her hands and, after a fractional hesitation, the imps rose and each took one of her hands.

"_____ out a war cry."

"This is my quite the story of a war cry, but I do need you ... can you handle it on."

The lamp cracked above. His face, it spun beside his ...

She was busy more than part of them in tears, but ... there's room in it especially."

"Of course ... turn the book self," said her ... her own ...

She stood up her hand, and with a movement of when the lamp came too and went and ... her head.

Chapter One

COPT HALL

Wednesday, 1 January 1941

NOAH SAT, WAN AND TREMBLING, IN THE drawing room of Copt Hall, staring first at Jack, then at Grace, then at Weyland, who sat next to her, holding one of her hands. Jack had asked her and Weyland to the hall first thing; Ariadne, Silvius, the Lord of the Faerie, and Stella were due later, but Jack and Grace had needed to speak to Noah beforehand. They didn't want to break the news of the White Queen, her daughter, before a room full of people.

Noah and Weyland had arrived almost breathless with excitement at the prospect of seeing Grace. Having discovered from Harry that Grace was at Copt Hall, Noah and Weyland had been ringing several times a day since the morning of the thirtieth trying to talk to their daughter. Either Jack or Malcolm had put them off, saying that Grace needed to rest, but that they could come visit soon.

Their joy at seeing Grace, at being able to hug her and exclaim over her and ensure for themselves that she was back whole and in fair (if thin and exhausted) condition was quickly dampened by the news of the White Queen.

"She's alive?" Noah whispered.

Jack glanced at Grace. "Alive" wasn't quite the word he'd use to describe her. "She can use a glamour to take form," he said. "But she's not back in flesh, Noah."

"My daughter," Noah said, dashing away some tears with a trembling hand. "I thought . . ."

Everyone knew what Noah had thought. Almost four thousand years ago she'd lost the baby girl when she was seven months pregnant with her, and the baby had not survived the birth. Then Noah had seen what she'd believed to be her daughter in her vision of the stone hall, but which had turned out to be Catling. Then, in the seventeenth century, when Noah had become pregnant to Louis, now Jack, she'd believed *that* pregnancy had been a rebirth of the daughter she'd lost.

But that girl had been the Troy Game, growing into flesh incarnate as Catling.

Noah had resigned herself to believing she'd never have the baby girl she'd lost so many thousands of years ago returned to her. Now, to hear that the girl had life in spirit if not in flesh, *and* had been communicating with Grace and Jack, was almost too much for Noah.

"Why not me," she whispered. "Why talk to you and not me?"

There was no answer for that, and Jack dropped his eyes, unable to look at Noah. He felt guilt and anger in equal degree: guilt that he'd conversed with the White Queen, and not Noah; and anger that the White Queen had not once thought to communicate with the mother who had wanted and loved her so greatly.

It was one more reason for him to distrust the White Queen.

He looked over to Grace, who was watching her mother with worried eyes. *Look out for the return swing of the sword, because it may take your head. Oh Christ.* Jack felt a terrible premonition of losing Grace.

"What the hell is she here for?" said Weyland, angry not so much at Jack, but at Noah's misery. "What does she *want*?"

"The others should be here in a moment," said Jack, glancing at Weyland sympathetically. Grace's long illness had brought Noah and Weyland much closer, healing the

rift between them. For this, at least, Jack was grateful. "When they're here," he continued, "Grace and I will go through what we know. I don't want to tire Grace out by going through it twice."

Ariadne and Silvius arrived in a few minutes, closely followed by Stella and Harry. They were all delighted to see Grace, although Jack noted Harry looked a little awkward with her (likely regretting his harsh words to her when he'd discovered Grace at the side of the road to Epping Forest), while Stella warmed to the point of almost effusiveness.

Ariadne had brought with her a large suitcase, which she put by the side of Grace's chair.

"Your clothes, my dear," Ariadne said, handing her coat to Malcolm (and giving him a broad smile as she did so), then sitting down on the sofa beside Silvius. "I packed everything. Well, most things. I admit to handing over to the Red Cross the worst of your fashion disasters, my dear. I've taken the liberty of replacing them with a few items of a more colorful nature." Her smile widened until it was positively lascivious. "Now that you're with Jack, of course."

"Ariadne . . ." Grace murmured, then gave up and grinned. "But thank you."

Malcolm served tea and coffee, then withdrew to the hall door to stand leaning against the jamb.

Everyone was quiet now, the new arrivals having noted Noah's misery.

"Grace has a long tale to tell," Jack said, "and of many strange things." He paused. "I asked Noah and Weyland here a few minutes ahead of the rest of you because, as you will hear, some of that story Noah needed to hear first. It is an extraordinary tale." He paused, gathering his thoughts. "There are better ways, perhaps, to tell this, and less bald means by which to impart the information she has, but the last thing I want is for Grace to exhaust herself by going through the same story over and over for individuals. The grouping of us here today represents the core group who must be, who *are,* concerned with the destruction of the

Troy Game. You all need to hear this and I hope that, like Grace and I, you come to the end of the tale with more hope in your hearts than dismay." He shifted a little in his chair. "As you can see, Grace is physically, emotionally, and spiritually at low ebb. The months she lay in a coma, and what happened to her during that time, expenditure of power she used to escape and then reach Noah and me on the twenty-ninth, have combined to leave her dangerously weak. Please, in however you respond to what she has to say, remember that."

Jack looked over to Grace, and gave a lovely, gentle smile. "Grace?"

She took a deep breath, and, in a soft but clear voice, related what had happened to her from the moment the bomb fell on Coronation Avenue.

Everyone listened in silence. No one looked away from Grace for an instant.

Until she revealed the identity of the White Queen.

Then every eye swung to Noah, now far more composed than earlier.

"My daughters have ever astonished me," she said, and Stella gave a small bark of surprised laughter.

"Certainly your daughters with Jack," she said. "Weyland has proved by far the better sire."

"And I am not going to argue that point," Jack said. He caught Grace's eye. They'd revealed much about the White Queen, but not what Malcolm—Prasutagus—and Boudicca had told them. Revealing her connection with the ancient druids would only muddy the issue, and further worry Noah.

"My half-sister," said Grace, "the White Queen, has been the one to construct this 'shadow' which has so puzzled us all."

Briefly Grace told the group what she had learned of the shadow: it was the shadowy potential of a new Game, a Game that could be used to destroy the Troy Game. She also told them that the White Queen had the final two bands (although Grace could not pinpoint the location), and that it had been the White Queen who had sat by her side at night through all those years, not Catling.

"Both Grace and I have seen her," said Jack. "I have spoken to the White Queen, to my *daughter,* as well, save at the time I thought her Catling and called her vile things."

Noah shook her head at this. "I had berated myself for not knowing Catling sat with my daughter at night. Now I discover it wasn't Catling, but my long-lost daughter. Come to visit with Grace, but not me."

"Mother," said Grace, "I think the 'daughter' part of her vanished millennia ago. She is the White Queen now, and has been for a very, very long time. I don't believe she even thinks of herself as your 'daughter.' "

"But why should the White Queen appear now," said Stella, "and reveal this 'Shadow Game' now?"

"I can answer that," said Jack. He explained that he and Grace were meant to dance the Shadow Game. "She wants us as its Mistress and Kingman."

There was a little silence, then Noah spoke. "I don't want to sound resentful," she said, "but . . . why wouldn't our daughter have wanted Jack and me to dance this Game she has made? That would make sense, wouldn't it? Not *Grace* and Jack?"

"Because," said Stella, "whatever Jack has said, there has never been much peace between you and him. You share a history of conflict that, whatever brief 'peaces' you conclude, is always shattered at some point. But Jack and Grace, on the other hand . . ."

She didn't need to finish, but already she'd said too much. Noah stiffened and looked away.

"Well," said Ariadne brightly, "what a little minx this child has turned out to be, eh? Do you think the White Queen thought of this all herself, or has she, in turn, been the pawn of someone else? The ally of someone?"

Noah sat back in her chair. "Weyland once said to me that he couldn't understand why, during that terrible night when my daughter and I both died, Mag only saved *my* life. If she had the ability to save the life of a woman who had been torn apart, then she should have been able to restore breath into my stillborn daughter. So, perhaps . . ."

"The White Queen has been in cahoots with Mag, with

the *land,* all this time?" said Harry, who until now had been content to listen, if with an expression of the utmost incredulity on his face. "I find that difficult to believe. Why keep it such a secret from—"

"The White Queen has existed in utmost secrecy," said Jack, "because it is the only thing that has kept her, and this strange potential for a new Game she has created, away from the Troy Game's attention. If the White Queen had gamboled out of the mists at *any* time in the past few thousand years, if she had made herself known to anyone over that time, then the chances are that Catling would know of her. She's been kept, or has kept herself, well away from the Troy Game, and I don't think that's a bad thing."

"But why keep herself away from *me*?" Noah muttered.

Grace glanced imploringly at Jack.

"Noah," Jack said, very gently, "we have only just learned of the White Queen, and none of us really know what she is about or what she truly wants. We know the potential for a new Game exists, we know that it has the capacity to destroy Catling, but we don't know how. Grace says this is a Game such as none of us have seen before. I don't think your daughter is snubbing you, or punishing you—God alone knows she has no reason to want that or to feel resentful toward a mother who loved her so greatly—but I think she is revealing herself only in snatches and only as the need dictates. All of us are brimming with questions, Grace and me included, and I think all of us are going to have to be patient for the answers.

"Grace needs to regain her strength," Jack continued. "We can do little until that happens. Then she and I need to discover what this Game is about, what its purpose is, *how* it can be used to destroy the Troy Game without destroying Grace at the same time."

"Wait," said Weyland. "Haven't you forgotten something? The imps? Their murders? What kind of Game is this that relies on blood?"

Jack and Grace exchanged another glance.

"We have not forgotten, Weyland," Jack said. "Grace and I approach the White Queen and this Game with the ut-

most wariness. We still don't know the connection between the Shadow Game, the imps, and the murders. We will find out all we can about this Game before we touch it."

"And how to do that?" said Silvius. "I remember how, when you'd first become aware of the shadow, and aware of its labyrinthine nature, you thought it would take years to walk it out, to discover its extent. Does that still hold true, or has the White Queen given Grace some clue?"

"Oh, aye," said Grace, a rueful expression on her face, "she showed me clues as visions while I lay unconscious in St. Bart's. However, those visions were so fragmentary, and there is so much I don't recall. But there was something . . ."

Silvius, along with most others, raised his eyebrows.

"She showed me a tall, thin man, crawling about crypts and ancient byways of London. He was dressed in the manner of a late Georgian gentleman. I do not know his name . . . but I remember seeing him arguing with a type-setter over the title of a book he had written."

"*And?*" said Stella.

"*Londina Illustrata,*" said Grace. "The book was called *Londina Illustrata.*"

"Then all we need to do, or all that Grace and Jack need to do," said Silvius, "is to discover the book, and perhaps all of the White Queen's secrets shall be revealed. How hard can that be?"

Chapter Two

COPT HALL

January to February 1941

Grace Speaks

ALITTLE HARDER THAN IT SOUNDED, AS IT transpired, but at least Jack and I could bury our disquiet about the White Queen by hunting for the book. After all, what harm could a book do?

Very quickly we discovered that *Londina Illustrata* had been written by a man called Robert Wilkinson in the early nineteenth century. The late Georgian period witnessed the emergence of a number of antiquarians and engravers intent on recording what was left of ancient London before it was lost forever to development. Wilkinson was on the outer fringe of this group, never achieving the same public recognition as men like John Thomas Smith or Thomas H. Shepherd, and thus never achieving the same depth of subscriptions needed to publish his work. Eventually Wilkinson didn't publish a book as such, but a collection of some two hundred folio pamphlets dealing with unknown London which he put out over a twenty-year period. Subscribers could collect these individual pamphlets and have them bound into a book, if they so wished, and if they were inclined to pay a book binder. Ever helpful, Wilkinson actually provided a title page for those who actually wanted to do this; in fact Wilkinson published so many pamphlets, he felt it prudent to issue two title pages. Subscribers could bundle the pamphlets dealing with monasteries, churches, and schools into the first volume, and the pamphlets dealing with everything

else (primarily, but not exclusively, the theaters of London) in the second.

Copies of the two volume *Londina Illustrata* abounded. Unfortunately, they were all different.

Twenty years is a long time to expect subscribers to collect every single pamphlet Wilkinson put out, to keep them, and then to decide they wanted to pay to have them bound themselves. Some subscribers died partway through the process, some only gained interest when Wilkinson got to the theaters, others lost pamphlets when they were moving house or to the jaws of ravenous babies and cats, or they mislaid one or two (or thirty or forty), or they simply missed acquiring a few of the pamphlets as they came out. Other collections were lost during the passage of time.

After all, Wilkinson was hardly a household name, no one thought these pamphlets were valuable, and, in the subsequent Victorian craze for modernization (involving the wholesale destruction of what remained of ancient London), who really cared about a few old musty pamphlets about the odd buried crypt or laneway?

Indeed, no one actually knew how many pamphlets there were in total, and we were faced with the realization that we might not recognize the "complete" *Londina Illustrata* should it be thrust under our noses.

Jack and Harry (who had the contacts) set themselves the task of finding that elusive, complete copy while I continued my convalescence at Copt Hall.

All they could hope for was that something had survived the wholesale bombing and firestorming of London, but, in the end, they encountered a different and far more frustrating problem.

Rather than having been destroyed (although some, indeed, had been) the majority of great collections of books and manuscripts had been removed from London in the year preceding, and in the months just after, the outbreak of war. The great collections of the British Museum, of the various record offices, of the book dealers and clubs and societies and public libraries of London, all of which might reasonably have been expected to have copies of

Londina Illustrata, had been scattered all over Britain. Many were not accessible, because they were either too far away, packed behind blast-proof concrete walls, deep in mines . . . or had been broken up to be stored in the attics and cellars of the great houses of the gentry.

And, unbelievably, no one actually had a list of what had gone where.

After all, everything had been done in such a rush.

One day Jack and Harry arrived back at Copt Hall so frustrated I could hear them banging car doors, and then cursing as jackets got caught in those slammed doors, from my bedroom on the first floor.

They thumped up the stairs, and came to sit on either side of my bed.

Jack tapped out two cigarettes from his pack, lit them, and handed one to Harry. If I had needed any indication that they'd had a bad day, this was it. Harry rarely smoked, and Jack tended only to do so when he was nervous or severely annoyed.

"No luck, huh?" I said, trying a smile to ease the tension. Jack and Harry had been searching for the damned book for more than three weeks now, and I think they must have harassed most librarians and book dealers within a hundred-mile radius of London.

Jack muttered something unrepeatable, and it was Harry who was left to explain.

"Someone suggested we try the Admiralty as all the sons of the gentry and nobility who served in the navy tended to leave their book collections, along with tidy sums of cash, to the place. So we went to the Admiralty. Their librarian checked his cards, and, yes, they actually had *twelve* different sets of *Londina Illustrata.* But their collections were removed into the country about six months ago."

"They waited," said Jack, and I could almost hear his teeth grinding, "until the bombs started to fall, and *then* decided to do something about it. Utter panic. *Witless* fools!"

Harry shot him a glance, and resumed the tale. "Indeed, utter panic. They had no plan about what to do, all they wanted was to get everything into the safety of the country-

side. So they requisitioned trucks from everyone they could think of. But they didn't have enough trucks, and the bombs were beginning to get closer and closer."

"So," said Jack, blowing a plume of smoke toward the ceiling, "they sent clerks rushing into the streets, to ask passing motorists to help."

"Scores of motorists stopped," said Harry, "and tons of books and manuscripts were loaded into the trunks and backseats of private motorcars and the trays of passing vegetable lorries."

"And no one, *no one*," said Jack, "thought to take down the names of these people, or ask them for their addresses. The stuff has just vanished into the barns and attics of innumerable private houses around the home counties . . . and no one knows where it is."

I didn't need to ask. The twelve sets of *Londina Illustrata* had gone into one or more of those private motors.

"Oh," I said.

Jack saw the expression on my face. "Don't worry, Grace. If Harry and I can't find a copy of this damned book then we'll just have to demand one from the White Queen."

I smiled for him, but I doubted the White Queen was about to pop a set of *Londina Illustrata* in the Royal Mail for us. In the weeks since I'd risen from my coma and come to Copt Hall I had woken on many occasions through most nights, and I'd never found her sitting by the side of my bed.

Neither had she manifested herself to me in any other fashion, or made it known how we might contact her. I had tried with my power, but it was at such a sad ebb because of my physical weakness and my exertions on the night of the twenty-ninth that I had no luck. Besides, I don't know if the White Queen would have allowed the contact, in any case. Having spent almost four thousand years at a distance, I do not think my newly found sister was going to become chummy all at once . . . if ever. I don't know what she wanted, and thought it highly possible that she had become so used to solitariness that she didn't want it disturbed.

She certainly showed little inclination to contact her

long-lost parents (save, of course, for those brief appearances she made to Jack over the past year).

Noah came and sat with me several days a week. She tried not to ask about the White Queen, but inevitably did, and I told her everything I knew. So much had changed for my mother—Jack's slow turning to me, my new place at his side as a Mistress of the Labyrinth, the return of a daughter she thought she had lost, but whom she had yet to touch—but I think she was very slowly coming to terms with it. For thousands of years Noah had fought her battles center stage; now (hard words, but I don't know how else to phrase it) it appeared I was to take that place.

How did I feel about this? Oh, my Lord, how my life had *changed* since Jack had returned to London. I had thought to resent and dislike him, *fear* him and all he could do to me, and, yes, he had turned my life topsy turvy, but it had not been as frightening or as disastrous as I had feared. Jack had taken my cage, opened its door, then shaken it violently and tipped me out. In doing so, he'd taught me to live, not so much through any action, but through his simple belief that I was capable of it. Jack had been the first person to really believe in me, to treat me no differently than anyone else, to rage and rail at me as he raged and railed at everyone else . . . and to smile at me, and laugh with me, to grant me respect, and, the greatest compliment, to learn from me.

How everything had changed. How *I* had changed.

The period that I spent convalescing at Copt Hall was a time of not merely gaining in strength, but in much reflection. It was also a time of growing. The first month, all of January, I spent mostly in bed. Jack sat most nights in the wingback easy chair by my bed, alternatively sleeping (and snoring softly as his head tipped against one of the wings of the chair) or, when he was awake, reading or watching me. I would often wake in the night, and see him there, and I felt so cared for, so protected, that I felt as if nothing could ever touch me.

During the days, when Jack was out and about, often with Harry, trying to track down a copy of *Londina Illustrata,* or trying to discover as much as he could about this new

Game, Malcolm sat with me. We talked about his wife, Boudicca, and what had happened two thousand years ago, and what had happened on New Year's Eve when Boudicca came to me, and on one day he asked me if I was afraid.

I smiled. "Afraid? No, Malcolm I am not afraid. I am at peace, mostly, with both the world and with myself."

"Not afraid of Catling?"

"No. What happens will happen. But she has no power to terrify or terrorize me now."

"And what of your sister, the White Queen?"

I fell quiet at that, because, to be frank, she did disturb me. I could not help remembering that night, so long ago now, when she'd asked if I would die for Jack.

And I had said yes. I would say it again now, but, oh, I wished I knew what she had meant by that.

Of course, Boudicca's little warning hadn't exactly calmed my disquiet, either.

"Be wary of the White Queen," Malcolm, said. "Trust what she says, but always be wary of it."

"Oh, come now, Malcolm! What kind of advice is that?"

He just shrugged, annoying me.

"I need to go to the bathroom," I said, irritated with him for unsettling me, and wanting to put a stop to the conversation, "and I need your arm to help me get there."

BY FEBRUARY I WAS FEELING MUCH BETTER. I'D gained weight, and my flesh had started to plump out from my bones. My strength had largely returned, and I spent more time out of bed than in it.

Even though it was cold, I spent an hour or two each day, wrapped well in a coat and scarf, my breath frosting about me, the frozen leaf litter crunching under my boots, walking Epping Forest with Jack.

These were good hours. Jack and I grew day by day into a deeper intimacy. It wasn't sexual—we had not become lovers—but something far greater: a sharing and trusting. An ever-deepening understanding and friendship. We explored each other in a way I think few people do, exposing

to each other our sins and our hopes, our frailties and the strengths we have made of them. We explored each other's powers, the depths and possibilities inherent in those abilities and in each other.

We *understood* each other, and we were completely, utterly, at peace with each other.

What we were doing was forging a partnership. This process had been in progress for at least a year, but it was solidified during the early months of 1941. By the end of February neither of us had any surprises left unknown to the other, only an infinity of possibilities.

Our intimacy was extraordinary, and I felt blessed by it. One day, when we were atop Ambersbury Banks, I turned to him, and tried to put into words what I was feeling.

"Jack . . ." I said. "Jack . . ."

I could have felt like a fool then, standing there with my face all pinched with the cold, my hands thrust deep into the pockets of my coat, staring at the man standing before me, and once I would indeed have felt like a fool. But today I didn't. I knew he would understand.

He did. He smiled, so gently, then stepped forward and kissed my forehead, then just gathered me to him.

We stood there almost an hour, not speaking, just standing close, the forest watching about us, the leaves frosting under our feet, fallow deer rummaging about in the trees for whatever nourishment they could find, and felt the land turn about us.

We'd both had disastrous lives, and we stood in a place where once the people of this land had met a disastrous fate at the sword of an invader.

We'd both been marked, one way or another, by the land, and those who had lived on it.

We both hoped then, more than anything, that we could walk away from this place of death, and this time turn all the disasters that had nourished us into something triumphant.

AT THE VERY END OF FEBRUARY HARRY SENT WORD
that a book dealer by the name of Lionel Sutherland was

making a brief trip back to London to see a relative. He was one of London's premier rare book dealers, but had fled, together with all his stock, some three or four months before the declaration of war (being a man of caution, Sutherland was taking no chances with what had taken him a lifetime to acquire). Sutherland had heard from various sources in the book world that Harry had been searching out a copy of Wilkinson's *London Illustrata* for friends, and Sutherland had what he claimed was "an almost" complete copy.

"The best you're ever going to get," was what Harry told Jack and me the man had said.

And Sutherland was bringing the set to London, if perchance Harry's friends wished to view it.

Jack and I looked at each other. "Almost complete" was not quite what we were after, but this wasn't a chance we wanted to ignore.

"When can we meet him?" Jack asked.

Chapter Three

COPT HALL

Monday, 3 March 1941

*J*ACK DROVE GRACE DOWN TO LONDON IN HIS Austin convertible, its cloth hood up against the cold, to meet Sutherland in a tea shop by the British Museum in Bloomsbury. Now that Grace was able to accompany Jack, Harry was staying behind at Faerie Hill Manor.

"How does it feel to come back to London?" Jack asked, glancing away from the road for a moment at Grace sitting still and introspective in the passenger seat. Every time he looked at her he couldn't believe the difference two

months' worth of rest and Malcolm's never-ending supply
of chicken soup and ham and cheese sandwiches had
made. She was looking better than ever he'd seen her, and
that was not only as a result of her physical recovery, but
also a wonderful sense of inner peace, a contentment with
both herself and her world, that Jack had never seen in her
previously. As far as he could tell, she rarely allowed her
doubts about the White Queen to bother her.

Grace tipped her head slowly from side to side, as if
considering what to say.

"I have barely given Catling a thought over the past two
months," she said. "Oh, we have talked of her, and of what
we might do with this Game the White Queen has gifted
us, but she has mostly been far from my thoughts . . . for
the first time in all my life."

"Catling has been very quiet," said Jack. "At least so far
as we're concerned."

But not for the Londoners. The city and suburbs had
been subject to some horrific attacks. While not as large as
that on the twenty-ninth of December, the air raids had
been extensive, causing heavy casualties, not the least be-
cause underground stations had been targeted, as also had
Buckingham Palace.

Catling may not have been visiting personally, but her
message was coming through as clear as day: *Finish me, or
people will continue to die.*

She might not touch Grace again, but both feared the
horrors Catling might visit on the Londoners, and they
hoped they could discover the secrets of the White Queen's
Game before Catling moved.

Eventually, as they were driving through the northern
suburbs of London, Grace sighed, and roused herself from
her thoughts.

"I hope this Sutherland has the set we're after," she said.

"If you ask me," said Jack, "it's a damn shame the White
Queen couldn't have left us a set where she'd know we
could find them."

Grace turned to look at him then, smiling gently.
"What? If we'd found a set in early January then we

would have lost these past two months of relative peace.
I'm not sure, Jack, if either of us would have wanted
that."

He flickered a glance her way, amusement shining from
his eyes. "I could stop the car right here, Grace, and we
could walk the rest of the way down to Bloomsbury. That
would give us an extra two or three days to enjoy each
other's company."

"Keep driving, Jack. I'm not sure that even you are
worth tired feet."

LIONEL SUTHERLAND WAS WAITING FOR THEM IN
the tea shop. Jack and Grace spotted him instantly when
they walked in: a well-built man in a superbly cut dark suit,
warm hazel eyes enlivening an otherwise bland, round
face, sitting at a table with a large parcel, wrapped in brown
paper and tied with string, sitting on the floor beside him.

He had a pot of tea before him, and as they walked over
was pouring the last dregs from it into his cup.

Sutherland rose the moment he saw them, reaching out
to shake first Jack's, then Grace's, hands. "Major Skelton?
Miss Orr? I'm very pleased to make the acquaintance of
two of Sir Harry's friends."

As Jack and Grace seated themselves, Sutherland sig-
naled the waitress for more tea and cups. "Do you want
anything to eat?" he asked as the waitress hovered about.

Jack and Grace exchanged a glance. "Do you have any
marmalade cake?" Grace said to the waitress.

She shook her head. "Tea cakes only, miss. And toast."

"Miss Orr would like a plate of tea cakes," said Jack
firmly, as Grace started to protest. "She's been ill and
needs feeding."

Grace laughed weakly. "You will make an elephant of
me yet, Jack."

"Sir Harry told me you'd been caught in the Coronation
Avenue disaster," Sutherland said. "This war has taught all
of us to treasure life."

"This war has taught all of us to live," said Jack, regard-

ing Sutherland with genuine warmth, and the faintest sense
of hope.

They chatted a few moments about the war (a subject
which had replaced the weather as a suitable topic over
which strangers could become acquainted), then busied
themselves with the tea and cakes the waitress set on the
table.

Eventually Jack turned the conversation to the issue at
hand. "Grace and I have been searching for a complete
copy of Wilkinson's *Londina Illustrata*," he said, finally al-
lowing himself a long, hungry look at the parcel still sitting
by Sutherland's chair. "Harry said you might have one . . ."

"Well," said Sutherland, pushing aside his cup and
saucer, "no one truly knows *what* the complete set looks
like. Wilkinson put out so many pamphlets over so many
years . . . every set is different."

"But you said this was almost complete," said Jack.

Sutherland finally had the parcel on the table and was
unwrapping it. "It is the most complete set I've ever seen,"
he said. "At least, it has more in it than I've ever seen."

Both Jack and Grace had their hands in their respective
laps, clenching and unclenching their fingers in nervous
anticipation. Both had yet to even see a copy, and, while
they had cautioned themselves against hoping too much
that this set might be the complete set they needed, neither
could prevent a surge of excitement as Sutherland finally
pulled the books free of their wrapping.

The books were large folio editions, twelve inches wide
by fifteen high, and each almost two inches thick. They
were bound in dull brown buckram, and had been stamped
with the logo of Fulham Methodist Friends Library.

"Got half their stock when the library closed their doors
several years ago," said Sutherland as he saw Jack looking
at the logo. "I sold most things on, but not these two books."

He pushed the books toward Jack. Jack took a deep
breath, ran his fingers over the covers, then slid the books
over to Grace. "You'll know. I won't."

Sutherland frowned at that, but watched as Grace
opened the top book and stared at the title page.

"It's the title page I saw," she whispered. Then, carefully, almost reverentially, she started to turn the pages.

The book, both books, were a hodgepodge of pamphlets dealing with every intriguing cellar, crypt, attic, kitchen, laneway, and sundry half-ruined house that Wilkinson had managed to come across in his rambles about London. There seemed to be no rhyme or reason to what had attracted the man, save that the construction was old and forgotten and therefore, in Wilkinson's eyes, worthy of record.

Grace ran her hands over each and every page, *feeling* rather than reading what was on it. The paper was thick and creamy, both text and the myriad wonderful full-page engravings still sharp and clear.

"Grace?" Jack muttered after a few minutes.

"Wait," she said.

Sutherland frowned again. "What are you looking for? Perhaps I can help."

Jack glanced at him. "An answer," he said, "and we don't know what it is."

Sutherland raised an eyebrow at that, but did not comment.

Grace finished with the first volume, set it aside, and set to looking through the second, her fingers flying over and through the pages. As she did so Jack leaned over her shoulder, intent on the pages as they flew past.

"It's a map," he said quietly. "A map of the key points of the Shadow Game."

"Aye," Grace said, her eyes and fingers still flying. But then, as she neared the end, her face became very still, her posture very rigid.

"Grace?" Jack said as she finally, slowly, closed the book.

She glanced at Jack, then looked to Sutherland. "There's a single pamphlet missing," she said.

"Dear Miss Orr," Sutherland said. "A single pamphlet isn't much."

Grace looked at Jack. "It is the one dealing with the heart of the labyrinth. Without it, we won't know the Game's intent and purpose."

But this is a map, Jack said to her privately.

Yes, she replied. *These two books map out the inner core*

of the labyrinth, not its full extent, but enough that we could extrapolate the rest. But the key to the dark heart is missing. Without that . . .

She raised her eyes to Sutherland. "But even though the set isn't complete, Mr. Sutherland, I wonder if we could purchase them from you? This is by far the finest set"—*the only set*—"that we've seen."

"They're yours," said Sutherland. "Sir Harry arranged purchase."

"Thank you," Grace said, sliding the heavy volumes into her lap and holding on to them as if they were a much beloved child.

"Do you have any idea," said Jack to Sutherland, "where we might find a complete set?"

Sutherland blew air out from his cheeks. "Well, Major Skelton, God alone knows where you'd find a better set. I've been in the business over fifty years and I've yet to see a more complete pair of volumes than that these here."

"You've *no* idea?" said Jack.

Sutherland sat back in his chair, thinking. "The only thing I could suggest, and this is so far-fetched it is no suggestion at all, is that Wilkinson alone would have had a complete set. Find his set, and there you have it."

"Mr. Sutherland," said Grace, "I expect you know our next question."

She was so sweet, so lovely, that Sutherland smiled at her. "Look, this is a long shot, and I have no idea how you'd gain access . . ."

"But?" said Jack.

"Most of these chaps were inordinately proud of their work. With good reason—Wilkinson must have put most of his life into *Londina Illustrata*. What they often did, once a book was complete, was send a perfect copy, the best copy they had, to the monarch. *Londina Illustrata* was completed the year Queen Victoria came to the throne. Your best bet is that Wilkinson sent her a copy as a coronation gift, perhaps hoping for a knighthood out of it. Or, at the very least, a bit of money. So, if there is a complete set remaining, then it

would be in George VI's private library . . . but unless you're a personal friend of the king's, I doubt very much you—"

He stopped, stunned by the wide grins on the pair's faces.

"Mr. Sutherland," said Jack, "you have no idea."

GRACE PUT THE TWO BOOKS IN THE CAR, THEN, before she could get in herself, and uncaring of the looks, Jack picked Grace up and spun her about in a circle.

"Damn it," he said, "I always knew Thornton would come in useful for something some day!"

He set her back to her feet and kissed her, and when finally she leaned back, and laughed, Jack thought she looked happier than ever he'd seen her.

"Thornton *and* the White Queen," she said. "My sister did leave us a perfect set, in the safest place possible, after all."

Chapter Four

LONDON

Early March 1941

ARRY APPROACHED GEORGE VI FOR THEM, but until he could arrange a meeting, Jack and Grace spent every spare hour they could studying Sutherland's set of *Londina Illustrata*.

It was an extraordinary collection of ephemera relating to ancient London. Wilkinson appeared to have had no rhyme or reason as to what he recorded in words and engravings. Yes, he wrote pamphlets on important churches and their crypts, but he also included pamphlets on strange underground kitchens, on long vanished water pumps, on

intersections with forgotten cellars beneath them, on gateways and priories and ancient walls and halls. Any London collector would have appreciated the set—both the descriptions and the folio engravings were magnificent—but to Jack and Grace they were extraordinary. Each turn of the page revealed new information, new meanings.

Somehow, likely under the subliminal direction of the White Queen, Robert Wilkinson had spent twenty years of his life mapping out the key points of the White Queen's shadow Game.

And here it was (save for that single, critical piece of information), in their hands.

Every pamphlet concentrated on one of the key, or cardinal, points of the shadow Game. Some were important landmarks—St. Paul's itself, the church of St. Alphage in London Wall, St. Paul Shadwell—but just as many of them were forgotten or ignored landmarks: a kitchen, a cellar, a water pump, a tumbled-down wall. Many of them had been removed, and only the power associated with them remained. Of the two Eleanor Crosses that had been built in London, only one remained at Charing Cross. The other, Cheapside Cross, had vanished long ago.

Wilkinson also mentioned key points that he didn't have time to cover, or that he felt had been covered sufficiently by other authors. All of Christopher Wren's spires on the churches he had rebuilt in London after the Great Fire of 1666, as well as all the public and private buildings he had planned and constructed.

Among the key points that Wilkinson mentioned, there were two surprises.

The first was Copt Hall.

"I wonder who suggested that," said Grace late one night as they sat in her bedroom, eating egg sandwiches and chocolate biscuits that Malcolm had brought them. "Boudicca or the White Queen herself?"

Jack had a hand resting on her shoulder, his thumb idly toying with one of her curls. "The Shadow Game is tied into Epping Forest," he said.

"Into your power as Ringwalker," Grace said.

"How long has the White Queen been planning this?" Jack said, his voice soft.

"Thousands of years," Grace said. "Some of these places were built . . . oh, during the Dark Ages."

And the White Queen had known he would become Ring-walker. Jack shook his head, not sure whether it was in wonderment or irritation.

The other surprise was a pamphlet on the building that had replaced Shakespeare's Globe Theatre in Southwark.

Skelton's Meeting House.

That caused Jack and Grace much thought and discussion.

"What is its significance?" Grace wondered.

Jack gave a wry grin. "Perhaps only to point out that so much of my history has been meaningless theater."

Grace smiled. "Look, the Meeting House was named after a Reverend Mr. Charles Skelton, a Dissenting Independent preacher. After his death the Meeting House was used as a mill to grind bones, and stone."

Now Jack laughed. "The mills of the White Queen grind slowly, but they grind exceedingly small," he said, paraphrasing the well-known proverb: The mills of the gods grind slowly, but they grind exceedingly small. "She's telling us that nothing has been left unplanned. Nothing to chance."

On another day, the Friday after they'd met Sutherland and acquired the books, they spent the afternoon walking about London, studying as many of the cardinal points of the Shadow Game as they could manage in an afternoon. They had wondered whether or not to be worried about Catling seeing them, but in the end they'd decided she would be able to gain little from their, to her, aimless wanderings.

"Do you remember that day," Jack said as they stood by the ancient water pump at the junction of Leadenhall and Fenchurch Streets, "the Sunday that your father drove us down to London after we'd listened to the declaration of war on the radio?"

"Oh, aye, I remember. I was trying to fade into the upholstery."

Jack looked at her. "You didn't want to be a nuisance, and I felt a pig at the way I'd been behaving."

"I was so scared of you."

"You were so . . ."

"Pathetic?"

"So not what I had expected from Noah and Weyland's daughter. Dear God, I had wanted to resent you so much."

She smiled, very slowly, very sweetly. "You brought me to this water pump to tell me that?"

"It isn't quite the place, is it?" Jack looked around. The junction was one of the busiest in the City, leading as it did to Aldgate and the roads to the East End.

"Soon, Jack," she said, and Jack looked back at her.

Aye, soon indeed. This relationship had been such a slow, sweet sliding for Jack that for the moment he didn't want the journey to end in either consummation or declaration. Neither of them had ever spoken of what they felt for each other, although that they did feel, and feel powerfully, was undoubted. Neither did either of them want to rush toward making love, although that they would was also undoubted.

Particularly now that they knew of the Shadow Game. To make it, as Kingman and Mistress, their union would need to be both physical and magical.

"Jack," said Grace, grinning, "what did you want to say when you spoke about that day my father drove us down to London?"

He laughed. "My mind had drifted!" He shared with her a brief fragment of where his thoughts *had* been drifting, and her smile broadened, but he returned to the original topic of conversation. "Harry and I walked around London, and this spot is where I first felt the presence of the shadow, although I had no idea what it was then."

Jack looked down, and tapped the pavement with his foot. Beneath the busy intersection, forgotten by all save those who had ever bothered to read *Londina Illustrata*, lay a twelfth-century crypt that had belonged to a now long-gone priory which had stood close to Aldgate.

It was one of the White Queen's cardinal points.

"What does it do?" Jack said softly, his foot still tapping at the pavement.

"We won't know until we have the key," said Grace, knowing Jack referred not so much to this single point but to the Shadow Game as a whole. *What was its purpose? How could it help them? How did it work?*

Jack sighed, giving his head a slight shake. Finding all these cardinal points, finding the map, was on the one hand exciting (particularly after so long of not knowing what the shadow was), but on the other singularly frustrating. None of the points made any sense, and formed no pattern, without knowing where they originated—where lay the heart of the new labyrinthine Game. It was impossible to work out the pathways of the new labyrinth without knowing the point at which they should start.

The dark heart of the White Queen's labyrinth.

Jack repressed a shiver. Every day his mind returned to Boudicca's warning, and he kept going back over every encounter he'd had with the White Queen, trying to guess at the subtleties of every word spoken, and he wished he had somehow understood then who she was.

The best marriage you will ever make is in my dark heart, she'd told him. Then Jack had thought she was Catling, and referred to Jack's "marriage" with Noah during the completion of the Troy Game.

Now he knew differently. It was not Noah he needed to make the marriage with, but Grace, and it would be in the heart of the Shadow Game, not the Troy Game.

But who would that marriage serve? Him? Grace? The land? Or whatever mysterious purpose the White Queen owned?

Would it save Grace, or would it murder her?

He reached out silently and took Grace's hand, and they walked up Leadenhall Street, passing over several more buried crypts and cardinal points as they went. Within half an hour, they approached St. Paul's.

They stopped well away from it, staring.

Most of the buildings surrounding the cathedral that had been destroyed on the twenty-ninth of December had now been cleared away, and St. Paul's now stood in a vast, open area. Parts of its outer walls had been blackened, but that

the structure had survived at all had been popularly labeled a miracle.

"I can't believe you and my mother got out of that alive," Grace said softly.

Jack squeezed her hand, but did not otherwise respond. Christ, the horror of struggling through the fires and collapsing buildings, and worrying about Grace trapped by Catling . . .

"Jack . . ."

"Hmmm?"

"St. Paul's is one of the cardinal points of the Shadow Game. It isn't . . ."

"It isn't the heart," he said. Between the end of December, when Grace had realized the true nature of the shadow, and the previous Tuesday, when they'd acquired the incomplete set of *Londina Illustrata,* Jack, as Grace and everyone else who had the training, had assumed that the new Game would be centered over St. Paul's. But it wasn't . . . St. Paul's was a part of the Shadow Game, but the heart lay elsewhere.

"I wonder what she has made," Grace said, still looking at St. Paul's, and Jack knew she wasn't referring to Catling.

"She's been lost in death for almost four thousand years," he said, thinking again of the murders. "I shudder to think what she may have made."

Chapter Five

THE ATHENAEUM CLUB

Monday, 10 March 1941

ON SUNDAY THE NINTH OF MARCH HARRY
had rung Copt Hall to tell Jack that the king would
meet with Jack and Grace at the Athenaeum Club
in Pall Mall late the next afternoon.

"He has the books," Harry said to Jack on the telephone.
"The Athenaeum is a private place to meet. The doorman
has been told to look out for you at four."

Thus, precisely at four, Jack and Grace presented them-
selves at the door of the Athenaeum, and were shown
through into a private room.

The king was already there, and he rose and shook both
their hands as they entered.

"Why do you want this book?" he said. "Of what impor-
tance is it?"

He looked worn and gray, and Jack thought that of
everyone caught up in this nightmare, George VI shoul-
dered the most care. He was in the unenviable position of
knowing what was truly happening to his country, yet being
unable to take any action that would affect the outcome. He
knew what was at stake, and yet was totally helpless.

"It is of the utmost importance," Jack said. He waved
George back to his seat (noting the irony that he was wav-
ing the king to sit, when it should be the other way around),
then he and Grace sat down in armchairs opposite. One of
the club's waiters had left drinks and sandwiches out, but
no one felt like eating.

Two large volumes, the same size as Sutherland's, sat on

a low table by the king's chair. Unlike the ones Jack and Grace had received from the book dealer, these were covered in fine calfskin, the boards tooled with gilt in intricate patterns, and the title and Wilkinson's name stamped in the raised bands on the spine of each book.

Jack, as Grace, gave them a long look, but then turned back to the king, and told him of what they had learned.

"A new Game?" said George, his face even grayer than when Jack and Grace had first come in. "Why?"

"It is designed to destroy the Troy Game," said Grace.

"And so then we'll be stuck with yet another Game?" said the king. "I am sorry, but I like the sound of none of this. Noah told me once, many years ago, of this daughter she had lost. To think that she has been drifting about, this unknown ghost, building a new Game . . . what manner of daughter, is she, then?"

"A very powerful one," said Jack.

"Powerful in *what?*" said George. "Evil? Revenge? Bitterness? I know what occurred surrounding that girl's untimely stillbirth. Murdered by hate, lost by a mother who, while desperate for her, had conceived her for all the wrong reasons, and by a father"—he shot Jack a flinty look—"who cared not a whit for either mother or daughter. And yet you expect me to believe she's hung about, filled with good will, making the enchantment that will right the wrongs created by everyone she has every cause to hate?" By this point the king was staring directly at Jack. "That's balderdash, man!"

"Sir—" said Jack.

"And you're telling me that *these* books"—the king's hand tapped the cover of the topmost book—"hold the key to understanding how this new Game works? So you and Grace can *make* it?"

"My sister," Grace said that deliberately, hoping to turn the White Queen from unknown potential evil into a knowable entity, "may be cold and distant, but I did not sense evil intent from her."

Now George turned his hard eyes to her. "Yet you have said she spent hundreds of years sitting by your bedside,

and you never once sensed any good from her, either. You hated her."

"I was convinced she was Catling," said Grace, now eyeing the books with some desperation.

"Perhaps because she exuded the same degree of malice?" said the king.

Jack leaned forward, speaking in a low but intense voice. "This is going to be our only chance," he said. "We have no other *choice,* damn it! We have no other means of destroying the Troy Game. None. And mean time the attacks on London and the rest of the country grow worse. How many have died now?"

"Don't you *dare* to impute the blame for that to me!" the king said.

"I'm sorry," Jack said, "that is not what I intended. And you are right. More than anyone *I* am to blame for this nightmare. Now I need to make it right. My only weapon, my only *chance* at a weapon, lies in those books. I have my doubts, too, sir, but I can't afford to ignore this Game. I can't afford not to *know* it. Once I know how it works and what its purpose is, then it will be my choice, and Grace's choice, and *your* choice, sir, whether or not we use it. The Shadow Game is as yet only potential, it doesn't exist as anything else. It needs Grace and me to make it reality. And I promise you, George, that we won't take a step toward making it reality without asking first for your permission."

George sighed, rubbing tiredly at his face. "Noah asked me for my permission before she burned London to the ground in 1666, too. Why me? What have I done to be thus burdened?"

"You are a good man," said Grace.

George sent her an expressionless glance, which more than anything else told the other two how low-spirited he was; then he sighed again, and tapped the books. "Read them here. Tell me what the key is."

Grace looked at Jack, then she rose, lifted up the top book, held it a moment, the put it aside in favor of the second volume.

This she picked up and took back to her chair.

Jack inched forward until he was on the very edge of his seat. "For Christ's sake, Grace, open it."

She looked at him, then returned her eyes to the book.

Painfully slowly she opened the front cover, and began to thumb through the pages.

Halfway through the book she stopped, and her eyes grew round as she stared at the engraving before her.

"What is it?" said Jack and the king together.

Grace opened her mouth, closed it, made a visible effort, then spoke.

"Sweet gods," she whispered. "I don't believe it."

Chapter Six

LONDON BRIDGE

Monday, 10 March 1941

Grace Speaks

ɔ COULDN'T BELIEVE IT BECAUSE IT MADE TOO much damned sense.

The single pamphlet that had been missing from Sutherland's set of *Londina Illustrata* was a pamphlet about the forgotten crypt under St. Thomas' Chapel.

St. Thomas' Chapel had sat almost in the center of old London Bridge.

I looked up from the book and met Jack's eyes.

The center of London bridge, where my mother had loved to stand and watch the water sprites at play, and where she and my father had given me the four Kingship bands to wear.

All this I shared mentally with Jack, watching the comprehension gather in his eyes.

St. Thomas' long-forgotten crypt, which had been built under the ninth pier of London Bridge.

I remembered my vision of the two remaining Kingship bands lying on an altar.

Oh gods . . . they were in St. Thomas' crypt.

"The crypt is still *there*?" said Jack.

"What is going on?" said George VI. "Grace, what have you read?"

I hastily told him what the pamphlet referred to, scanning the words as I spoke.

"Old London Bridge, the twelfth-century bridge with all the houses on it," I continued, "was demolished in the early nineteenth century to make way for a wider bridge capable of handling the city's growing traffic. Wilkinson was there when they demolished the ninth pier"—again my eyes met Jack's; nine was a number of such power—"on which St. Thomas' chapel had stood."

I took a deep breath, my fingers tracing the words. "The workmen found a stone floor deep in the pier, well below the water line, at the foot of a spiral set of steps. The center of the floor was of different stone to the edges . . . as if the steps had continued down."

I glanced up at the two men.

Both were staring at me: the king with fear, Jack with a reflection of my own excitement.

"The workmen took up the first layer of stone," I said. "Underneath they found bones—mixed human and donkey and cattle and raven."

"Witchcraft," muttered George.

"A warning," said Jack.

"Aye, a warning. There was a plaque there as well, which said DIG NO MORE. Wilkinson said the workmen refused to go any further—there was another layer of masonry beneath the bones. They took the human bones—Wilkinson said it was thought they belonged to Peter de Colechurch, the twelfth-century bridge warden who

designed and constructed London Bridge—then left the stone floor as it was, dismantling the pier to that level. It was below the waterline, flush with the river bottom. Jack . . . the crypt is still there, its entrance sealed."

Jack frowned, thinking. "The London bridge that replaced it—it only had a few arches, right?"

"Yes," I said. "The entrance and crypt would likely not have been disturbed."

"The White Queen's dark heart," said Jack.

"Her Game's dark heart," I corrected him, "but perhaps not hers."

WE LEFT THE KING IN THE ATHENAEUM AND WENT straight to London Bridge, leaving our new set of books locked in the trunk of the Austin.

It was dusk now, and cold, and Jack and I hunched deep into our coats as we walked briskly across the bridge.

When we got to the center we stopped, and, leaning against the bridge balustrade, stared down into the gray water.

For a long moment neither of us said a word, then Jack spoke, his voice flat.

"I don't feel a thing."

We should have felt it, particularly as we *knew* what we were looking for. Damn it, this Game was supposedly designed for Jack and me, its dark heart should have sung out to us, should have *screamed* to us . . .

I felt a sudden weight in my chest, as if my heart had swollen so greatly it could no longer beat.

"Jack—" I began but whipped about as I heard a step behind me.

It was my mother.

Rather, it was Eaving.

I so rarely saw her as Eaving that I shrunk against Jack for reassurance, then relaxed a fraction as she smiled at me, then at Jack.

Eaving walked to the balustrade and looked over, resting her bare hands on the icy stone, her long dark hair drifting

a little in the breeze. She wore only a diaphanous gown, but, cloaked as warmly in magic as she was, she didn't appear cold.

"It's not quite the same view as it was from the old bridge," she said.

"I imagine you were much closer to the water then," said Jack. I could feel his tension through the intervening layers of clothes. *Why was my mother here, and why as Eaving?*

"This is my home," Eaving said, still looking into the water as if entranced. "In this water I came into my true being. So long ago, when I walked as Caela."

Eaving sighed then, as if lost deep in memory, then looked at us, a gentle smile on her face.

"Yes, you are right," she said. "When I leaned over old London Bridge I was much closer to the water, and the old bridge had so many piers, twenty of them, that they blocked fully a third of the river. The water used to tumble furiously through, and the sprites tumbled with it, and had much merriment."

Now she turned to us fully, and the smile on her face became mischievous.

"But that is not why the view is not quite the same," she said.

We waited, Jack and I.

"They didn't demolish the old bridge and then build the new one atop its ruins," she said. "Didn't you know that?"

"Oh," I said, feeling unutterably foolish. I had lived in London during the time when the old medieval bridge had been demolished . . . had I been so absorbed in my misery I hadn't even known what was happening in the city about me?

"What did they do, Eaving?" said Jack, his voice tight. He was irritated at her for teasing, and I knew my mother well enough to know this was just the reaction she'd hoped for.

"Building a bridge takes years," said Eaving, "and early-nineteenth-century London was a busy port and city—no one wanted to be bridgeless all that time. So they built the new bridge alongside the old bridge, and, once the new was completed, they then started to demolish old London Bridge."

Jack muttered something, and I repressed a smile.

Eaving laughed, then nodded across the traffic to the eastern side of the bridge. "The old bridge, or whatever is left of it under the water, lies on the eastern aspect of this current bridge, some one hundred feet downstream. *That* is where I hung over the side, laughing at the water sprites, *that* is where Weyland and I gave the four bands to Grace to carry into the Faerie, and *that* is where your crypt lies."

"How did you know about the crypt?" said Jack.

"George called to me once you'd left the Athenaeum," said Eaving. "He is frantic with worry."

"And you?" I said.

She looked at me then, my goddess mother. "When you see the White Queen, deep within the dark heart, tell her I loved her."

Her voice broke a little at that last, and she stopped, collected herself, and dared a small smile.

"The water sprites will aid you," she said, "when you wish."

And then she was gone.

THAT NIGHT THE BOMBERS CAME, AND LONDON suffered one of the most terrible raids in weeks. Then, I thought it only yet another example of Catling's malignance.

Then, I had no idea what the White Queen had built, and of what horror.

Chapter Seven

COPT HALL

Friday, 14 March 1941

THEY HAD THE LOCATION OF THE HEART
of the labyrinth, and for five days Jack and Grace
did what hitherto had been impossible: they
traced out the lines of the White Queen's Game. They
begged and borrowed every book and scrap of information
they could about the building of the chapel on London
Bridge: Harry spent two days ferrying books from wherever
he could beg them—the king allowed Harry to raid his li-
brary, and Harry even managed to acquire books and manu-
scripts from the college libraries of Oxford and Cambridge.

Grace brought out the map she had made so many months
previously on which she'd drawn the various sections of the
Game (or the shadow, as then they'd called it) and spread it
out over the drawing room's floor. Then they took Wilkin-
son's *Londina Illustrata* and, item by item, marked out all
the locations he'd described or referred to onto Grace's map.

Then, knowing the precise location of the dark heart of
the Game, they began to trace out the parameters and me-
anderings of the Shadow Game. It was difficult and tedious
work—the Shadow Game was larger and more complex
than anyone had thought possible—but Jack and Grace did
not work alone. Noah and Weyland, as well as Ariadne and
Silvius, spent their days at Copt Hall, with Stella dropping
in for eight or nine hours on two occasions. Without them,
Jack and Grace would never have managed the task as
quickly as they did. They were all intimately connected
with the arts of the labyrinth, either as Kingmen or as Mis-

tress of the Labyrinth, and all could help in the unraveling of the mystery.

By Saturday, when they believed they had mapped out the majority of the Game, they sat back in their chairs and sofas and stared at the map, which lay spread out on the hearth rug between them.

Even Malcolm, who had brought in sandwiches and tea, stepped back and regarded the map, arms folded, eyes thoughtful.

"Can you understand it?" Malcolm finally said.

No one answered for a moment, then Ariadne and Stella (who had arrived a few hours previously after dawn) exchanged a glance, then looked at Jack.

Ariadne raised her eyebrow. "Can you, Jack?"

In his turn, Jack looked at Silvius, then at Grace.

"It's . . . twisted," she said, holding Jack's eyes.

He sighed. "Aye. Noah . . . what do you make of it?"

Noah stared at the map with troubled eyes. "I have never seen anything like it. I cannot quite understand it."

"Twisted?" said Harry. He'd been watching the expression on Jack's face turn from excitement to concern over the past few hours, and he didn't like it. "Jack, is this Game going to help us . . . or destroy us?"

If Harry had been hoping for reassurance from Jack, he didn't get it.

"I have never seen anything like this," Jack said, "nor had I ever imagined it." He looked again at his father. "Silvius?"

Silvius opened his mouth, but he didn't get a chance to speak.

"Just tell us what you *see,* Jack!" Harry said.

"It is a Game," said Jack. "A Game that uses the power of the labyrinth to entrap evil. In that it is no different to any Game that has been built previously, including the Troy Game. But . . ."

"Damn it, Jack!" Harry said, now edging forward in his seat. "What do you see!"

"I have never imagined a Game so complex or far-reaching in terms both of power and of physical range," Jack said. "What we see here is how far the Game extends

in and about London, but I suspect it travels farther out into the countryside . . . if the Game makes use of the London Eleanor Crosses, then why not also those extending into Hertfordshire and Northamptonshire? Christ, the White Queen has spent two thousand years building this . . . its intricacy is unbelievable."

"And is that good or is that bad?" said Harry.

Jack gave a small shrug, but Harry noted with some disquiet the glance he again shared with Grace.

"It is good insofar as it means that this Game is unbelievably powerful," Jack said. "But it is bad in that any Kingman or Mistress of the Labyrinth who tries to wield its power . . ." He broke off, not able to finish.

"Gods," whispered Ariadne, "any Kingman or Mistress who tries to work it will be killed!"

There was a short silence, broken by Weyland. "Of course," he said. "Has it not been feeding off death for the past eighteen months?"

"Weyland," said Jack, "we don't truly know that the imps were 'feeding'—"

"Damn you!" Weyland interjected. *"Look!"* He rose, moving forward so he could stab down at the map with a rigid forefinger. "What is it that you *don't* see? The heart of this new labyrinth lies under old London Bridge. Yes? Then what was the gateway to old London Bridge, eh?"

Everyone was staring at the map. No one answered.

"The church of St. Magnus the Martyr was the entranceway to old London Bridge," Weyland said, his voice much quieter now. "The road to the bridge literally led under its porch. Noah, how many times have you walked under the porch of St. Magnus to get to the bridge to watch the sprites at play? Gods alone know I've been under it a myriad of times." He paused, taking a deep breath. "The imps left the corpses of the women under the porch of St. Magnus, leaving them as close as they could to the heart of the Shadow Game, and tossed the women's wombs into the Thames to feed the Game. They not only knew what the shadow *was,* they knew where lay its heart. Please don't delude yourselves that these murders had nothing to do

with the White Queen or her Game. This is a vicious, black Game, Jack, and I do not like the idea of my daughter dancing it into existence."

Jack felt sick. He did not like the idea of Grace dancing it to her death, either.

"It is the Danse Macabre," said Silvius very quietly. "The Dance of Death. No wonder it is strong enough to deal with the Troy Game. What else could?"

Noah shivered, rubbing her arms. "You can't dance this, Jack. Nor you, Grace. Why? Why? It will kill you!"

"We'll all be dead sooner or later," said Harry, his voice harsh. "The Faerie is crumbling as we sit here and moan."

Jack lit up a cigarette, his hands trembling. He couldn't believe it. To come this far, to discover the extent of the Shadow Game, and then to learn its true nature.

A trap. A death trap. For the Troy Game, but also for himself and Grace. No wonder Boudicca had called the White Queen a double-edged sword. No wonder the imps had fed her Game living flesh.

It would slice their heads off on its return swing.

He glanced at Grace. She was very pale, but composed, and she smiled very slightly at him when she caught his look.

"We don't know it all yet, Jack," she said. "Perhaps my sister has left us an escape."

"But not one that's apparent here," said Jack. He drew deeply on his cigarette, then knelt down on one knee by the map, a finger tracing slowly over the lines that outlined the paths of the Shadow Game. "I'm torn between admiration for this Game's construction, and horror at what it actually is."

"Jack," Grace leaned forward, "perhaps we're not seeing this clearly. Yes, this is a Game of darkness and death, but, dear gods, think of *what* it is designed to trap! Maybe the Shadow Game is merely a reflection of its prey. Maybe . . ."

"All these maybes and perhaps," said Silvius, "don't change the fact that this Game will be a nightmare to dance. The power it will generate . . . gods . . . no one, not you, not Jack, not Noah or Weyland, not even Ariadne"— he picked up Ariadne's hand and kissed it as he spoke her

name—"could survive the power that will rope out of this Game's birth."

"Silvius is right," said Ariadne. "The White Queen has used Darkcraft to build this Game. Noah and Grace, who have had the Darkcraft bred within them, are first and foremost Mistresses of the Labyrinth. But their daughter and sister . . . I think her allegiance is first and foremost to the Darkcraft."

"I do not like the sound of *that*," said Harry. "I say again, as I have said before, why should we trust her? Even more now you tell me she has built this death trap, *why trust her*?"

Jack stubbed out his cigarette. "Because she's all we have, Harry, and this Shadow Game all we have to destroy the Troy Game."

Harry sat back in his chair, his eyes flat, his expression hard. " 'She's all we've got,' " he repeated. "And yet she has never shown herself to us—"

"That's not quite right, Harry," Grace put in. "She has sat at my side all my life and—"

"And never announced herself!" Harry said. "Curse it, am I the only one here with a suspicious mind? She has done *nothing* to earn our trust."

"She has kept out of Catling's way," Grace said quietly, her eyes steady as she regarded Harry, "and she has worked for this land's freedom. She is our only hope. Harry, I don't think either Jack or I, or *anyone* else present in this room can afford for the moment to ignore what she has done. Jack's right, the Shadow Game is all we have. It is our only hope. Somehow, we'll just have to learn how to use it."

Chapter Eight

The Savoy

Saturday, 15 March 1941

*J*ACK FELT AS IF HE WERE CAUGHT ON A never-ending emotional roller coaster. The elation of discovering the heart of the shadow labyrinth was so closely followed by the horror of realizing the power and dark cruelty of the Shadow Game that he had to battle to keep bleak despondency at bay. The group broke up just after lunch, Noah and Weyland returning to the Savoy, Harry and Stella to Faerie Hill Manor, and Ariadne and Silvius to Kensington. By early evening Jack began to feel that he needed to get out of Copt Hall, and away from any discussion of either the Troy Game or the Shadow Game. He also wanted some time alone with Grace, without Malcolm threatening to interrupt. So it was that, as soon as Malcolm had cleared away their supper dishes, Jack suggested to Grace they go dancing.

"Dancing?" she said, pausing in the act of rising from her chair.

"You like dancing."

She grinned, straightening up and brushing crumbs from her skirt. "That must have explained my complete enjoyment at St. Margaret's parish hall dance."

You most certainly enjoyed dancing atop Ambersbury Banks that night, Jack said in her mind, then spoke aloud. "*Real* dancing. Weyland used to take you dancing in the Savoy. You enjoyed that."

"Well . . . yes, but—"

"No buts, Grace. I need to get out. Come dancing with me. Let's get away from Copt Hall, just for one night."

She looked at him, and he could read her thoughts—
"Dancing" is not getting away from the Game—but after a
moment she nodded.

"Ariadne put a lovely dress into the suitcase of clothes
that she bought to Copt Hall," Grace said. "I can wear that."

WHEN, AN HOUR LATER, GRACE MET JACK AT THE
foot of the staircase, he had to take a deep breath to quell
sudden emotion that surged through his chest.

The dress she wore *was* lovely—an off-the-shoulder
ivory silk gown that hugged her figure and draped softly
from the hips to the floor—and the fur coat she had draped
over one arm and her carefully applied makeup made her
look far more sophisticated than he was used to seeing her,
but it was Grace's air of confidence and her overall poise
that so affected him. When first he'd met Grace she'd been
so lacking in self-assurance, so desperate to fade into the
background, that he could have never imagined then how
she might grow into the woman who stood before him now.

She stopped on the final step, one hand resting on the
banister, and Jack saw that diamonds glittered about her
wrist and up her forearm.

He held out his hand and, with a slight smile, she
stepped down and took it.

JACK DREW THE CAR TO A HALT ON THE VERGE OF
the road at the top of a hill just north of London. For sev-
eral minutes they sat there, the only sound the ticks of the
cooling motor, looking toward the blacked-out capital.

"Can you feel it?" Jack finally asked, his voice soft.

"Yes." Grace turned her head and looked toward the
east. "The Luftwaffe is sending a massive raid tonight.
They are not far away. An hour, perhaps."

"Do you still want to go?"

She turned her head to look at him, and in the dark of the
car he could not make out her expression. "I am not afraid,
Jack."

He didn't reply.

"Jack . . ."

"That Game will kill us, Grace."

"You were not afraid to die when you tried to complete the Troy Game with my mother."

Now he turned back to her. "I am not afraid for me, but for you. I will not do *anything* that will harm you, Grace." He was going to say more, but his voice had thickened during that last sentence, and now Jack swallowed, and silently damned whatever fates had led Grace to this point. What was the White Queen about, to save Grace with one breath, and then send her on the path to inexorable obliteration with the next?

"We don't fully understand the White Queen's Game," Grace said. "Who knows what is yet to be discovered?"

Jack gave a short, humorless laugh. "You are so young, to have so much optimism."

She smiled, and laid one of her hands over his as it rested on the steering wheel. "I have you, Jack."

"I have you." Dear God, he thought, *I am as likely to kill her as save her.*

Her hand tightened fractionally over his. "Jack, I am sure there is a way, and I am sure we will find it."

"I am so bloody useless. Nothing I do seems to—"

"Jack, for a man who worked so valiantly to persuade me to go dancing tonight, and who has then driven me to this lonely spot where he has killed the motor, then, yes, I would agree that you *are* bloody useless. Take me dancing, please."

"Grace . . ."

"Take me dancing, Jack."

He sighed, and started the motor, and Grace returned her hand to her lap.

As Jack drove, her head turned once more to the eastern skies.

The Luftwaffe was coming.

* * *

THE AIR RAID SIRENS HAD SOUNDED BY THE TIME
Jack and Grace entered the foyer of the Savoy ballroom.
Nonetheless, the sound of the Savoy's famous Orpheans
still filtered out from the ballroom, and the cloakroom girl
took Grace's coat and Jack's cap without a murmur.

"The hotel closed the ballroom for the first few weeks of
the raids," Grace murmured to Jack as they entered the
ballroom, "but after a while everyone got so used to the
raids that, as far as management is concerned, as long as
people remain to dance, then the Orpheans will continue to
play."

Heads turned as, following the maitre d', they threaded
their way through the tables about the dance floor. Jack
wasn't surprised. Grace looked so beautiful in her gown
and with the diamonds glittering up both forearms that he
felt privileged to be the one following her to their table.

As the maitre d' seated them, and signaled to a waiter to
take their drink orders, Jack gave a wry grin. "You look so
young and lovely and untouched, Grace. I should be the
last man with you here tonight."

She grinned. "Big bad Jack. Destroyer of maidens and
hopes and dreams. I shall have to keep my wits about me,
indeed."

He knew she was joking, but even so his stomach turned
over in guilt and not a small degree of desperation.
"Grace—"

He was interrupted by the waiter setting down their
cocktails.

"Jack," she said, before he could resume. "We are here
to dance. Please, can we dance?"

He took a sip of his cocktail, then a more healthy swal-
low. "I'll have every man in this ballroom tapping me on
the shoulder to—"

"I only want to dance with you, Jack."

There were any number of rejoinders he could have made
to that, but as Jack looked at Grace, and saw the certainty and
composure in her eyes, he suddenly relaxed. "A dance then."
He rose, took her chair as she stood up and, a soft hand in the

small of her back, guided her onto the dance floor. "Do you remember, Grace, how we danced atop Ambersbury Banks?"

Instantly the mood between them changed. She slid him a glance over her shoulder, and at the same time her movements became much more sinuous—her hips and shoulders gliding along almost as if they were fluid rather than flesh and bone.

They were on the dance floor now, and she turned into his arms. "I thought you'd never ask," she said, and she ran her hands up the sleeves of his jacket, pressing briefly each time they passed over one of his Kingship bands.

This is where we belong, Jack, on the Dancing Floor.

They fit together so perfectly. Jack remembered that night on Ambersbury Banks, how he'd felt she was his perfect match, but then she'd been unaware not merely of what he'd felt, but of how he'd reacted to her.

Not tonight.

Tonight Grace was in her element as a Mistress of the Labyrinth, and she was fully aware how perfectly, how *completely* her power slid into his, commingled with his, *danced* with his.

The dance floor was crowded, but for these first magical moments, it was as if no one else existed. Jack and Grace danced, not merely as man and woman, but as Kingman and Mistress, spinning harmonies and magic as they turned.

Every turn they made spun power.

Every step, every dip of the head, every slide of hip and shoulder twisted harmonies out of the earth and air and skies and cradled them in mystery.

Jack felt breathless, his heart was thumping so hard in his chest that he was terrified it would disrupt the harmony of their dance.

He had never known it could feel like this.

What he had achieved with Genvissa had been a jest. With Noah, a mere shadow of what might be.

There was a distant *thump*, at the farthest margins of his consciousness, and Jack realized that bombs were falling on London.

I hear them, too, Grace whispered in his mind, and she

moved slightly in his arms, tilting her head to one side, as if searching out the sound of more explosions.

Jack didn't worry about them. There was nothing for him at this moment but Grace, in his arms, dancing.

Twisting power out of the heavens.

The Orpheans were still playing, but now their music was underscored with a regular *thump, thump, thump* of bombs.

"Do you hear?" whispered Grace.

One of his hands ran the length of her back, tracing out the gentle bumps of her spine. "There is nothing for me but you," he said.

She smiled. He couldn't see it, for her face was tilted away from his, but such was the connection between them at this moment that he knew it. "The bombs, their rhythm, is ringing out the beat of the Orpheans' music," she said.

"Really?" he said, totally uncaring.

She relaxed against him, and for a long moment, Jack couldn't think at all.

"There should be something that we—" Grace began to say, but just then Jack's rhythm faltered and he tensed against her.

"Jesus bloody Christ," he said.

She tipped back her head, laughing at his cross tone. "What, Jack?"

"Your mother and father are here as well. I've only just seen them."

"Well, what of it? They live here, and both like to dance. I'm sure they came down for the same reason we did, to dance a while, and forget in the doing."

Jack was staring across the dance floor. The dancers had thinned out in the past minutes, possibly due to the increasing sound of bombs falling in the distance, and he'd only just seen Noah and Weyland on the far side of the dance floor.

"Damn it," he said.

"Well, then, you shouldn't have brought me here. Jack, forget them."

"Your father is looking murderous."

She laughed. "No doubt. His beloved daughter in your

arms. Leave it, Jack. The dance floor is big enough for all of us."

Slowly he relaxed and slid back into the rhythm of their dance. Once more Grace leaned in against him, her cheek against his shoulder, her body pressing lightly against his.

"You have better things to worry about than my parents," she said, and he laughed a little breathlessly.

"Oh, aye, that I do."

They continued dancing for several minutes. Couples slowly left the floor—somewhere in the distance bombs were pounding down; Jack could feel them almost in harmony with his heartbeat—and very soon there were only four or five other couples left on the floor with him and Grace and her parents.

"I guess this would be a really bad time," Grace said eventually, "to tell you that your father and Ariadne are here, too."

"I *don't* believe it."

"Well, look for yourself."

Jack glanced in the direction Grace was looking, and groaned. There was his father, debonair in the latest Savile Row dinner suit, dancing with an Ariadne resplendent in a figure-hugging red dress.

"Doesn't she ever wear any other color?" he said.

Grace laughed. "She knows what suits her. Ah, Jack, relax. Your father has been bringing his dates here for years."

"Ariadne is hardly a 'date,' " Jack murmured. He couldn't believe that Noah and Weyland *and* Ariadne and Silvius had decided to come out dancing tonight.

"Jack," Grace said slowly, her face now tipped up to his, both her hands in the small of his back, holding his against her, "feel the music, dance with me. Forget the others. Dance with *me*."

At that moment Jack thought he could have ignored Mount Vesuvius erupting a hundred yards down the road. He looked down into Grace's face, and smiled, and tightened his arms around her, and slowly they recommenced twisting harmonies out across the dancing floor of the

Savoy Hotel to the rhythm of both music and the largest
bombing raid to yet batter London.

*THE WHITE QUEEN STOOD ON THE DECK OF A BURN-
ing ship in St. Katharine's docks. The entire area east of
the Tower of London was ablaze, and the cargoes of wool
and oils in the ships in St. Katharine's docks had exploded,
adding further fury to the inferno.*

*The White Queen paid no heed to the flames. She stared
westward to where she could see three couples swaying on
the Savoy's dancing floor to the rhythms of the labyrinth
and the beat of the bombs as they pounded down on the city.*

*"Grace," the White Queen whispered, "don't you see?
Don't you understand? Jack? Jack? Don't you realize?"*

JACK DID NOT KNOW HOW MUCH TIME HAD
passed. He was aware only of Grace in his arms, of the
sweet harmonies they spun with their movements, and of
the power that danced through and about them. He thought
he could dance like this, with Grace, for an eternity, and
leave the rest of life behind, regretting nothing.

"Look at this," Grace whispered. "Everyone else has
gone, and there remains only you and I, and my parents,
and your father and Ariadne, dancing across the floor."

Jack did not care. In his world there was only Grace.

"Fancy," she whispered, the words barely reaching him,
"even the band has gone home, and we dance only to the
sound of the bombs."

That tweaked at something deep in Jack's conscious-
ness, but as soon as it disturbed him, it had gone, and Jack
thought nothing more of it.

"Three Mistresses of the Labyrinth," Grace murmured,
"and three Kingmen, if you want to count my father."

Jack remembered that day, a long time ago, almost a
year, now, when he'd asked Weyland if he had Kingman
powers. What was it that Weyland had answered? What?

Ah yes.

I could not do it prettily—perhaps you might offer me further training—but do it I could. Remember also that I would bring my Darkcraft behind whatever I could do as Kingman. I could be a very, very effective—and somewhat bleak—Kingman. Jack, why do you ask?

Why *had* he asked? Jack could not remember. There was nothing for him at the moment but the music and Grace.

But there was no music, there was only the distant sound of bombs and destruction.

"Grace," he said, pulling her to a halt as he stopped suddenly. "Let's get out of here."

THE SAVOY WAS DARK, ALL BUT CLOSED DOWN, but the cloakroom girl had left out Grace's coat and Jack's hat on a chair by the counter.

"Jack," Grace said, slipping her arms through the sleeves of her fur coat as Jack held it for her. "Why stop now? The dance was so perfect . . ."

He grabbed his cap, then took her hand and pulled her toward the door. "I was tired of sharing you with your parents and Silvius and Ariadne," he said. "I wanted to find somewhere to dance more privately." Jack had parked the Austin in the basement of the Savoy, but he did not lead her there.

Instead they walked down toward the deserted Embankment where they stopped and stared at the fires farther east in the docklands and the East End. The flames were reflected along the entire length of the Thames between where they stood and the docklands, giving the impression that the entire river was aflame. Overhead Jack could hear the drone of planes, and the sharp rattle of *ack-ack* arching up into the night sky.

"Listen to the music of the bombs," said Grace. "Listen to them dance."

Jack looked at her. She was staring at the infernos raging in the docklands, her head tilted to one side and her body swaying slightly as if she was, indeed, listening to music. He tugged at her hand gently. "Grace, come with me, please."

She turned her face toward him, and he saw the distant flames reflected in her dark blue eyes.

"No," she whispered. "Here."

And then she stepped forward, grabbing at the lapels of his jacket in both hands, and lifted her face to his.

He seized her, crushing her body against his, his mouth against hers. He'd kissed her before, but never like this, and never had he had her respond like this. He had a single moment of coherent thought, where he regretted with every fiber of his being that this hadn't happened within decent distance of a bed, then he was lost in her, in the heat of her body, the fervor of her mouth, the teasing touch of her hands which had now slid inside his shirt, the continuing magic of their shared labyrinthine power as it twisted about them.

Then, suddenly, terribly, she was pulling back from him, and once more looking to the east.

"*God*, Grace . . ."

Again her head tilted to one side, then she looked up, studying the clouds, and then, finally, back to him.

"The drone of the planes has gone. There are no more bombs."

He tried to catch at her, to pull her back into his arms. "*Grace*, please . . ."

"The raid has finished, Jack."

"Grace . . ."

She stepped forward and kissed him, very gently, very lingeringly, and with none of the passion she had displayed a moment earlier. "Not tonight, Jack. I'm sorry."

"Christ, Grace."

Again she kissed him, and he wished she'd stop that.

"Not tonight," she said. "Soon. But not tonight."

He sighed, wishing he could let go his arousal as easily as apparently Grace could let go hers. "When, then?"

"The next raid, perhaps. Then."

He studied her carefully, all thought of love-making now gone. "Why then, Grace? What is the importance of waiting for the next raid?"

"Didn't you feel it, Jack?"

He gave a soft laugh. "I felt many things tonight. Too many. It will take me a week or more to sort them out."

Once more Grace tilted her head to the east, then up to the clouds. "My shadow sister has built a strange Game, indeed."

"Grace? What do you know?"

She smiled, very slow, very seductive. "Why don't I show you," she said, "on the night of the next raid?"

He looked at her for a long moment. "I never thought I could wish so desperately for another raid."

She laughed, and took his hand. "Come. Drive me home. Malcolm has left sandwiches out, and I am ravenous."

Chapter Nine

THE THAMES AND SOUTHWARK, LONDON

Wednesday, 19 March 1941

Grace Speaks

'D FELT SOMETHING THAT NIGHT. NOT JUST arousal—*that* I felt as never before—but something that danced about the corners of my mind like a moth at a light that could never quite be caught in form and color. Something my sister was trying to show me, but I couldn't quite grasp.

But it had something to do with the bombs. Something to do with the pain and destruction and loss of life. Something . . . *something to do with the air raids.*

The Lord of the Faerie came to Copt Hall the next day and begged Jack to do something. The Faerie was now in desperate straits. During the previous night when Jack and I had danced to the music of the bombs, cracks had appeared in the sky and bleakness threatened to tumble through.

There were shadows of fingers, the Lord of the Faerie told us, groping at the cracks. None of us knew what awaited on the other side of the sky, what was attached to those shadowy fingers, and none of us wanted to find out, either.

Jack couldn't answer—what could he say?—and so I leaned over and took the Faerie lord's hand. "Soon," I said.

"That's not good enough," he said, snatching his hand away from mine and leaving the room.

"Grace," Jack whispered. "Please tell me what you felt last night?"

"I felt the touch of my sister," I said. "I felt hope."

He gave a bitter, brittle laugh, for the Lord of the Faerie's news, and his pain, was tormenting him. "Hope? From *her?*"

I was sitting next to him on the sofa, and I took his face in both my hands and kissed his mouth softly. "Hope, from me, then."

He rested his forehead against mine for a very long moment, then leaned back, his face a fraction more relaxed than it had been. "I want to sleep with you so badly," he said.

I knew he didn't refer only to sex, but to something much greater. It was comfort he wanted, the comfort of entwining his life so completely with another's that they became one.

I kissed him again. "Soon," I said.

Four days later, Hitler threw the entire Luftwaffe against London.

JACK DROVE US DOWN TO THE THAMES WHERE, IN a small dock in Southwark, we found a small rowing boat.

It was late at night, and the Luftwaffe had been overhead for over two hours.

London was ablaze.

I marveled that the city had sustained so much damage, and yet still there was material to burn. I marveled that the city still *lived,* and wondered what magic sustained it.

Not the Troy Game, surely.

The roar of the aircraft overhead, and the steady *thump thump thump* of the explosions was almost deafening, and yet . . . yet . . . yet still that moth hovered at the corners of

my consciousness. Still I could not quite grasp what my sister was trying to tell me, to tell *us*.

But, oh, the music. It thrummed through my veins with every blast, it thrilled through my flesh, it made me so aware of Jack that every beat of my heart was a scream to him.

I slid my eyes to where he sat at the oars, and saw him watching me.

Do you feel it? I asked him, and he nodded. Tersely, for I think he was hesitant and he did not trust his daughter.

I was excited, and could feel no fear.

Tonight something beckoned.

Part of that something was the heart of the Shadow Game. We wanted to find it, to see it, to know it. To see if it held any answers.

My mother had told us where to look, and in the end it was simplicity itself. We had to find a spot in the center of the river which lined up with the church of St. Magnus the Martyr on the northern bank of the Thames. I tried hard not to think of the deaths of those poor women as I looked at the church, but was unable to repress a shudder of horror at their fate.

By the time we reached the spot, the docklands of London were once again ablaze. I thought that they had burned to the waterline four days ago, when Jack and I had danced at the Savoy, but, no, there was yet further potential for destruction, and the flames reached a hundred feet into the night sky.

By this time Southwark was burning as well. The bombers had started in the east of London and then worked their way south, following the flames. We could hear them overhead, a constant drone of death and, unnervingly, we could also sometimes hear snatches of conversation from the German cockpits as pilots exulted or exclaimed or screamed for fighter protection.

We were becoming as one with the destruction.

That moth fluttered closer, and I began to make out its features.

"We're here," said Jack, and I blinked, losing concentration, and the moth fluttered back into obscurity.

I looked at the water. It was running with red and orange, the color of the flames on both sides of the banks, and it trembled with the force of the pounding explosions.

Thump thump thump . . . thump thump thump . . . thump thump thump . . .

And suddenly that moth was back, save now it swooped directly in front of my face, and I gasped in mingled joy and horror.

Joy at the discovery.

Horror, at all it meant.

Jack was staring at me. I leaned forward, grabbing his hands away from the oars.

Dance with me, I said.

Then, using all the power I had, and all the trust in me that Jack possessed, I summoned forth my Darkcraft and swept us both into the maelstrom dance of the bombs.

In that terrible place, that black, evil place of pain and fear and destruction, we found something completely unexpected.

A stunning new power source.

The pain and horror of the air raid.

No wonder the murders had stopped with the onset of the Blitz: the Shadow Game could gorge on the death the Luftwaffe dealt, and no longer needed the imps' aid.

IT WAS A VILE PLACE TO BE, AND WE EXITED ALmost so soon as we had entered. The brevity of our visit didn't matter, what *was* important was that . . . oh gods . . . even now I can't voice it.

It was too frightful.

Jack had gone white—even the wash of the flames over his face couldn't hide the fact he'd gone as white as a sheet—and I had to look away.

I looked directly into the crypt of St. Thomas' chapel.

I gasped, and out of the corner of my eye I saw Jack follow the direction of my eyes.

On the port side of our little rowboat the waters had opened up, as if they had become a frozen whirlpool. The

sides of this still whirlpool were not smooth; instead the water had formed steps leading down, steps in which the flames and continuing blasts from the exploding bombs reflected back at us.

There was a stone floor at the bottom of the whirlpool, glistening with a sheen of dampness.

Jack very slowly lifted his face to mine.

"It is the floor of the crypt of St. Thomas," I said needlessly.

"Grace," he said, "what did you just do? How did you—"

"Will you take me back to the shore?" I said. I didn't want to answer those questions just yet.

He glanced up at the sky, and then eastward. "The night is yet young for the Luftwaffe," he remarked, and I knew then that he was as attuned to that terrible Danse Macabre as I.

"I know," I said, and from the look in his eyes, I knew he understood what I wanted. We had to close that final bridge between us tonight, as man and woman, and as Kingman and Mistress of the Labyrinth. We had to do it tonight, while the power rang out about us. "The raid will go on for many hours yet."

Our boat rocked, and we both looked back to where a moment before the steps to the sunken crypt had been.

Now there was nothing but the gently lapping waters of the Thames, and the death and destruction mirrored in its face.

The crypt would wait for another night.

"Take me back to shore, Jack."

He hesitated a moment longer, then he put his hands back to the oars.

JACK HAD PARKED CLOSE TO THE RIVERFRONT, but I led him straight past the car into the back alleys of Southwark. The bombing was to the south and east of us; I knew now it would not touch this section of London where we were tonight.

He caught up with me, taking my elbow, pulling me to a halt.

"Grace, tell me that this isn't as terrible as I think it is. I don't want this night to be . . ."

Terrible.

Oh gods, here and now was a frightful time to have this conversation, but was there ever going to be a good time? I closed my eyes briefly, prayed for courage and the wisdom to find the right words, and began to speak of what we had both experienced in the rowboat.

"The Shadow Game is so powerful that for us to wield it would be to kill us."

He didn't respond, just stared at me as if he didn't want to hear any more.

"I said that I thought my sister"—his face twisted at that, as if "sister" was too generous a word to use—"may have provided a means for us to use it, and live."

He looked away, and I didn't blame him. My sister the White Queen *had* provided a means, a source of power for Jack and me that served two purposes: to protect us against the power of the Shadow Game; and to infuse that Game with such added power that it would be sure to destroy my *other* sister, Catling, the Troy Game incarnate.

The problem was that the means was so nauseating—the power of the air raids that battered London.

"Jack," I said as gently as I dared, "a Mistress of the Labyrinth and a Kingman use the twisting harmonies of creation to build a Game, and creation is and has always been a mix of the good and the appalling and the sheer unfair. That is what life is about."

"Don't preach to me about life."

The words were bitter, but the tone not, and so I pressed on.

"We have to use whatever power is available to us, Jack. We *must*. The Troy Game is too powerful to be destroyed with the gentle harmonies of daisies and peonies."

He gave a soft laugh at that, and I was never so grateful for anything in my life.

"Ah, I shouldn't complain," he said, "for who was responsible for the monstrosity of the Troy Game in the first instance? It is just that . . . that . . ."

And neither of us could speak the unspeakable at that moment. The murders had sustained the fledgling Game until the Blitz began, when the Game could feed properly. Even worse (if possible), if the White Queen had created the Shadow Game as a means to deal with the Troy Game, then she had also created the power source by which it fed and which the Game's Kingman and Mistress needed to access in order to work the Game.

My sister the White Queen was responsible for World War II. All this time we had thought to blame Catling, but it wasn't Catling's fault at all. The war and all its horrors were the construction of the White Queen.

That is what we both found so terrible. The only means to create the power by which to destroy the Troy Game was through the creation of such horrifying destruction and suffering.

Millions would die, *were* dying, all for Jack's and my benefit.

WE WALKED FOR A WHILE IN SILENCE. SILENCE between us, that is, for the dreadful sounds of the air raid continued—the screaming of the bombs, the crump of their blasts, the shocks of explosions, the roar and terror of the conflagrations to our east and north. The part of Southwark that we walked, in the west, had been spared the bombing, so none of the fires or bomb blasts were close to us.

Eventually Jack spoke. "Why don't you want to go home?"

"I want to be with you tonight, Jack."

He breathed in deeply. "Why not Copt Hall?"

"It can't be there. We need to use the power of the air raid."

Those words almost choked me, but I had to say them. Jack and I were not about to consummate our relationship, but also consummate the bonding of a Kingman and a Mistress.

We needed to use the power that the White Queen has given us. But, oh, what a loathsome way to cement a union.

He freed one of his hands from mine and cupped my face, kissing me gently.

"Do you think it would be the same between us," he said, "if I were just a soldier and you just a girl?"

"Yes," I said. "I think it would."

His face, his entire *being*, relaxed. "Aye, you're right. It would be the same."

"We need to do what we must if we are to destroy the Troy Game," I said. "It is our choice if we allow it to destroy us or not."

His hand moved against my face, so gently, and he gave a slow nod.

"If you had been Genvissa, or Noah, or even Matilda," he said, "I would have allowed the power to corrupt me. But you . . . you are the temple bell, and you will keep me true."

I winced. I hated that temple bell metaphor, and he laughed and kissed me again. "We need to find a bed," he said. "Soon."

WE FOUND A SMALL ROOMING HOUSE NOT TWO streets away. It was, remarkably considering the air raid, still open for business.

The proprietor was a small middle-aged woman with a tired face (not surprising, given the hours) and an air of world-weariness that must have come from the continual passage of strangers through her home.

She emerged from a trapdoor set below the stairs at the sound of the bell tinkling as we opened the front door—the house must have had a cellar which she used for shelter— and inspected us up and down, arms folded over her apron.

"You'll be wanting a room, then?"

"If you please," said Jack.

I bit my lip to keep from giggling. I knew what we must have looked like to her, a foreign soldier about to deflower the naïve English girl.

The woman pulled out a book from a drawer in the hall

table, opened it to a page marked with string, then picked up a pencil which hung at the end of the string.

"Your names?" she said.

"Major Jack Skelton," Jack said, his American accent more pronounced than it usually was.

"And . . . ?" said the woman.

"Grace . . ." Jack said. "Grace . . . what did you say your surname was, Grace?"

"Orr," I said, not able to keep the giggle inside any longer. Jack had a mischievous gleam in his eyes that I found immensely reassuring.

"And do your parents know where you are, Miss Orr?" said the woman, looking up from her book.

Now I really had to bite my lip hard. *What in the world did I say to that?* Incapable of speech now, I shook my head.

"Humph," the woman said. "Don't expect to get a ring out of this, young lady."

I suppose I could have drawn the sleeves of my coat up and shown her the diamond bracelets, but I contented myself with wrapping my hands about Jack's upper arm and gazing up at him adoringly. "I trust him entirely," I managed.

The woman harrumphed again, then glanced up as a plane passed particularly low overhead. "You sure you don't want to go to one of the shelters?"

"Absolutely not," said Jack. He winked at the woman. "The excitement, you know . . ."

Oh gods, what she must have thought of us! In the end she contented herself with frowning at both of us, took payment from Jack, wrote him out a receipt, then gave him a key to a room on the first floor.

"There's a bathroom at the end of the corridor, and don't forget to keep the blackout curtains closed."

That was a reasonably pointless piece of advice, I thought. With all the fires about the Luftwaffe would have absolutely no trouble finding London tonight.

We went up the stairs, and Jack unlocked the room.

It was terrible, a cheap soulless room that must have seen the passage of countless souls. An iron bedstead—which looked as if it had been purchased at a hospital

sale—stood against one wall, the bed covered with a pale green threadbare candlewick bedspread. There was a chest of drawers against a wall with a window draped in black curtains, and a wooden chair set against another wall, a chipped chamber pot underneath it.

The room was lit from a bare bulb hanging from the center of the ceiling.

We stood in the doorway, looking into it.

"Well," I managed eventually. "At least it has the advantage of not having a Malcolm likely to interrupt us with a plateful of sandwiches."

Jack turned to me with an arch expression on his face. "What manner of Mistress are you, then? What manner Darkwitch, that you would allow a ham and cheese sandwich to distract you from me?"

I laughed, loving him, and he closed the door, hung his cap on the hook behind it, then turned to me, putting both his hands on my shoulders. "I have made marriages in palaces in Greece and Europe," he said. "I wish I could do better for you than—"

I put a finger against his lips. "Shush." Then I leaned forward and kissed him.

When finally I leaned back, Jack turned out the light, then walked to the window, drew back the curtains and persuaded the stiff sash window to open, allowing the sounds of the air raid and the flickering glow of the distant fires to wash through the room and over our bodies.

WE MADE LOVE ON THAT DREADFUL BED—ON TOP of the bedspread because neither of us felt like crawling between the thin, cold sheets—and let none of our fears spoil it for us. Jack had set the tone with his jesting earlier, and we laughed at both surrounding and circumstance, and at ourselves, and with each other.

This despite that what we did was in no way just a simple coupling between a man and a woman. It was a marriage, but not the usual that people make. It was the union of a Mistress of the Labyrinth and a Kingman who were

soon to open a Game, and thus this love-making *was* the opening of that Game. We did not just use our bodies and our emotions to make love, but also the powers of the labyrinth. We twisted the harmonies out of our surroundings, from the shabby cheap room, from the creaking of the old house, and, most importantly, from the sounds of the aircraft, and of the explosions, and of the crackling infernos that raged to the east and north, and from the emotions that poured out of the city—the fear and horror, the pain and bewilderment, the desperation and panic.

We brought the vileness of the air raid, of the entire war, into our bed and into our bodies and used it to make our marriage—a marriage between man and woman, between Jack and Grace, between Kingman and Mistress of the Labyrinth, and between Ringwalker and Darkwitch. It could have been horrific, but we did not allow it to overwhelm us. Of all the marriages made atop that candlewick bedspread that night, the most important was between Jack and Grace. We were aware of all other unions, we reveled in the power we twisted out of the pain and fear of the air raid, but it was secondary to what we felt for each other.

We started it as Jack and Grace, and we ended it as Jack and Grace.

The Troy Game and the White Queen could twist and warp and manipulate, but they couldn't change who we were that night, nor what we made of ourselves.

WHEN, FINALLY, THEY SLEPT, THE WHITE QUEEN stepped into the room. She stood for a long time by the bed, looking down at their entwined bodies, her face white and cold and utterly expressionless.

Eventually she moved to where Jack had draped his clothes over the wooden chair. She leaned down a hand, hesitated, then picked up his jacket, rifling through his pockets until she found his wallet. This she carefully opened and withdrew the receipt that the woman had given him. She returned the wallet to its pocket, then dropped the jacket back on the chair.

The White Queen stared at the receipt, then lifted her eyes back to the couple. Very slowly, in almost crablike movements, she moved about the bed to where Grace lay.

She lifted the hand holding the receipt, then, very carefully, inch by inch, dragged it over Grace's ankles. Grace still wore her silk stockings, now tangled about her calves and ankles, and the receipt caught in them once or twice, dragging the delicate fabric against Grace's skin.

The White Queen froze as Grace murmured in her sleep, and shifted in Jack's arms.

They both stirred, and the White Queen drew back sharply, her eyes all black alarm.

But the couple relaxed back into sleep, and finally the White Queen, too, relaxed. She leaned back down, drew the receipt over Grace's ankles one last time, then vanished.

Chapter Ten

SOUTHWARK, LONDON

Thursday, 20 March 1941

ACK WOKE ONLY VERY SLOWLY. HE WAS aware that it was daylight, and that it was cool, but he did not open his eyes. He thought very briefly about slipping under the covers, but couldn't be bothered.

He was aware of Grace in his arms, her body laid against his, her back to his abdomen, warm and relaxed.

He didn't want to awake to any further awareness than this. The daylight, the bed, and Grace in his arms. It was, he realized, the first time in all his lives that he'd woken up in bed with a woman and not had his thoughts filled immediately with thoughts of another woman, or of power, or ambition, or loss.

He was content with all that he had in his arms, and he smiled slowly, and kissed Grace softly between the shoulder blades.

She stirred. His smile broadened a little, and he ran one of his hands over her abdomen up to one of her breasts, silently thanking Malcolm for all the good food he had fed Grace. She'd been so desperately thin, and now she—

Grace lurched upright with a cry of sheer terror.

Jack's eyes flew open. "Grace?"

She was staring down at her ankles, which she had somehow managed to slide under the bedspread at some point during the night, grabbing at them with both her hands.

"Grace!"

She cried out again, a formless cry of fear, then struck out with both her feet. Now the bedspread, as well as her stockings, was tangled around her feet, and Grace once more tried to grapple with whatever was wrong with her lower legs.

Jack leaned down, desperate to see what was amiss.

"She's tied me!" Grace cried, and Jack felt sick at the fear in her voice.

He pushed away her hands, managed to grab the bedspread and toss it to one side, then seized her stockinged ankles in both his hands.

God! It felt as if Grace's ankles were *manacled* under the rumpled silk stockings!

He turned back to her, and laid one hand gently along her cheek. "Shush," he whispered, and kissed her very softly. "Be still. I will see."

Grace was breathing heavily, her eyes wide and frantic, but she gave him a terse nod.

Jack kissed her again, then turned back to her ankles. Very slowly he smoothed away her stockings from whatever bound her ankles and then . . .

Sat back, astounded.

Around Grace's ankles were the remaining two golden Kingship bands of Troy.

Jack stared, hardly able to believe what he was seeing, then met Grace's shocked eyes.

"I thought . . ." she said, she looked back to her ankles.
"I . . ."

Jack was as incapable of coherent speech as Grace. He
ran a hand down her right thigh, over her stockinged calf,
and brought it to rest on the Kingship band around her ankle.

"She's been in here," he said hoarsely. "The White
Queen. As we slept."

"And bearing gifts," Grace said, her voice much firmer.
She pushed Jack's hand aside and slid the bands off her an-
kles. "When I woke, I thought I'd been bound. I
thought . . . oh, gods . . . I had not thought this."

Grace sat back toward the head of the bed, hefting the
two heavy bands in her hands.

Then she raised her eyes to Jack, still sitting toward the
foot of the bed.

Suddenly the diamond bands about her wrists and fore-
arms blazed into life.

Jack swiveled around on the bed, slowly, so that his feet
faced Grace.

His eyes did not once leave her face.

Grace moved forward on the bed. As she did so, she slid
the ankle bands over her hands so that they rested on her
wrists.

For an instant the diamonds and gold intertwined, blaz-
ing forth in shimmering fire, then the glow died down, and
there was only the gold over the diamonds.

Grace was on her hands and knees now, her eyes locked
into Jack's, moving catlike over the bed toward him. She
put both her hands on his ankles, then leaned forward, seiz-
ing his mouth in hers.

Suddenly she was all movement, her hands sliding up
Jack's legs, then up his body to clasp about his face, pulling
him forward into her embrace. She clambered forward,
wrapping her legs about his hips, pulling his face down to
her breasts.

He pushed her back to the bed, kissed her once, hard,
then sat back, examining the two bands, which now encir-
cled his legs just below his knees.

"What?" Grace said. "You prefer the bands to me?"

He glanced at her, grinning. "You're easier to catch than these bands."

She laughed, lounging back against the pillows as he ran his hands over the bands. "So how does it feel, Kingman, to finally have all six of your Kingship bands returned to you?"

"Would you like to know how it feels?"

"Absolutely."

Now his attention was all on her, and he slid forward on the bed toward Grace, his eyes dark with emotion.

"Not half as good as it felt to be with you last night," he said. He cradled her head in his hand, his face only inches away from hers.

"I'm sure that damned woman downstairs will be along eventually to hurry us out," he said, and kissed her, very slowly. "But not for an hour or two yet, I hope."

Chapter Eleven

THE CRYPT OF ST. THOMAS'

Thursday, 20 March 1941

BY TEN A.M. THEY WERE ON THE STREET, walking slowly back to where Jack had parked his Austin. While the Luftwaffe had long gone, the feel and sense and power of the air raid continued to hang heavy in the air. Fires still raged in the docklands and the East End, as well as in eastern Southwark and to the south. Dust clouds drifted over much of the city. Those survivors not yet in the care of the Red Cross or volunteer organizations wandered aimlessly through the streets, coated with blast dust, ash, and caked lines of blood. The sense of fear and desperation of what had been the heaviest raid on London to date had yet to dissipate.

Jack and Grace were in a somber mood. The earlier closeness and warmth had vanished, suffocated under the ash-laden air and the terrible silence of the air raid aftermath. They walked silently, nodding to the occasional person they met on the street, pausing now and again to stare eastward or northward at the towering columns of smoke rising from the docklands. Eventually they arrived at the Austin. Both stopped, looking at the car.

Neither moved to get in.

"Jack . . ."

He sighed, and lifted his head toward the river. Jack felt an appalling sense of impending doom every time he thought about St. Thomas' crypt and what might wait for them there.

"We need to go down sooner or later," Grace said very softly.

Jack continued to look toward the river. She was right, they did need to go down. What they had started the night before could not be stopped now. He felt his stomach turn over, partly in fear that they might not survive this, and partly in dread at meeting his long-dead daughter. The White Queen was all the guilt he had accumulated from the mistakes of his previous lives incarnate.

"Let's get it over and done with, then," he said, and held out his hand to Grace.

THE ROWING BOAT WAS STILL WHERE THEY HAD left it the night before. Grace sat down in the prow, then Jack climbed in and pushed off. As he settled down to row, Grace leaned forward and put a hand on one of his arms.

"It will be all right," she said.

"It has never been 'all right,'" Jack replied, looking past her into the cold gray waters of the river. "I can't see why it should start now."

The river was hardly deserted—barges and boats piled up and down—but no one took any notice of the man in American military uniform and the girl in her dress and coat in the rowboat. Jack and Grace used no power to cloak their movements. All of London seemed in shock, and the

sight of the two people in the tiny rowboat was not enough to jolt anyone into suspicion.

When they arrived at the spot over St. Thomas' crypt, Jack stowed the oars. The river breeze ruffled his short hair as he sat, looking at Grace.

"Let's do this," he said, and she nodded, then smiled.

"Jack, it will soon be over."

He took a moment to respond. "Do you know," he said, "after all this time, I find that so hard to believe." Jack's sense of impending disaster grew stronger by the moment.

She sat forward in the boat, making it rock, and kissed him gently. "It will soon be over," she said again.

He rested his forehead against hers. "I have such a bad feeling, Grace . . ."

"That's because we are sitting in the middle of a river, in a tiny, rocking boat, in a cold wind heavy with ash and the stink from the burning wharves, and neither of us have had any breakfast. You're feeling seasick, Jack."

I'm feeling heartsick, he thought, and wished that he could recapture, if only for a moment, the contentment of last night. But he would need to wait for that, wait until they came out of the dark heart of the White Queen's Game, and perhaps wait until it was all ended, and they were free of the Troy Game.

"Let's go down," Grace said.

THEY USED THE POWER OF THE LABYRINTH, AND twisted out of the air the residual power of the air raid. Within moments the water staircase had reappeared, this time with a convenient waist-high twisted column of water to which Jack tied the rowboat.

"What do you think passing boatmen shall see?" said Grace as she stepped over the side of the boat and onto the first water step. Surprisingly, it felt firm and dry beneath her foot.

"I suspect that they will see nothing but an abandoned rowboat bobbing around in the river," said Jack. "After last

night's raid, the odd boat floating free will surprise no one."

He stepped out of the boat himself, putting his hand on Grace's shoulder for balance and inching past her down the water staircase. "Let me go first."

They walked down the stairs that twisted down the circular water well. When Jack got to the stone floor, he held out his hand for Grace, and helped her down the final step.

Still holding hands, they turned to the left where stood a stone-arched doorway . . . and looked through into the long-forgotten crypt of St. Thomas'.

While Jack and Grace had read it had run the entire length of the chapel of St. Thomas', they were still surprised at its sense of space. They walked slowly through the door, still hand in hand, stopping a few paces inside, craning their heads to look at every aspect of the crypt.

The ceiling was fan-vaulted in stone, and very high, perhaps fifteen feet at its lowest, the peaks of the fans almost twenty feet high. There were two rows of columns running along the length of the crypt, supporting the fan vaulting.

At the far end of the crypt, the east end, was a semicircular wall into which had been fitted the altar. There were tall, fat candles burning on the linen-draped altar, and several objects lined up between them, although neither Jack nor Grace could make them out from this distance.

Standing to one side of the altar, hands folded before her, was the White Queen.

The instant that Jack and Grace saw her, neither could move their eyes away.

Her long black hair hung down her back, drifting over one shoulder, framing her cold, white face, but instead of the black dress she now wore a white one: sleeveless and loose fitting, it draped softly to her feet.

In her face, her eyes burned black, their intensity extraordinarily discomforting.

Neither Jack nor Grace knew what to say.

The White Queen inclined her head toward the altar, inviting them to walk closer to see what lay there.

Jack drew in a deep breath and led Grace forward.

They stopped a yard away from the altar, keenly aware of the White Queen standing only a few feet to their right.

"Oh," said Grace as she saw what the White Queen had laid out on the white linen.

A plate with four slices of marzipan pear on it.

A tray with a decanter of brandy and two glasses.

The receipt for the room Jack and Grace had shared the previous night.

"Do you remember these articles?" said the White Queen.

Grace nodded. "The marzipan fruit . . . it was Christmas night, and Catling had attacked me. Harry and Jack sat with me outside on the terrace of Faerie Hill Manor. The brandy and glasses are from the day I came out of my coma, and went to Copt Hall, and Jack washed me in the bath. The receipt from last night."

"Very good," said the White Queen. "What does this collection mean, do you think? Grouped like this?"

Jack turned a little toward her, at the same time raising one hand to Grace's shoulder. "It represents Grace's and my growing together. Our developing 'togetherness.' "

The White Queen laughed, although it sounded particularly humorless, and clapped her hands, three times, slowly. "Indeed! Did I not tell you that the best marriage you could ever make would be in my dark heart?"

"Our marriage we made last night," Jack said.

"Ah," said the White Queen, "but you made it using the power I spun for you out of this dark, forgotten crypt."

The power of the air raid. Jack wanted to address that, but Grace spoke before he could open his mouth.

"Why group these items?" said Grace. "Why collect them? Why place them *here*?"

"To give them power, of course," said the White Queen. "To cement your union the strongest way possible. Ah," she looked at Jack. "My father is uncomfortable. What makes you worry, father?"

"This," Jack said, waving his hand first at the altar and then about the entire crypt. "You. I don't know what you want. I don't like the power you want us to use. The war. God . . . did you have to—"

"Jack." Grace put a hand on his arm.

"Do you want the Troy Game contained or not?" said the White Queen.

"Yes," Grace said, her hand tightening about Jack's arm to silence him.

"Then use what I have given you," the White Queen said.

"Why are you doing this?" said Jack. "Why help us? God alone knows you have no reason to love—"

"I do not love you, nor care for you in even the least possible way," the White Queen said. "Please do not think I do this out of any familiar sentiment."

"Then why?" Jack said.

"Because I loathe the Troy Game," the White Queen said. "Because I wanted to live and couldn't, and it was all the Troy Game's fault."

"You don't blame me?" said Jack. "After all, I was the one who started the Troy—"

The White Queen stepped closer, and Jack had to restrain himself from taking a step backward. She placed a long, pale finger on his chest, and if Jack managed to restrain taking a step back, he could not stop his flinch.

"Oh, I blame you, father-Jack," the White Queen said. "And I loathe you for what happened to me. If only you had cared. Even a little. Just a tad. But now it is too late to think of what might have been. I need you to spring the trap for me. You're the only Kingman who can do it. I'm stuck with you. Please don't think that I built this Game out of love for you."

"Jack and I have studied this Game of yours," Grace said after an awkward moment's silence. "You have built exceedingly well. If nightmarishly."

"Why build a Game on murder and the horrors of war?" said Jack.

The White Queen regarded him for a long, uncomfortable moment. "But isn't that what you built the Troy Game on?" she eventually said. "What ever have I done that you haven't, Jack?"

Jack blanched.

"Well," the White Queen continued, "at least you've discovered how to use it."

"The Game is designed to destroy the Troy Game?" Grace said.

"No," the White Queen said. "My Game is designed to trap her. Contain her." One of her feet tapped at the floor of the crypt. "In here."

"Why not unwind her completely?" said Jack. "Why *not* destroy her?"

"Then *you* design a Game for that purpose!" the White Queen said. "Can *you* fix it so that the Troy Game can be destroyed? No? Can't do it? Then take what I offer and accept it."

She took a deep breath, visibly steadying herself. "The Troy Game is too powerful for you, and it is too powerful for me. But if I built right, and if you and Grace execute right, then we can trap it within this dark heart. If the Game is worked right then the Troy Game won't be able to escape. I built a Game to contain a Game. It was all I could do."

Jack felt Grace move slightly, and he looked at her.

"We'll take it," Grace said. "Thank you."

Grace was right, Jack thought, nodding to his daughter as acknowledgment of his own appreciation. The White Queen had managed far more than anyone else.

"But what I don't understand," Jack said, "is how this Game saves Grace. As I'm sure you know, she's tied by hex to Catling, and—"

"When I began to build this Game, thousands of years ago," said the White Queen, "I had no idea that one day Grace would exist, or that she would be tied to the Troy Game's fate. Or that Catling would tie everything that Grace had touched—you, the land, the Faerie—to her fate. During the execution of the final Dance of the Flowers, the intricacies of my Game *can* break Catling's hex tying everything Grace has touched to Grace's and Catling's shared fate, but it can't do anything else. So the answer to your question, father-Jack, is that my Game *doesn't* save Grace, although it will save the land, the Faerie, and you, and everything else and everyone else that Grace has touched—that part of Catling's hex was always the far weaker part and it will shatter apart during the final work-

ing of my Game. But the hex Catling put on Grace . . . that is too powerful for either me or for my Game. It's just one of those things. When Catling is trapped inside this dark heart . . . then so, too, will Grace be trapped."

Jack felt his world fall away. "No! I—"

"If you want her saved, father-Jack, then *you* do it!"

"I don't believe you," Jack said. "It doesn't make sense. Catling, and thus Grace, will be trapped inside your Game during the raising of the Flower Gate. Grace will be *inside* the dark heart."

With Catling, but this Jack did not say. He couldn't. The pain would have murdered him.

"And if Grace is inside the dark heart," Jack continued, his voice growing firmer, "then the Game can't be completed and Catling won't be trapped. So there must be a way to prevent Catling's hex dragging Grace inside the Game. There must. If Grace is to partner me to finish your Game, then she *can't* be trapped inside with Catling."

The White Queen shook her head, very slowly, her eyes never leaving Jack's face. "There is no reason why Grace can't continue her part of the dance when she is inside the dark heart of the Game. She can still partner you. Your powers can still connect. She will only lose power once the Game is completed. Then no one can reach her."

For one long, frightful moment, Jack could not believe, nor even comprehend, what the White Queen had said. The White Queen thought that Grace, once dragged into the dark heart of the Shadow Game with Catling, would continue to dance the enchantment that would trap her inside, with Catling, for eternity?

"Grace couldn't possibly continue a dance which would trap her for an eternity," he said. "She can't. No one could."

"I am sure Grace will do the right thing," the White Queen said. "If it is a choice between stopping the dance so she can escape, and thus allowing Catling to escape, or continuing the dance and making certain the world is free of the Troy Game's malevolence, then I am sure she will continue the dance. Won't you, Grace?"

Jack turned to Grace. She was staring at the White

Queen, her face ashen, and Jack was appalled to see once more in her eyes that terrible, haunted, lost look he'd seen when first he'd met her.

He slid an arm about Grace's waist, holding her against him.

Oh God, was this *his daughter's revenge? This her repayment for his lack of care so many thousands of years ago?*

"Then why sit with her at night for so many years?" he said to the White Queen over the top of Grace's head. "Why grow with her? Why—"

"I watched Grace because I needed to be sure," the White Queen said, very low, "that she was of strong enough character that she *would* continue to close the Game, even though she was trapped inside it. Imagine, father-Jack, I realized very early on that Grace would be your perfect partner, and thus the ideal Mistress to close out my Shadow Game with you. What you and she could do together . . . ah, the entrapment would be so *powerful*. But she was hexed to Catling! So I needed to sit with her, and watch what kind of woman she grew into, to make sure she would do what was right."

"That's why you asked me if I would die for Jack," Grace said.

The White Queen inclined her head.

"And why you set the shadow and imps to frighten her," Jack said, his tone wooden. "You needed to further test her courage."

"And if I hadn't had the right mettle?" Grace said. "If you'd doubted me?"

"Then I would have arranged that Noah," said the White Queen, "or perhaps Ariadne, would do as father-Jack's partner."

"You manipulative little—" Jack began.

"Jack," Grace said. "Don't. Please."

"Why make Grace a part of this if it will only condemn her?"

"If you regret not saving me, father-Jack, then redeem yourself by saving Grace."

Grace pulled away from Jack's tight embrace. "Jack, it is all right, please."

"It is *not* all right! Not! Damn you . . ." Jack stopped, unable to continue, remembering yet again Boudicca's words: *I am here to deliver to you a warning. Be careful. Look out for the return swing of the sword, because it may take your head.*

"Jack."

Jack dragged his eyes back to Grace. *Oh God, Grace . . . what had he done?*

"Jack," Grace said, her voice stronger and steadier than it had been. "We will manage. We will find a way."

Jack could hardly bear it. Now *she* was trying to reassure *him*.

"Save her," said the White Queen, "and you save me. We are both, in our own way, tied to the Troy Game. I by death, Grace by hex. Save us both, father-Jack." She paused. "But be warned. Catling is using the power of the air raids as much as my Game does, or as much as you can. She is strengthening the power of the hex that binds her to Grace. It may be that nothing *can* save Grace from her fate, Jack. Be prepared for that."

Jack was silent a very long time. He felt numbed, his mind unable to process even the most mundane of thoughts.

"This is the final tragedy," said the White Queen. "Just this one, Jack. Solve this, and there will be no more. Solve this, and you can walk away." *And I with you.*

Jack took a deep breath, shocked at how it shuddered in his throat. He rubbed a hand over his eyes, trying to force his mind back into logical thought.

"If Grace . . ." he said, then tried again. "When Grace and I open this Game, will Catling know?"

The White Queen shook her head. "This Game has been tied into her so tightly and so intricately, and has been created as her shadow, that I doubt she will feel the commencement of my Game." The White Queen gave a short laugh. "Your name for it is very appropriate, my Game shadows her every move, and she will feel little difference between it being potential, and being alive."

"Define 'I doubt' and 'little,'" said Jack.

"Pick a night like last night," said the White Queen, "a great raid, and the slight murmur, the almost undiscernible

shudder, that will go through her being as the new Game opens she will put down to the power of the raid. You may not like what I have done to make this possible, father-Jack, but it *is* the only way it will be possible. The war grants you both power and camouflage."

"But once the Shadow Game starts to wind the Troy Game in, and entrap it," said Grace. "*Then* it will be aware."

"Oh yes," said the White Queen. "And then you will need to be very, very careful. The night that you close the Game will be the hardest night of your lives. The Troy Game will fight with everything it has ... and that is a great deal of black power, indeed. Remember, Catling has been feeding, too."

Jack had heard enough. He increased the pressure of his arm around Grace's waist a little, thinking to turn for the door, but Grace resisted.

"White Queen," Grace said, "I have a message for you from your mother."

"Yes?" the White Queen said.

"Your mother loved you, very greatly. She wanted you to know that."

For a long minute the White Queen looked at Grace, her face expressionless.

"It was a long time ago," the White Queen said eventually. "Too long. It makes no difference now, as it made no difference then. I was a dream for her, nothing more. A hope. A fantasy. What I am now is nothing Noah could comprehend; all she would try to see is the daughter she lost. Tell her that I am sorry, but that she is meaningless to me."

Jack thought that would be the last thing he would tell Noah. "Does *anything* mean anything to you?" he said.

"Oh, yes," said the White Queen. "The Troy Game's demise. That is all I exist for."

Grace stared at the White Queen. "And when the Troy Game *is* trapped? What then for you?"

The White Queen gave a smile of infinite sadness. "Why, then I will be free, but who knows what that freedom might encompass."

* * *

MUCH LATER THAT DAY JACK AND GRACE SAT IN
the drawing room of Copt Hall. They had left the crypt,
climbed the water stairwell, got back in the boat and re-
turned to Jack's car.

They'd driven back to Copt Hall in complete silence,
both too wrapped in their own thoughts to want to talk.
Malcolm had met them at the door, taken one look at their
faces, and vanished back to the kitchen to make tea.

Now they sat, their tea growing cold, both staring at the
fire.

Jack was finding very little comfort in the flames. He felt
terribly responsible. More than anything he wanted to be
able to hate the White Queen, but he couldn't. She had
built a Game centuries before Grace had been born and
trapped. There was no reason to suppose that she could
also magically produce out of her hat the spell that would
shatter Catling's hold on Grace.

He dragged his eyes away from the fire to Grace. Oh
gods, he felt so guilty. Over the past year she had blos-
somed into such an amazing woman, so full of confidence,
and then to see it shattered so easily in that crypt at the
thought of being entombed for an eternity with Catling . . .

"I will find a way," he said, relieved his voice sounded a
great deal more confident than he felt.

Grace turned her eyes to him. She had recovered re-
markably from that terrible moment, having regained most
of her poise, but still there lingered that haunted air in the
shadows of her eyes.

"Jack, even if you don't—"

"I will find a way."

Tears filled her eyes, and he was instantly contrite and
filled with hatred for himself at the same time. *If only . . .
if only . . . if only . . .*

He rose from his chair, walked over to Grace's chair,
and, taking her hands, pulled her up into his arms. "I *will*
find a way," he whispered into her hair.

PART EIGHT

DANSE MACABRE

London, 1941

WHAT DO YOU THINK WILL HAPPEN?" SAID *Jim. He was sitting with his brother and the White Queen on the tomb of the Tradescants in St. Mary-at-Lambeth, both having returned from Europe the previous night. Once they would have sat on Old London Bridge, but that had been demolished a century ago. All of them sat with their arms about their drawn-up legs, chins resting on knees. Air raid sirens sounded dimly from the north and east.*

It was going to be a bad night.

The White Queen shrugged, more out of melancholy than disinterest.

"We'd like you to consider all the trouble we've been to," said Bill. "Indeed," said Jim. "We helped you put the finishing touches to your Game—"

"And we led Wilkinson by the nose to all the places you told us—"

"And whispered in his ear about what was important and not—"

"And then we went over to Germany and started whispering again, and—"

"I get the point," said the White Queen. "You've been very good. Veritable treasures."

"I mean," said Jim, "where would this country be without us?"

The White Queen burst into laughter, making the imps' eyes widen in startlement. "In a great deal of trouble, to be sure," she answered finally.

"But," said Bill, "all will be lost if Brutus-reborn can't manage—"

"Or his girl doesn't carry through—"

"Or if Catling"—Here both imps hissed as one—"gets wind of what's about!"

"Who's to say, then," said Bill, "that we won't get eaten up instead of Catling?"

"No one is to say," said the White Queen very quietly. "No one can tell. I certainly can't. We're either going to win or lose with this one, my fine black fellows, and from this point in there's nothing any of us can do about it."

"Nothing?" squeaked Jim.

"Well . . ." said the White Queen. "I do need several more rather fun air raids organized, if you could manage it."

"Just tell us when!" said Jim, and both imps brightened.

Chapter One

March to April 1941

Grace Speaks

FTER THAT TERRIBLE MORNING IN THE crypt of St. Thomas', Jack withdrew a little from me for a few days. He felt so guilty, and so helpless, and so desperate, and that made me feel worse. Jack kept protesting that he would find a means to break me free from Catling's hex, but, oh, the emptiness of those protests. He hadn't been able to do anything before, why could he now?

I tried not to think about what the White Queen had said. *I would do the right thing, and continue to ensure my own destruction, together with Catling's, once I'd been dragged into the dark heart of the Shadow Game.* If I thought about that, if I let even a single contemplation of it to scamper across my mind, then I knew I would succumb entirely to despair.

I couldn't think of it.

I couldn't.

So I had to believe Jack. There had to be a way, and Jack would find it.

He would.

He *must.*

For at least a week we kept apart from everyone else, save Malcolm. Harry was desperate to see us, no doubt to tell us of the latest disaster to befall the Faerie, and my par-

ents pestered, but Malcolm turned away all of them. I know my mother's creed and very reason for existence was to provide shelter, but that week Malcolm made a pretty damn good job of it himself.

After three or four days Jack and I began to spend hours each day walking Epping Forest, often well into the night. We rarely spoke, but we did not need to in order to communicate. After the shock of our meeting with the White Queen, we used those walks to draw gradually back together again. We might start out walking side by side, but by the end of the walk, after hours spent on the paths and under the trees, our steps would slow and we would link arms, and walk so close that our bodies bumped and touched in myriad different places. Spring had arrived, and the increasing warmth of the sun, and the bright green of new, vibrant growth pushing through the moldy leaf litter, increased our spirits until one day, without thinking, we laughed at a tiny fawn that had stumbled into our path and stood staring at us until his mother nudged him back into the undergrowth.

These walks helped as nothing else. Just being close to Jack, trusting in him, feeling his strength and determination, made me feel as if there might be a way, and I wouldn't need to spend eternity trapped with Catling . . . *No!* I couldn't even think of that. I couldn't.

I mustn't. I would go mad if I allowed that thought to intrude.

One night, after a long walk, when we'd felt closer than previously, we made love again, for the first time since we'd hired that little room in Southwark. Very gently, very slowly. Afterward, dozing in Jack's arms, I imagined myself lying in a glade in the forest on a warm summer's day, looking up through the forest canopy to the sky so far above, and every time that Jack moved slightly in sleep, so the forest moved very slightly about me. When I drifted into a deeper sleep my dreams took over where my imaginings had left, and I spent that night in the warm embrace of the forest, feeling more loved than I had ever thought possible.

In the morning, Jack rose, kissed me, and said that evening he needed to go out.

"Where?" I asked.

"To see Ariadne," he replied.

I sat up in the bed. "Jack? Of what did you dream last night?"

He stood the longest time, not answering, looking with unfocused eyes at the pattern of the bedspread.

Eventually he raised his eyes to me. "I dreamed of hope," he said.

Chapter Two

THE ROBIN HOOD INN, EPPING FOREST

Wednesday, 2 April 1941

THE ROBIN HOOD INN STOOD AT THE ENtrance to Epping Forest, to one side of a roundabout on the A11. Ariadne met Jack there in the evening, just after dusk. She had driven herself, and was drawing off her driving gloves when she walked in the door of the inn, pausing just inside to look about for Jack.

The five or six other patrons of the inn all turned to stare at her. Jack, sitting at a table in the shadows of a shuttered window, wasn't surprised. Ariadne cut an exotic figure in what was a fairly run-down establishment.

He didn't think the Robin Hood would see many like her.

Ariadne caught sight of Jack almost immediately and walked over. He rose, and helped her slip out of her ermine coat (only Ariadne, he thought, could have worn ermine to a casual meeting in a pub).

"A drink?" he said.

"Martini," she replied. "Dry."

Jack fetched her cocktail, then sat down on the other side of the table with a pint of ale for himself.

"I'm assuming a disaster," said Ariadne, taking a sip of the martini and leaving a smudge of her bright red lipstick on the glass. "I can't think why else you'd want to see me so fast, and alone. And . . . here."

She arched an eyebrow, and looked about.

"The Shadow Game's purpose is to trap the Troy Game within its dark heart—" Jack began.

"Which is under the remains of old London Bridge," Ariadne said. "I admire the concept, if only for its dramatic appeal. But we have not yet arrived at the disaster."

"The new Game does nothing to release Grace from the hex with which Catling has bound her. If Grace and I dance the Shadow Game, raise it into life, then it will trap Grace, with Catling, in this 'dank chamber.' For eternity. When Catling is dragged in, so also will Grace be dragged in."

"But that means that . . ."

"It means, Ariadne, that as Catling will be dragged in as the Flower Gate closes, then so also will Grace be dragged in, although the White Queen claims her Game can save the land and the Faerie. Apparently"—Jack had to pause to regain some control of his voice—"Grace can still complete her part of the Dance *inside* the Game's dark heart. The White Queen sat years by Grace's bed to make sure she could rely on Grace to do the right thing—continue the Dance even though she was trapped."

Ariadne looked at Jack, her scarlet lips slightly parted, her eyes wide. "Dear gods."

Jack gave a slight shrug: he didn't trust his voice right at the moment.

"I bred cruel daughters with Noah," he said after a few minutes. "Catling and the White Queen are true sisters, indeed."

"Well," Ariadne said quietly, and Jack thought it was the first time he'd ever heard her speak without a hint of affectation in her voice, "that *is* a disaster, and no wonder that you and Grace have cut each other off from everyone else. Noah is quite frantic. And no wonder you chose this ancient edi-

fice in which to meet. You didn't want to travel too far from Grace, yet you didn't want her overhearing our discussion."

"You should turn to writing detective fiction, Ariadne. You are too, too good."

She laughed softly, then took another sip of her martini. Jack didn't even raise a smile. "Ariadne . . ."

"I don't know how to help you, Jack, and I don't know how to help Grace. I would give anything to be able to help her. I have spent sleepless nights wondering how Catling's hex could be removed. I had a good opportunity to study that hex when Grace lived with Silvius and me." She paused. "Although possibly not the same kind of access I believe you might be enjoying now."

"Ariadne."

"Sorry. Jack, I don't know how to help. If I'd had the magic solution I would have applied it long before now. You know that. Why ask me now?"

"Because you're sly and devious and cunning, Ariadne, and I need all that to help Grace."

"Ah, and I thought you weren't the complimenting kind. Any chance of another . . . ?" Ariadne held up her empty glass. What Jack had told her had truly shaken Ariadne, and she needed time to think.

Jack rose, and fetched Ariadne her drink.

"Thank you," she said as he set it down before her.

"Ariadne," Jack said, "when the Flower Gate closes on a Game, it traps *everything* inside, yes?"

"Of course."

"The Shadow Game is powerful, stunningly so. Catling will be trapped inside so tightly that she could extend none of her influence outside it."

Ariadne paused with the glass halfway to her mouth. She set it down again without drinking. *And Grace will be trapped in there with Catling,* she thought. "And . . . ?"

"What if Grace *wasn't* in there with Catling? The hex would be broken as the Flower Gate closed. Catling's power would be confined to the dark heart of the Shadow Game. If Grace was still outside, then the hex would be broken."

Ariadne thought there was a hint of desperation in Jack's voice. "Maybe. But such speculation is pointless. Grace *will* be in the dark heart of the new Game with Catling."

Jack didn't say anything. One hand shifted his half-drunk glass of ale idly about in circles as he gazed at Ariadne.

"Jack?"

"Bear with me . . . I'm thinking this out as I speak. If Grace was on the outside when the Flower Gate closed, as the Shadow Game completed, the hex would be broken. So long as Catling remained trapped, then Grace would be free from the hex. Free."

His voice was more confident now, but Ariadne didn't understand why.

"Jack. Catling *will* drag Grace through into the dark heart with her. The Shadow Game will trap both of them. You need to break the hex *before* this Shadow Game begins to drag Catling through to its dark heart."

Jack was silent, studying Ariadne, his hand continuing to turn his glass of ale about in idle circles.

"For gods' sakes, Jack—"

"Just let me think aloud, Ariadne. If, as according to the White Queen, Grace can still dance the Shadow Game to completion while she is trapped in the dark heart with Catling, then she can also dance it to completion somewhere *other* than the dark heart. Somewhere safe from Catling."

"Well, theoretically, yes. But how are you going to get her away from Catling? Catling is not going to let go that hex. She will do everything in her power to drag Grace inside the dark heart with her, because she thinks it will be the only way to save herself. She'll be certain you won't complete the Dance if it means trapping Grace as well."

"Yes, yes, yes . . . but what if I *could* get Grace somewhere safe where Catling couldn't pull her into the dark heart with her? Answer me, Ariadne, please."

"Damn it, Jack. In theory, yes, it would work."

Jack had dropped his gaze now, and was staring at the table. As he'd been twisting his glass of ale, it had left concentric damp rings on the pitted, scarred wood.

"Jesus bloody Christ," he muttered. Then he looked up

at Ariadne with what she thought was an expression of mad hope, leaned forward, kissed her hard and briefly on her mouth, then strode out of the inn.

Jack drove through the night, through the forest, forsaking the road, using his power as Ringwalker to guide the Austin smoothly through territory it was never meant to traverse. His eyes were flat and unblinking, his hands rested white-knuckled on the steering wheel, his mouth moved silently, as if he rehearsed a speech in his mind.

He immersed himself in memory of the night he'd taken Grace dancing in the Savoy. Noah and Weyland had been there, and Ariadne and Silvius also, and the Savoy had witnessed the strangest of ancient spectacles, three Mistresses and three Kingmen, circling the floor of the ballroom to the soft music of the Orpheans.

Then something had tugged at Jack's mind, as if he should have learned something from this oddity. Then, he'd not grasped it.

Now he did.

Bloody Christ, this was so dangerous, *so* dangerous.

But it might just work.

It would be Grace's only hope.

Chapter Three

COPT HALL

Saturday, 5 April 1941

Grace Speaks

I DON'T KNOW WHAT HAPPENED AT THE ROBIN Hood Inn. Jack came home as if drunk, but with excitement rather than alcohol. I was waiting for him, sitting on the lower step of the stairs, and rose slowly as he came in the front door. He walked over, took me by the shoulders, stared at me a long moment, then smiled—so gently and sweetly it brought tears to my eyes.

"Go to bed," he said. "I want to sit up a while yet."

"*Jack.*"

"Don't ask, please. I have to work something out. Grace, I think I have something, but let me work it out."

"Jack . . ."

He cuddled me to him, rocking me back and forth, kissing the top of my head. "I think there's a way," he said, "but I need to nut it out. Please, trust me."

So I did. I went back to bed, where I didn't sleep, but sat up with Malcolm all night playing cards and refusing the biscuits he tried to press on me.

There were no answers in the morning. Jack spoke to me, and kissed me, and reassured me, but said he needed more time. He looked haggard with lack of sleep, but his eyes still shone with that wild, intoxicated excitement.

I left him to it.

Malcolm took care of me, keeping me still and reason-

ably calm, keeping me company, taking me for long walks in the forest and telling me druidic tales that were so strange that I think he made them up. He fielded the phone calls from my parents and from Ariadne and Silvius, and refused the Lord of the Faerie entry into the hall. He kept me quiet, and he kept a buffer of quiet around Jack, who emerged from his study only to use the bathroom or snatch a bite from the kitchen.

Jack stayed in the study until Saturday morning, then came out, kissed me again, asked Malcolm to ring my parents, Ariadne and Silvius, and contact the Lord of the Faerie, and ask them all to meet with us at the hall in the evening.

"I have it," he said. "Believe me."

Then he went up to bed, and slept through the day until the late afternoon, when he rose and bathed, and only emerged from the bathroom as my parents were arriving.

I wish he could have told me beforehand what he'd discovered, but it was only much, much later, when we were all sitting stunned about the fire, that I realized why he hadn't.

What he had to say was so incredible, so complex, and so *dangerous,* that I wouldn't want to have to explain it twice, either.

"WE CAN DO THIS," SAID JACK, LEANING FORWARD in his chair, his keen eyes shifting slowly about the group, "but it is going to take most of us, and it is going to take everything we have. *Everything.* Nothing can go wrong, and none of us can take a misstep."

We were sitting in the drawing room, the chairs and sofas pulled, as usual, in a semicircle about the fire. My parents were here, as Ariadne and Silvius, and Stella and the Lord of the Faerie. Malcolm had abandoned his usual listening post in the hall door to sit on the arm of my armchair.

"I want to go back over some things," said Jack. "I'm doing this so that everything is very clear in our minds. I want no shadows, no puddles of murkiness. I want everyone to walk out of this room tonight with our course of action so clear that you can have no question. Okay?"

Nods all about, and also a few shared glances of concern.

"Noah's and my daughter," said Jack, "who we know as the White Queen, has spent the past two thousand years building a shadow Game so powerful that it can trap the Troy Game. The White Queen requires Grace and me to dance this Game—to open it and to bring it to a conclusion. The only problem, as you all know, is that Grace is also bound by hex to Catling . . . to the Troy Game. Its fate is her fate. Grace will also be trapped inside the dark heart of the Shadow Game with Catling, for eternity."

Jack explained that while the weaker part of Catling's hex, that which also bound everything I had touched to my shared fate with Catling, could be shattered, the White Queen could do little for the original and far more powerful hex.

"Grace will even have to complete the final Dance of the Flowers of the Shadow Game inside its dark heart," Jack said, "as she will be dragged in with Catling during the process of raising the Flower Gate.

"On the face of it, bad news. Not what we want to hear. But it told me something else—that Grace can complete her portion of the Dance of the Flowers *elsewhere*. She doesn't have to necessarily be with me."

He reached out to me then, taking my hand and smiling at me with such warmth that my heart skipped a beat.

"What Grace and I share," said Jack, gently squeezing my hand, "is so powerful, and our abilities so perfectly matched, that we could almost be on opposite sides of the planet and so long as we remained perfectly coordinated, we would still be able to complete the Dance of the Flowers."

He gave my hand a final squeeze then let it go, turning back to the rest of the group.

"We need to get Grace somewhere safe," he said. "Somewhere so secure Catling's hex can't extend into it. She and I can begin the Dance of the Flowers together, but at that precise moment that the labyrinth begins to pull Catling into its heart, we need to get Grace somewhere where Catling's hex can't touch her. I don't know how to break that hex, no one else does, but I think we can move Grace to a place of safety—"

A *shelter*, I heard my mother whisper.

"—at the *precise* moment Catling is being pulled through into the dark heart, when Catling is disoriented and likely expending most of her energy trying to escape the Shadow Game.

"Noah," he looked at my mother, "I want you to use your powers as Eaving, as Mistress of the Labyrinth, and as Darkwitch, to construct a shelter for Grace. An enchantment whose only purpose is to shelter Grace during those terrible moments when Catling is being dragged into the dark heart of the Shadow Game before the Flower Gate closes on her for eternity. Can you do it?"

My mother's eyes were huge, and huge with the same thing I'd seen in Jack's eyes over the past few days—an intoxicating excitement.

"Yes," she said. "I can do it. I can construct a devising . . . something to keep her safe. *Yes,* I can do it." She thought for a moment. "It will be similar to a Game, but not quite. The devising will need to be danced by a Mistress and Kingman, which will tie it in with the labyrinthine forces involved in the Shadow Game . . . yes, yes, I can do it."

I saw Ariadne move slightly in a deliberate attempt to capture my attention, and I looked at her.

When I first trained your mother, Ariadne said in my mind, *I realized then she could do things with labyrinthine power that no one else could have ever imagined. She was born for this, Grace. She can do this for you.*

"And I will dance the devising with Weyland," said my mother. "With your father, Grace."

"No," said Jack. "Ariadne and Silvius will dance it."

Everyone's attention focused back on Jack, and Noah opened her mouth to protest.

"Let me speak," he said gently. "Let me show you what will happen."

He looked now at the Lord of the Faerie. "Coel, the Faerie is in desperate peril, yes?"

The Lord of the Faerie gave a terse nod. "You know it is."

"Good. Then Noah and I will go to Catling very soon, and we will say to Catling that we've had enough, we can-

not bear to see the Faerie perish, and we will complete her. She'll be wary of our promises—after all, we've done this before—but I think we can make her listen.

"Then, on the night of the next big air raid, Grace and I will open the Shadow Game."

I felt my chest constrict both with fear and with excitement.

"Catling won't realize?" Silvius said.

"I don't think so," said Jack. "The White Queen has made her Shadow Game well. It is so close a reflection of the Troy Game itself that, even when woken—and especially during a night of a massive air raid—Catling will think the slight reverberation of its waking as . . . oh, as nothing more important than a slight and distant wavering along the borders of her own existence."

Of course, Jack and I also needed the power of the air raid to infuse this Game with as much power as possible, but I hoped he and the White Queen were right about Catling not realizing what was happening.

"Eventually, within weeks, I hope, we will close out the Shadow Game, but at the same time as that is closed, so also must we begin to close the Troy Game, and Ariadne and Silvius must dance the devising to save Grace. Everything must be done at the same time. They are all interconnected."

"Of course," I said. "The Savoy, the night we were all there, dancing."

"Three ale rings," Ariadne murmured.

"Three sets of Kingmen and Mistresses, three labyrinthine enchantments, all danced virtually concurrently," Jack said.

"It must be my age," said Silvius, "but can you perhaps explain a little more clearly?"

Jack sat even farther forward on the edge of his seat, and pulled a lamp table close, lifting the lamp down to the floor. Malcolm had earlier served tea, and now Jack took three of the empty cups, and placed them atop the table side by side in a line.

"One night, three dances, three sets of Kingmen and Mistresses, three purposes," he said. He tapped the cup at the left end of the line. "The Troy Game." Then he tapped

the middle cup. "The Shadow Game." He tapped the final cup. "Noah's devising, designed to shelter Grace from Catling's hex. For the moment let's forget the devising and concentrate only on the Troy and Shadow Games."

His attention turned back to the first cup, the Troy Game. "Noah and I begin the Dance of the Flowers within St. Paul's to complete the Troy Game. We won't mean to complete it, but it will distract Catling from what *else* is happening that night." Now his fingers tapped the middle cup. "At *precisely* the same time as Noah and I begin to dance, Grace and Weyland begin the same dance over the top of the river crypt in order to begin the process of completing the Shadow Game."

"But my father and I can't—" I began, stopping as Jack glanced at me.

"Let me finish," he said. "The Flower Dances for the Troy and Shadow Games need to be danced concurrently, precisely in step. Two reasons. First, this way it is less likely that Catling will realize what's happening. Everything she feels she will think a product of her own completion. But secondly, and far more importantly, it enables me to transfer power smoothly between the two dances. Look . . ."

One of the cups had residue of tea left in it, and Jack dipped in his forefinger and drew a damp figure of eight about the two cups, so that they were each enclosed by interconnecting circles.

"Weyland," he said, "in partnering Grace you are my shadow, my proxy. You will still need to use your own power, and you will need to dance precisely what is needed, but you will also be acting on my behalf. While I will do enough with Noah to enable the raising of the Flower Gate in St. Paul's, most of my attention will be on Grace."

"How nice," said my father, "to be your proxy." There was humor underscoring his words, however, and Jack sent him a brief grin.

"Noah and I dance the Troy Game *almost* to completion," he said, "but before the Flower Gate is fully raised I transfer completely to Grace, Weyland moving to Noah's side. Noah, at this point you stop dancing, and I withdraw all power from the Troy Game and concentrate entirely on

completing the Shadow Game with Grace. This is a dangerous time for you and Weyland. Catling will realize instantly what is happening, she will flail and fight as the Shadow Game drags her into its dark heart, and the very first people she will flail out at is you and Weyland. Be careful."

"Grace will also be in terrible danger at this moment," said Ariadne, "as Catling will drag her into the Shadow Game with her. When do Silvius and I dance Noah's devising?"

"You start just before Noah and I abandon the completion of the Troy Game," said Jack. "You accelerate the devising to full strength as I move to Grace's side; by then Catling will know something has gone wrong, she will suspect the worst, and she'll be concentrating on Grace before all else." His finger now traced out a new figure of eight, enclosing the middle and last cups. "I will get an instant with Grace, in harmony, over the river crypt, before you and Silvius manage to enclose her within the devising Noah has created. Then, in whatever safe place the devising has moved her to, Grace continues to dance with me, the Shadow Game is closed, the Troy Game is trapped, and we're all safe."

Silence.

"Uh huh," said my father. "Very simple."

I didn't know what to think. It was horribly complicated. Three dances, enacted virtually simultaneously. One Game to trap another, and a devising to keep me safe so I could close off the Shadow Game with Jack in order to trap the Troy Game and avoid being trapped myself.

What a complex solution to trying to fend off the Troy Game. And we wouldn't even destroy it. Only trap it.

I hoped London Council had no plans for a major dredging of the Thames in the near future.

"Everything will need to be so carefully timed," said Ariadne. "Not a single step wrong, not a single dancer out of time."

"We did it that night in the Savoy," said Jack, "without even trying."

"And I?" said Silvius. "I will need the power of the

Kingship bands to dance Grace's Game with Ariadne. I'm assuming you share that power with me in the same manner you explained you will with Weyland."

Jack nodded, and his finger traced out the two figures of eight that connected all three cups: the Troy Game, the Shadow Game, and the devising Ariadne and Silvius would dance. "The power of the bands can extend through to all three sets of dancers. It will be easy enough."

"Sharing the power won't lessen it?" asked my mother.

"No," said Jack. "The Kingship bands provide clarification and guidance rather than real power . . . Kingmen draw and use power from the labyrinth in the same manner as do Mistresses. The Kingship bands just show us *clearly* how to direct that power, and where to direct it. I can share the bands with Weyland and Silvius with no harm."

My mother cleared her throat, edging forward a little. I knew her too well not to know she was about to broach a delicate subject.

"This sheltering devising you want me to make," she said. "Jack, if I devise it, then surely I should be the best person to make it?"

"There is no denying," Jack said, "that if you enacted it then it would be at its most powerful. But, Noah, Catling will expect you to be at St. Paul's in order to dance her final completion, and—"

"But there's no reason," said Noah, "when you swap with Weyland, when you and I *stop* dancing the Troy Game, that I couldn't then enact the sheltering enchantment with Weyland. There is no need for Ariadne and Silvius to do it."

Jack looked at her, taking his time, and I had to look away from my mother. I knew what he would answer, and I prayed that he found the tact to say it without destroying Noah.

"The devising will need to be started just before we stop, Noah," Jack said.

"But—" my mother said, looking ready to argue the issue.

"If the enchantment was for anyone other than Grace," Jack said, "then, yes, you could do it. But—"

Oh gods, that "but."

"—Grace is more comfortable with Ariadne and Silvius, and between them there lies no history of discord."

I had to close my eyes. My poor mother, why was it that somehow she always had to hear these small pieces of horror in front of an audience?

"There will be no second chances at this, Noah," Jack continued. "None. You and Grace love each other, but you are not close. I need Grace to be able to submit entirely and without question to the wielders of this devising." A pause. "I want her to be entirely comfortable with them."

Ouch.

"Besides," said Ariadne, too damn brightly, "Catling will surely be centering all her anger on you, and you won't have the chance to—"

"She'll be centering all her power on dragging Grace into the heart of the Shadow Game!" Noah said, her voice too loud and too hard. "She won't have time for anything else but that!"

I was watching my mother from out of the corner of an eye now, too embarrassed to look at her directly, and saw her swing back to Jack.

"Ariadne and Silvius can do it, Noah," Jack said, very gently, before my mother had a chance to say anything.

She deflated. Her mouth closed, she stared at Jack, then her back straightened. "Very well. If you think it worth the risk."

THERE ISN'T MUCH MORE WORTH RECOUNTING about the evening. Jack arranged for people to meet up as needed, Jack asked Harry to arrange a meeting with the king so that he, Jack, could ask George's permission for what he was about to do (as Jack had earlier promised George he would), then everyone left Jack and Malcolm and me to Copt Hall, and then, finally, Jack and I had some time together, alone.

He leaned back against the bedroom door as he pushed it closed, sighed, and rubbed a hand wearily across his face.

"Why do I always manage to say the wrong thing to your mother, Grace?"

"I don't think there was a right way to say that."

I had sat on the side of the bed, and now Jack came and joined me. He slid a hand behind my head, and tipped my face to his. "Are you scared, Grace?"

Oh, aye, desperately, and he saw it in my eyes.

"It is the best I could think of," he said. "I—"

I leaned forward and held him tightly to me. I knew it was the best he could do, and that was all I could ask of him.

"*Do* you think Ariadne and Silvius strong enough to work my mother's devising?"

"Ariadne managed to destroy the Aegean world all by herself, and Silvius has as much talent as I ever had. They can do it, Grace."

I let myself believe him. "You were right, Jack. I'd feel more comfortable with Ariadne and Silvius. With my mother there would always be the chance that our distance would intrude."

We were silent a long time, sitting on the bed, holding each other.

"I wish there were another way, Grace," he said.

With those words I realized he *wasn't* sure it would work, and I buried my face against his chest, and fought desperately to keep the blackness at bay.

Chapter Four

COPT HALL AND LONDON

Sunday, 6 April to Tuesday, 15 April 1941

OF THE SIX PEOPLE INVOLVED IN THE EN-
trapment of the Troy Game and the saving of
Grace, only Weyland needed any degree of exten-
sive training in the steps of the Dance of the Flowers. Even
then, he needed merely to shadow Jack, to be his footsteps
and body, and thus his training needed only to show him
the steps of the dance, and not to train him in the arts of
wielding its power. Jack could have taught Weyland the
steps, but he left it to Grace and Silvius.

Once Weyland learned the steps, then Jack needed to be
sure that everyone knew precisely what to do, and at what
point in time they needed to do it. But that needed to be left
until Weyland was ready. One of the first things Jack did
was to visit the king, explain to him what he wanted to do,
and ask his permission to go ahead. George was appalled at
the risk, but he finally nodded. Better to take the risk than
to submit the land to Catling's rule.

Noah concentrated on building the devising that would
shelter Grace from Catling's hex. For ten days after meet-
ing with Jack at Copt Hall, Noah isolated herself in a room
at Faerie Hill Manor.

Here, Noah sat in a chair, its back set to the closed door,
facing an open window. The room had no lights, no heating,
no stimulus of any kind save from the open window, and for
these ten days Noah took no sustenance save from her
power, nor did she move from, nor move within, the chair.
She sat, clothed in her power as Eaving, staring unblinking

out the window with sage green eyes shot through with lightning.

Exploring possibilities.

As Eaving, Noah's very purpose was to shelter. As a Darkwitch and a Mistress of the Labyrinth she could bring added (and far darker) power to her goddess powers which would entwine her devising with a twisted strength that would give it its best chance of success.

First, Noah had to think of a physical place of shelter. Grace had to go somewhere, and it had to be somewhere that already had a fortress nature. That nature would surely need to be buttressed, but if it were a natural fortress in any case, then its power would be so much more potent.

There was one place that shone out, but it had some massive problems. Noah kept returning to it, then discarding the idea almost immediately.

No, it had already been corrupted by Catling. She could already stretch her malevolent fingers in there.

So Noah tried to think of somewhere else, somewhere naturally *safe* from Catling.

And, over the three days, she came up with nowhere so suitable as her first thought. Even though it was corrupted, it was such a natural shelter, and one where Grace would feel so comfortable . . . somewhere where she would have no doubts, which would feel like home to her.

"If only I can protect it," whispered Noah, over and over. *If only I can devise some means to keep Catling's claws out of it.*

The Idyll.

When Weyland had originally constructed his Idyll atop the house in Idol Lane, he had, because of his secretive, close nature, instinctively made of it a fortress. Over the following years, as Weyland's relationship with Noah had developed, so the Idyll had grown, eventually touching the borders of the Faerie.

But with the gradual disintegration of the Faerie over the past year, the Idyll had retreated. Noah and Weyland rarely used it, and the Idyll had closed in about itself, try-

ing to isolate itself from what was happening within the rest of the land. Now, as originally, there was only one entrance. Weyland's house on Idol Lane had been destroyed in 1666, so the Idyll had taken as its single entrance the next best thing: the steps leading up the rebuilt spire of St. Dunstan's-in-the-East.

Noah could easily protect those steps, and the Idyll was so familiar to her that she knew she could just as easily devise a sheltering protection for it.

Indeed, the Idyll would embrace it.

Yet there was a problem. Catling had already penetrated the Idyll. In fact, it was the place where Catling had managed to hex Grace in the first instance.

For days Noah went over every possibility, tried to think of every complication, tried to think of somewhere else.

At the end of the ten days, Noah finally acknowledged that she had no choice. The Idyll was the best shelter possible for Grace . . . now all that Noah had to do was to create a devising that would shelter both Grace *and* the Idyll from Catling's hex. Noah needed to create a devising that not merely transported Grace into the Idyll (relatively easy) but would then seal the Idyll from Catling's hex (supremely difficult).

Moreover, Noah had to build a devising that Ariadne and Silvius could work.

"Damn you, Jack," Noah muttered tiredly as, finally, she rose stiff and exhausted from that chair. "Why not allow me to work this? Why *not*?"

ONCE OUT OF THE ROOM IN FAERIE HILL MANOR Noah went back to the Savoy, where she slept for eighteen hours.

Then she rose, bathed, ate—all under the concerned gaze of Weyland—then kissed her husband, and said she needed to speak with Ariadne and Silvius.

"I'll be back tonight," she said, and left him, still staring after her with worried eyes.

* * *

ARIADNE AND SILVIUS WERE AT HOME IN THEIR
Kensington apartment, and it was Silvius who opened the
door to Noah.

"Ariadne is in the drawing room," he said. "Come
through."

From the look on Noah's face, and the weariness in her
eyes, there was a great deal more Silvius could have said,
but he thought it prudent to leave it for the moment.

Ariadne rose as Noah entered, kissing her on both
cheeks, then offering her an easy chair in which to sit.

"Well?" Ariadne said as Noah sank down.

"I can build a devising," said Noah, "and I have a place
in which to shelter Grace—"

"Where?" said Ariadne.

"The Idyll," said Noah. "You have heard of it, surely."

Ariadne and Silvius nodded. "But I thought that Catling
could—" Ariadne began.

"I can build a devising to thwart her," Noah snapped.
"*My* only dilemma is, can you, *both* of you, control it?"

"We are not to blame for Jack's decision," Silvius said
softly.

Noah sighed. "I am worried for Grace, Silvius. You will
hold the life of my daughter in your care, and I need to
know if you can control this devising." She tapped a hand
over her heart. "I need to know *here*."

"We will do all we can," Silvius said, and something in
the steadiness of his gaze apparently answered some of
Noah's doubts, for she visibly relaxed.

"I am building this devising with everything that I am,"
said Noah. "Mistress of the Labyrinth, Darkwitch, and
Eaving, goddess of the land. The labyrinthine parts of the
devising both of you shall have no trouble with, and Ari-
adne none with that part of it constructed from the Dark-
craft, but as for that part of the devising constructed from
my powers as Eaving, then—"

"Noah," said Ariadne. "You forget that once I was Mag-

aLlan of this land. I may not have been particularly devoted to the land, but I learned well and true. If you bring into this devising the power of the land, then I can understand it, and wield it."

"And you forget that for countless centuries I lay in the heart of the labyrinth with the dying Og," said Silvius. "The power of the land is not as foreign to me as I think you assume."

Noah stared at them, then she smiled, and relaxed even further. "I had forgotten, both of those things. Ah, what is the matter with me? Maybe we have a chance, after all."

ON THE AFTERNOON OF FRIDAY THE ELEVENTH OF April, Jack and Grace were walking through Epping Forest when the White Queen appeared to them.

She startled them so greatly, suddenly appearing on the path as they turned a corner, that both jumped, and gasped.

"Next week," the White Queen said, not giving either a chance to speak. "Wednesday the sixteenth."

"What?" Jack snapped. "Should we expect the second coming then?"

To his and Grace's surprise, the White Queen's mouth actually twitched in a smile.

"You can expect a large raid that night," she said. "A very powerful one."

Grace glanced at Jack, then looked back to the White Queen. "You want us to open your Game that night."

"Are you ready?" the White Queen said.

"To open the Game, yes," said Jack.

Again the White Queen twisted her mouth in a smile, but this time it was humorless. "And when shall you be ready to finish it?"

"Soon," said Jack.

"You have a month," said the White Queen. "The best time to close it, and to trap the Troy Game, will be the night of the tenth of May."

"Another air raid," said Jack. "No doubt destructive."

"You need all the power possible," said the White Queen. "Are you not capable of handling it?"

"I am sickened by it," said Jack, "knowing what horror it wreaks."

"You cannot warn people," said the White Queen. "To warn them will be to warn Catling." Then she took a step forward. "Will you be ready, father-Jack, to close out my Game in a month's time? Can you do it?"

Without giving him time to answer, the White Queen swung her cold black eyes to Grace. "Are *you* ready, Grace? Ready to do what is needed, even though you will be trapped in the—"

"She will be saved," said Jack.

"Really?" said the White Queen, and then she vanished.

Really? The word rustled about them, twisting away on the wind, and Jack took Grace's hand, and smiled at her.

"Really," he said, his voice solid with certainty.

She did not return his smile.

Chapter Five

THE RIVER THAMES

Wednesday, 16 April 1941

THE LUFTWAFFE SWEPT IN JUST AFTER eight in the evening, over six hundred bombers, dropping parachute flares over the city. There was high but light cloud, and a low mist clinging to the river, and the flares drifted down brightly only to mute and blue as they finally fizzled out in the mist.

Ten minutes after the flares came the high explosives. The Luftwaffe had orders to concentrate on the docklands to the east of the Tower of London, and the wharves about South-

wark and Rotherhithe. Within an hour the docklands were ablaze, and great sheets of flame roared into the night sky in Rotherhithe as the Metropolitan Gas Works exploded.

Most people who were not part of the emergency response teams spent that night deep within shelters, praying that something would be left for them when they emerged in the morning. But there were nine people who preferred to spend the night within the thick of the raid, surrounded by clinging mist and ash and falling sooty debris.

Ariadne, Silvius, Stella, the Lord of the Faerie, Noah, Weyland, Malcolm, Jack, and Grace stood on the southern river bank just opposite St. Magnus the Martyr, which rose on the northern bank. All were dressed not as modern men and women, but in the robes of when they had first lived: Jack and Grace wore the attire of a Kingman and Mistress of the Labyrinth, a white linen hip wrap for Jack and a skirt of similar material for Grace. Jack's golden Kingship bands glinted in the light, Grace's diamond bracelets danced in the flickering lights of the fires.

Almost four thousand years ago, tens of thousands had witnessed the Dance of the Torches that had opened the Troy Game. This night there would be only seven witnesses to watch the Kingman and Mistress of the Labyrinth open a new Game.

There were no lines of lithe, beautiful dancers. There were no torches or ribbons or singing. There was no ambition or fear or hatred.

There was merely death falling from the sky, horror creeping along the river and bankside streets, and the small group of participants who had, between them, made such a nightmare of the original intent to build a Game to benefit London.

They waited until almost one in the morning, when the fires had built—and merged—to such an extent that the continually exploding bombs made no visible flash impression within the conflagrations. The mist over the Thames had almost dissipated, but enough remained that the river was shrouded in an eerie yellow and orange haze.

Jack looked at Grace, shared a silent thought with her, then he turned to Noah.

"Eaving," he said, using her goddess name, "I need your permission to—"

"Do whatever you need," said Noah. "Use whatever you wish. You do not have to ask my permission."

Jack nodded, then turned to the river. He took a step forward so that he was only some three or four feet from the water's edge, and very slowly raised one arm so that it extended out before him at shoulder height, his fingers reaching out over the water.

Around his shoulders, his marks began to writhe.

For long minutes nothing happened, then, very slowly, lights rose up from the river bed.

Tens of thousands of lights.

Water sprites, rising from the depths of the river, the lights of the firestorms reflecting in their copper-colored eyes.

His arm still extended, Jack turned his head very slowly toward Grace.

She took a deep breath, then stepped forward to his side. She lifted a hand, running it slowly over his shoulders, allowing her fingers to entwine with his marks, and ran her hand lightly down his outstretched arm until it lay over his hand.

The lights just under the water's surface, the water sprites, moved in what at first appeared to be an aimless and chaotic manner, but which within minutes resolved into a complex dance. When they'd finished, when the sprites had stilled with their eyes still cast upward to reflect the lights, they had formed a gigantic unicursal labyrinth just under the rippling surface of the water. The labyrinth was vast, extending from bank to bank and from the Tower of London down the river to Blackfriars Bridge.

Combined with the smoke and haze and mist, and the leaping light of the fires, the underwater labyrinth of light shone with an ethereal luminosity that was, even within the destruction of the air raid, one of the most beautiful things any of the watchers had ever seen.

"Grace?" Jack said very softly, and she smiled at him, and nodded.

She lifted her hand from his—Jack lowering his arm as she did so—and stepped a pace away from him.

"Behold," she said, softly but with such clarity that all heard her, "the Kingman stands before the labyrinth, here, on this night wrapped all about with mystery and magic."

As she spoke, both Jack and Grace twisted down from the sky the powerful harmonies of the air raid, the pain and the fear and the destruction and the jubilation of the Luftwaffe pilots, the roaring power of the fires, until it suffused their very beings, and throbbed through their bodies with every beat of their hearts.

We don't allow it to corrupt us, Jack. We only use it.

He gave a nod, and she continued.

"Here, this night, in this ancient and much beloved land, he will raise up a great mystery which will, in turn, lift from the land that which has corrupted it so that the land, and all who depend on her and live on her, may live better lives because of it." Grace's voice strengthened. "Here, tonight, we shall witness the rebirth of hope, and light, and watch as our Kingman consecrates the talisman which shall raise us from the tarnish that besets us!"

Grace raised up her arms as she spoke that last, and the light from the water sprites' eyes pulsed forth once, twice, then a third time.

Then she lowered her arms, and her head besides, and seemed almost to fade into the mist. Her task now was simply to keep watch, and to maintain, with Jack, the power they were spiraling down from the air raid.

Now Jack stepped forward. As he had, so many thousands of years ago when he had been Brutus, he danced into the labyrinth, save that this time he danced atop the water, his feet resting on the hands of the water sprites held just under the surface, rather than over the stone paths of the labyrinth he had constructed for the Troy Game.

He lifted his left hand high. When he had been Brutus, Jack had carried a ball of pitch in that hand. Tonight he held a similar ball of darkness, save that it appeared to

have been comprised of writhing darkness rather than pitch. His right hand Jack held out before him, his arm slightly curved, as if he held a woman within its bounds.

His body moved slowly and very sensuously, displaying its beauty as he danced deeper and deeper into the labyrinth, his feet making a tiny splash each time he set one down. With each dance step one of his legs lifted, its foot turned slightly outward, held, then lowered, moving the dance forward with measured deliberation.

With each dance step, his left hand, high above his head, moved a little, twisting the ball of darkness this way and that, his head moving slowly, deliberately, counterwise below his hand.

As that ball of darkness twisted first this way and then that in Jack's hand, so tendrils of darkness slithered out of the city, all from the northern bank, and vanished into the ball. The watchers on the bank (save Grace, who kept her head down, concentrating) winced every time a new tendril of darkness slunk out of the night sky, seeping its way into the ball.

Everyone knew what they were.

For over an hour Jack danced his way deeper and deeper into the labyrinth. He was too far away now for any on the bank to see the expression on his face, or to witness the trembling of his muscles, but Grace, standing so close, was clearly struggling to maintain control, not merely of the Dance of the Torches, but also of the malevolent power she and Jack were twisting out of the destruction around London. At one point Noah made a small sound, and moved as if she wanted to go to her daughter, but Ariadne whipped out a hand, and held her back.

They must do this alone, Noah.

So Noah restrained herself—barely—but her eyes did not leave the form of her daughter.

Eventually, Jack reached the heart of the labyrinth.

HE HAD DANCED HIS WAY THROUGH THE ENTIRE labyrinth on top of the river, but as he reached its center,

Jack found himself once more standing within the crypt of St. Thomas'.

For a long moment he stood, almost frozen in his dancing position, his left hand still held high, his right leg frozen in an arc.

Then he very slowly set himself in motion again, and danced the final few steps to the altar.

Here he stopped, standing upright, lowering his left hand until he held the ball of darkness in both hands, slightly extended out before him at waist level.

When he had been Brutus and dancing the opening of the Troy Game, a variety of evils and darknesses had followed him through the labyrinth into its dark heart. But the Shadow Game was constructed not to entrap evil in general, but only one evil, and thus the darkness that had accumulated in the ball Jack had carried represented only the evil which had created the Troy Game.

Jack stood before the altar of the crypt of St. Thomas', then, achingly slowly, his muscles trembling as if this cost him the greatest effort, Jack pulled out, one by one, objects from the ball.

The first object Jack pulled from the ball was an arrow, its tip stained with old, dark blood.

The arrow with which Brutus had murdered his father, Silvius.

Jack laid it on the altar.

The next object he pulled from the ball was a dark eye patch, encrusted with old blood like the arrow.

Silvius' eye patch, which he had worn through all those centuries when he had hated his son.

Then Jack drew forth from the ball a stunningly beautiful ruby and gold bracelet.

Cornelia's bracelet, representing everything she had once been.

One by one, Jack drew forth from the ball, and added to the altar, the sword with which he, as Brutus, had murdered Coel; Ariadne's flounced red silk skirt; Asterion's twisted horn dagger, its haft cracked with age, and its knife blade nicked and dulled; the necklaces and rings that Genvissa

had worn; and a cracked and terribly misshapen skull—what remained of Loth's malformed head.

Only then, as he drew forth the final object, did the ball vanish.

The instant it did, Jack heard a wail coming from the back of the altar, and he whipped about.

Grace lay there, her beautiful skin bloodied and bruised, her white linen skirt torn and dirty, her hair awry, her face twisted in such desolation that Jack thought his heart would fail.

She extended one hand toward him. "Don't leave me here, Jack! *Please, Jack, don't leave me here!*"

Jack knew what he was seeing. As when he had founded the Troy Game, he confronted his own fears and his own darknesses within the dark heart of the labyrinth.

And, as previously, Jack knew what he had to do in order to found the strongest Game possible.

He stared at Grace, hoping that she would read his love for her etched into his face.

Then he turned, and left her.

Chapter Six

EPPING FOREST

Thursday, 17 April 1941

JUST AS JACK TURNED HIS BACK ON GRACE, A bomber flying high overhead disgorged its last stick of high explosive for the night.

One of the bombs fell erratically, wildly, on a far different track than its fellows.

It struck the roof of the north transept of St. Paul's, bursting through, then hit the floor of the cathedral where it ex-

ploded, the explosion creating a massive crater into the crypt.

The White Queen's Game had taken its first bite.

CATLING SEETHED INTO LIFE. SHE HAD BEEN UN-settled the entire night . . . something was happening . . . but she couldn't define what it was, and wondered if perhaps she was mistaken. Maybe it was just the massive air raid which made her shudder so, or maybe it was the night-marish conflagrations within the eastern and southern parts of London that made her so edgy.

Maybe.

And maybe Jack and Noah were opening their move against her.

She crouched amid the dust and debris that filtered through the crypt, and snarled. None of the emergency workers or the members of the cathedral Watch could see her, but they could all feel the malevolence in the air.

They put it down to the bomb and the destruction it had wrought, not realizing for a moment what else inhabited the crypt with them.

Jack . . . Catling whispered.

JACK EMERGED BACK INTO EPPING FOREST. IT DIS-oriented him, because he had expected to appear back on the Southwark bank where he had left Grace and the others.

Why here?

Grace.

Jack couldn't forget the terrible image of her, despair-ing, in the crypt. He knew it was only a vision of what *could* be, he knew that Grace was either still at Southwark or on her way back to Copt Hall, but even so, he couldn't repress a sickening sense of loss that flooded his being.

He looked about. It was near dawn, a faint light tinging the eastern sky.

He was close to Ambersbury Banks, and thus close to Copt Hall.

Maybe Grace was waiting for him there.

He turned to the west, but before he had taken two strides Catling appeared before him.

Jack stopped, his stomach feeling as though it was rising up into his mouth. He knew instantly it was Catling rather than the White Queen. He swallowed, fighting down fear. *What did she want? Why was she here?*

"Dressed as a Kingman, Jack?" Catling said, taking a single, terrible step closer to him. "And with *six* of the Kingship bands now? I always knew you had them. But what is this? I smell residual power about you. What *have* you been doing tonight?"

She was very alert, very tightly strung, and Jack realized she'd felt *something*.

"Did you not feel the raid tonight?" Jack said, injecting anger into his voice. "Did you not *feel* the destruction and the terror? For all the gods' sakes, Catling, you are the one reflecting that destruction into the Faerie! That's where I have been, damn you, trying with every power I have to deflect your *cursed* malice!"

His voice broke a little on his last sentence: not through any skill of acting, but through sheer emotion and fear. All he wanted was to get away from Catling before she discovered the truth, get away from her before someone else (*Grace!*) happened upon them in the forest and uncovered unwittingly his lie to Catling.

All he wanted was to get away from Catling and get back to Grace and take her in his arms, and know that she was still safe.

Again Catling nodded, but Jack could see the mistrust in her eyes, and knew she didn't believe him. She smiled, so coldly it risked delaying spring by a month.

"Finish me," she said. "Delay as long as you will, Jack, for I cannot force you onto the dancing floor. But know that each day you delay I grow stronger."

Jack stared at Catling a moment, then gave a terse nod of his own, and walked away.

* * *

WHEN JACK GOT BACK TO COPT HALL GRACE WAS there, waiting for him.

Jack enveloped her in a tight embrace, holding her as close to him as possible.

"Thank God," he whispered. He knew now that if he lost her when they closed the Shadow Game, then he would not be able to live knowing she was trapped in its dark heart with Catling.

Chapter Seven

THE FAERIE

Friday, 18 April 1941

*J*ACK MET WITH NOAH AND THE LORD OF THE Faerie atop The Naked. The Faerie was now beyond the desperate. The hills surrounding The Naked were virtually barren dust, save for the odd tree here and there which had somehow managed to survive the desolation. The Faerie folk, those that had survived the desolation, were huddled in small groups about the slopes of The Naked, silent, blank-eyed.

"Look!" said the Lord of the Faerie. "Look!" He gestured to the devastated hills about him, fought to find words to speak, then shook his head helplessly. "We cannot survive much longer," he said eventually, his voice almost as lifeless as the Faerie.

Jack wondered if he should relate the conversation he'd had with Catling, then decided against it. No need to further worry anyone here.

"Have you built the devising yet?" he asked Noah. "Discovered somewhere to shelter Grace?" He'd barely seen Noah since the sixth of April, when he'd told the assembled

group of his plans. He knew Noah had spoken to Ariadne and Silvius, but he did not know the details of that conversation.

"Yes," Noah said. "The Idyll will be the perfect place to—"

"No!" Jack said. "Catling has already penetrated the Idyll."

"The Idyll has isolated itself entirely," Noah said. "As soon as the Faerie began to decay, the Idyll retreated. Remember, it is the essence of Weyland, and its very nature is to hide and isolate itself the moment it feels itself under threat. I know Catling penetrated the Idyll to hex Grace, but the Idyll is far more tightly shuttered now than it was then. And I have the devising that will keep Catling's hex from touching Grace. I *can* wall off the Idyll."

Jack said nothing, regarding Noah with a steady, probing gaze.

"Damn you!" Noah said, low. "Grace is my *daughter*! I will *not* risk her unless I think she has a good chance of being safe. *I can shelter her, Jack!*"

"I need more reassurance than that," he said.

"What more can I say? What do you want? A badge? A statutory declaration? Something written and signed on letterhead? We are *all* going into this blind, Jack. I have done as much as I can. I am certain it will work. There is *nothing* else I can say or do."

"For all the gods' sakes," said the Lord of the Faerie, "listen to you both! If this is the best the land can hope for, then gods help us!"

Jack took a step away, looking over the rolling hills, his entire stance tense, taking a few moments to calm himself down.

"I want Grace to survive," he said finally, softly, without turning around.

"We all do, Jack," said the Lord of the Faerie, "but the land must come first. Whatever happens to Grace, the land must come first."

"You want me to sacrifice her willingly?" Jack said, whipping about.

"Not 'willingly,' Jack" said the Lord of the Faerie, hold-

ing his gaze, "but I do expect you—and Grace—to do what is needed to save the land. The land *must* come first, the entrapment of the Troy Game *must* come before Grace. I know that. You know that." He paused, still holding Jack's furious gaze. "Grace knows that."

Jack stared a moment longer, then he turned, and walked away down The Naked.

Noah went to follow him, but the Lord of the Faerie caught at her arm. "Noah, how sure are you that your devising will work? How safe *is* Grace?"

"Not enough," she whispered, "is the answer to both your questions."

And then she, too, was gone.

CATLING SAT ALONE IN THE HEART OF THE TROY Game, feeling the labyrinthine powers of the Game swirl about her.

She was more certain than ever that Jack and Noah would launch an attack on her during the Dance of the Flowers.

Well, she was ready for them. Whatever happened to her *would* happen to Grace.

Catling's face contorted in a rictus of a smile. She raised her hands, revealing the red wool twisted about them. Her fingers began to move, layering the hex that bound her to Grace under new depths of malevolent constructions.

After a while, the wool began to scream.

"GRACE?"

She turned around from the fire in the drawing room, wondering how it was that the Lord of the Faerie had managed to get past Malcolm's watchful eye.

"He is upstairs, running your bath," said the Lord of the Faerie. "I did not knock. I just entered."

"Please," said Grace, "sit down."

"I will continue to stand, if you please," the Faerie lord said, his posture stiff, his words awkward, and Grace tensed in response.

"What can I do for you, Coel?" she said.

"Grace, if your mother's devising fails, if you are trapped within the heart of the Shadow Game, will you continue to—"

"Stop," she said, taking a half step back toward the fire. "Don't. Coel . . . for gods' sakes, we were lovers once, and—"

"I need to know, Grace. I am for the land, first and foremost. What we once did in a bed is beside the point. Will you continue to do what is right?"

"*Do* you have a heart?" she said. "Do you have even a faint shadow of one left?"

Something flickered in his face. "My heart has died along with the Faerie. I am not Jack, Grace. I would rather the land survive than you."

She blanched, unable to answer.

"Grace, please. Just answer the question. Will you continue the dance, even if trapped inside—"

"Yes! *Yes!* Damn you, Coel, get out!"

"I'm sorry, Grace," he said. "I had to—"

"Leave now," said Malcolm's voice from the doorway. "There is no place for you here."

The Lord of the Faerie turned, sent Malcolm an unreadable look, glanced once more at Grace, then left the room.

Grace now had her arms wrapped about her chest as if she were beset by terrible cold. "Malcolm, do you believe the White Queen when she says that she can, and will, do nothing for me?"

He didn't answer, not in words, just walking over and taking her in his arms.

Grace clung to him, her shoulders shaking.

Chapter Eight

THE SAVOY

Saturday, 19 April, to Friday, 9 May 1941

Grace Speaks

*J*FELT AS IF I COULD NOT GET WARM, NO MAT-
ter the trouble I took. Coldness enveloped me, as if as-
sessing me for long-term companionship.

I wondered if the dark heart of the Shadow Game was
cold.

Everyone that mattered, Jack and Malcolm foremost, my
parents and Ariadne and Silvius next, were brightly—and,
to my eyes, falsely—cheerful.

*Everything will be all right, sweeting. Here, let me hold
you, comfort you, reassure you.*

But all I could ever think about was Jack's lack of confi-
dence, which he let slip in a myriad small ways, and my
mother's likewise, and the Lord of the Faerie, standing be-
fore me, making sure that when I was trapped in the dark
heart of the Shadow Game with Catling I would continue
to "do the right thing."

How bloody *British* of him.

The land might be saved, and the Troy Game might be
halted in its tracks and entombed, but it looked to me like
everyone would be having their celebrations without me.

I felt myself slide back into the black hole of hopeless-
ness that had once ruled my life, and I couldn't do a thing
about it. Jack did his best. He bent over backward to be lov-
ing and kind and reassuring.

But there wasn't a thing he could do, either.

I was lost. I was certain of it, and that great, terrible weight of impending doom dragged about with me every waking moment.

I couldn't help but wonder what it would be like, trapped inside the dark heart, with a raging, vengeful Catling.

I TRIED TO BE CHEERFUL, AND BECAUSE JACK needed to spend time with my parents, and Ariadne and Silvius, he pretended to take that cheerfulness at face value. He spent most of the days at the Savoy, where Silvius and Ariadne joined him, working out the steps of the entwining Games with them, and making sure that Ariadne and Silvius understood, and could manage, the devising that my mother had made to protect me.

I went along every so often as well, mainly to practice with my father the steps of the Dance of the Flowers. Although Weyland would wield little power during the dance, he did need to mirror Jack's steps precisely, and in complete harmony with him, for the Flower Gate to begin to raise at the Shadow Game as well as at the Troy Game.

Jack was obsessed with timing. He berated everyone—save me—for lack of concentration, or application, or the occasional stumbling, which tore apart the critical sequence of events needed to ensure success. He snapped and snarled, he cajoled, he even wept in frustration, but in the end he had what he wanted. By Friday the ninth of May he said that he was as satisfied as he could possibly be.

There was one last thing we needed to do, he said.

We needed, all three couples, to go dancing in the Savoy's ballroom one last time.

IT WAS A REHEARSAL FOR WHAT WE'D NEED TO do—oh *gods*—tomorrow night, when the White Queen had told us a major raid was due. Where better than the dance floor of the Savoy's ballroom?

I should have been nervous, depressed (my fate would

be decided *tomorrow*) but instead I found the experience calming and settling.

All other dancers melted away as we took to the dance floor. Silvius, Weyland, and Jack were in evening dress, Noah, Ariadne, and I in svelte black gowns. I wonder what the watchers thought of us, three couples all dancing separately, but somehow so connected, so allied, that when one made a step, so also did five others.

It worked. It worked beautifully. I began dancing with my father, and Jack with my mother, but as the dance progressed then so Jack and my father changed places smoothly, effortlessly, missing not a beat or jarring our entwined harmonies. As Jack took me in his arms I saw the relief in his eyes, felt him relax against me, and suddenly, blindingly, I believed that everything would work.

It had to. This was too perfect to be an illusion.

Chapter Nine

ST. PAUL'S AND SOUTHWARK

Saturday, 10 May 1941

THEY STOOD UNDER THE DOME OF ST. Paul's. Around them wandered members of the cathedral Watch, uneasy and vigilant as the air raid above intensified; they did not see the man and woman standing so close together.

Jack and Noah stood facing each other, cheek to cheek, touching in a myriad of different places, taking comfort from each other's warmth. They were dressed as Kingman and Mistress of the Labyrinth, wearing little else save their white linen wraps. In her left hand Noah dangled a large spray of early spring columbines. They were peculiarly

still, their eyes downcast, their breathing slow and deep. Even the marks on Jack's shoulders were quiescent.

They were waiting, for the moment when they might start, and the other two pair with them.

They were communing, both with themselves and with the other two sets of dancers—Weyland and Grace at Southwark, preparing to step onto the labyrinth lit by the water sprites, and Ariadne and Silvius atop the ancient Keep within the Tower of London, where they could draw on the power of the ancient God Well deep below the structure's foundations.

They were deepening themselves with the land, preparing to pull behind them all their powers as Ringwalker and Eaving.

They were making peace with each other, marking both a start and an end. For almost four thousand years they had battled with each other and with the world about them. Now they would battle no more.

At precisely the same instant, each lifted their right hand and slowly, caressingly, ran it up their partner's left arm to the shoulder.

AT SOUTHWARK, SO ALSO DID WEYLAND AND Grace lift their hands to their partner, and at the Tower, so also did Ariadne and Silvius.

CATLING WAS DEEP IN THE DARK HEART OF THE Troy Game. She watched Jack and Noah above her, as if all the layers of rock and stone in between were transparent, and between her fingers the red wool twisted and frayed into a myriad patterns.

Catling muttered as she wove the wool, the words tripping unintelligibly from her tongue.

HIGH ABOVE, ON THE MARBLE FLOOR UNDER THE dome of the cathedral, Noah and Jack turned slowly away from each other, their hands dropping away reluctantly from

their partner's shoulder, walking—a movement so sensuous, so lyrical, it was more dance than walk—to opposite sides of the dome. As they had in late December, Noah moved to the eastern sector of the dome, Jack to the western.

Again, as in December, once they had reached their places, Noah stood still, her eyes on Jack, as he raised the labyrinth from the depths. Five months ago this had been difficult work for him, but now Jack had the six bands— and something else, Noah thought, although she couldn't quite define that "else." Jack had somehow grown in the past few months—not just in power, but in . . .

Serenity, Noah thought. He has grown in serenity and contentment. When they'd tried this in December, Jack had been distraught and unstill. Unsure.

Now, he was at peace with himself, and it showed in every movement, and in the ease with which he handled his power.

On the banks of the Thames at Southwark, Grace and Weyland mirrored precisely Jack and Noah's movements. As they turned away from each other, they moved on to the water, over the labyrinth surrounding the crypt of St. Thomas', their feet supported by the hands of thousands of water sprites who hovered just below the surface.

When Weyland had moved to the western sector of the water over which they danced, he raised his hands at precisely the same time as did Jack in St. Paul's, and, on command, as the labyrinth rose under the dome of St. Paul's, so the labyrinth rose from the depths under the water, lit by the eyes of the sprites.

Power flowed smoothly between Jack and Weyland; although it was Weyland standing on the water opposite Grace, it was Jack's spirit and power that acted through him.

ATOP THE ANCIENT KEEP IN THE TOWER OF LON- don, Ariadne and Silvius did not move. They remained close to each other, locked in contemplation as they continued to draw power from the God Well deep under the Keep.

Their time was yet to come.

* * *

DEEP IN THE DARK HEART OF THE TROY GAME,
Catling abruptly stilled.

"Something is wrong," she said.

Chapter Ten

St. Paul's, Southwark,
and the Tower of London

Saturday, 10 May 1941

ACK AND NOAH (SHADOWED BY WEYLAND
and Grace) danced about the perimeter of the
labyrinth, their movements slow, fluid, seductive,
their eyes not leaving each other. As she danced, so Noah
(and so, in turn her daughter, Grace) allowed single
columbines to flutter downward from the spray she carried.

They marked the external perimeter of the labyrinth, the
head of each spray of flowers turning so that it faced
toward the dark heart in the center of the labyrinth.

In St. Paul's, a seething blackness arose at the heart of
the labyrinth, which showed glimpses of something red
and twisting in its heart.

At Southwark, as Grace and Weyland danced about the
perimeter of the labyrinth, the waters opened over the crypt
of St. Thomas', twisting downward in a motionless vortex.

IN ST. PAUL'S CRYPT CATLING ROSE TO HER FEET,
her face ashen, her eyes glittering between incredulity and
anger.

"How?" she whispered as she saw before her a vision of the labyrinth rising under the Thames.

Catling had expected many, many treacheries from Jack and Noah, but not this.

Not a *new* Game.

HIGH ABOVE CATLING, UNDER THE DOME OF THE cathedral, and at Southwark, over the buried crypt of St. Thomas', the flowers that the Mistresses had scattered about the perimeter of the labyrinths now slowly started to slide toward the entrances of each labyrinth.

Each pair of dancers now moved toward the entrance of their respective labyrinth also, their movements still seductive and measured, their eyes still on those of their partners.

As they came to within ten paces of each entrance, the flowers slowly began to rise, weaving themselves into a gate.

"GRACE? GRACE?" SAID CATLING. "WHAT IS THIS you do?"

Catling had finally, devastatingly, realized what was happening—*there was another Game . . . how? How?*—and all she could think of was Grace. Not what Jack and Noah might be doing, but what Grace was doing.

Dancing the *closure, dammit,* of a new Game, one meant to trap Catling.

"You think to trap me?" Catling said, her voice stronger now. "You really think you can do *that*?"

Then, in her next heartbeat, Catling knew they could, for the Shadow Game sent forth the first of its irresistible, deadly siren calls, twisting its hooks into Catling's soul.

Tugging, gently for the moment, but Catling knew all too well how soon those gentle tugs would turn into an agonizing wrenching.

And all Catling could think of was Grace. *Grace* was dancing this Game.

"Don't you know what I can do to you?" Catling said,

and she raised her hands, the deadly tangle of red wool between them.

AS THE TWO FLOWER GATES BEGAN TO RISE, ARIadne and Silvius finally moved. In their minds' eyes they could see Grace as she danced with Weyland, and they concentrated on her with all their power. At the same time they began to dance. Although the rhythm of their movements was similar to those of the other four dancers, the dance they executed was strikingly dissimilar. They did not dance about a gigantic labyrinth, but instead executed a tight dance directly over the God Well, their hands constantly touching as they wove back and forth, and in and out, as if they were acting out the weaving of a gigantic basket.

IN ST. PAUL'S NOAH CAUGHT JACK'S EYES.

When, Jack? When? How much further should they allow their Flower Gate to grow? How much longer should they give Ariadne and Silvius to build the devising Noah had taught them?

Soon, he whispered back into her mind. *Very soon.*

She knows, Jack. Catling knows. I can feel her seething.

Jack did not reply to that. Aye, Catling knew. He could feel her anger as Noah could, coiling under his feet and through every fiber of his being.

He could also feel the direction of that anger. Not at him, or Noah, but exclusively toward Grace.

Every instinct screamed at him to move now, but he knew he couldn't. He had to wait, wait until they were all ready, until they were all attuned, until they were all at the peak of their dances.

He had to wait until Ariadne and Silvius were ready, and that would not be for a minute or two yet.

Meanwhile, the two Flower Gates continued to build, the Shadow Game increased its pull on Catling, and Catling . . .

All Catling seemed to be doing was channelling every ounce of malevolence she had toward Grace.

Jack hung on for as long as he could. Then, finally, he sent his senses scrying for Ariadne and Silvius, to make sure they were ready, then he looked at Noah, and with both mind and physical voice, said to her, *"Stop!"*

Several things happened at once.

Chapter Eleven

St. Paul's, Southwark, and the Tower of London

Saturday, 10 May 1941

ⱭACK AND NOAH STEPPED BACK FROM THE Flower Gate, withdrawing all their power from it.

The Flower Gate crumpled, the columbines scattering over the floor and blackening, as if they had been burned.

The next instant Jack's form glowed, distorted, and suddenly it was Weyland standing there. He blinked, then reached out for Noah.

"Quick," he said. "We need to get out of here."

AT SOUTHWARK, JACK APPEARED WHERE, BUT A heartbeat earlier, Weyland had been standing. He reached out his hand, grasping Grace's tightly.

The Flower Gate of the Shadow Game, before which they stood, shuddered slightly as the transfer was made, but then strengthened, its flowers forming an even tighter weave than previously.

About them came the sound of a thin wail.

Catling, perhaps, or the power of the Shadow Game drawing her in.

CATLING WAS NOW CONCENTRATING EVERYTHING she had on Grace. She was fully aware of what was happening—somehow a new Game had been made, its only purpose to trap her—but she also knew that she could concentrate on only one thing: either try to extricate herself from the clutches of the new Game, or to make sure that Grace would be pulled in with her. She couldn't afford anger now; better to leave that for later when she wasn't in so much danger.

Of the two Catling preferred the latter course of action. She wasn't entirely sure she could escape the clutches of the new Game (it was so powerful! From where had they discovered the knowledge to make something this powerful?), but she was certain, absolutely certain, that if she pulled Grace into the Game's dark heart with her then Jack and Grace (who Catling realized was partnering him in this Game) would not complete the Game.

Grace might continue her dance, but Catling was *certain* that Jack wouldn't. He couldn't bear to think of Grace trapped with Catling for an eternity. Jack may have convinced himself that he'd be able to close this new Game out . . . but Catling knew Jack better than he knew himself.

She knew he would never do it.

I have you, Grace, Catling whispered, very, very glad now that she'd put the extra effort into strengthening the hex that bound them.

But no need to close the hex just yet. No. Why alert anyone? Catling decided to wait just a little bit longer. Let them think they'd succeeded . . . then pounce.

AS GRACE AND JACK CONCENTRATED EVERY-thing they had on completing the Shadow Game, Ariadne and Silvius put their entire beings into the devising meant

to protect Grace. While the building of the devising took concentration and skill, and not a little effort, the critical factor was timing. It was better that Grace stay in sight of Jack, *with* Jack, for as long as possible before they spirited her away into the Idyll, but leave her there too long, and the chances that Catling would snatch her first increased by the second.

Ariadne and Silvius could push Grace from the Shadow Game into the Idyll, but they did not have the power to push her from the Game's dark heart into the Idyll. If Catling got her first, then Grace was lost.

They could feel Noah's power behind them. She wasn't interfering, but she was lending them all the power and support she could. Weyland was there, too, opening the Idyll for them, preparing the way.

Soon, Ariadne whispered to Silvius. *Soon.*

Then Catling struck.

THE SHADOW GAME HAD BEEN DRAWING HER closer and closer to St. Thomas' crypt. Catling had been resisting, and had slowed her approach, but she could not halt the movement.

If she didn't do something soon, then she'd be pulled into the Game's foul dark heart.

It was on the approach that Catling became aware of Ariadne and Silvius atop the Keep. She didn't know the precise nature of their enchantment, but she was well aware of its purpose: to protect Grace.

Thus, at precisely the same moment that Catling tightened her hold over Grace, she attacked Ariadne and Silvius.

THE ATTACK WAS NOT PHYSICAL, BUT POWER based. Ariadne and Silvius suddenly felt their power rock, as if something had slammed against it.

Then again, but more powerful this time.

The devising they had been building began to shudder.

* * *

JACK AND GRACE FELT IT AT THE SAME TIME. JACK saw Grace's eyes widen in fright, and he fought to keep himself calm. *Ariadne,* he commanded, *send Grace into the Idyll now. Now, damn you!*

It is too early, Ariadne said.

You have no choice. Do it now!

A heartbeat, a single heartbeat in which Jack stared into Grace's terror-filled eyes, and then she vanished.

The Flower Gate rocked, stabilized, and then, achingly slowly, the flowers kept on building.

Wherever Grace was, she was continuing the dance.

Ariadne knew that Grace had managed to get to the Idyll, and she could sense that Grace was continuing her part of the Dance of the Flowers there, but at the same time she realized that she and Silvius could not close out the devising. Somehow Catling had got her clutches into the devising, somehow her power was reaching into the Idyll as it had so many years ago when first she had hexed Grace, and Ariadne knew, with a deepening sense of horror, that Grace was not safe.

Jack, she screamed, *finish the Game now. Do it now, gods, do it now!*

Before she could say or do anything further, Ariadne felt her power tear apart completely.

Chapter Twelve

THE IDYLL

Saturday, 10 May 1941

Grace Speaks

COULDN'T REMEMBER PRECISELY WHAT IT had felt like when I'd been a baby and Catling had sent her imps into the Idyll to hex me, but I didn't imagine it could have felt any worse than this did, right now. Everything happened so fast, and so powerfully. Jack and I had been dancing the Flower Gate into its entirety, and had felt Ariadne and Silvius constructing my mother's devising. We could feel Catling, feel her anger and malevolence, but we could also feel the Shadow Game's grip on her, and sense her inexorable drag into the crypt of St. Thomas'.

Then Catling did what no one had anticipated—she attacked Ariadne and Silvius, and disrupted the smooth flow of their power. Ariadne screamed, Jack yelled, and suddenly I felt myself enveloped in the devising and was propelled into the Idyll.

I had no time for thought. I *had* to continue the Dance of the Flowers with Jack, had to get that Flower Gate up, but, oh, gods, I could feel Catling reaching into the Idyll. It wasn't just that Catling had disrupted Ariadne and Silvius' dance, it was that she'd somehow *strengthened* the hex that bound us.

I didn't think Ariadne and Silvius could strengthen the devising. They didn't have the power, and my mother's devising wasn't strong enough, in any case.

Catling was going to drag me out.

Oh gods, oh gods, I could feel the pull of the Shadow Game on Catling, and at the same time I could feel Catling's pull on me.

I went cold with dread. I also felt astoundingly sad, and I realized that the overwhelming emotion that I would feel when trapped in the dark heart with Catling would be this sadness. Not fright or terror or hopelessness.

Sadness, at everything that could have been. It was, I realized in a moment of blinding clarity, the feeling that enveloped many people at the moment of their death.

Sadness, at everything that might have been.

Voices surrounded me, screaming. My mother, somewhere, desperate. Ariadne and Silvius, in agony, as if Catling was devouring them.

Jack, frantic, but still dancing.

I continued the dance in harmony with him.

How heartbreaking, I thought, that I would still do this. How heartbreaking, that I would put duty first before struggling for my own freedom.

And how astoundingly heartbreaking, I thought, that Jack was continuing the dance as well.

We would both prefer to lose our future together than allow Catling freedom.

The only satisfaction I had was that I could, at the same moment, hear and sense everything else, feel Catling's incredulity and growing terror that Jack *was* still dancing, and that the Flower Gate was closing.

I could feel it close. I could see that last flower dropping into place.

And I felt myself being pulled out of the Idyll.

Catling had me. Finally, Catling had me.

Everything went black, and for all the time thereafter there was only . . . sadness.

That feeling which envelops so many people at the moment of their death.

Chapter Thirteen

SOUTHWARK

Saturday, 10 May 1941

*J*ACK FELT CATLING SEIZE GRACE, FELT Catling pull Grace, and knew that Grace was lost.

Noah's devising couldn't hold her. Ariadne and Silvius had not completed it, or the devising had not been strong enough to start with.

Catling had strengthened the hex beyond anything Jack had expected. Jack could feel it, he could taste it, and he knew that there was nothing left on earth, heaven, or hell that could prevent Catling from dragging Grace into the heart of the Shadow Game.

He screamed, even though he kept dancing, because he knew he could do nothing to stop Catling.

He screamed, even though he kept dancing, because he could feel Grace's horror and, worse, her resignation.

He screamed, because he knew Grace was continuing to dance as well.

He screamed, because he knew he could not save Grace, and that she was condemned to an eternity locked with Catling in the dark heart of the Shadow Game.

THE SPIRE OF ST. DUNSTAN'S-IN-THE-EAST EXploded. The high explosive bomb had dropped directly on the spire, and its detonation blew the entire structure apart. The rest of the building, the nave and outbuildings, caught alight.

Within two hours, the nave was a burned-out hulk, and the beautiful spire that Sir Christopher Wren had designed

*and personally supervised during its construction was a
pile of sooty rubble.*

Everything lay in rubble: hopes, dreams, and loves.
Nothing could be saved.

Chapter Fourteen

Southwark

Saturday, 10 May 1941

WHERE IS SHE? WHERE IS SHE?" NOAH HAD
her hands on Jack's shoulders, shaking him
slightly every time she uttered the word "is."

About them the rolling thunder of the air raid continued,
distant thuds and explosions, the roar and crackle of flame.

Jack appeared dazed. He didn't react to Noah's grip or to
her voice, merely stared with glazed eyes out to the water
where, only moments ago, he had been dancing with Grace.

But then everything had gone wrong. Catling had
snatched . . . "Jack!" Noah screamed at him.

To one side Weyland stood, looking almost as shell-
shocked as Jack. As Noah continued to shake Jack, Ariadne
and Silvius appeared, both leaning on each other, both
wearing devastated expressions.

Noah drew back one hand and dealt Jack a sharp blow
across the face. "Damn you," she hissed. "Where is Grace?
I can't sense her!"

Jack finally responded. He raised his eyes, looked at
each person one by one, and finally rasped, "She's trapped
with Catling. We've lost her."

Noah's eyes went impossibly wide, and she made a
sound partly between a whimper and a groan.

Weyland's mouth dropped open, very slightly, then he

moved, lunging the two paces that separated him from Jack and grabbing at Jack's hair, wrenching the man's head about. "Where . . . is . . . my . . . *daughter?*"

"She's trapped with Catling!" This time Jack roared the words, wrenching himself out of Weyland's grip.

"The devising—" Ariadne began.

"The devising wasn't strong enough!" Jack said. "And Catling had increased the power of her hex. *Grace is trapped with Catling!*"

"No," Noah whispered.

"Yes!" Jack said. "Yes, yes, *yes!*" He paused, then continued in a whisper. "Jesus Christ . . . *yes.*"

"Jack," said Silvius. He moved to his son's side, hesitated, then put a hand on Jack's shoulder. "Are you certain?"

Jack raised his face to his father, and Silvius needed no other answer than the devastation he could see in his son's eyes.

"Oh gods," Silvius whispered. "Catling took her."

"No . . ." Noah whimpered.

MUCH LATER, WHEN THEY WERE THE ONLY ONES left on the bank, Ariadne and Silvius turned to study London burning across the river.

"The Troy Game is gone," Ariadne observed. Her voice was listless, her shoulders slumped.

"Aye," said Silvius. "Grace must have kept on dancing, even though she knew she was trapped. She and Jack completed the Shadow Game and trapped Catling. The Troy Game *is* gone, but Grace is gone with it."

Ariadne was silent a very long time. Then, finally she turned to Silvius and allowed him to envelop her in his arms.

"How can any of us continue to live?" she said.

Epilogue

ST. DUNSTAN'S-IN-THE-EAST, LONDON,
AND COPT HALL

1971

A CROWD OF SOME TWO HUNDRED PEOPLE crowded into Idol Lane, spilling over into the churchyard of St. Dunstan's-in-the-East. It was a fine day, and the ruined church, despite its lack of a roof and its blackened walls, managed to look both beautiful and peaceful.

And, somehow, useful.

London had been so devastated by the war, and so much had been destroyed, that rebuilding had taken decades. In the immediate postwar period there had not been the money or the raw materials to rebuild St. Dunstan's. What finance and materials there were had gone into rebuilding homes and businesses and hospitals and docklands.

God's houses had been forced to wait.

When money and materials finally became available, some twenty years after the war, the ruins of many of London's ancient churches were bulldozed. As central London had been abandoned to business and finance, congregations of many of the churches had shrunk until there were

only a handful of worshippers left. Better to amalgamate parishes than to rebuild everything that had been ruined.

After hundreds of years, there was no one left for St. Dunstan's-in-the-East. The church came perilously close to being demolished to make room for an office block, but in the end the decision was made to make the leaning walls safe, and turn the churchyard into a garden and a place for contemplation.

Although the main body of the church was to be left a ruin, due to the efforts of a small, vociferous group of people—led by the Philpot brothers, who ran the White Queen Security Service in central London, and who personally put up the money—Wren's beautiful spire was finally rebuilt.

Today it was to be reopened.

By midafternoon the speeches drew to a conclusion. A curtain was pulled back to reveal a plaque. The crowd clapped, then broke into a myriad small, chattering groups as cups of tea were handed about.

Within the crowd the Philpot brothers shook hands enthusiastically with the Lord Mayor and the elderly gentleman who had been the vicar of St. Dunstan's during the war, leered at several young girls in miniskirts, and winked conspiratorially at the tall, black-haired woman with the white face standing at the back of the gathering.

Finally, after an hour, the crowd started to thin.

The Philpot brothers disappeared, the white-faced woman with them.

Workmen dismantled the small dais on which the dignitaries had sat, and took away the chairs and tea cups.

The final few stragglers went home.

The newly opened spire and the churchyard gardens were left deserted.

Dusk drew in. The City closed down. Night fell.

Then, very softly, almost hesitantly, there came the sound of footfalls, descending the stairwell within the spire.

THE KNOCK AT THE FRONT DOOR STARTLED MAL- colm. Hardly anyone came to visit these days. Noah and

Weyland, never. Silvius and Ariadne only occasionally, and their last visit had been two weeks ago. They would not have come back so soon.

Malcolm sighed, put down the dishcloth, and walked through Copt Hall to the front door, glancing up the staircase as he did so.

There was no sound from Jack, upstairs in his bedroom.

When he reached the front door, Malcolm peered through the glass set into the wooden panels, but it was so dark outside he could make out little more than a shape.

A woman. Malcolm frowned. Stella?

Then he opened the door, and his world stopped.

Grace stood there.

She looked wan, and too thin, and very tired, but it was Grace, and if her face was weary, and her eyes brimming with emotion, then she also looked very peaceful.

Malcolm could not speak. He stood, his mouth gaping, staring, unable to comprehend what he saw.

She smiled, very slightly, a little sadly. "Hello, Malcolm."

He managed one word. *"Grace?"*

"Oh, Malcolm," Grace said, and burst into tears. She stepped over the threshold and hugged him, only managing a tremulous smile when Malcolm lifted his own arms and hugged her fiercely back.

"How?" said Malcolm. *"How?"*

"The Idyll saved me," Grace said as, finally, she stepped back, wiping the tears from her eyes. "Catling had me. The hex was so damned strong. My mother's devising was never going to hold me. But the Idyll . . ." She took a deep shuddery breath. "The Idyll had been breached once before by Catling—the day she sent her imps to place the hex on me. The Idyll never forgot it, nor ever ceased to resent it. When Catling reached in again, this time to use the hex to drag me into the dark heart of the Shadow Game with her, the Idyll . . ." She gave a small laugh, as if she could hardly believe this herself. "The Idyll lost its temper. That's the only way I can describe it. The Idyll lost its temper, repelled Catling, and . . . and undid the hex."

"What?"

"The Idyll knew how to unwind the hex, because it had seen how it was applied in the first instance. No one else. The Idyll understood the hex." Grace paused. "And having repelled Catling, and having undone the hex, it then blew apart St. Dunstan's-in-the-East's spire, destroying any way in or out, making *certain* Catling could not reach back in once more—but neither could I reach out to anyone to let them know where I was. It was my father who created the device that saved me, not my mother. Malcolm, *is* the Troy Game trapped?"

"Yes, and all this time we were sure you were trapped with it." Malcolm stared at Grace, still barely able to believe she was standing before him. "But you have been trapped in the *Idyll*?"

She nodded. "And it was only today that the spire was reopened. Only today that I could leave. Malcolm . . . how is Jack? Is he here?"

"Gods, Grace. It has been terrible. He thought—we *all* thought—you were in the Shadow Game's dark heart. We didn't . . ." His voice broke and he hugged Grace tightly to him once more. "The past thirty years have been terrible," he whispered.

"It has been *thirty years*?" Grace said. "My God, how has Jack managed?"

JACK SAT IN THE WINGBACK CHAIR BY THE BED-
room fire, staring unseeing at the flames.

This was the only way he could bear to live now—alone save for the ghostly presence of Malcolm, isolated, unthinking.

If he thought, then his existence became a hell, because shadowing every thought was the knowledge that Grace lived tormented in the dark heart of the Shadow Game. That while he lived and breathed and ran the forests, while he drew in breath and drank whisky and screamed at the stars, Grace lived shuttered away with Catling.

Always before him was that haunting vision he'd experienced on the night Grace and he had opened the Shadow

Game—Grace, lying bloodied and bruised on the floor of St. Thomas' crypt, a hand held out to him, her eyes pleading.

There came a soft knock at the door.

"Go away," muttered Jack.

A lengthy stillness, then the soft knock again.

"Go away, curse you!" Jack yelled, and threw the empty whisky glass against the door.

It shattered, and Jack thought he heard a breath on the other side of the door.

Malcolm, probably, wanting to offer him some damned druidic counseling.

"Go away," Jack whispered.

There came this time, not a knock, but the soft laying of a hand against the door, and then a forehead, and finally a cheek, wet with tears, pressed against the wood.

Jack couldn't hear it, only sense it.

"Go away," he whispered one last, futile time, then he rose, walked over to the door, and opened it.

Glossary

ACK-ACK: antiaircraft fire from London's defenses.

ALBA: ancient, and now vanished, city on the banks of the river Tiber in Italy.

AMBERSBURY BANKS: an ancient hill fort situated in the northern region of Epping Forest.

ANCIENT CAROL: that which is sung by the CAROLLER within the REALM OF THE FAERIE to welcome in both dawn and dusk.

ARIADNE: ancient MISTRESS OF THE LABYRINTH in Knossos on Crete at the GREAT FOUNDING LABYRINTH. She was the half-sister of ASTERION, the Minotaur, and also his lover. She betrayed him to Theseus.

ASTERION: the ancient Minotaur who inhabited the GREAT FOUNDING LABYRINTH in Knossos on Crete. Murdered by Theseus, and recalled from death by ARIADNE, in this current life he is known as WEYLAND ORR.

BANKS, NOAH: once CORNELIA, spoiled princess of MESOPOTAMA, Noah is now EAVING, goddess of the waters, DARKWITCH, and MISTRESS OF THE LABYRINTH. She lives with WEYLAND ORR (ASTERION) and their daughter, GRACE, at THE SAVOY in London.

BOUDICCA: queen of the Iceni, a British tribe, in the first century C.E., wife of PRASUTAGUS.

CAMULODUNUM COLONIA: the Roman name for Colchester.

CAROLLER, THE: the songstress who carols in the dawn and the dusk in the REALM OF THE FAERIE. See STELLA WENTWORTH.

CATASTROPHE, THE: after Theseus left ARIADNE, she responded by destroying much of the ancient Aegean world in revenge. This is known as the Catastrophe.

CATHEDRAL WATCH, THE: volunteers from among the staff and clergy of St. Paul's formed a Watch during the war in order to act as firefighters in case bombs hit the cathedral.

CATLING: the TROY GAME incarnate. The Troy Game took flesh as Catling in *Darkwitch Rising*.

CHAMBERLAIN, NEVILLE: prime minister of Great Britain from the late 1930s until May 1940.

CHURCHILL, WINSTON: prime minister of Great Britain from May 1940.

CLEMENTS, VERA: a nurse at Guy's Hospital.

COEL: a man of the Bronze Age and a friend and lover of CORNELIA. He now lives as HAROLD COLE.

COLE, HAROLD, BRIGADIER (RETIRED): the LORD OF THE FAERIE, who once lived as COEL, as Harold of Wessex, and as Charles II.

COPT HALL: an ancient and now ruined house on the northwest outskirts of Epping Forest. Sometimes spelled as Copped Hall.

CORNELIA: wife to Brutus when the TROY GAME was first constructed. Now she lives as NOAH BANKS.

DANCE OF THE FLOWERS: one of two dances involved in creating the TROY GAME, the Dance of the Flowers needs to be performed to close the Game and bring it to its full strength.

DANCE OF THE TORCHES: the magical dance that was used by Brutus and Genvissa to establish the TROY GAME.

DANCING FLOOR, THE: literally the labyrinth as it is carved into rock or stone. The MISTRESS OF THE LABYRINTH and the KINGMAN use the dancing floor to raise the Game from the labyrinth. Dancing floors—labyrinths—could be found in many medieval European cathedrals.

DARKWITCH: a woman who uses the dark power (the Darkcraft) found in the heart of the labyrinth.

EAVING: the goddess of the waters who takes the mortal form of NOAH BANKS. In the Anglo-Saxon language,

Eaving meant "shelter," or "the unexpected haven from the storm."

EAVING'S SISTERS: in *God's Concubine* and *Darkwitch Rising* EAVING was reborn in Caela (now NOAH BANKS). She drew fiercely loyal women about her who became known as Eaving's Sisters and who live in this life as Matilda, Ecub, and Erith, taking back the names of their first lives.

ELEANOR CROSSES: when Eleanor, the first queen of Edward I, died in Nottinghamshire, her husband was so distraught he built magnificent crosses at each place that her corpse rested on its journey back to London. Two crosses were erected in London: at Cheapside (this has now gone) and at Charing Cross (which still remains).

EPPING FOREST: the surviving remnant of the great forests which once spread over southeast England. It is situated just to the north of London.

FAERIE HILL MANOR: the home of Sir HAROLD COLE situated in EPPING FOREST.

FAERIE, LORD OF THE: an ancient being who watches over the REALM OF THE FAERIE. He is often confused with the Green Man, an ancient mythical figure in English village culture closely associated with the forests, and with the Maytide celebrations. Figures of the Green Man, or the Lord of the Faerie, can be found carved into the decorations of a myriad English (as European) cathedrals and churches.

FAERIE, REALM OF THE: the faerie world, which exists side by side with the mortal world. Governed by the LORD OF THE FAERIE who is HAROLD COLE (Harry) in this life.

GEORGE VI: King of England. George lived as JOHN THORNTON in his previous life, when he was NOAH BANKS' lover.

GOG: one of the legendary giant protectors of London, closely associated with the Guildhall (you can still see him there); his brother is MAGOG. Once a SIDLESAGHE.

GREAT FIRE OF LONDON: in 1666 central London was destroyed by a massive conflagration that was started by NOAH BANKS in an effort to halt the progress of the TROY GAME.

GREAT FOUNDING LABYRINTH, THE: the original labyrinth in Knossos on Crete, where was imprisoned the Minotaur ASTERION, and where ARIADNE betrayed him to Theseus.

GREAT MARRIAGE, THE: the formal union between the STAG GOD and the goddess of the waters (see EAVING), signifying that forest, water, and land exist in harmony.

GREAT ORDEAL, THE: whenever a woman is trained as a MISTRESS OF THE LABYRINTH, she must undergo a final test to determine whether or not she is capable of controlling the powerful sorceries of the labyrinth. It is the Great Ordeal, and not all novice MISTRESSES OF THE LABYRINTH survive it.

HAMPSTEAD HEATH: lying in the northwest of modern-day London, the Heath comprises eight hundred acres of parkland and woods; Parliament Hill rises in its southeast quadrant.

HERNE, WALTER: Loth reborn and a clergyman within the Anglican Church.

IDYLL, THE: During the seventeenth century, when WEYLAND ORR lived in a house by ST. DUNSTAN'S-IN-THE-EAST, he constructed in the attic a magical faerie world that he called the Idyll. Only he, NOAH BANKS, and later their daughter, GRACE, had access.

IMPS, THE: see PHILPOT.

INDENTURES: house and property deeds of sale and transfer in Britain were traditionally called indentures, and, until the early twentieth century, were usually written on vellum.

KINGMAN, THE: the TROY GAME is constructed and controlled by two people, the MISTRESS OF THE LABYRINTH and the KINGMAN. The KINGMAN was traditionally the king or ruler of the city that needed to be protected by the Game. In TROY, the original KINGMAN was Aeneas, and his descendant Brutus later took on the role.

KINGSHIP BANDS OF TROY, THE: when Brutus originally constructed the TROY GAME with Genvissa, he used the power of the ancient and magical six Kingship bands of Troy he wore about his limbs. But when CORNELIA killed Gen-

vissa, and ASTERION threatened to invade, Brutus took the Kingship bands and hid them about London as part of a protective enchantment. Ever since then both Brutus-reborn and ASTERION have competed in the effort to locate them. In book II, *God's Concubine*, Caela (CORNELIA-reborn and NOAH BANKS in this book) took them and hid them in different locations about London. Possession of the bands enables the wearer to control the TROY GAME.

LLANGARLIA: the ancient name of England during the Bronze Age (about 1500 B.C.E.).

LONDINIUM: Roman name for London.

LONG TOM: a SIDLESAGHE, and a close friend of NOAH BANKS. In medieval and early modern England, individual standing stones were often called Long Tom.

MAG: goddess of the waters in ancient LLANGARLIA, now reborn in NOAH BANKS as EAVING.

MAGOG: one of the legendary giant protectors of London, closely associated with the Guildhall (you can see him there); his brother is GOG. Once a SIDLESAGHE.

MAKRIS, SILVIUS: the father of Brutus—now JACK SKELTON. Once murdered by his son, and trapped in the dark heart of the labyrinth for thousands of years. Now reunited with his son.

MALCOLM: servant at COPT HALL.

MESOPOTAMA: In the Bronze Age Mesopotama was a Dorian city on the river Acheron on the west coast of Greece. It was ruled by Pandrasus, who was CORNELIA's father.

MISTRESS OF THE LABYRINTH: the TROY GAME is constructed and controlled by two people, the MISTRESS OF THE LABYRINTH and the KINGMAN. The Mistress is an ancient office that derives from the GREAT FOUNDING LABYRINTH in Knossos on Crete. In previous lives Genvissa, reborn as Swanne (now STELLA WENTWORTH), has been the Mistress of the Labyrinth.

NAKED, THE: the greatest of the holy sites within the REALM OF THE FAERIE, and the site of the LORD OF THE FAERIE's throne.

OG: see STAG GOD.

ORR, GRACE: daughter of NOAH BANKS and WEYLAND ORR. In *Darkwitch Rising* Grace was hexed by CATLING, who tied their fates together.

ORR, WEYLAND: ASTERION reborn, husband of NOAH BANKS and father of GRACE.

PEN HILL: one of the ancient sacred VEILED HILLS of LLAN-GARLIA. Pen Hill has now vanished underneath the nineteenth-century urban sprawl (and waterworks) of London.

PHILPOT, BILL AND JIM: WEYLAND ORR'S IMPS, whom he first created in the eleventh century to torment NOAH BANKS and STELLA WENTWORTH (once Caela and Swanne). Jim and Bill are now far more independent, running their own private investigation agency in Southwark.

PRASUTAGUS: British druid-king of the Iceni. Husband of BOUDICCA. He died circa A.D. 60.

RINGWALK, THE: the medieval term for the path of the stag through the forest.

RINGWALKER: the name of the current STAG GOD, JACK SKELTON.

SAVOY, THE: a famous hotel situated on the banks of the Thames on the Strand. It takes its name from the medieval palace which once stood on the spot.

SIDLESAGHES: ancient magical creatures of the land who often take the form of standing stones within the STONE DANCES.

SILVIUS: father to Brutus, murdered by Brutus in the forests outside ALBA in Italy almost three thousand years ago. See also MAKRIS, SILVIUS.

SKELTON, JACK: once Brutus, who, with Genvissa, began the TROY GAME during the Bronze Age, Jack is now also RINGWALKER, the STAG GOD of the forests. Previously he had lived as William the Conqueror and Louis de Silva.

ST. DUNSTAN'S-IN-THE-EAST: one of the medieval churches of London. It stands in Idol Lane near the Tower of London.

ST. PAUL'S CATHEDRAL: situated in the heart of London, St. Paul's is the heart of the TROY GAME. The cathedral that stood during World War II (and which stands now) is

that designed by Sir Christopher Wren to replace that destroyed by the GREAT FIRE OF LONDON in 1666.

STACEY, ROBERT: concierge of the private resident's lobby at the SAVOY. Stacey is a SIDLESAGHE.

STAG GOD: one of the ancient gods of the land of LLANGAR-LIA, the Stag God is particularly associated with the forests. For aeons he was known as OG. In the previous life JACK SKELTON assumed the powers of the Stag God and took the name RINGWALKER.

STONE DANCES, THE: the ancient circles of standing stones that dot the British Isles.

THORNTON, REV. JOHN: see GEORGE VI.

TROY: the fabulous city of Troy sat on the western shores of Anatolia (modern-day Turkey). Paris, son of the Trojan king Priam, stole away Helen from her husband, Menelaus, king of Sparta, precipitating the Trojan War in which the city-states of Greece united against Troy. Although it survived a long Greek siege, Troy was eventually destroyed due to a combination of hubris, the betrayal of the gods, and Greek cunning. Those Trojans who survived the destruction scattered about the lands of the Mediterranean, either as refugees or slaves.

TROY GAME, THE: the ancient protective sorcery which draws on the power of the ancient labyrinth in order to protect a city. In *Hades' Daughter* Brutus and Genvissa constructed the Game, but were unable to complete it when CORNELIA murdered Genvissa. Now the Game has taken on a life and power of its own, and wishes only to be completed by the KINGMAN and MISTRESS OF THE LABYRINTH.

VEILED HILLS, THE: the six sacred hills of LLANGARLIA, clustered above the Thames River in the area now known as London. The six hills were: Tot Hill (where now stands Westminster); the Llandin, the most sacred of the hills (now called Parliament Hill); PEN HILL; Og's Hill (Ludgate Hill); Mag's Hill (Cornhill); and the White Mount (Tower Hill).

VERULAMIUM: the Roman name for St. Albans.

WENTWORTH, STELLA: once Genvissa, who started the TROY GAME with Brutus, Stella is now the CAROLLER (she who sings in the dawn and the dusk in the REALM OF THE FAERIE), and lives as the LORD OF THE FAERIE's lover.